MAXIM JAKUBOWSKI was born in England but educated in France. Following a career in publishing, he opened London's famous MURDER ONE bookshop. He has published over 70 books, won the Anthony and Karel Awards and is a connoisseur of genre fiction in all its forms. His recent books include ten volumes in *The Mammoth Book of Erotica* series, as well as *The Mammoth Book of Pulp Fiction* and more recently *The Mammoth Book of Pulp Action*. Other well-received anthologies include: *London Noir*, three volumes of *Fresh Blood*, *Past Poisons*, *Chronicles of Crime* and *Murder Through the Ages*. A regular broadcaster, he is the crime columnist for the *Guardian*. His fiction includes *Life in the World of Women, It's you that I want to Kiss, Because She Thought She Loved Me, The State of Montana, On Tenderness Express* and *Confessions of a Romantic Pornographer*. He lives in London.

Also available

The Mammoth Book of Awesome Comic Fantasy
The Mammoth Book of Best New Erotica 3
The Mammoth Book of Best New Horror 14
The Mammoth Book of Climbing Adventures
The Mammoth Book of Comic Crime
The Mammoth Book of Egyptian Whodunnits
The Mammoth Book of Elite Forces
The Mammoth Book of Endurance and Adventure
The Mammoth Book of Explorers
The Mammoth Boom of Eyewitness America
The Mammoth Book of Eyewitness Battles
The Mammoth Book of Eyewitness Everest
The Mammoth Book of Fantasy
The Mammoth Book of Fighter Pilots
The Mammoth Book of Future Cops
The Mammoth Book of Great Detective Stories
The Mammoth Book of Haunted House Stories
The Mammoth Book of Heroes
The Mammoth Book of Heroic and Outrageous Women
The Mammoth Book of Historical Whodunnits
The Mammoth Book of Humor
The Mammoth Book of Illustrated Crime
The Mammoth Book of Journalism
The Mammoth Book of Legal Thrillers
The Mammoth Book of Literary Anecdotes
The Mammoth Book of Locked-Room Mysteries and Impossible Crimes
The Mammoth Book of Maneaters
The Mammoth Book of Men O'War
The Mammoth Book of Mountain Disasters
The Mammoth Book of Murder and Science
The Mammoth Book of Native Americans
The Mammoth Book of Private Eye Stories
The Mammoth Book of Prophecies
The Mammoth Book of Pulp Action
The Mammoth Book of Roaring Twenties Whodunnits
The Mammoth Book of Roman Whodunnits
The Mammoth Book of Science Fiction
The Mammoth Book of Sea Battles
The Mammoth Book of Sex, Drugs and Rock 'n' Roll
The Mammoth Book of Short Erotic Novels
The Mammoth Book of Tales from the Road
The Mammoth Book of the Titanic
The Mammoth Book of UFOs
The Mammoth Book of Vampires
The Mammoth Book of Vampire Stories by Women
The Mammoth Book of War Correspondents
The Mammoth Book of Women Who Kill

THE MAMMOTH BOOK OF

Best
New Erotica

Volume 4

Edited by Maxim Jakubowski

CARROLL & GRAF PUBLISHERS
New York

Carroll & Graf Publishers
An imprint of Avalon Publishing Group, Inc.
245 W. 17th Street
New York
NY 10011-5300
www.carrollandgraf.com

AVALON
publishing group incorporated

First published in the UK by Robinson,
an imprint of Constable & Robinson Ltd 2005

First Carroll & Graf edition 2005

Collection and editorial material
copyright © Maxim Jakubowski 2005

ISBN 0-7394-5174-X

Printed in U.S.A.

Contents

Contents vii

Acknowledgments

WINGS by Amanda A. Gannon © 2003 by Amanda A. Gannon. First appeared in *Scarlet Letters*.

MEMORANDUM by N.T. Morley © 2003 by N.T. Morley. First appeared in *Good Vibrations* Magazine. Reprinted by permission of the author.

BLUEGUMS by O'Neil De Noux © 2003 by O'Neil De Noux. First appeared in *City Slab* Magazine. Reprinted by permission of the author.

PET SHOP GIRL by Lisette Ashton © 2003 by Lisette Ashton. First appeared in *Forum*. Reprinted by permission of the author.

LILITH BROKEN TO BRIDLE by Molly Weatherfield © 2003 by Molly Weatherfield. First appeared in *The Big Book of Hot Women's Erotica 2004* edited by Marilyn Jaye-Lewis. Reprinted by permission of the author.

EVERYTHING BUT THE SMELL OF LILIES by M. Christian © 2003 by M. Christian. First appeared in *The Bachelor Machine*. Reprinted by permission of the author.

TEN MINUTES IN THE EIGHTIES by Alison Tyler © 2003 by Alison Tyler. First appeared in *Wicked Words 8*, edited by Kerri Sharp. Reprinted by permission of the author.

A DAY WITH THE BERNSTEINS by Charlie Anders © 2003 by Charlie Anders. First appeared in *Suspect Thoughts*. Reprinted by permission of the author.

BASSAI DAI by Zoe Constantin © 2003 by Zoe Constantin. First appeared in *Clean Sheets*. Reprinted by permission of the author.

THE END OF DAPHNE GREENWOOD'S TRAVEL CAREER by Tara Alton © 2003 by Tara Alton. First appeared in *Scarlet Letters*. Reprinted by permission of the author.

CRY OF THE LOOGAROO by John Edward Ames © 2003 by John Edward Ames. First appeared in *Hot Blood XI:Fatal Attractions*, edited by Jeff Gelb and Michael Garrett. Reprinted by permission of the author.

UNDER THE FROG BRIDGE by Debra Hyde © 2003 by Debra Hyde. First appeared in *Scarlet Letters*. Reprinted by permission of the author.

EYE OF THE BEHOLDER by Mark Timlin © 2003 by Mark Timlin. First appeared in *The Erotic Review*. Reprinted by permission of the author.

INDIGO WHITE, BURNT UMBER by Cheyenne Blue © 2003 by Cheyenne Blue. First appeared in *Clean Sheets*. Reprinted by permission of the author.

WHEN CALLS ED WOOD by Tom Piccirilli © 2003 by Tom Piccirilli. First appeared in *Leather, Lace and Lust*, edited by Sage Vivant and M. Christian. Reprinted by permission of the author.

THIS HURTS ME MORE THAN IT HURTS YOU by Stephanie Schaeffer © 2003 by Stephanie Schaeffer. First appeared in *Clean Sheets*. Reprinted by permission of the author.

EYEWASH by Michèle Larue © 2003 by Michèle Larue. First appeared in *The Big Book of Hot Women's Erotica 2004*, edited by Marilyn Jaye-Lewis. Reprinted by permission of the author.

THIS FAR INSIDE by R. Gay © 2003 by R. Gay. First appeared in *Scarlet Letters*. Reprinted by permission of the author.

FEEL THE PAIN by Michael Bracken © 2003 by Michael Bracken. First appeared in *Flesh and Blood: Guilty as Sin*, edited by Max Allan Collins and Jeff Gelb. Reprinted by permission of the author.

THE SUMMER OF GRANT LEE BUFFALO by Maxim Jakubowski © 2003 and 2004 by Maxim Jakubowski. First appeared in *Suspect Thoughts* and in a revised version in *Confessions of a Romantic Pornographer*. Reprinted by permission of the author.

LOOK AT ME by Riain Grey © 2003 by Riain Grey. First appeared in *Clean Sheets*. Reprinted by permission of the author.

CASHMERES MUST DIE by A.F. Waddell © 2003 by A.F. Waddell. First appeared in *Leather, Lace and Lust*, edited by Sage Vivant and M. Christian. Reprinted by permission of the author.

THE ARB by Nicholas Urfé © 2003 by Nicholas Urfé. First appeared in *Scarlet Letters*.

THE KEY by Sage Vivant © 2003 by Sage Vivant. First appeared in *Naughty Stories A to Z*, vol 2, edited by Alison Tyler. Reprinted by permission of the author.

TOO BAD by Cara Bruce © 2003 by Cara Bruce. First appeared in *Suspect Thoughts*. Reprinted by permission of the author.

SPRING PICTURES by Donna George Storey © 2003 by Donna George Storey. First appeared in *Scarlet Letters*. Reprinted by permission of the author.

NICK/NICOLA by Mark Ramsden © 2004 by Mark Ramsden. Reprinted by permission of the author.

THE PERMANENT by Catherine Lundoff © 2003 by Catherine Lundoff. First appeared in *The Big Book of Hot Women's Erotica 2004*, edited by Marilyn Jaye-Lewis. Reprinted by permission of the author.

NO SOLACE FOR THE SOUL IN DIGITOPIA by John Grant © 2003 by John Grant. First appeared in *Live Without a Net*, edited by Lou Anders. Reprinted by permission of the author.

SWIMMER'S BODY by Patrick Califia © 2003 by Patrick Califia. First appeared in *Suspect Thoughts*. Reprinted by permission of the author.

COMMUNION by Lisabet Sarai © 2003 by Lisabet Sarai. First appeared in *Sacred Exchange*, edited by Lisabet Sarai and S.F. Mayfair. Reprinted by permission of the author.

CONTENTED CLIENTS by Kate Dominic © 2003 by Kate Dominic. First appeared in *Leather, Lace and Lust*, edited by Sage Vivant and M. Christian. Reprinted by permission of the author.

THE LESSONS by Nola Summers © 2003 by Nola Summers. First appeared in *Clean Sheets*. Reprinted by permission of the author.

NUDE IN MAGENTA by Debra Gray De Noux and O'Neil De Noux © 2003 by Debra Gray De Noux and O'Neil De Noux. First appeared in *Hot Blood XI:Fatal Attraction*, edited by Jeff Gelb and Michael Garrett. Reprinted by permission of the authors.

DOING THE DISHES by Rachel Kramer Bussel © 2003 by
Rachel Kramer Bussel. First appeared in *Best Women's Erotica
2004*, edited by Marcy Sheiner. Reprinted by permission of the
author.

AVRIL'S NAME by Thomas S. Roche © 2003 by Thomas S.
Roche. First appeared in *Erotica Writers and Readers Association*. Reprinted by permission of the author.

All efforts have been made to contact the copyright holders,
either through their last-known email address or care of the
editors who published them. Should anyone who could not be
reached thus wish to make themselves known, please contact
Maxim Jackubowski c/o the publisher.

Introduction

Maxim Jakubowski

Another year, another bountiful handful of erotic stories covering the whole gamut of human sexuality, fantasies and entertainment. This time, our tales come laced with wit, desire, danger, irony and dollops of lust given a free rein and most definitely out of control.

The popularity of erotic writing keeps on growing and in the twelve years I have been editing these groundbreaking anthologies, I have never been faced with such an embarassment of riches.

To select the stories included here I have read over 1,500 stories – some from direct submissions, some previously published in rival anthologies (a few of which were only available to US book club members) or single author book collections, and yet others from countless magazines and websites. This represents an increase of almost 40 per cent on the previous year and proves a fair reflection of the current boom happening in the realm of the literary senses.

And yet again I am particularly proud to be able to introduce a brace of new authors who haven't appeared in previous volumes in the series together with many favourites whose imagination and talent show no sign of drying up.

As ever, I am amazed by the variations our erotic writers spin on what is commonly (and mistakenly) thought of as a subject where the limitations in sexual positions and sexual combinations lead to a dead end. They all manage to be sexy without resorting to vulgarity and their characters come alive as real people and not cardboard characters with sexual bits attached. Emotions as well as humour banish the spectre of mere pornography and the ensuing results are both fascinating and enchanting.

After months of reading erotic stories, I must confess I am already looking forward to seeing next year's offerings and how they will invariably bring new angles and dimensions to a subject that will never cease to live in the hearts and genitals of men and women: desire, lust, curiosity, call it what you will.

Adam and Eve (and the serpent, of course) have much to be blamed for.

Enjoy this delicious apple of a book . . .

                                        Maxim Jakubowski

Wings

Amanda A. Gannon

"I want wings," Sara said, laying the sheet of paper on the glass. "Black ones." The case held glittering rows of body jewelry and pierced anatomical models like strange orchids.

The man behind the counter looked at her design, the swords of the black feathers slashing down the paper, stark and gorgeous, then turned an experienced eye to Sara. He, with his several facial piercings and close-shaven head, looked like he belonged here. Sara, in her work clothes, with her black hair pinned up smartly, did not. She returned his stare evenly.

"That design's going to take a while." His voice carried a faint but pleasant Texas accent.

"How many times will I have to come in?"

Again, that appraising look. His eyes were agelessly dark. Bird's eyes at once naïve and wise. "Maybe four or five. Is this your first tattoo?"

She glimpsed the flash of a bead as he spoke. A pierced tongue. The sight intrigued her. She shrugged. "What you see is what you get." Her ears weren't even pierced. He leaned back, plainly surprised. *Well,* she supposed, *I don't really look the type, do I?*

"Ma'am, that's a *big* tattoo, for the first time."

"Yes," she agreed. She'd expected this. She didn't want to *try it* and she didn't want to start small. She wanted her wings. "When can we start?"

He ran a hand over his near-naked skull. "Umm. Thursday afternoon? If I put you in at close, we can spend more time at it, no interruptions. I don't want to rush."

"Yes. At close. I'd like that."

He nodded and pulled up a daily planner, flipped it ahead a few pages, and hesitated, pen needling the page. "I'm sorry. Your name?"

"Sara."

He grinned, and it transformed his face. He was very handsome, beneath the twenty-first-century-primitive gloss of beads and rings. Sara felt silly for not having seen it before. "I'm John."

She'd looked at samples, of course, in the studio and online. John's work was more than that of a competent copyist with a tattoo gun. His designs lived. Breathed. Which was why it surprised her that this lip-pierced puppy with his faint Texas drawl and his old/young eyes had produced them. He looked no more than twenty-two.

They agreed on a price, and she left the design with him. She told her husband over the take-out she grabbed on the way back from the studio. "I'm getting my wings. Thursday."

Alex looked sidelong at her through his fringe of hair. He was thirty-five, just starting to go gray. She liked it. "You went?" She nodded mutely, already afraid. He smiled at her. "I know you want them. And I can't wait to see. Those big black wings under all those good-girl clothes."

"I can't wait either." But her smile was dry.

"You can do it, Sara. You've wanted this."

She hugged herself. Her husband didn't have any tattoos. Not one. No earrings, no hidden piercings. Alex was an accountant, for God's sake. He was *normal*. He couldn't tell her what to expect.

When she didn't answer, he came over and kissed her softly, running his fingers through the uncoiling black spirals of her mane. "Come on, baby. What're you scared of? These are your *wings*."

"I don't know how to fly."

They both laughed, but Sara had her doubts, rooted deep, and pricking her like quills.

On Wednesday night, as they made love, Alex turned her over, pressed her down into the blankets, and ran his fingers over the flawless skin of Sara's back. The touch raced down her spine like liquid light, cold and hot. She felt his cock brush the back of her thighs and she expected him to enter her, but he didn't. He bent, instead, mouthing the channel of Sara's spine, tasting her sweat, savoring the smooth, unmarked skin. As Alex kissed from her shoulders to her hips, she caught the scent of her own fear.

Alex's fingers rubbed at the very core of her, stroking, skilled. His tongue drew darts over Sara's marzipan skin. When she felt Alex's strong arm snake about her waist and pull her back, when she felt his lips describing the delta of her tailbone and the smooth split-peach furrow of her backside, when she felt Alex's darting tongue press against her asshole, then lower, to the sticky paradise of her pussy, it was John she thought of.

She grabbed Alex's hair as though clutching at an anchor, and ground back. This moment mattered, not the future, a week, a day, an hour from now. And certainly not that boy ten years her junior, with his gifted workman's hands and his silver-tipped tongue. Alex twisted to his back and settled Sara over his face, leaned up as though thirsting for her. Sara ground down, leaning on the brass headboard for support and panting through clenched teeth. Alex's clever, probing fingers and wicked tongue made her feel the aching hollowness of her body. Sara caught herself thinking of John again, and what he'd do to her. The needle. The touch of his hands. Dreading the pain, and longing for it. Longing for her wings.

Alex pulled her down, strong hands on the smoothness of her hips, and she mounted him, rode him hard. Her fingers traced the scratchy stubble on his cheeks and chin, her nails raked at the hair on his chest as she pushed herself down on him. And again, thoughts of the studio boy intruded, his firm young body, his strong neck. She'd seen tattoos under his shirt, like the tails of long, black snakes.

She finally bent back and parted her thighs wide, affording Alex a glimpse at his cock as it disappeared into her wet folds. She licked a finger and pressed it down through the narrow line of her pubic hair, pressed it to the top of his shaft, then rubbed at her own burning button. She arched, thrusting her hips out, riding him, offering him the sight of her own lovely, shameless body mounted atop him. Her breasts bounced as she drove down, and when Alex reached up to stroke them, she forced herself into his hands, urging him on with rough little cries.

Ambushed by her own pleasure, she arched, breasts thrown out, shoulders back, her nails digging into Alex's belly as a swan song forced its way out of her throat in one long, silvery cry. For a brief, fluttering moment, she hung between earth and sky. Then Alex overturned her, pinning her, nailing her to the mattress, his sweat sliding against her skin, her body opening and yielding to him even as her mind wandered away, wandered over smooth, black-painted skin. Alex came inside her, kissing her, but her mouth was lax beneath his. Her mind was off, wandering. Guiltily, she called it back.

When they lay beside one another, cradled like kittens, Alex kissed Sara's shoulder. "I thought you were going to take off."

"I nearly did," Sara replied, taking Alex's hand and kissing his fingers, tasting herself. She sighed, tired but restless, and annoyed with herself for her fantasies. She closed her eyes and wriggled back against Alex. "I love you."

The electronic bell beeped twice. The reception area was empty and silent but for the hum of the Coke machine. Her first time in, Sara had expected blacklight posters and incense, but the inside of the minimalist studio smelled only faintly of glass cleaner and new carpet, and was more meticulously clean than a doctor's office. It scared her a little.

John came out of a door behind the counter and blinked at her. This time he wore a short-sleeved shirt, white, and she could clearly see the thorned vines of tribal designs crawling from beneath his sleeves and up the back of his neck. The sight heated her.

"Hi," she said. "We're still on, right?"

"You bet," he said, stepping around the counter. "If you're ready, I'm ready."

"Didn't think I'd show?"

He shrugged. "A lot of people lose it at the last minute." Then he grinned at her sidelong, an unsettlingly disarming grin. "I knew you'd show, though. I could see it in your eyes. You're not scared."

"Yes, I am," she said, correcting him with a slight laugh.

He smiled with those *eyes*. "You only think you are." He opened a door on one side of the waiting-room and gestured her inside.

This room was better. A big padded table with a headrest, like the ones used by chiropractors or masseuses, dominated the floor. Beside it was a comfortable stool, and a standing stainless-steel tray. The room was obviously a renovated clinic, complete with cabinets and drawers, but some attempt had been made to make it look colorful. Sheets of tattoo flash covered the walls – everything from fifties cheesecake to modern biomechanical. And other furniture: a copy machine, a stereo, the little oven of the autoclave.

Beside the stool crouched the air compressor, its snakelike tube winding up to the tray. The tattoo gun looked like a sci-fi prop, all black and silver, a cross between an airbrush and a hypodermic gun.

John lay a couple of towels over the table. "You can put your shirt there," he gestured to a clothing rack just behind the door. "I'll give you a minute to relax." He left her to wrestle with her fear as he prepared his tools to the sound of Paul Oakenfold. Her last chance to back out.

She stripped her shirt off and stepped out of her shoes. He looked up, grinned once at her, the skin at the corners of his eyes wrinkling, so friendly, and she felt a sudden dread go through her like a knife at the thought of what he was about to do to her. She swallowed.

"You can leave that on if you want," he said of her black satin bra. "Just unsnap it in back."

"No," she said. "I won't be able to drive back in it."

He stole another glance at her – and why shouldn't he? – but didn't stare. She lay face down on the table and fidgeted. When John showed her the unopened package with the needles in it, she nodded, lips pressed tight. He lay them out and fitted the first into the gun. The ink, as he poured it into tiny, disposable wells, smelled heady and strangely organic.

"Can you pull this down?" he asked, tugging gently at the waist of her velvet skirt with two gloved fingers. The wings' lowest points would come almost to her sacral dimples. She bared more flesh, felt him looking at her, though he said nothing.

He transferred the design to her very carefully, smoothing the onion-skin paper to her dampened flesh. When he peeled it away, she looked at the outline in the full-length mirror, using a hand-held glass to see over her shoulder. John's reflection regarded her with dark eyes. His gloved hand rested on the gun. Was he thinking of her, the way her body looked just now under the harsh light, or was he, too, seeing her as she would be, when he was done?

Sara nodded. "It'll look fantastic." She settled onto her belly again. "Let's do it."

The air compressor snarled, and the sound of the gun as he depressed the button was a sharp, ratcheting buzz. He let her get used to the sound before he began. "I'm going to lean against you with my left arm a little." His voice was smooth and soothing. "Are you ready?"

She took a deep breath. "Yeah. Give me my wings."

She glimpsed his smile as he leaned over, his weight comfortable across her lower back, and then she felt his breath across her shoulder, cool on her skin, still damp from the disinfectant. The gun purred behind her ear. He spread the fingers of his left hand, drawing the skin taut between his thumb and forefinger. His right hand hovered above her.

"Here we go."

The first line stung. The second burned. "Is that all?" she whispered, surprised by how little it hurt.

"Yes," he whispered back, over the needle's wasplike drone. "That's all."

And he inked her in lines of fire, the music spiraling and dancing behind the burr of the compressor. Sara watched John's face in the big mirror as he bent over her. Once, he slid a curling lock of her hair off the design and she watched his face grow serious as he ran a gloved thumb quite deliberately up the nape of her neck. The contact was like a shock to her. He went right back to work, eyes intent, utterly absorbed. His voice came as a surprise.

"This is a really beautiful design."

"Thank you," she said. "It's my work. I paint, when I'm not typing."

"You could do flash, you know. You have an eye for it."

His needle blazed a stop-starting scarlet trail over her shoulder and down, down, down. The arch of the alula, down the coverts, then the long, knifing burn of the left wing's first primary. She gasped. The flesh on her lower back was so much more sensitive. He put a gentle hand on the small of her back, just above her tailbone. "*Easy.*"

"It's worse, there," she gasped, her throat tight.

"It is," he agreed.

But he spread the pain out, to help her manage it. He spent a long time outlining the delicate feathers high on the wings before he traced the second primary and back up, a sizzling cut across her naked skin that sent tingles racing to her fingertips. She panted a little. Her shoulders were one burning mass, as though she wore a coat of fire. He dabbed at her side with a bit of gauze.

"Am I bleeding?"

He showed her. "It's only ink. Your skin is taking it really well. I think you were meant to have these." She could hear the smile.

"I was," she said.

The hum and buzz lulled her, and she could feel the steady vibrations through his arm or hand as he leaned on her. It soothed her, the weight of his body against hers, the gentle touch. She could feel him breathing, slow and calm. By the time the music ended, she was nearly drowsy. *It's the endorphins*, she thought dreamily, but when he stopped for a break, she found herself alert.

She took the water he offered her, sitting up on her forearm to do it. Her nipples dragged the rough towel. John stretched.

"Do you need to quit for the evening?" she asked as he changed gloves and dried his hands. The gun looked heavy.

He shrugged. "I'm all right for a while, yet. You know, you're handling this well."

She looked at him. "It doesn't hurt as bad as I thought."

"Nope," he agreed, with a smile as lopsided as her wings.

She smiled back. "Keep going."

The outline alone took three hours. But they finished both sides in one night. "How do you feel?" he asked, taping gauze over the burning, incomplete pinions.

She smiled. "Good," she said, the word woefully inadequate. How to explain how it felt – the smooth lull of the gun, the constant burn of the needle? That it freed her, somehow? She looked at his upper arms, the gorgeous tribal spirals. She didn't have to explain, she suddenly understood. She didn't have to say anything. He knew.

"Can I see them?" she asked softly, embarrassed. She was holding her shirt over her breasts, feeling at once self-conscious and stupid for feeling that way, when what he'd done to her was far more intimate than a simple look at her naked body.

"Mine? Oh. Sure."

He pulled his shirt off, not shy in the least about this act of exposure. The designs were exquisite, though perhaps not as exquisite as the young and healthy muscle beneath. His skin was very smooth, only slightly tanned. A mantle of black interlace covered his shoulders, nearly as large as her own design. More wound down his upper arms. The small of his back echoed the design on his shoulders, disappearing under the worn-white rim of his jeans. Another, smaller design started just beneath his navel and slid down. She could barely see the top of it.

The sight of it sent a pulse through her, and her nipples hardened traitorously. How must he have looked as it was being applied, holding himself still, trying not to arch under the gun? How had his face contorted? And would his face look the same in the grip of pleasure?

"So beautiful," she whispered. Beneath her skirt, her sex was wet. And her skin *burned*.

She paid him in full that first night. There was never any question. She'd come back.

Two weeks later the itchy welts had faded, leaving her with the tracery of feathers like lacework splayed to either side of her spine. Alex spent an hour following them with his finger once it was safe to touch them.

And when they made love that night, Sara thought of John

again, had to bite her fingers to distract herself from thoughts of his face as Alex bent over her, all his attention bent to her burning, itching skin. He mounted her from behind, this time, sliding into her roughly, *taking* her. He wanted to touch her feathers, but she stopped him. The pain was still too recent, too new, the memory too intense. His touch, reminding her of it, threatened to cheat her of her pleasure. So he clung to her hips and crashed against her as she gazed back at him, her black hair tossing as though in a wind. When her orgasm broke upon her, she reached back and tugged sharply on the hair above his cock, and he used her even more fiercely. "No," she rasped, her voice husky with her cries. "I want to taste it."

So he fed it to her, and she took his length down, lapping herself from him, driving her tongue into the slit at the end of his cock to gather the sea-salt drops that welled out there. She let him jerk it into her mouth, and when he came she let the bitter fluids collect there so that she could swallow it all at once. She looked up at him, and he drew a line up her spine with one finger.

"I love them already," he whispered. "Big, beautiful wings."

"I love them too," Sara replied. "Am I your angel?"

"A fallen one," Alex replied, smiling.

She smiled back. "Not yet."

The next time, she wasn't at all shy. She removed her shirt and lay on the table, watching John as he completed the little rituals without which the ceremony would not be complete.

"Those are hawk wings," he said, pressing his hand over the tracery of her primaries. "Or eagle wings. Like fingers."

"Yes," she agreed. "I'm no dove."

He laughed and took the gun in one gloved hand. "Let's make them black."

The fill needle was a cluster of small points bound into a group, and it felt less like being scratched than being branded. It was a raking, grating pain, and this time she dug her fingers into the sides of the table.

"Should I stop?" John asked immediately.

"No," she grunted. "No. Keep going. It – it *burns*."

He raked her again. Did he take pleasure in this part of it? her suffering for his art? "It's not going in as deep, you know. Most people say the fill needles hurt less."

"*I* don't."

Sara gritted her teeth. He burned her, seared her black. When he was done inking each feather, she felt it, whole and distinct. She knew exactly where they all were. She could count them. Like real wings, indeed. When he gave her a break, she found herself sweating. Her arm was stuck to the vinyl of the table where it hung over the towel.

"You're doing great."

"How much further?"

He showed her.

"I want you to finish that one tonight."

"That's a lot."

"I want it done. And tomorrow – the other one. I want them to heal evenly." She knew she was pushing, but he did it. Three hours went by, the seconds inked in fire. He taped gauze over it in squares when he was done, working gingerly around the screaming-sore flesh. She drove home leaning forward in the seat, feeling the pain less than the phantom weight of his touch. It seemed she floated somewhere between street and sky.

Alex let her be. Sara was spacey, distant, from the endorphins. He understood. She didn't. She kept feeling John's hands on her body every time she closed her eyes. His weight on her back. His smell covered her, close as her own skin. That night, her sleep was broken, uncomfortable. She lay on her belly, the sheet piled around her hips, and dreamed of tongues sharp as scorpion stings, of fingers that pricked like thorns.

The last session, three more hours of pain. She lay on the bench, trembling already. John said nearly nothing. He seemed strangely tense. Sara felt on edge as well. The smell of the ink this time was like ozone in a storm. And when he filled in the last feather, close in near her spine, it felt as though her wings were made of fire.

"That's it," he said. "You're done."

She rose shakily, half-fell. He caught her with one arm,

careful not to touch her back. Her breasts pressed against him. She righted herself. "Sorry."

"Why don't you rest here for a while before you try to drive?" he suggested. She nodded woozily. He let her lie on the table while he cleaned up and closed the shop, turned off the lights outside and in the outer rooms. He brought her some juice from the machine.

"Here. The sugar will help."

She drank greedily. And when she felt she could rise, she did. Her shirt scratched over the taped-down bandaging and she winced. "Thank you."

He only smiled.

"They're beautiful," she added, knowing it was true, even though they were hidden.

"Yes," he agreed. "They are."

She stepped up, drunk with endorphins, and felt the piercing in the hollow of his lower lip with two fingers. He shied, but she quickly kissed him, parting his lips with her tongue, moving her hand to the side of his neck, which was warm and firm and very smooth. She dug her thumbnail against the flesh of his throat and explored his mouth. His tongue rose to meet hers and she felt the little ball on its post pressing firmly against her tongue, her lips. She licked it, caught it in her teeth and sucked at it as he made a brief, surprised sound of protest. Then he laughed, his fingers grazing her belly, and pressed his mouth firmly to hers.

"I won't see you again," she said, breaking the kiss. She touched her back, lightly. "These – were all I wanted."

"Yeah," he agreed after a moment. "I think they're all you need."

"But I'll remember you. Thank you. For giving me my wings."

He grinned. She let go of him and left.

"Two weeks?" Alex sounded incredulous. Sara shook her head. She should've told him over the phone, so he'd have time to get used to the idea before coming home. "Darling, you don't have to wait!"

"I want to," she said. "It hurts, right now. But even later – I can't do it on my back, and I don't want you to have to look at it while it's peeling."

"They're your wings. They're gorgeous and *I want* to see them. Peeling or not."

"Please, Alex. I'd rather wait." She rubbed a hand over her face, then smiled through her fingers abruptly. "I want to save it. Surprise you."

Playful. Playful he could apparently handle. "I don't get to see before then?"

She bit her lip, shook her head so that her hair rained down into her face. "Nope."

"What about doing it in the dark?"

"Cheating."

"Witch," he said, grinning. "My balls will fall off."

"I never said you had to keep *your* clothes on," she whispered. "My mouth is fair game. Just watch the shoulders."

He laughed, richly, warm. Oh, she loved him. Absolutely.

And every day of those two weeks she took his cock in her mouth and pressed her hands to him, imagining smooth, black-inked skin beneath her fingers. An idle fantasy. It kept her hunger keen, like a hawk's. Alex's thighs bore the marks of her talons.

But alone, alone it was another story. In the dark, her husband asleep, she'd squeeze her thighs together and think of him, and think of her wings. At night, surrounded by shadows, it seemed they enfolded her. Superstitiously, she did not even pleasure herself. Her denial sharpened her other senses. Denied satisfaction, she found continual desire.

After two weeks to the day, her skin began to peel. The punished flesh lifted in tissue layers and dropped to the floor of the bath as she ran the sponge over herself. Like the shedding of a snake's skin. She molted every last, clinging tatter. And when she looked in the mirror at her new skin, she gasped.

They stretched from her nape down to her hips, long drapes of shadow, her black hair a curling cloud above. How lovely they were. Truly alive. She ran her fingers over them, shivered. They shrouded her, black as the pinions of Lilith herself. She went to bed in an old shirt, as she had for the weeks before, and didn't tell Alex. She kept her secret under the jersey knit, where nobody could see. Just for tonight, it would be hers. Just for tonight.

She climbed into the Rover parked outside the firm's downtown office, ducking the rain. Her shoulders were tense from long hours of deskwork, as though her wings were trying to push free. She shrugged her shoulders and started the car, then let it idle, the wipers flicking back and forth.

Temple Tattoos' carport dripped rain. She ran into the little airlock of a room between the parking and the reception areas, shook herself like a damp crow. The place looked empty, as usual, but the muted TV in the corner played a cooking show, staticky with the rain. She pushed her way inside, the beeper dinging into the silence.

"John?" Her voice sounded too loud.

"Yo," came the reply from behind the closed door. "Just a minute."

She waited, hands clutched in front of her, in her black slacks and sensible shoes. She should've redone her makeup. Her hair was kinked and frizzy from the rain.

He came out after a moment, unsnapping a pair of latex gloves and dumping them into the trashcan by the door. He seemed surprised to see her. A twenty-something boy with roached, purple hair and a cup of water in one hand followed John, looking pained and thoughtful.

"Sara. Let me give him his care sheet and I'll be with you."

He took the boy to the counter and discussed aftercare for oral piercings with him, but his eyes strayed to Sara. She had not moved, or spoken. After about a minute, she went into the side room, expecting John to call out after her. He didn't.

She sat on the table, feeling its padding slowly sink beneath her weight. Her fingers dug into the vinyl. The room's smells, the tick of the wall-clock, all reminded her. Her hands trembled with the memory of pain. How quickly she'd made the association, like a trained animal. She flexed her fingers and waited.

The door beeped, thumped closed. John came in a few moments later. "Hi," he said, like an old friend. "It's good to see you back."

She looked at him, in his black shirt and ratty blue jeans. "Is something wrong? How's the tattoo?" He sounded anxious, now. An artist afraid for his work.

She hugged her shoulders with both hands. "I dreamed about them, you know," she said, softly, looking at the spotlessly clean floor. "Before. I dreamed of flying when I was a little girl. And then I dreamed the tattoos, a year ago. It was so real."

"Is it – is it what you wanted?"

Again, a long silence. He came a step or two closer. She looked up at him through thick lashes, let her hands slide down her arms. "It's what I needed. I wanted to thank you. It's why I came back. And you should get a chance to see them, I think. They're so lovely."

She stood, saw him put one foot back as though to step away. Was he afraid? No. He was reaching for something – a camera, an Olympus digital. "Please?"

Rain drummed outside, long trance rhythms. She nodded.

She shed her coat, left it piled on the floor like a castoff skin. She unbuttoned her red blouse slowly, not looking at him, then pulled it off. When she looked up, he was staring. She grinned, then turned and flicked her hair over her shoulder. Her slacks hid the tips of the primaries, so she pushed those down, too, stepped out of them and her shoes at once. The bra she removed impatiently, and the panties. She stood naked, her skin pale and smooth, save for the char-black wings. She looked over her shoulder at him as he took the pictures. He stared hungrily, jaw clenched, and when the last one had been stored in digital limbo, he set the camera back on the countertop and stepped within arm's reach. Sara snared him, hooking an arm around his neck and pulling him in. Warmth radiated off him, nearly burning her. His hands found her breasts, cupped them, squeezed. With ungentle fingers, he pinched her nipples and hauled her against him, bent to her suddenly open mouth as she gasped. He licked at her, the bead on his tongue tap-tapping hers, or clicking against her teeth, pressing under her lip, under her tongue. She caught it longwise, holding him prisoner, his breath panting into her open mouth as she forced her hand down the front of his jeans, grasping. His cock was hard, hot in her fist, like an iron bar. She squeezed it, felt it throb.

"Get these clothes off right now." Her voice came out husky. She leaned back against the table, taking in the sight of him as he shed his clothing, young, strong, no scars or blemishes beyond the ornaments he wore. And there was something innocent in that, too. A wholehearted belief in, but not vanity of, his beauty. The tattoo under his navel, an inverted tribal are, stopped just above his patch of darkish pubic hair. His cock stood up at a stiff forty-five degree angle, strongly-veined. A horseshoe-shaped barbell thrust up through the frenum and out the tip. The hanging beads gleamed like droplets of quicksilver.

"Turn around," she whispered, and sat up on the table to watch.

He colored slightly, perhaps not used to being ordered, but he did it. His shoulders belonged on a sculpture. The firm column of his back, deeply furrowed by his spine, shamed anything she'd ever seen. And the black darts of his tattoos, the patterns like tangled thorns and bones, accenting his outline, beautifying him.

She sighed. "Come to me."

And he came, witched into her spell. He stepped up and took her knee, forced her thighs apart. She leaned back, mouth open, gladly showed herself to him. The glossy thatch of hair cresting her mound, no more than a feather-stroke above the firm little lips, still closed about their secret. His hand, so eager, went to her sex and pinched it, squeezing the lips tight together until Sara felt moisture trickling out. He trapped the firm pink berry of her clitoris between her folds and worked his fingers back and forth, until it slipped like a bead under the skin. She spread her legs wider with a little moan and he pulled her sex wide with both thumbs, opening her to the room and the air and his own dark and bottomless hungry gaze.

He leaned in and kissed her, and only then did she think of Alex, a brief guilty flash that ended when John pushed his middle finger into her, thrusting it deep so that it tapped the entrance to her womb. After what they'd shared, she the canvas, he the magician wielding the burning brush, these physical intimacies seemed inevitable.

Wings fluttered in her belly and she uttered a wordless cry, bucking her hips against his hand until he pushed another finger into her, curling them both up to cradle the bone and rub against that bitterly tender place inside her, the one she never seemed to reach alone. She felt her wetness welling out over his fingers, felt her heart pounding.

His tongue ravaged her mouth. His free hand roamed over the smooth hills of her breasts, over her rippled belly, her taut flanks. At his touch on her spine, she shuddered away from his grip, which only pushed her against him. He dropped his mouth to her collarbones, her breasts, his tongue and teeth punishing her nipples. She arched into his mouth, and his fingers pressed against her spine, stroking her firmly, stroking the feathers so new they still felt embossed on the skin itself.

Sara reached down and wrapped her fingers about his shaft. It throbbed in her grip and she moaned, pressed her thumb to the bead on the end of his cock, then thumbed the lower bead, working the shaft of the barbell in his flesh until he bit her lip in frustration, shoving against her hand. She pushed with her thumb in the space between the beads, pushed so hard she felt the steel shaft move under her fingers, and he gasped helplessly.

Slowly, drawn down by the weight of her lust, she slid from the table, folded to her knees on the hard floor. Her fist she kept carefully clamped around his cock, pumping it, the skin sliding along under her fingers. Eager, curious, she bent her head and pressed her tongue to the pierced flesh of his cock. It was hot, soft under her tongue, and salty already with the fluids leaking from the tip. She sucked at the end, sucked at the warm bead. The shaft slid more freely now, wet from her tongue. She dug her tongue in around the piercings, under his cock, where the flesh was so soft and tender, then around the slit in the end. He was hard as slate, and his thighs trembled under her touch. His cock throbbed between her lips and she let it fill her mouth, loving the salty taste of him, and the smell, all man.

His fingers brushed her shoulders. When she looked up, she saw him staring down at her wings as they spread beneath him.

She used her mouth, incarcerating him, drawing at him mercilessly. Even when he tried to warn her, to urge her away with
small sounds, with his hands on her neck, her shoulders, she
did not cease until he erupted into her mouth, surprising him
as much as her with the force of it. Most of it she swallowed.
She pulled back, leaving a hanging thread to drop from his
piercing. For a moment, she sat on her haunches and looked up
at him, then she rose and pressed her body against his, feeling
the sweat that'd sprung to his skin.

He bore her back against the table's tacky edge, his fingers
seeking the core of her, pressing through the hair and between
her lips, opening her again. She sucked at the piercing in his
lip, tugged at it with her teeth. His cock was coming hard again
against her thigh. She moaned, spread herself out, needing
him. A wild thing's growl built in his throat as he looked at her
smooth, well-fleshed body lying before him. He turned her by
the hips and shoved her belly-down against the edge of the
table. His thigh nudged hers together, the heel of his hand slid
up her spine and stopped between her wings, held her down
firmly as he sank himself into her in three rough strokes. Her
wetness spread quickly over him and down, slicking her thighs
where they pressed tight together. She gasped and would've
ridden back against him but he held her still, forced himself
into her urgently. Her back arched, her fingers sank into the
sticky padding of the table's sides. A grating cry ripped free of
her throat, jarred loose by his thrusting.

He took handfuls of her black hair, stilled its furious tossing
and yanked her head back. She arched like a bow, bent by the
force of him. He bit the side of her neck. Hot breath panted
harsh against her throat. She turned to mouth his lips, her
kisses drunken with lust, his mouth soft under hers. His hands,
hands capable of such delicacy and skill, snaked around,
described her belly, her breasts, and instead of pain gave
pleasure, teasing until the aching lilt of orgasm began, turning
her to pulsing fire where she engulfed him. She shrieked when
it broke like a storm over her, leaving her trembling and
alarmed. When had it ever come so quickly or so hard?

She'd slid forward on the table, which was slick with her
sweat. He pulled free and shoved her up further, until she had

hold of the headrest and watched nervously behind her as he climbed up. Yes, there was room for two. He forced her hips down until she was glued to the tabletop, and he entered her like that, her legs stretched back, him straddling one of her thighs, rubbing full-length against her like a snake. His lips caressed the roots of her wings even as his hand twisted cruelly in her hair, forcing her head down.

When he leaned back to run his hands over them, she squeezed, bent and pushed against him, every muscle in her body tensing, trying to lift him along on the ever-rising crest of her own passion. The days of healing, of pain, had sensitized her. His fingers on her skin burned white fire down her spine. She ground herself back against him, his touch pure electric torment. His fingers dug into her shoulders, raked down the tingling welts of her wings, and she came again, mastered by her pleasure, lost in it, and yet somehow riding the storm, floating above it.

He lost his rhythm, thrown off by her own desperate grinding. His sweat dripped onto her back, his panting was harsh and jagged, painful-sounding. He was going to come.

"Out," she gasped. "I want it all over me. I want to feel it."

He made a sound somewhere between a whimper and a snarl, then slipped from her, leaving her gasping and empty. She twisted her head around to look as he jerked his shaft. When he came, it splashed all over her, the white streams interrupted, broken by the piercing. It fell on her in droplets like hot rain, sizzling her skin, filling the channel of her spine and running to puddle between her wings. Its smell, rich and animal, reminded her of the smell of tattoo ink. She smiled under the curtain of her hair.

He fell down beside her on one hand, panting. She sighed, murmured, wordless sounds of need fulfilled. His fingers stroked her back, then rubbed, working his semen into the black lashes of her wings. Her skin shuddered, and she felt as though her pinions were stretched wide, limp and trembling after bearing her through the storm.

"Don't you want another one?" Alex asked, stroking her back. He was still breathless. It had been a good romp. Sara flexed her shoulders.

"What? Another tattoo?"

"Some people get addicted. Go back again and again."

"Oh," she buried her face in the crook of her arm and smiled. "No. I'm done. I have what I needed. Sorry to disappoint."

But three weeks later she walked in again, the beeper announcing her. John was cleaning the glass cases. The hiss of the spray-bottle ceased when Sara walked in, as if he knew. He turned, and their gazes locked.

"Back for more?" he asked, smiling that *smile* at her.

"You do piercings, too," she said, a statement, not a question.

He nodded, standing.

She tapped the glass case with her nail, indicating a pierced latex model of the female labia. A bright gold post went through the clitoral hood, one bead resting firmly against the clitoris itself. Her smile threatened to crack her face. "I want *that* one."

He grinned. "Good choice. How about Tuesday?"

"No," she said. "Now."

Memorandum

N.T. Morley

Notice of Disciplinary Action
To: Audrey Chivas, Executive Assistant
From: Tabitha Kelly, Office Manager
Date: 1 September
Re: **Violation of Office Dress Code**
cc: All Staff

It has been brought to my attention, Miss Chivas, that you have violated our office dress code on numerous occasions since being hired by the firm on 10 August. When you accepted employment at our firm you read and signed a copy of our office policies and procedures document, including our office dress code on page 14. Nonetheless, you have continued to violate our dress code.

I have listed the documented violations below; each was brought to my attention by a senior partner in the firm.

1) On 11 August, your skirt was measured by Mr Armando Stern to be eight inches above the knee. On that day, you also wore pumps with four-inch heels, a clear violation of article 8 of our office dress code. A first-level warning was issued.
2) On 12 August, your silk slacks were sufficiently snug that Mr Stern was able to see your panty lines, and his comments on their visibility met with, by Mr Stern's report (and as I witnessed first-hand), a careless dismissal of Mr Stern's concern. That is wholly unacceptable. Furthermore, on that day your leopard-print brassiere was quite

visible through the tasteless lemon-yellow top you wore. Again, this behavior is unacceptable.

3) On 15 August, your skirt was, as estimated by Mr Spankett, six inches above the knee. Miss Chivas, I would like to point out that such a skirt is decent by perhaps four inches. I was out sick with bunions that day, but I have a reliable report from Mr Stern, Miss Beck in Accounting, and George, our Federal Express delivery person. In addition, Mr Spankett was kind enough to provide a Polaroid he took that day, and I am appalled. I have enclosed said Polaroid here. Coupled with the four-inch heels you wore that day, not to mention the blatant display of what could only have been a push-up brassiere underneath your rather filmy blouse, this outfit presented a wholly unprofessional picture of our firm. A second-level warning was issued at this point.

4) On 22 August, your dress was black in color, decent, again, by perhaps four inches, and was coupled with knee-high lace-up boots with the Doc Martens tag clearly visible at the back of your calf. I admire your forward-facing fashion sense, as I admire your attempt to be accepted by the "in" crowd. But we are a place of business, Miss Chivas, not a Marilyn Manson concert.

5) On 23 August, though your skirt was of acceptable length, your red lace panties were clearly visible underneath when you bent over during your rather ill-advised and lengthy session of filing in the lower drawer in Mr Grimm's office. Polaroid enclosed.

6) On 25 August, you showed up to the office with your hair in pigtails, a white blouse thin enough to show your brassiere underneath, and a plaid skirt which came, again, eight inches above the knee. When asked to retrieve a file from the bottom drawer of Mr Harshass's desk, you reportedly turned away from him, bent over fully without kneeling, and displayed your white panties to him most shamelessly. Again, Mr Harshass thoughtfully provided a Polaroid, which I have enclosed. A third-level warning was issued, resulting in your being docked a day's pay, to which you responded with a shocking display of disregard for the

disciplinary process, stating (and I quote): "Ah, mother-
fuck, I guess I'll have to make up the difference giving
blowjobs down on the waterfront."

7) On 26 August, when working a Saturday to help Mr Stern
prepare for a client meeting, you arrived at the office
dressed in hot pants, a halter top and platform clogs. Again,
as reported by Mr Stern (and demonstrated by the enclosed
Polaroid), your panty lines were clearly visible under the
shorts, though you didn't see fit to wear a bra under the
halter top. I should perhaps clarify here that our office dress
code is to be followed even when the position demands
weekend work.

8) On 28 August, you returned from taking your lunch hour in
the company gym without changing out of your exercise
clothes, shamelessly displaying the fact that you wore a
white leotard that had become rather moist with sweat, and
therefore almost entirely transparent. A fourth-level warning was issued, resulting in this memorandum.

Miss Chivas, let me take this time to commend you for your
excellent work on many other fronts. Your willingness to help
out with client meetings has been quite admirable and has led
to a number of important accounts being exceptionally ser-
viced by this office. The senior partners have repeatedly
commented on your willingness to lend assistance in whatever
way is needed. However, your interpretation of the company
dress code clearly needs extensive correction, which I offer
forthwith:

1) As stated in our policies and procedures document, skirts
for employees who measure five feet three inches (as you
do) are to be no less than eight inches above the knee;
measured from the torso, hems are to remain decent by no
more than two inches or (preferably) less. Heels on all shoes
worn to the office will be no less than six inches, except on
casual Friday, when five-inch heels are permitted.

2) Silk slacks, as you well know, are to be worn without panties
underneath (except on casual Friday, when a thong may be
worn). Furthermore, you know quite well that employees

with D-cup or smaller breasts (yours were measured to be a C-cup) are not allowed to wear brassieres. On that day, this undergarment entirely disguised your nipples, which should have been erect and clearly visible throughout the day, as stated on page 16 of our office policies and procedures document. Also, animal-print clothing is strictly forbidden at this time. If the firm institutes a "Trailer Trash Thursday," you'll certainly be the first to know. Lastly, when Mr Stern offered his rebuke of your wearing panties with these slacks, proper office behavior and our specific policy required you to remove the offending panties immediately in front of him and feed them into the office shredder.

3) Again, a skirt six inches above the knee is decent by perhaps four inches and therefore a full two inches longer than is permitted by our dress code. Additionally, I must reiterate that heels are to be six inches, not one bit less. Lastly, wearing a blouse as see-through as you wore on that day, Miss Chivas, you should have known better than to wear a push-up bra. While I admire your desire to display your breasts as attractively as possible, you know full well that such displays of your fetching knockers are required by our dress code to be much more blatant than is provided by a push-up bra. If you are in need of some support, Tamiko in the mailroom has volunteered to provide you with her particularly skilled incarnation of breast bondage. Simply visit her on the third floor before you report to work.

4) Our policy clearly states that black outergarments are unacceptable, as they do too much to camouflage what lies underneath. Furthermore, wearing flat-soled boots is well beyond the scope of acceptable dress at our firm.

5) While red lace panties of the style you wore might be, arguably, allowed to slide on a casual Friday (given their little red hearts and bows on the sides), again, panties are expressly forbidden on all other days. Additionally, Mr Stern found your shameless display entirely distracting, as he was attempting to spank his secretary Julia at the time.

6) While your kinky little schoolgirl fantasy is commendable, I made it quite clear in your job interview that the only

schoolgirl who belongs at Stern, Stern, Grimm, Spankett & Harshass is a *shameless slut* of a schoolgirl. While your skirt was quite attractive, it was entirely too decent for the office, and wearing a brassiere is unacceptable in all circumstances regardless of how visible it is through your blouse. Furthermore, shamelessly displaying your white panties to Mr Stern strikes me as another example of your willful disregard of our policies. As mentioned in earlier paragraphs, Miss Chivas, you should have been entirely nude under that pert little outfit of yours.

6a) As a supplementary note to Item 6, I should like to remind you that any income you derive from giving blowjobs down at the waterfront should be provided to me in cash (and preferably not in wadded-up little $1 bills) for laundering through the corporate account. We can't be too careful about those IRS sons-of-bitches, Audrey, now can we? They certainly don't appreciate the value of a good blowjob the way our firm does.

7) I should perhaps clarify here that our office dress code is to be followed even when the position demands weekend work. I applaud your adhering to our dress code by eschewing a brassiere under your halter (which would have been unflattering in any event), but you violated our dress code in two ways: first, by wearing panties under those skintight little hot pants (did you get them at Next to Nothing? I've been thinking of picking up a pair of those myself) and second, by failing to wear high-heeled shoes. Your platform clogs, while presenting an admittedly cute '70s trailer-trash picture of your whorish little bitch self, Audrey, were again inappropriate for the office, even on a Saturday.

8) As you know, the co-ed company gym is to be used only when fully nude. I should note that you looked adorable with your nipples poking out of that tiny little leotard thing, but please, in the future, remember to strip naked before mounting the stationary bicycles – and don't forget to wipe down your equipment afterwards.

Audrey, please let me reiterate that your job duties on other fronts have been performed with great skill and enthusiasm.

Mr Stern frequently comments on the quality of your oral skills, and his secretary Julia particularly likes the way you always come when she spanks you. I, myself, have had the distinct pleasure of feeling you up on numerous occasions, and your juicy little cunt never fails to open right up to my mercilessly thrusting fingers. Furthermore, you look particularly eye-catching when you lift your skirt, drop to your knees and take it doggy-style; I think all of Stern, Stern, Grimm, Spankett & Harshass's partners will agree that you have the finest ass in town, and you never hesitate to give it up. Mr Spankett, in particular, has commented that if you weren't a shameless little cocksucking whore he'd love to take you home to Mother.

But I must take this opportunity to ask you to reflect on whether full-time employment as a paid submissive in a private brothel for poontang-obsessed billionaires is truly your long-term career goal. While I admire your love of spankings and your unthinking devotion to taking it in those filthy little holes of yours whenever possible, not to mention providing orally for any rampaging hard-on that appears in front of you regardless of the identity of its owner, I question whether the willfulness and cheek you've shown in your tenure here isn't indicative of an unwillingness to wholeheartedly adopt a submissive posture. Perhaps you are what educated office managers call a "smart-assed masochist."

In that event, despite your disciplinary record, I question whether you wouldn't do better assuming a leadership role at Stern, Stern, Grimm, Spankett & Harshass. Julia and Tamiko have both expressed the desire to feel that firm hand of yours on their behinds – in Tamiko's words, to "See if that horny little cunt can give as good as she can get." I concur. Your impressive showing in the recent catfight with Antoinette over who would get the last Pixie Stick in the company snack room certainly displayed a propensity for uninvited dominance, and once you had the little slut in a headlock you did show an estimable appreciation of the finer points of forced cunnilingus, not to mention great skill at the old "pile-driver." Furthermore, your skilled application of your throbbing sex to the little bitch's mouth despite her crocodile tears really demonstrated an ability to turn any administrative situation to your advantage. The result was a full acceptance of her defeat by Antoinette; in fact, the girl saw me immediately afterwards and when I threw her over my lap for disciplining I only had to spank her three times before the little vixen exploded in sobs of orgasm.

In short, you show a talent for exerting your own will, even in the face of resistant employees. I think you would make an excellent apprentice for me, Audrey.

Should you prove open to such an altered career path here at Stern, Stern, Grimm, Spankett & Harshass, I must caution you that along with the vastly increased salary and many career perks (frequent tongue-jobs from your subordinates being not the least of them) comes a great deal of responsibility. It will require improved commitment on your part, not to mention an intense program of mentorship in which I will teach you a great deal about administering punishment to horny little sluts who think they know it all.

Audrey, I hope the choice is clear.

Please report to my office at 5:00 p.m. for further discussion of this matter.

Cordially,
Tabitha Kelly
Office Manager

Bluegums

O'Neil De Noux

"My problem is," the man from New York explains, "I can't understand what they're saying."

I cover the receiver so he can't hear me laugh.

"They have the strangest accent," Noonan adds.

"It's probably a Cajun accent." I lean my freshly shaved face in front of the black, revolving fan perched on the corner of my beat-up mahogany desk. My aftershave tingles in the fan's breeze.

"Anyway," Noonan continues, "it's all in my telegram. If you can get those people to confirm Adam Kinzer died an accidental death, we'll be set."

"I have your telegram right here." I open the yellow Western Union telegram and press it flat on my desk.

"You don't have much of an accent," Noonan says.

"I'm from the city."

"Right." His voice is sarcastic as most New Yorkers tend to be. They live in the only real city in America, right? Center of the fucking universe, right? "Actually, you sound as if you've lived in Brooklyn."

"No, just the French Quarter," I answer. "And Bywater."

"What?"

"I've lived in New Orleans all of my life, except in the army." No need explaining how we don't have southern drawls here, except in the movies where we all sound like we're from south Alabama or like refugees from a French bordello.

"You're a vet, huh?"

"Fifth Army. I fought in the sideshow. Italy." That's what General Mark Clark facetiously called the Italian campaign.

Pressing the receiver between my chin and right shoulder, I instinctively rub my left arm where the round from a German Mauser smashed through my humerus outside Monte Cassino, sending me home early from the bloody mountain campaign. Kesselring's Gustav Line was one helluva sideshow.

"I think I spelled the name of that village right in my telegram," Noonan adds. "You guys actually have villages down there?"

"Bayous too and even swamps."

Noonan laughs for a second, then reminds me Mr Kinzer's daughter should be at my office at ten o'clock. My electric wall clock reads nine-forty.

"Any questions, you have my number." Noonan hangs up without saying goodbye.

I do too and pick up the telegram. Dated yesterday, September 16, 1948, it's from Empire Insurance Agency, New York, New York, authorizing two days work and reasonable expenses.

The village is called Cannes Brulee. I pull a Louisiana road map from my desk drawer but the village isn't listed in the index. I hope Kinzer's daughter knows where we're going.

Leaning back in my chair, I adjust the holster on my right side to let the weight of my snub-nosed, nickel-plated Smith & Wesson .38 rest on my hipbone. I prop my hands behind my head, close my eyes and imagine Kinzer's daughter as a long, cool blonde in a tight-fitting dress unbuttoned in front to show a hint of white, lacy bra. Getting out of New Orleans for a couple of days with a woman like that would soothe the likes of this thirty-year-old ex-cop, ex-G.I., half-Spanish, half-French, southern boy, struggling to make it as a private investigator. For the record, I'm six feet even with standard issue, Mediterranean brown eyes and wavy, dark-brown hair.

I hear a car door close outside, hear the outer door of my building open, hear light footsteps, high-heels I'm sure, hear the squeaky knob of my office door turning. I pull my legs down as a tall, dark haired beauty peeks in.

"Mr Caye?"

I stand and wave her forward.

"Call me Lucien," I tell her as she crosses to the stuffed chairs in front of my desk. She's in a lightweight suit; navy blue waistcoat and snug, tan skirt the exact color of the new tan suit I'm wearing.

She has a round, Cupie-doll face with bright green eyes and a wide mouth that looks sexy as hell, with that deep crimson lipstick. She's about five-nine, taller in heels, but still has to look up at me. Nicely built, she has a creamy complexion, like a porcelain doll. She's in her mid-twenties. No wedding band.

"I'm Ann Kinzer," she says nervously.

I point to a chair but she doesn't sit.

She tells me she knows the way to Cannes Brulee. It's on Vermilion Bay, south of Abbeville. She says she's ready to go immediately and would I mind driving. I follow her nice, round hips out into the sunny, September morning.

Parked behind my dusty, pre-war Desoto is a new '48 Cadillac with the new-style two piece, curved windshield, wide rear window and tail fins that remind me of a P-38 fighter plane.

Ann passes me her keys and climbs into the front passenger side, crossing her long legs as she settles in the seat, skirt just above her knees. I hurriedly dig my over-night bag from the trunk of my Desoto, put it in the Caddy's trunk, next to her pink Samsonite suitcase and climb behind the steering wheel.

Catching a whiff of her light perfume as we pull away from the curb, I take us up Barracks to Rampart and over to Tulane Avenue. The Caddy's engine is so quiet I can't tell if it's killed as we wait out a red light.

"My father was an executive for Western Union here in New Orleans." She pronounces each syllable, Or-lee-uns. An up-town girl. "He went fishing down on Vermilion Bay. He goes there often."

Not anymore.

Taking a right on Tulane, I go up to Clairborne Avenue and take it through the city, passing beneath the towering oaks along the neutral ground dividing the lanes of the wide avenue. New Orleans is such a mix of architecture, from the narrow streets of the Quarter, streets lined with lacework balconies through the bustling central district with its concrete high rises along Tulane

Avenue to the wide mansions dotting Clairborne Avenue. I watch the passing buildings and houses, the street workers next to Charity Hospital, dogs playing tag along Clairborne.

Stopping for the light at Clairborne and Carrollton, I see a streetcar conductor moving inside a streetcar at the end of the line. He's flipping the backs of the seats around for the return trip toward Canal Street.

Ann looks out of her window as we drive and I'm not about to try small talk on a woman who just lost her father. It isn't until we're atop Huey Long Bridge, high above the swirling water of the muddy Mississippi, does she speak again.

"He liked to get out on his own. He'd take his fishing gear on a bus and stop where he thought he'd get some peace and quiet."

The flat scenery along Highway 90 is one, long monotonous succession of scrub oaks and other swamp trees. I settle back and let the Caddy roll along the two-lane blacktop.

Outside New Iberia, as we pass along the wide grasslands of the Cajun prairie, I tune the radio to a Baton Rouge station with a soft-voiced reporter who tells us how the Allied airlift into Berlin just set a new record by flying seven thousand tons of supplies in defiance of the three-month-old Russian blockade.

I turn the dial until I stumble onto the ABC network and the familiar sound of a gong, followed by the wild chattering of Chinese gibberish before the announcer yells, "T-e-e-e-r-y and the Pirates!"

My God, *Terry and the Pirates*. Haven't heard one of those in a long time.

"Leave it, please," Ann says and we listen to the recording of the old show. Not bad, actually, with Agnes Moorehead as the Dragon Lady in China of 1937.

Turning left on narrow Louisiana Highway 14, we head through green fields of sugar cane, taller than the car. As the radio show ends, Ann turns off the radio, looks at me and says, "I think something bad happened to my father."

Sure. He's dead. Can't be much worse.

Her lower lip trembles. "I think something evil happened to him in the swamp."

"You know something I don't know?"

She shakes her head and looks out at the last cane field before
we pull into the small Cajun town called Abbeville, parish seat
of Vermilion Parish.

All morgues smell the same: formaldehyde with an ammonia
chaser. The coroner, Dr Louis Simone, a thick man with
handlebar moustache and dark, Cajun complexion, sits behind
his cluttered desk and waves us to the two chairs in front. He's
in a white, doctor's smock.

"De ting is, I just finish the autopsy report on your daddy's
death." Simone opens a drawer and pulls out a folder, which he
extends toward Ann. "But you know he body's not here. It's at
the Bultman funeral home in N'Awlins."

She looks at me and I take the folder which contains the
autopsy protocol for Adam L. Kinzer, white male, forty-nine,
of Versailles Boulevard, New Orleans.

"I want to tank you for all the details you give me on de
phone," Simone tells Ann.

"Excuse me," I say as I read the manner of death. "What
exactly is death by misadventure?"

Simone watches Ann as he answers, "It mean how somebody die from where he not supposed to be."

"By accident?"

"O'course. He accidently die in de swamp."

I look back at the report for the cause of death, which is
listed as, "Massive loss of blood and tissue."

"He didn't drown?"

"Mais no. He got tore up."

From the corner of my eye I see Ann stiffen.

"By what?" I ask.

Simone takes a deep breath and looks up at the ceiling before
answering. "When someone from de big city or like a Yankee is
killed by a gator, we don't put dat down cause it'll scare people.
Dey tink we live in some sort of primitive area or sometin'. We
call it *Death by Misadventure.*"

Ann gets up and walks out.

I stand, but have to ask Simone, "An alligator ate him?"

"Not all of him, but some."

Ann is waiting in the car.

As I approach, I read the Sheriff's report that is also in the file. It seems Mr Kinzer was out on the swamp in a rented pirogue. The pirogue came back by itself to where it was rented, a place called Magnolia Alley. Apparently, Kinzer's body had been found at the edge of Vermilion Bay by two men from Oregon on a fishing trip. The men left town the next day.

Sitting behind the steering wheel, I look at Ann who stares straight ahead.

"I'd like to head south now, to Cannes Brulee."

We take another two lane blacktop out of town and are immediately surrounded by towering cypress trees dripping Spanish moss. The road is elevated as we drive through a wide marsh, but there are dips which must flood when it rains hard.

Ann looks even more pale and I try not to stare.

"He wasn't bitten by an alligator," she says suddenly.

She uncrosses her legs, points her knees my way and re-crosses them. In the quiet Caddy I hear the sexy sound of her nylons rubbing together.

"We had a doctor examine him at Bultman's. Something else bit him."

I slow for a curve in the road and we move past several old plantation homes, not big ones like Tara, but smaller ones in dire need of repair. One on the left has been painted recently and Ann points to it.

"Pull in here."

As I turn into the oyster shell driveway, I spot a blue sign nailed to a cypress tree. The sign reads: *Welcome to Magnolia Alley*.

Ann reminds me this is the hotel where her father stayed as we park between two of the largest magnolia trees I've ever seen.

The hotel, converted from an antebellum plantation house, has a wide veranda surrounding the entire building. The lobby is quaint with furniture from the Great Depression, straight-back sofas, wicker ceiling fans and a bare light bulb Edison made, himself.

An ancient black man leads us upstairs. He wants to carry our bags, but I won't let him. My room is surprisingly big and clean with a view of the rear of the place, a wide yard leading straight to a deep, cypress swamp. Ann's room is across the narrow hallway.

The dining room downstairs is nicer than expected. After a couple bowls of crab gumbo (I have two and Ann only picks at hers), we walk around to the back of the place.

Ann steps off the veranda and walks briskly across the lawn, straight for the swamp. I follow until she steps around the first cypress tree and starts down a narrow trail of slightly higher ground.

"Where are you going?"

"To find the Chula." She doesn't slow down and I have to follow. Mosquitoes immediately attack me and I swat at them.

"The what?"

Ann looks back at me as I catch up. "The Chula's a who, not a what." She takes my hand and leads me along a well-worn trail into the swamp. There are other trees here, berry trees and huge, moss-covered oaks with vines wrapped around them like snakes. The swamp smells of decaying wood and stagnant water, the air thick with humidity.

"Who is the Chula?"

Ann lets go of my hand and stops a moment. She looks around, then takes a fork in the trail moving to the right.

"Don't laugh," she says. "The information came from a woman in Treme who knows about these things." Ann pauses and points to a tall, dead cypress. "Two hundred yards beyond that is a bent oak."

Ducking under a huge spider's web, I follow Ann and can't help wondering about some woman in Treme, the oldest Negro section of town, known for its voodoo rituals a long time ago.

Jesus! What have I gotten into?

Ann points excitedly at the bent oak and moves around it to a trail of wooden planks that becomes a footbridge over water leading to a shack. No, it's a flat-bottom houseboat at the edge of a wide body of brown water.

Just as Ann is about to knock at the screen door, a shrill voice calls out, "Y'all come in, now."

I step in first, Ann holding my left hand with both of hers. My eyes take a few moments to adjust to the darkness in the small cabin, which smells of boiling crawfish. A black cauldron simmers over a fire in a small fireplace on the far side of the room. A shadowy woman sits on a rocker in the darkest corner. Her eyes seem to shine.

She leans forward and the sunlight from the door illuminates the reddish, craggy face of an old woman. Her white hair is short and frizzy and her mouth far too large for such a tiny face. She's part Negro and part Indian, I'm sure.

"What you want?" she asks.

Ann inches around me and takes in a deep breath before asking the old woman if she's the Chula.

"O'course. But that ain't what you want, is it?"

Squeezing my hand, Ann says she wants to know what happened to her father.

The Chula extends a gnarled hand and says, "Gimme five dollar."

Ann digs a bill out of her purse and passes it to the old woman who crumbles it in her hand and holds it tightly. She leans even farther forward and stares intently at Ann.

"Sometin' bad happen to you daddy."

No kidding. He's dead.

Ann begins to shake and I pull her close, feeling her breasts pressing against my side, smelling the perfume in her hair. I feel something else too – my heartbeat.

The Chula turns her gaze to me, staring without blinking for a long minute until I break her stare with, "What does Chula mean? It's Indian, isn't it?"

"Means Fox in Choctaw. I yam part Choctaw and part African." The old woman looks at Ann again and adds, "You daddy die in de swamp, didn't he?"

Ann nods slowly.

The Chula closes her eyes. "He were wearin' a plaid shirt and dem dungarees. He were in a pirogue, fishin' wit de cane pole."

Ann lets out a high-pitched noise and presses herself even tighter against me. I wrap my arm even tighter around her waist, feeling the line of her panty along the side of her hip.

"The coroner says he was killed by an alligator," Ann blurts out.

"No," the Chula replies. "No. No. No." She shakes her head and opens her eyes. Craning forward, she whispers, "Bluegums got him."

Ann lets out a sound as if the air is being sucked out of her lungs.

The Chula stands and moves to a purple curtain. She opens the curtain to reveal a window so dirty light barely shows through. She looks out the window.

"Bluegums," she says. "Dey got him."

Ann shivers in my arms and when I look down at her face, her eyes are shut tightly.

"What are Bluegums?" I have to ask.

Her voice is distant and gravely. "When de slaves come from Africa, some escape into de holds of de slave ships. Lived off de rats in de holds. Learnt how to be real quiet in de leaky holds wif dem stones."

"Stones?" Ann whispers to me.

"Probably ballast. In the holds of the sailing ships, they used stones for ballast."

"Dat's right," the Chula says as she moves back to her rocker. "When de Bluegums live in de holds of ships, dey turned white, whiter den white folk. In de ships gone to New Orleans, some Bluegums escape into de swamp." Her voice became a harsh whisper, "Dey so white, dey almost shine at night. Dey all white, except for de big, blue lips and gums."

Jesus! She's giving us five dollars-worth all right.

"They killed my father?" Ann asks.

Before I can answer, the Chula says, "Dey eats men."

"Yeah. I'm sure." I chuckle. "And they only come out at night."

The Chula nods.

"They eat people?" Ann asks in a quavering voice.

"Dey eats men. Dey don't eat womens."

Ann is so pale, I think she is going to pass out.

"Dey do de unspeakable to womens who get caught on de swamp at night and de womens, dey never be the same again, no."

I shake Ann and she blinks up at me.

"It's a fairy tale," I tell her. "Come on. White zombies with blue gums?"

"Dey ain't zombies. Dey people. Dey a different race."

Give me a break, lady. I get Ann's attention and tell her that we're due back on planet earth about now.

"Yeah," the Chula agrees. "You betta' go now, afore it get dark."

Ann moves stiffly as I lead the way out.

It's twilight by the time we reach Magnolia Alley, just in time for supper. I eat two heaping helpings of the best crawfish bisque I've had in years. Ann eats a little. Even she can't resist the succulent, spicy crawfish.

We go out on the veranda after supper and walk to the back of the plantation house turned hotel.

"I wonder what they used to grow here," I say aloud.

A Negro maid, mopping the back steps of the veranda, stops to tell us there used to be sugarcane and cotton around here but the swamps done took it over.

Ann and I sit in rockers outside the back door. The swamp is extra dark now. The croaking of frogs and incessant buzz of crickets is drowned momentarily by the rising call of cicadas that flows out of the swamp in singsong waves.

Ann kicks off her heels and flaps the top of her waistcoat. "It's so hot," she says.

I hand her my glass of ice water and she pours some of it down the front of her blouse and says, "That's a little better."

She hands me back the glass and lifts her dress up, way up, all the way to her garter belt and loosens her right stocking, lifting her knee, pushing the stocking off to let it drop next to her shoes. Then she unfastens her left stocking, letting it drop. She leaves her dress up and leans back. As I stare at her legs she lifts the dress and flaps it, giving me a nice view of her sheer, white panties.

"That's cooler," she says, but now I'm hotter, much hotter.

"We can't go back to New Orleans yet," Ann says as she unbuttons her waistcoat to reveal the white, silky blouse beneath. Wet now, it's so sheer I can see the lacy bra.

"Why not?"

She turns those green eyes to me and they glisten in the yellow porchlight. "We have to see them ourselves, otherwise the Sheriff will never believe us."

I look into those eyes and I swear she doesn't look crazy. She just sounds that way.

"If *I* saw one I wouldn't believe us," I tell her. *Come on, now, Bluegums?*

She bites her lower lip as she looks away and I remind myself she's just lost her father.

A low-pitched howl echoes from the swamp. The sound rises and sounds like a wolf.

"What is it?"

"Probably a red wolf," I tell her. "Pretty rare, but still native to south Louisiana. There's one at the Audubon Zoo. Kinda small with a reddish-brown coat."

Ann uncrosses her legs, stands and walks down the steps to the lawn and keeps walking. I catch up just as she arrives at the swamp's edge. I swipe mosquitoes from my face as we stand there for long seconds. These mosquitoes buzz as loud as dive-bombers. Ann lets out a long breath and tells me she saw something.

I don't ask what and feel better when she turns back to the hotel.

I follow those round hips up the stairs into the hallway.

"You gonna be all right?" I ask when she turns to me outside her room.

She nods, steps forward and puts her hands atop my shoulders. She leans up, turning her head to the side and gives me a feathery kiss, softly, very softly. Her lips linger against mine for several heartbeats before she pulls away, turns and unlocks her door and goes into her room. I hear her set the lock.

Finally catching my breath, I go into my room, leaving the door open so I can see her door. Not bothering to turn on my light, I pull the straight-backed chair around the foot of my bed. I kick off my brown and white Florsheims, prop my feet up on my bed and watch her door.

Just before midnight I stand and stretch, take a hurried bathroom break and turn on the radio on my way back to my chair. I catch the end of a radio play and at midnight, the eerie notes of an organ come over the radio. A deep, male voice melodramatically tells me to stay where I am, because this is a time for mystery. He says this is the haunting hour.

I listen to a radio play called "Bird of Death." Something about men haunting carrion crows in a marsh. No it's a murder case. Something about a will, a short cut to making a lot of money. The deep voices are soothing and I get drowsy. When one of the actresses uses the word *"land-a-goshin!"* to the pernickety old man, it's time to turn the radio off.

Moving to the window, I look out. The moon is high now, illuminating the back lawn in a bluish hue. I open the window wider, and a warm breath of air slips through the screen into my stuffy room.

Stripping down to my boxers, I climb into bed. I'm a light sleeper and concentrate on the hall. Hopefully, I'll hear if she opens the door. No. I don't think she'll creep in here. There was something else in her eyes, something spookier than the creepy organ music on that radio play.

I wake with a start and realize I'm hearing something.

A long, low howl echoes outside.

I get up and move to the window. She's there, at the edge of the lawn. Her long, white gown glimmers in the moonlight, her raven's hair hanging loose below her shoulders. She turns to one side and I see her face in profile, her lips dark, her skin nearly as white as her gown.

Ann turns back to the marsh and starts down the trail we took earlier.

In the time it takes me to dress, hurriedly shoving my gun back into its holster, racing down the hall and down the stairs like a maniac, she's disappeared into the swamp.

Ten steps down the trail, I realize I can't see a damn thing. But I keep moving forward. A branch slaps my face and I slow down in the darkness. Ahead, I see a pale light. Stepping closer, I realize it is splotches of moonlight filtered through the openings in the canopy of trees.

I see her for an instant. She runs between a stand of trees, about thirty yards from me. Rushing forward, I trip over a root and stumble into mush. When I climb out, I've lost my left shoe. The chilling howl echoes again and I freeze, reaching instinctively for my gun.

The insects are silent.

I squeeze the checkered, walnut stock of my .38, holding it in the standard, two-handed police grip. Something moves behind one of the trees where Ann disappeared, but I don't aim at it, keeping my muzzle down in case it's Ann. It's a human form, but not in a white gown.

The hair stands on my arms and my heart thunders as I raise my gun slowly. The form moves behind the tree. A noise to my left turns me that way and I see the white gown floating a good distance away now.

I move that way, watching carefully.

The trail narrows as it sinks into an area with no trees. It's lighter here and doesn't look as wet. I keep moving forward until I reach another stand of trees. Easing around a towering oak, I catch a movement to my right and turn as a tall man steps from behind another tree. The moonlight catches his white face and I gasp.

Clad only in tattered pants, the man is a good half-foot taller than my six feet. Long arms dangle to his knees, he has a wide nose and thick, bluish lips and deep-set eyes. It takes a few seconds for me to realize he's inching toward me. I raise my weapon and he stops and then bolts away too quickly for me to do anything but finally let out my breath.

Bluegums! Jesus, what have I just seen?

My legs are wobbly as I move in the direction I last saw Ann. The trees are wider apart now and the trail easier to follow in the moonlight. I seem to be moving in a circle. It doesn't take long for me to be back between the trees.

Maybe Ann went to the Chula's.

I can't tell which is the way to the houseboat. I'm lost. I don't even know the way back to the hotel, but I know if I keep moving forward I'm bound to run into something. Stepping on damp ground, I realize I've lost my other shoe.

A noise off to my right pulls me that way, through more trees to an open area of water glistening in the moonlight. I hear the sound again, like a low moan. I follow the water, still moving to my right.

A flash of white across the water catches my attention. It's Ann, white gown flowing as she moves away from me, disappearing between cypresses.

I shout her name and try to follow, moving into water that's over my knees. A sudden movement in the water to my right causes me to jump back as something large slithers away quickly. Gator? Cottonmouth?

I move back to dryer land and look around. Shoving my revolver back in its holster, I work my way around the water. Sweat drips into my eyes, mosquitoes the size of pterodactyls feast on my arms and neck, slimy things cling to my stocking feet and I press on.

A white face appears from behind another cypress. I reach for my gun and it pulls back. I spot another tall, white figure in the distant light. It could be the same pallid-faced man. I keep seeing them peering from the shadows.

Finding higher ground between two oaks, I stop and listen but can only hear the call of insects. I wait. Eventually, a pale light seeps across the land. A splash behind me turns me in time to see three Bluegums standing there, staring at me.

I pull out my gun just as a piercing howl echoes through the swamp.

The Bluegums duck and dart away in separate directions.

I try to follow the closest, but he's gone in seconds. Then, I hear her again, a cry. Or, is it a moan? I hurry, but the sound fades, then comes again and sends a chill through me because I can't tell if she's crying for help or from something else. It sounds more like a cry of pleasure.

I stumble and realize I'm moving in circles, but I keep moving, trying to locate the moaning. Minutes slip away into maybe an hour, maybe longer.

I move back to the dryer land and move off, away from the cypresses. Suddenly, I step on a wooden plank. I recognize the bent oak and quickly move to the footbridge leading to the Chula's houseboat.

The Chula is sitting in the same chair. She rocks forward as I stumble in and leers at me with those glittering eyes.

"Ann!" I gasp. "She's lost."

"No. She ain't lost, no." The Chula points to a door in the far corner of the room. "She in dere, takin' de bath."

"What?" I move to the door, open it to a small room filled

with yellow candlelight. Ann, her back to me, sits in a white tub. She is humming as she lathers her arm with soap.

"Ann," I call out, but she doesn't respond. "Ann!"

She turns and smiles at me, then lathers up her other arm.

"Are you all right?"

Ann nods.

"You come back in here," the Chula calls out. "Leave dat girl alone."

I fall back into the main room. The only place to sit is on the small bed across the room from the old crone's rocker. I sit heavily on the edge of the bed and look back at the Chula, who is watching me pretty closely.

"She'll be fine, dat one," the old woman tells me. "But, you don't look so good."

I run my hands through my hair and pull out leaves, sticks and a small pine-cone, of all things. Sitting back, I feel the heat of the room on my face and I'm so tired I fight to keep my eyes open.

Ann comes out of the bathroom wrapped in a brown towel. She comes right for me, as if in a trance. She leans down as if to kiss my lips, but continues forward and collapses on me.

"Jus put her in de bed," the Chula says as I roll Ann off me.

The towel opens and my face is just inches from her silky mat of pubic hair. I wrap the towel around her as Ann rolls on her back, her eyes staring at me with a faraway look, a look of passion from some distant fire. She's breathing heavily and so am I.

"She still in de sex trance, right now, yeah."

I look back and the Chula waves me toward the foot of the small bed. I sit at Ann's feet, adjusting the stiff member in my pants as I sit.

"She's dreaming about them stickin' in her, yeah." The woman cackles, then adds, "She had de semen all dripping from her when she come by. But she clean up nice, yeah."

"They raped her?"

"Ha! She had de sex wit' dem. She *like* it!"

I watch Ann's pretty face for long minutes. She seems . . . so peaceful.

"You get sleepy; you go ahead and lay down with her, boy. She ain't gonn' bite you, no."

I recline across the foot of the bed. The weariness tugs at me and I feel myself drifting to sleep.

Something touches my face and I wake with a start.

Ann stands next to the bed. She's naked and the bright morning light falls across her round breasts, flat stomach and long, silken legs. Her small nipples are erect and their pink areolae seem to glow in the light as she leans them toward me.

She grabs my belt and unfastens it, working my pants down, then my boxers, yanking off my socks. I sit up and pull off my shirt, taking a second to see if the old crone is watching. The Chula isn't there.

Climbing on the bed with me, Ann kisses her way from my chest to my throat, to my mouth. We kiss softly, letting our lips caress before opening our mouths to let our tongues take over.

I cradle her breasts and knead them as she moves atop me. We kiss, a deep, long, heart-pounding kiss. Ann reaches down and guides me into her, shuddering as I slip inside. She gasps and lets out a little cry before starting long, rhythmic grinding. We fuck there on the old crone's bed, in the middle of the swamp where her father died.

My God, she's so hot and so loving. She rises on her hands and her face is radiant with pleasure. With her eyes closed and her hair bouncing back and forth Ann is so beautiful I can't help but stare at the fine lines of her gorgeous face.

The sensations seem magnified, the pleasure is so intense. Maybe it's because of our narrow brush with death, maybe it's being here in the Chula's cabin. Or maybe it's simply Ann, the beautiful, passionate woman.

Our hips grind as we both reach for pleasure. We climax together and Ann settles on me, kissing my face and neck, telling me I was wonderful, talking dirty to me. She tells me she wants to get under me, to feel me atop her.

I roll her beneath me and we kiss until I'm ready and we make love again, we melt into one another again and the heart-pounding rapture is so intense.

I've never lost count before, but when I wake up to the old crone's cackling, I realize I don't know how many times Ann and I fucked on that rickety bed.

We both look at the Chula who is back in her rocker, sinewy arms folded across her lap. I notice the sun isn't as bright outside.

"Now ya'll know de secret of de swamp, mais, yes you do."

The Chula points to Ann, who sits up behind me. "She gonna need more screwin', yeah." Ann climbs over me and heads for the bathroom without saying anything. I hear the bath water running.

"You join that gal in de tub. You betta hurry." The Chula looks out the open door. "It gonna be dark soon, yeah."

I climb into the narrow tub with Ann and we wash off, but I'm in a hurry and get out quickly to dress in the front room. It's still daylight out, but the light is beginning to fade.

When Ann steps out in her white gown that is brown from the knees down, the Chula tells her she now knows what the women around here all know.

Ann stares at her.

"You want some good sex? Some wild-ass, animal sex, you do dere yourself and de Bluegums give you a good screwin. Just like the way the white slave owners used African womens for dere lust, Bluegums do de same to white womens, who love it!"

I stand and buckle my belt as the old woman lets out a high-pitched laugh.

"De best fuckin' you ever gonn' get. Can't have no baby from dem. Can catch no disease from dem cause dey ain't human, zactly. Dey a different breed. Bluegums got dere own womens, back in the deep swamp. Dey make babies wif dem, but dey come out for us womens too."

I don't know what I'm going to do with this girl when we get back to town, besides reporting to Mr Noonan that her father died an accidental death. I do know I'm holding on to her as long as she wants.

We pick up our pace to hurry back to civilization before dark. What did Dr Simone say? Something about living in some sort of primitive area?

Jesus, we have to get back to New Orleans!

Pet Shop Girl

Lisette Ashton

"There you are." He spoke without surprise and Cindy got the impression he hadn't just expected her to be waiting in the pet store for him had he known she would be there.

She glared at him, her expression a mixture of annoyance, contempt and adoration. She had waited – not because she needed to, and most definitely not because she wanted to – but because he was her master and she was his slave. Regardless of when the instruction was given, or how it interfered with her life away from him, it was her duty to obey. "Yes, master," she replied stiffly. "Here I am."

"Give me your coat."

She glanced nervously around and, when she looked back at her master, she fixed him with a silent plea. There were shoppers and staff nearby, emptying shelves and slowly re-stocking them and, because this store was local for both of them, Cindy knew there was a danger of their relationship becoming public knowledge. She didn't want to take off her coat and beseeched him with her eyes. Fervently, she hoped he would sympathize with her unspoken wish.

He kept his hand extended and repeated the request.

Not disguising her reluctance, Cindy unfastened the belt from her trench-coat and pulled it grudgingly from her shoulders.

Like the expert in human nature that he was, her master seemed to understand her brightest hopes and darkest fears. He knew she dreaded public embarrassment and yet he appreciated that the prospect excited her beyond belief. Those few times he had reprimanded her within earshot of others – a sharp word spoken too boisterously, his hand tightly encircling her wrist while his eyes spat venom, and the obvious implication when he loudly called her a slut – they had all been exercises in the most exquisite form of torture. Even something as simple as the instruction to remove her coat, and the mortifying fear that someone would see what she wore beneath, was enough to send her pulse racing with loathsome arousal. From past experience she knew the worry that a passer-by could notice, or the horror of friends or strangers discovering her servile vocation, were only matched in magnitude by the relief that came when she realized her subservience remained a secret.

"I have a gift for you," he explained.

Her antipathy melted and, for the first time since she had received his summons, Cindy smiled. It was easy to forget the torment of the previous two hours since he had called; her haste in concocting an excuse and escaping from the office; the inconvenience of her quick rush home to shower and reapply makeup; and the nuisance of having to change into the uncomfortable outfit he expected her to wear. She brushed aside her memories of the pains that had come from struggling into the rubber lingerie – the agony of fastening the stockings' clips to her over-stretched labia, the discomfort of tying herself into the waspish corset, and the punishment of donning the six-inch stilettos – and she beamed for him.

"You have a gift for me? Really?"

He nodded.

Eager and excited, she blurted, "Where is it? What is it?"

He stepped away, beckoning with one commanding finger, and Cindy hurried to follow him down the aisle. Each step was a lesson in torture, the six-inch stilettos straining the muscles of her calves and inner thighs. It was impossible to walk normally in the footwear and she knew her gait was little more than an elegant hobble.

But the shoes were only a minor source of discomfort.

The micro-mini was painfully tight and obscenely revealing while the whalebone corset pinched her chest and squashed her breasts more effectively than the cruellest tit-bindings with which they had experimented. Her nipples, stiff with the arousal that always precipitated her meetings with the master, rubbed painfully against their rigid confines.

Yet it was the rubber stockings that caused her the greatest suffering.

The rubber stockings were an accessory that Cindy simultaneously loved and loathed. They clung beautifully to her legs, sculpted every curve with a polished, glossy lustre and the micro-mini displayed them to a glorious perfection. But, because they were secured to her labia, held in place by torturous clips that bit incessantly at her sex and mercilessly tugged downward, they made every step an exercise in anguish and constantly sparked her body with conflicting explosions of pleasure and pain. However, because her master had summoned her to follow, and because he was being generous enough to present her with a gift, Cindy tried to walk without complaint. It didn't matter that her body was aflame with perpetual torture. All that mattered was that he had been thinking of her.

"Now, stand still," he instructed.

Relieved to obey this command, Cindy did as she was told.

He was a good twelve inches taller than her and, even with the addition of the crippling heels, she only found herself on eye-level with his broad, manly chest. Standing so close to him, able to inhale the sweet perfume of his fresh sweat, she basked in the nearness of her beloved master.

With a broad smile, he revealed the gift. It was a short length of supple black leather, decorated with stainless steel studs, and equipped with a shiny, simple buckle. Not waiting for acquiescence, acting with the commanding authority of her undisputed owner, he encouraged her to step closer and looped the collar around her throat.

Cindy stood rigid, basking in the caress of his fingers against her neck, and shivering with gratitude. She considered the soft flesh beneath her jaw to be one of the forgotten erogenous zones, a sensitive expanse of skin that responded to every subtle kiss and caress more acutely than most other parts of her body. Cindy knew her own neck was extremely receptive to any stimulation and that made the collar seem even more special. Just as her master knew that she wanted to keep her servility a secret, he had also known exactly which gift would best please her. The collar reaffirmed their master and slave status and, sitting snugly against her throat, its presence was a constant reminder that he had been thinking about her.

"You can't ever take this off," he said firmly. "Not without my permission."

She touched the gift, her fingertips sliding from leather to steel. "I wouldn't want to take it off," she told him. With honest gratitude, she whispered, "Thank you."

She wanted to say more but a shopper was walking past, casting a curious glance in their direction. Cindy's master acted with his usual haste and forethought, his hands holding her cheeks, his cuffs concealing the collar, as he lowered his face to hers. His kiss, while only a ruse for the sake of discretion, gave her the opportunity to thank him properly. She explored his mouth with her tongue, pressing herself freely against him and revelling in the discovery of his swelling arousal. She gasped eagerly when she felt his pulse twitch against her and Cindy tried squashing her body closer. Their mouths remained locked together for a long time after the stranger had walked by. When the master eventually broke the kiss Cindy could see her eager smile reflected in his eyes and knew she appeared breathless and wanton.

"That collar isn't the only gift I have for you," he confided.

She stared at him puzzled and not sure she had heard correctly. It was touching that the master could treat her to one present but, Cindy thought, the idea that he had organized a second was more than any slave deserved. She started to shake her head, trying to tell him that he was being too generous, but the master was already producing a longer length of leather. Identical to the first gift in colour and style, fashioned from the same, supple black hide, and decorated with matching studs, the leash clipped easily onto the metal loop that hung close to the collar's buckle.

"The same rule applies to this leash as I mentioned for the collar," he said solemnly. As he spoke, he tugged her gently toward him. "You can't remove either unless you have my permission."

Her legs ached from the tension of trying to hold still and she happily stumbled in the direction that he pulled. She knew that no one else would appreciate the collar and leash he had given her but, in Cindy's eyes, that only served to make their meaning more personal. If it had been appropriate she would have happily embraced him and smothered him with a thousand grateful kisses. She almost wanted another stranger to walk past so her master would be forced to conceal her gifts as he had done before. Even though she dreaded the concept of any living soul learning of her servility, she would have happily faced that danger if it meant her master would kiss her again.

"Do you like them?" he asked.

She almost laughed at the understatement. "No. I don't like them. I love them."

He nodded approvingly and pushed a coin into her hand. "This is your final present," he said quietly.

Cindy glanced down at her palm, not sure what she was looking at until she studied it closely. The steel disc was drilled and fitted with a split ring so it could be attached to her new collar. The side she could see had been engraved with her name and, when she turned it over, she saw the master's address and phone number were printed on the reverse. His name was written under the words, OWNER'S DETAILS.

No longer caring about etiquette, and after taking a glance around to make sure no one was watching, Cindy pushed herself into his arms and hugged him. Her corset-flattened breasts pressed eagerly against his chest and her yearning for him had never been stronger. Coming to a sudden decision, confirming their mutual arousal by casting a quick glance into his eyes, she lowered herself to her knees. His erection pulsed hard against the tight constraints of his pants and she could see the shape thrusting at the fabric. Lovingly, she traced a finger over the swollen lump.

"Cindy?" he asked curiously.

She cast another glance around, just to confirm that no one was watching, then unzipped him. His length sprang through the slit immediately and she had a moment to realize she hadn't misjudged his excitement. The bulbous glans of his erection was a dusky purple and glistened with a smear of pre-come. The shaft was solid and hard and, before she could allow her fears of discovery to overwhelm her, Cindy pushed her mouth over the end.

"Are you sure we should be doing this here, Cindy?" he asked quietly.

Concentrating on her task, she didn't answer. She worked her mouth back and forth along him, sucking gently and languishing in the thrill of his taste. His pulse beat firmly at the back of her throat and, each time she tried to swallow him, she was reminded of the pernicious weight of the collar that hung around her neck.

A part of her wanted to recoil from what she was doing – they were in a public place and the danger of discovery grew greater with every passing second – but Cindy knew she had to show him her gratitude. As always, the fear of being found out, even the niggling worry that someone might surreptitiously notice, added to her spreading wetness. Her inner muscles trembled and her clitoris throbbed with a desperate urge for stimulation. Still revelling in the shameful prospect that would come from discovery, Cindy guzzled greedily along his glistening shaft.

He tugged on the leash, pulling her face briefly away, and she was stung by the fear that they had finally been found out. She cast a panicked glance around, grateful to see that there was no one observing them, and then wrapped her mouth hungrily around him again. Attacking his flesh with renewed fervour, she licked and sucked until his explosion spattered against the back of her throat. His seed was rich and thick and sickeningly noisome.

Swallowing each mouthful, her tightening throat constricting with the gentle pressure of the collar, she kept him in her mouth until he was totally spent. Remaining on her knees, she tucked his flailing length back into his pants before easing herself from the floor and smiling warmly for him.

"That was very kind of you," he said, fastening the name tag to the buckle of her collar. "And I'm sure you know I appreciate the gesture."

She wondered if he knew how much she appreciated everything about him, from the thoughtfulness of his gifts to the consideration he showed in keeping their relationship so discreet. He continually teased her with the threat of exposure, summoning her to assignations in public places like this shop, then firing her with a need to do something outrageously private and run the risk of discovery. But he always kept the secret of their relationship and Cindy was confident that he always would. Even in a public place like this one he had managed to dress her in a collar, leash and name tag without anyone noticing. He had even filled her with the grateful urge to openly take his erection in her mouth, and no one was any the wiser.

"Come this way," he said abruptly.

"Where are we going?" She was reluctant to walk toward the door without her coat because she could glimpse a concentration of shoppers queuing at the checkout. She tried to retrieve her coat from his arm but he deliberately kept it out of her reach.

Smiling indulgently he tugged gently on her leash. The collar pulled at her neck, making the name tag jangle musically, and she was forced to stumble toward him. "You can have your coat back once we're outside," he allowed. "But we have to pay for your gifts at the checkout before we can take them home."

Cindy's fingers went to the collar and she flushed crimson at the thought of the torment that lay ahead. She could picture her master leading her to join the queue while he still held the leash. She could imagine him artlessly exposing her secret to everyone in the queue, and making no apology or excuse as the girl behind the counter scanned the three items they were purchasing. Eyes growing wide with panic, Cindy scrabbled for the buckle and implored her master. "Please, sir," she began hastily. "May I take this off?"

His smile was thin as he reminded her, "Not without my permission."

Lilith Broken to Bridle

Molly Weatherfield

The two men trotted their horses down the path. It was early morning in April, not a fashionable hour for riding in London in 1890, and they encountered few other horsemen. But coming toward them, visible in the distance because her horse was galloping down over a rise, was a woman on a large chestnut, her own long mane of hair – chestnut as well – tumbling over her shoulders, loosed by the speed at which she was travelling.

"Unusually good seat for a woman," the older of the men commented. "Almost as though she were part of the animal. Damned unusual."

The younger man murmured something under his breath, which the older one took as agreement.

Damned unusual indeed, Lord Robert Arthur Ashleigh, 12th Earl of St Bartlemas, murmured to himself again, his eyes flooding with a warmth he hoped his companion wouldn't discern.

He'd begun to notice her the previous summer, galloping by with her hair tossed and her face flushed. Her horse was harnessed in the fashionable "bearing rein" style – head much too high for comfort, probably bridled with the knobbed "gag bit" as well. Cruel to the animal, he'd thought, showy and unpleasant; she was clearly a shallow, fashionable, most irritating young woman. He'd forced his thoughts brusquely to other things – the statues he was casting in bronze in the barn of his country house at Overton. And the beautiful roan mare he was exercising.

But he'd had to admit she was striking. Slender, upright, a

marvellous, fearless rider. It had taken him an additional
month to observe – because he'd tried so hard not to – the
odd symmetry between herself and her stallion. For she was as
extremely and compactly corseted as the horse was tightly and
smartly harnessed. Why – he'd found himself wondering idly
from time to time – why lace herself so tightly when she'd be
slim with no corset at all? It couldn't be comfortable to ride in
that condition.

But it had only been idle speculation until a tedious rainy
afternoon late in August. Trapped in his sister's back parlour
and leafing through a copy of *The Englishwoman's Domestic
Companion* (that's how hideously bored he'd been), he came
upon a letter to the editor describing the "delightful sensation
of feeling the tightly borne up horse spring under you when
you are equally tight-laced." Signed by a Lady Catherine
Andrews.

The London humidity was oppressive. His breath came
raggedly.

But there was some benefit to be gotten from a sister who
knew all the town gossip and delighted in sharing it. He had no
difficulty learning that the Lady Catherine was "of unim-
peachable breeding, a little withdrawn since she was widowed
in that horrid boating accident a few years ago. But utterly
devoted to her little boy. He's really her only occupation,
except for riding. I hear she's a terribly smart rider. Rather
pretty, I suppose, if you like that very severe look.

"But why do you ask, Robert? Lady Catherine isn't the sort
to interest herself in a lazy lord who sculpts in a barn. Actually
she doesn't seem to care about men or marriage at all – not that
she hasn't had offers. Well, she's rich enough, I suppose, not to
have to . . ."

The weather was clearing. He needed to take the roan mare
for a ride.

Of course she wasn't out that day. Or the next. And then he
had to go to Overton to attend to some repairs.

"And should I go ahead and tear down that small shed near
the barn – where we used to keep the donkey cart when you and
your sister were babies, sir?"

That had been the plan he and his steward had agreed upon. But no, he said. No, he'd changed his mind.

"Very good, sir. And if you don't mind my asking, what do you intend to do with that shed?"

"Remodel it, Wright. A personal project."

"Not into a new donkey shed?"

"Oh no. A folly, Wright. A folly was what I had in mind."

He worked night and day on the folly, servants and tenants staying away at his instructions. He'd get back to the bronzes some other time. And now that it was finished – shiny and painted, the leather and gleaming metal hung just as he wanted – he had to face the possibility that he'd never use it.

But there she was, on the paths. It was autumn now, the leaves ruddy in the crisp air. Wait, she was dismounting, her brow knit. She bent over her horse's leg, whispering, patting and comforting him.

He walked his horse over to her and asked if he could help.

Her dark eyes were large and liquid above a straight nose, a pointed chin.

"Oh no, thank you," she said, "Lucifer just has a stone in his shoe that I can't get out. It will be a long walk back to the stables, though."

Sorry, Lucifer. And thanks.

"You can ride my horse and I'll lead him back," he offered. But she wouldn't dream of leaving Lucifer when he was in pain.

And so they led their horses back together.

"You haven't been out for a few weeks," she said. He wouldn't have minded if she'd said it flirtatiously, but she didn't.

"I noticed you," she explained, "because you ride well, and because you're handsome, and because you obviously disapprove of my riding style."

He nodded, not knowing how to answer.

"There's cruelty, you know," she added, "and there's . . . cruelty."

"But can a horse tell the difference?" he asked.

She paused before responding.

"I think," she said, "that Lucifer loves me. Or pities me, more likely. In any case, he indulges me."

He cleared his throat. *Say it, idiot. Before you lose your nerve entirely.*

His voice surprised him by sounding quite natural.

"Actually, I've been considering . . . your riding style. I've recently acquired a new mare. And I've been doing some research. But I need a bit of help."

"Help?" She smiled and met his eyes.

"She's a magnificent chestnut," he said, "slender and high-strung, and with extraordinary character, I believe. I've resolved to start training her tomorrow."

Her black lashes swept over her cheeks.

"And you want my assistance."

"If you had the time," he murmured. "And the inclination."

She looked up at him again, for a longer moment than either of them had expected.

"I do have the time, Lord Robert. And do you know, I believe I have the inclination as well."

She'd been silent, but pleasantly so, on the way to Overton the next morning.

Ah, she said, stepping out of the chaise, it's good to move again.

She made polite compliments on the house and grounds. He thought the house had never looked so venerable, the grounds so lush, as with her striding through them in the austere black and white of her riding costume.

No, she didn't want any tea, thank you. Perhaps later, afterward.

They walked out past the barn to the folly, which was a small trim stable hung with shiny tack. There was a little training ring next to it, its fence painted bright white. He'd enjoyed building the fence.

"And the mare?" she asked, smiling.

He didn't answer.

"What's her name?"

"I call her Lilith," he answered. "The first woman," he

added before he could stop himself. "Well, *really* the first woman," he said.

The look she returned was calm, amused.

"How will you begin?" she asked.

"I need to make sure her tack fits," he answered. "I've never bridled her." Were her breasts swelling slightly over her corset? Her white stock front was so crisp it was hard to tell for sure.

"I don't know," he added, "if she'll submit willingly." And yes, a sigh escaped her, though her mouth retained its curve.

A moment of stillness. He turned to examine a riding crop hanging from a nail; slowly, he ran a black-gloved finger down its length.

And when he turned back, she'd begun to unbutton her coat, She undressed quickly, pausing only to hang each garment on one of the brass hooks mounted in a row on the wall. The sky was changeable, shadows sweeping through the little stable's open doorway. The lights and darks of her body shifted balance and combination with each garment she removed.

The jacket of black wool faille shrugged off her white shoulders. The white stock unwound from her long white neck. She'd stepped quickly out of the narrow skirt and lace pantaloons, revealing white thighs above black boots laced to her knees, taut white belly over dark triangle. He'd taken the riding crop down from the nail and was balancing it in his right hand.

"Part your legs slightly," he said. "And then turn to show me your hindquarters."

"My *hindquarters*?"

One said *derrière* to a lady. Or perhaps, in certain situations, *arse*. Her voice was husky, savouring his inappropriate word. A small dimple deepened at the right corner of her mouth.

He flicked the riding crop at her left flank.

"You won't be able to speak," he said, "after I've bridled you. But even now, you must respond silently and immediately to my commands." He hit her again and she turned to display the white, curved rump thrust out by her corset. It looked wider than it was, in contrast to her constricted waist. His fingers tightened around the riding crop.

She'd wear a tail, of course. He'd exercised some ingenuity designing that apparatus, with the help of a very understanding lady in London who'd been under his protection for some time.

But he didn't want to get ahead of himself.

He slapped her rump with his gloved hand, to communicate that she was to turn again to face him. She'd lowered her eyes, thick black lashes casting shadows on her flushed cheeks.

He put the crop into his boot and wrapped his hands around the waist of her corset. He wouldn't need the measuring tape in his pocket; his hands would never forget her waist's span. Or the other distances: small of back to top of the corset's bust; curve of hips beneath. Next time she visited, there would be a leather corset, with many cunning rings and buckles, to be used for . . . well, for all sorts of things.

So much to do. He cautioned himself to take his time. But he couldn't help the next impatient gesture. He'd waited quite long enough to see her breasts, thank you; he cut away the chemise from over the top of the corset with a penknife. Champagne goblets, just as he'd hoped, the nipples pink, erect, obedient: they stood at attention, swelling proudly beneath his gaze. He'd mount silver bells on clips with little spring mechanisms. He'd adjust the clips with jeweller's tools; they shouldn't bite, just pinch a bit. Cling to her flesh to fill the air with clear, shivery jingling as she moved.

She breathed calmly, eyes still lowered. How must it feel, he wondered, to accede so completely to the gaze of another?

"Outside." He prodded her to the door. "Where the light is better."

The clouds had passed, the sun glared on the bridle in his hand, the knobbed, arched metal bit that could make a horse froth at the mouth.

He raised her chin with the riding crop until he saw the bit reflected in her eyes. Or perhaps the spark he saw was fear instead. Well, she'd be a damned fool not to be a little afraid. But she forced herself to be calm, to relax and even to part her lips.

And to send him a haughty glance.

Fear had made her imperious, as he'd rather hoped it would.

Still, it wouldn't do. She gasped – and then softened – at his hard swipe against her thighs.

Oh yes, much better.

But how could he bridle her with all that hair coiled at her nape? He pulled out the pins, sending the hair tumbling almost to her waist. He brushed it with a wire currycomb into a tail at the top of her head, tying it clumsily with a leather thong. She'd need a groom, he thought; delightful and diverting as all this preparation seemed to him today, in time he'd find it tedious.

And her eyes? Calm, wary. If anything, they'd softened a little more as her mouth opened, moistened to receive the bit.

He adjusted the straps, pulled the buckles. He hadn't attached the blinkers yet; he wanted to watch her eyes as the bit settled to the soft roof of her mouth, the panic as she realized that the pain wouldn't go away. That every tug of the reins would make its demands on her in the same harsh language.

He stroked her hindquarters gently – he'd taken off his glove and was using a bare hand – he stroked her arse and breasts as she stamped her feet in terror. He played with the reins, pulling to the left and right. And upward too, communicating that she'd be required to keep her head smartly erect, her chin eagerly raised.

She stamped and shuddered, dancing, careening, trying to pull away. She knew better, of course, than to create this unnecessary pain for herself, but her fear was genuine – fascinating for both of them. He slapped her arse and shuddered in momentary wonder as her whole body flushed, her pink nipples turning deep brown. Sensing his arousal even through the monstrous veil of pain, she made a valiant, clever, sidelong feint, pulling one of the reins out of his hand.

He grabbed it back, jerking her head up and then suddenly relaxing his hold. She lost her balance and tottered forward. He pulled straight downward, and she sank to her knees in front of him.

"Head down." His voice was soft: no anger, merely the slightest suggestion of disappointment. He nudged her forward, the sole of his boot pressing her upper back and shoulders toward the ground, "You will learn to obey my hands on the reins." Her hindquarters rose as her shoulders sank to the ground.

He prodded her with his boot until she reversed position, skittering on her knees to present herself for punishment. Hindquarters. White and vulnerable. Never chastised.

"You will walk" (a swat of the riding crop).

"And trot and canter" (another).

"Prance and bow" (a third).

"As I direct you" (two more).

"And you will *never*" (a particularly stinging one, for emphasis) "oppose your will to mine." He gave her the other four strokes in measured silence.

She gasped and sobbed behind her bit. But she remained still beneath the blows, receiving them, he felt, with pride and generosity, the dark ropy-looking welts rising on her buttocks.

He pulled her to her feet, holding the reins loosely now with one hand and prodding her lightly to turn toward him. Proud. Calm. Broken to bridle and needing only the lightest touch to indicate his will. She was his.

Or was she? He trained her to pull carts, to preen in the dressage ring. She trotted all over the property, head high and proud, silver bells jingling, mouth exquisitely responsive to his hands' subtlest tug at the reins. He engaged a groom to wash and feed her, to brush her hair into a tail as elegant as the one that streamed from the cleft between the fresh stripes on her rear.

She liked his sculptures, too – often after she'd dressed herself they'd walk over to the barn and discuss how his work was progressing. And sometimes, when her son was on an overnight visit to cousins or grandparents, she'd stay the night in her little stable, sleeping soundly on straw and eagerly lapping oats and water from her trough. She had done so last week, in fact.

But no, Lord Robert, she'd said – and, to his shame, she'd had to say it more than once – she had no intention of marrying again. The boating accident, the loss of Edward (oh no, Edward hadn't been a horseman – his talents had lain . . . elsewhere) . . . she didn't think she'd ever recover from it.

Perhaps, she'd added, he shouldn't be spending so much

time with Lilith. Well, a handsome, talented, charming and awfully rich man like him should marry.

But she'd had a lovely, a delightful time this afternoon, no it hadn't hurt too much thank you, just enough, just the perfect amount. Her mouth had curved, its shy dimple flickering at the corner.

As it did this morning, in accompaniment to her cheerful greeting that wasn't it a lovely day Sir Robert, before she spurred Lucifer away.

The older man gaped. "Didn't know you knew her, Robert."

To which the younger one smiled sadly. "I don't. Not really," and galloped up the hill as though his life depended upon it.

Author's Note: Lady Catherine's letter to *The Englishwoman's Domestic Companion* is patterned on one that really did appear in the July 26, 1890, edition of the *Family Doctor*, a household periodical of the late Victorian era. The paradoxes of control of self and others, as well as the erotics of imminent rebellion under tight rein, were discussed with remarkable candour in these magazines, and are not my invention at all.

Everything but the Smell of Lilies

M. Christian

She is wearing spandex pants decorated with the bold black and white icons of half a dozen Tokyo corporations. Her hair is in dreads, spiced with glittering watch parts. Her shoes are new and intelligent, contouring to her feet as she runs out of the crowd towards the place. Her poncho is tiger-striped, the newest Eurotrash fad, and the bystanders can see, as she pumps those strong legs in those black and white spandex pants, that she doesn't have a top on, and that her nipples (flashing out from under the red and black of the poncho) are only covered by crosses of black electrical tape. She is a mix of black and something else. All can see – even in the midnight glare of Broadway's brilliance of neon, lasers, fluorescents, and headlights from blurring cars – that her skin is a brown – like stained wood. Her face is high-cheekboned, her lips dark brown, her eyes hidden behind mirrored image-intensifying glasses.

She is running for her life: down the street, through the sidewalk crowd – panic in her strides and panting breaths.

It is drizzling, like static. The muscle at the door to the place don't like it because it messes up their radar goggles. The clients don't like it because it gets their furs and leathers all wet. The street drek don't like it 'cause it pisses off the money and the muscle and they usually take it out on whoever is closest and can't afford to fight back. The limos come and go, a high-class and costly river of black plastic and steel. The rich's banter is light and sparkling above the rain and it blends, as only it could in the twenty-first century, with the chatter from the muscle's narrow-band radios.

She runs through the crowd, pushing street drek and citizens aside, glancing back over her shoulder at every opportunity. Panic lights her muscles, and she looks for someone to . . .

The words finally come out in an oscillating scream as she slams against the first ring of genetically enhanced, neurochemically boosted, electronically hot-wired thugs. True to their purpose and few remaining authentic brain cells, they smash back – surrounding her with dense muscle and squealing radios and pushing her back into the crowd.

Her hands are grasping claws, her nails draw blood in a triad streak down the face of one of them (who didn't blink against his conditioning), and her legs hammer against his ballistic-nylon pants. Her scream sounds like some kind of a weapon and the few cheap, off-the-shelf guards pull their own and track the high windows around and up – unable to distinguish one crazed woman from an armed assault squad.

Then an arm snakes out of the crowd and with a clean, sure swipe slices her throat ear to ear.

The city is big, but not so big as to make the woman's throat opening up and a fine fanning spray of arterial blood commonplace. The muscle reacts first, being now freckled with potentially dangerous infected blood, and draws and aims . . . at nothing but the already twitchy street. At the sight of the weapons being quickly drawn and dropped to street level, anyone who has any kind of survival skills instantly turns and runs. To a streetful of people used to sudden urban violence, turning and running is called a riot. Luckily for the muscle and the few really innocent bystanders, the riot had a place to go: down the street like water down a cascade, away from the Men with Guns, away from the dangerous Blood, away from the Rich People being thrown into their cars by their over-reacting bodyguards.

The street is nearly quiet very soon after save for the wailing of an approaching ambulance, called in a moment of rare altruism by one of the suits, and the last foaming, crackling bubbles from the woman's throat.

The ambulance, one of the new Matzitas, arrives with a pulsing Doppler scream, parting the few bystanders who linger over the cooling corpse of the woman. Pulling up to the low curb, it clamshells open and coolly – as only micromechanicals and smartpolyplastics can – reaches out and touches her with the preciseness of Japanese manufacture. Like-born, the medic steps from the uncoiling and undulating machines, orchestrating their movements with a palm-sized control unit.

Screened, probed, touched, sampled, sniffed, smelled, she is neatly picked off the cold and dirty sidewalk and swallowed into the ambulance's expanded interior.

Leaving behind the bodyguards giving statements to bored cops, the impatient suits, and the hungry stares of the onlookers, the ambulance closes with her and the medic inside and screams away.

Death is too easy for me. See it every day. No, that's not the truth: some days I sit in the hospital bay with the warm and humming ambulance and just wait for it. But the deaths I do see – the leaking, shrieking, whining, crying ones – reach beyond their occasions to swallow me, even when I do nothing but sit in the bay and watch teevee. One of those deaths can last days for me, stretching beyond its instant.

It's easy to die, when you're like me. I mean it's easy to die, period, man. Slip in the tub, get iced for your wallet, the new strains, acts of God – all of it man. Easy as pie to lie down and croak – and it's easy when you're like me to get right back up again.

I try not to get used to it, try not to have them stretch so far that they start to die in my dreams, when I eat, when I'm away from the ambulance. But I've been at it too long – they die in slippery, out-of-focus dreams and even when I sit down for dinner, soup becomes blood, meat becomes . . . meat. I look into everyone else's eyes and expect to see the things I've seen reflected back at me, but I don't. I don't know what they see, but it sure isn't what I see – what feels like every day.

Like me, yeah. Painful, sure, but you just gotta lie back and think of the money. Isn't that how it always is? Fucking for money, getting fucked for money – I just happen to get fucked over for money, that's all. The big fuck, maybe, but still . . . I'm a whore. A whore with a specialty, that's all. A real specialty.

I look at people differently, I guess. You do that when you see them dying, when you see them hurt and crying. I don't see them as they always look – smiling, laughing, getting angry . . . kissing or touching. . . . I see them broken and leaking, discovering that they're meat and bones and blood. I see them in pain. Had a few girls in my life, even have two myself, now, but it's strange to see them, hear them and even crawl into bed with them when you see the things I see. I keep expecting them to break, to leak, to cry. I see it all the time – so often it doesn't seem right that they aren't hurting or dying.

Morley rigged it, the sick bastard. "There's a need, babe, a need we can fill." Yeah, you bastard – creeps like to fuck dead girls, so what do they need? You fucking guessed it. Problem is your usual dead chick will get all, kind of . . . unappealing after a point, right? What you need is a dead chick who can get up and walk out when the John's finished. What you need is me – or me after Morley.

Sometimes, the most real women I see are the ones who are lying still and cooling in the ambulance with me. The rest of them, the rest of the people I see, are just waiting to see me.

"Just rearrange you a bit," he says and gives me to his pals with the machines, the plastic parts, the implants. Technique noir, black tech, nasty bedroom tech. I remember one of them, this fat Chinese with skin like cheese – a clicking and whirring part of his face looking me over with God knows what: radar, microwaves, frigging sound for all I know. I remember him for the clicking and the whirring, and how he only spoke a few words of English. He also fucked me, I'm sure, while I was zoned under his machines, under his knife. My pussy smelled bad the next day, something that could've been come leaked out – smelled an awful lot like cheese, too.

Like this one, here: they look so peaceful, so rested and still. Their skin is so cool, so smooth. Even with the blood . . . but I can fix that, a little swipe with disinfectant, a dab or two with a biohazard absorbent towelette. Such a long wound, a thin slice from ear to ear. Clean, must have been a fractal knife, or a monomolecular wire. Still, she is beautiful. Striking. Frozen at the peak of her beauty by the knife, or maybe that wire. Her face is like a magnet and I have a hard time doing the routine things I'm supposed to do. The implant and blood-screen fall away because of my entrancement. It's all I can do to sit in the back and let the ambulance drive itself to Mercy. She has high, sharp cheekbones; a nose with just enough of an upturn; lips full but not cartoonish. She has such a natural, wild look, this one has. I can see her not lying, cooling, chilling, in the back of my ambulance, her negative signs showing on half a dozen flat-screen monitors, but rather running under a hot sun some-where, naked and warm, wild grasses shushing by her fine, perfectly turned legs, not-too-big, not-too-small breasts bob-bing and swinging free and bare under the same glowing sun. She isn't a casualty, a DOA, a street drek; she is a primeval forest huntress, a priestess of a land long ago paved and sterilized.

I'm a corpse. I'm a professional victim, a stiff for hire. Pull my string (okay, slit my throat, strangle me) and I do my little number. And while I'm down there on your floor, on your bed, you can do whatever you want to do to me. Special job, as only Morley's dark doctors could have done. Don't know all of it myself – one lung gone for a refillable tank of air (so no breathing), blood now flowing through the back of my neck so my throat can get sliced or crushed if you like that kind of thing. On cue I get all cold, my nipples get all stiff, my cunt chills, my eyes lock up (in case you like to see your reflection in them when you fuck my stiff self) and I'm dead. Everything but the smell of lilies. Pay in advance, don't break the rules, and you can kill me, fuck me, and go back to the wife and kids. It's a living, dying is . . .

So beautiful. So natural she looks, even cooling and stiffen-ing. She is a statue, an image on clear water. I try to be quiet, watching her, so as not to wake her. The image of her, quiet and still and not really, truly dead is so strong it's almost enough to dissipate the clean wound across her throat, the whining instruments all crying *she's dead* and the few specks of blood that remain on her poncho. Carefully, so as not to wake her, I move the poncho aside to better see her breasts – and so lovely they are: just the right size, somewhere between a nice cleavage and too small. They are fine, tight cones of deeply tanned skin. I can't see her nipples, covered as they are by crosses of tape (a recent style). I notice as I move the poncho that her pants end a bit below her navel, that her navel is pierced with a steel ring, and that she has the tiniest of bellies – a gentle rise to her stomach that seems so perfect on her. It adds something to her, this little belly does – when everyone can look like anyone (with enough money, of course) this little pot brings her right down to me, in the ambulance. She is a woman, a wild and fiery woman – all heat and hunger. Dead yes, but more alive than most of the meat I haul to the hospital.

Doesn't help that I like it. Yeah, Morley, make me into a dying doll. Yeah, you freaky creep, remake me so I can die on cue. Wouldn't work, you knew, if I didn't get off on it, too – maybe not croaking for every fat, rich slob, but – shit – I dig stepping into even the weirdest fuck's fucked-up trip. I don't get off, really, about lying here all dead, brain still clicking away but body faking being all cold and still, but I sure as shit do when I watch them hump my stiff body. That's what gets me off, man, that's what Morley saw as he sucked my toes and came in my shoe – that I come when you come from doing your weirdest shit. I get off watching them all – yeah, Morley, too – dig down in their weirdest shit and make me do it. That fucking makes me come . . .

My still little angel. *Justine Moor, 27, type B+* the info from the ident card in her slim little wallet going past my eyes, into the mind of the ambulance. I watch her still chest, her fixed and dilated eyes. Even with a clotted line across her throat she is more alive than anyone I have ever seen. She is more alive, more vital, than Ruth or Vivian, than the other attendants at Mercy Hospital, than the doctors, than the people who flash by the window of the speeding ambulance. She is immobile, chilling but more alive than anyone, than me – I can't resist.

She pulls me down to her with the force of her dead aliveness and I stroke the cool belly, run my quivering fingers up her sides to her lovely, pert breasts. I glide my hand up to cup them, to hold one like a still pillow, her nipples powerfully erect beneath the crosses of tape. My breathing is a hammer in my ears and my cock is painful iron in my uniform pants.

Yeah, Morley sure can pick them. "Justine," he said with that smile, that voice, "become a hardwired dead girl, a chilling and stiffening hooker. A corpse for rent." Slice my throat, strangle me, fuck me – pay me. Pegged me, looked right into these eyes and picked just the right job for a fucked up rent-a-corpse like me. Like tonight, man, Morley comes right up and says "– die for me, babe." Sure, no thought, no problem, man. I die for clients, right? So why shouldn't I die for my fucking pimp? Some bent job, some need for a diversion – what better than little me doing the poor street drek routine, right up to the suits and their rented guns, then Morley with his straight-edge right on cue to slice my pretty throat. Just another Saturday night for me. All I gotta do is get to the damned hospital, turn myself back on, get up and get out. Morley's got his distraction, I got my money. All is right with the – what the fuck? What's this guy doing? Shit, man, of all the fucking ambulances I gotta get one with a perv. Fucking-A, man, just my luck. Shit . . .

So still and quiet. So perfectly frozen. Carefully, I remove the tape from her breasts. Her nipples are hard – little fingers, not thumbs. Deep brown like chocolate babies, wrinkled and hard like tire rubber. I taste one, the right one, and it reminds me of a pencil eraser dipped in chilled water. It seems to fill my mouth – the fear, the excitement, the humiliation making the universe balloon till there's just me, the background whine of the ambulance, and this dead girl's nipple in my mouth. My hand moves without me to cup the breast, to feel the weight of it, to gently squeeze to know its shape: it is a firm breast, a young breast. Not warm, no, but soft like silk with a thick African-mixed skin. Her skin has the weight of a black woman's but the color of coffee with way too much cream. As I lick and suck at her glorious nipple, my cock aches with the feverish pounding that fills my head and pushes the whine of the ambulance's electric motor to somewhere in the deep background. I hear the sound of my lips sucking and kissing her breasts and nipples. I hear my hammering heartbeat and the hurricane of my breaths going in and out.

What a fucking freak, man. What a professional, roaring, twister! The guys who do me know I can snap out and sit up, right? This guy ain't one. He's a corpse fucker and I'm his girlfriend, man. This guy ain't playing a fucking game with a specialty hooker. I almost switch my heart back on and take a nasty ol' breath and sit up and sock him one, right? But then I remember Morley, with his cold eyes and his jailhouse tattoo of chains going around his neck (one link per year) and I remember those chilling words: "Just give me enough time." And I'm fucked, I'm screwed, "cause it ain't been enough – not nearly enough – so I gotta lie down like the nice little stiff that I am. At least the guy knows how to suck a tit – dead or not.

I burst into flame, then. The heat of me blasts through my head and my cock and my lips. I kiss and lick her other nipple, squeeze and knead her other tit. She is cold under me, like from an ice water bath, but I am flaming, smoking from my lips and cock. Roughly, more rough than I would even have been with Ruth, Vivian – anyone breathing – I grab at her pants and give them a hard pull down, relishing in the smoothness of that glorious little belly. I get them down, and for the first time see her cunt. It is a glorious cunt, precisely shaved like hair was never there: a coffee-too-much-cream triangle padded with a delightful layer of so-soft skin. Her lips are tucked inside, so all I see is a faint brown crease, that delicious mons, and the hint of pearly clit. I struggle with her pants, stretching and pulling at the elastic stuff till I realize they are not coming off over her shoes. I quickly take out the safety shears and slice them away, leaving her strong legs and glorious cunt free. Now that I have completely fallen in, I am feverish and panicked: it is a long trip to Mercy, but not that long. I have minutes but not all that many. But, still, she is here, and my panic only adds an edge to my straining cock . . .

Fuck, fuck, fuck, fuck – not only a fucking corpse fucker but a fucking corpse rapist. Shit, shit, shit! I almost pop my cork, blink and tell him to get the fuck away from my cunt when I remember again Morley's cold eyes and stay down. How many ambulances, man? How many tricks in this city? And I pick the two on the one night when I can't screw up. Great. Just great. Oh, man, not the fucking pants, man, they aren't cheap – oh, well. I'll get Morley to get me some others when I – oh, Jesus, this is one sick fuck, man, one sick fuck . . .

I can't resist. Even dead her pussy is wine, a pure lovely vintage. In the cramped inside of the automatic ambulance, I get down between her strong legs and part them just enough – just enough to get my face down to her cunt, spread her lips and taste her. Her clit is big, her juices are chilled. Not white wine, red – not blood, just served cold, chilled. Her lips are so soft, like fine silk and I explore her cunt with my tongue, feeling her tiny inner lips, the hard cleft between her clit and her cunt proper. I slide my hand under her hard ass and squeeze, feeling the softness there, too, but also the relaxed, dead muscles that I could tell would have been iron, knotted steel when she was alive. Somewhere along the way I reach and grab my cock, start to roughly yank at myself, driven by the high-octane of her and the whine of the ambulance that I am sure, at any second, will drop as we enter Mercy's medical bays. My fear and disgust and excitement ram into me and make my cock an iron, burning rod at my waist.

God, he's a fucking freak! My cunt's sopping, man. I'm dead and he's licking my corpse cunt, teasing my clit and I'm fucking coming. Can't move, can't until I pop my programming cork and climb all the way out of my "zombie" act, but that doesn't stop my clit from jangling like a bell. The comes echo and bounce around inside me. Can't cry, can't scream, can't grab the fucked-up freak's ears and jam his maniac face down hard onto my clit but, fuck, fuck, fuck I can damned sure fucking come. Can't scream, man, can't jerk and yell and cry and all that damned embarrassing stuff I do normally when someone's going after my clit like trying to dig the pearl out of an oyster, but I sure as fuck am coming and coming all over the place: I can feel it ripple and surge and tear and buck my brains out. My eyes are for crap anyway when I'm dead but now they're strobing and flashing all these gorgeous colors and all I can think, all the words that I can get to run through my head are that I hope he's so weird, so fucking bent, that he fucks me – cause I really want to get fucked, like, real fucking bad.

I want to fuck her. My cock hurts, and the one place, I know, that will make it feel so much better is the cold, wet and stiff confines of her cunt. With the taste of her still on my tongue and all over my face, I fuss and mutter with my belt and pants, finally getting them down as the ambulance rolls neat and computer-assisted into a high-banked turn and I know I have maybe five or ten minutes before the bay, before Mercy, to finish. My cock is finally out, and I clumsily position myself and move her cool legs out of my way. Despite the pain I feel from my cock, the horrible tension, I resist just sinking myself into her – wanting to make it last just so much longer until I taste her dead cunt with my cock . . .

Fuck me fuck me fuck me – fuck! I hate when they fucking tease! Get it in me you sick fuck, I scream in my paralysis, in my cooling and immobile jail cell of my reengineered and redesigned body. Fuck me, you sick fuck!

I sink myself into her. Her cunt is cool, but not cold – maybe my own heat warming her, maybe her core temperature is still pretty high. But you can't think of medicine and science when you fuck . . . fuck a corpse. I push myself in and feel her froth and juices swell around my cock, feel her tight yet loosening muscles surround and squeeze my cock. I think two things as I fuck her, my mind split by excitement and a cramping shame: I think of this beauty I am making love to, think of her incredible body, her nipple that I again put in my mouth and suck and kiss and nibble, and I think of fucking a sucking chest wound, of a sultry corpse, or a graverape. My cock is ramming, hammering into her beautiful cunt, into this delicious corpse and I tighten and spasm and jerk and scream as it all starts to come out . . .

Fuck fuck fuck – that's it, I've reached my top. How many fucking (fucking fucking fucking) times is a fucking corpse supposed to come, man? Fuck Morley and his rip, fuck him and me as his little distraction for the guards and the suits, I think the magic word, twitch that nerve-cluster I didn't have before Morley got his black medical hands on me, and I come up and out with a rush of heat, a screaming wave of fully reactivated nerves. I pull myself up and out of the grave, restart my heart, take a deep, painful, breath, feel my skin awake with an S/M crash of blasting pain (imagine your whole body falling asleep then waking up) and I scream into his face as he fucks me. I put my legs up and around and lock them behind his back, in that special place guys have just for this kind of thing and I fucking ride his own screaming bucks. He lets go of my nipple and gives me the cutest look of pure lust and fear I have ever seen, but the sick fuck doesn't stop fucking, doesn't stop jerking himself into and out of my now-warming, now steaming honey-pot. He screams and yells and keeps fucking then jerks and squirms . . .

I ain't done yet, man, I ain't at all done yet. I push and pull on his stiffening and quivering muscles until I've had my own – and it comes like it has never come before: a fucking torrent of good stuff crashing down and all over me and I scream like I never screamed for Morley, for a client (when they're into murder), I scream the best scream I have ever screamed, bucking and clawing at his cooling back until I can't move any more . . .

The ambulance arrives at Mercy. It whines, fading to a simple warning burst of sound as the medicals pour from the hospital's service bays. Nestling into its sockets and data-ports, it opens organic and precise, spilling out its gurney into their waiting arms.

With technological precision, the body is brought into an emergency suite and the hospital sets to work with an array of micro-surgical tools resembling a squirming, undulating, chrome palm frond. Fluids are pumped, charges are sent, nanomachines are injected, and even a cloned and altered heart the size of a large orange is mated to his body. These and many other (as many as his body and minimal medical insurance can stand) attempts are made but in the end, after some four or so minutes, his body is simply dumped into the hospital's vast and frightening organ storage facilities for recycling – and his next-of-kin is automatically sent an apologetic videomail message.

Walking home through a drizzle that is creeping towards a hard rain, she doesn't feel any of it. Some stare at the pale gash that runs from under one ear and across her throat to end at her other ear – but since it closely resembles a new young fashion statement, most dismiss it casually.

Justine doesn't think all that much as she walks the three miles back to her capsule apartment, but once she thinks very, very clearly, cleanly: *Morley, Morley, Morley . . . I hope it was a good score, a grand score. You owe me, you motherfucker and you owe me big . . .*

You sure can pick them, Morley; next time I get to fuck a corpse – next fucking time, man, you get to be all cold and stiff.

Hope you like playing the corpse, man. Cause I just developed a new – hmm – taste . . .

Ten Minutes in the Eighties

Alison Tyler

For ten minutes in the eighties, I was beautiful.

I've been beautiful since, but never like that.

Never again.

Before those magical ten minutes took place, I not only *wasn't* beautiful, I was hardly noticeable. Simply put, I was just another lowly freshman at UCLA, one of 40,000 others who called the campus home. Shy, insecure, terrified – those three adjectives fit me perfectly. In a land of voluptuous vixens and bottle blondes I had no idea that, with my sleek build and darkly mysterious features, I was far more than pretty. It never occurred to me that men would – and did – find me attractive or that all of the things girls lay awake at night and hope will happen to them would eventually happen for me.

Rather than put myself in a position to be rejected I didn't give the guys a chance to approach. I kept my peers at a safe distance by creating a mood of constant motion. I hurried to class, spent hours studying in various libraries around campus, and used my free time cultivating miscellaneous interests as a deejay at the college station and a flunkey on the student paper. I was a good girl all year long until the end of spring finals, when I finally let down my guard and got drunk with the rest of the students on my dorm floor. With no prior drinking experience I downed five beers in one hour, and wound up, to the great surprise of my dormmates, making snow angels on the cool turquoise-and-white tiles of the bathroom floor. Five beers will knock out any lightweight. And at five foot three, and 105 pounds, I was a lightweight.

In the morning I experienced my first-ever hangover. For

hours, I lay on the slim twin bed and stared at the ceiling, willing the rushing sound in my head to subside. When I eventually took a chance at walking upright, I realized that I'd missed the cafeteria's sole Saturday daytime meal. If I wanted to eat I'd have to wait until six p.m., or fend for myself. Miserable, but yearning for sustenance, I took a taxi a mile off campus to the nearest grocery store. For a long time I wandered aimlessly up and down the aisles, filled with an overpowering craving for something, *anything*, but not knowing precisely what. After choosing two items with the care that some women use when buying expensive jewelry, I took my place in line at the checkout. My self-prescribed day-after cure was a bottle of tomato juice and a can of Pringles (the only things in the whole store that seemed even mildly appealing).

It was while I was standing there with my red plastic basket in hand that I started to become beautiful.

I didn't know the transformation was happening right away. All I knew was that the handsome, dark-haired, forty-something man next to me in line was staring at me, his head angled so that he could look at me over his shades. I felt myself flush, pale skin turning scarlet, embarrassed because I had on the clothes I'd worn during the festivities the evening before, the clothes I'd ultimately slept all night in: faded blue jeans, a rah-rah-style University T-shirt in Bruin colors, and a thin navy blue hoodie. My turbulent raven curls had escaped from their standard ponytail style, falling well past my shoulders to reach the middle of my back. Purple smudges of fatigue made my brown eyes look even darker than usual. I hadn't bothered with makeup of any kind.

Nervousness made me bite into my bottom lip. I felt overexposed beneath the fluorescent lighting and underprepared for a confrontation with a stranger. I tried to look extremely interested in the multitude of processed foods filling the fat woman's cart in front of me, but I felt the man staring relentlessly, and so I slowly turned to face him. As if encouraged by my action, he took a step closer to me and, in a low, soft voice, he whispered, "You have a look."

The way he said the words gave me an unexpected wave of confidence. Or maybe it was the lack of sleep talking. I don't know precisely why, but I met him head on and said, "The drunken, slept in my clothes, barely post-hangover look?"

He shook his head. "That's not it. Something else. Something special."

I bit my lip again, harder this time. Here was a true Hollywood-style line, but I was no Hollywood starlet. Flustered and confused, I looked down at my white Keds, looked out the window at the half-filled parking lot, looked up at the bars of ugly lighting. Suddenly it was my turn to pay for my groceries, and I fumbled in my pocket for my folded bills, then grabbed the change and my small paper bag of supplies and started to leave the store. The man abandoned his own few items on the gray conveyor belt and hurried after me.

"Where are you going?" he asked, his hand on my shoulder. I didn't flinch away from him, but I pulled back, surprised by the power in his touch.

"Back to campus. I have a cab over there—" I gestured to the far corner of the parking lot. The blacktop glittered where shards of broken glass had melted into the oily asphalt.

"Tell him to go. I'll take you." He hesitated, as if he could sense the insecurity that had cloaked me for so many years, as if he could actually feel it. "Anywhere," he promised, "I'll take you. Wherever you need. Wherever you want to go."

I looked at him carefully. Here was the exact situation my parents had spent my entire teenage life worrying about and doing their best to protect me from. I was going to take a ride with a man I didn't know. And all their warding off of evil spirits did nothing to stop me. For some reason I obeyed his command, paying off the cab and following him to the expensive, shiny silver sports car parked nearby. The car gleamed like foil in the bright sunlight.

"You should never accept a ride with a stranger," he told me severely as he opened the passenger door. "Especially a stranger in Los Angeles."

"I know."

"Then why are you choosing to ride with me?"

I smiled. I had been given the perfect answer. "You have a look," I said, and he laughed as he got into the driver's side and then slid an unmarked cassette into the tape deck. "I'm a music producer," he told me. "I just heard this tape for the first time. The boy's going to be huge."

It was Terence Trent D'Arby's "Introducing the Hardline According to . . ." and that music is embedded in my mind as a soundtrack to what happened next. The man drove me to his house high up in the Hollywood Hills where the movie stars live. He led me through the huge, well-decorated rooms, all the way to the mammoth patio in back. There, he gently took my clothes off my body and had me touch myself while he watched. And I was beautiful. For ten minutes in the eighties, I was so beautiful it was hard to handle.

I'd never done something like this before. Technically, I was a virgin. I'd had some kissing experience in high school, some backseat petting at a local drive-in theater, but shyness had kept me pure. Now, in the heat of the day, I touched myself while a stranger watched. I ran my hands over my body. I let my fingertips graze my nipples until they stood up hard and erect. I kept my eyes on the man as I let one hand wander lower, reaching to touch my pussy while he watched. The pool behind him was a true, aqua blue. The sky above matched that Technicolor brightness. Standing there on the tiled deck, looking out at his multi million dollar view, I put on a show with my nakedness and my roving touch.

"That's right," he said, nodding, his voice hoarse as if he were as surprised by my actions as I was. "Do that."

He was seated on a deck chair, with his hands on his thighs, his sunglasses low down on his nose so he could look at me over the rim. I felt power in being naked. Felt a power in the way he drank in every touch of my fingertips on my stripped-bare skin. It was as if he were touching me as well. When my fingers found the wetness coating my lips, he sighed before I did. I closed my eyes and leaned my head back, arching my slim hips forward, running my hands over my hipbones. The tiles were hot under my bare feet. The air was still and clear. My hair tickled against my naked back. My eyelashes fluttered against my cheeks.

I knew that he wouldn't touch me. Not unless I invited him to. Not unless I asked. But I didn't. I didn't need anything from him except his gaze. Because the way he stared at me –

that's what did it. That was the magic that made me beautiful. I used my fingers to spread my nether lips wide apart. I ran my thumbs up and down over the ridge of my clit, first my right thumb, then my left, then both together, vying for control, until I knew that I was seconds away from coming. I touched myself harder, my eyes closed tighter, my whole body flexed as I waited for the change to take me away.

My mind was filled to bursting with images. I saw myself relaxing with a beer the night before, letting my guard down for the first time ever. I saw myself the way this man must have seen me, unwound, let loose from the tight confines I'd kept myself in all my life. I saw myself opening up, from the split of my body, from the cages within. This picture of freedom brought me to the brink. For me, there was nothing more freeing than standing naked in front of a total stranger – a man whose name I didn't even know – and letting him see everything.

He said, "Oh, God," when I came. He said the words for me, so that I didn't have to, and then, as if my pleasure had released him, he took off his sunglasses and came closer, on his knees on the patio, so very close to me, but he still didn't touch me. "Oh, Jesus," he said, as I brought my fingertips to my lips and slowly licked my own juices away.

"Don't stop," he said, and I knew from the sound of his voice that if I chose to, I could ask him for things. That he'd give me whatever I wanted. But all I wanted from him was his gaze. "Do it again," he said, "please make yourself come again."

With my fingers wet from my mouth, I parted my pussy lips for him, but this time, I slid two fingers deep inside myself. He was close now, his breath on my skin, and I pushed forward with my hips again, feeling his hair softly tickling against my naked thighs. I let him watch me from inches away as I fucked myself. I let him see everything, the way my clit grew so engorged with the heat from within. The way I worked myself hard with my fingers, thrusting my wrist upward against my body, slamming my hand inside me when the need grew stronger and then stronger still. I used only my right hand this time, my thumb rubbing back and forth over my clit, and when I felt the climax building, I put my left hand on his head and twined my fingers through his thick, dark hair, grabbing onto him, anchoring him as I came a second time.

"So beautiful," he said in that same low, steady voice. "You have this look, this god damn beautiful quality. I knew when I first saw you—"

I picked up my clothes from around me on the tiles and I dressed carefully, not hurrying. I felt as if I'd never hurry again, never be nervous again. When I was ready, he drove me back to my dorm, as he'd promised he would. Delivered me back in perfect condition, unmarred and unhurt, although I wasn't the same person. Not at all. I'd transformed under his gaze. I'd changed.

I guess, sometimes that's all it takes, one person's gaze, one person's opinion, to make all the difference. Like the way he'd said that D'Arby would be big – a single person's opinion, summing up a powerful truth. It happens all the time in the media, the way it happened for me that time in L.A. In fact, just this weekend, I read a five-star review of Trent D'Arby's latest CD, and the reviewer wrote: "For ten minutes in the eighties, D'Arby was on top of the world."

And for almost those same exact ten minutes, I was beautiful. For the first time in my life, I was so fucking beautiful it was hard to handle. Yeah, I've been beautiful since. But never like that.

Never again.

A Day with the Bernsteins

Charlie Anders

"Actually," I stammered, "I've never . . . taken a man in my mouth before. I was hoping you'd . . . coach me."

There. I'd said it. I wanted Mrs Bernstein to tell me how to suck her husband's cock. I wanted her to run her fingers through my hair and whisper encouragement. Good boy, that sort of thing. She smiled, as if she understood.

I tingled from my nipples and my crotch as I knelt before Mr Bernstein's big rocking chair. He grinned down at me, maybe a little nervous himself. To my right, Mrs Bernstein perched on a stool. "Unzip his fly, Tom," she told me. "You're going to do all the work here. John's just going to enjoy himself." The hardwood floor chafed my knees. I glanced around the spartan cabin fearfully for spectators before focusing on John Bernstein's fly.

Both Bernsteins were stocky, but in different ways. Mrs Bernstein's torso started wide at her shoulders, broadened at the bust, and barely tapered to her waist. She wore a baggy one-piece green cotton dress. Her gray hair twined around a pencil. Mr Bernstein started with burly shoulders, too, but descended to a slight paunch. Mrs Bernstein's wily grin contrasted with her husband's seriousness. I lusted after both of them.

Bernstein wore briefs under his tight jeans, so wresting his penis free proved challenging. "Don't act like you're digging up a potato," Celia Bernstein counseled. "Half of a good blow job is presentation. Coax it out." I made myself slow down and slide the briefs away from his cock.

Mr Bernstein's cock, already half-hard, reached full size in my hand. Smaller than mine, and circumcised, it twitched as I ran a finger along its underside. "Lick his balls," Mrs Bernstein said. "Ever so lightly, like a kitten." The trembling in my chest and stomach grew as I obeyed; I'd chosen well when I'd asked the Bernsteins to fulfill my fantasy of being dominated by an older married couple.

He moaned as I tongued his scrotum. I worked my tongue up until it was on the base of his shaft; his moans grew. I felt a hand grab my hair. "Did I tell you to lick his cock? Wait for orders, boy!"

I started to apologize, but Mrs. Bernstein cautioned me not to let my tongue leave its task. I worked his balls for a while until she told me to move on. "Take the head in your mouth. Suck for all you're worth." Mr. Bernstein was as surprised as I was.

I sucked really hard until I felt her grip my hair. "Stop."

"Good boy." I felt her big fingers run through my hair. "Keep 'em off guard. Now lick the shaft with that kitten tongue of yours." She cooed praise as I licked, then after a while sent me back to sucking hard on the head. Slowly, I took more of Mr. Bernstein's cock in my mouth. Then back to licking. Mrs. Bernstein stroked the back of my neck with one hand and tickled my crotch with the other.

The blow job went on for what seemed like hours. Mr. Bernstein got more and more worked up, but didn't quite come. I felt entranced by Mrs. Bernstein's bossy whisper. She only occasionally touched my cock, but I stayed rock hard.

By the time Bernstein's unexpectedly sweet come poured over my taste buds, my jaw ached and my tongue was sore. But I lied when Mrs. Bernstein asked if my tongue needed to rest. "I'm fine," I said.

"Gargle." Mrs. Bernstein handed me a tiny cup of mouthwash.

We left the wilting Mr. Bernstein in his chair. Mrs. Bernstein led me to a smaller room. There, she perched on the bed, kicking her Birkenstocks onto the floor. "Kiss my feet," she said. "And maybe I'll let you eat me."

The hugeness of her feet only lent their wriggling more sensuousness. I licked between each toe on her left foot, then over the arch and under the instep. After I repeated the process on her right foot, she grabbed my hair and guided me on a grand, unhurried tongue-ride up her leg. She hitched up her big green dress as we went.

The only thing sexier than a big beautiful woman is a BBW with a bush that floods down onto her thighs. I got lost in Mrs. Bernstein's bush. Her snatch was a pleasant surprise when I stumbled on it, deep in the thicket. It smelled like a fresh-baked olive loaf.

"Remember the kitten tongue?" Mrs. Bernstein said.

I nodded.

"Well, forget about it. I want dog tongue. Up and down, then in circles. Until I tell you to change." I followed directions. Her hand flailed around, brushing my head, her mound. My tongue got so sore I had to prop it up between my teeth.

Mrs. Bernstein quivered. Both her big hands pressed my mouth onto her clitoris. She wailed. Her orgasm came on like a hellfire sermon. I didn't dare stop licking.

"Come up here," she hissed. "Grab a condom."

I'd been hard for an hour and a half, and every passing minute had ratcheted the tension in my balls. Sliding inside Mrs. Bernstein was so blessed I could have come immediately. But she bit my ear and growled, "Don't come until I tell you."

A novice at BDSM and bi-sex, I knew how to last a long time at conventional het sex. I had self-control. I'd learned to vary my thrusts and hold back my orgasm. After a few hundred missionary thrusts we switched to doggy style, and I lost count. Mrs. Bernstein came twice, tightening and shuddering around me, before she growled permission for me to come. I pushed myself deep in; I heard my own voice descanting over Mrs. Bernstein's grunts, and for a moment I was oblivious to everything but the tingling of my whole body. I collapsed, falling over sideways and landing curled up on the foot of the bed.

"God," Mrs. Bernstein said after a time. "That was amazing. I haven't been fucked like that since the fall of the Soviet Union. You're so much better than my husband." She raised her voice. "Hear that, John? You should ask him for pointers. He may be a sub, but he's twice the lover you are. God. What was that, an hour and a half?"

I sat up, startled by the unwanted praise. I felt cast out of my appointed role, and the feeling only worsened as I saw Mr.

Bernstein standing in the doorway. He held a tray of crackers and spread. His face looked calm, but calm as if he didn't trust himself to express the rage he felt. He was dressed, and he looked at our naked bodies with something like contempt. "Paté?" he said after a long pause, holding out the tray.

We ate in silence, Mrs. Bernstein and me still naked. The three of us sat around a glass-topped table eating off little plates that were almost saucers. After we'd eaten, I resumed my submissive role and did the dishes.

On my way back from the kitchen, I ran into Mr. Bernstein. His arms were folded. He stared at me, his unshaven jaw clenched and his brown eyes cold. "My turn again," he said. "Come."

Mr. Bernstein sat in a big armchair. He gestured for me to lay face down. I obeyed, naked against his denim lap. He brought his palm down on my butt. Then he hit the same spot harder. Then he hit another spot with a hairbrush he hadn't let me see. The strokes got harder and fiercer – but occasionally he'd lighten up, remembering his wife's dictum: "Always keep them off guard."

I bit my lip. The pain went from a sting to a burn, and then to a nerve-racking throb. I barely felt Mrs. Bernstein touch my chin with one finger.

"Stay away," Mr. Bernstein said in between strokes.

Mrs. Bernstein ignored him. "You remember your safe-word, right, Tom?" I nodded. We hadn't done a great job of negotiating the scene ahead of time, but we had agreed on a safe word: "Soufflé."

The beating continued. My cock chafed against Mr. Bernstein's jeans. I heard myself sob. The truth was I didn't want to use my safe word. I hadn't exactly asked for what was happening, but I was lost in it. It was the escape from control I'd dreamed of when I'd discovered submission. I lost myself in the terror, the inevitability, of this large man spanking me brutally.

I heard myself bawling. I felt my skin ablaze. By the time Mr. Bernstein said, "Beg me to stop," I think I was already begging. His command only made me beg louder. I felt like a blubbering kid.

Mr. Bernstein lifted me off his lap and stood up. He dropped me face down on the armchair and leaned over. He pulled a lever. The backrest slid backwards, leaving my face about a foot from the ground and my butt highest in the air. Mr. Bernstein asked Mrs. Bernstein where she'd put the condoms and the lube.

I felt a prodding at my sore ass, and something slid inside me. I felt like I was being stuffed. Mr. Bernstein thrust deeper. The pain kept company with the pleasure. Deeper and harder. I cried out, tears and sweat on my face. His thrusts became spasmodic. He roared. He grew more and more violent and arrhythmic. Then he stopped.

I lay face down, sobbing. Mr. Bernstein pulled out of me and walked away without speaking. After a moment, I heard water running in the bathroom. I ground my face into the backrest, ashamed of my tears.

"Come here." I turned to see Mrs. Bernstein on the rocking chair. She beckoned. I crawled over. She clasped my head to her breast. "I know that was hard for you. I hope you got something out of it."

"It's not that . . ." I sniffled. "It's . . . you treat your husband cruel. He treats me cruel in turn. What's the point?"

Mrs. Bernstein chuckled. "God forbid your exploration of domination and submission should lead to an actual lesson about the nature of power." She patted my head, in a different way than she'd patted it when I was sucking Mr. Bernstein's cock.

"Don't laugh at me." I'd stopped crying. "I just don't understand why you . . . why you treat him like that."

"Hard to say." Mrs. Bernstein hugged me against her chest, rocking back and forth. "The patterns seem to come from the spaces between the decisions, not the decisions themselves. I never made up my mind one day to be a bitch. Maybe I could do better by John."

She grabbed my cock. She pumped it to full erection, then lay me on the floor and took me in her mouth. No games this time. Instead, she worked her lips and tongue up and down me until I shot. She kept me in her mouth until I was completely soft, all the while brushing my stomach lightly with her wide, strong fingers.

Bassai Dai

Zoe Constantin

Bassai Jhoon Bee

Swing both hands around as you raise your left foot. Clasp the right fist with the left hand, and breathe out hard as you thrust fist and foot down. The Bassai ready stance.

Anna vented a sharp breath. Ready. Of course she was ready. Even so, it took her a full minute before she finally dialed the karate studio's telephone number. Rain spattered against her office window, and her hands shook momentarily, in spite of the non-regulation space heater under her desk.

Two weeks ago, she had hung up before the first ring. Last week, she had shredded the paper with the studio's phone number. It didn't matter. Her memory, her stubborn, unreliable memory, still retained every digit.

Make the call. Tell him you want a second chance.

A second chance to prove herself competent. To confront her failures. To prove herself immune to . . .

Anna winced away from that last thought. She punched in the last number, and the line clicked. In the brief dead space before the phone rang, she mentally recited her opening line. *Hello, Master Sengor. It's Anna Kubrick.*

Two years since she last spoke with him. Would he recognize her name? Would he remember why he had dismissed her from his studio?

"Sengor's Academy of Karate."

His voice. Dâvûd's. Anna's cheeks turned hot, then cold. In class, he snapped out commands in a guttural tone. When he spoke privately with a student, like now, his voice reminded her of dark blue silk, cool and smooth and soft. There was the faint accent from Turkey, his homeland, and France, where he studied. That interlude in Belgium. All the familiar slips and slurs and a lilting intonation.

Anna shook away thoughts about dark blue silk and launched into her speech. "Master Sengor, it's Anna Kubrick. Do you remember me? I saw your ad in the newspapers, and I wondered if you had openings in your class. Your red belt class."

The phone line crackled. Outside the rain pelted harder against the window. Anna waited, aware how loud her breathing sounded; aware, too, that a full minute passed before Master Sengor spoke again.

"No," he said. "I'm sorry. I have no openings for a red belt."

"But Master Sengor . . ."

She broke off and closed her eyes. Control. That was the key.

Lowering her voice, she said quickly, "Please listen. I'd like to come back. I started practicing again. Strikes. Blocks. Forms . . ."

"Which studio?"

His abrupt question silenced her a moment. "Wilcott Academy. In Redding."

"I know the studio. Why come to me then?"

Because you taught me first. Because you sent me away. Because I want . . .

"It's because of Bassai," she said. "I'm still having trouble. You know me better. I think you can help me through that last part."

A longer silence followed, during which the air seemed to draw tight around her. Eventually, Master Sengor released an audible sigh. "Come tonight at nine o'clock. Wear your uniform."

Her breath trickled out. "So you'll take me back as a student?"

"No." Then, "We'll talk tonight."

The line clicked off. Anna stared at the receiver, her mind blank with surprise, before she remembered to return it to its cradle.

Shi Jak

Begin the form. Lean forward, hands clasped and twisted to one side, until you cannot balance any longer. In that moment between falling and not-falling, you leap. Land with ankles crossed, left hand against the right arm, right hand fisted in a block. An attack that resembles a defense.

Anna peered through her rain-streaked windshield, trying to remember if Andover Mountain Road twisted right or left ahead. She wore a thin T-shirt and her karate pants underneath an exercise suit. Jacket and belt waited, neatly folded, inside her gym bag, along with her sparring gear. The jacket cuffs had started to fray, and the Sengor Academy logo had faded, but the red trim looked as crisp and bright as new.

I lied to him, she thought.

A small lie. A temporary one. But what if Dâvûd Sengor called the Wilcott Academy? He'd find out she had never signed up for classes there. She intended to, however. Just as soon as she proved – to herself and Master Sengor – she had overcome her difficulties with Bassai Dai.

You can do it, she told herself. *You can master the goddamned form.*

Except she hadn't, the last time she tried, and she never knew if one particular distraction had contributed to that failure.

Bassai Dai. Master Sengor had always pronounced the name with a pure Korean accent, perfected from decades of teaching. The name meant *Penetrate the Fortress,* he had said. Like the Eight Key Concepts, or the poem at the back of her Gup manual, the name was more than poetry. *Bassai* meant destruction of pride, of self-deception. She also remembered their last talk before he dismissed her.

"You are a red belt now. You are in training for Cho Dan. A part of that training is to break down the barriers you've built within yourself. I think . . ." She remembered how his glance had shifted to one side. "I believe you should discontinue your studies here."

His voice had sounded gentle, almost sad. After weeks of

struggling with the Bassai form, she had expected him to be strict. She had not expected to be dismissed.

Yet today, he had agreed to talk. To teach. Why else the order to wear her uniform?

Go to class. Master the form. Move on.

A dim yellow glow appeared ahead, signaling the tiny strip mall where Master Sengor had his studio. Anna eased the car to a stop, careful of the slick roads, and turned into the driveway. At this hour, the parking lot was empty except for one other car, an ancient blue Thunderbird, whose windows reflected Anna's headlights and the red neon from the studio. She pulled into a space two down from Master Sengor's car. The studio was lit; a dark figure waited motionless at the window.

"Shi Jak," she murmured, then gave a soft laugh.

Inside, she bowed to Master Sengor, who bent his head in reply. Sengor was just as she remembered. Dark hair clipped short. Lean brown face. The ghost of a beard along his jaw. His master's belt tied just so. Still, he seemed tired – the corners of his mouth turned down slightly, and a few faint lines showed beneath his dark brown eyes.

Those dark brown eyes were observing her just as closely. Self-conscious of his gaze, she turned away. Like Master Sengor, the studio had changed little. The same photograph of the Grand Master hung between the Korean and American flags. The same scuffed mats made a checkerboard of red and blue. Racks of bow staffs, punching shields and sparring gear occupied one side, while mirrors lined the other. A few more certificates and trophies crowded the glass case, but these were small details. She breathed in the scent of old sweat, plastic and leather.

A metallic rattle made her jump. Master Sengor had adjusted the blinds to slant upward, leaving only strips of night sky visible through the slats. Good. She didn't want any chance passer-by to witness this class.

"We'll start with stretches," he said. "Then some basic moves, just to evaluate your training. You have your uniform?"

No other greeting. No wasted pleasantries. She nodded. "Yes, sir."

She removed her shoes, then slid off her exercise jacket and pants, conscious that Master Sengor was studying her with the same cool look she remembered from class. *Yes*, she thought, *I've worked out. I've kept in shape.* He said nothing, however. When she had finished tying her jacket and belt, he gestured for her to follow.

They took their places at the front of the studio and faced the flags, Anna standing two paces behind Master Sengor.

"Cha Ryut. Bay Ray. Ba Ro. Muk Nyum."

Stand to attention, hand over heart. Return and meditate. Bow to the flags, to the Grand Master's photograph, and then to Master Sengor. After the formal opening, Master Sengor led her through a short set of warm-up exercises and stretches. The sequence came back easily, and she found herself relaxing.

Don't get too comfortable, she reminded herself. *This is temporary.*

"Stand ready."

She brought her fists together.

"Stepping out left leg – low block, reverse high punch. Once more. Now high block, reverse middle punch. Again."

He took her through the basic blocks and strikes, then moved quickly to combinations. Kicks followed, from basic to jump to spinning kicks. Master Sengor had begun with English commands, but after a dozen moves, he switched to Korean, so that she had to think fast. If she flubbed a technique, she stopped, bowed, and repeated the move correctly. He offered no encouragement, but she had expected none. She was a red belt, a third Gup. She was supposed to be beyond coddling.

By the time he called out Ba Ro, her cheeks were flushed, her breathing uneven. At his signal, she turned to the right and adjusted her uniform, then faced him again with a bow.

"So," he said. "You want to study Bassai."

His voice was uninflected; she could read nothing in his expression except a faint weariness. She resisted the urge to lick her lips. "Yes, sir."

A pause followed – long enough that her stomach fluttered – before he nodded. "Very well. We'll go through the form by my count, just to see what you remember. Bassai Jhoon Bee."

He rapped out the last phrase, taking her by surprise. Anna

blinked, then brought her hands around to meet in front of her face. Left hand over right fist. The Bassai Jhoon Bee.

Master Sengor smiled dryly. "Good. You remember that much." A briefer pause, then, "Shi Jak."

This time, she was ready for the command. Anna rose smoothly onto her toes, twisted left, and leaned forward. Just when she tipped beyond balance, she jumped and landed with legs crossed and her arms swinging up to the proper position.

"Hap." He signaled the next move.

Spin around. Two inside-out blocks, left and right.

"Hap."

Move by move, he took her through Bassai. She had practiced alone for weeks before she called; even so, there were blank spots in her memory. Master Sengor said little, except to give hints when she obviously had forgotten a step. Throughout, Anna was aware of his unblinking gaze. That look, that quiet intensity, had come from his early years. Plucked from one culture into another, he had learned how to observe in silence, absorbing every minute detail – or so she guessed. Master Sengor seldom spoke about his past. What bits she knew, Anna had gleaned from chance comments, a difference in tone or expression, the photos he kept in his back office.

At the last move, Soo Do Mahk Kee, Anna faced front and held her position. A trickle of sweat ran down her back. Her leg muscles burned from holding the stance, and a strand of hair had worked itself loose from her braid.

"Ba Ro."

With a sigh of relief, Anna returned to the resting position.

Master Sengor regarded her a few moments. "Not bad, not good. You're right – you're still rough with the last section. When did you start classes at Wilcott?"

Anna brushed the hair from her face, shrugged.

Sengor's mouth quirked into a smile. "I see. Well, you made a few mistakes. We'll go through it again, slower this time. Bassai Jhoon Bee."

Did she hear a different tone in his voice? She didn't have time to speculate, because he was motioning for her to begin. This time, he paused after each segment to review her mistakes, or to correct her stance. Eyes front, he reminded her. Hips turned just so. Hands lifted higher, so that she looked over her knuckles. "Like so," he said, adjusting her hands with a touch as light as moth wings.

The touch called up those distracting images that had assailed her during class, after class, in her dreams. His hands brushing her skin, each caress leaving a fingerprint of his scent. His warm lips . . .

Sengor had stepped back and was studying her. Belatedly, Anna wondered if her expression had betrayed her thoughts.

"Dasi," he said mildly. "Again. Your count this time. And remember what I said about keeping your eyes upon your opponent. Imagine him well – how tall, how heavy, the way he moves."

Imagine. Yes.

She started over, concentrating on each movement, and conscious how awkward she looked. Sengor kept silent for the first half dozen techniques. As she settled into the form, however, he began a running commentary: Twist your hip and block together in one fluid movement. Feel your feet – don't look at them. Do not hesitate. Do not glance down. Commit yourself to each movement. Don't anticipate the next one.

Leaping into the middle punch, Anna stretched too far and landed off balance. Her foot twisted, pain lanced through her ankle, and she hissed in pain. *Please, let it not be a sprain. Not now.*

A hand touched her shoulder. "Are you injured?"

Anna cautiously flexed her foot. It twinged, but already the worst had subsided. "I don't think so."

"Stand up, and we'll see."

He grasped her wrist and pulled her up. For a moment, she was close enough to sense the heat radiating from his skin, and catch the scent of his aftershave, mixed in with sweat. Anna had the swift and vivid fantasy of leaning forward and kissing that generous mouth.

Sengor released his hold and glided back. "How is your ankle? Too bad to go on?"

Cool. Aloof. Dispassionate. Just as she ought to be. Nevertheless, her skin still tingled, as though he'd marked her wrist with his touch. Anna shook her head, not trusting her voice.

"Very well. Please start the form over."

His continued coolness acted to steady her nerves. Anna drew a deep breath and closed her eyes a moment to focus. It came to her that she was choosing the wrong approach, but she didn't know another way. A soft tread brought her attention back. She opened her eyes to find Master Sengor in front of her, observing her closely. She had not noticed before how thick and dark his lashes were.

"Think of eliminating all boundaries," he said softly.

"Imagine all defenses gone. You, yielding them. You, offering your pride, your self, to the void."

Blue silk rippling in the shadows. Yes. That she could imagine. But she had come to rid herself of those fantasies, not to indulge them.

This close to Dâvûd Sengor, however, and her resolution wavered. Even if he meant surrender to Bassai, she could do both, in the privacy of her thoughts. Surely that harmed no one, including her.

Anna returned to her starting position and performed the Bassai Jhoon Bee. Her gaze flickered toward Master Sengor, then back to the wall.

Shi Jak.

She tilted forward into the first sequence. Surrender. Attack. Two opposites held in balance.

She pivoted around into the next two blocks. She could tell, even without seeing herself in the mirrors, that her movements were stronger, sharper. Chop. Punch. Block. Back fist. When she sprang into her first Soo Do block, her bare feet hit the mats with an audible thump. Her uniform snapped in time with her side kick; her sharp exhalations marked each sequence. All the while, Master Sengor's gaze followed – dark, impassive, unreadable.

Surrender was the key. What had existed as words and rules became understanding, and her thoughts divided into parallel streams. On one side, Bassai Dai. On the other, her desire.

Another series of Soo Do blocks. Then fists drawn together and pushed up high. Lunge forward into the double-fisted strike. Leap into the middle punch. Pivot and shift into the knife strike.

Anna imagined Dâvûd's fingers tracing a path over her cheek, down her throat to its base, one thumb resting there. A momentary pause – she could feel his pulse beating against hers – then the first hungry kiss. Yes, she could imagine it well. The scent of his body would be intoxicating, the taste of his mouth, his skin would fill her senses.

Jerk the hand back. Breathe in slowly as you raise the left leg, slide it down to stand with feet together. Pause.

Kiss upon devouring kiss, each one followed by a caress, his and hers. His mouth upon her breast, his palms cupping them. Her mouth nibbling his chest and shoulders and arms. Her hands pulling his body closer to hers. With quick deft movements, he would untie her uniform and slide the jacket free, while she tugged his trousers over his lean hips.

Swing into the wheel kick. Back fist. Another with open hand. A flurry of punches, a change in stance, twist and thrust two fists into a double strike.

Anna's belly tightened. Her breathing shifted. Her eyes saw two figures, one of her teacher, one of her lover. Her body moved through the twin acts of sex and Bassai.

Penetrate the fortress, he had said. *All defenses gone.*

She had come to the final sequence – for her, the most difficult part. Anna pictured tumbling with Dâvûd onto the mats. Mouth fastened against mouth. Her legs opening up. Her voice babbling, *Please, oh please, yes, now.* Her hands running over his back, between his legs, guiding his penis into her vagina, already slick with sweat and desire. One smooth gliding motion and he would be inside. Break down the barriers. Yield.

X-block. Back fist. Sink low, lower still. Double knife strike.

A deep ache gripped her sex. Anna groaned, and strained to draw him even deeper. More, more. She thought she might be babbling. She didn't care. Dâvûd buried his face into her neck. He was murmuring in a strange language, but though the words were foreign, she understood his meaning. Come to me. Closer, closer, my love. Yes. There, exactly there.

Another back fist. Sink down low. Lower. Spring into the

middle Soo Do block. Spin into the second one. The third, the last one, a block that is an attack.

Dâvûd threw back his head and groaned. Anna's body arched toward him, pushing as hard as she could. For a long moment, their bodies went tense and still, before Dâvûd sank onto Anna's breast, his mouth covering hers in a kiss.

The dream broke. Anna held her position, gaze to the front. Her uniform was patchy with sweat. More sweat pooled at the base of her neck, between her breasts. That was the last requirement of the form, to remain still until the teacher released you.

"Ba Ro."

With the last of her self-control, Anna performed the Bassai Jhoon Bee. Her legs trembled. Had he seen the dual dance? Had he recognized himself as her partner and her opponent?

"Very well. Yes. I could see the fortress broken."

Master Sengor's voice was softer than usual. She could guess nothing from his tone, however. *It doesn't matter*, she told herself. *You proved yourself competent. You can leave here with all your doubts resolved.*

Not quite. She needed one last confirmation. Keeping her voice level, she asked, "Will you take me back as a student?"

"No."

For a moment, she didn't comprehend what he said. When she did, her heart gave a lurch. "Why not?"

"For the same reason as last time."

"But you said . . ."

"I said you should discontinue your studies here. I never meant for you to give up karate." His gaze veered to one side, just as before. "It would not have been right for me to continue as your teacher. Or perhaps I misunderstood."

It was the same as before. The same refusal. The same . . . Had *she* misunderstood?

Her pulse thrumming, Anna heard herself say, "Oh no. You understood quite well."

"Ah." Dâvûd's gaze finally met hers, and his mouth, so serious a moment before, softened into a pensive smile. "Did I?"

Surrender, she told herself. Abandon pride and self-delusion. She had come here with too much of both.

Anna lifted one hand to caress his cheek. "Kay Sok," she whispered. "Begin Match."

Dâvûd shook his head, still smiling. He leaned forward and brushed his lips over hers, a sweet brief kiss. "Let us try again," he murmured, his warm breath tickling her face. "Your count."

Shi Jak.

The End of Daphne Greenwood's Travel Career

Tara Alton

It started with the pen. I wouldn't call it a stupendously fancy pen, but rather a clumsy, space aged like missile from a hotel vendor visit, where sales people fob off cheap little gifts so you'll book them. If you click the pen, different chain names spin around in a tiny display on the barrel. It belonged to my team leader, Pam. She loved that pen. Pam also loved to think she was hot shit because she had a degree in travel from a university, while the rest of us have travel school certificates under our belts. I would say she's not a team leader because of this. She's a team leader because she doesn't mind sticking her head up our boss's ass.

What have I done with this pen? I've moved it a few times so she had to look for it, stuck it in my mouth, licked it, doodled penises with it and took it into the bathroom. Why? Let's just say I had sexual relations with it. I know it wasn't consensual, but who is the pen going to tell? Besides the little bugger was so uptight I didn't even come. Still, I got some satisfaction planting it back on Pam's desk, watching her face when she realized it was sticky and trying to figure out what it was before she wiped it with one of those antibacterial wipes for anal retentives.

Pam left me a chastising note on my desk about someone whom I like to call Passenger Thirteen. Why Thirteen? I like to think that this row of seats on an airplace is the travel agent's row of hell. If a passenger pisses me off, I put him in that row. Well, this guy really yanked me around over a trip to Des

Moines, so every time since I've tried to deposit him there. Apparently, he wasn't too happy about being in a middle seat again either, but it wasn't my fault since the rest of the seats were under airport control. Well, they weren't, but we won't tell, will we?

I crumpled up Pam's note, tossed it in the trash and picked up my book. Between calls, management doesn't care what we do as long as we are ready to take a call. Some girls knit. Some read fashion magazines. Some write bills or clip coupons. I read porn. Not outright crotch shot magazines, but rather anthologies of porn pretending to be erotica, but there are still a lot of muffs and cocks bouncing around, only in a more civilized manner.

Reading about a girl who was having an erotic thrill ride on a cable car in San Francisco, I started to get all squirmy. I thought I might have to go to the bathroom to relieve myself in that special way, when Passenger Thirteen rings in. On and on he went about being in the middle seat again. It's uncomfortable, blah blah blah. *Well you shouldn't have been such an ass to me about Des Moines*, I wanted to tell him. My gaze swept back to the open page of my book. He was doing what to her? Could I slip a finger under my skirt?

Looking up, I realized Pam had on her head set and her eyes were on me. She was monitoring me, the bitch.

"I'll definitely try for the aisle seat next time," I said to him. "I'll do that. I will."

The operative word there was *try*.

The moment I hung up, Pam put down her headset and wrote something down. That night, I threw her pen away.

The next day, I watched her look for her pen, and I felt the thrill of a job well done. I had wrapped it in several layers of toilet paper and stuffed it in the sanitary disposal bin in the bathroom. It was long gone.

Actually, I was feeling quite good over all because I forgot to wear underwear, and the seam of my tights was riding up into my crotch.

Suddenly, Miranda, Pam's boss, strode over to me. I thought she was going to say something about the pen, and I quickly concocted several stories about where I saw Pam with it last, but instead she hauled me into her office and chastised me about my clothing.

Apparently I'd forgotten it was a client walk through today, and I'd worn a short corduroy skirt, a slightly ratty, white cotton blouse and my regulation black tights, instead of business attire, which meant a suit. After giving me a long lecture on the difference between business and business casual, she released me to my desk.

Feeling like my neck had been whiplashed from nodding to convince her I was listening when I really wasn't, I tossed myself down on my seat. Oh great. Now my keyboard tray was stuck. I couldn't pull it out to do my travel agent duties. I called the maintenance man, Ayad. A lot of girls thought he was thick because of the language barrier, but I thought he was adorable.

Moments later, he was under my desk, fiddling with my tray. I kept checking him out. Was it warm in here?

"Do you want to know why I wear dark tights all the time?" I asked him.

He looked up at me. I tried not to imagine him giving me that look between my legs in the bedroom.

"Tattoos. I have tattoos of flowers on my legs," I said.

He paused, a blank look on his face. Did he even know what a tattoo was? How could I explain it?

"Do you want to see what I'm reading?" I asked him instead and showed him my book. He flipped through the pages. Now, I got a reaction out of him. He raised an eyebrow.

"You read this at work?" he asked.

I nodded, happily. He shook his head, handed me back the book and checked the batteries on his cordless drill. Surely what I had to say was more interesting than that piece of cheap plastic crap.

"I'll let you in on a secret," I said in a low voice. "I'm not wearing panties."

Slowly, I opened my legs. He looked.

"You're still wearing something over your legs," he said.

"But nothing underneath. Use your imagination."

He shrugged and peered in closer. Just when I thought I had him, Miranda approached us. I clapped shut my legs.

"The clients are walking through," she said. "You can either put this on or you can go wait in ticketing."

She held up the cast off sweater from the closet. No one knew who it belonged to. It had been in there forever, and for good reason with its light blue knit and ruffled collar.

I wasn't wearing that sweater, so I chose ticketing, a cave of a room where underpaid employees who got bad grades in travel school shuffled ticket stock together. Pam breezed by with a smirk at me.

That bitch. I had to do something else to get her back. Plus, Miranda was on my shit list as well because she told ticketing I could help them for a half hour if I showed up. I wasn't about to stamp parking coupons with our logo as instructed by a timid girl with a set of chin whiskers, so I set out to find a suitable box for my next project.

An empty staple box became my voodoo box. I drew hex signs all over it with a black magic marker, and by the end of the day, I had acquired an earring of Miranda's and a miniature green frog eraser off Pam's desk. I loved the way they rattled inside it, sort of like little bones.

The next day, I decided to add someone else to my voodoo box. Crystal. She had been sexually harassing me for the longest time, and I was finally fed up. You wouldn't believe the things she said to me, like: I love it when you wear purple. I like it when your hair is all wild like that.

Women don't say things like that to one another. They say "cute skirt" or "nice blouse." Also, she's always brushing up against me or stroking my arm. I've tried to put her off by talking about how much I like men whenever I'm near her, but it's not working. The last time, I told her how much bone I had in me that weekend, but she said all I needed to do was to make love to a woman.

I was in the lunch room, chewing on a hangnail in front of the vending machine as I contemplated what I should steal from her desk for my voodoo box, when she made an appearance. Ayad came in as well to stuff his lunch in the fridge.

Crystal leered at the candy bars.

"You wouldn't believe how much I like eating boxes of goodies," she said. "Especially a mound."

I rolled my eyes and let out a deep breath.

"Listen, I like guys," I said. "I like a good, hard cock, and you don't have one. Stop hitting on me, or I'll report you for sexual harassment."

With that said, I bought a package of old-fashioned caramel creams, shot Ayad a look, who had his eyebrow raised at me once more and flounced back to my desk.

She must have told her little group of friends what I said because for the rest of the day they all kept giving me dirty looks. Give me a break. I saw them waiting for me in the hallway after work, like they were in Junior High, waiting to beat me up. Little did they know I had a secret weapon. The fish eye. Yeah, I got some crazy genes in my gene pool. My mom, for example, was truly nuts.

I whipped it out, glared at them, and strode past them like shit wouldn't even stink on me. They didn't say a word.

The next morning, no one was waiting for me in the hallway, but my water cup looked odd. It was one of those plastic tumblers you get at the dollar store, but the water inside it had a yellowish tint. I smelled it and took it straight to Miranda.

"Someone pissed in my cup," I said.

She smelled it.

"Probably the cleaning people," she said, handing it back.

I looked at her, waiting for her to say something else, show some indignation at this appalling act, but she acted like the matter was already closed.

Disgusted, I went to the sink to pour it out when Ayad came by.

"How are you?" he asked.

"I'm being sexually harassed by Crystal, and someone pissed in my water cup," I said.

I tossed the cup in the trash.

"I'm pretty sure she did it," I said.

I realized he wasn't making eye contact. Rather, he was looking down at my tights.

"How is your drawer?" he asked.

"It's still sticking," I said. "You never did finish fixing it."

He followed me back to my desk. It was like he had never left. As he adjusted the screws, I kicked off my shoes and rubbed my foot slowly up his leg. I dug my toes in his crotch and wiggled them around. Then I pushed the ball of my foot up his chest where he took my foot in his hands and bit my big toe. He ripped the seam, his tongue touching flesh. I nearly fell off my chair.

Miranda stopped by my desk. Thank God she could only see his legs and tool box.

"There are calls on hold," she said. "Can this wait?"

Once more abandoned to a sticky drawer and a throbbing mound, I watched him gather up his tools and leave. Reluctantly, I put on my headset, feeling buzzed from the flirting. Across the office, I realized Crystal was watching me. Her hunger for me simmered in her eyes. Why shouldn't she want me? I was hot stuff.

I should make love to a woman.

I always felt bad about the austerity of my desk when everyone else had their trophy photos all over the place because of this innate need to prove to the world they are loved. Finally, I had a photograph to bring in to work. Last night, I visited my childhood friend who happens to be a stripper. One of her friends gave me a lap dance and we took a picture.

I showed it to Crystal, who at first looked so pleased I had walked over to her and then so sheet white at what she saw. I don't know why. Everything was covered. My hands were on my pretend girlfriend's thighs, her tits in my face, but that was it. Like a proud mother of a freakish sense of justice, I displayed the photo on my desk.

Word of it zipped around the office like a plague. It took no time at all for Miranda to stomp over.

"Take it down," she ordered.

I wrested up an expression of mock indignation.

"Everyone defends Crystal," I said. "So I took her up on her advice. She told me to make love to a woman so I did. This is my girlfriend. I'm allowed to have pictures of my loved ones on my desk."

Miranda snatched it down and opened my drawer to toss it in. Her gaze locked on my voodoo box.

"What is that?" she asked.

I did the only thing I could. I acted like I had never seen it in my life.

Acting as if it was covered in rat shit, she picked it up and opened it. Her earring and the frog came tumbling out. I'd never seen her speechless before. Mostly it involved her turning quite red and acting like she couldn't swallow.

Of course, she felt compelled to go through the rest of my desk.

The sanctity of my travel agent's rights being violated, I stormed off, spotting Crystal's cigarettes and lighter left on the water cooler. As quick as a bee, I snatched them off and headed for a smoke in the storeroom to calm my nerves.

I spotted Ayad, bending over as he looked at a wall socket. He did have a fine ass. I thought about my toe poking through the hole in my tights, his tongue on my skin. Suddenly, my legs felt unsteady. I sauntered over to him.

"Does your mouth taste like toe cheese?" I asked.

He looked up at me, a hint of smile on his mouth. I gave him a come hither look. He stood up. I shrugged in the direction of the conference room. Like someone with their pants on fire, which they were, I scooted inside and held my breath. Would he follow? Would he be up for it? For a moment, the suspense was stupendous. He appeared in the doorway. I shut the door behind us, letting out my breath, a little more than dizzy now.

Jumping on the conference table, I kicked off my shoe. My big toe poked out.

"I think I need to file a lawsuit. Someone ripped my tights," I said.

It was sort of romantic, the way he looked at me with lust in his eyes, his package standing out and how he got down on one knee.

The moment he put my big toe all the way in his mouth, I nearly passed out. A giggle escaped me that shook my rib cage. He ripped open my tights further, working his tongue between my toes. It was the best foot massage ever. All these knots in my shoulders relaxed, and I felt my body melting into the table.

He pulled my foot out of his mouth and stood up.

"Now I have toe cheese on my breath," he said.

"Yes. You do," I replied smiling.

I waited for him to do something else to me. Anything.

Really. For a second, I thought he might turn around and leave, that maybe he was just a foot guy, but he ripped my tights a little more.

"I think these need to come off," he said.

I couldn't get out of them fast enough. They got caught twisted down my legs. He helped, yanking them down. Thank God, I hadn't worn my old cotton panties, but my blue sparkly ones instead. He didn't even bother pulling those down. He unzipped his pants, pushed aside the thin fabric and entered me. God, he felt big. I was either tighter than I thought, or he had a really big dick.

I tried to hang onto him, but he was fucking me too hard. So I flopped back on the table, let him pull my hips to him and went along for the ride. I was just about ready to start pinching my nipples when I heard the conference room door open.

To my horror, I saw Miranda standing there with the nicest looking man I ever saw, tall, dark, brooding, oozing masculinity and mystique. He was New York and Ayad was a suburb outside Detroit. I couldn't believe I was checking him out with another man's dick in me.

"Oh my goodness," Miranda cried out.

Like I was suddenly made of battery acid, Ayad zipped up and jumped away from me. Sheepishly, I pushed down my skirt with an oops I accidentally fell on the table, devil may care, attitude.

Miranda didn't buy it.

"Ayad, I would have thought better of you. Getting caught up in her shenanigans. This has to be the most appalling thing I've ever seen here. You're treading on thin ice, Mister."

Ayad shot by her through the doorway, deserting me. Suddenly I wasn't so impressed by him, big dick or not. I picked up my tights and my shoes, very aware that the slickness of our love was beginning to trail down my thigh.

"And as for you . . ." she started to say to me.

"Yeah. I know," I said. "Daphne Greenwood is a screw up."

"Exactly. See me in my office in fifteen minutes."

They were still in the doorway. I had no choice but to squeeze by them. Good looking man was looking highly amused. Glad I could make your day, I wanted to say to him. Instead, I got a whiff of him. Damn. He smelled good.

"I'm so sorry, Mr Andrews," Miranda said. "This will never happen again. The girl is plain crazy."

I shot a glance back. That was Mr Andrews. Passenger Thirteen!

I still had Crystal's cigarettes and lighter. Why not have a smoke before I faced the firing squad? Now I needed it more than ever. I was so pissed off at Ayad for abandoning me, and I was terrified Miranda was going to have a Daphne Greenwood ass buffet when she got a hold of me. She had plenty of chafing dishes filled with my misadventures – a picture of me with a stripper, a voodoo box with one of her earrings in it and me screwing the maintenance man on the conference room table.

Behind me, I locked the storeroom door and stood by the vent, where I lit up. A cigarette never tasted so good. In the corner stood an old vending gumball machine. It must have come from the lunchroom at some point. That was soon going to be me – empty, forgotten.

Cigarette still in hand, I adjusted my panties. My tights were useless. Everyone was going to see my tattoos. Another thing for Miranda to yell about. Great, why not just parade around naked. I try to fit in. I do. And look what happens.

I could talk my way out of this. I could tell her that the stress of being sexually harassed by Crystal had made me doubt my heterosexuality, so I took up with a stripper, had a breakdown and I had to screw Ayad to find myself again. It wasn't my fault. It was Crystal's.

I was using the fabric of my tights to sort of clean between my thighs when my cigarette fell from my hand and landed in an open box of file folders.

At first, I thought nothing happened. The stupid thing disappeared. Maybe the fall had snuffed it out. I poked around in the box. Nothing. Maybe I should just dump the whole thing out, but the box was huge. Pulling out some of the folders occurred to me, but then I saw it. A wisp of smoke. The box was smoking my cigarette. All that angst from travel agents and travelers was inhaling. I wasn't sticking my hand in there.

How on earth was I going to put it out? There wasn't a fire extinguisher in here. What did fire need? Fuel? Air? The door looked pretty air tight. Being the good citizen I was, I fled the room and shut the door.

Please go out. Please go out. I glanced at the crack at the bottom of the door. Blast it. Smoke. Then there was this sound like a whoosh and an intense crackling. Orange light joined the smoke at the crack.

What do I do? I wasn't about to leave the building without my purse. As calmly as I could, I walked back to my desk. I didn't see Miranda. She must still be in the meeting with Thirteen. Just as I sat and opened my drawer to get my purse, I heard the fire alarm go off. Everyone leapt up.

"This isn't a drill. We have a situation on the third floor, please leave the building."

Anyone who was on the phone got to say there was an emergency and hang up on the client. The one time we get to do that, and I missed it.

Down the three flights of stairs I traipsed with the others. You could smell the smoke now. Once we were outside we were supposed to meet in a designated spot in the parking lot, far from the building, in case it blew up or something.

You would have thought it was a national emergency or something with all the fire trucks that pulled up, even the kind with the long ladders.

I stood away from the others, including Pam, Crystal, and Crystal's friends. Not on purpose or anything. It just happened that no one else stood with me, not even Ayad, who was shooting me dirty looks from beside a tree. *It takes two to tango, buddy*, I wanted to call to him. You're the one who had my toe in your mouth. I couldn't believe his dick had just been inside me and now this. He was the owner of a seriously defective character.

Miranda finally came out, wearing a fire marshall red vest. She must have stayed behind to make sure everyone was out. How very brave. She shot me a look that could have burned Lycra off a hooker.

I managed a wan smile in return. Not in a million years was she going to believe my sexual harassment breakdown story. Not after today. Especially if they found out who started the fire. I'd never get out of my crappy trailer or get a better life. I didn't belong here. It was so obvious with us standing out in the open. No one else was standing apart. What had I been doing at this place? Torturing myself trying to fit in. Who was I kidding anyway? I wasn't an office girl, a travel agent. I never traveled because I couldn't afford the hotels or the food even with a free airline pass.

Someone cleared their throat behind me. I turned. It was him, devastatingly handsome him.

"Passenger Thirteen," I said.

"Thirteen?"

"That's what I like to call you. A nickname of sorts."

He looked mystified.

"Haven't you noticed you frequently end up in row thirteen?" I asked.

"Oh, that. Actually I probably deserve it. I can be quite abrasive sometimes."

How had I ever been shitty to such a fine man?

"You probably shouldn't be speaking to me," I said. "I'm a doomed woman."

He smiled, obviously not heeding my warning.

"That was some meeting you were having in the conference room," he said.

"You liked that?"

He nodded. "You could probably do better with your choice in colleagues though," he said.

I glanced at Ayad.

"You can see someone's true colors when the chips are down," he continued.

"Or when the skirts are up." I blushed. I was so blatantly flirting with him. Hysterical flirting.

"I probably won't be booking your travel any longer," I said. "I think I'm all through here."

I was debating going back inside to get my things when the fire was out, but it was all crap wasn't it. I realized Thirteen was looking at my legs.

"Nice tattoos," he said.

"Do you want to see a picture of my pretend girlfriend?" I asked.

He looked at it. For a moment, I thought shock was registering, but then I saw that same bemused look I saw in the conference room.

"This is a very interesting photograph," he said. "I think we should get together sometime."

"You do?" I asked. "Even if I'm working as a waitress at a strip club? Because that's what I'm going to be doing next."

He nodded. I heard Miranda shriek. The fire was out. With a fireman in tow, she headed over to Crystal. I saw something glint in his hand. I knew what that was. I'd left it in the storeroom. The lighter!

Thirteen got out a scrap of paper and a pen to write down my phone number.

"Nice pen," I said. "I know a lot of uses."

The sexual tension between us was crackling. I never wanted to fuck someone so bad in my life. All that conflict on the phone between us had been like some sort of intense foreplay. I knew he was feeling it. I could see it in his eyes.

He raised an eyebrow at me.

"I have a lot more pens in my car," he said.

And just like that, I trotted off after him toward his car, like a dog in heat. Miranda caught sight of us.

"Where do you think you're going, missy," she called out.

I waved her off and caught up with him.

"This could cause you problems," I said.

"No. It won't. I wasn't going to use your travel agency any longer anyway. That's why I came in for a meeting."

His expensive car was parked in two hour parking. The moment I got inside with him, I forgot all about the pens. He was as horny as I was. Over the console, he pulled me into his lap so I straddled him. Pushing my panties aside much like Ayad, he was inside me lightning fast. I was really tight today, or he was big as well. Very big.

"Don't you think it's perverted you met me with another guy's dick in me and now you're screwing me?" I asked.

"Yes."

"And you don't care about sloppy seconds."

"No."

I shoved my tongue down his throat, licked his tonsils, and

bumped his uglies with a passion I never knew. The moment I came up for air, I realized the entire office was watching us with open mouths, Miranda, Pam, Ayad, and Crystal. And there it was. The end of my travel career.

Hitting the window button with my elbow, I leaned out my head as Thirteen was grabbing my hips and ramming me into him. He was quite the fucker.

"See Crystal. I do like a lot of bone," I called out.

Cry of the Loogaroo

John Edward Ames

"Feature this: A dark, dank, fetid, wildly overgrown place dominated by alligators and snakes, by tall tupelo trees marching on stilts that, on closer inspection, turn out to be exposed roots. Imagine a dripping, insect-humming monotony of sound that's eerily akin to the uneventful stillness of a mausoleum. This is a place where death is lazy, primitive and anonymous, and thus, vastly more terrifying in its pitilessness."

I gave a little fluming snort as I switched off Libby Mumford's microcassette recorder.

"Fetid?" I repeated, watching Captain Breaux. "The hell's that mean?"

He shrugged one beefy shoulder. "I look like a dictionary? I think it means stinky. This chick's got a nice voice."

"Nice everything. In fact, she's a certified traffic hazard. Most of these award-winning female-journalist types look like constipated librarians. Not Libby. She was a model before she got into photojournalism. Here, check her out."

I opened a folder on my knee and handed him a color glossy of Libby Mumford; she was running along a beach somewhere, damn near butt-naked in a yellow bikini thong.

Breaux, who normally has all the élan of a deep coma, loosed a sharp whistle.

"She's a tidy little bit of frippit, all right," he allowed, visibly impressed.

Libby was a blue-chip *chica* all the way, pampered and sleek and boob-enhanced. Breaux took in the shoulder-length platinum hair, eyes the soft blue of forget-me-nots, skin tanned to the exact shade of sunlit honey.

"Yeah-boy," he added, handing it back to me. "That's something to wrap your leg around. Where'd you say she's from?"

"Houston."

"What, she's with one of the crap sheets there?"

"Nah, she's freelance. But not a scoop merchant, just fluff and feature stuff. Specializes in travel pieces and photo features for the Sunday supplements. Also writes hot romance novels under the name Deanna Chambers. But when she disappeared last week, she was working on a series for *Eros* magazine called 'Hot and Haunted America' – which her editor described as—"

I glanced down at the notes on my flipback pad.

" '—a showcase for some of America's most colorful and steamy regional-bogey legends.' "

Breaux, negligently sprawled on a swivel chair behind a messy pecan-veneer desk, raised one hand like a traffic cop to stop me. He was a huge and sloppy rag-bag of a man with a lopsided mouth and big pouches like bruises under his eyes.

"Yeah, well let me guess: our hot little infobabe caught wind of the scuttlebutt about Shrieking Swamp, uh? Figured being diddled by an 'invisible sex fiend' might be more of a rush than the politically correct coffee-shop weenies who usual *schtupp* her?"

"Somehow I doubt she went there to get laid," I assured him from a deadpan. "But yeah, she knew about the stories, her editor confirmed that."

"He the one reported her missing?"

I nodded. "After she failed to check in by phone."

He pointed at the microrecorder. "How'd you get that?"

"Search and Rescue turned it in. It's all they found."

"Play some more."

I switched it on. Her throaty contralto voice again filled Breaux's cubbyhole office on the second floor of the New Orleans French Quarter Precinct Building.

The recordings were obviously made at intervals as time passed and her location varied. For a few minutes there was more of the same tour-guide stuff; just verbal notes of her physical impressions, ideas she obviously intended to help her when she wrote her article later.

"Vast Honey Island Swamp has formed around the mouth of the Pearl River where it empties into the Gulf of Mexico along the Louisiana–Mississippi border. Since the earliest days of settlement in the Deep South, this remote area has played host to French, Spaniards, Creoles, Arcadians, various Indian tribes, pirates, runaway slaves, criminals and deserters from countless armies.

"Where I'm standing right now, however, is actually the one-thousand acre 'inner circle' of Honey Island, a taboo place known to locals as Shrieking Swamp. It is this area, so the well-established legend goes, that's haunted by a mythical demon known as the *loup-garou* or 'loogaroo' to locals, a distinctly American variation of the European werewolf."

Breaux raised a hand, and I switched the recorder off again.

" 'Well-established legend' my sweet ass," he repeated, his tone mocking the words. "It's pure horseshit being shoveled by a bunch of redneck chawbacons. Did you say this dizzy broad went in there alone?"

"She hired a local Cajun guide who took her onto Honey Island. But he refused to go into Shrieking Swamp, so she made him wait while she took the boat in alone. He claims she never returned."

"You've put him under the light?"

I nodded. "He's got no priors, and we can't poke any holes in his story. He also volunteered for and passed a polygraph."

"Mm . . . well, the way this chick looks, *some*body fucked her and killed her, you can make a book on it. That or the silly little twat fell into some quicksand. Either way, by now she's fermenting in a 'gator hole, end of story."

It never took Breaux long to get into his hardass riff. He was a gruff old coot, notorious for his impatience when subordinates failed to produce, and he could be a pig-headed son of a bitch when his hems were flaring – as I suspected they were now judging from the way he fidgeted in his chair. Made me wonder how many solvable investigations he had closed down just because his asshole was on fire.

"That's pretty much what I thought, too," I assured him. "But there's more on the tape, you need to hear it."

I thumbed the microcassette back on.

"In the case of Shrieking Swamp, however, the loogaroo tale has taken an . . . interesting deviation from the usual reports of violent, killer attacks. For this loogaroo does not kill or injure – reportedly, it sexually ravishes its victims. It is an invisible, supernatural sex fiend, and according to its supposed victims, it is either male or female depending on the gender of the person attacked. In fact, I talked to a husband and wife who were attacked simultaneously, only a few feet apart, and each one reported the attacker as 'of the opposite sex.'"

"Screw this," Breaux interrupted again. "Why do I need to hear this shit? It's the same old doo-dah we been hearing for years now. You a cop or one of the fuckin' squirrels?"

"You need to hear some more," I insisted.

"And *you* need some serious couch time, Savoy."

But he piped down when I turned the recording back on.

"I could no longer avoid this story once it became a persistent rumor. Oh, it never makes the air waves or establishment print media, not even locally in Louisiana or Mississippi. But it's creating a growing fascination on the Internet. Yesterday I interviewed a Tulane University graduate student in anthropology who claims to have been 'ravished' by the sex demon of Shrieking Swamp. She has developed an interesting theory that the 'loogaroo' angle developed back in the earlier days because attack victims were too scandalized to openly report the sexual nature of their bizarre experiences. Some cover story was needed to explain torn clothing, scratch marks, and bites left by the—"

"Shut that fucking drivel off," Breaux growled.

"It's coming up," I insisted. "Just listen."

"—and I've also interviewed folks who live near Shrieking Swamp, for no one actually lives *in* it. And most of them concur: the eerie sounds emanating from the swamp seem much more like gasps than shrieks; howls of ecstasy, not terror. And as another attack victim admitted to me: 'Once you've had it, you may well wander back in for more. I have and so have others who—"

Breaux heaved himself out of the chair, nearly 300lbs of pissed-off precinct captain angling around his desk and bearing down on me like the Apocalypse.

"Savoy, you *and* this broad are so full of shit your feet are sliding. I said turn that fucking thing—"

A sharp gasp sliced into his threat, and Breaux froze like a hound on point, staring at the microcassette recorder.

"What? Oh, good heart of *God*! What's happening to me?"

Her voice had suddenly grown a few octaves sharper. Her breathing, barely audible to this point, became rushed and heavy panting.

"I don't understa—oh! *Oh!* What's—wha-wha-what's—*oh!* Oh, my God, oh, *OH*! That—oh, Christ, yes, *yess*, that, *that*! Jesus God, *YES*!"

There was a sudden rush of frenzied noises: clothes being ripped, undergrowth rustling as if she were thrashing around, groans and moans and sharp little yipping cries even a Vestal Virgin would know were sex noises. And a steady, rapidly increasing noise like dozens of cats hungrily lapping milk.

Her voice was hardly recognizable as human now, escalating to a shrieking pitch that seemed as much pain as pleasure.

"Yes, yes, *yes* . . . ahh, ahh, *ahh* . . . do that, do it, do it, faster . . . lick me, *lick* me, I . . . oh, I'm going to . . . oh, Jesus, I'm going tooo exx-*plode*!"

And she did, a banshee cry welling up so loud that, even on the tiny speaker, it seemed to fill the office.

The recorder went silent, and I thumbed it off again, watching Breaux.

He looked shell-shocked. I watched him return to his chair and slack into it, scrubbing his face with his hands as if trying to wake up. For a minute he refused to even look at me, studying his office as if seeing it for the first time. His eyes went first to the framed prints of Louisiana shore birds lining one wall, then to the old print sampler he'd swiped from a now defunct Basin Street brothel: IT TAKES A HEAP O'LO-VIN' TO MAKE A HOME A HOUSE.

"She could've faked this, Cap," I finally remarked. "Publicity, whatever. If she did, she's one hell of a porno actress."

Breaux mopped his glistening face with a handkerchief.

"The best," he conceded. "Christ, I got a Viagra hard-on just listening to her."

He looked at me, and I could tell he didn't think she faked any of it.

"It's like the way you never confuse TV voices with real people talking," he told me. "There's just this difference you can always tell. Same with fake sex noises versus real. Neal, am I fucking bonkers here, or did Miss Libby get her little muff licked eight beats to the bar?"

"There's one last recording before the tape goes silent."

I flicked the recorder on again and fast-forwarded past some empty tape.

"Though few of us can name it, we all search for something transcendent, something that takes us out of ourselves. Sex, when it works right, is the ultimate no-mindedness. For me it has never worked right. Until now. Until this place. Until . . . you. Now I have sloughed my old self as surely as a snake sloughs its old skin."

I turned the recorder off, watching Breaux closely.

"Very weird," I volunteered.

"I know *that's* real," he agreed. "Shit! I'm fed up to *here* with that freakin' swamp. At least a dozen people have disappeared there over the past ten years. And each time the department takes it in the shorts."

"French Emma's curse," I said, mainly just to piss him off. And I succeeded. I watched a vein over his left temple swell until it looked like a hyperventilating worm.

"You sorry-ass dipshit," he growled at me. "Since you think it's so funny, Sergeant Savoy, I want your ass in that swamp tomorrow. You know that area, check it out good. And keep this fucking recording under wraps. I shit thee not – if the media bozos get hold of this, I'll have your guts for garters."

"French Emma's curse" is part of the tourist-oriented local mythology in southeastern Louisiana. French Emma Johnson was rumored to be an avid practitioner of Obeah, sometimes called Cajun Voodoo, a hybrid of African and Southern American black magic. She was also the most notorious "landlady" in Storyville, the infamous yet legal New Orleans tenderloin that thrived, adjacent to the French Quarter, between 1898 and 1917, when the U.S. Navy razed it as a public-health menace to the military.

Emma's "sporting house" was the first to be leveled. Not only did she lose a fortune in this raid, she became the whipping girl for the blue-nosed crusaders. She was literally run out of town after her head was shaved to shame her. Forced to flee penniless into Honey Island Swamp, she reportedly laid a strange curse on her tormentors: "Long after my bones rot in this swamp, the siren's song will endure like an angel with savage weapons."

Of course the voodoo angle was a crock, and I never met one local who seriously believed it. But there was no denying that Shrieking Swamp, the remote heart of Honey Island, had become a black hole into which people simply vanished forever, prompting the rubes to make up the "cry of the loogaroo" crap. There was never even a hint of any crime, and because the area was a virtual sinkhole of quicksand pockets, it was natural for the authorities to assume accidental deaths with no hope of recovering bodies.

But Libby Mumford's bizarre tape recording suggested it might not be that simple.

Her strange final message to the world, complete with sounds of orgasmic overdrive, had lit a fire under me to solve this long-standing mystery. Ever since I was a kid I had hunted and fished along Honey Island's meandering bayous, so I had no trouble guiding a borrowed pirogue deep into the dark, tangled swamp. A pirogue's shallow draw and flat bottom allow it to float in only inches of water, and there's no current to fight in a swamp, only mudbanks and submerged tree roots.

The sun, only rarely visible through the dense overgrowth, nonetheless seemed to remain stuck high in the sky as if pegged there, radiating a merciless furnace heat. Thick humidity clung to my skin like wet cloth. Eerie fingers of sunlight poked through the thick canopy of trees, and I became almost hypnotized by the powerline hum of insects, the only sound besides my paddle slicing through the dark, still water.

"Libby! Libby Mumford!" I called over and over into a megaphone.

But my words simply disappeared like stones into a well, and after a while I gave up calling her name – each time I disturbed that breathing stillness, I felt like I was shouting swear words in church.

Uneventful hours ticked by until at last I was following the final bayou that snaked through Shrieking Swamp on its eastern edge. I decided to paddle through the next dog-leg bend, then head back to my car for the hour-long drive back to New Orleans. I was halfway through the bend when I heard it – a keening, ululating noise I couldn't even find the vocabulary to describe.

You really *can* be "shocked to the marrow," just as surely as your blood really can carbonate with fear as mine did at that moment. The noise did not seem human or animal, but hell-spawned and demonic, and yet it literally and instantly aroused me, my erection so hard that it throbbed painfully against my restraining jeans.

The pirogue glided through the bend, and I spotted Libby Mumford.

She was lying on her back along the muddy bank of the bayou, completely naked, both shapely legs raised into the air and spread wide as she writhed and wiggled like a *mambo* who'd been mounted by the *loa*. The honey-colored skin was splotched with dried mud, the platinum hair tangled with leaves and twigs.

"That!" she cried out in a voice distorted by intense lust. "*That*, oh yes, *do* that! Do me deeper, harder, oh yes, your big cock is tamping my shit! Yesss, like *that*!"

Her taut round ass began flexing and releasing like a blowfish, her pelvis thrusting up rapidly from the ground, and her nipples were swollen so stiff they looked like little chocolate thumbs. She was so amped up with passion that every breath included a slight groan. Clearly she was enjoying the fuck of her life.

Or *thought* she was. Because in fact she was all alone on that muddy bank.

I was witnessing some kind of insanity. Yet, all I could feel was my own demanding lust. My cock throbbed like there was a tourniquet around it, and I could hear my pulse surf-crashing in my ears.

"Like *that!*" she howled, thrashing like a gut-hooked fish. "That's it! Yes, yes, *yes*, I'm going to – oh, Christ, I'm gonna – *anhh!*"

In my time I've watched a few babes get their rocks off, and if I'm lying, I'm dying – Libby climaxed just then, a shuddering, screaming orgasm that left her gasping, spent, and weak.

Don't get me wrong. The objective cop in me knew damn well that even a PERK – a physical-evidence recovery kit – would've turned up no signs in her vagina of actual sexual intercourse. Yet, "real" it was. Beyond the swamp's fungoid stink of rot and decay, I could detect another odor staining the air: the faint bleach smell of spent semen.

"Libby!" I called out, starting to paddle toward the bank.

She sat up quickly, and I received another jolt when she looked in my direction: her lips were visibly swollen, as if from passionate kissing.

Her glassy-eyed glance touched me and slid away. She scrambled to her feet and turned to flee into the swamp.

"Libby, wait! I'm a cop! Dammit, stop!"

For a moment she obeyed, but when she looked at me again her eyes were mutinous.

"I don't need any cops!" she flung back at me. "Just leave me alone! *Don't* take this away from me, please don't!"

"Take what away? The hell you talking about?"

I had stood up to leap ashore. She pointed toward my crotch. I didn't have to glance down to know there was a huge furrow along my left thigh, the outline of my raging blue-veiner.

"That! You felt it, too, didn't you? Come back if you want the best sex of your life!"

"Wait! You can't survive in this—"

But it was no use. She had already disappeared like a frightened rabbit.

"What, I gotta pop you on your snot locker just to get a freakin' report out of you, Neal?"

Breaux stared at me across his bomb-rubbled desk, that lopsided mouth of his twisted into an impatient scowl.

I opened my mouth to reply, but the words snagged in my throat like half-chewed bread.

"Well, Jesus Katy Christ!" Breaux exploded. "You *did* search the swamp this weekend?"

I nodded.

"As much of it as I could," I qualified. "But it'd be easier to bite your own teeth than for one man to search that entire swamp."

Breaux's eyes puckered with suspicion. "That dog won't hunt, Sergeant. What are you holding back?"

Again I opened my mouth to report, but I felt like a snake trying to get started on loose sand. Since Saturday I hadn't been able to shake the retinal after-image of Libby's gorgeous body thrashing around like a downed power line. *Come back if you want the best sex of your life.*

"All right, I get it," he essayed next, changing tactics. "You didn't find out jack shit, did you?"

Holding back was one thing. But in twenty years of being a cop, I'd never lied to a superior yet.

"I saw Libby," I finally told him.

Breaux's eyes bulged out like wet white marbles.

"You saw her *alive?*"

I nodded, thinking: oh, she was sure-god alive, all right. More alive, probably, than any other woman on Planet Earth.

"Did you talk to her?"

"Sure. She told me to leave her alone. Then she ran off."

"And you let her?"

I shrugged. "How could I stop her? Honey Island is public land, after all, and she's broken no laws I know of."

I watched him turn the problem back and forth for a while, studying all the facets and angles.

"I spoze you're right," he finally ceded. "It ain't none of our picnic if some pert skirt decides to play Jane in the jungle. So what do we do now, sit and play a harp? This chick's got family looking for her."

I said nothing for perhaps thirty seconds, hearing Libby's urgent voice in my auditory memory: *You felt it too, didn't you?*

Since Saturday I'd been trying to convince myself I had only gotten aroused at sight of her in sexual ecstasy. But it was more than that, different somehow. As if I had wandered onto the periphery of an area of electrically charged particles. And as if, had I gone any closer to her, *I* might have been "mounted," too.

"I think I should go back," I finally replied. "Try to find her and talk her into resurfacing. Hell, how can she survive there?"

Breaux approved this with a nod, shrewd eyes studying me like a bug under a magnifying glass.

"You do that. Just one more question: has this got anything to do with that porno soundtrack she left behind? Or the last comment we heard on her tape recorder? All that doo-dah about how fucking is the 'ultimate no-mindedness?'"

I shook my head. "Hell if I know."

"Who's the 'you' she's talking to?" he added, eyes piercing me like a pair of bullets.

"Nobody I know," I answered truthfully.

He watched me a few seconds longer, trying to read the unspoken subtext but drawing a blank.

"You bolted to that chair?" he finally growled. "Get the hell outta here, and don't come back without Libby."

The next day, when I made my return trip to Shrieking Swamp, one part of me intended to carry out Breaux's order. Libby, I told myself repeatedly, needed help. Sure, she had begged me not to "take this away from me." But heroin addicts felt the same loyalty toward their sickness, too.

Another part of me, however, rejected this supposedly noble impulse of mine. Piss on the humanitarian schmaltz about "helping" – she had invited me back for the best sex of my life, and naturally I assumed she meant with her.

And *with* her is how it turned out. As in "in the presence of."

I returned to the very same spot where I had last seen her. For hours I waited, slapping at bugs, until the waning sun was replaced by a moon bright enough to make shadows.

I could hear the nocturnal predators coming to life, slithering and splashing all around me, and still no sign of Libby. Bored and dejected, I started to drag the pirogue back into the water, intending to return to my car.

"You came back," a voice behind me said softly.

I whirled around. Libby stood there in the buttery moonlight, wearing a muddy and torn *brisa del mar* dress. Her platinum hair gleamed like quicksilver.

"Yeah, but I'm not sure why," I admitted.

"You're about to find out why," she assured me, starting to unbutton her dress.

She let it fall in a puddle at her feet, naked now, and the sight of those huge, high-thrusting tits on such a slim girl sent blood surging into my cock.

"You get naked, too," she ordered me, and I didn't require any further persuading to peel off my clothes. I expected the mosquitoes to eat me alive, but oddly, there was no longer an insect in our vicinity.

"Not too close," she told me when I started toward her.

"But I've been thinking about you since Saturday."

"About *me*?" Her laughter was softly melodic. "You still don't understand. But you will. Oh, you *will*. Be patient."

A few minutes passed in a strange, communal silence. She hadn't even asked my name, and yet, I felt as if we were already close – closer, even, than lovers.

"You're here," she said abruptly, joy sparking her tone, and it was clear she wasn't talking to me this time.

Soon I heard urgent sucking noises and watched in slack-jawed astonishment as both her nipples stiffened in the moon-light. Whimpering, she sank to her knees, her breathing suddenly ragged and hoarse.

I was on the verge of stepping closer to take her right there in the muck. But invisible hands seemed to grip my shoulders and propel me down onto the ground. My first reaction was abject fear, but that quickly passed as the incredible pleasure took over.

Moist heat flowed over my erection, the unmistakable feel of a hungry mouth pleasuring me. An invisible tongue swirled all around my swollen glans, invisible teeth raked along my length with just enough pain to hurt so nice. A hot, tingling pressure began to build between my asshole and my balls, and it felt like every nerve ending in my prick had been raised to the fifth power as a pleasure receptor.

Whoever or whatever was sucking me into a spastic frenzy never did take any recognizable form. Yet, the "substance" was all there: a feminine odor like honeysuckle and lilacs, even the tickle of long, silky hair brushing my belly while this . . . demonic nymph teased me to the brink of explosive release.

"*Lick* my cunt!" Libby screamed from only a few feet away. "Faster, *faster*, yes, like *that*, you fucking stud!"

I managed a quick glance in her direction. Her legs were raised, drawn back to expose her sex, and the wet slapping sounds of a good tongue-lashing were unmistakable. Her pleasure-glazed eyes met mine in that eldritch moonwash, and watching each other had a powerful booster effect on our lust.

Her sharp cry of orgasmic release was followed almost immediately by my own. Both of us came so violently that we went limp and comatose afterward, floating on a sea of dazed bliss.

But that supernatural blow job was only the beginning of my initiation into the erotic addiction that had already claimed Libby. I came to with my erection back in full force. A tight velvet glove seemed to slip over it, I felt invisible vaginal walls parting, and for hours Shrieking Swamp lived up to its name as Libby and I were both fucked with savage sweetness while the moon crept toward its zenith.

It's been several months since that night, and I haven't left the swamp except for brief trips to a little Cajun grocery store near the mouth of the Pearl River. I live with Libby in an old shack built on stilts, somebody's long-abandoned fishing camp. It's primitive: a rusted hand pump for water, no toilet, and when it rains the place leaks like a perforated bladder.

Search parties have come through a few times, and we hid in a giant deadfall until they left. Neither one of us ever wants to leave our invisible lover.

It's weird, but neither of us wants to fuck each other, either. Oh, sure, we've bonded, all right, grown inseparable. We even sleep together naked in the shack's old leather-webbing bed. And we love watching each other in the throes of carnal abandon. But Libby was right when she claimed that "normal sex" pales in comparison to what we now have.

But all is far from bliss. We bought a battery-powered radio.

Late one night, when it was too hot to sleep, we were listening to some stump-screaming evangelist: "My friends, the Devil is sailing on a sinking ship, and the place where he reigns is called Doomed Domains."

After that we tossed the radio out. It was a reminder that we ourselves are doomed – doomed and damned. For neither of us doubts that whatever holds us in thrall is demonic. We simply aren't strong enough to resist it. We have willingly immersed ourselves in the destructive element.

There's shame – and fear. When lust becomes your drug, you must constantly up the dose. Each night the sex becomes more savage, more physically punishing. What will our ravenous libidos demand by this time next year – if we even live that long?

The darkness within us all is deep, and for some it makes demands like a stomach that must be fed. I only know one thing for sure about Shrieking Swamp: whatever lurks there lusts there, and now it lusts within the two of us.

Under the Frog Bridge

Debra Hyde

During the first weeks of spring, everyone around me complained about the winter that wouldn't end, but I kept my mouth shut. I said nothing when sleet hissed against our windows, when the snow pack melted and the river frothed mad, or during the countless gray days of pounding rain. Even five inches of snow from an early April nor'easter didn't compel me to speak. Saying anything would jinx me.

All that changed mid-May. In its usually chaotic way, the southern New England weather swung from intolerable to temperate, pushing people from sweaters to tank-tops practically overnight, proving, I suppose, how native nutmeggers can't escape that locally indelible Twain-attributed saying, "If you don't like the weather, wait."

But wait, I could.

Unfortunately, forty-eight hours into the 70-degree days, my luck ran out. Standing at the kitchen sink as dusk neared, I heard them from the window, spring peepers, they who herald the first warm nights of spring. In the seasonal wetland behind our neighborhood, they sprang up, tiny creatures no bigger than a fingernail, always heard but largely unseen. They would signal my fate, a fate I'd meet under a man-made shrine that, ironically, worshipped their kind.

When John came in from hauling the trash to the curb, I knew I was doomed. The smirk on his face told me so.

As Friday turned toward twilight, the temperature slid from hot to comfortable with forecasters predicting a clear night. Spring birdcalls faded with the sunlight and in the void between light and dark, those spring peepers rose again in choir. Unlike the birds that dominated the daylight, their sound was not diverse; it lacked the distinction of a mockingbird among crows. No, the spring peepers croaked in cheeping, high-pitched unison and, lone soul that I am, I didn't welcome them. If anything, I wished they'd croak deeper so they could sound more like the doom I anticipated.

My fate arrived hours later, once darkness had fully wrapped itself around my world. John came to me, collar and leash in one hand and a small duffle bag in the other. He motioned me to follow him to the couch where he dropped the bag at his feet as he sat down. He opened it and drew out my clothes.

"Strip," he ordered.

He needn't say more; I knew the drill. I peeled off my common, everyday clothes and stuffed my trembling body into the uniform of the night: flannel shirt, leather chaps, and a custom shaped, leather underwear that hid my crotch and the roundness of my ass but left one thing accessible: my asshole.

In the dark, only that hole matters.

Once I had dressed properly, Master strapped the collar to my neck and the leash to its O-ring. He picked up the duffle bag and rose with a "time to go." As we moved to the front door, he turned off the lights, both inside and out. To my immediate relief, we left our house under the cover of darkness. It was unlikely that anyone would see us like this, the leader and the led, bound by collar and leash.

As we walked down our driveway and along the street, my relief dissipated and the anxiety that comes when John does this to me flooded me. The cover of night was not enough to protect me from what was to come. If anything, it facilitated the inevitable.

The walk to the bridge is brief, just a "down the hill, cross the street, turn left" jaunt. Little in the way of living things moves about this time of night, rarely anything beyond a stray car of teenagers trying to make curfew or the bark of a keen-eared dog. All too often, I long for something to halt our steps, something that would deter us from the bridge, but I'd yet to see so much as a cat cross our path.

East of the bridge, John found the trail down and pulled me

by the leash to follow. I stepped over the guardrail and watched my steps down the narrow footpath. The ground was soft and my boots sank slightly into a near-muck that had not yet grown slippery. The air smelled of moldering leaves, a rank odor that said last autumn's detritus had yet to give way to its final decomposition. Soon, the smell of lube and human bodies would overtake my senses. I cannot say which odor I find most detestable – or more morbidly attractive.

Where the footpath met flat ground, a puddle of water greeted my steps. Wet, everything was wet with spring. My time indeed had run out.

We walked along level ground until a gravel slope encroached on us and forced us toward the train tracks. I stumbled as John trotted me over the tracks and toward the bridge's first footing. There we settled into the obscurity of darkness. I could hear the river running just yards beyond us and the rush of its waters spoke of spring runoff, too swift to host those little frogs of dusk.

John dropped the duffle bag, knelt before it and rummaged through its contents. A cursed word of frustration, then the tiny beacon of a penlight shined down. Onto the hood.

The hood obscures me, but it also shields me. It muffles the sounds of that which gets done to me. It soothes me with its musty scent and renders me anonymous so I need not focus on how vile I am. It saves me from the worst of what occurs to me.

The first time John did this to me, the hood kept me from a panicked flight. It soothed me the same way it might comfort a horse being led from a barn fire. It kept me manageable and in my place.

That's not to say it freed me from all anxiety – I was well aware of why I was there, even then, that first time – and when the man stepped up to me, I flinched at his nearness. As rich as the smell of my hood was, it could not overcome the smell of this man. He was feral with the need for release. Yet he hesitated.

"Man or wo—" he tried, but John interrupted.

"Does it matter?"

No answer.

"I told you I'd bring a hole to fuck. An asshole. Here it is, take it or leave it."

John can be such a sarcastic dick when he bullies people.

I tried not to think about what was happening to me when I heard the tear of wrapper and the grumbling that came with it. I tried to go blank as the man's dick pushed into me. I struggled to divorce myself from the snorting beast he became as he arched over me, furious in his intent and desire.

I imagined the spring peepers instead, hearing them in the idle of my mind. *Fruelings*, my late grandmother had called them, *fruelings*. Such a sweet word, it celebrates the very sense of spring as it rolls off the tongue. Like that other word my grandmother would use, *liebeskind*. But that word had dark beginnings. "Nothing good will come of this," she had hissed to my mother when first she held me, before she welcomed me into the family with her kisses and her cooing. *Liebeskind – me*, the child tainted by an accident and abandonment, cherished despite the shame.

As the cock shuddered within me, I choked on my shame, knowing that that man's orgasm had fulfilled my grand-mother's old world prediction.

In the safety of daylight, after that first time, I walked to the bridge to marvel at it and at what had occurred beneath it. Built just before the stock market's bust had robbed Connecticut of income, it connected two disparate sides of the small city I called home, and the Department of Transportation had spared no expense in making the bridge a notable landmark. Over each footing sat a giant thread spool, sculpted from stone and bare of thread, marking the city's glory as a one-time thread manufacturer. At each end of the bridge, upon two taller and more majestic spools, sat eleven-foot tall bullfrogs. There they perched, each copper green with bulging gold eyes. Crouched on three legs while a hind leg stretched luxuriously down over the spool, each looked upwards towards the sky, but not quite at it, vacant and dumb.

The state of Connecticut had pompously named the bridge "Thread City Crossing" but everyone around town called it what it was: the frog bridge. And beneath the clean lines of its design, hiding under its commemorative presentation, lay evidence of the city's less savory reality: the waste of lives lived marginally measured in booze bottles, discarded needles,

cigarette butts, and condom wrappers. Amid which I had
croaked plaintively while an anonymous horn dog had fucked
my ass.

And yet I wait for another one of these clandestine and dirty
encounters.

You'd think I'd be ready for whoever approaches me, but
experience has not brought me any ease. I still stand there,
tensing in the dark as I wait to see whether cock or fist or toys
will be used on me.

Yes, some men like toys. Voyeurs, they touch themselves as
John shines his penlight on me, on the whole aching ordeal. I
hear them when they come, and for reasons I've yet to fathom,
I find the sounds of masturbation always more lurid than those
of sport fucking.

Footsteps. I hear them now, muffled but close. Code words
are spoken and John's hand is at my neck, pushing me to bend
over. I hear a zipper, a condom wrapper, twin sounds of
ripping, of things being readied. Cold lube slathers my hole.
John's finger slides into me, prepping me.

The anonymous taker steps up to me, but I'm startled when
I feel a slight, small hand on my hip as the man presses into me.
What enters me is slender and long – the guy must be skinny, I
think – but it feels different, lacks something, and I'm at a loss
to say what.

My asshole, however, says something of its own. It rejects
the cock, protesting in painful spasms. Skinny Guy doesn't
notice; he just keeps pushing and it pisses me off. All I can do
behind the hood is howl and although it feels futile, John
recognizes the tenor of my complaint.

"Hold up there," he tells the trick. "Stop pushing. Rectal
spasms."

Skinny Guy heeds him and, as they wait for me to settle
down, John talks shop with the guy. "First time out since last
year. It tends to panic at the first fuck of the season."

It. Damn, that word, *it.* The sound of which stuns me and
makes me stupid. Stupid enough that my asshole opens right
up.

I know why John does this to me, why he brings me here.
Once, between tricks, he told me how in the years before men

had to worry, he'd bring "his boy" to the bathhouses. How he'd bend the guy over and let cock after cock take his ass, how used the hole would look, by night's end, all stretched and weeping white. He told me he kept his boy naked the next day so he could "test the burn" with dry fingers. He recalled the rent parties he staged, where people would pay for an evening cluster fuck. There, he could take instant photos, capturing anonymous, tight shots of holes, cocks, and mouths.

John brings me here, does this to me, because he misses those days.

Skinny Guy starts up again, fucking me at a slow, steady pace. He utters an "oh yeah, nice" and his other hand comes to rest on my hip. The voice is gruff but shallow, lacking just like the hands.

But the dick that reams me knows what to do and wastes no time going about its business. It plows me, stretches me. Sometimes it grazes a nook of bliss, sometimes it hits a cranny of discomfort.

But Skinny Guy isn't wham-bam rhythmic like the others who've used me. He mixes it up. He grinds his pelvis, cork-screwing his dick into me. He fucks slowly; he fucks fast. When he goes deep and holds it there, I sense that he loves his dick far more than he enjoys my ass.

The variety of movement he foists on me begins to over-whelm me and I want to escape the sensations. I seek refuge. But where can I go?

I think of frogs, again, but this time of their past. I think about that night in 1754 when a sound so terrifying rose up that the village folk feared that if the French and Indians weren't descending upon them, then Judgment Day had. Morning's light revealed that it was neither men nor God who had waged war, but frogs. Hordes of them. And they had battled to the death over a millpond as it went dry and their amphibious screams had sent people spiraling into fear.

Whereas me? I only had a cock up my ass.

Still, I want the frogs to scream for me, to sound the alert, to save me. I long for them to rescue me on this my judgment day.

It won't happen though. The water moves too fast for all but those stoic and stupid copper frogs. No, I won't be rescued and

I can't scream in death knell fervor either because my suffering is a myth and a myth is never the truth and my truth is darker and deeper than any mass frog extinction ringing out in the black of night. Because deep down inside, I like what happens to me. I may fear it, I may tremble before it, but ultimately I like it.

The dick pulls out and the void left in its wake is mysterious and confusing. I'm not certain an orgasm was had. But Skinny Guy says "nice hole" and pats my ass. It's the only acknowledgment I receive. No farewell, no clumsy inquiry about whether I'm tucked forward or tapped shut.

As footsteps sound and recede, it dawns on me. The small hands, the underdeveloped voice, the dick that didn't quit with orgasm, he – he who had me – understood all too well how concealment works, how anonymity can mean something other than the obvious. Dysphoria, it would seem, seeks its outlets in camouflaged appearances and finds its solutions in unusual realities.

In the hour just before darkness lifts, I lie in bed, unable to sleep. Outside, the birds haven't waited for daybreak; they chatter in the dark. House wrens, finches, even the occasional robin make noise. A brief ruckus in the tree outside our bedroom window tells me that even baby birds need an a.m. feeding.

But these sounds will fade as the breeding and brooding subside in the heat of summer. So, too, will one of two things that croak, namely that which sings sweetly, collectively, historically. The other won't be that lucky. It will protest and plead in falsetto and false struggle every time it's taken out and made anonymous.

But at least by then the days will be long and the nights, short. And maybe June will be as rainy a month as the entire winter was white.

Whichever, I'll take my comforts where I find them.

Eye of the Beholder

Mark Timlin

I'd been sitting on the floor inside the walk-in closet for over an hour before I heard the key in the door of the hotel suite. I'd slid in like a ghost using a duplicate when I knew she'd left to meet him, and before I went to my hiding place I wandered around for a few minutes picking up things here and there: a used glass, an item of soiled underwear that I'd put to my face to smell her musk. I wondered what the hell I was putting myself through again. She'd left her portable CD player on repeat, playing an old Joni Mitchell album that I'd always liked, and I nodded my head in time to the music.

Inside the closet her clothes hung close to me and I could smell old perfume, old makeup and just the hint of sweat. But that might have been from me. It was hot in there and I had only cracked the sliding, mirrored doors an inch or so, just enough to see the king-size bed lit softly by the bedside lamps that she'd left burning.

The two of them had been drinking and were noisy as they came in, straight to the bedroom, where I was waiting. No messing with niceties like a schooner of sherry or an after-dinner mint. I appreciated that. The closet was getting warmer and warmer by the minute, and as they entered the room I squinted through the gap to see them both, and what they were going to do to each other.

The woman was tall and blonde in a leather coat with her hair piled up on top, and they'd obviously been having such a good time in the bar that some of it had come loose and strands hung around her face. Even so, she looked great, and even better when she did something to it at the back and it fell to her shoulders. Her hair had always been beautiful: shiny, lustrous, the colour of butter melting in the sun.

Lucky bloke, I thought as they stood by the door and kissed. She had the face of a Hollywood star on a movie poster and blue eyes that said, "Come to bed, and I mean right now".

He was taller, older, florid, ugly, as it goes, and I felt my spine contract at the sight of his face. He was big, but not fat, in a pinstripe suit cut to make him look slimmer, a blue shirt, striped tie and black slip-on shoes. When they broke away from each other he slammed the bedroom door behind them, as she slipped off her coat to reveal the inevitable little black dress. She tossed her coat over a chair and he threw his jacket down and grabbed her again. She didn't object when he kissed her once more, and neither did she object when he spun her round and pulled the zip of her dress down to her waist and peeled it off her shoulders so that it fell to her feet like a pool of ink before she stepped out of it.

Underneath she was wearing tart's gear, whore's kit. But by Christ she did look good in it. Black fuck-me shoes with five-inch heels, black nylons that gleamed in the light with thick bands of double black at their tops, then pure white thighs, the colour of fresh milk, slashed by the black bondage of suspenders, lace briefs just see-through enough to give a hint of the goodies underneath, and a black lace bra that her breasts hardly needed for support but to flaunt their beauty. To tease. Her tummy was flat as a billiard table, her waist was tiny then flared into rounded hips and when she turned round she shook the twin peaches of an arse to die for.

I could see he appreciated the sight as the front of his pinstripe trousers tented, and when she turned back she reached for his cock straight away. She seemed to be pleased with what she found and she knelt down and unzipped him, reached in and pulled out his prick. It was long and thick, gorged with blood, and she spat on her fingers and rolled back the foreskin before taking it in her mouth, both of them groaning with pleasure.

It was getting hotter in the closet as I watched, and I felt myself harden too and I hated myself for it.

"Wait," he said, and she stopped for a moment, releasing his

prick. He kicked off his shoes, undid the button on his
trousers, and pushed them and his boxer shorts off, looking
comical in shirt-tails and socks. No one ever knows how silly
they look having sex.

As he tugged off his tie and pulled at the buttons on his shirt,
almost popping them off the material in his haste, his cock
hardened even more as she took it inside her soft mouth again
and she put her fingers in the bush of his pubic hair and
gathered his balls into her hand. Bitch, I thought, as she sucked
on his dick like a baby at a tit. Bitch. Just you wait. It didn't
help that my cock was now unbearably hard and all caught up
in my underwear, and in the position I was in I couldn't adjust
the damn thing to get it comfortable.

Anyway, after she'd feasted on his prick for a few minutes
she let it slip out of her mouth and it was all shiny with spit and
they went over to the bed and really got down to it after he'd
pulled off those stupid socks. First, off comes her bra and by
God she's got a pair of tits. He held them in his big hands and
started sucking on each nipple until they were as pink and hard
as pencil erasers, and she started wanking his cock in her hand
and I was worried he was going to come all over her and I'd be
stuck in that damned closet until he could get it up again. But
she knew just how to get him to the peak of orgasm before she
let him slip back.

He was loving all that, squeezing her breasts and rolling her
nipples between his fingers, making her cry out half in pain, half
in pleasure. After a minute or two he went for the main event,
running his hand down her belly and inside her knickers and he
obviously liked what he found as I could see his fingers were
slippery with cunt juice, and he took a big lick and then kissed
her again, a long, lingering snog, and at the same time pulled her
pants over her hips and down those long legs and let her kick
them off. She opened her legs wide and I could see that her cunt
was shaven close to the skin which somehow made her look even
more naked, like a young girl, even though she was still wearing
the suspender belt, nylons and those shiny black shoes. So now
was the time for them to start fucking. The man lay on his back
and she climbed on top, her favourite position, and she guided
his prick up inside her and slid down hard.

Come on, I thought, get on with it. We haven't got all day. But she took her time, riding him like a jockey, her head thrown back, eyes closed, her hands clenched tightly in the hairs on his barrel chest, until she froze solid, gripping him tighter inside, and came with a whoop. They stayed like that, a human tableau, for a moment that seemed to go on for ever before she rolled off onto her side, her cunt opened to my eyes, all red and wet and raw inside before she leant up on one elbow and looked directly at the closet door. I imagined she was looking straight into my eyes but she gave no sign that she could see me or anything else after her climax. Maybe she was admiring herself in the mirror, or maybe she just didn't give a damn.

But the man wasn't going to allow her a rest. His fat, red cock was still erect. Still ready to shoot his spunk up into her belly. Good job, I thought, as he grabbed her again and stuck his face between her legs, slurping like a pig at the trough, then with dripping lips, covered her face with her own juice and threw her down onto the bed. I waited until he climbed on top and pushed his cock deep inside and started to move. As he rose and fell I could see her cunt bulge from the girth of his knob and his huge balls banging against the crack of her arse, and I swear I could smell the stink of their sex clear across the room.

They both began to moan as they approached climax, she for the second time, he for the first. Hers a slight whimper from the back of the throat and his harsher, louder, just as I had expected, and was waiting for. There was no chance they could hear as I gently slid the closet door open, its runners carefully greased earlier. I stood up slowly, the surgical gloves on my hands hot and damp inside, much like her vagina, I thought, but dismissed the thought immediately. On rubber soles I crossed the carpet silently, and just as he was beginning on the short strokes I tapped him on his big, bare, suntanned shoulder with the silencer on the end of the .22 automatic I held tightly, but not too tightly, in my right hand.

He stopped in mid-thrust and turned his head with a look of astonishment on his heavy features.

"Hi. How's it going?" I asked, "Having a good time?"

"What . . . ?" was the only word I let him say before I stuck the barrel of the pistol in his ear and fired once. The report was no louder than a virgin's sigh, but I could imagine the small, powerful bullet ripping around inside his skull, scrambling his brains into a bloody mush, as his eyes almost popped from their sockets from the pressure within his head. He collapsed onto the woman's body.

She screamed a small scream then, not as loud as the one she'd made when she'd orgasmed a few minutes before, and tried to heave his dead weight off herself. I put the smoking barrel of the gun to her forehead and smiled a smile I was glad I couldn't see, and she flinched as I knew she would when my finger tightened on the trigger again.

We stayed like that for a brief moment before I said, "Come on," in a voice I hardly recognised as my own, as I eased off the pressure and removed the gun from her face. "We've done what we were paid for, let's get this place cleaned up and get out of here."

"You didn't even let the poor bastard come," she said as she pushed at his torso and I helped her roll him over, his almost flaccid cock popping out of her cunt like a cork from a bottle. "You could've at least let him do that."

"Fuck him," I said, "No one comes into my wife but me."

Indigo White, Burnt Umber

Cheyenne Blue

I'd walked too far. The Landcruiser was an indistinct blot on the wavering horizon, hulking down among the saltgrass and low dunes on the southwestern shore. The water licked ankle-deep, clear, white and warm. Curls of silt oozed between my toes; I sank slightly at every step. Beside me, Jeremy was intent on small discoveries, head bent, studying the water.

"Look, Petra." His thin face was alight with enthusiasm. "There's shield shrimp here! Lake Eyre hasn't flooded this far in nearly thirty years, yet the shrimp survive."

The biologist in him. I nodded absently, more interested in finding words to describe how the light moved and danced in this place. Indigo white, burnt umber. The artist in me.

This trip through outback Australia was supposed to re-concile those differences. Re-establish our common ground, rekindle our relationship. I liked to think it was working. Away from the petty annoyances of our shared lives and mundane routine we would reconnect our friendship and our love. Our Friday night sex was as predictable as his Wednesday night Star Trek re-run. And when I snapped at him over the laundry, when he growled at me for the umpteenth time about the misplaced car keys, or when our debate about Sunday night take-out turned into daggers drawn over Indian versus Thai, we both knew we had to do something. Twelve years of married life has to count for something, doesn't it? Doesn't it?

We both came home with travel brochures the next night, and for a week we fenced around the destinations. He sug-gested Turkey, I parried with India. He talked about Russia, which would be a frozen wasteland in November, and perversely I held out for Iceland, which would be floating on the ocean like a giant ice cube. He moved south and in rapid-fire succession came up with Chile, Peru, and South Africa. I countered with Japan, New Zealand, and Bolivia. We were at stalemate. The gaudy brochures were stacked in toppling piles on the coffee table, spreading over the floor like a shiny, multi-colored sea. And we fought bitterly and venomously over what was supposed to cement our marriage.

When he came up with Thailand, it was all I could do to stop myself shooting off a snide comment about the sex trade.

My shoulders slumped. Suddenly it all seemed so petty, so silly. Slowly, I extended a hand to him as he sat in a defensive posture on the couch next to me.

"Jer-bear." I used the pet name I hadn't voiced in years. "Let's start again. Let's pick somewhere together." He grasped my hand and gave me a tentative smile, and I knew it would be all right.

We made love that night, a slow meshing of our bodies, the ritual undulations of the dance that we hadn't bothered with in a long time. Our Friday night bonk didn't count: a few minutes exercising of the bedsprings, a quick release for him, then he'd dutifully bring me off with his fingers. No, that night we made love as it should be done; slowly, wanting to give pleasure, not just scratch an itch. I went down on him for the first time in over a year, stretching my mouth over the rubbery contours of his cock, so familiar but so strange for the absence. I sucked him, insinuating a finger up between his buttocks to tickle his rectum, something I'd never done, only read about. His surprised tightening and then his groan of appreciation told me it was welcomed.

He didn't quite go down on me; his mouth just hovered over my inner thigh as his fingers pushed their way up inside me. But my climax was sharp and intense, full of the heady rush of feeling, the pooling of heat deep in my belly.

The next day we went to the travel agent together.

Hand-in-hand, we perused the brochures lining the shelves, and then we booked a flight to Adelaide, Australia, and reserved a Toyota Landcruiser, fitted out for three weeks' camping.

Of course we argued again after that. We fought on the plane, quietly and viciously in our seats at the back, hissing at each other in an attempt to keep our disagreement from the other passengers. We fought again in Adelaide, when the hotel didn't have the king-size bed we'd requested. And we argued vehemently when we saw our vehicle. The rusty old Toyota was smaller than our full-size SUV back home, yet we were expected to live within its battered shell for three weeks.

But when we turned north toward the Flinders Ranges and wheeled through the wine country, our differences were forgotten. We saw the strange landscape burning in the late spring sun and the narrow strip of bitumen leading off like a promise into the distance, hazed and floating in the strange muted light of this place.

Jeremy stopped the truck in the middle of the road, and we grasped hands over the gear lever. It was partly for reassurance; this was all so strange, so new, and, if I was honest, thrilling. I don't know how long we might have stayed there, but a pickup truck swerved past, honking. The aboriginal driver yelled something, and a beer can bounced off the Landcruiser to roll around in the middle of the asphalt. We looked at each other and laughed.

"I guess we're one tinnie from Adelaide," I said. The great Australian measurement of outback distance: one can of beer per hundred kilometers.

"Well, it's a four tinnie drive to Wilpena Pound from here," Jeremy said, "so we better get moving."

We had no plans beyond exploration. The distances drew us on inexorably towards Australia's center. Leaving the purple ranges behind us we pushed forward across a land as flat as Kansas.

Small things held our attention. I spent an hour in a dry creek studying the patterns of bull ants as they marched across the shifting sands, trying to match the colors to the paint charts in my head. Burnt ochre, titanium white, sienna. Jeremy watched a parade of processionary caterpillars, nose to tail, proceeding in an unbroken line across the road. *Chrogaster lunifer*, he said, an Australian Notodontid.

Jeremy found a book on geology abandoned in a pub and

chanted the names of the rocks as I drove. Argillaceous and calcareous slates, metamorphosed schist and gneiss, sandstone, limestone, granite. The unfamiliar words became a poem, and I'd chant along with him in a singsong voice, banging the rhythm on the steering wheel. He also had a book on desert flora and fauna he'd purchased in the information center at Wilpena Pound. Entranced, he'd turn the pages for hours as we rested in the evenings, our backs against the dusty shell of the truck, the land spread like solitude in front of us.

We soon learned to camp like the locals, stopping beside the road, pulling in behind stunted drooping gum trees, or granite outcrops. Initially we were worried, but no one ever bothered us. All too soon we were in the heart of the outback, way beyond the black stump. Still following our noses, we turned onto the wide dirt Oodnadatta Track.

William Creek, population four, had a light aircraft parked in the middle of the road outside the pub. The pilot was downing a beer inside.

"G'day." The barman wore the universal uniform of the outback male – shorts and singlet. Bare sunburned arms and thick stubby legs. He slapped two beers down on the counter without being asked. "Which way youse headed?"

We looked at each other. "To Lake Eyre," said Jeremy. It hadn't been discussed, but Lake Eyre, the great salty inland sea that covered much of the center of Australia, seemed a fitting place to go. Jeremy had read aloud to me about its dry saltpans and sand. Rivers that drained to Lake Eyre never made it to the ocean.

The barman craned his neck to see out the door of the bar. "One of them rental vehicles," he said. "She'll be right, mate."

We looked at each other in bewilderment. The rusty old truck had done us well so far. We'd even grown rather fond of it. "Right for what?" I asked.

"You'll be going out the back of the pub, into the lake that way," the barman explained. "There's water in the southwest corner of the lake, first time in . . ." He scratched his head, and took a long swig of his own beer, ". . . maybe twenty years or more."

I sensed Jeremy's excitement. He leaned forward on the bar. "How far?"

"Only 'bout a hundred kays or so. But she's rough. It's a three tinnie drive."

Actually it was a four-tinnie, two potty-stop drive. We set up camp behind low dunes just as the sun was setting. We seared steak on the camp stove and washed it down with more beer from the William Creek pub. The wind sprang up, a light circular breeze that stirred the sand at our feet, rustled the thick dune grass and tickled my skin like a lover. To the east were the dry saltpans of the lake. I couldn't see water, but I fancied I could smell it. The air was fresher, not the crackling desert air of the Flinders Ranges. A flock of cockatoos wheeled among the clouds of insects, their cries harsh in my ears.

We made love that night, sweating in the stuffy camper, our skins sticking clammily together as Jeremy lay over me, pumping a steady rhythm that made the camper bounce and sway. At the first shudder of my orgasm the clack and clatter of small insects paused for a suspended moment before resuming, louder than ever.

Jeremy dragged me out at first light and handed me a mug of coffee and a hunk of bread slathered with peanut butter. He waited impatiently as I ate, then threw the dirty dishes into the truck and, taking my hand, led me out onto the lake.

We walked slowly, holding hands like lost children. The cracked saltpan became softer, the air stiller – so silent that the world seemed to be holding its breath. I looked back and saw the dunes already starting to shimmer in unreality. When my feet started to sink, I pulled off my shoes and left them. I could pick them up on the way back.

And then we were out there, so far that the Toyota was indistinct, so far that the light hurt my eyes. The horizon was gone, diffused into the sheen of the lake, absorbed into the sky which floated like a parable above our heads. Jeremy walked by my side, stooping to study the life he found. My eyes were on the absence of horizon, on the floating white light that filled my vision. Titanium white? There was no color and all color. In our solitude there was only light.

When we happened upon our abandoned shoes again, we realized we were lost, circling aimlessly. Out here in the few

inches of bloodwarm water, there were no footprints, no
landmarks to help us navigate. Just the great, white light.

Jeremy looked at me, one eyebrow raised. "I think it's that
way," he said, pointing in what appeared to me to be a random
direction.

"No." I was positive he was wrong. "This way."

We stood locked in stalemate. "If we had a coin, we could
toss it," Jeremy murmured.

I revolved slowly, searching the light for clues. Nothing. We
were alone and lost; the light swelled around us in a subtle
diffusion of color. And so I reached for Jeremy at the same
moment he leaned towards me. Our arms closed around each
other, a haven of comfort, and our lips met, tentatively seeking
the familiar.

He kissed me slowly, a melding of lips and tongues that we
knew well. His hands reached down inside my shorts, cupping
my buttocks, pulling me against him. I wasn't surprised that he
was already hard, pressed between us rigid through the thin
cotton. He was already seeking between my legs, his fingers
raking the hair, probing the wetness inside me. I felt a shell
pink flush rise.

I pulled off my T-shirt and bra and let his mouth close over
my nipple. I wove my fingers through his hair and threw my
head back. Through closed eyelids the white burnt my eyes,
the brightness creating floating patterns of threads. He stroked
me harder than normal, fingers insistent on my clit. The
pressure and friction bordered on discomfort, but the light
encompassed us now, seeping through our skin, illuminating
our bodies from within. It was the light that mattered.

Our clothes were gone. Jeremy's skin shimmered, the harsh
sun bleaching him to his bones. Titanium white, skin pale. We
were down in the water now, on our sides, hips sinking into the
yielding lake bed. I raised my thigh, he slipped in between; no
more foreplay, no more skating, gentle movements. He fucked
me hard, gripping my buttocks, forcing me up against him,
holding me as if he feared he would split me in two. Open-
mouthed he panted into my face, pushing his way up me. I
clenched hard, feeling the smooth sides of his penis advance,
retreat, thrust forward, withdraw. And I came hard, a fierce

strong orgasm, shuddering around him, milking his cock with muscular walls as he pressed his way further inside me, white heat within me, white light around me.

The mud of the lake bed clung like cement. A heavy, pale mud, it streaked our skins, matted my hair. Yellow ochre, streaked sienna. We picked a direction at random and started walking toward where we hoped the truck was. It wasn't visible; there were no features to guide us, so we just walked into the shifting distances, trusting that we would get there. The soft, slippery lake gripped my feet, sucking me in. The mud dried to powder on my thighs and cracked on Jeremy's chest.

I stopped to examine the desiccated corpse of a water bird half submerged in the salty water, its gray feathers caked with silt. Poking it with a toe, I watched with detached interest as a couple of the small shield shrimp moved in the ripples I created. Their chitinous casing well adapted to their harsh life.

Beside me, Jeremy paused, his eyes straining for a horizon. I waited for his worried words. We were totally alone, lost in the bleached landscape.

"See that darker patch on the lake, Petra?" he said. "Who would have thought the wind was indigo white?"

When Calls Ed Wood

Tom Piccirilli

The cats were up in the pomegranate trees again wailing their scrawny asses off next door. They did it at least twice a week, but by now I'd grown used to their prolonged screeching. It reminded me of ambulance sirens in New York and even made me a little homesick.

Monty's place had two main floors, an attic and a mother-in-law apartment around the rear. The landlord and his wife lived in the house proper, but they were always on the run in Mexico from drug dealers they'd burned in East LA. Monty Stobbs stayed in the attic, and I lived out back directly below his window. He wouldn't waste time walking down all the stairways and would just call me on my cellphone.

I'd left New York after having a couple of shows presented off-off Broadway. They were both well-received by critics but didn't draw enough of an audience to stay afloat for long. Monty Stobbs had been hustling the same backers that the director had been hustling, and he'd invited me to come stay with him in Hollywood to write him a screenplay.

I wasn't naive enough to believe it might amount to anything, but for the first time in my life I was desperate enough to fall into the starry-eyed Hollywood trap. I was being evicted and my wife had left the year before. She'd taken the kid, the dog, and the goldfish, but she'd left me with a case of crabs. The fuckers were so big I could identify them well enough to give them names, and after the cream started to work and they died off, I fell into sobbing fits. So there wasn't much holding me in New York.

The script had started off as a joke, which is bad in Hollywood. Nobody at the major studios has a sense of humor, and the small production companies are always looking for the next Ed Wood, something so awful it'll be a hot property in video units and when it shows up on late night cable. Manufactured cult films.

The script was called *Critter From Beyond the Edge of Space* and the pages smelled like beer. I'd drink myself into oblivion every night trying to figure out how I'd gone from writing my historical novel about the Trail of Tears to this piece of shit in front of me.

My phone rang and I picked it up. "What?"

"Listen, you need to rewrite a little."

"Monty, why don't you just shout out the window, you're using up minutes."

He said, "Put in some big-titted sorority girls."

"There's already four milkmaids and the Swedish Women's Volleyball Champions, for when the bus goes off the road outside the haunted house where the alien is residing."

"I know but we need sorority girls too."

"How many?"

"Let's say three to be on the safe side. Can you do it?"

"Sure."

"We're going to start filming tomorrow."

It was the sort of thing I should've been expecting but Monty slid one by every now and again. "The hell are you talking about now?"

"I found some backers and we're going to get enough footage to bring to a production company and get a budget. I've got our actors coming in tomorrow to film a few scenes."

"I'm holding the only copy of this unfinished screenplay, Monty. What kind of actors are these?"

"The best kind, they do whatever you tell them. One more thing, put in a bathtub scene."

"We've got two shower scenes already."

"Yeah, but Zypho the alien is gonna take a bath with one of the girls. Toss it in."

There was a time I would've shrieked louder than the cats next door about something like this, but I couldn't rouse myself enough to care much. I glanced over at the unfinished manuscript of my novel and fought back a sigh. "Sure."

When I was frustrated I usually went upstairs to the kitchen and baked. My grandmother had taught me how to cook before I hit my teens. I'd seriously thought about going to gourmet school and becoming a chef. On days like these I really regretted some of my life decisions.

Most screenwriters would've just drank half a bottle of JD down and been done with it. I made two apple pies and a lemon meringue with crust so light it nearly floated out the window.

My cellphone rang. "Hello?"

"Are you baking again? Knock that shit off, Betty Crocker, and get to work!"

I went back to my desk, sat at the keyboard, and in twenty-eight minutes I'd added three sorority sisters who were in a van coming back from feeding the homeless when they were side-swiped by the bus carrying the Swedish Women's Volleyball Champions, just outside of the haunted house where Zypho the man-eating alien had crash-landed.

One of the sorority girls has been going through dumpsters behind ritzy restaurants trying to feed a homeless family of five, and that's why she needs a bubble bath. Rich girl learns all about the harshness of poverty. Washes the street off her skin but not her soul. Further symbolism and morality lessons ensue before Zypho eats her brain.

Sleep was rough in coming. I was irritable, nervous, and the pies hadn't taken off the edge. Finally I drifted off. In the morning I got up early and ran downtown to make copies of the script. Who the hell knew how many people Monty had coming to the house. By the time I got back he'd rearranged the furniture, set up the lights and had the DAT and Sony VX-1000 digital video camera out and waiting.

I handed him the script. He took thirty seconds to flip through it and then said, "Perfect. You're a genius."

Working for Monty had completely shattered my self-esteem but he was somehow also good for my ego.

Monty said, "All right, these are just establishing shots we're doing today. Two of the sexy scenes to get the red-blooded assholes at the studios to kick in for a budget. We'll get the rich sorority girl in the bathtub scene done." He stopped and put a hand on my shoulder. "Very deep there, man, I like the social commentary. The underlying everyman feeling, the struggle of the masses, the clashing cultural order."

"Thank you."

"Maybe you can add a sub-plot, like at the end she goes back home and has a confrontation with her wealthy father, makes him start paying the migrant farmers more money."

"She gets her brain sucked out on page forty-three."

"Oh," Monty said, "right. Well, that's fine too."

"And we'll do the scene with the other two topless girls lost in the attic where the ghost of the insane eighteenth-century vicar is about to get them."

"They're not topless in that scene, Monty."

He grabbed the script from me, turned to the scene, pulled out a pen, and wrote in the words *naked bobs*.

"Naked bobs?"

He wrote in another "o" making it *naked boobs*. "There, that ought to do it. Anyway, the shoot shouldn't take more than the afternoon."

I hadn't been in Hollywood that long and still didn't know my way around the business much, but I had a feeling that Monty wasn't following so-called established channels.

I heard a car pull up in the driveway and Monty let out a giddy laugh that sort of scared me. I didn't mind him being sleazy but when he got silly I feared that anything could happen.

"Here are our sorority babes," he said. "Don't worry, they're all over eighteen."

They sure were. Two women walked in. The youngest one was forty-two and kept showing everybody photos of her first grandchild. I recognized both of them as models in men's magazines who'd been on the downslide for two decades. I had a nostalgic tug, remembering that I'd first beat off to layouts of these ladies twenty-five years earlier. I offered them some pie.

Monty handed out the scripts and the middle-aged sorority babes sat back and studied their roles.

Then Lauren St John walked in and I nearly dropped my lemon meringue.

Lauren St John had been one of the fantasy women of my youth. I'd seen her in *Doreen Does Newark* and *Indiana Bone and the Temple of Cum Sluts* and I'd flogged myself into a bloody little puddle. Over the past few years she'd worked her way into B thrillers and grade-Z horror flicks. She was closing in on fifty and looked barely a year or two older than when she'd taken on three foot-long schlongs in *Temple*. I was intimidated as hell, horny as fuck, and even sort of star struck, wondering if I should ask for her autograph.

Her tits were 42DDs at least and she did this thing where she clapped them around a guy's face until he was almost unconscious. I remembered the protruding thumb-thick nipples and how men and women had suckled on her through her films. Her blouse had the top three buttons opened and I could see the beautiful curves of her tanned breasts and the beginning of a huge black lace bra. My breathing hitched and I started to hiss through my teeth.

The long fiery hair had dimmed to a smoky brown. There were lines in that lovely face but there were lines in everybody's face. I wasn't thirty yet and had more gray hair than my father did at sixty. Her body still looked wonderful beneath a pleated business suit. It was such a dichotomy to what I was used to seeing that I found it even more sexy than if she'd showed up in a bikini. She turned a white smile on me that glowed with sincere affability. It was so beautiful that it nearly brushed me back a step. She held her hand out and said, "Hello, I'm Lauren."

"Hi, I'm Thomas."

Monty rushed over holding a diving suit and a mask covered in plastic tubes and elastic hoses. "The hell is this?" I asked.

"Your Zypho suit."

"*My* Zypho suit?"

"Well, somebody's got to wear it. I'm the cameraman so you get to be the monster. Get down to your skivvies and I'll help you on with it."

"Excuse me," I said to Lauren St John. Monty ushered me into the bathroom. He'd been busy in here cleaning up, I noticed. The tiles had been scrubbed, the glass doors to the stall were sparkling and the tub shined. A large jar of bubble bath sat on the counter. A citrus scent pervaded the shower.

"Damn, Monty, I didn't know you could clean like this when you wanted to. And you break my ass for baking?"

"All right, so I was a little anxious, but the bathroom needs to be clean for Lauren's tub scene. Christ, man, those tits are gonna make us a million bucks!" He plugged the drain and let the water run.

I undressed and climbed into the alien outfit. It was a tight-fitting rubber getup that zipped up in the back and was way too tight. I could barely move at all and after Monty strapped the mask on me I couldn't see much either. I clunked around the bathroom waiting for Monty to help me out of there when I realized that he was gone and Lauren was in there with me.

"Are you okay, Thomas?" she asked.

"Uhm, well – actually –"

She took her skirt off, her blouse, and folded her clothes neatly and placed them on the counter beside her purse. My cock tried to spring to attention but the suit was so tight that it was like trying to get hard against a brick wall. It hurt like fuck, but I didn't mind much as Lauren slowly slid her bra off her shoulders. My Christ. Those beautiful tremendous tits fell free and I gulped so loudly it sounded like a gunshot. They were creamy and luscious and perfect to behold, with enough bounce that as she turned they swung low and rose again as she breathed, brushing us back.

She drifted over and stood in the tub and I was shocked at how beautiful she still was. Lauren grabbed the bubble bath crystals and dumped half the jar into the bath. She got in and sat and began soaping her immense tits. They were still so firm that you could put a pencil under them and it wouldn't stick.

Monty ran back in with the DV camera in one hand, holding an arc lamp in the other. "You're Zypho, critter from beyond the edge of space!"

"Monty—"

"Now go on, get in the tub and feel her up with your tentacles of unholy love."

"Monty, I can barely see anything."

"What's to see? Wave your arms around . . . wait, we have to set this up here . . . we've got to get your tentacles into her nostrils for the brain-sucking scene."

"Holy Jesus Christ."

I waved my arms wildly around and pretended to attack Lauren St John and slurp her brain out of her head. I felt certain I was trapped in an Ed Wood movie – in a flick struggling to be as good as an Ed Wood movie – and that Tor Johnson was about to swing his bald rounded body toward me any second. My legacy to the world was going to be Zypho from the planet Anianibr and it left a black depression gnawing in my chest. The only saving grace was that Lauren was so sexy I was starting to get a woody even through the rubber suit.

"Hey, what's the matter?" she asked.

"What?"

"You tensed up."

"Oh, sorry. I think I'm feeling a tad embarrassed."

"Perfect!" Monty shouted. "It's a print. A little editing and we're good to go. Great job, you two!" He rushed out and I slumped forward, too despondent to do much more than lay there.

She moved beneath me and my hard-on kicked up into high gear. Even if I didn't have a foot-long schlong it got her attention.

I couldn't help myself any longer. I put my hand on her left tit and hoped she wouldn't scream. Even ex-porno starlets can get offended. It was like reaching out and touching paradise. Huge and soft enough to hold up my weight. I prayed she wouldn't scream rape or grab a can of mace out of her purse. I kneaded the areola and toyed with that nipple and grunted where I lay on top of her.

So my hand was on her tit and I couldn't stop thinking of the cops breaking in and sending me up to share ten years with a cell mate named Bubba Raul. It was a precarious situation.

"Uhm," I said.

"It's all right," she told me. "Just take these plastic things out of my nose."

"Oh, sorry."

I tried pulling the mask off but it was connected at the back of the neck to the body suit. "Can you get the zipper down?"

"No, it's stuck."

"Shit. There's no hole in the suit."

"You can't get it out?"

"God damn."

"Can you reach my purse?"

I lurched blindly, managed to find the purse, and handed it to her. She rummaged around for a second and came out with a box-cutter that I could see even through the pinhole-sized punctures I had to look through.

"Jesus Christ! What's that for?"

"Protection. I live in East Hollywood too." She drew out the blade and then kneeled in front of me.

"The fuck are you doing?"

"I'm going to make a slit in this rubber."

"For Christ's sake be careful!"

"I will."

Suddenly her hand snaked in. I was down to about a quarter-mast, but I thought that was pretty good considering the circumstances.

"It's all right," she said.

"Look, I'm not about to make the mistake of thinking that adult actresses are any more promiscuous than anybody else, so—"

"Are you really this cute and embarrassed or are you just pretending?"

I thought about it. "No, I'm really this cute. Well, under the suit anyway."

My breathing became ragged and I knew it wasn't just because of the ten pounds of rubber mask around my head.

Lauren hiked her knees up. I leaned into her, plunging inside so easily that it almost startled me. "That's it, Thomas," she whispered.

"God yes."

"Oh, Thomas."

I liked her using my name. It gave me a warm hitch under my heart.

"Can you see me at all?" she asked.

"I can feel you."

"This is the first time I've ever fucked a creature from outer space," she whispered.

It wasn't the truth. I'd seen her hump some guy in a costume almost as ridiculous as mine in *Alien Anal Attack* fifteen years ago. I didn't blame her for not remembering.

She kept our movements slow, rocking lightly as I pushed harder. She was wonderfully tight and had great muscular control. Her tits floated atop the suds and kept pointing at me. She reached beneath the water and raised them high, pointing those giant nipples at the eye-holes in the mask. She poked at me with them and then started doing the thing where she swung them hard and let them loose. I grunted and fucked her savagely, groaning with the heat and the fact that I was going at it with one of my ultimate fantasies. Her tits bounced wildly and slugged me in the forehead, the shoulder, the jaw, really letting me have it as she squealed and cried, "That's it, keep at it!"

Like I would stop. She gasped as I kept at her, finding the rhythm and enjoying how her tits bounced each time I rammed her. Soon she began trembling beneath my body. Lauren clung to me and drew her nails across Zypho's rubber chest. I reached under her ass, grabbed her hips and pulled her further onto me until I was embedded as deeply as I could go. She grunted at the force of my penetration and said, "That's it, Thomas." Whoever would've thought that hearing your own name would be such a turn on? Lauren climaxed again, shuddering so hard that I heard her elbows crack.

I felt my own climax coming on. She did too and urged me on, whispering, "That's it, that's it, like that, yes." She growled a little and it drove me nuts and she kept slapping me with her tits and I was every stud she'd ever fucked on film. She let me be the best and I was so thankful I tried kissing her through the mask. I held on to her nipples like two joysticks as I rode her until I creamed.

She froze for a moment and said, "What's that sound? That yowling."

I still had lights dancing along the edges of my vision. "What? Uh, those are the cats next door stuck in the pomegranate tree again."

I gave her three or four more shoves and then came, letting her milk me and I quivered and shook. I rested atop that chest and never wanted to leave. She held me for a while, worked at the zipper, and finally managed to get me out of it.

"What a workout," she said. "But I'm not done yet."

Already I was at half-mast again. "Neither am I."

"Where's your room?"

"Around back. Let me check on Monty first and then—"

"Then I want to look at your face when I fuck you until you pass out."

"Oh boy."

It sounded like a fine plan to me. We got dressed and left the bathroom and sat on the couch together, chatting about films and our lives and feeding each other slices of pie. We made out for a while until I realized Monty and the other sorority babes had been missing for a long time.

We went upstairs to find out what had happened on the rest of the shoot.

I'd been wrong. That yowling hadn't been the cats that time. Monty and the two actresses has been doing something pretty funky and unholy up in the attic. All three were in a daze and it looked like Monty's left shoulder had been tugged out of the socket. It was a good thing he was double-jointed. He popped it back in. His cellphone rang.

I said, "It's probably Ed Wood calling to tell us that we've bumped *Plan 9 From Outer Space* as the worst movie ever."

Monty got a faraway look in his eyes and said, "Wouldn't that be something?"

This Hurts Me More Than It Hurts You

Stephanie Schaeffer

I was in college the first time a man asked me to spank him. It was in the dorms at Columbia. I was fooling around with a sophomore after consuming quite a bit of alcohol, and as soon as we got naked he handed me an ordinary leather belt and told me to hit him across the butt with it.

"Really?" I asked him. "Are you serious?"

"Please," he said. He rolled over and presented his ass.

I was coming down. I had a headache and needed to pee. "I can't do this," I told him. I got up, used the toilet and washed my face and when I returned he was passed out on his roommate's futon.

But oddly enough, even though the initial thought of it had repulsed me, over the years it became the thing I fantasized about the most. Spanking. Not being spanked, but being the spanker. I liked to fantasize about spanking men.

With each rotation of my hips, I'd visualize applying an enthusiastic hand to the eager behind of some deserving date. Tantalizing my swollen clit with a lubed finger, I'd picture different implements – the back of a hairbrush, a leather paddle, a thin birch rod – until I settled on the one that was most stimulating. I'd also imagine various guys: my last e-date, some hot movie celebrity, that sophomore in college and how differently things could have gone if I'd just smacked him with his belt like he'd asked. Now, envisioning some beau's blushing cheeks never failed to bring me to climax.

An ex-boyfriend of mine, Elliot, started making a regular

appearance in my spanking fantasies of late. A typical Elliot fantasy progressed as follows: while rubbing myself tentatively through my thin cotton panties, I visualized the faces Elliot used to make when fucking, only in my imagination he was making them while I spanked him. Then, I'd plunk his sore ass down in a chair and suck his dick. At this point my underwear was down around my knees, thumb circling my clit with fervor. As my fantasy self straddled him and fucked him until he came screaming, my thighs would be pressed around my hand, urgently squeezing the finger up my pussy as I came along with him.

I hadn't thought about Elliot in a sexual way since before we broke up last year. It was that old cliché of us being at different points in our lives. I was in my mid-twenties and had just started graduate school. Elliot, at 31, had recently co-founded a small computer consulting start-up. He was putting in long hours at the company. It was his baby, his anchor, his sweat and blood, and his availability was limited. Our courtship consisted of 15-minute coffee dates at odd hours of the day whenever he could fit them into his agenda. He was a proficient lover, particularly adept at oral sex, but only when he could find the time, which was scarcely once a week.

We'd had an amicable split. By the time he mustered up the courage to feed me the "I don't have the time for a relationship right now" line, I'd already gotten involved with a fellow graduate student at the university who had more time on his hands and shared my interest in Kierkegaard.

I still ran into Elliot quite often at my favorite study spot, The Local Mocha. His office was nearby and he stopped there morning and night for his caffeine fix. We'd become friends, of sorts, having a coffee together from time to time. I'd taken up with the online dating scene after Rolf, the grad student, had moved to Minnesota to pursue a community college teaching opportunity, and Elliot always liked hearing about my most recent romantic escapades. He laughed at my stories of stand-ups, one-night stands, and threesomes gone awry. I thought it was his way of living vicariously.

Elliot hadn't dated anyone for a while, but recently he'd begun seeing Kara, an emaciated, elongated 19-year-old with fuchsia hair and modeling aspirations. I was surprised by his choice but didn't say anything. Our conversations mostly centered on his work and my bad dates.

Now Elliot had started showing up in my fantasies and all this masturbation was getting in the way of my school work. It was a Monday night. The lit review I had procrastinated on all weekend and just barely finished was due at 8:30 a.m. the next morning. My printer, I had just discovered, was all out of ink.

With a frustrated sigh, I popped the disc out of the drive and headed off on foot to the copy place near The Local Mocha. When I got there, the storefront was dark. I glanced at the posted hours. 9 a.m.–9 p.m.

"Fuck," I said, aloud.

"Problem?" It was Elliot. I wondered momentarily what he was doing there until I remembered he'd told me his office space was on the block. He had a Local Mocha to-go cup in his hand, probably his usual double espresso.

"I have to print out this paper for class tomorrow, I'm all out of ink and this place is closed," I said.

"You can use the printer in my office," he offered.

His office, it turned out, was in a building just two doors down on the third floor. I waited as he rummaged through his pockets for the keys. He unlocked the door and ushered me inside. We were alone. His partner, clearly the one with a greater sense of the concept of work/life balance, had already gone home. The office had that distinct buzz that offices always seem to have.

I followed Elliot to his computer station and handed him my disc. As he fiddled with the computer, I surveyed his work-space. There was a snapshot of him and Kara on the desk amidst some papers. It looked like it had been taken at an office party or similar function. Little bitch looks like she just swallowed a lemon, I thought.

"How's Kara?" I asked.

"Fine," he said.

He bent over the desk to turn on the printer. His gray wool pants stretched tight over his ass. I could tell there was a nickel in his back pocket, and something that looked like it could be a gum wrapper. I traced the curves of his butt with my eyes. It was all I could do to prevent myself from reaching out and swatting those cheeks.

"What is it?" he asked, catching me looking at him and straightening up.

"I'm just looking at your ass," I told him.

He stared at me, expressionless.

"It's nice," I said.

This time he looked amused.

"So is that," I added, looking pointedly at his crotch.

Now he was more than amused. "It's pitching a tent," I told him.

"That it is," he said. We both admired his hard-on.

"Bend over the desk again," I told him.

"Why?"

"So I can see your ass."

He bent over as I asked, playing along.

"I'm going to spank you," I said.

"What?"

"I'm going to spank you."

He didn't object. I took this to be an assent. I smacked his butt. He didn't flinch. I slapped his ass again, harder. And again.

"Take off your pants." I wanted to feel his bare skin, to see my handprint vividly branded across his fine expanse of ass, but he took my order to mean punishment was over.

He turned around and embraced me. His dick was as hard as a board. We fucked right there on the desk. I left a sweaty butt print on the cheap veneer finish.

I didn't see Elliot around the next couple of days. He didn't call either. I don't know why I expected him to. I didn't even know if he still had my telephone number. Still, it bothered me a little.

Feeling restless late one night, I did an Internet search, typing in "spanking." All I found were a bunch of sites containing photos of barely legal women dressed ridiculously as Catholic schoolgirls, sprawled over the laps of some pervy looking older men, tears running down their faces as their fannies got slapped silly. Not what I was looking for.

On Friday of that same week I went to Chez Arlene to hear

my friend Scott's band play. I was chatting with Scott on the smoking patio between sets when Elliot came in with Kara. He didn't acknowledge me. Kara had on a pink halter top and stretch jeans and looked like she hadn't eaten for months. She was chattering on about something – I couldn't decipher what – and Elliot placed his hand patronizingly on the small of her back as if to encourage her along inside, away from my vicinity.

We didn't speak to each other throughout the course of the evening. I drank a beer and left after Scott's last set, furious. I thought about the stripes I would leave on Elliot's ass the next time I saw him. I contemplated making him count after each stroke.

Over the weekend I scheduled a meeting with another e-date. I thought I might as well since it didn't look like things between me and Elliot would go any further. Mitch was a lawyer, mid-thirties, new in town, never married, no kids. We agreed to meet at 2 p.m. on Sunday at The Local Mocha.

My date looked pleased to see me, but his strait-laced hunter green polo shirt and white shorts made me cringe. After exchanging pleasantries we ordered two coffees and sat down at a table near the window. "So you went to Georgetown?" I asked Mitch, making conversation. "What was living in D.C. like?"

Elliot came in and ordered a double espresso. I saw him do a double-take at me and my date. Mitch was answering my question, but I wasn't paying attention. Elliot got his coffee to go and left. Through the window I watched his ass as he walked across the street. He was wearing corduroys, and the fabric was worn a little on the seat.

Mitch and I continued with the small talk. Over refills, the subject of S&M came up.

"My ex-fiancée liked to get spanked," my date said, lowering his voice and leaning forward, preparing to evaluate my reaction. "Do you?"

"I like to do the spanking," I said.

"Oh," he said, surprised, disappointed. "But quite frankly what you really want is some dashing gentleman to take you over his knee and—"

"No," I said, "not really."

Mitch cleared his throat and fiddled with his coffee stirrer. Our date ended shortly after that.

At home later that night I tried to read, but I couldn't concentrate. I felt bored and lonely. I checked my e-mail and I had some responses from interested e-dates, but the experience with Mitch had left me feeling drained. I didn't have the energy for more "getting to know you" chitchat.

I was preparing for bed when the doorbell rang. I looked through the peephole. It was Elliot.

I opened the door and he stood there looking at me with a coy smile on his face. "I've been bad," he said.

I closed the door and followed him into the bedroom. He was already in position, bent over the bed. I lowered his trousers and boxers, exposing his ripe peach ass. Removing the belt from his pants, I set it aside for later. Elliot waited in anticipation.

I smacked his bare butt with my palm open and fingers spread, not too hard at first. I was just warming up. He braced himself, wanting more. I reached for the belt, holding the buckle away at a safe distance and gripping the strap in the middle for tighter control.

It came down across his bottom with a satisfying snap. I admonished him as the leather tongue licked his behind.

"You've—" *snap!* "been—" *snap!* "a really—" *snap!* "bad—" *snap!* "boyfriend!" *Snap!*

Elliot clenched his stinging buttocks, pressing himself against the mattress in an attempt to alleviate the agony of his stiff cock.

His ass was glowing red. I let him cool off for a minute before searing his butt with another succession of lashes.

I lay the belt down. Gently I ran my fingertips over his tingling skin. He quivered.

I picked up a hairbrush and softly rubbed the smooth wooden side over his bottom in a circular motion. Elliot sighed and relaxed a bit. Swiftly, I dealt two sound whacks to the center of each rosy cheek. Elliot yelped. He clutched at the bedsheets as I paddled away. His ass was now scarlet. Just looking at it made my own cheeks flush in empathy. I stopped to finger myself. My pussy was hot to the touch.

I caught Elliot looking at me expectantly so I went for the belt again, crisscrossing his backside with the leather strap. I could tell it stung, but he took it like a man.

I leaned back against the wall, eyes closed, rubbing the leather belt tip underneath my panties, against my clit. I came almost immediately, like warm butter melting down my thighs. I opened my eyes. Elliot hadn't strayed from position.

The spanking had left marks. Not severe, but marks nonetheless. I went to the kitchen for ice. I returned and Elliot was still face down on the bed. I could practically see his ass throbbing. He raised his head up and watched me as I went over to him, cup in hand. I put an ice cube in my mouth and ran my chilled tongue over his hot tender skin. He murmured. Gently spreading his cheeks, I lapped leisurely around the circumference of his asshole.

I turned him over, cushioning his sore bottom with a pillow. His dick bobbed in the air. Transferring the melting ice to the inside of my cheek, I took the head of his penis into my mouth and sucked. Elliot moaned. Soon he pulled out of my mouth and came, splattering my chest and throat.

"Thanks for the pearls," I told him, and he laughed.

He didn't stay long. It wasn't even half past ten when he got up and reached for his clothes.

"I gotta go," he said. "Early meeting."

I watched him dress, his back to me. Across his butt was belted out a constellation of little red stars.

I was at The Local Mocha the next morning when Elliot came in with Kara. His walk seemed a bit stiffer than usual. Some friends invited them to sit down at their table, but Elliot said he preferred to stand. "I have a meeting at the office in ten minutes," he explained.

Elliot stood in line waiting for his double espresso. While Kara was in the ladies room, I walked up to him to say hello. I knew she'd be in there for at least twenty minutes, checking her make-up.

I pinched his butt and he winced. "Nice ass," I told him.

He smiled. "I'll call you tomorrow," he said.

Amsterdam

Simon Sheppard

Late afternoon, when things change.

Tall, maybe six-five. Thin, almost skinny. Not bad looking, but short of handsome. Just his type. The thin man looked at him and stroked his crotch.

At this time of day, the Web wasn't crowded. Maybe two dozen men, most stopping by on their way home from work. For a drink, a quick fuck, shelter from the raw February wind. All sorts: older guys still in good shape, younger guys with hungry eyes, tired men significantly past their prime. A chubby guy with a North English accent joking with the bar boy. A Japanese tourist still gripping his indecipherable guidebook.

Everyone in the bar's rear room was staring up at the video monitor, where a blond hunk shoved his latex-gloved hands up the butts of two kneeling men with wide-open assholes. Everyone except the thin man, who was staring not at the monitor, but straight at him. He felt his crotch swelling against his winter camouflage pants. Staring straight back, he grabbed at his thickening dick.

The thin man walked to the stairs and went up toward the darkroom, never looking back.

He gulped down the rest of his Dommelsch and headed for the stairs. Just above his head, the blond hunk was still punch-fucking a stretched-out hole.

Up the stairs, opposite the direction of the "Exit" arrow, white diagonal against black wall. Out one door, then back inside through another. At first the darkroom was impenetrably black, but in seconds his eyes had adjusted. The dim shape of the thin man was leaning against a wall directly in front of him, waiting. For a few long seconds, nobody moved.

The thin man turned, walked down a dark hallway. He followed. At the end of the hallway, a room with a toilet on the left, a still darker room on the right. The thin man leaned against an invisible wall. They were inches apart. They could feel each other's hot breath. The thin man reached down with both hands, grabbed both dicks, squeezed.

He put his hand around the thin man's narrow waist. Slid his hands beneath his shirt. Scabbed-over nipples. Amsterdam, he thought, must be the tit-work capital of the world. The thin man let go of his cock and raised his hands behind his head. He slid his hands to the thin man's belt buckle, started to undo it. The thin man pushed his hips forward and moaned.

Freed of jeans and briefs, the thin man's average-sized, uncut dick stood stiffly out. From somewhere down below, the muffled beat of neo-disco. He grabbed the thin man's cock with his left hand and stroked, sliding foreskin over dickhead. His right hand found the guy's ass and gave it an exploratory slap. The thin man groaned for more. He grabbed the thin man's hips and turned him around so he was facing the wall, hands still behind his head. He started slapping the guy around in earnest now, each whack of hand against flesh echoing through the darkroom. The thin guy writhed appreciatively, pushing his butt out for more. When he reached around for the thin man's cock, it was dripping wet.

He shoved the man over to a bench and forced him down onto his knees. Not "forced," really, since the thin man quickly lowered his head to the bench and hungrily shoved his butt in the air. Even in the room's near-darkness, the white flesh of his ass glowed softly. A dark crack down the middle. The smell, rich, slightly revolting, rose to his nostrils like an aphrodisiac.

The action had gathered a small crowd: a couple of the older guys, the Japanese tourist. He'd built a rhythm, whacking one butt-cheek, then the other, then a slap right down the moist, hot crack. Somebody's hand reached out to the bottom boy's ass. Rude motherfucker. He pushed the hand away, reached between the skinny thighs and grabbed hold of hard dick.

WHACK! The thin guy pulled away. He pulled him back by the dick. Slapped him again, hard.

"Pull your pants up and follow me to a *hokje*." He headed down the hall to one of the small, dark cubicles with locking doors. The thin man followed him in. He closed the door and clicked the lock shut.

A few minutes later, the lock clicked open. The thin man walked out alone. The Japanese tourist, still hungry, hesitated for a minute, then walked in. Tripped over something on the floor. Something heavy and soft. Bent down, peered into the darkness. Opened his mouth and screamed.

But by then the thin man was gone, fading into the grey drizzle shrouding the Sint Jacobsstraat.

Late afternoon. I'm walking down the Sint Jacobsstraat, across the Damrak to the Warmoesstraat, past Mister B and the Argos, over to where the tourists feed the pigeons on Dam Square. I stop for a paper cone of frites. I'm not hungry, of course, but the hot fried potatoes with mayonnaise get the taste of blood out of my mouth.

Amsterdam is a brown city. A brown, old city. And I was old when these buildings were new. A tired, cold city. As I am tired and cold.

I've been careless. Leaving that boy in the bar back there. Unforgivably careless. In all my years, my centuries, I've never done such a thing. They're going to get me. Now they're going to get me. And I don't care.

He walked into the Argos. Past the chains hanging from the ceiling, the Satanic animal head hanging by the bar. Just past midnight, not yet crowded. Down the steep, familiar stairs to the darkroom in the basement. Plenty of guys hanging around already. That one, the one illuminated by the light from the stairway, he looked interesting. Faintly familiar. Tall, maybe six-five, and thin, almost skinny. Sharp cheekbones, eyes hidden in shadows; he would do.

He walked over to the thin man, looked up at his face. The thin man's expression gave nothing away. He reached up, stroked the man's hair. The thin man put his hands behind his head and leaned back against the wall. As though he was waiting to get blown. Or slapped. He reached down, undid the guy's zipper. Already hard. "Come to a cabin," he said, in English, to be safe. The leaning man didn't move. He repeated it, in Dutch, but there still was no response. He slapped the guy's hard dick. The tall, thin man writhed in pleasure, and he did it again, harder. "Yes," the man said. "*Ja.*"

He grabbed the thin man's dick and pulled him into one of the wooden cubicles, locking the door behind them. He unbuckled the man's belt, pulled his jeans down to his knees, then ran his hand up a thin, solid inner thigh till he felt the soft, warm ball sac against his fingers. He flicked a forefinger at the man's balls. The man moaned and shoved his crotch forward. He slapped the man's balls with the palm of his hand. "Good?" he asked. The man nodded. "Poppers?" Another nod. He shoved a small brown bottle under the man's nose, then took a hit himself.

Within seconds, they were tearing at one another, kissing so hard that he could taste blood in his mouth. He unbuttoned his fly, pulled out his dick, grabbed a cock in each hand, and stroked. The thin man grabbed him by the throat, tracing his veins with cold fingertips.

My hands are on his throat. My lips are on his neck. I want to strike, I'm ready to bite down. I can taste him. I can taste him already. And then he moves his hand from my cock to the back of my head, presses my face into the hot hollow of his neck. In a husky voice he whispers, "That's it. That's right, fucking kill me, man," And I'm overcome, not by feelings of lust, but of sudden, irrational tenderness. It's so unexpected. Unasked-for. I don't want to leave him there. I don't want to leave him at all. I run my tongue from his neck, along the hard ridge of his jaw line, over his stubbly chin, back into the warm, sweet cave of his waiting mouth.

The thin man, Theo, hurried from the bar. "HEY, WAIT UP." The boy who said he wanted to die. Theo hesitated, then turned around. In the dim light of the cold, windy street, the boy seemed fragile. "Where're you off to?" The boy spoke Dutch with a Slavic accent.

"Home."

"Mind if I come along?"

"What's wrong with your home?"

"Okay, okay, sorry." The boy turned to go. The seat of the boy's jeans was thoroughly ripped-up. The flesh of his ass looked tender and pale.

"You really want me to kill you?" Theo's voice was tender, too. Tender and pale.

"I want you to take me home with you."

"My bike's over there."

"Mine, too."

They unchained their bicycles.

"I live over by the old docks." Suddenly, despite his hunger, all Theo wanted to do was sleep, sleep with this boy in his arms.

"Let's go, then."

And they pedaled off into the black, raw, welcoming night.

It's morning now. The boy is curled up, asleep beside me. How did this happen, this compromise, this need? How could I have let him get this far, come into my apartment, into my life?

Christ, I'm starving.

Milos woke, stretched like a cat, smiled at Theo. "Coffee?"

"None made."

"I'll do it. You just stay there." Milos's skin was translucently pale, revealing blue veins coursing with blood.

Milos climbed out of bed and walked off to the kitchen. Theo couldn't take his eyes off the boy's ass, the way skin and muscles shifted as he moved. The boy was fleshy, not plump exactly, but fleshy, as though he were happy with his body, at home in his body. Milos's dick was still hard as he switched on the coffee maker.

"It'll take a few minutes. Come back to bed." *I could do it now*, Theo thought. *I could do it right now.*

Milos bounded back toward the bed, his dick bouncing crazily. He kneeled by the side of the bed, grabbed Theo's wrists and guided the thin man's hands to his throat. Theo's hands slipped around his neck. He bent to kiss Theo's lips. "Squeeze harder," he whispered into Theo's mouth. The grip grew tighter. He wrapped his hands around Theo's hands and pressed them into his flesh. His dick had gotten so hard it almost hurt. His breath was coming in gasps now. Blood pounded in his head.

Theo was out of bed now, kneeling on the floor, kneeling between Milos's naked thighs, his knee pressing hard into the Slavic boy's soft balls and hard dick. He pressed Milos's head back till the boy arched his back, groaned, fell backwards against the cold floor. Theo threw himself onto Milos's squirming body, dick against dick, hands still around his new lover's throat. He took Milos's lower lip between his teeth, bit down hard, made blood flow. The dark, metallic taste filled their mouths like a sudden shock. They came, both came, brutally, desperately, ecstatically. Theo loosened his grip, stroked Milos's beautiful face, wiped the tears from his eyes.

"I'm hungry," Milos said.

"You're welcome to the kitchen, but I'm afraid you won't find much to eat."

While the naked boy was rummaging around in the hollow cabinets, Theo reached for the remote and switched on the TV. A too-handsome blond man was reading the news. "Police are still searching for the killer of a man who was found murdered in the darkroom of a popular gay leather bar this week . . ."

None of this is simple. I wanted it to be simple, the relationship of predator and prey. Instead, I have this, this boy here, someone to – God, I don't know, look after? – just when I've become so tired, so fucking weary. Just when I've begun to sow the seeds of my own destruction.

Unless, of course, he himself is part of the process.

On the third morning, they were lying entwined in each other's arms when the doorbell rang. Theo struggled out of bed and pulled on a thick woolen robe.

Pieter was at the door. "Mind if I come in? It's freezing out here."

"It's not a convenient time, Pieter. I'm sorry, but you could have called first."

"Who's this, then?" Pieter's pale blue eyes were staring at

Milos, who'd gotten out of bed and was standing a few feet behind Theo, naked, one hand loosely cupped around his dick.

"Pieter, this is Milos." Theo's voice was dead. "Milos, Pieter."

"Is he one of us then? Have you had him yet? No?" Pieter walked over to Milos, reached for the boy's ass, and kissed him on the cheek. "Well, don't worry dear, he will."

Pieter turned on his heel, walked out the door, and was gone.

"What did he mean, 'one of us'?" Milos asked while he was pulling on his pants, preparing to go out in search of breakfast.

"Perhaps I should tell you," Theo said. *This has gone on long enough*, he thought.

I told him. I told him everything. He didn't say a word. I don't even know him well enough to be able to read his face. So I don't know.

He's out now, gone to get some breakfast for himself. He's lucky that his hunger can be assuaged so easily. Has he gone to the police? No, I doubt it. Will he be back? I have no way of knowing. Do I even want him to come back? Outside the windows, the gulls are swirling above the half-frozen canal. Do I even want him to come back?

It was already early afternoon when Theo heard the click of the key in the lock. Milos locked the door behind himself and just stood there, the chilly light playing on the angles of his face. For a moment they watched each other in silence. Then Milos knelt at Theo's feet, reached into a little bag he was holding, and pulled out an old-fashioned straight razor. He opened the gleaming blade and held it against the skin of his forearm. Looking deep into Theo's eyes, he drew the razor across his flesh, leaving a gleaming red line in its wake. He offered his wound up to the tall, thin man standing above him. Theo leaned down, put his lips to the blossoming flow, and nursed gently. As he sucked at the upwelling blood, he felt the boy's body shudder, tense, then shudder again. It was not till he drew his lips from the wound that he realized that Milos had used his free hand to unbuckle his jeans and take out his cock. His half-hard dick, shiny with cum, still rested in his fingers.

"Had enough?"

For now," Theo said. "For now."

Milos pressed his hand against the gash to staunch the flow. "I love you," he said.

Theo stared out of the window at the flocks of gulls diving, wheeling, diving again.

Sometimes I think back to the great days of Amsterdam. Down by the Montelbaanstoren, desperate men with nothing to lose boarded ships that would take them to the edge of the world. I would watch them sail off, and wonder how they felt as they looked back at the cozy brown city they might never see again. Maybe the way I do when I look into this Slavic boy's eyes.

Another day passed. Theo was feeling faint with hunger. He offered Milos some of the hashcake he'd bought at the gay *koffieshop*, waited till the boy was asleep, then slipped out and bicycled to the Web. He found a boy that was to his liking, very young, short and slight, with a nose ring and a dazzling smile. It was easy to get him to go to the darkroom, easy to get him into a cabinet, easy to pull the clothes from his body until the boy stood naked before him, thin almost hairless, with a small, almost delicate hard-on. *Delicate, that's what he is*, Theo thought as he slipped his hands around the boy's thin neck. He knew that this was stupid, doing this here, so soon after the other one. Even so, he pulled the boy closer, till he could feel the boy's body heat, till the skinny young boy began jamming his hard little dick against his leg.

"Please let me suck you," the boy gasped, reaching for Theo's crotch. The naked boy kneeled. Theo watched as the kid opened his fly, gulped down his cock. A thousand miles away. The boy seemed to be a thousand miles away. A bony white shape in the airless gloom. Skinnier even than he was. But not, despite his voracious cocksucking, anywhere near as hungry.

In a few short moments, Theo's hunger was sated.

Milos's heart. I lie here undreaming, watching him sleep. Deep within him, within his fragile, mortal body, his heart pumps, steadily, erotically, sending life through the network of his veins. His heart, his secret heart.

I want to reach inside him, into his soft ass, slide my hand up into him until I grasp his heart, feel its mindless beating. Hold his life in my hands. Feel the coursing of his lifeblood against my fingertips.

But do I want to love him? Do I want him to love me?

"The police were around to my place, asking questions."

"They haven't been here yet."

"They will be." Pieter was sprawled in Theo's living room, sipping strong black coffee. "You're the one, aren't you, Theo? You're the one who did it. Stupid of you."

Theo stared at the square of moonlight on the floor.

"You've ruined a good thing, brought trouble to the rest of us, too." Pieter's pale blue eyes shone in the semi-darkness.

"You're angry, then?"

"Not really angry, Theo. But if trouble comes, I won't be there for you, none of us will. You do understand, don't you?"

"Of course I do."

The front-door lock clicked open. Milos walked in, arms loaded with groceries.

"Ah, I see the dream boy is home," Pieter sneered.

"Why do you hate me, Pieter? Is it because you're jealous?"

"How wrong you are, boy. I knew Theo long before you arrived on the scene, and I'll know him long, long after you've gone."

"Why, then?"

"Because Theo is acting like a damn fool, and you're a part of that. You're a threat to him. A threat to us all. You think you understand. Maybe you even think Theo loves you. But you understand nothing, nothing at all. You're just a little fool, a young, young fool."

"I think you've said enough." Theo's voice was flat, expressionless, lacking passion, maybe lacking conviction. "I think you'd better go now."

"Maybe I'd better. But when this all comes crashing down, you'll remember what I've said. Though it will be cold comfort to you then, Theo." Pieter smiled grimly. "You may not believe this, but I wish with all my heart that I turn out to be wrong."

He was at the door, wrapping a long woolen cape around his shoulders. "Take good care of Theo, little boy. He's in trouble. Big trouble." He opened the door. The cold night blew in. And then Pieter was gone.

I haven't been able to sleep. I walked the frozen streets till dawn, till mid-morning. My wanderings have led me here, to the Rijksmuseum. To the long hall that leads to *The Night Watch*, hordes of tourists squinting at Rembrandts. Over here, to one side, almost ignored, hangs *The Jewish Bride*. It's an astonishing painting, one of Rembrandt's finest. A light seems to glow from within the couple, he placing his hand upon her breast. Over her heart. Their hands meet in unutterable tenderness. The light remains undimmed, through all the years since it was newly made.

And this tenderness, it makes me want to weep. Only I can't weep. Because I'm closed off, forever cast out from the tenderness of this couple, this simple love. And so I can't weep, because I can't feel. Not like they feel. And so whatever else I'm trying to feel is turning to bitterness, to anger. I can see why that man took out a knife and slashed *The Night Watch*. If I had a knife . . .

If I had a knife . . .

"Where have you been?" Milos asked. "The police were here looking for you. They said they'd be back later."

Nothing can kill me, because I'm not alive. Not in the way other people are. Not in the way Milos is, warm, feeling, hot blood coursing through his veins, blood that he kneels to offer me. His heart is a work of art, a work of art of unutterable tenderness.

When I told him I had to go, he said he wanted to come with me. To escape. There's no place to escape, I said.

He stripped himself naked for me. His dick was already hard. He begged me to put my hands around his neck. To squeeze hard.

His heart is a fucking work of art.

When the police arrived at the apartment by the Oosterkerk, they found the door ajar. They called out; no one was home. They pushed the door open. In the middle of the living room floor was a pool of blood, three, maybe four feet across. It had been shaped into the form of a heart, a wet valentine. The outer edges of the heart were drying to a duller brown, but the center of the heart was still shiny, wet, red.

On the wall above the heart, someone had thumbtacked a post card to the wall. A reproduction of a painting. A Rembrandt: *The Jewish Bride*.

So fucking tired. So fucking weary. So very, very old.

Nacht Ruck

Karen Taylor

I first saw her at an auction. I wasn't the only one who stared; she had brought a buggy alone.

She loosely wrapped the reins around the hitching post, next to a line of buggies and wagons, moving among the horses with an assurance I'd never seen in any woman. Then I saw the limp, and knew that no man would have married her.

She was greeted, and I saw her nod to a few of the women. I followed her into the barn, watched her settle in front of Mama, adjust her white prayer cap on her greying hair, and pull work out from the basket she was carrying. I moved closer to see her hands busily braiding strands of black horsehair. Mama bent forward from her seat, talking to her briefly. They chatted, and I saw her hands never stopped moving. She caught me staring and when I started, she smiled. Mama beckoned to me and I moved to her side, shyly. Mama introduced me, and she reached her hand out to shake mine. Her hands were calloused around the outside, from the base of the palm to the second joint of her little finger and on the inside of her index finger. To my surprise, her palms were no more calloused than my own. Her fingers were small and fine, the tendons prominent against the back of her hand, rising from the skin near the wrist to disappear above the knucklebone. I was sorry when she released me, and when I touched my hand to my face, it smelled of lanolin. My eyes followed her hand back to its work in her lap and I noticed her index fingers bent slightly back toward her hand. I wondered if it was from work, her age, or some infirmity.

Mama said something about getting a basket of laundry from

the woman's buggy, and I remained. She asked me about the book in my hand and laughed when I showed her: *Mirror of the Martyrs*. I still preferred the inspirational book to any worldly literature I had tried. I told her I sometimes imagined my own body pressed to death by rocks, stretched on the rack, flogged with nettles, wanting to know if I, too, could bear the tortures our Amish heroes had done so many centuries ago. She nodded, knowingly, her fingers twisting the horsehair in her lap.

I asked her if she missed not having a husband. She laughed merrily, her eyes dancing. I sometimes miss having children, she said. But not the other. I wanted to ask her why. But I thought I knew – and color flooded my face in a rush of heat. She saw it and, gently, her hand covered mine. We stood there silently, until Mama returned. The woman smiled at Mama, and asked that we meet at the market the following Saturday, asked if I could help her pack up and bring her work home. She can stay the night, the woman said, as she returned to the work in her lap, her hands busy plaiting the strands in her lap. I watched the tendons flex beneath the skin, and trembled.

The rest of the auction was a blur. I didn't dare return to the barn, and joined my friends under the big elm outside. Nearby was a group of boys from our church, some of them smoking cigarettes. We ignored them and watched the grown-ups going in and out of the auction barn while we giggled and gossiped under the tree. It was summer, and all of us were trying our parents' patience. We were all the age of *rum springa*, the years between childhood and before baptism, enjoying our years of freedom before joining the church and giving up our worldly adventures. Sarah and Amy were going to a non-Amish friend's house that afternoon to watch a video. Hannah had cut some of the hair from around her face and was daring me to do the same. Last week Josh had actually purchased a truck from a boy who had joined the Church, and took us all over to LaGrange, to play miniature golf. Katie whispered to us that after the miniature golf party, she and Grace and some of the boys stayed on to drink beer. One had gotten so drunk he passed out in his buggy and only got home because his horse knew the way. I gasped appropriately, but was privately relieved that Josh had dropped me off before the evening went too wild. Liquor was not my form of rebellion. My rebellion was much more secret, and only today had I ever met anyone else who even suspected. Even as I was thinking it, I saw the woman limp back to her buggy, free the horse from its post, and struggle in. The whip flicked across his flanks, and I flinched. Had she seen me? I thought I saw her smile as she drove past, but maybe it was just a wish.

I could think of nothing but her for the week. My chores were a mild distraction; watching the younger ones, walking them to the one-room schoolhouse I had attended until eighth grade, free after that to go about real world learning, as my Mama would say. The youngest children I would meet at noon and walk home to have the lunch I made for them. But the rest of the day's chores were different each day. Monday I helped Mama bake the pies and breads for the market. Tuesday morning I was up before dawn firing up the gasoline-powered washing machine for laundry, getting the clothes on the line that stretched from the house to the barn early enough so Mama and I could pack the baked goods in the buggy and Papa could drive us to town by nine. Wednesday my sisters and I weeded the garden and plucked the sweet peas for shelling in the shade on the porch. That night I promised Mama that I'd get up early enough to do the extra laundry she had brought home, and I dreamt all night of lying in those sheets.

I was up before dawn on Thursday, washing *her* sheets, *her* quilts, caressing them as I hung them in a pleasing pattern on the line. I returned to the kitchen, helping Mama bake another batch of pies and bread for the weekend, and making several dozen cookies as well. Friday I stayed home while Papa took Mama to the market, because the baby was not feeling well. I fixed up a basket to hold the laundry I'd be taking with me on Saturday, filling it with sweet pea, rose petals, lemon balm, and other scents pulled from the flower garden. I packed a carefully folded black dress, black stockings, white apron and black prayer cap. And in the bottom of the basket, I placed my *nacht ruck*, my nightdress, for bundling.

Bundling started centuries ago when unheated houses led hosts to double up with their guests for warmth. The tradition evolved into a form of courting for those of us in our *rum springa* years, the only time boys and girls are allowed to be alone together before marriage. It is so fixed in Amish tradition that in my grandparents' day, a preacher who once spoke out about it in Shipshawana was silenced for nearly five years. It was because of this tradition that I was not yet ready to give up my *rum springa* years and join the Church. Truly, I suffered from the sin of vanity. I wanted to be seen in my *nacht ruck*, my bundling dress.

I had finished my *nacht ruck* over a year ago, when I turned sixteen, even though there was no boy I fancied, and none that fancied me enough to suggest calling after dark, to tiptoe into my room and spend the night with me, and come down for breakfast the next morning to meet my folks. By the time I was sixteen I was pretty sure there would never be a boy I fancied like that. But I had made a dress anyway. It was a ruffled, pale lavender color, its capped sleeves exposing my arms almost to the elbow. Pink ribbons at the sleeves, collar and hem were unbelievably indulgent, the result of work secretly done over the past winter. The buttons on the bodice were an extravagance that only highlighted the worldly nature of the dress – something that would never be worn once I joined the church. The *nacht ruck* represented my freedom, and I wanted more than anything to wear it for someone. I thought about her that night, and secretly touched myself after my sister fell asleep next to me, silencing myself in the down pillow so as not to wake the little ones.

I woke early on Saturday. The whole family went to the open market off County Road 12 where Mama and I met Aunt Fannie, who was already setting up her quilts to display to the tourists. I took the younger ones over to our cousins' wagon, where the chore of babysitting would be distributed among relatives, then helped Mama unpack her appliquéd pillow shams and her pies and cookies. *She* was already there, in a stall selling decorated saddlebags, horse brasses, fancy show bridles, and two or three riding saddles. She was talking with an English man, but her hands were busy, braiding strands of leather that were attached to a hook on her display table. I turned back to Mama and Aunt Fannie, helping to arrange the quilts and shams. When I turned back to her stall, the man had gone, as was one of the saddles. She was looking my way. I ducked my head, quickly sitting next to Mama.

It was nearly noon when Mama and Aunt Fannie sent me away, told me to make myself useful. I approached her stall with a picnic basket, told her I had made lunch. She smiled, and asked me to join her. I unpacked fried chicken, pickled eggs, homemade bread, and apple butter, and some Jell-O salad. We ate silently, but whenever I dared to look at her she was watching me, smiling that secret smile. After we finished, I packed up slowly, and watched her hands return to plaiting the leather, which she was gently pulling against the heavy brass hook, keeping her plaits under tension. I finally asked her what she was making and she told me: a lash for the end of a buggy whip. I flushed, and nearly dropped a plate. She chuckled softly and asked me to meet her at her stall in a few hours. She reminded me to bring the laundry. I picked up the picnic basket, and fled.

Late afternoon, Mama pointed the woman out to Aunt Fannie, told her that I was to be helping her that evening. They spoke of the polio epidemic in the 1940s, how it killed her brothers and sisters, how she was lucky to have survived. Mama admired her courage, her determination not to make herself a burden to our community. Aunt Fannie sympathized for her childless state but marveled at her skills with leatherwork and with the horses. They told me I was being a good Christian to spend time with her. But they didn't know that Christian duty was not my intent. They hadn't seen her hands work that leather.

She had sold another saddle; the horse brasses and fancy bridles fit neatly into the unsold saddlebags. I carried these, and she took the other saddle and my basket and limped to her buggy. I stepped up, sat next to her and we were off, down the county road. I kept my hands clasped in my lap, looking at her sideways. I'd never been in a buggy with a woman driving before. She was silent, calm, keeping the buggy on the gravel shoulder, finally turning off into a long dirt road. Twitching the reins, she turned the horse into a lane leading to a small house with a small barn at the back of a cornfield. She pulled the horse to a stop outside the barn, then stepped out of the buggy. Nodding to me to take the bags to the house, she began to unhitch the animal. I dropped the bags on the porch and turned in time to see her lead the horse to a water trough inside a makeshift corral. I met her at the gate after she poured some grain into a feed box. When she turned and looked at me, I felt my knees turn to jelly. Her eyes were light blue, almost grey, and they pierced me through. She smiled again, and touched my cheek. I closed my eyes. When I opened them, she was limping toward the barn. Hastily, I followed.

The smell of leather and cut wood permeated the barn, and I stood in the doorway, inhaling the rich scent as my eyes grew used to the dim light. Aside from a stable near the front, the rest of the space was a workshop. Two long tables were covered with cut leather, half-formed into what would become more wares by the next week. Racks of tools I couldn't name were hung on one wall, the other long wall holding oak and hickory poles that I knew would be used for buggy and wagon hitches. Mysterious stands and arched wooden shapes stood farther back in the dusty light and as I watched, she placed the unsold saddle on one of the forms. Beyond the forms was a smaller room, and I made out hides of leather on racks, some in bright, worldly colors. An odd bench with a piece of wood sticking through its center stood near one of the tables. Another small bench and a plain pine stool with castors seemed to be the only regular furniture. A sense of calm, decades old, permeated the room.

I stepped to a long counter filled with leather straps and carefully braided buggy whips. I picked up one of the straps and pressed it to my face, inhaling the scent of leather and lanolin. As I rubbed it against my lips, she walked toward me, smiling that deep, secret smile. I handed her the strap. Please, I thought, or perhaps I said it aloud. Either way, she accepted my offer, settled herself on the workbench and invited me to join her. I gathered my skirt, pulling it high behind me, and bent across her lap.

Her arm rose and I moaned even as the leather struck my buttocks. She slapped it against me again, harder, and my fists bunched the fabric of her dark green dress. She was as wonderful as I dared hope. The leather strap beat steadily across my buttocks and thighs, my cotton undergarments no protection, nor did I want any. The strap was surely leaving welts, and my face was streaked with tears. The pain grew intense and my sobs more ragged, but she did not stop, and I did not struggle to avoid the leather's sting. It was all that I could have dreamed.

After a long while she stopped, her strong hands caressing my reddened and sore buttocks, tracing the marks she had made. I thanked her through my sobs of pain and ecstasy. She said nothing, waiting for me to calm myself. Then she bid me stand before her. I refused, kneeling instead to look up into her eyes. I offered her more. Her eyes shone with pleasure, and I was overjoyed.

She reached out and touched my face, dampening her fingers with my tears. She stroked my cheeks, brushed her lightly calloused fingertips across my eyelids. Her hand traced my hairline, and she chuckled at the cut strands peeking out from beneath my prayer cap. Last week I had played with my hair in front of the small hand mirror in my room, finally trimming some of the locks, wondering if the extravagance of cutting my hair would please her. Slowly, she worked the fingers of both hands under my cap, and gently pulled it from my head. No one, not even my mother, had seen me without my head covered since I was ten and old enough to dress myself. No Churchwoman would ever be seen this naked. I trembled, closing my eyes as I felt her remove my hairpins, letting my pale blonde hair loosen and fall around my shoulders. My nipples were pressed hard against my dress as her fingers carefully untangled the strands, and I remembered her plaiting the horsehair. I raised myself on my knees and reached to the table. I retrieved a buggy whip, the lash newly repaired, and a fresh horsehair popper dancing on the end. Please, I asked again. Her eyes danced as she untangled her fingers from my hair, and stood.

I stood up as well, and pulled my navy blue dress over my head. With a deep breath, I removed my cotton undershirt, then bent to take off my black shoes and dark blue stockings. I folded my clothes carefully on the bench and she set my prayer cap on top of them, the hairpins resting inside.

I could not see her face as clearly in the light filtering in from the afternoon sun, but I heard her sigh, and hoped that was a good sign. She reached out and traced my breasts, tickling the nipples with those strong fingers. She caressed my shoulders, running her hands down my back to my buttocks and massaged them. A spark of pain reignited from the strapping and I sighed, turned to kiss her, but she stopped me with a finger to my lips.

She pulled long leather reins from a hook in the wall and wrapped first one, then the other, around my wrists. My arms were pulled wide, and tied to two braces in the shed. She stood before me, her green dress slightly wrinkled, her grey hair carefully tucked into the white, pleated prayer cap. In her hand was the buggy whip. She kissed me on the lips, for a long time, her tongue tickling its way between my teeth, filling my mouth slowly until I hungrily sucked at it. She pulled away and I gasped, feeling myself grow damp. I wanted to touch myself; I wanted her to touch me. But when she flexed the whip through the air, and the horsehair popper cracked, my desire changed again. I closed my eyes.

The whip touched lightly on my bare shoulders. I flinched, but it was more a reaction of surprise, the sting over almost as quickly as it had begun. I sighed, and heard her echo the sigh behind me. The whip touched my shoulders again, leaving nothing for a split second until the sting began. I gasped, surprised at the delay of pain. And I heard the whip whisper through the air. The ends flicked my shoulders, and I cried out. The whisper, the moment of nothing followed by the flood of shock and hurt. The lash whistled before landing on my already reddened buttocks, making me yelp in surprise and pain. Again the whip sang, and again the pain stung me deeply. She made it dance across my shoulders and back, tickling and biting, sometimes cracking the popper to surprise me, mostly letting the whisper of leather through the air be its only announcement. Yes, I thought. And maybe she heard me.

I opened my eyes, and looked into hers, but the light and my exhilaration were playing tricks and I couldn't focus. I wanted her to touch me, and I arched my body forward. Instead, she stepped a few feet away, then flicked her wrist. The whip caught my left nipple. I jerked back against the bonds, yelped. She flicked the whip against my right nipple, and I twisted in my restraints, trying to escape the stinging pain. The whip snaked across my bare thighs, leaving angry red marks. I twisted again as the lash whistled through the air, touching my breasts, my stomach, my thighs, making me dance. It was too difficult to think, and my face was hot, flushed, streaked with tears when she glided around me and once again brought the buggy whip down on my shoulders. I sobbed in agony, my voice breaking as I struggled to free my wrists from their leather bonds, hoping to shrink my body, to make it a smaller target. My legs were burning and I could hardly breathe, I was choking on my tears. The whip touched down on my body like an angry wasp, and I struggled like a beast until I was too exhausted to avoid its evil sting.

And then she was upon me, her hands caressing and exploring me, nimble fingers untying my wrists and helping me stumble to a low bench. Blinded by my tears, I groped for her hands, sobbing anew when I felt their cool touch. I caught them then, and pressed my lips to the palm of each. I was sniffling, and she kissed my eyes and forehead while I held her hands, worshipping them with my kisses and my tears. When I had quieted down, she picked up my clothes and began to limp to the house, with me following behind.

She had a washtub half filled with cool water in her kitchen, and I stood in it while she brushed me down with a rough cloth, rubbing the sweat from my body and massaging a comfrey and herb ointment into my buttocks and shoulders. While I dried myself near the stove, she stepped back out to put the horse in the barn. I lit a kerosene lamp while I watched her brush hay off her skirt before coming back inside. In the lamp's soft light she pulled off her prayer cap and her green dress, and stepped into the tub. I watched her strong hands rub the cloth across her shriveled breasts, under her arms, between her legs. She threw a towel across her back and I saw the strong muscles flex as she pulled it back and forth vigorously, then, still naked, picked up the basket filled with fresh laundry, and limped into the small bedroom. I followed with the lamp, set it on a bedside table, and helped her pull the scented sheets across her bed and drew the heavily appliquéd quilts on top. I was smoothing the bed when she drew the *nacht ruck* from the basket, the fabric rustling in her hands. I stood frozen as she examined it. Her fingers plucked at the pink ribbons, fondled the row of buttons at the bodice, traced the careful stitching I had done in blue. She reverently moved to my side, and helped me pull the soft fabric over my head.

She stared at me for a long time, her eyes seeming to shimmer with tears. She bade me turn this way and that for her and I enjoyed the feeling of the fabric swirling about my ankles. She touched the sleeves, smoothed the fabric over the bodice, retied some of the ribbons, arranged my hair to fall softly over my shoulders to brush the collar line. I glowed under her attention. Finally, she nodded her approval. Together, we turned down the bed and slid under the freshly laundered sheets, I covered in lavender silk and satin, she completely naked. She pulled me to her, her hands caressing the dress's silk, fingering the buttons. I kissed her lips, her neck. She shivered, then gathered my head to her breast and pressed my mouth to her nipples. I sucked eagerly, my tongue tickling the tiny nipples, feeling her move against me. Though she kept one hand pressing me to her breast, I felt her other hand move between her legs, and I suckled harder, using my tongue and teeth as she groaned, her body bucking against me. I tentatively reached to cover her hand as her fingers slowed. She clasped my tit, then pushed my mouth gently away from her nipple, rolling onto her side to slide her hands across my *nacht ruck*. She gathered the fabric in her fingers, pulling the dress up above my knees, then sliding one of her hands under, trailing her strong fingers across my thigh. We both gasped when she touched me between my legs, the wetness there a surprise to me and a delight to her. My dress was pushed gently to my waist and she disappeared beneath the covers, where I felt her kissing my thighs higher and higher until her lips touched me where her hands had been. I cried out as she kissed and licked me, astonished at the strength of my response. I rocked against her, and felt a deep energy gather in my womb, expanding until it pushed me hard onto her mouth and I was crying out with pleasure, my hips thrusting against her. She rose from beneath the quilts and I threw my arms around her, kissing her, tasting myself on her lips. She pulled the *nacht ruck* back down, covering my legs again, and was stroking the fabric when I fell asleep in her arms.

The smell of coffee woke me the next morning. I could see her in the kitchen, dressed in a black dress, a spotless white apron, her grey hair pulled up and tucked into a starched black cap. I joined her in the kitchen, still wearing my *nacht ruck*, and set the table. She pointed to a chair. When I sat down, she pulled out a beautiful silver-backed brush and drew it through my hair. Carefully she pulled the brush through, its soft bristles caressing my scalp, then pulling away as they glided down to my shoulders. I counted one hundred gentle strokes, my hair shining from the attention. It fell softly against my shoulders; she caressed my face, smiling as her fingers tangling through the cut locks around my face. She asked me to stand for her again and pulled some of my hair forward so it fell softly against my shoulders and breasts, the blonde strands glowing against the lavender material. She retied some of the ribbons at my throat and sleeves and smoothed the silk down once more. Sighing, she told me I was beautiful. I told her I loved her and her eyes filled suddenly with tears and she turned away to rescue the eggs she was scrambling for breakfast. We ate breakfast in silence. I glanced at her while we ate; she was serene, her eyes as soft as a dove. She motioned for me to wash up while she went out to the corral and brought her horse around to the carriage. When I had finished the simple task, I returned to the bedroom and carefully made the bed, pulling the sheets tight and brushing out any wrinkles in the quilts. With a sigh, I pulled the silk gown over my head, and picked my clothes up from the rocking chair. I watched her out of the window while I pulled my stockings on and pulled the clean black dress over my head, fastening the apron on with straight pins. She was buckling the harness onto the horse, and I watched her competent hands tighten and fasten the buckles. I turned to the bureau to peer at my hair as I pulled it into a tight bun, using the hairpins in my weekday prayer cap to fasten it into place. I pulled my Sunday black cap over the bun, tying its ribbons in a bow under my chin. I folded my dark blue dress carefully and put it in the basket that I had used to bring her fresh laundry. I began to fold my *nacht ruck* as well, but stopped. I looked again out of the window; she was petting the horse and offering it something to eat. I watched the horse nuzzle her palm, heard it nicker. I turned away from the window and back to the bed. I carefully laid my *nacht ruck* out on the quilt, spreading it on the side of the bed where I had slept. Then I gathered up the basket, and went out to join her.

Eve Scales the Wall

Maria Dahvana Headley

I like titty bars. I like to go to them for anthropological reasons. That's what I'll tell you.

I'll tell you about the clear plastic platform shoes containing maybe goldfish, but I can't quite see and if it is a goldfish it could be fake, and I'll tell you about Her scaling a pole, whipping upside down, her lip-gloss catching the light and blinding me, her body suddenly a mermaid figurehead clinging to the prow of a ship, arched and painted. I'll tell you about the waves of men, or rather the waves of men's hands not quite getting there, and their breath warming the air, and the chairs emptied of asses as the men crane to get a better view of her marvelous mortician-quality rigor mortits. I'll talk until you're blue in the balls, and I'll tell you a million reasons I might like titty bars, though none of them would be the whole truth.

Here you are at the girly bar on the corner of Cinnamon and Wythe. Its claims to fame are the things that used to happen here involving guns and molls and blood and guts, but now they just consist of watered down drinks and women wearing two or three sequins and a hell of a bikini wax. I'm here too. I'm at a velvet banquette having a tête-à-tête with a man I don't necessarily want to be lovers with. I'm here because he's bought me dinner and dared me, and though by now this dare is dull, it's better than sitcoms.

I'm here to tip the stripper, slipping myself over the edge of her platform, his dollars in my hands. A surprisingly simple investment, singles, wads of paper adding up to not much, but feeling like salvation. I'm here to tip her so that as he tipples he can watch my nipples tilting from the top of my t-shirt, and then he can watch her do stripper things such as kiss me full on the mouth, or take the dollars from my cleavage to hers in an arcane yet titillating transfer operation, or bend over all the way backwards in an X-rated limbo and bite the bucks from my beaver. The latter only in certain clubs that allow that kind of thing. For the record, most clubs allow most things as long as you're a pretty girl and not too bull-dyke-like.

The man I don't necessarily want to be lovers with is making his zipper gnash its teeth. And I'm tipping the girl. Who is not really blonde, but brave, because her bush is dyed too.

I haven't forgotten you. You're in the corner. Are you bored, broken up with, busted? One of those things. I don't care which. You're in a fairly good suit missing the tie. You have a company card. You have balls enough to submit your receipts for reimbursement. You've poached egos, you've slid in ID, and the percentage of your actions you're willing to take responsibility for is approaching double digits as you mature. You like titty bars. Right? Why do YOU like them, if the question's on the table? I know you asked it first, but I don't play by the rules. You should be able to tell that. I drink bourbon. Straight. You're drinking light beer. You're a wuss in creep's clothing. You have made a joke to the bartender about girls who drink drinks like mine, who are on their third, a joke about slinging me over your shoulder and carrying me away. Good luck. You're like every guy I ever meet, greet and complete a frazzled, foolish fantasy for. I know you. Don't bother giving me your name, I'll only pawn it in the morning. And don't leave your wedding ring on the bedside table. I'm making a wedding ring quilt. Sort of chain mail. It's 6 by 8 feet and it's three-quarters done.

I almost graduated from a respected university. I've taken courses in things you've never thought of. I read Virginia Woolf, James Joyce, and Proust. For fun. And I like titty bars. A dichotomy isn't it?

So, the velvet banquette, you sweating in the corner in the jacket you'd rather not drop in something questionable, flashing lights specially timed to obscure cellulite, sparkly thong panties stretched over the pricking promise of puissant pudenda. Me, bent over the platform, my breasts pressed against the stage, my skirt riding up behind me, and Her wrapped around the pole, 10 feet up, whirling by the hook of one high heel, a pornographic merry-go-round.

She's why I come. Or not she exactly, but girls like her. This is nothing new for me. I come to this bar often. They're the same everywhere you go. This Bar in Singapore, or This Bar in Milwaukee. They've been converted from finger steak restaurants and bowling alleys and daycare centers. In them, you'll find girls in stretch vinyl chiffon sequin rubber plastic tassels candlewax chocolate whipped cream gothic naive whorish schoolgirl kneesocks pulled up to there and demi bras cupping 800 sizes of mammary, all these various versions of the voracious vestal vulva, shaking their things for profit just as they have ever since Eve noticed the figleaf was backless. And thank you God (in case you need to hear a prayer from these lips that have never uttered your name save for in the heat of heavenly sin), these girls are good to look at. God (in case you'd like me to go down on my knees and for once not do it with my mouth full), give me a long-legged stripper braided around a pole and listen to how well I can speak in tongues.

Wonderful things I have seen, speaking of miracles:

1) Happy Hour. South Texas, 1997. The face of Christ appears in the 5 o'clock shadow of the shaven pussy of a 17-year-old-stripper. Following hubbub and criminal charges of exploitation of the faithful, stripper is sent straight to the electrolysis chair.
2) Salt Lake City, 1994. Another bush story. Impervious Stripper lights her bush on fire as part of an incendiary act entitled "Moses." Fire department comes.
3) Georgia, 2001. Stripper with a sense of humor glues two cream-filled pastries to her nipples in lieu of pasties.
4) Asses and tits and glittered eyelids from here to eternity, mother–daughter duos, 4 feet tall to 7 feet tall, Amazons and Tinkerbells, handstands, batons, girls capable of fucking baseball bats, fruit bats, and battery-powered behemoths.

Do you actually think I'm capable of making this shit up?
I haven't forgotten you. You're not really in this story, but I
know you're still there, balancing on that cracked vinyl or
buttery leather barstool, leaning on that splintered formica or
Italian marble counter, shuffling your sheaf of singles or
bundle of billions. You're the guy. We're here to entertain
you. You're the reason God made pussy out of Adam's rib.
Forgive the religious imagery. I took a lot of theology courses
before I didn't get my degree.

The lights change, the shift rolls over, the new girls are fully
dressed and the naked ones who've come off the platforms are
roaming the audience like gunslingers, fingers twirling, spurs
jangling. Lone hens in flocks of crowing birds, visiting cock-
tables and roosting there. I go back to my velvet banquette and
my tête-à-tête with the man who will never be my lover, and
brood over how to be rid of him. He's still throbbing over the
possibility that he'll get to go home with me and one of the
naked girls, but he hasn't asked the right questions, and I
haven't let him know that I'm hooking my thumb in the
waistband of my panties, slipping them off and leaving them
wet and exhausted beneath the table. He claims to be a career
soldier, but has somehow missed basic training and every
subsequent opportunity to learn how to shoot his gun. I am
here for the strippers. And the new one, you like her too, I
notice, is a redhead with seamed stockings and a 1950s black
dress.

Is it the bliss of constant renewal, perpetual undress, the
blessed press of freshly naked flesh? Heaven for the attention-
deficient, girls whose names and features you need not recall
tomorrow, bounty, outlay, spreading thighs and flashing eyes,
moans and sighs and no goodbyes. Could anything be more
satisfying than the titty bar? Certainly not the having of the
things you're thinking you want. Certainly not the pulse-
pounding pursuit of Prurience and her minions. In the titty
bar, you don't have to move, apart from hand to wallet, hand to
drink, hand to cock. You can recline, and imagine that for five
bucks your grapes are being sweetly peeled. You can watch us.

The redhead unmakes her New Look silhouette, standing on
her hands and twisting her ankles around the pole. Under the

mourning dress is a merry widow. Her legs are crossed and, despite her upended pose, she is demure. Have I mentioned how I love titty bars? The music is loud and electronic, someone is claiming this girl is actually a stockbroker, and all I can hear is my pulse playing *In-A-Gadda-Da-Vida* on my eardrums. She winds her way up the pole, arched and upside down, stripes of white thigh showing between her garter belt and her stockings. She flips over, holding herself tight against the metal, and those of us with the right angle see that between her legs she's wearing nothing. She pulls herself up the pole, slowly, slowly, her pussy spread against it, and with one hand unzips the dress and lets it drift to the floor.

And there you are, leaning forward slightly, boredom requited, mouth a little open. The expensive suit missing the tie is crumpling and you don't care, your elbow is in beer, and you let it soak, you've got one foot on the floor and the other half raised in a step in the right direction, but you won't be taking it yet. You're scared. This is the stripper that doesn't exist. I admit it. You do too. She's not real. There are no strippers like this stripper. She's the one we've all been waiting for. She's the one that makes us wander from town to town, to all the titty bars in the country, the one that bent over us in the night and left lipstick on our faces, the one whose smell of sweat and perfume lingers on the fleece of sheep that, leaping, sent us sleep.

And her red hair glows in the lewd light, libations flow so fast it's trite, and all of us sitting here ignite with something like the firefly's torch, undrownable, quenchless, our blazes desperately blinking and signaling to the constant shining thing that is her body.

She is a bonfire in a snowfield and the ice in our drinks relents.

She puts one foot on the floor and leaves the other stranded against the pole, kicked over her head. Her garters imprint her flesh, her stockings slide smooth against the air, and she unsnaps one of the buttons holding them up. The music is gone by this point. We can all hear each other breathing. We're calculating which of us will get there first. None of us can move.

Do you remember the story? About the princess at the top of the glass mountain. And the apples she rolled down the mountain to suitors, who, if they brought the apple back, could win her. I can't remember how Prince Charming finally made it. I can only remember all the hopefuls who skidded bruised and despondent to the bottom. I may be making this story up to some extent. In one of the anthropology courses I analyzed it, cannibalizing from feminist tomes, but I have no recollection now of how to get to the top of the glass mountain. I only know how to fall.

This is why I love titty bars. Do you agree? We descend on love like mosquitoes, frantic desire relieved after one long suck.

Her stockings are gone now. She's barefoot, which is against the rules. Strippers are supposed to wear platform slippers made of clear plastic, but none of us are complaining. She's looked us each in the eye and crawled on hands and knees across the platform. She's strung a stocking around the neck of the never my lover man, and drawn his glazed face toward hers. She's flicked her pink tongue over his lips. We're ruined. We sit in soiled clothing, peanut shells crunching under our feet, strings of drool suspended from our chins. We've nothing left but want. I can see the freckles on the tops of her breasts as she bends over our banquette. She slips her hand into the lace and jiggles the flesh, pushing the strap over her shoulder.

The room is a collective moan. You are on your knees, suit be damned, cellphone be lost, wallet be stolen. You're the guy. We're doing this for you. If you can believe that, you may also be able to believe that she loves you and only you. Believe it. She is the sexiest stripper on the face of the earth, and she doesn't exist. She's made of smoke and sawdust and sympathy. She puts her nipple in my mouth, and I suck. Because she's the stripper that doesn't exist, her breasts are real, and because I don't believe in boob jobs, so are mine. She holds my tits in both hands and runs her thumbs over my nipples.

You, being male, will not understand how calculated it is that I am the only woman customer in the room. I will get all her attention, I will be loved, and you, being male, will love it. Hands from here to infinity grab wallets, hundreds of dollars flick forth, and the stage is showered with satisfaction. You may also not understand why it is more satisfying to feel her lips against mine, to feel her breasts against mine, to feel the merry widow's lacings in my hands, and to untie them, than to be kissed by the man I never came with. His maleness does not mean he is a man. I would rather crisscross the country, kissing strippers, than do almost anything. The stripper that doesn't exist is everywhere in the dead of night, as soon as the drinks are strong enough and the cars outside have stopped honking and they've called last call, she'll come out of her dressing tomb and start spinning in front of us. Music box ballerinas don't dance when the box is closed. I open my legs to her hand, and together we circle the pole. Something in the abandoned college education says mayday, mutters about ribbons and spring and possibly sacrifices to a virgin god, but I ignore it. Have I forgotten you? I'll let you lay your cheek on the stage and look up at us, as we weave together.

I love titty bars. I love them for my knee between her knees, and for the dress lying spread across the floor. I love them for the wire in her bra, and the glitter of greed in her eyes as the men in the room hang upside down and shake, emptying their pockets in bright rivers of coin and credit, whimpering for more and more and more and then some. The floor is knee deep in tips within moments and you feel the forty thieves must have a hideout here. She and I are still pole dancing, and we will be nightly. They know me at this bar. I'm here all the time. In Egypt and Miami and Paris and everywhere. The stripper that doesn't exist trails around behind me, always arriving before I do, always ready with the fake eyelashes, always wet and bent over backward. She can swallow swords and eat fire and fuck snakes and God, can she shake.

I'm not going to give you the satisfaction of putting you back in the story. You're the guy. You're always here. If you're quiet you can watch us get into my car, see us drive away, read the motel sign on the highway telling us to Sleep Tight and see us stumble out and go into our room. You can squint through the keyhole and see what happens when the stripper that doesn't exist kneels in front of me and rubs her face over my bush, and you can hold a glass to the door and listen to us gasping and moaning and breathing into each other's bodies. You can watch the end of the story becoming the beginning.

American Holidays

Mike Kimera

1. Memorial Day

"So what was your best?"

"Best what?"

"Best erotic experience."

Mark is a sex bore. He talks about it so much it's a wonder he gets time to do it.

"Mine was with two Swedish twins in a sauna," he says, leaning toward me conspiratorially. "I'd added a day to a Swiss business trip to get some skiing in and these two and I were first back to the hotel from the piste. Well, you know how the Europeans are with saunas, everyone together and no clothes allowed. Just one of these girls would have been amazing – snow white hair, all-over tan and sleek body – but twins! I thought I'd died and gone to pussy heaven."

I hate men who say pussy like that. Like a woman starts and ends at her cunt. But I've known Mark since grade school, so I give him some latitude. Turning slightly away from him, I look toward the lake where my wife, Helen, and Barbara are sunning themselves. They are the best of friends, and they tell each other everything. I want to sit quietly beside them and listen to their talk. Instead I am standing next to Mark at the BarBQ pit, burning burgers.

"So anyway, the shock came when the first one took me inside her. In the heat of the sauna her pussy felt cool. No shit. Cool pussy from an ice maiden in a sauna. How sexy is that! *Then*, when her sister joined in . . ."

I think Mark is making this up. Maybe the twins were real.

Maybe he even saw them in the sauna. But I want to believe that he doesn't cheat on Barbara on his business trips.

I am a little in love with Barbara. Helen pointed it out to me one night as we drove back from dinner at their house. She said that she'd noticed that Barbara is always the last person I look at in a room, and that I avoid being alone with her, both sure signs of my attraction. Denial would have been pointless; Helen knows me too well. After a few seconds of guilt-ridden silence, Helen pulled the car over to the side of the road, and right there, on a tree-lined suburban street, where nice neighbors repaint their picket fences every spring, she fucked me. She didn't say a word. Mouth on mine, she freed my cock, pushed aside her panties and rode me. I came like a boy. She grinned at me, held my face in her hands and said, "If you ever call me Barbara while we fuck, I'll cut your dick off." Then she drove us home.

Only when Mark says, "Your turn," do I realize I've missed his sauna-sex story, and he is now waiting for mine.

"Come on Pete", he says, "even a terminally married man like you must have had *some* erotic adventures. 'Fess up."

An image of Helen blossoms in my mind. She is nineteen and has just let me fuck her for the first time. She'd insisted that we use her parents' bed. "It will make up for all the times I've had to listen to them screwing," she'd said as she led me into the master bedroom. I am lying on my back, wrists still tied to the headboard, sated and happy, watching her between half closed eyes, pretending to be asleep. She is sitting at her mother's dressing table, brushing her long black hair. The sun streaming through the window behind her seems to me to be a kind of halo. She leans her head to one side so that she can push the comb through the full length of her thick glossy hair. This causes one small upturned breast to push off the silk robe that Helen has "borrowed" from her mother, and to stretch triumphantly up towards the sun. I am hypnotized by the play of light on her hair; the smooth movement of her arm as she wields the brush and the slight but attention-grabbing movement of her silhouetted breast. She puts the brush back on the dressing table, looks at me and smiles. Many times since, I have returned to that moment of still happiness, crowned with the love in her smile.

"Well?" Mark says.

"Sorry Mark," I say, "nobody seems to want erotic adventures with me."

I mean it as a playful way of changing the subject. Mark takes me literally.

"I don't know," he says, "you're not bad looking. I know Barbara thinks you're sexy. You just need to read the signs."

"I think the food is ready now," I say, gathering the half-burnt/half-frozen products of Mark's culinary skill onto plates.

"You must have been tempted. At least once," Mark says.

"I'm happily married Mark. Temptation is easy enough to overcome."

"Ah yes," Mark says, "I'd forgotten about the 'Peter Brader, man-of-steel' act."

I start to walk back toward the lake, hoping to bring an end to the conversation before we get into a fight. Mark has always taken my abstinence from casual sex as a personal affront. Briefly I wonder if he thinks it's all an act and I'm just refusing to share the details with him.

"Barbara really does think you're sexy, you know."

I stop and look at him. He laughs.

"No need to look so horrified. She's not going to rape you or anything. But she told me that she admires your serenity. Isn't that a great phrase? Admires your serenity."

I try for a wry smile but Mark is already striding ahead of me, so it is lost on him.

"OK girls, the hunters have returned with freshly charred dead animals for their women to feast upon," he shouts.

Sometimes I think Mark is locked in a parallel dimension. The "girls", both in their late twenties, exchange pained glances at Mark's return, but he either doesn't notice or doesn't care.

This meal is a tradition amongst us going back eight years, to when we were both newly married couples. Every Memorial Day we drive out to the lake and have a barbecue on the public beach. Back then we slept in our trucks and drank beer with our burgers. Now we rent a large cabin and sip Pinot Noir. Sometimes I think the burgers are the last talisman of the days when we had more hope than history.

I have my head in Helen's lap. She smells of sunshine and cotton. I relax, content to listen to her telling Barbara stories about the people in her office. I have never visited Helen's office. I am reluctant to have reality superimposed on the vivid images I have of her colleagues. Barbara and Helen used to work together, and Helen introduced Barbara to Mark.

When Barbara laughs at the punchline of Helen's story, it is a raucous laugh that seems to escape from her. I turn my head slightly, knowing that Barbara will have one hand in front of her face. Helen feels me move, recognizes the reason and, unseen by the others, pinches my earlobe as she pulls me back to my original position. I look up at her. She mouths the word "later" and I shiver at the thought.

Despite Helen's admonition, I find myself wondering about Barbara's laugh. It reminds me of Miss Honeychurch in *Room With a View*, whose passionate nature is discernible only by the way in which she plays piano. With a stab of guilt, accompanied by a sudden erection, I have a flash of Barbara coming as raucously as she laughs.

On our second year out here, we almost got into a group thing. We'd stopped talking and started kissing, still in couples but with each couple acutely aware of the presence of the other. I left the decision to Helen, who in turn looked to Barbara. Mark was thinking with his cock and pushed up Barbara's T-shirt to take her nipple into his mouth. The discomfort on Barbara's face was obvious.

Helen grabbed me by the belt and said, more loudly than she needed to, "Come on Peter, I need a bed to tie you to."

I was happy to leave. Barbara smiled her gratitude while trying to keep Mark's fingers out of her shorts. Civilized man that I am, I still could not erase the sight of Barbara's stiff nipple topping a small neat breast that just demanded to be taken into my mouth. Helen knew what I was thinking. When she rode me she held my nipples between her fingernails and used them like a bridle. I was sore for a week but my cock was made of ivory that night.

The scene was never repeated. Barbara confided in Helen her embarrassment at how Mark fucks her. I was puzzled when Helen passed on the remark. She just laughed and said, "Well, you've seen him dance haven't you?" Mark thinks he dances like John Travolta, but he looks more like Fred Flintstone. He dances vigorously, with his eyes closed, paying little attention to either his partner or the rhythm of the music. The magnitude of the criticism made my balls retract.

I am constantly amazed at what women tell each other. Men brag, women tell the truth. It's a frightening thought.

A tinny rendition of the James Bond theme fractures the silence. Mark has brought his cellphone, even on Memorial Day. Barbara glares at him, but he turns his back on her and takes the call. Mark uses an earpiece on his phone. He says he doesn't want to fry the brain cells that survived the drugs. He looks demented as he paces in a circle, apparently talking to himself.

We overhear enough of the conversation to know that he has been summoned back to the city by some European emergency that he must respond to at once. I wonder at that – it's 9 p.m. in Berlin right now. It occurs to me that I have just seen a piece of performance art. Maybe Mark doesn't make his adventures up. Perhaps there is someone waiting for him even now in a city center hotel room.

To my surprise, Barbara lets Mark go without complaint – she just sits and watches as he takes the car, leaving her behind like luggage that we will forward to him later.

"I'm going to lie down in the cabin for a while," Barbara says once the car is out of sight.

"Are you OK?" I say. Dumb question. Helen digs her fingers into my side to tell me to shut up.

"No Peter, I'm not OK, but I'm trying to get used to it. Not everyone has a marriage like yours. I live with a man who never touches me, but who tries to fuck anything female that can move without a zimmer frame. He doesn't even have the tact not to embarrass me in front of my friends. So I'm trying to preserve my dignity by not letting myself cry until I get back to my room."

Barbara's eyes are wet, but she is standing straight and her voice is strong and clear. She holds my gaze until I look away, then she picks up a bottle of wine and heads back to the cabin. Helen follows her. They talk quietly but passionately. I can't hear what is said. Then they hug in that way that women do, halfway between a caress and a handshake.

Helen waits, head on one side, hands on her hips, for my questions. I don't ask any. She looks at me for the longest time. I seldom know what she is thinking. She moves to stand in front of me, tilts my head down towards hers and says, "I love you, Peter Brader."

We give Barbara an hour before we return to the cabin. I head into the kitchen to clear away the debris of our meal. Helen goes to check on Barbara. I have just loaded the dishwasher when I hear Helen say, "Come here, Peter."

I know from her tone that we have started to play. I am surprised, but out of long habit I go to her and wait, eyes downcast, for her instructions. I love surrendering to her like this. My cock is already thickening and my heartbeat is elevated. It is so exciting not to know what will happen next. Even so, I am concerned. Surely she's not going to take me here, in the main room. The thought worries and thrills me at the same time.

"Strip, Peter."

Helen has never done this before. On our Memorial Day weekends she has always used the bedroom for our fucking.

I don't look at her or speak as I strip. I feel exposed standing there, my cock sending semaphore signals of desire to my mistress.

"Put your hands behind your back," Helen says.

The steel cuffs Helen produces from her bag are cold against my wrists. They make me feel pleasantly helpless.

"Peter, I want you to stay hard as long as you can. Let me help you," She ties a soft leather strap around my balls. My cock trembles at her touch. She grins and plants a chaste little kiss just underneath the head.

I wait for her to undress. She doesn't. Instead she reaches into her bag and pulls out a scarf. Standing behind me she blindfolds me with the scarf. I feel her breath on my neck. Her teeth sink into my earlobe as her fist closes around my cock. I groan.

"You wanted Barbara today, didn't you," she says.

I nod.

"Say it. Tell me what you were thinking"

"I wanted to know how she sounds when she comes," I say. She lets go of my cock. A cool finger probes my anus.

"So you prefer her to me?"

"No. I love you. I need you."

"But . . . ?"

"But I like Barbara."

"Would you like her to fuck you?"

"Yes," I say. I think I know where Helen is going with this but I can't believe she really means it.

Helen kisses me; a deep, slow kiss, exploring my mouth with hers. Except it is not Helen. Helen is still behind me.

The kissing stops. Before I can speak Helen presses against my back and whispers, "It will be OK, Peter. Trust me." I nod my head slightly and she whispers "Thank you."

I understand the blindfold. It gives us the option to pretend that none of this has happened.

No one is touching me now. I wait. I assume the women are undressing. I wonder if they are touching. Suddenly it occurs to me that over the years they may have done more than just touch. My mind doubts that this is true, Helen would have told me, but my cock goes with the image and twitches ludicrously.

A hand, strong and purposeful, pushes on my shoulder, signalling for me to kneel. The floor is hard on my knees. I won't be able to do this for long. I recognize the smell of Helen's sex, seconds before it is pressed against my face. She holds my head and rubs herself against me. My tongue presents itself for use. She presses her labia against my mouth until my head is forced backwards. She rubs me in a figure of eight against her sex, then she is gone.

Seconds later another sex is pressed against my mouth. To my surprise it smells and tastes just like the first. Maybe I can't tell the difference between Helen and Barbara. Maybe Helen is returning to confuse me. The message is clear enough: stop trying to analyse, go with the flow, be the moment, let the sex flow through you. That message is at the heart of my sexuality, and I recognize it as their gift to me.

Hands guide me to lie first on my side and then on my back. Cushions are placed under my head and my butt. Care is taken to ensure that I am never touched by both women at the same time. I could let myself imagine that there is only Helen or only Barbara, but now is the time for feeling, not imagining.

A mouth suckles my nipple. The sound of it is loud against the eerie silence that possesses us like a spell. The tongue moves down my belly slowly, skilfully, until it reaches my pubic hair, then it goes away. A hand, warm, strong, grips my cock around the shaft. The palm of a second hand rubs my precum over the head of my cock, making me wriggle and moan. It takes effort not to come, but I control myself.

Attention shifts from my cock to my mouth. Swift butterfly kisses that make me smile. Then tickling. Tickling that goes on until I am giggling helplessly with tears wetting my blindfold.

I am allowed to get my breath back, then I am mounted. My cock slides into ripe wetness that grabs at me eagerly. Hands on my chest. Thighs around my legs. Deep forceful strokes, followed, after the shortest of times, by a tremor of passion that passes through to my bones. She falls forward onto me, sweat-slick breasts sliding over me, teeth nipping at my neck.

Then she rolls off me, leaving my cock straining for relief, my body demanding stimulus. Both are granted by the mouth that envelops my cock and the swollen labia that descend upon my face. I lick eagerly at first, then become distracted by the play of teeth and tongue and lips upon my cock.

I break the spell of silence, begging to be allowed to come. The mouth releases me as she slides down my body and impales herself on my cock. She does not move, but she squeezes me with her cunt, milking me irresistibly. She is moaning now, but quietly, as if she were gagged. Her hands are on my ankles; her cunt is pressed hard against my pubis. When I start to come, her grip on my ankles tightens and I hear a groan that starts in the back of her throat and becomes an explosive "Fuck!" She stays on me until my cock softens, then she lets it slide out.

I am exhausted. Cool fingers undo the leather around my balls. My cock is patted gently, like a Labrador being rewarded for performing a favorite trick. I find it hard to focus. My awareness always ebbs after I come.

I am being helped up and led somewhere. A bed. Fresh clean linen. The bed feels so comforting after the hardness of the floor. My hands are uncuffed. My arms are massaged vigorously and asexually. Scarves are used to tie my wrists to the headboard.

I am ready to give way to sleep when I hear that unmistakable buzz followed by the smell of lubricated latex. My asshole clenches in anticipation.

"Spread, Peter," Helen's voice. A calm command she knows will be obeyed.

The vibrator is slim and has a slight curve. It is perfect for stimulating the prostate. I relax and let it slide in, wondering who is holding it. My tired cock starts to rally. I think I hear a giggle from beside the bed, but I am distracted by having my balls sucked one after the other.

My brain is fuzzy. I want to sleep. I want to fuck for ever. I turn down the noise in my mind and focus on the cunt that is now raising and lowering itself on my cock. I have no control over the pace. I am a flesh dildo. I am happy.

With the vibrator in place I manage to stay hard until after she comes. I am rewarded with a skilful handjob that drains my balls and takes the last of my energy.

I hear Helen say, "You can sleep now Peter," and I know the game is over. As sleep washes over me, I think I hear a different voice say, very quietly, "Thank you."

I sleep late. When I awake my hands are free, the blindfold is gone, my ass is sore and my memory is confused. Before I can get out of bed, Helen and Barbara, both fully dressed and looking refreshed and relaxed, bring me breakfast on a tray.

"Good morning sleepyhead," Helen says. "We've brought you something to build up your strength."

"Do I need building up?" I ask.

Helen ignores the question and hands me a glass of cold OJ. Barbara is standing at the foot of the bed. She is smiling, not broadly, but persistently. I doubt she is aware of it.

"Barbara is going to come and stay with us for a while," Helen says.

I look at both of them. Helen posed it as a statement, but we all know it was a question. The silence continues while I think about it.

"It's only until I decide what to do about Mark," Barbara says, "Helen thought I could stay in the guest room for a while."

I think about how long I have known Mark and yet how little I really like him. I consider how comfortable Helen and Barbara are together. I remember the carefully anonymous passion we shared last night. I know that if I say yes, it will change things for ever in ways that I can't yet predict.

"I'm sorry about you and Mark," I say to Barbara, "but I'm glad you're coming to stay. I'm sure we'll work something out."

The look on Helen's face tells me I've done the right thing. I don't know if last night will be repeated. I trust Helen to work that out. I do know that I am still naked under the bedclothes and that I desperately need to use the bathroom.

"If you ladies will excuse me," I say, "I have some urgent business to attend to, privately."

Helen grins and leads Barbara by the elbow, saying, "A man's gotta do what a man's gotta do," in a terrible John Wayne accent.

Barbara picks up the theme and says, "Yep, and there are some things a man must do alone." They are both laughing as they leave the room.

I'm still not sure what I've just agreed to, but however it turns out, it won't be dull. I head off to the bathroom, whistling happily.

2. Independence Day

"So how often do you fuck my soon to be ex-wife, Peter?"

Peter looks the way he always looks, calm to the point of not being there. I wonder if he even sees me.

"Is she good? Does she moan for you? Or does the frigid bitch freeze your dick off?"

I don't want to be saying this. I don't plan it. It just comes.

"Or maybe it's your bull-dyke wife that she has between her legs?" I hear myself say.

My mouth fills with blood, my jaw is on fire and the floor of the bar is much closer than it was. The bastard hit me.

By the time I make it to my feet he's gone. People are trying not to look at me. No one offers to help.

Who would have thought Peter would know how to punch? I

knew he was the silent type, but I didn't think he was the violent silent type. Shit, this is a man who lets his wife tie him to the bed before they fuck – not exactly Mr Macho. I haven't seen him hit anyone since grade school. And then he just walks away like he's John Wayne and I'm a bit part player from central casting.

So much for trying to arrange a meeting with Barbara for tomorrow. Just once I wish I could keep my smart mouth shut. My wife's been living at Peter and Helen's since she left me on Memorial Day. Great sense of timing she has. We've all been friends for years, Peter, Helen, Barbara and I. At least I thought we had. Now I wonder when I became the odd one out; an unfortunate addition that arrived whenever they invited Barbara anywhere.

I'm sure there's nothing going on, Barbara is just staying with them while she sorts herself out. At least she hasn't tried to throw me out of our house. I should be grateful, but you know how it is in the dark hours of the night. I keep imagining them in a continuous three-way. If Peter wasn't so terminally monogamous and Helen wasn't such a control freak, I could almost believe it.

All I'd wanted out of the meeting today was to arrange to see Barbara face to face. She won't talk to me on the phone, but Peter agreed to meet me here. We used to do a lot of drinking here once. Well, I did. I don't think I've ever seen Peter really shitfaced. So I get him here and insult him badly enough that Peter the placid actually hits me. Good job!

I decide to stop being the bar-room floorshow and go to the restroom to clean myself up. The man in the mirror looks older than me, he hasn't had enough sleep, and his bottom lip is split just below the left incisor. My shirt is history, blood all over the collar. I'm meeting Kirsten for lunch in an hour. "Welcome to the fucked up life of Mark Grady," I say. Even my reflection in the mirror doesn't smile.

My cellphone goes off and the "Mission Impossible" theme tune, my latest choice of ring tone, bounces around the restroom. This strikes me as absurdly appropriate. "Your mission Mr Grady, should you decide to accept it, is to get a life." I start to laugh, way too loudly. I'm still laughing when I answer the call.

"Well, you sound like you're having a good time," Kirsten says, "did you start to party without me?"

"Not exactly."

"Listen Mark, I know it's a bummer but I'm going to have to blow you off for lunch today."

"Why?" I say, sounding petulant even to my own ears. I hate the but-mom-you-PROMISED whine in my voice.

"I've got to work, Mark. To get things done before the holiday tomorrow."

I hear a male voice I almost recognize calling out impatiently, "Come on Kirsten or we'll lose our table."

I pretend I didn't hear that and put a leer into my voice to say, "I'd rather you were blowing me than just blowing me off."

"So would I," Kirsten said, "in fact, didn't I do that this morning?" I don't know if she's being humorous or genuinely can't remember.

We always have sex in the mornings. In seven years of marriage with Barbara she never once woke up wanting to fuck. Kirsten does it like it's part of her morning exercise routine; a warm up before she goes jogging.

The first time we spent the whole night together I was delighted to wake with my cock already in Kirsten's mouth. She likes to be on top. She does what she calls "the jockey". She tells me it's very good for her pelvic floor. She squats over me so that only the palms of her hands and the inside of her cunt are touching me. Then she rides me. She squeezes me like she's making orange juice with my cock. She looks wonderful up there: fit, young, tanned, little tits that don't move when she fucks, topped by nipples so hard you could hang your coat on one. I was in heaven that first morning.

But here's the thing: she does it every morning. Great, right? Wrong. Some mornings I want to sleep. Or to cuddle. But Kirsten has a schedule and she's never late. Last week I timed her by the bedside clock. The fuck takes eight minutes. Every day. Exactly. If I'm slow to rise, she grows impatient. I think that if I couldn't get it up one day, she'd just use her vibrator and then go jogging. But listen to me, I'm fucking an ambitious intern who does sexercises on my cock each morning and I'm feeling sorry for myself? Loser!

"Mark, you there? You've gone all quiet. Listen, I have to go, I'll be late this evening but we can spend all day tomorrow together, OK?" She hangs up before I can reply.

I put my phone away, look at my bruised and bleeding face in the mirror once more, and wonder how the hell I let all this happen. "I coulda been a contenda." I mumble at the bum in the mirror. Not funny. Not funny at all.

Outside the bar I have difficulty getting a cab to stop. Too much blood on my shirt. So I indulge myself. I'm good at that. I walk three blocks in the noon heat to my favorite hotel and I rent a room for the afternoon. I love luxury hotels. All life should work the way they do. From the comfort of my room I order a fresh shirt from the hotel store, some paracetamol for my aching head, and a good room service meal with a decent bottle of wine.

I pour myself four fingers of J&B and relish that first-taste-of-the-day moment. Ah, that's better. So Peter hit me. I can cope with that. Maybe even use it to get some sympathy from Barbara. The day is definitely getting better, until my phone goes off and it's Anthea the Hun, my boss, looking for me. I made a pass at Anthea once, before she was my boss. Bad mistake.

Anthea comes from that mix of Norwegian and German stock that produces blonde amazons that can work in the fields all day long and then drink you under the table at night. We'd been working late together on an important project. We got along very well. We had had some Chinese delivered to the office so we could work even later. The meal felt relaxed and fun. It also felt sexy. Something about watching Anthea's powerful jaw suck down those noodles made my flesh tingle.

We were in the little kitchen area, the only people on the entire floor. We'd been laughing at something. Anthea bent over to dump her cartons in the trash and I couldn't resist it, I ran my hand up the inside of her leg. She was wearing stockings. Who would have thought it? I love stockings. I love that transition from the rougher surface of the silk to the smooth warm flesh of the upper thigh. It gives me a hard-on every time. Then I got a bit carried away and let my fingers rush upwards and push into her.

The effect was dramatic and unexpected; she clamped her thighs around my hand and then turned rapidly on her heels. I was pulled off balance and ended up on the floor. Anthea stood on my wrist and pressed hard enough to hurt. I was pinned to the floor, wondering how I got there, and trying hard not to look up her skirt. She looked wonderful from that angle. If it hadn't been for the pain I might have enjoyed myself.

The idea of fun ended the moment I heard her speak. "They told me you were a hopeless lech," she said, "but I thought they were wrong. You're bright. You have a nice wife. You don't need to screw around."

She sounded very angry and I found myself wondering if she was stronger than me.

"I'm sorry," I said, "I just . . ."

"You just thought you'd shove your fingers up my cunt. Did you think I'd like that? Or that I'd be a good sport and put up with it anyway? Or do you just see me as a cunt on legs, a slot to be filled?"

I didn't know what to say. I hadn't meant any harm. I mean things had gone too far too fast, but it's not like I raped her or anything. But I'd really pissed her off and she looked scary. She took her foot off my wrist and I went to get up.

"*Don't* move," she said.

I lay still.

"I hate shits like you Mark. I could have you fired, you know that don't you. But then I'd be the ballbreaking bitch who her co-workers can't work late with in case she accuses them of rape."

"Anthea, look, I . . ."

"I'm talking now. You're listening. I'm going to teach you a lesson Mark. And then you're going to leave. Show me your cock."

Nothing she said could have surprised me more.

"Come on Mark, get it out. Show me what you were thinking with."

"I don't want . . ."

"Or should I get it out for you? Maybe I should just unzip you and find out what you're made of."

She bent toward me and I found myself shuffling backwards on the floor.

"Just a quick feel," she said. "A compliment really. What's the matter Mark? Be a good sport."

She reached for me again. I was frightened. She looked like she could kill me. I bumped into the cupboard behind me. Instinctively, I covered my cock with my hands, unable even to speak.

Then she stood up straight and looked down at me. "I want you to remember this Mark. I want you to remember just how it feels. Tomorrow, you're going to phone in sick. You'll stay sick for a week and I'll finish this project alone. Do you understand?"

I nodded. She left. I did phone in sick. She got a promotion for completing that project. We worked together from time to time after that, but always in a bigger group. She never mentioned it again, but there was always some hostility there.

When she was made head of my section, I knew she'd fire me. She called me into her new office. Before I could speak she said, "I'm not going to fire you, Grady," she never calls me Mark any more, "because you are going to work your balls off for me aren't you. And I will make sure you get the bonuses that go with that. OK? Good. You can go." And that was it.

I've worked for her for six months now, and every week I wish I had the courage to tell her to stuff her job. One moment of weakness and she crucifies me.

So, as I answer Anthea's call on my cellphone, all enjoyment of the hotel fades. Jesus, even my balls retract slightly. I hate her for making me feel like this.

"Why aren't you here Grady? Did you quit and forget to send me an e-mail? Just let me know where you want the stuff from your desk sent and I'll have it couriered over."

"Bitch," I think to myself, but I put a smile in my voice and say, "Hi Anthea. I was just about to call in. I'm not feeling too good. I think I'm coming down with something. Good thing tomorrow's a holiday."

"You poor thing," she says, "which is it, the booze getting to you, or the intern wearing you out?"

"Look, I came in above target last month, didn't I? I always make my numbers. I can afford the time."

"So far, Grady. You've always made your numbers so far. But try looking in the mirror some time. You look like a man who's losing it. I don't have losers on my team. Are you hearing me?"

I really want to come up with some smart remark; to tell her how wrong she is, but a small voice in my head is whispering to me "loser, loser, loser." I empty my glass of J&B in one swallow to try and make the voice go away.

"Yes Anthea, I hear you," I say. I sound resigned and a bit pathetic.

"One more thing Grady," she makes me wait three seconds, wondering what the sting will be. "Happy fourth of July," she says. Then she hangs up.

Shit. Not good. Not good at all.

I strip and head for the shower, wondering when the damn painkillers will kick in. I love showers. It makes me feel I can start everything again from the beginning. Clean, wrapped in a bathrobe so thick and soft it cuddles me, I pour another three fingers of J&B into my glass and I feel better.

I start thinking about tomorrow, Independence Day. I always have a BarBQ at my house. Barbara does the cooking, so the guests survive OK. I get to go round making sure everyone has enough to drink. Barbara's parents moved down to St Pete's in Florida two years back and mine are both dead now, so it's a friends and neighbors deal mostly. No one stays long, but lots of people drop by. I think having the game on the projection TV on the patio helps. I call it Al Fresco's Sports Bar. When I told Kirsten that, she asked who Al was.

It's not that Kirsten is stupid, in fact she's very bright, but she's into numbers and the markets and good health and doesn't have time for a lot else. The first thing she said to me was, "I really admire your portfolio."

It was late on a Friday. Kirsten had been on staff for a week. I'd noticed her. She'd noticed me noticing and hadn't seemed to mind. So, Friday she comes into my office just as I'm going out and hits me with the portfolio line. I don't know what to make of it, but she's young and pretty and standing very close, so I decide to smile and wait.

She steps slightly closer, too close for normal conversation but not close enough to touch. "I've been told you have the biggest one in the office." No doubting the tone there. She looks me up and down, slowly. Then she says "maybe we could stay late one night and you could show it to me?"

"How about Monday?" I say.

"I'll look forward to it," she says. She stepped back and then turned to walk away. I enjoyed watching her walk. When she got to the elevators she looked back over her shoulder. "I hope you and your wife have a great weekend." To me it seemed like she'd just offered a no-strings-attached fuck. I couldn't believe my luck.

That night I took Barbara to bed early and fucked her hard. She was delighted that, for once, I did the asking. That made me feel bad. We don't fuck much and I felt like a shit when I saw how pleased she was. But I was a shit with a hard-on and hell, if I could win points and get off at the same time, why not? Well, because it's the wrong thing to do and I'd feel bad about it later is why not. But with me, now always wins out over later, so I fucked her anyway.

She was a little dry at first, but once we got going, she lubed up just fine. We did it doggie style, my favorite. When I was in the rhythm, slamming into her and making those flesh-slapping noises that are sort of nasty and exciting at the same time, I closed my eyes and imagined Kirsten in her place. I dug my fingers into Barbara's buttocks and wondered how Kirsten's smaller, rounder ass would feel. I came hard deep inside Barbara. It was good. At least for me. I knew Barbara hadn't come yet. I knew I should've done something about that. What I actually did was to pretend to fall asleep. I do that real well. I wish I had really slept, then I wouldn't have had to lie there listening to Barbara trying to cry silently.

Shit, I hate it when I make myself think about stuff like this. It's like part of me just wants to keep rubbing my nose in it and say "bad boy". Well fuck that. We all do stuff we shouldn't. It's part of being human.

I'm glad when room service interrupts my thoughts by

bringing me my meal. They know how to do this here: real linen tablecloths, heavy cutlery, and crystal glasses. For an hour I manage to lose myself in tastes and smells and textures. The wine is full-bodied and mellow. I probably shouldn't have drunk the whole bottle, but I enjoyed every sip.

Food is a passion of mine. I don't cook but I love to eat. Barbara is a great cook. I sometimes think food is the closest we ever came to satisfying each other's desires.

Now I'm back on Barbara again. That keeps happening to me. It won't do me any good. Deep down I know she's right to divorce me. The thing is that my mother-in-law was right, she is too good for me.

I lay back on the bed, wine glass resting comfortably on my belly, and pull out the mental picture album labeled "Barbara and Mark: the early years."

The couple in the album are young and inexperienced. Young Mark has learned how to make the quiet and mysterious Barbara laugh. Her laugh is a wonderful thing. It knows no inhibitions. It fills him with a warmth, close to lust, that he thinks for a while is love. He will do anything, no matter how absurd, to provoke that laugh.

In the early pictures, Barbara is always laughing, one hand in front of her face, as if trying to cover up accidental nakedness.

In the wedding photos, Barbara has a faraway look, as if she cannot quite believe that she has gone through with the wedding. Young Mark looks as though he has just won the lottery.

I know I am going through these memories because I am drunk. For all my practice, I have never learned to be a happy drunk. Alcohol makes me too honest with myself.

I go to the bathroom and splash my face, hoping to drive away the ghosts of my marriage. They refuse to leave. I know what they want. They want a confession. I look in the mirror above the sink and say the words that will lay the ghosts.

"I am a lousy fuck and I'm sorry."

This is what I'd always wanted to say to Barbara and never could.

Barbara, in those early years, was a good lover. She wanted to fuck the way she laughed. She was uninhibited and enthusiastic. And she intimidated the hell out of me.

I'd mainly done one-night stands and orgy fucks before. I'd never had to try and fuck the same woman night after night. It's not that she was a bad lay, the opposite in fact. But when we had sex I had this image of her as a powerful car that I never got out of first gear. She was patient. She got into foreplay. She read me erotica. She dressed up in sexy lingerie. She shared her fantasies. And every single thing she did made me shrivel up a little more.

Eventually, in the third year of our marriage, she stopped all the fancy stuff and settled for my clumsy, short-lived fucks. She even faked orgasms. And, dumb-fuck that I am, I didn't notice. I thought I'd cracked it. I was walking around thinking "first I learned to make her laugh, then I learned to make her come."

The bubble burst when I came home early one afternoon. I heard her as soon as I came through the door. She was moaning. A deep, low, continuous moan that I could not mistake. "So this is what she really sounds like when she comes," I thought. I was angry. Some bastard was fucking my wife in our bed and making her come better than I could. I moved up the stairs quietly, looking forward to my dramatic entrance. The moans were subsiding as I reached the bedroom door. I went in via the bathroom, which has doors to the hall and the bedroom. Barbara was on her belly. Her face was buried in one of my sweatshirts. She was alone. The room smelled of sweat and sex. Her fingers were still trapped beneath her cunt. When I realized what I was seeing, I left at once. I didn't want her to know that I knew she preferred her own fingers to me.

My drinking increased after that, and I started to chase women. I hoped that one of them would prove to me that I was a good fuck after all. None of them have. Oh, most of them enjoy themselves, but they aren't looking for the same thing as Barbara. They fuck me because they like fucking, and I'm safe and generous and no worse than average. Barbara fucked me in the hope that we would fly together. She is the swan who married the penguin because he made her laugh.

OK, so now I'm getting maudlin. Penguin! Jesus wept, where do I get this stuff.

I should get dressed now and go home and wait for Kirsten. But what I want is to talk to Barbara. I want to tell her that I miss her and that I don't deserve her and I want her back. With the certainty of the very drunk, I know this is the right thing to do.

I dial Peter's number. The gods are on my side; Barbara answers.

"B," I say, "it's me. Mark."

"What did you do to Peter?"

"What? Nothing. Listen. I have something to say."

"I saw his hand. Did you hit him?"

"Yeah, real hard. With my chin." I'm laughing and I want to stop but I can't.

"You're drunk aren't you?" She sounds sad, not angry. "Is she there with you, listening?"

"Who?"

"Who? Can't you remember her name now?"

"Oh, Kirsten. No she's coming later. Listen. I wanted to tell you . . ."

"I don't want to hear it, Mark. I'm not listening to you any more. It hurts too much."

"But . . ."

"Tomorrow is Independence Day, Mark. Take it as a sign. From tomorrow we are completely independent."

She is almost crying now. I can hear it at the edge of her voice.

"Please B, I just want . . ."

"Goodbye Mark."

She hangs up.

I feel 100 years old. The phone stays in my hand because I can't think what to do with it. I listen to the drone of the dial tone and it seems to be singing the song of my life.

Anger helps. Anger is good.

I throw the phone away.

"Bitch," I think.

I say it out loud, "Bitch."

Then, "Heartless, man-eating BITCH."

That's better; much better.

The hotel arranges a taxi for me. Soon I will be home.

Maybe Kirsten will want to fuck when she gets in. Or maybe it can wait until I get my eight minutes tomorrow morning.

3. Labor Day

"You OK?"

The concern in Peter's voice makes me smile.

"Yeah, I'm fine. Just taking a moment you know?"

His stillness in the doorway calms me.

I stand, check my hair in the mirror and say, "I'll be out in a minute and I'll be the life and soul of the party, honest. After all, it's a holiday right?"

He says, "You've done the right thing, Barbara," like it's not a non sequitur. Then he leaves.

I hope I've done the right thing. I hope it with all my heart.

There has been so much change in my life, in such a short time, that I feel giddy. I sit back down, composing myself, staring at the woman in the mirror, looking for signs that she has changed.

When I was a child I used to love to play blindman's buff; to be blindfolded and turned round and round and round until all sense of direction was lost and the only way left was forward, into the arms of whomever I could catch. These past months I've been playing that game with my life. Now it's time to take off the blindfold and seize what I have found.

God, I sound like some New-Ager peddling re-birthing seminars. How Mark would laugh at that. I can imagine the "commercial break" voice in which he would say, "Tired of the old you? Give birth to a new and improved one after only five days at our woodland retreat!"

I've always sneered at the idea of such fundamental change. You are who you are. You don't suddenly become someone else. But maybe, sometimes, we settle for not being ALL of who we are. We shut down the parts that don't fit. We grow, but we grow stunted, like plants raised in a too-small pot. At the beginning of the summer it came to me that my life had become pot-bound. So I smashed the pot.

God knows, Mark had already put a few cracks in it, with his

serial seductions of silly girls. But in the end it was me, not
him, who shattered our marriage beyond hope of repair.

When he abandoned me, in the middle of a Memorial Day
BarBQ with our best friends, so that he could go and fuck his
latest Barbie, everything suddenly changed. I didn't get angry.
I got cold and still and then I cracked, like an iceberg snapping
off from a glacier and sliding into the sea. One moment Mark
and I were connected, the next we were separated by an
unbridgeable stretch of despair and disappointment.

I think I might have frozen for ever on that day. Gone into
shock and never come out. But Helen and Peter rescued me,
right there and then. They took me into their hearts and, for a
while, into their bed. I know that sounds bizarre and weird, but
it didn't feel that way. I've known them both for ever and I love
them in my way. Helen, so brave and fierce and full of energy.
Peter, her rock, her keel, always there for her, always calm and
true. Being with them felt like coming home. Like rejoining my
family. Except, of course, I don't fuck my family.

But now it's time to leave. The summer, that started so
badly, is coming to an end. It's Labor Day today. Helen and
Peter are having a little party to wish me well in my new job in
big bad Chicago. All my friends are waiting out there and yet I
can't bring myself to leave this room which has been my refuge
from having to deal with the reality of divorcing Mark and
learning to live on my own.

I know I should despise Mark. Everybody else does. But I
can't. He's weak, not wicked. I know all about being weak. I
was weak for years. In a way, my whole married life was a
result of weakness.

I let Mark marry me because he wanted it so much. He was
the first man in a long time to see past the cloak of invisibility I
had wrapped myself in. The dowdy clothes, the shyness, the
lack of makeup, didn't put him off. He wanted me and he
wanted to please me. That was flattering. He found ways to
make me laugh. That was endearing. And he was always there,
like a faithful hound waiting to be taken for a walk. All I had to
do was look at him for his tail to start to wag. That, in the end,
turned out to be irresistible.

It's not that I didn't love Mark, I did. I still do. But the thought of him never made me wet. When we kissed it was nice rather than good. When we fucked it was urgent rather than potent. I told myself that things would get better; that we would learn how to please each other; that we had plenty of time. But that isn't how it worked out. Things got worse, not better. We never talked about it, but it was always with us; an absence of the passion that should have made our marriage grow.

In the end, that absence became the center of our marriage. We walked around the hole it left in our lives every day, until it became our habit to circumnavigate sex, at least with each other. Mark found solace in sport-fucking shallow, undemanding women. I let my fingers release what I couldn't suppress.

I wonder sometimes if things would have been different if I'd been a virgin when I married Mark? But I wasn't. Not by a long shot. Todd had seen to that.

"You thinking of Mark?" Helen says. "You look upset."

I didn't hear her come in. I knew she would want to see me alone before I left. I have, I realize, been avoiding it. Now she is here, looking at me in the mirror, and I can't read the expression on her face. She can do that sometimes, just switch her face to neutral. It's disturbing because she is normally so expressive. Mark christened her "Helen, the face that launched a thousand quips."

"Actually, I was thinking of Todd," I say.

"Todd the impaler? What brought him to mind?" Helen moves closer to me. Her face has softened a bit. She knows Todd is a difficult subject for me.

"I was wondering if being with him screwed up my marriage."

My voice sounds like I'm on the edge of crying. I didn't expect that. I hate that I cry so easily.

Helen is smaller than me. When she hugs me, I have to bend slightly to put my head on her shoulder. She leads me to the bed and we sit for a moment, next to one another. She holds both my hands within hers and, suddenly, I see her as she was when we were both in our first year in college.

She was my first adult female friend. She told me everything about herself. No embarrassment. No restraints. It was infectious. And one night, when we were sitting on her bed in her room, I started to tell her about Todd. I hadn't told anyone about Todd. She let me talk. For hours. I think that Helen performed an exorcism that night.

When I had finished she said to me, "You are a good person." It felt like a blessing.

If I had been prettier earlier, I would never have gone with Todd. Up to my senior year in high school, I was the invisible girl. The one everyone wrote "I hope you have a great summer" to when they signed my yearbook, trying to remember who the hell I was.

The summer before my senior year I had a growth spurt. I grew three inches, lost some weight, and acquired a waist and hips. Suddenly I had long legs and a good ass. Barbara the boring became Babs the beautiful over night.

My mother was so pleased that she bought me outfit after outfit. "I've been waiting to take you shopping for such a long time," she said. In the store I became the center of attention. My legs were applauded and I was encouraged to buy skirts that would display them. I went back to school feeling wonderful.

It didn't last long. I'd broken one of the prime rules of high school. I'd tried to move out of the slot that my peers had allocated to me. My best friend, Alice, felt slighted by my new look. My studymate, Carl, suddenly became tongue-tied and uncomfortable. But the toughest reaction came from the wannabe-prom-queens. They started to call me Babs the Booty. They said I looked like a slut. But I wouldn't give in. I wouldn't sacrifice the look of pride on my mother's face just to fit in at high school.

So now I looked good but no one talked to me. Then the boys found me. They weren't bad boys. They were polite and nice and muscular and I ached for them. I hadn't dated much so I wasn't really sure what to do. I knew enough not to fuck on the first date. But the second seemed reasonable. And the boys wanted it so badly. And they were so nice to me. And besides, the sex was good. Sometimes very good.

I was Barbara the Queen Bee, surrounded by a group of adoring drone-boys. We went everywhere together. We had fun. And at the end of the evening one of them would take me home and on the way we would park and I would find out one more time just how good it felt to ride a fresh strong cock.

Looking back now, I think I went a little crazy for a while. The thinking me was switched off. I stopped being shy and introverted and tried hard to live in the now. The now where I was beautiful and the boys were eager. I was aware that they didn't love me. I knew I didn't love them. But it felt so damned good.

I'd been Queen Bee for about a month when Todd Rawlins showed up. Todd was two years older than me and had been the star of our football team in his senior year. If it hadn't been for a knee injury, Todd would have made it to college on a sports scholarship. Instead he was working at his daddy's Chrysler dealership.

Every girl in school knew three things about Todd: he drove a brand new LeBaron Convertible, he partied hard and he had the biggest dick in town. One Friday night the drones and I were coming out of the bowling alley and I was teasing them about who would get to drive me home, when Todd pulled up next to us in his killer car. No "hello"s. No "baby you look good"s. He just said, "Get in," and I did.

Once we were away from the boys, Todd was nicer to me. He told me how he'd heard that I'd become hot and said he'd decided he had to take a look for himself. I asked him if he liked what he saw. He told me that he hadn't seen it all yet and that he'd let me know later.

In a way I was still a virgin until Todd fucked me. I mean, I'd had sex, lots of it, but I'd never been possessed by it. Never had it take over my whole mind until I was just a set of nerve endings surfing on wave after wave of orgasm.

That first time, he took me to woods and we parked. He led me out of the car and made me sit on the hood.

"I got something for you baby and you're gonna like it a lot," he said.

I nearly laughed at that, but realized in time that no joke was intended.

Then Todd unzipped and took out his dick. It wasn't fully hard yet but it was already bigger than most of the cocks I'd had inside me. My cunt contracted and my mouth went dry. I wanted to see it stand and I wanted to feel it stretch me. That dick of his brought out desires that I didn't even know I had.

"Told you you'd like it," he said, "they all do."

I wasn't listening. I was spreading my legs and pushing my panties aside and staring at his dick and wondering if it would tear me. There may have been a small voice saying "why are you fucking this dick", but even if I had heard it, my only answer would have been "because it's there! Now shut up bitch and let me fuck."

The first fuck, he just grabbed me by the back of the knees, spread me so wide that it hurt and rammed it home. Nothing had ever made me feel so full. It hurt but it hurt good. He pounded away at me so hard I thought we'd dent the car. I was breathless and stunned. Not ready to orgasm yet; still amazed at how full I felt; almost afraid to move in case I hurt something.

Then he came and I thought "Shit no, not yet!"

I must have said some of that aloud because Todd grinned at me and said, "We ain't done yet baby. You feel anything getting smaller down there? All we've done is get you nice and lubed."

It was true. He'd come, but he was still hard. I pushed against him gratefully, eager to chase my orgasm. But he pulled out.

"Time to say hello properly baby," he said.

I didn't know what he meant.

He stepped back from the car and said "On your knees, baby. Come and show Mr Pecker here your deep appreciation."

I wish I had laughed then. I wish I had told him and Mr Pecker to fuck off. But I didn't. I got on my knees and I took him in my mouth. It was bitter tasting and unpleasant but sort of compelling at the same time. There was just so damned much of it.

I didn't have a lot of experience with giving head. The drones and I had skipped that part and gone straight for the main course. It must have showed.

Todd said "Jesus, girl, mind those teeth," and took Mr Pecker away from me.

I thought it was all over then, but Todd wasn't done. He bent me over his car and took me doggy style. You wouldn't believe how deep he could get like that. And he was slow, now. No hurry at all. It went on and on. He made me come the first time just from the way his cock moved. The second time he got me there by working on my clit while still going with that slow deep stretching in and out movement. My third orgasm was triggered when he spurted inside me.

My legs were shaking when he pulled out. I couldn't move off the hood of his car, even though I could feel his cum running down my thigh. I'd never come three times one after another like that. My mind had gone away completely, a bit like the way you lose your hearing after a gun goes off. I wanted to sleep right there.

Todd guided me back into the car. We drove to my house in silence. I don't think I could have talked even if I'd wanted to. When we reached my house, Todd just waited for me to get out.

I struggled onto the curb and he said, "You have a great cunt baby, but you've really gotta learn to give head. See you tomorrow."

Then he drove off.

I lay on my bed thinking about what had happened. It was shameful. I knew that. Todd was using me and I was letting him. My cunt was sore. My legs ached. My pride wanted to say, "Screw you, Todd Rawlins." I fell asleep still undecided about whether to see him again.

I was late for school the next day. By the time I got there everyone seemed to know I was one of Todd's girls. Not Todd's girl. Just one of them. The drone-boys all found reasons not to be available that night. My ex-best friend told me I should be ashamed of myself.

After school, Todd was there with his shiny car and his big smile. We did it all again. The only difference was that I nearly threw up on him when he tried to push Mr Pecker down my throat.

At the time it seemed to me I was out of options. I couldn't go back and I didn't know how to go forward so I just let Todd go on fucking me. It lasted a whole month.

My cunt was sore by then. My mind was working loose from the corner I'd tied her up in and was shouting "stop this nonsense right now young lady." I gagged her because I didn't want to hear it.

It ended when Todd called me and asked me to come over to his house. He said his parents were away and he wanted to show me something special.

I went because I couldn't figure out how to say no.

When I got there the door was open so I went into the family room. Todd was on the big sofa watching a porno movie. Amy Shanks, universally known at school as Amy Skanks, was on her knees sucking his dick. I must have just stood there looking stunned.

Todd said "Hi baby. This is what I wanted to show you." Then he turned to Amy and said "Do it baby."

Amy looked at me. She held eye-contact while she lowered her mouth on to Todd's dick. She swallowed it. All of it. It made her throat bulge but she swallowed it all. Todd placed his hand on the back of her head and started to move her up and down on his dick.

"Amazing isn't it?" Todd said. "And Amy here is gonna show you how it's done. Come on over baby and get a better look."

My mind finally broke free of her bonds and all I heard was her shouting "Run, Barbara and don't stop until you're home in bed."

I don't remember getting home. I don't remember anything until I woke up the next day. Then it all hit me. I was a slut. I had been a slut for months. Everybody but me knew that. And my grades. My grades had seemed so unimportant while I was slutting around but now I knew that they were dropping enough to put college at risk. I stayed in bed all day. And the next day.

Finally I told my Mom that there was a problem at school but I didn't want to talk about it. I think maybe some of the neighbors had already been talking about it, because Mom quickly sorted things out without any questions. She arranged private tuition to rescue my grades. I worked hard. I made it to college.

But I still had a secret. The secret was that I had wanted to be fucked like that. I'd enjoyed it. I wanted more of it.

My mind was firmly back in control now and she tried hard to banish Miss Libido. She made me dress in baggy clothes and to stop even talking to boys. I became invisible again. But at night, before I fell asleep, my fingers would find my cunt and I would think of Todd and wonder if I would ever find anyone who could make me come like that ever again.

Helen is waiting for me to tell her what's on my mind.

I manage a smile.

"Remember when we talked about Todd that night? You were wonderful. And then you introduced me to Mark," I say.

"Yeah, sorry about that," Helen says, "he seemed like a nice guy at the time."

"He was a nice guy at the time."

We are both smiling now and I can finally say to Helen the thing that needs to be said.

"Helen, about Peter . . ."

Helen's smile goes. I feel her stiffen.

"I'm so sorry," I say.

"It's over now," Helen says. She removes her hands from mine but manages a smile that almost reaches her eyes. "No harm done," she says, moving toward the door. "Now stop moping and come and join the party."

No harm done. I hope that's true.

The day Mark left me, the day when I could have shriveled up and nursed my sense of worthlessness, Helen rescued me. She knew that I was attracted to Peter. She'd told me that he was a little in love with me. We'd laughed about that. Imagine quiet Peter harboring a passion for Barbara. That was back when Helen and I would trade stories about our husbands. When I still felt married. Before the lack of passion in my life made me feel dried up and useless and unlovable.

By the time I reached that Memorial Day BarBQ it was painful for me to watch Helen and Peter together. I was like a starving beggar pressing my face against the window of a restaurant, tormented by the sight of food but unable to look away.

When Mark left the BarBQ with some insultingly see-through excuse, I headed back to the cabin to cry and to feel sorry for myself.

Helen stopped me. She spoke softly. What she said surprised me. "We love you Barbara. You deserve better. Let us care for you. Let me share Peter with you. Be with us for a while."

I could tell that she was sincere and that what she was saying wasn't springing spontaneously into her head. I knew what "share Peter" meant. Something in the way that Helen said it left no doubt.

Above all else, this felt like an act of friendship. I accepted it, my numb distress starting to be replaced by a sense of dislocation from reality.

The sex was fun.

Helen likes to tie Peter. I'd known that for a long time. Mark was always going on about how odd that was and how Helen "had Peter's pecker in her pocket." I couldn't quite imagine it.

That night, Helen tied and blindfolded Peter and then we both . . . played with him. My memory of it is so clear. Time slowed down. I tried not to look at Helen. I was at such a high level of awareness that reality was too vivid to be anything but a dream. Peter surrendered himself to us. We took him in turns, never speaking, always preserving the convention that it COULD have been just the two of them in the room. But we all knew. And we all wanted it.

My orgasm was like a return to sanity. It sounds an extravagant claim, but it healed me. I felt, for the first time in a very long time, happy.

I moved in with Helen and Peter after that. I had my own room. There was no more sharing. But there was love and support and a space to learn to be me again.

Things might have been fine if the walls had been thicker, or if Helen had been less noisy when she came, or if Peter had not been just a little in love with me. I lay there at night and listened to them having sex. I could tell they were trying to be quiet, but there would always be that last moment in which Helen lost control. I would close my eyes and try to remember Peter being inside me. I would try to come when Helen came.

After a while we all started to become less comfortable with each other in the mornings. We took care to dress before coming down for breakfast. I tried not to watch Peter's every move. I tried not to yearn for him. I failed.

Later Peter told me that he couldn't get me out of his head. He said the blindfold had meant that he was never sure when it was me and when it was Helen he was with. He felt like he should have been able to tell. He felt like he wanted to experience the difference.

One evening, Helen went to fix us some drinks. While she was out of the room Peter and I accidentally looked into each other's eyes. We'd each being trying to sneak a quick look at the other. We were still looking at each other when Helen came back. We broke contact guiltily. Helen just stood there. No one spoke.

I wanted to leave or to apologize. I felt as if she had walked in on us fucking.

Helen handed us both a drink. Then she said "It's OK. Really. I'll sleep in the other room tonight."

Peter started to rise from his chair to protest. Helen stopped him with a glance that I couldn't read but which brought him to a complete halt. Then she was gone. She took my room.

I was standing too now, staring at the closed door between Helen and us.

Peter and I turned toward each other. I was uncertain. I wanted Peter. Really wanted him. He was so close and so alive that I thought sparks might jump the small gap between us.

I reached up and stroked the side of his face. He was very still. I kissed him.

It was as I had imagined it. Soft lips. Warm. Accepting. Except that it felt wrong. It felt like betrayal.

Peter didn't kiss me back but he didn't resist. I know that if I had continued he would have let me. To please me. To please Helen. But I stopped.

Still we didn't speak. I took Peter by the hand and led him, quietly, into my room. Helen was curled up in a ball facing the wall. She didn't hear us come in. I said her name. She turned and looked at both of us. There were tears in her eyes. I held Peter's hand out to her. She jumped up off the bed and hugged him. When I left, they were kissing fiercely, as if they were sucking in oxygen after almost drowning. I went for a drive.

They were in their room when I came back and everything was quiet.

The next morning I declared my intent to look for a job. Here I am, five weeks later, ready to move to one.

"B. Are you in there B? Come out, come out wherever you are." It is Mark's voice calling from the garden. He sounds drunk. I rush out. The last time he and Peter met there was trouble. I expect to see Peter dragging Mark away, but it is Helen, little Helen, who is blocking Mark's path.

"B. Please B."

I put my hand on Helen's shoulder and she lets me step in front of her. She continues to glare at Mark.

"B. I'm drunk. I'm sorry I'm drunk but I've got something important to say to you."

Mark looks ill. His clothes are dirty and his complexion is pale. I wonder how long he has been drunk this time.

He staggers toward me, reaching for me. I stay still and he stops short.

"I know you're going away. The lawyer told me. I want to tell you . . . to say . . . to let you know that I love you B. I've always loved you."

He was crying now. He looked lost. I assumed his nympho intern had left him. He looks like he wants me to take him in my arms as I have so many times before.

Everybody at the party is looking at us. I step forward so that I can speak directly into Mark's ear. His arms fold about me as I say, "I know you love me, Mark. I love you. But it will never be enough will it?"

His face turns toward me. He seems suddenly sober. I wait for the tantrum or the insult. Instead, he says quietly, "Good luck in your new job, B." and walks, a little too precisely, toward his car. Helen sends Peter after him to drive him home.

The party doesn't last long. Mark has taken the edge off it. By the time Peter gets back people are already leaving. It's getting dark earlier already. Summer is over and Fall, "Season of mists and mellow fruitfulness" is here.

The last of the guests leaves just before sunset. I stand and watch the slow ignition of the sky. Peter and Helen come and stand on either side of me. I take their hands.

I don't know who Barbara will become in Chicago. I hope Barbara the Bold, ready to make her own future. But right here and right now, she feels like Barbara the Blessed.

4. Hallowe'en

"You can't do this to me, Anthea."

Mark is more pathetic than fierce. The smell of alcohol preceded him into my office. He looks slightly jaundiced. His cheeks and chin sport small islands of stubble that managed to evade his razor this morning. I'm surprised he can keep his hand steady enough to shave.

"I'm not doing it to you, Mark," I say. "You're doing it to yourself. You've lost it. Look at yourself. How long can you last between drinks now, Mark? An hour? Two if you really try? I'm giving you a simple choice: either dry out or ship out."

For a moment I think he's going to tell me to fuck off. I almost wish he would.

When we first met, before his long-suffering wife finally left him, he was a maverick. He always had a comeback ready. I liked him. He reminded me of Davey, my younger brother. Or at least how Davey would have been if he hadn't wrapped himself around a tree riding that motorcycle of his.

I've never found it easy to talk to men. Somehow it always turned into a conflict: the strong ones saw me as a challenge, someone to put down either by bedding or ridiculing; the weak ones were afraid of me and their fear made me despise them and despise myself for feeling that way. I built a shell around myself. I out-manned them; being tougher than the strong and ruthlessly removing the weak.

I thought Mark was the exception, that for once I could drop the macho crap and make a friend. I liked the way he smiled and he was easy to talk to. Then, one evening, when we were working late, Mark pushed his fingers between my legs. I wanted to kill him. I felt betrayed. Stupid really, he wasn't to know that he reminded me of my dead brother.

Mark works for me now. I should probably have fired him, but I always hoped that he'd pull himself together and be the guy I wanted him to be. Now he's sitting on the other side of

my desk with nothing to say. Oh shit. He's crying. Not big
sobs. More like his eyes are leaking.

Part of me wants to hug him and help him, but most of me
just wants to slap him. How could he fuck up his life like this?

Of course I can't do either of these things. I'm the boss,
Anthea the Hun they call me: strong, logical, unemotional.

I look at my watch. Mark is my last chore before I head
home. It's Hallowe'en tonight and I have things to prepare. I
let my eyes rest on the picture of Drazen and his daughter that
I keep on my desk. The picture is supposed to remind me of
home, give me a smile in the middle of the day; increasingly it
just reminds me that I spend too many hours at work and most
of them are wasted on cleaning up the messes other people
make. Time to clear up my last mess of the day.

"I'm going to leave these details with you, Mark. If you want
to keep your job then I will get a phone call from the clinic on
Monday saying that you've checked in. If you want to continue
to drown yourself in booze, then just clear your desk and don't
come back. This is your last chance Mark. Choose wisely."

Why do I always sound so pompous when I'm doing something unpleasant?

Even though it's my office, I get up to leave. I want to be
home. I want to be somewhere where I don't have to be in
charge and where I can let people love me. Mark starts to cry
quietly as I leave. I pretend not to hear him and keep moving.

The express elevator, a perk of my executive status, is softly
lit and lined with mirrors, presumably so that executives can
maintain a positive image. I stand in the center of the elevator
and stare at the infinite number of Antheas that head off in
each direction. I don't recognize them. I don't want these
uptight, asexual women to be me.

Perhaps it is the shock of seeing the wreck Mark has become,
or perhaps it is the news I want to give to Drazen tonight, but I
feel a strong need to change the images in the mirror. I reach
up and release my hair, letting it fall around my shoulders. My
hair is thick and soft, I love the feel of it against my face, the
taste of it in my mouth. My hair is my freedom, my sexuality.
Which is why I bind it so tightly at work, but why I refuse to
have it cut.

I bend forward at the waist, letting my hair fall forward over my head. It is almost long enough to touch the floor. Then I flick myself upright, casting my hair behind me like a mane. The images in the mirror, with their legs apart, shoulders back, hair shining in the massaged light, seem more recognizable now. I wave to myself just as the deferential tone sounds to let me know that I have reached the ground.

I opt for a limo rather than taking the train. I tell myself that it's because I'm late and I need to hurry home, but I know that what I want is the privacy.

In the car, I settle back against the leather seat and slip off my shoes. I will be home in less than an hour, but I need Drazen right now. The wireless earpiece of my cellphone (Anthea the Hun always has all the latest boy toys) is hidden beneath my hair. I say, "Drazen" and the speed dial starts.

"Anthea." A statement, not a question. Drazen's voice, soft and calm, slides into my ear and makes me shiver. In his mouth my name is "Ann-Tea-Ah" and immediately "the Hun" is left behind. I remain silent, waiting.

"So . . ." he says, "you can be overheard, but you want to play. Soon, I hope, you will be home, but then there will be other things before . . . I understand."

I can hear him walking through the house. He will go to his studio. Soundproofed and secure. I recognize the noise the door lock makes as it snaps shut.

When he speaks again he is more relaxed. His voice is still soft but it has an energy to it suggesting the confident strength and controlled arousal of a predator stalking his prey.

"You are in a car. No, it is quiet enough to be a limo. I can hear your breathing, Anthea. Press your shoulders back against the leather seat. Keep your thighs together. Tight together. Squeeze. Close your eyes and remember how it feels when your thighs close against my beard, when my tongue dips into you. Remember the smell of your arousal, the soft drizzle of your juices onto my chin. Remember how hard it is for you to stay still, how much you want to move, to grind, to rock, to press, to drive yourself down upon my tongue until it impales you. Remember all of that but keep a calm expression on your face."

I look forward at the rearview mirror. The driver's eyes are on the road, but if he looks up he will see me.

It feels as though Drazen is behind me, breathing into my ear, as if it is him I am pressing into. I want to open my legs, just a little, slide a finger along my thigh, draw small circles on my mound.

"No touching, Anthea. Keep your legs closed and your mind open."

I smile. I know he will be imagining me smiling.

"Stretch your legs. Feel the muscles at the back of your thighs tense. Keep them tense. Can you smell yourself yet? Do you think your driver can smell you? Not yet perhaps, but soon."

My face flushes at the thought. I check the rearview again. The driver looks up, then looks away.

"You will feign sleep, Anthea. Let your beautiful head rest against the leather. Hold some of your hair across your mouth. Keep it in place. Remember how my thumb feels, pressing against your lower lip, my fingers resting on your cheek, how good it feels to dip your head forward and feel the thumb press into the roof of your mouth."

I bite down on my hair as the first little contraction hits. Memory flares. The first time that he fucked me in a public place it started like that, a small dip of my head on his thumb, my face scarlet with embarrassment, my sex damp with need. It ended with me bent over the back of a park bench, Drazen behind me, pushing slowly and calmly into my ass, as if anal sex was a normal pursuit on a Sunday morning stroll in the park.

"Good girl, Anthea. Good girl."

His voice is stroking me. Soothing me. I hear him unzip his fly and a small moan escapes from me.

"Shh, Anthea is sleeping. She cannot see how hard I am at the thought of her, cannot smell the musk of that arousal."

I love the smell of him. The taste of him. The fascination of playing with his foreskin. The strong scent that rises when I roll back that soft skin.

"In her sleep Anthea will reach beneath her respectable executive jacket, open one button of her pressed and spotless white blouse, push aside the cup of the plain white cotton bra and let her breast rest in the palm of her hand."

Slowly, shifting to one side as if in sleep, I let my hand slide onto my breast.

My nipples are so sensitive that I can hardly bare to have them touched. Before Drazen, my lovers had always been too rough: pinching and biting when they should have been caressing. I had begun to think that I was a freak with hair-trigger nipples that would be constantly off limits.

Drazen, with his pianist's hands, showed me how wrong I was. He would stand behind me, his mouth on my neck, my breasts cupped gently in his hands, just the underside of them resting against his skin, lifted slightly but with no pressure. Then his thumbs, light as butterflies, would graze the tip of the nipples, coaxing them, letting them rise, working them until they throbbed, finally pushing them back firmly into my breasts and biting down on my neck until I was wriggling with pleasure.

"Anthea is dreaming. In her dream my cock slides, slick and stiff, out of her mouth. She guides it to her breasts. Uses it to draw a wet circle around her nipple. Laughs when I flinch with the extremity of the sensation. Rubs the underside of the gland over the stubby arousal of her nipple, then squeezes the head of my cock until the slit opens. She looks up at me, her eyes on mine as she pushes her nipple into the slit, fucking me and fucking me and fucking me."

Drazen's voice has a ragged edge now. He will be touching himself. His eyes will be closed as he remembers how I took him that night. The first time I really took the initiative.

"Stroke the nipple, Anthea. Slow strokes. Persistent strokes. Suck on the hair in your mouth. Squeeze your thighs. Sweat for me inside your executive suit in your oversized limo. Come for me. Come hard. Come silently. Come for me, Anthea."

And I do. Not at once. Not on command. It takes maybe a minute of silent struggle. I can hear him breathing hard into my ear, listening to me, sniffing at me through the phone line. The come is a sunburst of warmth spreading up from my stomach, exorcising the tension of the day.

"Good girl, Anthea. Very good girl. Now come home to me."

The line goes dead in my ear.

I open my eyes and sit up straight. The driver's eyes flick away a little too quickly when I look into the rearview. I realize that I am smiling. "Ann-Tea-Ah" smiles a lot.

I open the window, even though the day is cold. I don't want my smell to stay in the car.

I am nearly home now. We've left the freeway behind and are driving slowly through tree-lined streets. I can see jack o' lanterns on porches. They are all grinning at me. I grin back.

Drazen was my New Year's resolution. It was part of project APT GAL (Anthea's Plan To Get A Life) that I dreamed up when I found myself alone in my house on New Year's Eve. If I'd been sober when I put the plan together, I'm fairly sure that step one would not have read "Take piano lessons". Nothing might have come of it except for the card I saw the next day on the notice board at the convenience store. It read "Drazen Bebic: Piano Teacher".

For some reason, "Piano Teacher" had summoned up an image of a kindly old man wearing spectacles and an old brown cardigan and speaking with a Professor Von Duck accent. Drazen was nothing like that. First there was his hair: thick, jet black, and brushed straight back so that it seemed to cascade to his shoulders. Then there was his beard, short, precise, somehow emphasizing the sensual softness of his lips. But most of all there were his eyes, dark but filled with light, and hard to look away from.

He was at least fifteen years older than me and I'd only just laid eyes on him but, by the time he stepped forward and shook my hand, my palm was already damp. When he touched me, my nipples hardened. No one had ever had that effect on me before. Then he said my name, "Ann-Tea-Ah" and I understood what gives cats the urge to purr.

He sat me down in front of the huge piano that dominated his tiny apartment. I felt like Jane Eyre, asked to play for Mr Rochester, and knowing that every note would diminish her in his eyes. Yet I'd been good at the piano once, back before work spread itself across my life like a gorse bush, leaving room for nothing else, so when, standing so close behind me that I could smell his cologne, he said, "I would like to hear you, Anthea." I started to play.

He listened and watched. There was nothing flirtatious, but I had his complete attention. I played quite well once I got started. Enough to demonstrate some technique at least. He didn't tell me to stop, so I played every piece I knew. When I finished I wondered why I'd ever given up playing. I was good and this was fun.

"I would like to know what it is that you want, Anthea." Drazen said.

I had turned to face him, waiting for praise or at least coaching, wanting to look into his eyes again. His question surprised me.

"I want to play the piano."

"Ah, I had hoped that perhaps you wanted me to teach you."

"?"

"You already play the piano. But you play with these . . ."

He reached out and picked up my hand, holding it gently by the tips of the fingers. My skin prickled where it touched him.

"When you could be playing with this."

He held me by the wrist and placed the palm of my hand against my chest, between my breasts. The contact wasn't overtly sexual but I felt naked in front of him. The surprising thing was that my body was clearly happy about that. My mind was offended.

I shook his hand off my wrist and stood up.

"I'm leaving now", I said.

Drazen bowed his head. I'd never seen anyone do that in real life before. His eyes stayed on me during the bow. I couldn't read them but I didn't want to look away from them. I had to remind myself that he had been rude to me and that I wasn't going to stand for it.

"Are you always so . . ." I realized that rude was the wrong word. He'd been polite but, ". . . personal with your students?"

"What is life if it is not personal, Anthea?"

That was pretty much the question I'd been asking myself on New Year's Eve.

"I'm going now."

He stepped back and to one side so that I had a clear route to the door.

I didn't leave. It was Anthea the Hun who wanted to leave. The rest of me wanted to stay. I sat down.

"I'm sorry," I said. "You caught me by surprise. I'd like to stay."

He didn't look surprised, but he did smile.

"Then I'm glad that I 'caught' you at all", he said.

And he had caught me. We became lovers within the week. But even in bed he was my teacher. He taught me to listen to the now, to surrender to the needs of my body in order to feed my soul. Another man talking like that would sound ridiculous, Drazen just sounds truthful.

Months afterwards, lying in his arms after sex, I asked him about the day we met. I wanted to know what he thought of me then.

He lifted my chin off his chest to make me look at him and said, "I thought then, what I think now. That I want you. That, if you will let me, I will take you. That sometimes life is worth living." I knew then that he loved me.

"We're here, ma'am", the driver says.

There are no lascivious looks, no innuendo. I smile at him and tip him more generously than usual.

Anja is waiting for me when I get home. She has the same grave face as her father, one that is transformed when she smiles.

Anja is doing her best to find a place for herself in America, but she has a solemnity about her that is not normal for an eleven-year-old American girl, but she is strong, a survivor. She has survived the war in Bosnia, the death of her mother, her exile in America. Seeing her standing there on the porch, her face lit by the huge jack o' lantern that I helped her carve last night, I want to rid her of her ghosts. I want to see her filled with joy.

"Hello, Morticia," she says, holding out her hand in a formal invitation "come and meet Gomez."

Tonight we are, at Anja's insistence, the Addams Family. She will, of course, be Wednesday.

Drazen is already in the double-breasted pinstriped suit that is his concession to costume. I wonder if he was wearing it when I called.

"Gomez, mon cher, mon amour," I say in a voice I hope is like Anjelica Huston's.

"Ah Trish, you spoke French," he says on cue, taking my outstretched arm and kissing his way from the back of my hand up my arm to my neck. I glance sideways at Anja/Wednesday, wondering if she approves, fearing that moments like this summon the spirit of her mother. The edges of her mouth are slightly upturned. I take that as a warm approbation.

When Drazen's head is at my neck I twist sideways, plant a quick kiss on his cheek and say, "Thank you, that was delicious." Then I send him away so that Anja and I can change.

Anja has prepared everything, the clothes are laid out on the bed, the wigs are on the dressing table. It is all I can do to slip away and shower before she sets about her work.

There is an intimacy in dressing each other that is like nothing else. It is a recognition of trust and an offer to reveal and to transform. The costumes emphasize this. I never wear black at home, yet now I am wrapped in it like a shroud.

"How do I look?" I ask as the wig goes on.

"Believable," Anja says.

Not quite the comment I expected. I wonder how I normally look to her. There is a short silence during which I grow nervous in front of this child.

Then she hands me the makeup bag and says, "Make me look sad, but scary."

It doesn't take long.

"Gomez" declines to walk the streets with us. Waving a thick cigar, which I know he will not smoke, he says, "My dears, the two of you are frightful enough, three of us could prove fatal."

By the standards of the day our costumes are sedate, yet at every door Anja makes a killing. She never once steps out of character, extorting treats because, from her, the threat of tricks seems so real.

I let her walk ahead of me, keeping to the shadows, arms folded across my breasts whenever we reach a house. Watching

Anja, I see her father, his stillness, his confidence. I wonder which of her gestures belong to her mother, Sanja.

I realize that I am jealous of Sanja for having Drazen before me. Crazy to be jealous of a dead woman, and yet tonight I feel as though, at any moment, I might meet her.

When Anja's sack is full we return home. She is so serious that I am uncertain whether she has enjoyed herself or whether this has all been a bizarre experiment in which she has tested the sanity of those around her and found them wanting. Yet when she sees Drazen on the porch, she runs to him.

"DaDa" she says, holding up her sack, "look how much they gave me."

"You must have made them tremble, little one."

"No, it was Anthea, standing in the shadows like a threat. She was perfect."

Drazen looks over Anja's head at me and smiles. I feel as though I have won a medal. I wait for Anja to turn and thank me, but she grabs her sack and runs into the house.

"Happiness still catches her by surprise," Drazen says. "She wants to go and hug it to herself in private."

He takes my hand in his, rubs his thumb against my palm and says, "You understand that I'm sure."

I almost tell him then, but I don't want to do it in my costume so I wait. Dinner comes and goes without me finding the right moment. Anja gets permission to sleep in her Wednesday outfit because, as she explained very seriously, "it is still Hallowe'en until morning," and then Drazen and I are alone.

I go into the bedroom to change out of my Morticia costume. Drazen follows me. Leaning against the door frame, he looks at me, waiting for something.

I want to tell him. But not yet. "I need to think some more", I tell myself. "Coward", I reply.

"Come to bed," Drazen says.

"I have to do some work first, I'll be back later."

I can see he doesn't believe me, but he makes no comment when I go back downstairs.

I sit at my laptop, pretending to work, trying to find my courage. I make some coffee and go out onto the back porch.

The moon is full tonight. It sits in the sky, large and round and proud. It occurs to me that the moon and I are both pregnant, except that I don't show yet.

This is what I need to tell Drazen. So what's stopping me? We aren't married. We've never really talked about the future. A man with a past like Drazen's can be forgiven for living in the present. I don't want to drive him away and I don't want to force him to commit. And I don't know how I feel about being pregnant.

I know exactly when this baby was conceived. It was on the anniversary of Sanja's death. Drazen had never talked to me about how his wife died, but then I'd never found him crying before. I held him and let him cry.

"They hurt her, Anthea, before they killed her; they spent a day hurting her. And I couldn't stop them. I didn't even know what was happening until they dumped her body at my door."

I rocked him, holding his head to my breast.

"She was my life, Anthea. And they killed her."

There was nothing to say, so I stayed silent.

After a while he looked up. His eyes had no strength in them, only sorrow. I kissed them one at a time. Then I kissed his mouth, again and again, small healing kisses.

I put his hand between my legs. I don't know why I did it. Words seemed so inadequate. I gave him what I had. The sex started slowly. I sat astride him and pulled him into me. Then I carried on kissing him. He stopped crying. He held me so tightly that it left bruises. Then he started to fuck me, fiercely, passionately, as if fucking me was the only thing that kept him alive. He clung to me even after he had come. I still hadn't spoken to him, but now it was me who was crying.

I think he was saying good-bye to his wife that night. I know he was choosing me, choosing life. It turns out that we were also creating one.

I shiver in the cold and realize I have been outside a long time. Drazen is asleep when I reach the bedroom. The moon is washing his face with silver. He looks older, more vulnerable. I want him so badly it frightens me.

Time to choose: trick or treat?

I stroke his face, following the moon, then I sit astride him.

He doesn't wake until I kiss him. I place his hands on my breasts and rock gently on his cock, which is lying flat against his belly. I lift my hips and he slides into me. So good to have him there. So good to have him.

"There is something I need to tell you," I say.

Drazen puts his finger across my lips, pulls my head down to him. He pushes upwards, slowly, without urgency, until he is all the way in.

"What shall we call the child?" he says.

5. Thanksgiving

"You want me to sleep here?"

"Well, this is where you slept when you lived here, Helen. Why should it change now? I thought you'd be pleased to have your old room back."

I try to read my mother's face. She must be doing this deliberately. And she must know that I can see what she is doing. But she still has that innocent, not-quite-connected-to-planet-earth look that she uses to avoid any minor questions about her decisions that my father might be rash enough to voice.

I stare in disbelief at the single bed that I slept in as a child. It's a very narrow single bed.

"I know that you prefer to ignore the fact that Peter and I are married, mother, but he is my husband and I expect to have him in my bed. We can't sleep here."

"Really, Helen, I have no idea where you get these impressions from. I have no opinion about Peter. As I said at the time, who you chose to marry was up to you."

What she'd said at the time was "Are you sure you want to marry Paul, dear? He's such a bland man. I can see the advantage of having someone manageable, but marriage needs a little spice if it's to last. I've always preferred to wake up to Huevos Rancheros, the problem with Paul is that he's just so . . . oatmeal."

I'd stood there, with my hands balled into fists and my jaw clenched, trying to quell the desire to hit her.

"His name is Peter, mother," I'd spat out.

"You see, dear, not even his name is memorable. Ah well. It is your decision of course."

Now, seven years later, I find myself having to bite back my anger one more time. My mother is talking. I'm trying not to strangle her.

"I didn't think that you and Peter would mind being separated for one night. I've given him the fold-down bed in your father's den. He'll be perfectly comfortable. I had to give the guest bedroom to Troy and Dianna; after all, they have the baby to think of."

The baby. Of course we should be thinking about the baby. My younger brother (what kind of mother calls her kids Helen and Troy?) produced a grandchild right off the bat. I of course committed the sin of putting my career ahead of my duty to deliver grandchildren, although even that became Peter's fault in my mother's mind. "If Peter has a problem, dear, I can recommend an excellent clinic." My mother had left that helpful tip on our answerphone in the second year of my marriage. Peter played it back to me when I got home from work.

I don't resent the fact that Troy and Dianna got the big bed. I resent the implication that Peter is so bland that I won't even notice his absence.

"I want him here with me, mother."

Even I can hear how petulant I sound.

"Well, if it's that important to you, dear, I'll ask your father to move the fold-down bed in here. I'm sure he won't mind. Although of course he has only just set everything up in the den. But then your father always makes sure that his little Helen gets what she wants, doesn't he?"

I don't believe it. She is still jealous of the fact that Dad will do things for me.

"There won't be a lot of room in here. You'll have to fold up the bed before you can open the door. But, if that's what you want . . ."

Oh God. It is always like this. A constant trickle of words that erode my will. I either have to get angry or to shut down and give in. Giving in is easier. If I push her now, the topic will come up at dinner. And again in the morning. And the next time we come to the house. If there is a next time.

"Never mind, mother. Peter can stay where he is. Let's just concentrate on getting dinner ready."

"Well, if you're sure, dear."

How did this woman live so long?

"You look tense, Helen. Why don't you take a moment to freshen up? Dianna is changing the baby in the bathroom but you can use the suite in the master bedroom. I'll be in the kitchen when you're ready."

And then she is gone. The relief is physical, like when your ears pop at altitude.

I don't really need to freshen up, but it gives me a reason to delay going downstairs. Nothing has changed in my parents' bedroom. The huge wrought-iron bed with the chintz canopy over it is still there. I used that bed the first time that I fucked Peter. I used it because I liked the headboard, because I wanted revenge on my mother for all the times I'd had to listen to her thrashing in this bed in the middle of the night, and because I wanted to see if good, nice, sensible Peter Brader would do what I wanted him to do.

I sit on the stool by the dressing table and summon up the memory of a nineteen-year-old Peter, lying on this bed with his wrists tied to the headboard; so calm and trusting that, except for the impressive erection he was saluting me with, he might almost have been ready to sleep.

Other boys I'd known had only pretended to submit. They'd made comments as I tied them to establish that it was all a game, and as soon as they'd come they'd started to fret at their bonds, demanding to be let free. Peter didn't do any of that. He just waited for me to use him. But his serenity wasn't passive. Somehow it managed to amplify everything I did. The harder I fucked him, the harder I wanted to fuck him. His cock was my lightning rod, calling me forth, daring me to spend myself on him, taking everything that I could give and leaving me discharged and sated.

Afterwards I'd left him tied to the bed while I sat and brushed my hair. A beam of sunlight was shining down on him, highlighting the sweat on his muscles and the small scratches and bites I visited on him. He looked happy, even grateful. I'd shown him my wildest side. I'd sworn and fucked and bitten and scratched and shouted my come with my head thrown back and he hadn't pulled away, he hadn't been threatened. He was waiting for more. He was waiting for me. For the first time in my adult life I felt as if I'd found a home.

Peter wasn't my first fuck, but he was my first lover. Actually, he is my only lover. To me that is a statement of how rich my life is rather than how narrow my experience has been.

"Helen dear, if you've finished up there, you can help your father lay the table."

The sound of my mother's voice makes me feel guilty and furtive and childish. I get off the stool quickly. Why does coming home always turn me back into a little girl? And why do I hate that so much?

There are six of us at dinner, but there is food for at least a dozen. The conversation is stilted at first. Troy and Peter have the mandatory road-number-filled review of the drive to my parents' house, even though I actually did the driving. I ask Dianna about the baby, revealing my ignorance of modern childrearing with each question that I ask. Mother fusses over Dad, ensuring that he gets the best slices of meat, touching his hand when she passes him things, keeping his glass full. She always makes sure that he knows he is the center of her attention. Dad catches me watching them and gives me an unapologetic grin. This is how the world is, that grin says, and it's too late now to change it.

As the wine flows, words become easier for everybody but me. I feel as though an invisible barrier has settled between me and everyone else. I watch, but I don't speak. Peter fits in so well. He is a good listener. People relax when they talk with him. When they talk with me it is as if they are always just a little on their guard. Dianna is talking to him now. Peter isn't talking to her about the baby. Somehow he has learnt that she paints, and within a few moments the woman I could barely exchange a word with is sharing her passion for abstract art. As the courses go by, I drink and eat more than I should. I want to speak to Troy. I want to sit and exchange deep truths with him, except that those truths remain just out of reach of my words so

I remain silent. By the time we reach dessert I am quite drunk. It seems to me that Peter has abandoned me. Everyone has abandoned me.

"I think you might want to have a little lie down, dear."

My mother is leading me back to my little, virgin bed. I'd protest, except that I can't find the words. And I'm tired. Very, very tired.

I wake with a fierce thirst and a vicious headache. It's dark. I've slept through the afternoon. I groan in self-pity. I've made such a fool of myself. I know that mother will be secretly pleased.

I want Peter. Except Peter isn't here; my mother saw to that. Sitting up is not pleasant, so I lie down again.

The room hasn't changed since I left it seven years ago. I've changed so much since then that it seems incongruous for me to be occupying the same space that I did then. Peter is responsible for most of those changes. Living up to how he sees me, using the quiet space he provides for me to seek refuge in, has changed who I am.

Who would I have been without Peter?

Back before Peter, I'd never really been that comfortable with boys. It wasn't that I was shy; it was more that I saw them too clearly and I didn't like what I saw. For them, girls were trophies to show off to other boys. I used to imagine them at swap meets, talking to each other about girls like they were baseball cards: "Had her. Had her. Had her. Want her. I'll swap you two Heathers for an Alicia." But the worst thing was that, when it came to sex, they all seemed to want to be in charge although very few of them seemed to know what to do.

I knew enough about my own body to know what I wanted: where and how I wanted to be touched and for how long. I also knew the kind of body I wanted to do the touching: tall, lean, strong. Unfortunately, most of those bodies seemed to come with the supersized ego option as standard.

I tried a few anyway. It wasn't hard to get their attention; I was attractive enough in a petite, androgynous sort of way, the challenge was to stay in control. The first couple of attempts were an education.

"Tall 'n' Lean #1" put his hands everywhere but he didn't

know what to do with them. And he got irritated when I moved around. I was supposed to be his bendyfucktoy, something he could pose for his convenience. His dick was nice: smooth and hard; but he wasn't interested in me touching it for long, he wanted to "slide it home". I moved to climb up on his lap but he wanted me on my back. He wasn't in me for long before he came. Then he asked me if I wanted to go get a burger. I realized I'd just had the sexual equivalent of a drive-thru meal: smells good, is over too quickly, and lies like a lump in your stomach afterwards.

"Tall 'n' Lean #2" wasn't interested in entering anything other than my mouth. He wanted me on my knees, looking up into his eyes. I had no objection to the idea in principle. It was corny but it had a sense of theater to it. What turned me off was him placing his hand on the back of my head and using my mouth like an extension of his hand. I've seen drains unblocked with more finesse. I had to grab his balls to make him stop. I thought he'd be angry with me, maybe even try to hit me, but he actually whined like a little boy, "What did you do that for?" It was the question I was beginning to ask about sex as a whole.

I decided to do some research before seeking out "Tall 'n' Lean #3". I went to Barnes and Noble to see what kind of books I could find on sex. I'd done the "Insert Part A into Part B" manuals and the *Joy of Sex* hippy-type manuals but they didn't give me what I wanted. They were too much like cookery lessons and not enough like good food. I moved on to the erotica section and found *The Story of O* and *The Taking of Sleeping Beauty*. They definitely got my attention. Hours of it. The thing was, I didn't want to be O or Beauty, I wanted to be the person doing things to them. Well, not them in particular. I wanted to be doing things to "Tall 'n' Leans". I'd lie in my narrow little bed, exhausted from my reading or listening to my parents having sex in the room next door, and I'd think about what it would be like to have that kind of control. Then I got to thinking about how I might make it happen. As it turned out it wasn't that difficult but it wasn't that much fun either.

I found "Tall 'n' Lean #3" in a karate class. I'd signed up because I wanted to be able to protect myself, and because I figured the boys there would be more disciplined. He was beautiful, his sweat smelled good, he was a black belt, and he was older than me. I waited for him in the parking lot after class. I had decided to be direct.

"Would you like me to fuck you?"

He didn't look stunned, offended, or even pleased, just curious.

"Are you sure you mean it that way around? Most girls want me to fuck them."

"I'm very sure."

His eyes licked slowly over my body. Then he smiled.

"OK," he said, like he was agreeing to grab a pizza, "but I have a question."

"?"

"What's your name?"

I blushed at that. It hadn't occurred to me that while I'd been noticing the muscles in his forearm and the tight curve of his butt, all he'd been paying attention to was his karate technique.

My parents were away on one of their pagan weekends. Sex was the bedrock of their marriage; you only had to look at the two of them together to see that. The pagan weekends gave them the opportunity to concentrate on fucking each other's brains out without worrying about making a noise.

I'd decided to have a mini-pagan weekend of my own. I brought "Tall 'n' Lean #3" back to my house. I was more than a little nervous. He didn't touch me or hassle me, but there was a confidence behind his eyes that was unsettling. I took him into my dad's den and gave him the speech I'd rehearsed.

"OK, here are the rules. I want to fuck you. I want you to do what I tell you while I fuck you. If you don't do what I tell you, the fucking will stop. Do you understand?"

It was supposed to be my first step to establishing mastery over him. He sat on the edge of my dad's desk, like he had a right to be there, and said, "That speech would work better if you said, 'I am going to fuck you. You will do what I want.' You have to sound like you mean it."

He slipped off the desk and on to his knees in front of me without breaking eye contact.

"Tell me how to serve you, Mistress."

In theory this was just what I wanted. But he was laughing at me. It was gentle laughter, but laughter all the same.

"Shit," I said.

For a second he looked surprised. He thought I was giving an instruction.

"I so wanted to tie you to my dad's chair and tease you and fuck you. But it's not going to work, is it?"

He stood up, lifting me like I weighed nothing at all and placed me on dad's desk. I felt a little bit of panic and a lot of excitement.

"Your dad's chair? How old are you, Helen? No. Don't answer that. You're a pretty girl, Helen, and a brave one. You know what you want, but you don't yet know how to recognize who can give it to you."

I'd known he was a little older than me but I hadn't expected him to talk to me like I was a child. Who did he think he was, my camp counselor?

"Well, why did you come here then?" My eyes were hot with embarrassment.

"You sounded convincing in the parking lot. And I don't mind switching from time to time."

"Switching?"

"I'm a Dom, Helen. I normally do the tying up."

"You think I'm stupid, don't you?"

"No. But I think you need to learn to recognize a sub when you meet one."

Then he kissed me. It was a slow kiss, passionate but friendly. It made me wonder what it would be like to be tied up by him. To let him do whatever he wanted. Then he wasn't kissing me anymore.

"Gotta go, Helen. My name is Jon, by the way. I'll see you at karate next week."

I picked up a book from the desk and threw it, but it only hit the door closing behind him. I was mad at Jon for the rest of the day. Then I started to think about how things might have gone wrong: about the risks that I'd taken; about how gentle he'd been. Gentle and strong. I could see why women would let him tie them.

Mike Kimera

Jon and I became friends but not lovers. He gave me things to read and told me about his life. I left the "Tall 'n' Leans" alone for a while and concentrated on getting to college. I'd gotten through two more "Tall 'n' Leans" in college before I met Peter, both of them one-night-stands, both of them left me feeling hungry and somehow cheated.

My head is feeling better, so I check my watch. Somehow it has reached 10 p.m. I've missed Thanksgiving and they've all forgotten about me. I hug my sense of hurt to me tightly. It serves me right that I've been abandoned. You see, I made a mistake. Such a big mistake. I gave Peter away to my best friend. I was so sure of him, you see. So certain that I was what he wanted. I thought I could lend him out. Share him with a friend.

It started out OK. Barbara was sad and needed comfort, so I tied Peter and blindfolded him and then I shared him with her. It was fun. It felt human and loving. I was so proud of all of us. But the thing is, I get jealous. Just the way my mother does. I hate myself for it, but I can't help it. I'd invited Barbara to stay with us, to join the Peter and Helen household. I knew they liked each other, but I was too vain to think it through. And then I saw how Peter looked at her. How he wanted her. It was my doing, not his. Peter followed my lead, trusting me to do the right thing, and I gave him away.

Except Barbara gave him back. Barbara gave him back. I don't know if he'd have come back on his own. I must still be a little drunk. I've spent months carefully not thinking about this and now I'm crying into my pillow, afraid that Peter hasn't really come back to me. I know that I'm not worthy of Peter. I'm not really the person he deserves. For weeks now I've been watching him, wondering if I'm living in a charade; whether Peter would rather be with Barbara but is just too nice to leave me. Maybe my mother was right to put him on the other side of the house.

"Helen?"

Peter is standing over me. I didn't even hear him come in. I sit up on the bed, conscious of how red my eyes must be and how strongly I must smell of drink. I want to get up and hug him but I can't make myself move.

Peter has brought the toy bag with him. I didn't even know he'd packed it.

He places the toy bag on the bed beside me. Normally I choose the toys, but this time it is Peter who opens the bag. He takes out the strap-on. It's a complicated affair. The strap that goes between my legs will push a dildo and a buttplug into me and leave a long thin curved black latex cock jutting out from my belly.

"I'd like you to use this. I want us to make some noise."

Peter wants me to fuck him, and he wants everyone to know it's happening. Joy spreads through me like liquid sunlight. Peter wants me.

He's been watching me figure it out. When he sees my smile start, he kisses me. I am Sleeping Beauty being brought back to life. Except I'm going to reward my prince by reaming his ass as hard as I can.

I take the strap-on from him.

"Strip, Peter," I say.

He sheds his clothes calmly but quickly. He is already hard. I make him wait while I shrug out of my clothes, then I stand with one leg on the bed and tell him to tool me up. I mean to sound stern but I can't keep the joy out of my voice.

Then it starts for real. Peter lubes me slowly and thoroughly and straps me tight. With both holes full and a strong black cock thrusting in front of me I feel powerful and as randy as hell.

"Get on your back on the bed, Peter, and hold on to your ankles."

I love the sound of that. Love the calm excitement with which he obeys. He doesn't ask why he's on his back when he should be bent over. He does what I tell him.

I spread lube over my mock-cock, place my finger and thumb around the base of Peter's erection and push hard into his anus.

"Keep your hands around your ankles, Peter." Then I make the noise he's been waiting for: in my best rodeo tones I shout "YEEHAW" and we're off.

I ride him hard enough to make him buck on the bed. I keep his cock in my hand like a joystick or perhaps a saddle horn, squeezing it as I pound him. The harder I push into him the deeper the dildo rises into me. When I'm close, I slap his hands away from his ankles, lift his feet up over my shoulders and fuck for depth. The bed is bouncing now.

"Wank, Peter. Wank hard."

His hand moves eagerly on his cock. I am so close that I'm groaning as I grind into him. The heat of his sperm splashing onto my belly pushes me over and I growl my come at him.

I pull out of Peter's poor abused asshole and collapse on top of him. I feel strong and whole and loved.

Peter holds me gently and whispers, "Welcome back, Helen."

It turns out that the bed is not too narrow if we lie like spoons. As I fall asleep, I remember that I'm still wearing the strap-on, but I'm too tired to move.

We are both sore the next morning but that doesn't stop us grinning at one another.

"Do you think they heard us?"

"Your parents' bedroom is next door isn't it, Helen?"

We both laugh.

At breakfast I wait for my mother to say something. She discusses the weather and asks if we really have to leave straight after breakfast, but makes no mention of our exploits. As we say our goodbyes, mother hugs Peter and says something to him. I miss the exchange because I have a crying baby in my arms at the time.

When I've driven as far as the freeway, I ask Peter what my mother said.

"She told me, you were lucky to have me."

"What did you say?"

"I said that you would always have me and that I would always give thanks for that."

I try to imagine the expression on my mother's face when she heard that. I decide that it would probably be one of approval. *Thank God for Peter*, I think to myself. Then I start to look for the next rest stop. I want a quiet place where we can do a bit more thanksgiving.

Bodies of Water

Cecilia Tan

*Her skin is more sensitive now, she's sure of it. As the water
trickles over her back, she can feel every drop, each rivulet tracing
a line down her back like a fingertip caress. Water never felt like
this before, not even in the most luxurious shower.*

She remembers the shower at Argyropoulos's palazzo. One of
Steve's rich investors, taken in by the adventure of treasure-
hunting, he had not only bought in to the expedition company
but insisted the team stay at his palatial home while they were
landside. She barely remembers what the bathroom looked
like, only that the shower was such a luxury – hot water, dry
towels – after three weeks on the ship sifting through sand-
covered artefacts and always being damp.

It was one morning when getting out of that shower she had
seen the blue speck on her skin, just glimpsed it in the mirror
on the underside of her arm. No, no it can't be . . . she thought
to herself. It was blue like a spot of spilled ink, just like
Jackie's, just like Karros's. She refused to believe it. In a
few hours she would be back on the ship, and they would be
that much closer to solving the mystery of the wreck. The fact
that Karros was in a hospital in Athens and Jackie was on her
way to the CDC in Georgia affected her only slightly. Not
when we are this close! she thought. She felt sure they were on
the verge of a breakthrough.

The wreck was a mystery, and that was what mattered most
to Lydia. When she had gone into archeology she had thought
she would be sifting dust in an Egyptian desert or hacking
through the Yucatan jungle. But there was pioneering work

being done in undersea archeology, and her fiancé Ambrose had hooked them up with Steve to do a few voyages. No matter how much he claimed he wasn't a treasure hunter, Steve still hoped for a large haul of gold to pay back his stockholders with. Ambrose hoped for prestige and fame. But Lydia just wanted the answers to questions history had left for them.

Her arms are crossed over her chest, but the water flowing down her back feels so good she wants to reach up into the stream. She lowers her hands, her fingers sliding over her skin, and she shivers in delight. She has never been comfortable in nakedness, but now she forgets modesty as she leans back to let the water spatter onto her breasts. She reaches up and spreads the water between her breasts, over her nipples, her neck and lips.

She had argued with Ambrose over the origin of the wreck. That morning at the palazzo, before they had set sail again, he had picked a fight with the other archeologist, a young man named Tomson, Will Tomson, who had speculated that if they couldn't find evidence for a Mediterranean culture who whaled, who was to say the cargo came from the same place as the ship? Ambrose had practically bellowed at the man, "What sort of twisted logic is that? You'll never get anywhere with thinking like that, my boy. You'll spend your life on one wild goose chase after another. Simplify!"

Lydia had been pretending not to hear the exchange, putting sugar into her coffee with slow deliberate spoonfuls, and stirring so that the spoon did not clink against the side of the mug. But when it had come to that she had stood up, and approached their table.

Ambrose had put his hand around her hip as she came over, proprietary as always. But he took it away again when she said, "It very well may be that our explanation is going to be a complicated one. Where did the whale oil come from? Where did the ship come from? They may well be two different answers." As she walked away, she could feel Ambrose's usual daggers in her back. She would pay for defying him later, she was sure of it. But no matter the consequence, Lydia could not allow an incorrect or foolish statement to stand.

And they certainly had to consider every option. This wasn't like the Spanish galleon they had recovered off the continental shelf last year, doubloons and rare artefacts and a diary clearly revealing the date of her voyage. No, this wreck was older than any ever found, probably 3,000 years or more, and nothing they had brought up yet had matched their body of knowledge. There were amphorae and other jars they expected to be full of olive oil. But some were found with their seals still intact, and when opened they were found to be whale oil. Some of them were strangely fragrant, as if perfumed to last over centuries, millennia. The scents of some civilization older than any they had previously encountered. Staggering.

Almost as staggering as the news that came to them after the ship had set out to sea once again. Lydia had been standing on the deck of the ship, her hands gripping the railing. The sun was hot but the spray was cold and damp as they headed back to the deep water where the wreck lay. She barely felt the pitching and yawing of the converted trawler as it sliced through the waves, her eyes fixed on a far spot on the horizon. The answer was out there, somewhere.

Tomson disturbed her reverie with a hand on her elbow. At first she was glad to see him. He was such an inquisitive fellow, so delighted by every puzzle, every discovery. But his face was closed, now. "Jackie just radioed in."

He sounded like he was choking as he said it. Lydia saw the distress on his face. "What is it? Is it the blue fever? What did they find?"

"Karros died in the hospital, some kind of pneumonia-like symptoms, but they weren't sure if it was related to the skin condition or not. But the CDC thinks it's some kind of infectious agent. They've got Jackie in a bubble."

For a moment, pure human emotion took over. "Oh, poor Karros . . ." She crumbled and he put his arm around her, held her for a moment. She coughed up a few tears, though she mostly held them back. But then she straightened up and looked into Tomson's eyes. Like the ocean, their blue was brighter in the sun. "What do they want us to do?"

"For now, stay out here, and tell them if we have any more cases of it. We shouldn't try to land anywhere, that's for sure."

She watched as his eyes roved the horizon like hers, and she felt their hips touch as they both leaned on the railing. "It's just lucky we were out here when the news came," she said.

"Why do you say that?"

"Because now we have no reason to stop operations," Lydia said. "We can keep digging."

Tomson nodded and a relieved almost-smile warmed his face. "I'm so glad you feel that way about it. Steve wants to keep going, too."

"Who doesn't?" Lydia asked, already suspecting the answer.

"Your partner," Tomson answered. "Ambrose thinks we should head straight for the mainland and all get ourselves into a hospital right away."

"A hospital didn't do Karros any good." Lydia stared back into the blue. "Do you feel it, Will? We've barely begun to investigate, but we're on the verge of something quite extraordinary."

"You sound quite sure of yourself."

"It's rare I find something so totally outside of my knowledge base." Lydia liked the way her voice sounded when she said that, at last finding that note that reminded her more of a professor than of a student. "Whatever we find, they'll be rewriting the history books, I'm sure of it."

Will Tomson nodded then, and they both watched the sea roll under the ship for long minutes.

She opens her mouth to let the water dribble in, letting it run down her chin and over her closed eyelids. Her lips tingle where it touches, and she lets the tip of her tongue emerge. She touches her wet cheeks with her hands and then brings them together in front of her mouth – she looks like she is praying. She has never felt anything quite like this before. It must be the fever. Her chest heaves as she breathes, the water falling faster now, over her face, her breasts, and down her belly. Water, who would have thought water would be the key to it all?

Ambrose had fought her bitterly that night in their cabin. "You'll get us all killed. Crazy woman . . ."

She had held her ground as much as she could. "They've

ordered us to stay in quarantine. And no one else is sick. There's no reason to stop the expedition. For all we know, Karros's pneumonia wasn't even related."

Ambrose rumbled like gathering thunder. "It's still too dangerous. I'm not handling anything that comes up from the wreck and neither are you."

"What do you mean . . . ?"

"You're my wife-to-be and you're mine to protect. You're not going near it. Let little Willie do it."

She tried to deflect him by teasing, but it was a mistake. "You sound like those old Egyptologists, running from the curse of the mummy."

"I'll have to tell the others that you're not feeling well, that you have a headache." He left then, and she realized what he meant, as he bolted the door from the outside. The converted trawler was all steel – there wasn't even a porthole for her to shout through.

She beat futilely on the bulkhead door for a few moments and then sat back on the pallet bed, unable to believe that Ambrose would really keep her locked in there for long. He was touchy, she knew that. She had known it even when he had proposed, that he had a temper, fits of ego and irrationality. But he had courted her so earnestly, with flowers and dinners, and always on his best behavior, shaking hands with her father and asking his permission . . . how could she say no? All those years, college, graduate school, the Yucatan, she had never had time for a companion. Ambrose had seemed ideal in some ways. They could work together, live together, grow old together. He was what they called "old-fashioned" and she had liked that, at first. Before all this talk of protecting and property.

She licks the water from her lips. They had been chapped from sun and wind but now they feel like rose petals, the water droplets beading on her face like dew. She cranes her neck down to lick the water from her breasts, and leans back again to let the water rain down her midsection, pooling in the triangle of her crotch, her bush half-wet like a shore plant in a tide pool.

That night Ambrose had brought her dinner, canned stew heated in the galley with some crackers. He unbolted the door and swept in with the bowl in front of him, placing it on one corner of the bed with a flourish. So pleased with himself. The ship rocked slightly, but the seas were calm and there was little danger of spilling. "I thought you might be hungry," he said.

"Not really," she replied, just to annoy him. His face said he was expecting praise, as if he had forgotten she wasn't really ill, forgotten that was a lie he had invented.

But then, she thought, she really was ill. While he had been gone she had examined the underside of her arm – the spot had grown bigger. There was another spot in the small of her back, as well.

He shrugged off the annoyance and came over to sit next to her. He took her hand in his. "Lydia, my dove, please don't be angry. You have to realize how irrational you can be sometimes. It's better this way – you'll see how it will all work out. You'll be glad . . ." He was leaning toward her, to kiss her. She pulled back almost involuntarily, as if he were the one with the contagion. He pressed forward more, his eyes closing, until their lips met.

She allowed him to kiss her for long moments, until she broke away saying, "That stew smells good."

He straightened, remembering his pretense for being there. "Of course. Here you are." He stood up and she gathered the bowl to her. Then he left, and bolted the door behind him.

She ate the stew, but didn't taste it. She ate it because she supposed it was better to be fortified than not, but her mind was elsewhere. What was Tomson doing right now? He might be opening a basket brought up by a remote right this minute. The wreck was so deep human divers, even in submersibles, couldn't reach it. But machines, guided from the deck with video monitors, could go anywhere. She felt sometimes that it was her hands, not the robot's, picking through the wreckage, lifting an ancient astrolabe out of the silt, peeling apart the remnants of a wooden carton to find whatever lay inside.

She hesitates a moment, the rapture frightens her a bit, and she questions what is happening. But pleasure is a reassuring thing, it feels right rather than wrong, and she gradually separates her knees. Pooled water cascades between her legs, and her mouth quivers as the trickle touches a place she has only let Ambrose touch when he fumbles to insert himself in her. Unlike his hard knuckles the caress of the water opens her, and she feels an outflow of her own juices come forth to meet the cascade of water.

Lydia had been locked in the cabin two days when someone came to the door while she was sleeping. The knock woke her, a muffled voice.

"Open the door!" she shouted, her voice hoarse from sleeping. That sounded like Tomson. She banged on her side of the door.

With a clank the door came open, and Will Tomson stepped in with a wrench in his hand and a puzzled look on his face.

She grabbed him by the hand and pulled him down the corridor to the dark, empty galley. The room was lit only with the orange emergency light above the door and they blinked at each other. "Will, you have to tell me, what have you found?"

"Lydia, wait a minute, were you trapped in there?"

"That's not important right now. Please Will, what's been going on?"

"That's why I came looking for you. I found something you're not going to believe." He shifted the sack on his back to the table, opened it carefully to reveal what looked to Lydia rather like a book. It looked to be some kind of leather, and Tomson folded it open once, then again like a road map, to reveal several sheaves of skin.

"How could something like this survive in the water all that time?" she asked, even as she began to take in the drawings and symbols.

"Have a look at this," he said, taking out his flashlight and flooding the table with white light. The pages were blue. "Tell me, please, Lydia, did Ambrose lock you away because you've been infected?"

She shook her head. "No, to keep me from being infected. But Ambrose be damned, do you realize this is a map?" In human measure of time, the coastline of Spain and Portugal looked essentially the same. But this showed some land one did not see in the modern era. The drawing detailed a tiny map-size city, and a route from the mainland to it. A route that they had followed to arrive at the site of the wreck.

He nodded and turned the sheaf over. "And it looks like an instruction manual, as well." On the other side were drawings of a man and a woman, the odd-shaped whale-oil jars, and more. Lydia was reminded of the safety instruction cards in airplanes. The final picture in the sequence, if they were reading the correct direction, was of the two humans swimming with two dolphins.

The other page also had a sequence of pictures on it. Lydia felt almost dizzy as she looked at them. "Can I be interpreting these correctly?" she thought. It appeared to tell a story of a city being engulfed by the sea, the same drawing of the city as on the facing sheaf, with the water level going up and up and up.

"It's not possible," she said, her voice so low Tomson was not sure she spoke. "A lost civilization? Who had the know-how to make a book that would not decay after thousands of years under water?"

Tomson put his hand on hers. "That's not all. We got word from Georgia."

"Oh no, not Jackie."

"She's alive. They said she's almost completely blue now, though. Antibiotics, antivirals, they aren't effective. They are assuming now if it's an organism, it's something like a prion, something they haven't seen before. They say her cellular structure is changing. Not just on her skin. They are seeing changes in her brain."

"What sorts of changes?"

"Cognitively she still appears the same, but they are seeing increases in activity in some very unlikely areas . . ." Tomson was blushing red again. "I have some theories . . ." He shook himself a little. "But this is the important thing. They're keeping her alive by keeping her wet."

Lydia's hand went to the small of her back of its own accord. "Oh my."

Tomson grimaced as he saw it. "Lydia, there's something else you should know."

She heard the tremble in his voice and looked up from the diagrams. He was unbuttoning his shirt, his head down, his blond curls hanging over his eyes as he pulled the garment out of his pants and opened it.

Lydia could see the blue creeping up out of his waistband, climbing his stomach and up his chest.

"I won't be able to hide it from the others much longer," he said. "It's spreading upward and outward."

Almost without thinking, she reached a hand toward him and touched the skin of his stomach. It felt smooth, hairless, soft. He gasped and she pulled back. "Did that hurt?"

"No, no . . . it's just, very, very sensitive." He quivered then, as if her touch reverberated throughout his body.

She rubs the water on her thighs, splashing up handfuls of it from the puddle around her. The pleasure is unlike anything she has felt before. She rolls over now, letting the water run over her back, then rolls over again, letting it bounce off her stomach. She lets her knees fall apart and invites the droplets to fall there, as well. She is soaked now, wet over every inch of her skin, and she reaches for the jar.

We must keep away from Ambrose. That was her only thought as she and Tomson made their way to the hold where the recovered objects were prepped. If she was reading the diagrams correctly, then what Tomson needed to survive was there. She located one of the jars with the curlicue top as shown in the drawings, and opened it. The scent of some extinct flower filled the small room, and the slight motion of the ship made her grip the jar tighter.

Tomson pulled his shirt completely off and Lydia stood close to him. She dipped two fingers into the jar and came up with a dab of something with the consistency of honey. She smeared it into his back where the blue part of his flesh met the pink, and began slathering it upward. As she watched, she could see the blue edge beginning to spread. "It's working," she said to him. "The ointment is encouraging the blue to grow."

He trembled under her touch and when she tried to come

around the front of him he shied away. "Let me do it," he said, holding his hand out for the jar.

She knitted her brows in puzzlement, but then saw the embarrassment on his face. She turned away as his trousers dropped, but she could still hear the sounds he made in his throat. He could not stop himself as he covered his legs and private parts, and then huddled away from her, hiding his crotch with his hands.

"Now we need to wet you down," Lydia said, her eyes still averted by studying the diagrams. There were hoses with small nozzles here, made for rinsing away sediment on artefacts. She turned the spigot on one and brought it over to where he was sitting in a ball.

He cried out as the water hit his back. "Not too hard!"

She reduced the flow to a dribble and let the droplets spatter softly over him. He moaned and then sighed, the tension seeming to go out of his body as she wet him. He let her run the water down his chest, and she saw that he had been hiding a rampant state of turgidity from her. His eyes were closed now, and she watched his penis curiously. It was thoroughly blue, standing up like a finger of coral, and he whimpered a bit when the water sprayed it.

"Will," she said in a hushed voice. "What do you know about dolphins?"

He lay back into the puddle and let out a long breath, his shyness gone. "A bit. Why?"

"Do you think it's possible that the transformation taking place here is to make us more like them?" Lydia began to untuck her own shirt. "To survive the day when our home is overrun by water?"

Will sat up and blinked water from his eyes. The blueness was creeping up toward his neck and she wondered if they would remain the same color when it reached them. "No one will ever believe it."

She shook her head. "I believe it." She turned to show him the spreading patch of blue on her back, her shirt hiked up. His wet fingers traced the edges of it and she knew then why he had moaned. His hands reached around her then, and she felt his cheek pressed against the small of her back.

"I'm sorry, Lydia, I just can't help it . . ."

"It's all right, Will." Dolphins, she thought. "Help me with it, now."

He helped her to shed her clothes and then handed her the jar, so she could slather herself. But then she came to her back, and he helped her with that as she had with his. And then she tilted her head back and waited for the water to come down.

She opens her eyes to see him standing above her, the hose still in his hand. She reaches up and pulls him down to her, wanting the feeling of his water-slick skin against hers. Their still-red lips meet, and she feels like they are drinking each other. She laps at his mouth, her hands buried in his curls, as his hands run up and down her back. She licks him, licks at his cheeks, kisses his eyelids. His mouth answers, making its wet way down her neck, to the delicate nipples, standing erect from the water and from rubbing against his so-slick torso. He rubs them with oil, his thumbs brushing across the tips, and then he lowers his mouth to them, wetting them, his tongue lapping at the flower scent mingled with the taste of her skin.

His tongue follows the trail of water down her belly, down to the triangle between her legs. She is wet and slick there by more than just oil and droplets from the hose. As she reaches her hands down to spread her lips apart some part of her knows she has never blossomed this way for Ambrose. Will's fingers dig into the jar of oil and he slicks her from anus to clitoris with the fragrant stuff. Lydia writhes under the touch, her hips rising up until he sinks his fingers deep into her, the pleasure rippling outward from her center. She clings to his neck, wanting skin on skin, wanting wetness on wetness.

She wraps a leg around him and almost before either of them realizes it, he mounts her. Every part of her is slick, both inside and out, and she sucks in a breath. No, it was never like this with Ambrose. She reaches a hand between their pumping bodies, curious to feel if something else in her anatomy has changed. The breath keeps getting deeper, and her fingers slide over her clitoris, fundamentally unchanged and yet . . .

The intensity of it makes her want to cry out, and yet she does not want to exhale. Breathing has become a secondary thing to the urgent need between her legs, and she clings to him hard with three limbs, the fourth a moving blur between them even as he speeds up the rhythm of his own motion.

And then suddenly she feels him break loose, she feels the burst of hot salt liquid inside her, and her own pleasure cascades throughout her body, rippling from one end to the other. They cling together as the spasms quake through their muscles, and then, as one, they exhale.

They sit up slowly in the puddle on the floor, the hose still running, and look around them. Lydia looks down at her own body – the blue is everywhere their bodies touched, and spreading. She clasps Will's hand in her own. "Do you feel like you are coming down with pneumonia?"

"Actually, my lungs never felt better."

She nods. "Mine, too. In fact, all of me . . ."

Before she can finish, the door swings open to reveal Ambrose. He flicks on the light. There is not even a moment for anger to register on his face before horror and fear set in. "Get me out of here!" he shouts, as he runs down the corridor. That sets Will and Lydia to laughing. A short time later, Steve calls on the intercom and they tell him about the oil, the water, and the change. "You're safe if you don't handle the jars," Lydia tells him. Her hands are touching Will as she speaks. His are exploring the hollows under the arms, under her breasts, anywhere he might have missed. Lydia's voice is breathy as she speaks. "We're safe so long as we stay wet. Are we still at anchor?" she asks. Steve's voice through the speaker says yes. "Good," she says, and takes Will's hand again. "We're going for a swim."

Dregs

Claude Lalumière

According to an old folktale, nightmares once covered the night sky, blotting out the stars. When those creatures of darkness invaded our dreams, the night sky opened up and the stars revealed themselves.

I found the book that contained that particular story at Lost Pages, one of my favorite teenage haunts. It wasn't the only bookshop I frequented, but the books I found on its shelves were . . . unique. What I mean to say is that I never saw any of these books anywhere else. Not even in secondhand bookstores – the patrons of Lost Pages apparently valued its treasures too much to hawk them off in such a fashion. Or perhaps the secondhand bookdealers were too canny to let such books onto their grimy shelves once they acquired them from those desperate or ignorant enough to sell them.

Bizarre bestiaries. Dictionaries of dead, obscure languages. Maps to lands that may never have been. Essays on religions with names I had never encountered elsewhere. Obscure mythologies. Accounts of wars no history teacher had ever mentioned. Such were the wares of the bookshop that fed my teenage dreams.

I left my home town after high school. I took my first trip overseas, and, shortly after that, went to university in another city. Lost Pages was left behind, like a passing fancy of adolescence.

My parents had offered me a two-month-long voyage abroad for, as far as I could tell, two reasons – only one of which was voiced. One, they felt they could afford this luxury because, unlike most of my graduating class, I showed no interest in automobiles; most of my classmates were rewarded with a shiny, fashionable car for coming out of high school alive. The other, unspoken, reason was that my mother and father worried that I was spending too much time in my own head. They often commented, with varying degrees of tact and concern, on my lack of friends. They judged – as it turned out, wisely – that being dropped alone in the middle of foreign lands would make me take notice of the world around me.

And so I did. I stood next to the sea at dawn, inhaling its pungent aroma. I walked through streets too narrow for automobiles, yet bustling with human activity, loud with unfamiliar languages and cacophonic sounds that swirled through my ears. I ate delicately spiced foods, enjoyed an undreamt-of variety of meats, greens and fruit. I wandered city avenues where lovers danced and kissed in the moonlight to the tunes of street musicians or their own hearts.

And there was so much more that I experienced. This whirlpool of exotica awakened in me many unfamiliar lusts.

Two weeks into my trip – on a hot summer night periodically lightened by an elusive cool breeze – I was in a port city whose hectic nightlife clustered in a busy quarter next to the docks. Club music blasted through open doorways, mixing with the sounds of outdoor performers. The women wore short, tight dresses, advertising their physical charms to potential suitors. The men, overdressed in the heat as was the fashion, sweated the night away dancing athletically, careful never to let their eyes wander from the women they coveted.

I was mesmerized by the nimble performances of these dancers, the precision of their movements, the sway of their hips and shoulders, the sweat spraying from their brows as they swirled to the rhythms of the dance music.

I was tempted to dance myself, but there was no one I wanted to impress or seduce. It was a notion I could barely contemplate. My new experiences had yet to include sex – I had never even masturbated! The sexual energy that, unknown to me then, was yearning to break free was intensifying the self-consciousness I felt over my awkward body. Not being a fashionable young man, I was dressed to be comfortable in the heat: thin cotton pants and a T-shirt. My awareness of my appearance emphasized the sentiment that I was a child among adults. I remained a spectator.

As the evening wore on, I grew increasingly frustrated at my inability to join in the festivities. I felt cheapened by my voyeuristic role and I was tortured by an inner conflict – the desire to abandon myself to the surrounding merriment clashing with an unshakeable fear of embarrassment. Burdened with self-loathing, I decided to make my way back to the inn where I was staying, hoping to calm down enough to fall asleep.

I had been in this city for three days. Each succeeding night, I was further entranced by its vigorous night life, by the soulful music, by the simmering sexuality.

That night, as I walked back to the inn, I was overtaken several times by an extreme dizziness and had to brace myself against walls or lamp-posts to keep myself from stumbling. I was not tired – quite the opposite! I was a nervous mess: exhilarated by the intensity of my experiences and angry with myself for my cowardice.

A block or two from the inn, while I was suffering another bout of dizziness, my hand failed to find a steady purchase, and I fell. A young man – he looked about my age – rushed to my side and helped me up. The contact of my rescuer's hands on my bare arms as he bent down to help me caused me to suffer the most intense bout of dizziness yet.

I took a deep breath and, with the stranger's help, I got up and steadied myself. He looked vaguely familiar: slightly taller than I, dark eyes, olive skin smooth and dry despite the heat, strong sharp features, a pronounced nose, stylish black pants and white shirt. I was dazzled by what I took to be a trick of the light: highlights of green, blue and brown shimmered in his dark hair. Probably I had seen him at one of the clubs, or in the streets among the strollers and dancers.

His gaze locked with mine as he asked me something in a language I could not understand – he spoke so fast I couldn't even be sure which language he was speaking. He seemed genuinely concerned. I tried to mime that I was all right, livening up my risible performance with a few simple words in my own language.

He laughed at my antics. I surprised myself by laughing along with him. I was such a serious young man. Laughing at myself was a novel experience. It lifted a heavy burden from my shoulders and somewhat attenuated my feeling of self-loathing.

Looking at my companion, I remembered the handsome men dancing to seduce the eager young women watching them. I was overcome with a vision of my new friend dancing as I had seen those men dance: his hips and shoulders swaying confidently, his seductive smile directed towards me, his eyes never straying from my body . . .

The next thing I knew his lips were closed over mine, his tongue exploring my mouth, just as my own tongue was tasting his warm, wet mouth . . .

I panicked. I shoved him away from me. The dizziness was stronger than ever; I felt I would faint as easily as dust catches in the wind, but I struggled not to succumb to this weakness and ran to the inn.

Inside my room, I fell into the chair, closed my eyes and took long, slow breaths. Eventually, exhaustion conquered my restlessness. I got up and started to undress, eager to climb into bed.

Taking off my pants, I was startled by the sight of my erect penis. Of course, I'd had erections before, but I'd never paid any attention to them. This one, huge and dripping, refused to be ignored. At that moment, it occurred to me that I had felt its pull all evening.

Nevertheless, out of naivety and habit and ignorance, I still neglected it.

Why had I never masturbated? Even now I can't really say. Not out of prudishness, and certainly not out of some strange belief that it could be evil or bad in any way – I simply didn't.

I crawled into bed, determined to fall asleep – despite my over-engorged penis – and put this troublesome evening behind me. Tomorrow, I thought, I would check out and head for another city. I was compelled to flee. I was too young to know that no matter how far I fled, I could not escape myself.

The erection made it difficult for me to get comfortable. Nevertheless, I did succeed in falling asleep quickly.

I awoke trembling with violent pleasure, and, before I could
take stock of the situation, an inner explosion sent aftershocks
of ecstasy rippling through my body. I was unable to make out
any distinct sensation. My sense of touch was now so acute that
all contact with my skin – air, sheets, anything – contributed to
the sensation of being enveloped by a warm sea of delicious
comfort, like a foetus blissfully floating in its world of amniotic
fluid.

Slowly, I regained the ability to distinguish sensations. I felt
my back bathing in a pool of sweat. I felt the cool breeze from
the open window next to my bed. I felt a warm mouth around
my spent cock.

My fellator was the gorgeous young man I had met earlier in
the streets. His kiss had been my first. And now he had given
me my first orgasm.

He must have sensed a shift in my posture; he took his
mouth off my penis and straightened up to look at my face.
There was enough moonlight coming in from the window for
me to make out his seductive, mischievous smile.

I recalled how he had so easily succeeded in making me
laugh at myself. Again, looking at him towering over me, I
could not help but recognize the comical nature of my behavior
earlier that night. What a burlesque figure I must have cut!
Running scared from my own body, from my excitement, from
its fulfillment, from my new friend's beauty, from the possibilities his body offered me.

As he smiled at me, I burst out laughing. Instantly, he was
infected by my outburst. He leapt on me, and we hugged as
fiercely as we were laughing.

After hours of exploring each other's bodies, we lay silently
in bed, my head on his chest while he stroked my hair. The first
light of dawn was seeping through the window. He kissed my
forehead and disentangled himself from me. I closed my eyes,
savoring the lingering sensations of his touch.

I heard him fumble around the room and, moments later, I
felt his hand on my stomach. I opened my eyes to see him
offering me a drink from what I took to be a bottle of wine. It
was transparent, clearly revealing the amber fluid within.

Seeing me hesitate, he took a sip himself. Overcompensating

for my timidity, I grabbed the bottle away from him, more roughly than I'd intended. I kneeled on the bed and, theatrically, raised the bottle to my mouth. I swung my head backward and let the dark liquid cascade down my throat. I nearly gagged as a result of my eagerness to show off. Rivulets of amber flowed through the burgeoning hair of my adolescent chest. He snatched the bottle away from me before I spilled the entire contents.

I coughed to regain my breath, but found myself dizzy and drowsy. The shapes around me were losing their definition. Once more, my seducer kissed me. His tongue playfully explored my mouth as I felt his fingers gently tighten around my scrotum.

I did not lose consciousness; but I could no longer differentiate my body from my surroundings, nor my self from the world.

I saw fabulous creatures burst from exploding stars. Was I myself one of many laughing monsters frolicking amongst the flames of the sun? I witnessed great migrations of majestic undersea beasts. Was I the great primeval ocean in which they thrived? I underwent uncounted metamorphoses, limbs turning into wings turning into tendrils turning into leaves turning into ripe fruit turning into stone turning into molten lava turning into dark ambrosia trickling down the throat of unfathomable deities turning into a thin old man wracked by ceaseless physical pain turning into a glowing snake changing colour with every flick of its tail while negotiating a path through high and dense grass turning into a pantheon of gods smashing planets asunder for their amusement turning into a stomach growling to be fed turning into a baby suckling at its mother's teat turning into a host of dark shapes writhing in the sky. I was a silent, stunned spectator to this torrent of hallucinatory visions, if visions they were.

My companion kissed my chest, and then rose from the bed. He drank the amber liqueur down to its dregs. He looked at it longingly, then bent down to kiss me. I tasted his tears. He carefully left the bottle on the night table. Did his feet and hands turn into claws? Did scales sprout from his flesh? Did his moist mouth take the shape of a beak? Did wings with feathers of green, blue and brown rise tall above his shoulders? Did he fly through the ceiling and into heavens as strange as those I had just glimpsed?

I lay in bed immobile, listening to the furious sound of beating wings.

When I could move once again, I stared at the empty bottle. Were it not for the evidence of that bottle I might have dismissed the events of the last twelve hours as feverish delusions. No, my erotic adventure had been real enough; the delightful tingling that lingered on my skin and the musky smell of sweat and semen attested well enough to that. But as to what came after I drank the mysterious liquid. . . . Had my lover slipped me a powerful hallucinogen? To what purpose? Stupidly paranoid, I immediately convinced myself that he had robbed me.

I sprang from the bed in search of my pants. I found my wallet undisturbed. I rummaged around the room and calmed myself down. Nothing was missing. It would be many years before I made any sense of my bizarre encounter.

I enjoyed the remainder of my holiday more than I had previously anticipated, as I eagerly explored myriad new worlds of taste, smell, sound, beauty and sex. I returned home only briefly. University was a few days away.

My parents immediately noticed a change in me. I was more alert. My eyes were brighter and I smiled much more easily. My parents deluged me with questions about my trip.

Ordinarily, I would have fled from such a barrage of attention. But I knew they were only happy to see me, and that they would miss me once I was gone to university. Also, I was very grateful for their gift to me – that vacation that I couldn't have known how much I needed. Of course, I would answer their questions, but I also knew that I could not be entirely candid.

They asked about the empty bottle I had brought back as a souvenir. I answered coyly that it was to remind me of someone special. They did not press the issue, not wanting to embarrass either me or themselves. Their thoughts were transparent. They were imagining some exotic girl, nice but not too nice, who had deflowered their shy son. The reality would have shocked them, as, in fact, would the extent of my sexual escapades. So I gave them a nice, polished version of my travels: enough details for them to know that their idea had been a success. But I was also vague enough to let them understand – by omission – how much of one it had been.

Yes, I had kept the bottle. It was not quite empty. There were some dregs, some few lingering drops. I had carefully sealed it and packed it. It escaped customs unquestioned and unbroken.

I was both tempted and scared to sample the liquid again, even in the tiniest amount. I did not know what to make of its effects – if indeed it had been responsible for my vivid hallucinations – and I was loath to waste it. I thought of diluting the remains in water. Drinking the result only occasionally, slowly learning to understand the visions it bestowed upon me. It was too soon. I put the bottle away, intending to leave the decision to a later time when I would have the leisure to think properly.

The few days between the return from my voyage and my departure for university went by with alarming rapidity. Did it occur to me at the time to visit Lost Pages? I can't remember – but even if it had, I would not have been able to find the time to go. And how could I have known what to look for?

To facilitate my preparations, my mother had already packed most of my things. My clothes were neatly folded into old suitcases. All of my books had already been stored in boxes, ready to be shipped to my dormitory.

In this new life, my time and mind were now occupied with my studies and the string of tedious jobs I had decided to take in order to afford an apartment that would secure me the privacy dormitory life failed to provide.

I taught myself to cook and used my lovers, mostly men but also the occasional woman, as guinea pigs for my culinary experiments. As time wore on, the dismal failures grew farther apart, and my guests grew to eagerly anticipate the food I prepared for them. I was discreet and avoided permanent entanglements. I attracted – and was attracted to – those who yearned for an intimacy that would not shatter their daily lives or their other, more public, attachments.

I rarely returned home to my parents. They saw me for

some, though not all, of the customary holidays and family events. Those visits were short and never included enough time to visit my old haunts. It was as though my previous identity had been supplanted by a new one that recognized no continuity with the past. Everything I had experienced before university – more precisely, before that summer trip that changed everything – might as well have happened to someone else.

Eventually, teaching assignments supplemented the scholarships I earned, and the two sources of income allowed me to quit migrating between minimum-wage jobs to support myself.

One night a young woman – a mischievous student whom I had met the previous semester while teaching an undergraduate survey class – noticed the bottle on a shelf among other knickknacks nestled between piles of books.

On the floor of my living room we were naked, the sweat of sex clinging to our cooling bodies. We were laughing at everything and nothing until the laughter escalated into a wrestling match, into a bout of mutual tickling. I had her pinned down between my legs, mercilessly digging my fingers into her ticklish belly, but, in a surprise manoeuvre, she managed to squirm and jump away from me.

She ended up on the far side of the room, staring at the bottle. She called me over to her. "Look at how the light catches it." She pointed with one hand and squeezed my buttocks with the other. "It's beautiful."

At the bottom of the bottle, where light hit the amber liquid, miniature rainbows danced. If I tried to concentrate on any particular aspect of this tiny spectacle, it hid from my sight. I had to absorb the phenomenon in its entirety, or not at all.

Why had I never noticed this? Had this effect been going on unnoticed all these years?

How could I know? I had found it simpler to ignore my memento. I suppose I passively cherished its presence, but I had yet to pursue – or even to contemplate pursuing – my investigation of its contents. A council of unacknowledged, intertwined fears sat at the heart of my negligence: that my life of pleasure would be shattered by the revelations that awaited the conclusion of a successful investigation; that there were no answers to be found; that the liquid would turn out to be nothing more than wine or some other mundane beverage; that I had those many years ago lost my grip on sanity and been besieged by delusions; that my great moment of epiphany rested on an instance of madness; that the foundations of my personality were too shabby to withstand close scrutiny; and more, many more. However, this personal insight was still in my future, some time later than that evening, when I stood in my living room, my naked body pressed against my lover's soft back, as we both stared at the contents of my precious bottle.

It seemed, to my neglectful gaze, that the dregs were somewhat more substantial than I remembered. Hadn't there been but a few drops? There was now a pool at the bottom of the bottle.

"Tell me the story," said my lover, tucking a stray strand of her blonde hair behind one ear.

"What do you mean?" Unsuccessfully, I attempted to resume our tickling match.

"Stop it! There must be a story! What are you hiding? Tell me. Tell me!"

It dawned on me that I had, unconsciously, tried to avoid her question. I had never told anybody the story behind this bottle. Of course, since my parents upon my return from my fateful voyage, no-one had thought to ask.

I had never told anyone.

Suddenly, I felt the tremendous weight of this secret. In her curious, smiling face, I sensed the potential for release and relief. To finally relate the events that changed my life.

I must have been silent for longer than I realized. She was gently stroking my chest. I noticed her looking at me, worried.

"Yes," I said.

"Yes?" she whispered back at me.

I led her into the bedroom, and, then, I told her.

I told her everything. My whole life. She listened to my ramblings, paid attention to every word. She never grew impatient – or at least was sensitive enough to my needs not to show it if she did. Somewhere in this great mess of a narrative, the bottle's story came out. I omitted no detail, no matter how utterly embarrassing or unbelievably fantastic.

Why did I trust her so when I had never allowed myself to open up to anyone in this fashion before? Because I needed to. I do not mean to undermine or diminish the depth of her empathy or her curious intelligence, and certainly not the quality of her companionship. No doubt all of these aspects of her self combined to trigger my realization of this great need, this great chasm, in my life. My need may not have necessarily been to share with her, but without her I would not have been able to acknowledge – much less satisfy – it.

I can't remember how or when, but my confession segued into sex. There is no clear dividing line in my memory between the two. It was all communion – I thought I understood that word more deeply than ever before. I lost myself in my lover and became one with her.

I also can't remember when sex turned into sleep. One moment I was intoxicated by my lover's smells, our smells, the pungency of our bodily secretions . . . the next I was waking up, sweetly serene, to see her eyes scrutinizing my face.

I took her hand and kissed it. "I—"

"Don't say . . . don't say anything. Shh." She placed her fingers over my mouth. Her eyes avoided mine. "Don't."

We had been hugging in silence for a short while when she said, "We should get going. We both have busy days today." I grabbed her wrist and looked at her watch. She knew that my next class was to start in fifty minutes. I prided myself on my punctuality. I would not make my seventy-five students wait.

I found myself irritated that she knew my schedule. I wondered – silently – about her own affairs. What did I know of her? I became ashamed of myself, ashamed at my self-ishness, my egocentrism. Did I ever enquire into her daily grind? Did I ever show any interest in the details that made up her life? I hid that lack of interest under a veneer of sophistica-tion, under the idea that we met not to encumber each other with the boring minutiae of our quotidian routines, but to escape into an oasis of sexual delight. But wasn't all that a petty excuse to forgive myself for the lack of interest I exhibited in my friends and lovers? I was such a peacock. I was embarrassed; I now saw myself as a clumsy, transparent, ridiculous jester. As someone whose relationships didn't matter, didn't mean anything. As someone who didn't matter.

I fled to the bathroom, using the time as a convenient excuse. Any feeling of communion had been shattered. I heard her walk around the apartment, heard the clinking of a belt buckle as she was getting dressed.

"Gotta rush! See you soon!" she shouted from two rooms away. In my agitated, self-engrossed state, I failed to fully register the uncomfortable and distant timbre of her tone. I heard the door open and close.

I focused my mind away from introspection and, instead, on the busy day ahead of me. I washed and dressed in a precise hurry and managed to step into my classroom a few seconds early.

That day was interminable. Illusions had been destroyed, and I was in no shape to deal with the wreckage. I yearned to see her, yet dreaded the prospect. I needed and feared her. Was it brave to stay alone? Was it cowardly to not call her, or anyone? Alone, I could hide from eyes that could penetrate my thin carapace. With a lover, I could lose myself in the waves of erotic fulfillment. No matter what I did, I was hiding.

That evening, I was too restless to read or work. I couldn't find any comfort in music; the familiarity of my record collection irritated me, and the radio was intolerably banal. I ate incessantly, stuffing food – raw vegetables, crackers, baking chocolate . . . whatever I could find – into my mouth continuously as if the slightest respite would allow some unnameable threat to invade my innards.

It was only nine o'clock when I decided to go to bed.

Beforehand, remembering the previous night, I felt compelled to walk to the shelf where rested the memento from my coming-of-age voyage. I stared at the pool of liquid at the bottom of the bottle, dazzled by its luminous effervescence and haunted by ambiguous memories. I tipped the bottle and let the spectacle of liquid and light cascade up and down the sides of the glass. I uncorked the bottle, brought it to my nose and smelled its contents. I was no longer the inexperienced, ignorant youth who had first encountered the liquid years ago.

Nevertheless, I still could not identify the fragrance that escaped from the open bottle.

I closed my eyes and savoured the exotic aroma. My lips caressed the mouth of the bottle as I recalled – with both wonder and unease – how I had come to possess it. The dampness shocked me. I clamped down on the memories and emotions the taste evoked as firmly as I recorked the bottle. I licked the liquid from my lips.

And I suddenly felt awake and vigorous. And aroused. So aroused, it pushed everything else from my mind. So aroused, it hurt. I decided to take a shower and masturbate while enjoying the hot steam.

In the bathroom, I saw him in the mirror. His beautiful face. The subtle, mesmerizing colours running through his hair.

But he was wearing my clothes, was standing where I stood.

I had turned into a doppelganger of the mysterious lover who had left only that bottle behind – exactly as he'd looked all those years ago, when he'd kissed me.

I collapsed, tears storming out of me. And then I felt my head explode and the bathroom vanished around me, to be replaced by—

I am a boy, looking at myself everywhere in the world. I am everyBODY in the world. I gorge on my own flesh, my arm disappearing down my throat. HE is nowhere. I am dancing. There are many of me. I am a boy. I am a girl. I am a man. I am a woman. I am dancing. With each whirl I take off a piece of clothing. The boys, the girls, the men, the women, I, I and I take off my clothes. I and I and I and I have sex. I MAN insert my penis in an anus BOY in a mouth GIRL in a vagina WOMAN. I WOMAN rub my vulva on the stomachs of myself BOYGIRL-MAN lying on the ground. I laugh and cry. I am reading a book. Every page is a mirror. I see myself but I do not look like me. I am handsome. I am beautiful. I am charming. I am elegant. I am strong. I am vulnerable. I am everywhere and it is me. It is my body. I am not me. I am a boy. I look down MY HEAD TURNS AND SPINS and there is a boy licking my anus, but it is not him. It is not me. He looks up at me. Smiling and laughing, laughing and crying. He kisses me. I taste semen in his mouth. I take off my penis and offer it to him. I run. There are many people. None of them are me. None of them are him. They all laugh, but they do not cry. I shout: WHO ARE YOU? WHY ARE YOU NOT HIM? Still, they do not cry. Where is he? The sound of beating wings. I can see myself IT IS NOT THE BODY OF A BOY running, my cloven hooves hitting the pavement, the amber blood coursing through the thick veins bulging from my hairless naked body, the lack of genitals at my crotch, the huge mouth with thick amber lips and big white teeth gaping from my belly, my full breasts covered with thick amber veins bumping against my chest. My head is spinning out of control. I am not him. On the one side, below the ring of eyes crowning my head, a penis and scrotum protrude from my face, flapping around. On the other side, a wet vulva opens deep down into my throat. I cannot cry, no tears will come. I am not a boy. I hear the furious din of beating wings. I do not see him. The black shapes come and smother me THE BODY THAT IS NOT A BOY. There is no sound. Swirling rainbows erupt from the darkness. There are bodies everywhere. Of every shape. I recognize no body.

I woke up with a debilitating headache, having no idea how long I'd slept – if I'd slept at all – profoundly disgusted by my . . . hallucination? . . . nightmare? . . . Whatever that had been. I was terrified by its oppressive self-loathing. And what was I to make of the monstrous hermaphroditic creature "I" had turned into? Cold dread spread through my bones.

I had fallen on the floor, and I could feel how I'd bumped my head and elbows. Reluctantly, I propped myself back up. The mirror told me I was myself again. Not a monster, and not my mysterious lover either.

It was that bottle. That strange liquid was some sort of drug that produced powerful hallucinations. Of course I had never turned into anything or anyone else.

Ignoring my aches and bruises, I stomped to the shelf where I kept the bottle. I picked it up, considered smashing it, or just throwing it away. Instead, I put it in a box in the broom closet, refusing still to deal with it decisively.

I spent the rest of the day dawdling – doing this and that, not really accomplishing anything, distracting myself with little pleasures: listening to favorite records, re-reading cherished stories. In the end, it was another long, dreary day. But I managed to dismiss that frightening vision as nothing more than the result of that awful potion combined with my fragile emotional state.

A few days later, I ran into my young blonde lover at the university; but her eyes avoided mine, and I had to acknowledge what, I suddenly realized, I already knew. Ah well . . . I claimed not to want serious attachments, didn't I? I'd promised her sexual fun and ended up needing emotional comfort.

I broke off all my sexual liaisons and for a year or so mainly kept to myself. I needed that year to redefine my identity, to dig within myself, to discover the tools with which to rebuild myself.

I put the bottle – its contents and its disturbing visions – far from my mind.

I took to solitude rather well. It reminded me of my childhood, when I spent days locked in my bedroom, content with my books.

Eventually, I made new friends, or rather acquaintances. I met no-one significant. I shared lunches, occasionally went out to the theater and such. I surprised myself by staying celibate. My sex drive had simply faded away.

Years passed. I took a position as Associate Professor in my department. The bottle once again receded to a neglected corner of my consciousness.

I was flying to my home town, dreading a family event that I couldn't avoid – a cousin's wedding – when my parents died in a fire. The house burned down – a kitchen accident, the investigators said. The street was sealed off; my cab had to drop me off a block away. It was an impressive, angry blaze. After it had spent its fury, nothing from the house was salvageable. I was told my parents died quickly.

The wedding wasn't postponed. I didn't go.

Mom and Dad had always been so kind to me. Ours had been a peaceful and supportive household. I didn't have a single resentful memory and yet I found myself unable to grieve. Not numb, not sad, not even relieved; just – and I hate to admit this – indifferent.

A year later, I used the money from the estate to buy a new house. I was charmed by the building upon first seeing it. The deal was quickly concluded and within weeks I left my old apartment. I successfully coordinated the ground floor in a few days, making it fully operational and pleasing to inhabit.

The upstairs of the house remained in complete disarray. I had been renovating, organizing, and unpacking for weeks, but I just couldn't seem to make things jell. I was too excited at the prospect of creating this dream space. I wanted to do everything at once, with the enthusiasm of a teenage boy, but the dwindling energy of a man nearing forty. The box now before me had not been opened in years, judging by the brittleness of the packing tape. A box my mother had packed many years ago when I had left my parents' home for university. Despite the mess around me, the pull of curiosity and nostalgia overwhelmed other concerns, and I excitedly tore open the box.

It was filled with books I hadn't seen in years – all books I'd purchased at Lost Pages. They had such sensationalistic titles: *The Transfiguration of Gilgamesh*, *Antediluvian Folktales*, *Intrigues and Scandals of the Lemurian Court*, *The Trickster Among Us*, *City of Saints & Madmen*, *Great Migrations of Extinct Branches of the Genus Homo*, and so forth. Just the kind of thing to excite a lonely boy's imagination. The more scholarly titles on the shelves of Lost Pages, many of which featured names and words – not to mention languages – that were, to me, alien and unrecognizable, had always intimidated me, though the serious young boy I had been would never have admitted it.

Antediluvian Folktales exerted a particular pull on me. Why had I never unpacked these before? They'd lain forgotten for so long. I grabbed the folktale collection, and the shop's distinctive bookmark fell out. Ignoring the huge task before me, I opened the book and started reading. I completed the first half-dozen short tales, and I started remembering when I'd first read the book at age fourteen, in late August, just before school started. And then an image lodged itself in my mind, from a story I now remembered for the first time since then. I flipped through the book impatiently, trying to find a particular passage to confirm my memory. On my fifth or sixth run-through, I found it: ". . . the rich fullness of his wings, the shifting colours of his feathers, the bright sparkle of his scales, the sharpness of his beak . . ." I felt my heart beat anxiously against my chest. I had to take several deep breaths to calm myself down. I returned to the beginning of the tale, "Why We Dream Nightmares."

Long ago, in the time before the Earth had taken the shape of a globe and so night was night and day was day throughout the world, the Shifpan-Shap flew every night, battling nightmares with their mighty weapons. After the sun disappeared over the horizon, the nightmares covered the whole sky with their great number, determined to descend into the dreams of women, men, children and animals. Every night, the Shifpan-Shap fought them to a standstill, never letting a single nightmare break through their ranks. If only one of them entered the realm of dreams, the war would be lost, and nightmares would plague the land of dreams forevermore. In those days, the night sky was pitch black; no stars could shine through the dense darkness of the attacking horde of nightmares. When the morning sun rose on the horizon, the nightmares cowered back into the dark embrace of their creator, Yamesh-Lot, who yearned to rule the land of dreams.

Every morning, the Shifpan-Shap uttered a great cry of victory, mocking the retreating nightmares and rousing humanity and other animals to wakefulness. The Shifpan-Shap then flew back into the city of Shifpan-Ur – the lustre of their green, blue and brown feathers revealed by the morning sun – to rest and prepare for the next night's campaign.

One of the Shifpan-Shap, Behl Jezath, was a proud and fierce warrior. Many of the Shifpan-Shap admired his youthful beauty, and the delights of his body were much coveted. Although Behl Jezath knew the love of many, he had only love for himself. Often he would hover over still water to glance at his reflection. How he admired the rich fullness of his wings, the shifting colours of his feathers, the bright sparkle of his scales, the sharpness of his beak, the smooth girth of his phallus!

Behl Jezath grew older, as all Shifpan-Shap did in those days. His wings became sparser, his scales lost some of their sheen, his beak acquired a certain bluntness and wrinkles appeared on his phallus. Before, his splendid beauty had been so dazzling that it outshone his great vanity. Now that his beauty was dimming, the harsh glare of his pride drove his lovers away.

Embittered, the ageing Shifpan-Sho spent more and more time away from his people. In broad daylight, he flew far from Shifpan-Ur. From high above he spied on the women, men and children that the Green Blue and Brown God had entrusted to the Shifpan-Shap's protection. The lustful eyes of Behl Jezath fell on the young men just old enough not to be called boys. He saw them play with their burgeoning genitals, enjoying themselves and each other.

The Green Blue and Brown God had forbidden the Shifpan-Shap from fornicating with mortal animals, upon punishment of having their wings torn from their backs, but Behl Jezath's lust was overpowering. Day after day he flew high in the sky spying on the young men, lusting after their muscular bodies and their smooth phalluses, tempting himself with this forbidden passion.

One day, Behl Jezath decided to hide behind some trees, near a spot where the young men often gathered for their sex games. He wanted to be close to the young men. He wanted to be able to smell their muskiness and to see their beautiful bodies up close.

The young men came as expected, and the hidden Shifpan-Sho smelled their young manliness and admired their muscular bodies. Their proximity was intoxicating to the old warrior. Behl Jezath took his wrinkled phallus in the palm of his claw and rubbed himself to ejaculation. So intense was his pleasure that his wings unfurled in splendid glory. He uttered a great shrill cry. The young men scattered in fear.

Behl Jezath flew away, back to Shifpan-Ur to rest in preparation for that night's battle with the nightmare legions of Yamesh-Lot. And as he had been doing with increasing frequency, he dreamed of the young men and the sex games he yearned to play with them.

That night, a nightmare embroiled in close combat with Behl Jezath smelled the lingering aroma of his dreams. The nightmare whispered into Behl Jezath's ear and said to the Shifpan-Sho: "Warrior! My master, Yamesh-Lot, can make your dreams come true. Let me go to him now and let us meet again tomorrow night in this very spot. I will bring you the means to fulfill your dreams."

The lust coursing through Behl Jezath's veins was very powerful and he let the nightmare return to its dark master.

The sun rose. The nightmares retreated. The Shifpan-Shap uttered their cry of triumph and returned to Shifpan-Ur to rest in preparation for the next night's battle.

Behl Jezath could not sleep all day, restless with anticipation.

The following night, the nightmare returned as promised, clutching a bottle. The creature whispered in the old warrior's ear: "Let me pass and you can take this bottle, the cornucopia of ambrosia. This drink will transform you into your heart's desire. One sip, and you can disguise yourself as a young human male – or whatever you desire – veiled from the wrath of the Green Blue and Brown God and free to enjoy the bodies of young men. As long as one drop remains, it will forever replenish itself. This bottle is Yamesh-Lot's gift to you, warrior, if you let me pass and enter the realm of dreams."

Behl Jezath replied: "How do I know this is not a trick, nightmare? You could easily be lying in order to win the war for your dark master."

The nightmare immediately answered: "Warrior, I propose a test! Form a clear picture in your mind of your heart's desire, and I will let a drop of the ambrosia fall on your tongue. One drop will transform you only for a short time, but it will be enough for you to believe in the power of this beverage."

Behl Jezath agreed to this test. In his mind's eye, he saw himself as a young Shifpan-Sho with his wings rich and dense, his scales bright as little suns, his phallus smooth and large, for that was his true desire.

The nightmare let a drop fall on the tongue of the ageing Behl Jezath. The Shifpan-Sho felt his wings fill out, he could see his scales glitter even in the darkness of night, and his phallus was restored to its full girth.

He remembered the smell of the young men and his newly-young body was filled with lust for them. Then, the effect of the one drop of ambrosia wore off, and the body of Behl Jezath regained its true age.

The nightmare said: "Well, warrior, that was the effect of only one drop! Are you convinced? Are we agreed?"

Behl Jezath hesitated, but only for a moment. "Yes," he said. "Yes, we are agreed, nightmare."

The next day, the Green Blue and Brown God was furious with the Shifpan-Shap for letting a nightmare into the land of dreams. He punished them by turning them all into immortal skeletons, forever denied all sensual pleasures. When the Green Blue and Brown God meted out his punishment, Behl Jezath was hidden from the god's view. He was disguised as a young man, trying to find other young men with whom to play sex games. However, the young men no longer played sex games amongst themselves. Their new nightmares taught them to fear such things. Frustrated, Behl Jezath flew back to Shifpan-Ur. His punished brethren saw his unspoiled form. They knew then that he had betrayed them to Yamesh-Lot, and they banished him from their midst for all time.

And so it came to pass that Yamesh-Lot won the war over the land of dreams. However, his nightmares no longer covered the night sky and the shining stars were the source of new dreams for humanity, dreams outside the reach of the dark lord.

Trembling slightly, I sat on the floor, silently but nervously pondering this story. After a while, I calmed down again and read the rest of the collection. There were no other references to these characters, to this tale. In an appendix, the author quoted some sources and suggested further reading for each story. "Why We Dream Nightmares" had but one reference: *Ambrosia: The History of a Cornucopia of Transformation.*

I picked up the bookmark, remembering the many hours spent at Lost Pages. I knew I would not find the volume anywhere else. The book was on the shelves of the shop, waiting for me. It had to be.

It would have to wait, I thought. The next few days were filled with engagements from which I could not, in good conscience, extricate myself. I suppose I could have called the bookshop in advance to make sure they had the book, or to ask to have it put aside for me, or to ask to have it delivered to me. But I needed to visit the place once again, to find the book myself.

I knew in which box to find the bottle. I took it out and held it up to my face. The pool of liquid was now several centimetres deep, the bottle nearly half full.

Three days later, tense and anxious, I was on a plane to my home town. The last time I'd been there was to settle the last of my parents' affairs, about eight months ago.

As I had hoped, I found the book at Lost Pages.

Inside the bookshop, I recognized the young boy who had once been the shopkeeper's assistant, now grown up. He appeared now to be running the place with an assistant of his own, a girl in her early teens. I did not attempt to identify myself to him as a long-lost customer. I quickly made my purchase, promising myself to return one day and take the time to enjoy the experience. This short trip was an indulgence my schedule could barely accommodate.

I took a cab to the airport. The terminal was bustling. Long queues writhed in irritated impatience. Indecipherable announcements fizzled from unseen speakers. Porters and travelers crisscrossed the huge room every which way.

A hand brushed against mine. I was aroused by the intensity of that elusive touch. I looked around, in vain, hoping to find the source of this furtive sexual thrill.

Frustrated, I joined the line for my airline and eventually secured a boarding pass. My plane was scheduled to start boarding in fifty minutes. I settled on a bench and savored the anticipation of cracking open my new acquisition, eager to find answers to questions I'd long neglected.

About ten minutes later, I suddenly felt very dizzy, as if all the blood was rushing out of my head. I had to brace myself on my neighbor. At the contact, he turned his head toward me.

His face was beautiful. He now appeared to be about my age, but how could I not recognize the features of the boy who had been the first to kiss me? His greying hair had lost some of its luster, but I thought I could still glimpse a hint of green, blue and brown.

Staring at the bulge in my pants, he laughed. I noticed my conspicuously large erection.

I regained my composure – partly because of the pleasant nostalgia his good humor called up, but also because I recognized the comical nature of my situation. I chuckled, but then a spiky chill tore down my chest.

I knew who he was, now. What he was.

I opened my mouth, ready to . . . interrogate him? Plead with him? Or . . . I never found out what I would have said. He placed two fingers on my mouth, tenderly silencing me. He looked hurt. No. Something else. Some emotion I couldn't grasp. I longed to know him better, to understand his every gesture, his every expression.

He seemed to shrug off that feeling, and he smiled. He gave me a look – of deep compassion, perhaps? It made me feel overwhelmingly lonely.

I realized then how, these past few years, I still hadn't learned to care about anyone. I still protected myself against intimacy. Now, I was overcome by how much I wanted to care about him, care for him. It suddenly seemed so obvious to me that I'd spent all these years trying to recapture the transcendence I'd felt when he'd seduced me and, failing to ever again reach those heights of ecstasy, how I'd shielded myself against my inevitable disappointments.

He clamped his hand behind my neck and gave me a fierce

kiss. He released me, and nodded upwards, silently telling me that I should go. My flight was being called.

I looked into his eyes, but they refused to yield any answers. Stifling tears, I nodded back, got up, walked towards the gate. I didn't look back. I was afraid to see in his eyes the gaze of a stranger. The sound of beating wings drowned out the ambient noise around me. Did I imagine that?

I told myself that it was his wish that I leave.

Two days later, here I am in my house, in this upstairs room that I have yet to organize to my satisfaction. The book, *Ambrosia: The History of a Cornucopia of Transformation*, is closed. I have studiously read every word. I wondered how the author found all that information, and I felt a surge of envy at his ability to uncover so much about my seducer's mysterious life.

The book mentions many of the identities Behl Jezath adopted and speculates on many more. It describes years, centuries, millennia spent in solitude – hiding and fleeing from the pride of his youth and its consequences. It tells of epochs wiped from human memory. It details how his continued life depends on the bottle of ambrosia, the memento of his terrible moment of weakness.

What will happen to him now? Why did he give me the bottle? Why had I been such a coward at the airport? I—

I stare at the bottle. It rests on the little table next to my armchair. The light from the window catches the slowly rising pool of ambrosia. Rainbows dance and swirl, flowing and erupting from the amber fluid.

Tonight, I'll sit on the roof and look at the stars. If it's overcast, I'll close my eyes, feel the chill of the early autumn wind against my cheeks and dream of the furious beating of multicolored wings.

At Long Last

Madeleine Oh

This was it.

As the train slowed, I snapped my novel shut, and pulled my suitcase from between the seats. In a few minutes we'd be face to face after thirty years. Was it curiosity or obsession that had me haring up to Scotland to see the man who'd shattered my twenty-two-year-old heart when he married my cousin, Penelope?

Why was I here? To see how the years had treated Alec? Did I hope he sported a massive beer gut? Sagging jowls? Perhaps recovering from a triple by-pass and double hip replacements? Sitting in a wheelchair pushed around by his brand new trophy wife?

If he looked the same as he had at twenty-five, I'd rail against the injustice in the world. He didn't. But he wasn't the one who recognized me.

"Jasmine Waters! May I call you Jasmine?"

It was Emily, wife number two. One of my faithful readers.

"Of course you may. It's my name."

"But it seems so . . . You being so famous and—"

"You must call me Jasmine. Alec does." She all but blushed. How deliciously English and young she was, like a fat, ripe plum, ready to drop off the branch into my hand.

"He calls you Jazzikins."

He would. He had. Couldn't call me Jazz or Jasmine the way everyone else did. He had to make up a special name that still had the power to tweak my soul. Standing beside her was my old heartache himself. "Hi, Alec."

A man who left his wife with an autistic teenager and a senile mother-in-law had no right to thrive on it. But heaven help us all, he was still gorgeous! His dark hair was half-way gray, but it looked good on him. And as for the laughter lines, where had they come from? From smiling to himself as he walked away from his responsibilities?

"Jazzikins!" His smile was so sincere, I wanted to spit. "Fantastic to see you!"

I held out my hand before he had a chance to even think about hugging me. "Alec. It's good to see you." That wasn't a lie. I was satisfying my curiosity and, to be truthful, he was as easy on the eyes as ever. He still had a smile to invoke impure thoughts in virgins' minds. It had in mine. He'd just never delivered.

"Jazzikins." I restrained a wince. "After all these years." He grabbed my hand and pulled me into a hug before I could evade, planting a great smacky kiss on my left cheek. While I took a deep, cleansing breath, he stepped back, looking me up and down as if contemplating purchase. "I still can't believe it! You're here, and all because of Emmsy. Who'd have thought it?"

Thought what? That I could write? That his wife could read? That he was incapable of using anyone's full name? I made a point of *not* snarling. "How could I not come? Invited to Scotland by a loyal and ardent reader?" He'd better not think I'd spent all day in a train for him. But he did.

"Alec," Emily put a hand on his shoulder. Marking her territory, perhaps? "Let's head for the car. I bet Jasmine wants to kick off her shoes and have a drink."

I decided I might like her, even if she had supplanted my cousin, and hoped her idea of a "drink" entailed something more than a cup of tea. I couldn't help wondering what Alec had told her about me. Was I his ex-wife's cousin, the sister of a school friend, an old, lost love? Most likely, none of the above. Maybe he never remembered breaking my heart.

His dark green Jaguar was an improvement on the 2CV he owned the last time I'd ridden with him. His transport might have changed but his laugh hadn't, neither had his voice, nor the way he drove too fast and slid through lights as they changed. He made a very Alec crack and Emily laughed, throwing her head back a little, shaking her long, chestnut-colored hair and showing the vulnerable expanse of her long, pale neck. I'd always longed for a long neck. Still, I had bigger boobs, but she had Alec.

Did I honestly care now? Come to that, had I ever really been in the running? I'd fallen for him like a felled oak. And got over him, or so I always told myself. I wasn't the type to do unrequited love. But I'd hurt. Standing as bridesmaid at Penelope's wedding was an agony I hoped never to repeat. Now was payback time! Alec owed for breaking my virgin heart, leaving a gaping hole in my cousin's life, and for the handicapped son he'd abandoned. Penelope wouldn't seek revenge. She was far too kind and up to her eyes with providing care. Simon missed his father desperately, Alec's mother was too senile to realize he'd gone, and poor Penelope was ageing daily.

But I was here, and willing, and as we settled in the living room overlooking the garden, I prepared to settle the score. One way or another.

Trouble was, I liked Emily. I could hardly fault her for falling for Alec, I'd done the same when I hadn't been that much younger. And she was a fan. She had every one of my books in hardback, and all but kissed my hands when I gave her an advance copy of the new one. Hard to hate a woman who admires your work and mixes a mean G & T.

By halfway through dinner, I seriously thought about smashing Alec's face into his tiramisu as he pontificated about local politics, the virtues of his new car, and the tremendous responsibilities of his job. How many more "Jazzikins" and "Emmsies" and "old things" was I prepared to endure? It was the last that got to me the worst. He had two years on me and I didn't have gray hair. Thanks science.

Emily was far more tolerant than I. That's what love does to you. But I caught the occasional spark of irritation, and the glances of female complicity she shot my way.

I grinned back as her dark, gray eyes flashed amusement and, when she hugged me for helping load the dishwasher, I squeezed back. Her body was warm and soft and her breasts pressed nicely against mine. She was my height, her body firmer and her breasts higher but we fit together, the old and new loves of Alec Carpenter.

"How's the coffee coming along, girls?" he called from the sitting room. Emily looked ready to give him hot coffee where it hurt.

It was an odd after-dinner conversation. Emily wanted to talk about my books. I was more than happy to oblige. Alec didn't exactly sneer at mysteries but he came darn close. Then he committed the cardinal sin, "How much do you make on a book?"

"Tell me what you earned last year and I'll tell you what I made."

He declined the invitation with an irritating laugh. "Oh. Jazzikins! You've changed."

In more ways than he could guess.

I broke up the evening by pleading weariness. Emily kissed me goodnight with a promise of tea in the morning. Her lips were warm and ripe and young. Hugging her was a joy. I looked forward to my early morning cuppa.

She brought it wearing a short, pink robe with satin rosebuds scattered over the yoke. It suited her, bringing out the highlights in her dark hair. She blushed deliciously when I told her so. Alec had seldom told me that I looked beautiful either. She sat on the edge of my bed and I watched her firm nipples underneath the thin cotton. I'd found my revenge. I just had to find the means.

Alec handed it to me at breakfast.

Emily was annoyed.

I was thrilled.

"Why this weekend? Didn't you tell them you had a visitor?" Emily gave him the closest thing to a pout I'd seen yet.

"Never mind." Time to smooth amicable oil over the marital waters. "If Alec has a crisis at work, he needs to go."

Emily muttered disagreement.

"I knew Jazzikins would understand." I got Alec's best smile and heartfelt regrets. He did both really well. "I feel terrible mucking up your weekend when you've come so far."

"You haven't mucked it up. Emily and I will frolic together in the fleshpots of Aberdeen." Emily's face brightened. Alec glowered. No other word for it. I gave him my sweet smile. "She'll look after me, I'm certain," He looked worried. He should. "You go take care of your crisis. Don't bother about us." I sure wasn't going to bother about him, and if I had my way, neither would Emily.

He streaked off in his Jaguar. Emily and I set out in her little Fiesta. Size was of no importance.

"Take me on the tourist tour," I asked. "Show me the sights and all the bookshops. We can stop somewhere for lunch and somewhere for tea and somewhere for a drink, and if we really feel like it, another somewhere for dinner."

She giggled like a schoolgirl let out of boarding school. We visited the bookshops and had coffee in a dark-paneled café where we sat close in a corner, and she confided in me that Alec worked terribly long hours. She took me to the rose garden and the maze. We got nicely lost and held hands muddling our way out.

She drove to the beach. "It's almost deserted," I said looking at the great crescent of golden sand. "No one's swimming."

"Too damn cold! This is the North Sea."

It wouldn't stop me. "I've got to put a toe in after coming this far."

I left my shoes in the car and ran across the beach. Emily hesitated a few seconds before following me. The tide was out. I zig-zagged over the hard sand, glancing over my shoulder. Emily followed, cutting off corners trying to catch up. I let her, just as we neared the water.

"Chicken?" I teased as I jumped in. Emily hadn't been kidding! An icy wash hit my ankles. She stared. I took a step deeper and held up my skirt.

"Never!" She followed me, and gasped. "This is ridiculous!"

I wouldn't argue. We ran along the water's edge, keeping to the firm sand. My toes were tingling with cold as I out-ran Emily again. The girl was no marathon runner, that was for sure, so I slowed to take her hand and made a beeline for the car.

By the time we got there, my feet were numb and turning red

and my calves stung from salt water and North Sea wind. Emily was shivering. "Alec will never believe we did that!" Her right eye watered from the cold, but she grinned.

"Does he need to know? Do you tell him everything?"

She shook her head. Slowly. "Not everything."

Smart girl.

We wiped our feet on Alec's cricketing sweater. The closely knitted wool warmed our skin as it absorbed the damp and the sand. The sweater was unwearable by the time we were finished. Emily shook her head at it. "He'll throw a wobbly when he sees that."

"Let's save him the worry, then." I took the sand and salt encrusted heap and tossed it toward the beach, the wind caught it momentarily, whipping it higher before it fell, wet and heavy, on the sand.

Emily watched it arc up and fall. I wasn't too sure of the look on her face. Regret? Shock? Worry? Until she smiled. "I doubt he'll miss it until next summer." A wry smile twisted her mouth. She took my hand and squeezed.

I pulled her to me. Slowly. Giving her time to draw back. I wrapped my arms around her and dropped a soft kiss on her forehead. "I'll never tell," I said.

She kissed back, a soft whisper of skin on my chilled lips. The warmth of her breath was lost in the wind but the heat of her body wasn't. We stood, arms entwined, warming each other against the wind. It wasn't enough. Emily shivered.

"We need to get out of the cold," I said, "Where's the nearest place for a drink?"

The all-but-deserted bar of a vast Victorian hotel.

Dark lincrusta covered the walls and the rings of generations of damp glasses marred the oak tables. Emily ran her fingers up and down her glass. I raised my drink and savored the best single-malt whisky the bald-headed bartender had to offer. Watching Emily over the rim of my glass, I drank. The old codger's best was pretty good. I took another taste, holding the whisky in my mouth and working it over my tongue before swallowing.

Emily's manicured nails tapped the side of her glass. She hadn't tasted it beyond a first sip, when I'd proposed our mutual health. "Drink up."

"You want to go home?" Her eyes were dark with unspoken wants.

"I think we both need a nice, hot bath."

Her full lips parted. Slowly lifting her glass, she tilted it and drank half down with one swallow. I expected her to choke and splutter but she just smiled. "That's good." Her glass made a dull thud on the table as I nodded.

"I never settle for less than the best you can have . . . or give," I said. Her hand rested on the table, palm down. I covered it with mine. Her skin was still cold. Emily moved so our fingers meshed. There was no mistaking the look in her eyes. She would appreciate what Alec had refused.

She bit her lower lip with one very, white tooth. "I'm glad Alec is at work."

"So am I." I swigged the last of my whisky almost as fast as Emily did, ignoring the burning as I swallowed.

We were back in the house in minutes and upstairs in seconds. On the landing, with its ornate railings and decorative cornice, I paused. Her room or mine?

She settled that. Emily dragged me into the bathroom. Squeezing my hand, she leaned over the claw-footed tub. Steam rose, misting the gilt-framed mirror as she stood upright, and hesitated.

I didn't. I released her hair from the pale-blue scrunchee. As she shook her head and ran her fingers through her hair, I unbuttoned her blouse.

Did she and Alec share this tub? How hard did he get seeing her firm breasts swelling above her pink lace bra? Did he lust after her young body? Who was I kidding? They were married! They did this every night. Except when he hared off to save the day and left her alone. But Emily wasn't alone now and she hankered for me. Her nipples weren't hard from the cold.

I unsnapped her bra and cupped her breasts. They were round and soft and tender. I pushed aside the lace, slipped the straps and her shirt off her shoulders, and unsnapped her jeans. She wore a pretty lace thong that matched her bra. They ended up together on the floor. Her legs were long, her thighs smooth and her tummy flat. Her breasts hung high and firm with nipples the color of the inside of a Venus shell. I'd looked like that once, back when Alec had rejected me. Now I had crepe thighs and a soft belly but, along with the cellulite, I'd gained experience and I knew what pleased women.

I eased my hands up her flat belly to her breasts and watched her face. My mouth curled with anticipation. Emily smiled back. I didn't wait any longer. Cupping the back of her head with my hand, I pulled her face to mine. I started soft and slow, just a brush of lips on lips but she opened her mouth and swallowed the kiss and my breath. Her lips were moist and as eager as a virgin's. Hell, she most likely was one with a woman. I kissed back, trailing my other hand down between her shoulder blades and holding her steady in my arms.

As I broke off the kiss, I whispered. "Get in the tub." Like a good child, she obeyed. As she stepped in, I couldn't resist skimming my hand over her smooth thigh.

"Are you coming in?" When I nodded, she reached for a bottle and poured fragrant oil into the bath. The room was now filled with lavender-scented steam. I dropped my clothes on the tiled floor and joined her.

Perfumed water rose to our breasts as I sat down. Brits may not have figured out about ice in cold drinks, but they have bath tubs right. As I soaped Emily's breasts with scented foam she closed her eyes, sighing as my fingers trailed lower. I soaped her all over like a child, having her kneel up as I washed between her legs and down her thighs.

After I rinsed her with a damp wash cloth, she washed me with a touch that left me impatient and ready. Damp and heated, we patted each other dry with warm towels that wrapped us from shoulders to knees.

Emily raised her fingers to my face. "Jasmine," she said, her voice tight and her eyes bright with curiosity and need.

"Come on!" I grabbed her hand and led her down the hallway to the room I'd slept in last night.

She tugged me in the opposite direction.

She pulled open the door and pulled me inside. After all these years I was, at long last, ending up in Alec Carpenter's bed.

I grinned as I yanked back the covers and pulled Emily beside me. She tumbled onto her belly and the smooth expanse of her back and lovely curvy butt inspired me. "Don't move! I'll be back in a minute."

I was down the hall to the bathroom and back with a jar of lavender lotion in less time than it takes to tell.

"What are you doing?" Emily asked, looking over her shoulder as I walked through the doorway.

She hadn't moved.

"Pleasuring you." I squeezed out a dobbit of lotion and rubbed my hands together to warm it, before easing my palms across her shoulders and down her back to the curve of her waist. She sighed with pleasure so I reached for the lotion again. I anointed her. Kissing her neck and shoulders as I stroked lotion into her back and arms. Fluttering my tongue on the soft pale skin behind her knees as I massaged her thighs and butt. She went limp under my touch. Lovely. But I didn't want her too loose. I needed her sweating with want as her body arched under me and her eyes blazed her need.

I rested a hand on the curve of her hip and nudged. "Roll over."

Emily didn't need asking twice. She flipped onto her back, giving me an uninterrupted view of her delicious breasts. I ran my tongue up from her rib cage to her nipple and felt her excitement as I worked it between my lips. She gasped as I pulled it into my mouth and let out a slow moan of contentment as I worked my lips to her other nipple.

"Don't stop," she whispered as I pulled away.

"I won't," I promised.

I could smell her arousal over the scent of lavender, but I took my time, running my fingertips over her curves and tasting her skin. As I rested my hand on her bush, she was whimpering with need. I spread her legs with my shoulders and opened her with my fingertips, reveling in the scent of her sex. Gently I breathed on her moist flesh, and ran the tip of my tongue from fore to aft. Her head came off the pillow with a jolt, and the eyes that met mine were as wide as her cunt.

"Jasmine!" It came out on the tail of a gasp. "There? No one ever . . .!"

Can't say I was surprised. Alec always was a selfish bastard but. . . . "Shhh." I didn't say anything else. My tongue was busy.

She was sweet and fresh as morning and as ready as sunrise.
I'd hoped to take longer but in minutes she climaxed with a
series of little cries and frenzied jerks as frantic hands grasped
my hair.

She was still gasping, her breasts rising and falling with each
pant as I eased up the bed and took her face in both hands. I
kissed her very gently, letting my lips linger before opening her
mouth so she could taste the joy I'd given her. She was halfway to fainting when I let her go. I settled for gathering her
close, delighting in her warmth and scent and, I have to be
truthful here, thrilled that I'd upstaged Alec.

Nasty of me. Bitchy of me. But in the circumstances . . .

"Jasmine?"

"Yes?" I smiled at her as I ran my hand over her hair.

"You haven't come?"

I shook my head. It could wait. I was enjoying a different
satisfaction.

Emily disagreed. Propping herself on one elbow, she bent
her head to my breast and carefully worked her way down.
When she reached my cunt, she delved in with the enthusiasm
and ardor of a convert. I came three times before she finally
paused and I insisted we take a nap. She might not need a rest
at her age, but I did.

We slept the day and night around, waking as the early sun
streamed in through the open curtains.

After a slow morning loving, Emily lent me Alec's toweling
robe to eat breakfast in. We sat in the bay window, sipping
coffee and spreading butter and tart Seville marmalade on
butteries. These were heavy, fatty pastries I'd have disliked in
anyone else's company but now they tasted of Emily.

We were debating the wisdom of more coffee or back to bed
when Alec walked in, clothes rumpled, hair on end and eyes
red from lack of sleep. I was scared he'd smell the sex on us,
but all he seemed to notice was food. Muttering a couple of
sentences about idiot crews who don't maintain equipment
properly, he wolfed down the remaining four butteries, and the
better part of the second pot of coffee that nice wife Emily
fixed. Seemed Alec had not enjoyed the past twenty-four hours
as much as his wife and I had. He wobbled off to bed to restore

himself, so that put paid to an encore. But there were other times. I was a patient woman.

"So glad you two get on so well together," Alec said that evening as we walked down the platform to my sleeper. "Some people have been unbelievably snooty. Peter hardly talks to me now."

Can't say I blamed Peter. He was bound to take his sister's part. Heaven help me! Had I really loved this man? He was so self-centered, patronizing and just plain thick! I had, once, when I was young and equally thick but now I was well and truly cured.

"Nice of you to ask Emmsy to your book signing in Edinburgh," Alec went on, as I hugged her goodbye.

"It'll be nice to see someone I know." I gave a wave and hopped on the train. "I'll let you know the date." Something good had come out of the hurt of Alec Carpenter. I was going to insist my publisher added Edinburgh to my next book tour. They wouldn't need to provide any escort. I could arrange that. I settled back in my seat. I was a trifle torn, between genuine fondness for Emily and our promising affair, and the thought that Penelope might get a kick out of knowing I'd made Alec a cuckold. And the fool would never know.

Underneath Your Clothes

Elizabeth Coldwell

I only noticed it because I dropped my pen. Otherwise I would
have never known there was a secret life being lived so close to
me. As I scribbled notes on the draft report that had been left
in my in-tray for approval that morning, the red ballpoint
slipped from my grasp and I had to go crawling under the desk
to retrieve it. It was as I was beginning to shuffle out backward,
knowing there was no dignity in the view this presented but not
wishing to bang my head on the underside of the desk, that the
pair of legs directly in my eyeline crossed at the ankles and I
caught, for the briefest of moments, a flash of something
utterly unexpected. Where I would have expected to see bare
white skin above the top of the short charcoal-grey sock, I saw
instead a smooth expanse of sheer black nylon. The legs were
under the desk opposite mine. Michael's desk.

I shook my head, convinced I must have bumped it without
realizing. There was no way I could have seen what I thought
I'd just seen. Michael played a lot of squash; he must have
damaged his ankle and be wearing some kind of support
bandage. Yeah, right, if they'd started making support bandages in ten-denier nylon. But not Michael Hodgson: not our
project leader; the quietest, straightest man in the department.
There were other men in the company who I could quite easily
believe might indulge their feminine side at work, like Johnny
in the marketing department, with his glossy, shoulder-length
blond hair and pouting, almost girlish features, but not
Michael.

But then, how much did we really know about him? After all,
he had only joined the department a month or so earlier, to

oversee and troubleshoot when the project had started running over budget. Janice, the departmental secretary, had subjected him to a prolonged bout of questioning when she had noticed the absence of framed family portraits on his desk, but all she had managed to find out was that he was in his early thirties, had joined the company five years earlier, and was single. It wasn't that Michael was unfriendly; he was happy enough to chat about something superficial during coffee breaks. He just seemed to feel that, as he was only going to be working with us for a matter of weeks, it was no basis for making permanent relationships.

I knew part of the reason Janice was being so nosy; I was single, too, and she was checking him out, none too subtly, on my behalf. She couldn't understand that I was quite happy being on my own – I needed time and space after Greg had walked out on me so suddenly – and she definitely didn't share my view that it was never a good idea to start an office romance. I had seen too many of those go sour in my time to want to make that mistake.

I had to admit, though, that the thought of Michael in tights intrigued me. He was certainly my type – I've always had a weakness for men with green eyes and toffee-colored hair – but it went deeper than that, tapping into fantasies I'd had for a very long time. Fantasies I had never dared to share with any of my boyfriends. If I had ever suggested to Greg that I might want to see him in my lingerie, that picturing him in stockings, his hard cock straining against a pair of silky panties, was enough to get me wet, he would have left me a damn sight sooner than he did. As far as I was concerned, dressing like that wouldn't have made him any less of a man; it would have made him more horny, more desirable. But he would never have understood that, and I would never have been able to explain.

I said nothing to indicate I had seen anything the least unusual under Michael's desk, but that night I lay in bed and gently frigged my pussy to the image of a handsome, green-eyed man with long, tights-clad legs and a hugely erect cock. A cock that I touched and licked through the thin film of nylon that covered it, till he groaned and his come oozed through the fine mesh, onto my greedy, sucking tongue . . .

And it would have stayed as nothing more than an image if Michael hadn't accepted an invitation to Janice's birthday drink. I'm sure he would have turned it down and quietly slipped away after work on Friday night like he usually did if it hadn't coincided with his last day in the department. We had finally put the project to bed, and even Michael was in the mood to celebrate.

The pool table was unoccupied when we walked into the White Lion, and that's when we knew it was going to be a good night. Eddie went straight over and placed a row of coins on the table's edge, making it ours for the next hour or so. Normally, it had already been claimed by the lads from the building site across the road – the White Lion was the only establishment in the area that tolerated their work boots and site clothing – but tonight they were nowhere to be seen. We liked the pub for the same reasons they did; it was more relaxed, less of a yuppie pick-up joint than the wine bars and pavement cafés that catered to the after-work crowd who spilled out of the waterside office blocks. And even if we were still dressed in our double-breasted, skirt-suited corporate armor, at least we could take off our jackets, unbutton a few buttons and have a good time, knowing we were unlikely to bump into any of the company's big bosses or, worse, their gossipy PAs.

While Eddie was racking up the pool balls, Michael took a contribution from the rest of us and went to the bar, returning with a couple of bottles of champagne and half a dozen glasses. Janice was slotting money into the jukebox, punching in the numbers of her favorite slow, raunchy rock songs. The look in her eye told me she was planning on drinking too much, flirting too much, and trying to entice one of the boys to go home with her. She usually succeeded; even though she was never looking for more than a one-night stand, there was no one who could resist the combination of her generous cleavage and sultry, smoky voice. Except perhaps Michael.

It was Janice's idea to divide the six of us into male/female teams: herself and Eddie, Louise and Tim, Michael and me. I couldn't decide whether she was still trying to set up the two of us, but I was happy enough with the plan, particularly when

Michael, quickly realizing just how useless I was at pool, decided to give me an impromptu lesson. Standing so close behind me I could feel the warmth of his body pressed against my own, he took hold of my hands and directed them into place on the cue. But as he helped me line up my shot, all I could think of was that glimpse of sheer nylon. Was he dressed like that now? I wondered, barely managing to drag my attention back to the cue ball. With his help, I somehow sunk the shot, but we still lost the game quite easily, leaving the remaining two couples to take each other on.

I found myself studying Michael as he poured the remnants of the second bottle of champagne into all the glasses on the table. With his tie off and his normally neat hair ruffled up, he looked unbelievably gorgeous, and I knew that if I didn't do something, in a couple of hours he would walk out of this pub and, in all probability, out of my life. I couldn't let him go without telling him I knew about his little secret, and just how much it turned me on. Alcohol made me bold and loosened my tongue. The words spilled out of my mouth before I could stop them. "So tell me, Michael, are they stockings or tights?"

Any other man might have thought I was speculating about Janice as she bent over the pool table, her skirt riding so high that if she was wearing stockings, their tops were dangerously close to coming into view. But Michael knew immediately what I meant; his face went pale as he said, tight-lipped, "How did you find out?"

"I dropped my pen," I told him. "I had to go under the desk to get it back – and that's when I saw them."

"And what are you going to tell everyone when I go back to head office?" he said. "That I'm a pervert, a freak? Janice will love spreading that juicy little piece of scandal when she finds out." He broke off as Tim wandered over, clutching more champagne.

"Anyone for a refill?" he asked, sloshing more drink into our glasses without giving us a chance to refuse. Not that I would have refused; I needed as much Dutch courage as I could handle if I was going to get out of this situation without making a complete fool of myself.

I took a deep breath. "She's not going to find out, because

I'm not going to tell anyone anything," I said. "And if you want the truth, I don't think what you do is freaky or perverted. If you must know, it makes me really horny."

There was a long moment's silence, compounded by the song on the jukebox coming to an end. Now I definitely had blown it. I reached for my handbag. "Maybe I should just wish Janice a happy birthday and go."

Michael put his hand on my arm. "Don't go, Lorna. Repeat what you just said."

Knowing I had nothing to lose, I said, "What, that the thought of you wearing stockings, tights, whatever they are, makes me horny?

He drained the rest of his champagne in one gulp. "You can't know how long I've waited for someone to say that to me. It's always felt like this dirty little secret I've been carrying around, ever since the first time I tried on a pair of my sister's old tights. Don't get me wrong, Lorna, I don't go the whole hog. I don't wear dresses and I don't spend the weekends as Michelle, or anything like that. And I'm not gay. I just like the feel of nylon against my skin."

"You've got them on now, haven't you?" I said, praying I was right.

He nodded, and I felt a rush of liquid heat to my pussy.

"I want to see them," I told him.

"What, here?" he asked.

"No. Preferably at my place, and preferably with you wearing absolutely nothing else." This wasn't me talking, this was the champagne, but I still knew I meant every word of what I was saying.

"Okay, let's go," he said.

At that moment, Janice wandered over, slightly unsteadily. Her face was flushed and beaming, and her blouse was open far enough to reveal the tops of her plump, freckled breasts, cradled in a white lace push-up bra.

"Are you having a good time?" she asked. "Because I'm having a fucking fantastic time!" She lowered her head to mine, trying to be discreet, but the amount of alcohol she'd drunk had taken her way past discretion, and her voice was loud enough to carry across the room. "Do you think Eddie's fit, Lorna? I think he's really fit. He's got a great arse when he bends over to line up a shot."

I smiled indulgently at her and then glanced across at Michael, wondering how we could best make our excuses and leave before one or both of us lost the courage to act on our erotic impulses.

Janice seemed oblivious to the looks that were passing between Michael and me. "You know, I've always had a fantasy about getting fucked on a pool table," she slurred.

Most women I knew had; it seemed almost compulsory, like fantasizing about being fucked by a fireman, or inviting your boyfriend's handsome best friend to join you in a threesome. I knew exactly how she pictured herself; splayed over the table, her hands gripping the edges; skirt up and panties off, while Eddie ploughed into her from behind. Her imagination would no doubt add the cheering audience, the encouragement for her lover to get her big tits out on display, or slip his cock into her arse. It was a horny image, but it wasn't my idea of a good time. My fantasies took me to a darker, stranger place and now I had found a man who shared them, I was eager to make them a reality.

"Well, why don't you ask Eddie nicely, and see what he says?" I suggested. I got to my feet and gave her a gentle peck on the cheek. "Enjoy the rest of your birthday, Jan. Michael and I have had a good evening, but we really should be off."

As we made our way to the door, I wondered how long it would take Janice to twig that we were leaving together, or whether she was too wrapped up in her own fantasies to realize. We stepped into the frosty night air just in time to see the friendliest sight in the world: a sleek, black cab coming down the street with its "FOR HIRE" sign blazing. We hailed it, and when it slowed to a stop, the driver pulled down the window and I gave him my address.

The cab sped through the city streets, almost deserted now that the offices and the shops that relied on them for trade were shut for the weekend. Michael and I sat close together, his hand resting lightly on my stomach as I leaned into his body. There wasn't enough light for me to see the gap between the cuff of his trouser leg and the top of his sock, but I knew that if

I could, I would have a glimpse of sheer nylon. The thought, combined with the feel of Michael's fingers stroking me almost absentmindedly, was enough to keep me wet all the way to my flat.

The mechanics of paying the cab fare, stumbling up the stairs to the second floor, and turning the key in the lock seemed to happen without my being aware of them. I was on autopilot, heading for the bedroom and almost dragging Michael with me.

"Slow down, Lorna," he said in an amused tone, but I could tell he was just as impatient as I was.

I threw myself onto the bed, kicking off my shoes. Lust and hunger pulsed through my veins. "Strip for me," I ordered him, my voice steady and confident. As Michael shrugged off his jacket and then turned his attention to unbuttoning his shirt, I rucked up my skirt, spread my legs, and began to touch myself lazily through the gusset of my panties. His eyes seemed riveted at the sight as his shirt joined his jacket on the floor. Shoes and socks followed, and then he was reaching for the belt of his trousers. I wanted to slip my finger into my panties and stroke my clit directly, but that would take me too close, too soon, and I wanted to truly savor the sight with which I hoped Michael was about to present me.

As his trousers slithered to the floor, my breath caught in my throat. This was every hot, dirty fantasy I had ever had come to life. My eyes trailed upward from the crumpled garment pooled around his ankles. The fine, blond hairs on his legs were almost invisible beneath mesh of a denier much finer than I could usually wear without laddering, but that wasn't what drew my attention. Michael wore no underwear, and the tights, sheer to his waist, clung to his already erect penis and balls. His excitement was evident, dampening the nylon in a halo around the head of his cock. It was a beautiful, magnificent vision, more erotic than anything I had seen in my entire life.

Now that I had what I had dreamed of for so long, my self-assurance seemed to melt away. Need made me weak, robbed me of the ability to speak. In the end, I just opened my arms and beckoned Michael onto the bed with me.

Our mouths met, wet and hungry, and we kissed as our

hands roamed over the other's body. Michael was tugging at the buttons on my blouse, almost popping them in his eagerness to undress me. I, in return, was stroking the long contours of his back before my hands settled on their real prize; his muscular buttocks, wrapped in their delicate second skin.

Stripped of my blouse and bra, I was aware of Michael's hands cupping my small breasts, thumbs rubbing my nipples till they peaked. But at that moment, my pleasure seemed like it could wait. Like an excited kid on Christmas morning, all that mattered to me was playing with the beautiful present, wrapped in tights, that knelt before me.

Kids, though, always want to tear the wrapper off in their haste to get to the goodies inside. Not me: as far as I was concerned, the wrapping was the present, just as much as the gorgeous, erect cock concealed beneath it. I touched Michael's cock through the nylon, skimming along its length with light, spidery strokes that made him moan. The soft hairs of his balls prickled through the fabric as I caressed those, too. And then I bent my head and did what I had done in my fantasies; I began to lick his thighs, my tongue moving ever closer to the hot, throbbing length of flesh that waited between them. I could taste salt on his skin, smell the muskiness of his genitals, trapped and magnified by the artificial fibers of his tights. I could have breathed in that scent forever.

The nylon was turning slick and wet as I mouthed it, my saliva mixing with the juice that leaked from the tip of his cock, but I would have happily kept licking him until he climaxed. Michael, however, had other ideas.

"Lorna, I want to come inside you," he said urgently. He reached for the waistband of the tights, about to pull them down, but I caught hold of his hands and shook my head.

Using a fingernail, I carefully poked a hole, close to the seam that ran between his legs. Grinning at a surprised Michael, I ripped downward until there was enough room to pull his cock through and out into my eager clutches.

I quickly removed my skirt and panties, leaving on only my hold-up stockings, and then I clambered over Michael, straddling him. Grasping his cock firmly, I placed it at the entrance to my pussy and lowered myself, taking him inside me inch by inch. My eyes never left his as I began to move, rising and falling slowly. He reached up and played with my nipples as I rode him. Our nylon-clad thighs slithered together, and I could feel the material at his crotch rubbing against my pussy lips every time our groins made contact.

It was all too much for both of us. He was groaning and bucking his hips frantically; I snaked a hand between our bodies and quickly rubbed my clit, feeling the spasms of orgasm starting to pulse through my sex. Michael cried out, and I knew he was coming. The tension that had been building within my body suddenly broke, and I followed him.

I slumped forward onto his heaving, sweaty chest. His hands stroked along my back as our breathing slowed.

"I'm sorry I ruined your tights," I murmured.

"That's okay," he replied. "You'll just have to buy me some more – as long as you promise to ruin those, too."

"Don't worry, I intend to," I said, feeling his cock begin to stir beneath me again. "In fact, if you're interested, there's a supermarket round the corner that stays open all night – and I do believe they sell their tights in packets of five . . ."

Meat and Potatoes

Geoff Cordner

Eddie moved into a squalid little single on Gardner just below Sunset, straight down the street from the Guitar Center and around the corner from Rock'n'Roll Ralph's. His wife called him from Vienna the day he moved in. He didn't even know his number yet, so he couldn't figure out how she got it.

"Hi, Eddie?"

"Alicia! How are you? Where are you?"

"I'm in Vienna, Eddie," she said. "I'm good." She paused. "I'm really sorry about your mother." Her voice sounded like it always did, hesitant, soft, and repentant. She was taking a long time between sentences.

"Eddie, you gotta minute?"

"Yeah."

"I got your letters, Eddie."

"Yeah?"

"Well, it's kinda hard for me to say this, but I've been thinking . . ."

A long silence.

"Eddie," she said in that soft, repentant voice. "I hate you. I really hate you. And I just wanted you to know that."

A week later, Eddie met Lisa. Lisa was a meat and potatoes kinda gal. A big-boned, heavy-breasted blonde; she looked like a farm girl version of a Ralph Lauren model; she had a solidity that those models don't; she had muscles, she was sharp, but hers weren't patrician angles. She and Eddie had nothing in common but sexual attraction.

It was meat and potatoes sex. She'd show up, they'd buy some beer, they'd fuck, they'd order in Thai food from Pink

Pepper, they'd fuck again. When they were both too tired, she'd leave. They never went out, they never rented a video. They never really even had a conversation. They just drank beer, ate Thai food and fucked. She always paid for the beer and the food. Eddie marveled at how nonchalantly she'd take cash advances at the Seven–Eleven ATM. He couldn't even afford the $2 surcharge.

He had three pieces of furniture in his apartment. He had a mattress, a TV, and the Sophia Loren set. He found the mattress in a dumpster behind the Veterans of Foreign Wars Thrift Shop in Glendale, kinda near the old house he lived in for a month with his first wife before she threw him out. He got the TV in trade from North Hollywood Bud, who didn't have any money but had a lot of TVs. The Sophia Loren set came from Out of the Closet Thrift Store on Fairfax, and as far as Eddie could tell it wasn't a set at all since none of the pieces matched, but the weird Russian Queen refused to sell them separately. The Queen kept waving his arms around in a dramatic fashion while sputtering out an impassioned monologue in some language Eddie was pretty sure wasn't English, and the only thing Eddie could understand was "Sophia Loren, Sophia Loren, Sophia Loren", who seemed to somehow be at the center of this incomprehensible torrent of words. Besides his car, the only other thing he owned was a spare car door. He'd bought a '63 Dart from Nicky, who'd once played drums for the Cramps, and Nicky insisted on giving him a spare door, just in case. Most people had a spare tire, but not Eddie. He got stuck with a spare door. He didn't even know how to change a fuckin' door for Chrissakes. The door was in the kitchen, propped against the stove.

As far as Eddie could figure, he'd come back to LA to die. He hadn't wanted to come back to LA and he didn't want to die, but that's just the way it was. He felt totally ripped off. His mother had just died, and with her went the past. It didn't sound like Alicia was coming back, and with her went the future. Eddie had an unconventional notion of time. The way he figured, the future had already happened; it just hadn't happened yet, and so that bitch Alicia had stolen something that was rightfully his. The present was nothing – just a bridge between what had already happened and what hadn't happened yet. The present was nothing, and suddenly that was all he had – nothing – stuck on a fucking bridge from nowhere to nowhere.

"I hate you Eddie. I hate you. I just wanted you to know that." That fucking bitch, that soft voiced, hesitant, repentant bitch. She and God had fucked him. Fucked him. This was desperate shit. It was fucking sad what they'd done to him.

Eddie didn't fuck Lisa. She fucked him. And that was okay. The way things were, getting fucked was pretty much what Eddie did. He was used to it. His role in life was just to lay there and take it. At least he enjoyed getting taken by her.

Eddie couldn't start drinking until three in the afternoon, and this was starting to give him trouble. The reason he couldn't start drinking until three in the afternoon was not because he couldn't afford it, although he really couldn't afford it, but because of the whore. The liquor store was on Sunset, all the hookers lined the sidewalk looking for some business lunch action, and there was this one whore on the corner, next to Resurrection Guitars; she looked about 18 tops, but a worn out 18, tottering around on her high heels with a desperate jones, somehow managing to look funereal in skintight fluorescent lycra. "She's on loan from the dead," Eddie thought to himself, "just like I am," and he'd shudder.

Right about noon he was about to enter the liquor store, looked behind him and saw the whore on her corner underneath the Resurrection sign. This guy walked by with a puppy, and she squatted down and started playing with it; the puppy jumped up and licked her face, and she came back to life, became the little girl she should've been, she was alive, her flesh had color, she was happy, she laughed, she was youth, it was achingly beautiful. Eddie stood there slack-jawed; he felt a yearning surge of hope. And then the guy tugged the leash and pulled the dog away and that tug of the leash robbed her of everything she had left. She stood and she sagged and she withdrew into herself with a psychic death rattle that swelled into a monstrous pulse of raw desperation; Eddie could see it surging across the street and down the block, straight toward him. "Oh fuck," he said, "Oh shit! Jesus fuck! Shit!" His eyes were popping outta his head. He barely ducked into the liquor store in time. He struggled to regain his fake cool, bought a six-pack, strolled into the back parking lot as quickly as he could and guzzled one down just outside the door. Whatever it was that just happened was too fucking close for comfort. Eddie was sure he'd barely escaped death. Now he had to stay inside until the whore was gone, no matter how bad it hurt. She was death.

He was still kinda shaky when Lisa came over.

It was meat and potatoes sex. She was the meat and potatoes and he was the plate. She'd push him on his back, grab his head and mount it. There was no seduction. She always had coarse stubble – everything about her was coarse, even her beauty, and she really was beautiful. His face would get abraded. She'd grind and push and rub and grind and push and after a while she'd come with a grunt and a gasp and a hard sudden thrust, and after the second or third time he figured out to push forward on her ass at the crucial moment so that his nose would slide into the wet softness of flesh and not be smashed by the stubbly hardness of bone. Her substantial clit would slide down the bridge of his nose, which would end up deep inside her; he'd feel engulfed, and she seemed to like that.

He couldn't sleep without being fucked. He'd doze off for a few hours and then wake up in a pool of cold sweat. The sheets would be soaked, the mattress he pulled from a dumpster behind the Veterans of Foreign Wars Thrift Shop in Glendale would be soaked, it smelled bad, and in the morning he'd drag it onto the back porch and let it air out and dry in the sun. He was too depressed to eat and he couldn't afford to anyhow; what little money was left over after buying beer was needed to wash the sheets again before Lisa came over.

The mornings were getting harder. He couldn't summon up any of the anger that used to get him out of bed. The anger used to fuel him, and the alcohol was the oil that kept the shit from seizing, but Eddie wasn't very fuel-efficient any more; he was running on fumes, he was burning oil.

He relied on her for everything. He didn't even like her. He thought she was vulgar. Her breasts were too big. He wasn't really into blondes – he thought they had no class. But she brought him food and beer and fucked him, and he needed that. "Oh man, I hope I'm not falling in love. She's so not my type." Lisa was his sustenance.

He always thought of her in terms of food. She had a substantial clit that would swell up in his mouth. He preferred to think of it as one of those baby carrots because he was more or less a vegetarian, but in his mouth it was a little piece of meat. She would thrust it in there. He could almost give her a little blowjob. She would fuck his face. He'd get stubble burn.

Eddie didn't believe in God, and was starting to hate Him too. Eddie sat on the floor of his apartment, rolled in a ball, rocking back and forth, bloodshot eyes all bugged out, arms wrapped tight around his knees, pouring sweat, gazing up at the ceiling, beyond which were the Heavens, and mutter "Chickenshit asshole." He wanted to scream "FUCK YOU GOD!" but didn't for fear of drawing attention to himself. It was too embarrassing. The Marshal had been by two nights ago with eviction papers. She seemed almost apologetic when she handed them to him, and Eddie was grateful for that. It wasn't her fault, she was just doing her job and he was just doing his, getting fucked up the ass by life. It was the fault of his landlady. Fat ass bitch. She was just bitter because she couldn't get laid. Bitter fat ass man hating bitches. More of God's handiwork. And of all the guys in town, she had to take it out on him, probably because he was an easy target. He'd already decided he wouldn't fuck her even if his life depended on it. "I have principles," he said to the TV, and then muttered "Not that they're doin' me any good." He rolled his eyes to the ceiling. "Cocksucker."

She'd sit on his cock, he'd feel the heavy flesh and the hair stubble and get hard, she'd smirk and stuff him inside her and start pounding. She'd lean forward, dig her fingers hard into his shoulders or biceps or pin his wrists, her blonde hair covering all of her face but her open mouth, gasping, intent, sweat would roll down her face, sometimes she'd catch the drops with her tongue, or they'd drop onto his face or chest or slide down between her heavy breasts; it was a hot summer and she'd be soaked, her hair would be wet and if she tossed her head back drops of sweat would fly across the room. She'd pound and push and grind and then come with a grunt and a gasp and a hard sudden thrust. She'd lean forward and kiss him with her sweat-soaked mouth, and her sweat-soaked breasts would rub against his chest, and then maybe she'd slide forward, he'd pop out of her, she'd sit heavily on his stomach or chest, take a long slug of beer, look down at him and smile.

Here's what God should've done. He should've taken Eddie aside and admitted he'd fucked up. He should've said "Eddie, all that church crap? All that turning the other cheek, do unto others, that shit? Forget about it. I was young and that was just wishful thinking." Eddie would've nodded, because it made perfect sense, and because, hey, God was speaking and you gotta listen. "Eddie, forget about doing good, standing up for what you believe in, what's right and just. I fucked up. That shit will get you nowhere. You gotta sell out hard and fast, Eddie. What you gotta do is this: drink, shoot dope, lie, steal, fuck your best friend's wife up the ass and make him watch while she squeals and begs for more, make him call you Sir and thank you and suck your cock clean when you're done. Enjoy using it while it's there and leave before it's gone." But God never sat Eddie down for this little man-to-man, and Eddie wound up being the guy sucking his wife's shit off someone else's cock, metaphorically speaking, so far. What very little dregs of anger and hate he could muster he directed at God. "Chickenshit asshole," he muttered.

Pounding away, she seemed completely absorbed in her own pleasure, but she knew just when to ease off, slow down, slide long and slow so that he could feel the stubble rub against the head and then the shaft of his cock on the downstroke, and always, always the grunt and the gasp and the hard thrust down, beefy bone and stubble slamming against him, jamming him as deep inside her as she could pull him, and then a muscular vaginal squeeze that held him hard and fast and he'd come. She was milking him. She was a farm girl. And then she'd sit there, sweat-soaked and heavy, look down at him, take a slug of beer and smirk while he twitched and shuddered beneath her.

Eddie sat on the floor rocking back and forth. He'd glance at the ceiling, mutter "fuck you," glance at the clock to see if the whore was still there, 10 minutes since he'd last checked, two hours to go, glance at the damp wad of beer money, and then rock some more.

She was a meat and potatoes fuck. Nothing fancy, but all he had for sustenance. She brought him food, she brought him liquor, she took him inside her and pounded him until she was nearly satisfied and he was nearly spent and then with a grunt and a gasp and a hard thrust, she'd suck him deep inside her meaty sanctuary and consume him.

Eyewash

Michèle Larue

The three of us sat on the back seat of an Ambassador, bumping along the road from Madras. Our reward was to be Mysore, where the Indian driver ultimately set us down. One of my friends, big-boned and Irish, led us into the first hotel that came along, the Sapphire, next to the bus station. Corrupted by Indian fatalism, we let her make all the decisions. At dawn, the bus drivers tested their engines beneath our windows before venturing out on to the streets. Kate, the Scot, lit her first *Beedee*. Our skin was oily, our hair lusterless, we were haggard and marked from the road. We needed to move upmarket.

Built for some British Vice-Consul, the Lalitha Mahal Palace was the best in town. In a dining room done up in the manner of English pastries, Kate began finding fault with the waiters' baggy trousers. She came from a family of penniless aristocrats and had latched on to the Irish Laura, who didn't seem to mind paying her way. They both had the same scapegoat: the English. Kate was into females, but Laura paid no attention to her overtures, she was a man-eater who couldn't go three days without a fuck. Whenever sex was in short supply, she had a change of personality.

Then the bonze came in and our laughter froze on our lips. Athletic-looking, holding his shaved head high, he looked the diners over with mischievous eyes as he strode to a tableful of Americans. A childlike shoulder protruded from his saffron robe. Kate and Laura commented on his physique and asked my opinion.

With tears in their eyes from the spicy food, they went over the games they might play at his expense. Kate would lift the sacred robe with her teeth – "100 per cent cotton, soaked in musk!" – Laura would tickle him with the feather tips of her earrings – "Only ten quid at Harrod's, darling" – and finish with his bare feet, so appetizing in those sandals, with their well-cared-for toes. Then together, they would lick his buttocks – "Butterscotch, dearie, but zero calories." The texture of his skin was anybody's guess.

The program included exploring his anus with a finger, and Laura held out the copper-green nails she stuck on with Crazy Glue. Kate would make comments on the boy's expressions while Laura burrowed into him with her ring finger. Would he keep that serene expression that they both envied so much? One thing would lead to another and the next vile act would be tasting his anus. They would suck their greedy fingers right under the bonze's nose, and soon a makeshift dildo would take their place, such as the penlight bulging through Laura's pants pocket.

They finally decided on a banana; Kate would stick it in, but which orifice? They argued. First the mouth, to get it wet. No, no, the asshole first, "It's so much more humiliating, dearie!"

My religious sensibility kept me from taking part in this deluge of pornography. Whenever one of them sought my approval, I would answer with a cowardly nod. To keep the fantasy alive, Kate kept ordering fresh pots of tea from the waiter. Beyond the range of their cocky voices, the living statue shone forth.

Later I learned that the monk lived in a nearby camp of Tibetans. He was a political messenger, pleading the refugees' cause to foreign benefactors. Kate led the way out of the restaurant and managed to touch the saffron robe. A flicker of amusement lit up the lama's pupils. Surely that dazzling sparkle was meant for me . . .

Out in the street, I put my hallucination down to collective hysteria. Kate resolved not to wash her hands for the rest of the day.

En route for Blue Valley, we passed an elephant with her baby, then a busload of Japanese. An Indian army colonel was waiting for us on a wildlife preserve, in the middle of the unspoiled savannah of my dreams. The camp included a few permanent bungalows. During dinner, an officer wearing a blazer jacket told us of the elephants' mating season and their sexual excitement, the *musth*, when they trampled everything in their path. Late that night, in spite of the fire in a ditch, a troop of them destroyed the lamps outside and beat on the walls of our bedrooms with their trunks.

The next part of my dream materialized the next day. Perched on the back of a tame elephant, I photographed wild animals in their natural state; on the other hand, the idea of wild beasts terrified my two friends and they kept to the camp day after day. There was a private courtyard, safe from prying eyes, where they could strip to sunbathe. In the end, they got an urge for colonial nostalgia, just like their English "enemies," and set off for Oloon, a tea-growing town in the hills. After a week of safari I'd had my fill of bears and buffaloes, and set out for Mysore, where we were to join up again.

The windows of my hotel looked out on a ruined palace in an unattended park. By noon, the heat was stifling and I went for a swim at the Lalitha Mahal Palace. Feeling relaxed from the pool, with my hair still wet, I glimpsed a saffron robe going round a hallway turning. I met my rickshaw driver at the entrance. As we drove slowly over the dry lawns, the bonze appeared and waved to us. He was taking an elderly monk to the bus station. Sitting in the middle of the seat, the young lama took advantage of the first turn we took to put his arm around my waist. At the bus stop, I loaded sweets into the old man's bag and we helped him to his seat.

Lobsung, for such was the bonze's name, came back to the hotel with me. No sooner had he come into the room behind me than he'd seized upon a pair of binoculars lying on the bed. Braced against the balcony railing, he was peering at the ruin across the way when he burst out laughing. I took my turn at the binoculars and saw across the lawn a tiny monkey hanging by his rear legs from a children's swing. He was holding a kitten coiled in his long tail and buggering it as he swung. We could even hear the feline mewing. The monk's laughing mouth blew cool air on the back of my neck. He pressed his chin into my flesh, began rummaging under my blouse with one hand while the other stroked my belly with juvenile awkwardness. I was dying to slip my fingers inside his robe, imagining the warm gap between his cool skin and the cloth.

I showed him how to kiss. After that, I had to slow him down. He'd have licked my tonsils, so hungry was he for a woman. He peered down my cleavage: the virgin wanted to see everything there was to see on a female.

He sniffed me and I did likewise. He had a sharp, woody smell, his skin tasted salty. He gave me the impression of someone who'd been told about sex and was busy checking out his second-hand anatomic knowledge. His breathing was slow and abdominal. "Working on his *chi*," I said to myself while his girlish hands stroked my thighs.

The moment the idea of *chi* entered my mind, all my thoughts focused on Lobsung and his breathing honed in on me. His mauve lips chanted weirdly into my vulva. The buzzing of a fly. Or sometimes the throbbing of a trombone. He blew his breath into my sex and sucked it out, humming all the while. He drew muted sounds from my nether parts, cavernous echoes of his own melody. I had become a Tibetan bagpipe. Blasts of hot air, gusts of wind, a Buddhist hurricane, blew my dress away like a Montgolfier balloon.

Now his rangy body emerged in turn from the folds of orange. His legs grew thin at the ankles and his penis hung pointing at the floor. Without further ado, he sat down on top of me and began rubbing his perineum and buttocks against my belly. Then he came into me from above. Only our internal muscles moved, exchanging a series of voluntary contractions.

He was attentive to my sensations, and waited until the time was ripe to move his organ in the proper way. My pleasure peaked each time he stopped. Orgasm was not a goal in itself, but a point of no return, a killjoy both of us were determined not to reach.

To make the pleasure last, we drew apart. He lay on his back and worked on his energy, breathing slowly through his nose, not breathing at all for long stretches of time. Propped on my elbow beside him, I watched.

After our first "climax of delight," we began to explore further. With this man, pleasure involved different levels of intensity, stages to be negotiated. It was my turn to sit on top, with my legs wrapped around his hips. My belly shuddered electrically and I opened for him all the way. He lay with his eyes shut, motionless inside me, his firm hands resting on my shoulders. Then he withdrew. Wrapping a towel around himself, he went to the window, had a look at the monkey, and giggled.

He wanted me to sit on him again, but the other way round, facing his feet. This time there was a whole succession of tiny movements and muted vibrations rose to my skull: the Will to Pure Pleasure by osmosis. A Bengal light began to sizzle in my head. Nirvana lasted a long time, but in the end I couldn't keep up with his tantric apprenticeship and collapsed on top of him, worn-out before I could come. Lobsung muttered something in his language, more like onomatopoeia than words, and went to sleep with a smile on his lips.

In the cool of the morning, I went looking for my two friends near the bus station. By telepathy or bush telegraph, the desk clerk at the Sapphire predicted that "the English ladies" would be a day late.

Back at the hotel, I saw Lobsung in the ruins across the lawn, weightlessly leaping between the windows. He did a double somersault, landed on his feet in a martial stance, went on to do forms. Then he levitated on the veranda steps. I remembered Kate's horrified expression when a child stuck his fingerless hand through the car window for a cigarette and Laura's cynical remark: "Eyewash!"

I was on my way back to the hotel when I saw two silhouettes hobbling up the road with familiar-looking giant-sized suit-cases rolling behind them. My friends were on the verge of exhaustion. From a distance, they'd taken me for a boy in my baseball cap.

The Oloon–Mysore "express" had broken down in the middle of the wildlife sanctuary. Neither Laura nor Kate had left the bus for fear of elephants. They'd been terrified to see several passengers actually go off into the bushes to answer the call of nature. And when they opened their sponge bags, a horde of monkeys had swarmed into the bus through the open windows and made off with their cosmetics! At the Sapphire, they asked the desk clerk for their old room back.

The final blow fell later that evening when they came to see me in my hotel in a state of extreme nervous fatigue. The peace and quiet, the panoramic view from my window, made Kate hysterical. She took it out on Laura for having chosen the Sapphire, but Laura wasn't listening, she was gaping at the saffron robe on a chair.

My head bounced off the wall from the slap she gave me. She grabbed me by the hair and Kate pitched in with a kick to my kidneys that knocked me to the floor, then she kneeled on me and squeezed one of my breasts in the crook of her elbow. They dragged me over the linoleum and called me a hypocrite.

When they finally left me alone, I looked for the bonze's robe. It was gone. The bathroom door was banging in the evening breeze. On the windowsill, a tiny monkey with knowing eyes stood swaying on its paws. I thought to myself: "That wasn't fair: two men ganging up on a girl."

This Far Inside

R. Gay

The words *I Love You* entered our vernacular after a month of dating and now, a year after getting married, they seem to have disappeared, and I am left not knowing how to communicate with my wife. It's not that we don't talk. She asks me how my day was, and I return the favor. On Sunday mornings, she asks for the crossword. Occasionally, we argue about her sister, Candace, who seems to have permanently moved in with us. But we don't really talk. We only say the things we think we are supposed to say. Late at night, when she thinks I'm sleeping, my wife will stand on the balcony of our apartment chain-smoking and crying, or staring up at the stars. I'll stand in the shadows of the curtains, with a sheet wrapped around me, staring at her, wondering what she's thinking. Sometimes, I start to open the door, move toward her, but something always holds me back because she looks at once so sorrowful and so peaceful in these moments I know they are meant to be solitary.

Ursula and I met during law school, and although we are complete opposites, I have always been drawn to her. Perhaps it's the current of irresponsibility that touches everything in her life, or the way she laughs, or the way she always carries a tin of Altoids to hide the fact that she can't quit smoking, although she has been trying for three years. More than anything she reminds me of how tangible and messy and wonderful life can be. I'm the first to admit that I'm an overly conventional person. I believe that rules exist for a reason and I find a value in conducting myself responsibly. I enjoy ironing because it relaxes me and serves a decent purpose. I never make hasty decisions because I don't believe in regrets.

Before proposing to Ursula I took a long time to actually go through with it. I had the ring hidden in the back of my sock drawer for six months. I weighed the pros and cons of spending the rest of my life with this woman, and when all was said and done, I knew marrying her would be a decision I could never regret.

Ursula is staring at me right now, trying to figure out what I'm thinking. I smile at her and reach across the table. She looks down at my hand and pauses before meeting me halfway. Slowly she smiles back, and we sit in silence until she asks me what I'm planning on ordering.

"Filet mignon with roasted portabello mushrooms," I say.

"Good choice," she replies, and I can't tell if she's being sarcastic or not.

"And you?"

She wrinkles her nose. "I was thinking lobster tails and veal marsala and the chicken piccata."

My jaw clenches, but I nod and smile wider. She does that, ordering two or three entrées, just in case she's not satisfied with one or more. She likes options. And so do I, but three entrées seems a bit extravagant. We aren't eating at a Chinese restaurant where we can fill the table with steaming dishes, our chopsticks meeting over chop suey and beef and broccoli. But I say nothing, because when I married her I also married her many quirks.

When our food arrives, Ursula immediately pushes the chicken piccata away.

"What's wrong with it?"

She shrugs. "I don't like the way it looks."

I lean forward, carefully inspecting the dish. "How so?"

"Not enough color."

I arch an eyebrow as I eye the pale veal practically quivering on her plate in a pool of equally pale marsala wine sauce. "I see. Well, hopefully the lobster and veal will be more colorful to your lovely eyes."

Her cheeks redden slightly, and I can't help but notice that they are similar in hue to the lobster tails, four of them, artfully placed along an oval plate. We eat in silence. Although the restaurant is crowded it feels like the place is so quiet that I can hear her chewing, the sound of the linen napkin gliding back and forth across her lips. Sometimes silence is deafening.

At home, I stand in the bathroom, plucking my nose hairs. It's a chore, but I hate staring at my reflection in the mirror only to see the wispy blond hairs waving from the air flowing through my nostrils. It's distracting. Ursula is sitting on the edge of our bed, left leg crossed over right, watching me, an amused expression on her face. In the next room Candace is playing the same U2 album that she has been playing for the past three months. I hate U2. I didn't before, but I do now. I'm not even sure what a Joshua tree is.

"Why are you watching me?" I ask her, wincing as I pluck the last hair, and begin wiping the counter clean.

"Because when I imagined things I'd see my husband doing, I imagined watching him shave, take a piss, shower and whatnot. I never thought I'd see him pluck nose hairs, so I'm absolutely fascinated and repulsed at the same time."

I frown, flicking a stray hair off the mirror. "Thanks. Glad to know."

She pats the bed and leans back. "Don't be grumpy. Come get naked with me."

I arch an eyebrow and turn to face her. Her bathrobe has fallen down her shoulders and she is naked, arm muscles taut and stretched behind her. The shaft of light from the bathroom leaves half her body in shadows, and there is something intriguing and erotic about seeing her like this. Later, I am alone in bed, sweat cooling against my skin. I can see the curves of Ursula's body in the sheets next to me, and it's strange but I feel her presence more in these shadows than I have sitting right next to her lately. I slide out of bed and tiptoe to the window. She is sitting on the balcony, hugging her legs to her chest. I can only see one side of her face and it is streaked with tears. I place the palm of my hand against the glass. And I stand, still.

I remember my childhood in sounds, not words, because my parents' relationship lacked a verbal vernacular. They were creatures of silence and they communicated in an intricate way that made up for all the thoughts and feelings that went unsaid. I remember the sound of my mother rushing to finish dinner each evening before my father came home, the way she would

hum, how the humming would get louder the faster six o'clock
approached, and the catch of her breath as she heard him in the
doorway. I remember my mother's laughter, low and husky,
like whisky pouring over ice as she greeted my father. The hum
of her sewing machine for hours on end and the sound of her
left foot tapping against the wall as she worked. I remember the
sound of my father's briefcase landing against the hallway tiles
and the way he cleared his throat to let us know that he was
home. He and my mother would dance to Frank Sinatra every
night before they went to sleep.

And when I got older, I remember the sound of my father's
oxygen cart, the wheels always in need of oil; the hiss of
oxygen pouring into his lungs hour after hour, the sound of
his old Zippo lighter clicking against his thigh as he longed for
just one more cigarette. And my mother, gently patting his
back when he was attacked by a coughing fit, or the way she
would click her tongue when she was worried about him,
worried that sooner rather than later she would no longer hear
his sounds. But I don't remember the sounds of their voices,
because in my memory my parents never spoke to each other.
It was as if, day in and day out, they slid around each other,
only invisible words spoken between them. And now I think
that's why the silence growing between Ursula and I feels
familiar. But it is a familiarity I am uncomfortable with,
because in that silence I don't hear the things I heard between
my parents' silences.

The next morning Ursula ignores the alarm, but I jump out
of bed, pulling the sheets and blankets off her before getting
ready. After I'm dressed, I sit on the bed next to her adjusting
my tie. Getting the knot to look the way I want it to is a skill I
have yet to acquire.

I pat her thighs. "Babe, it's time to get up."

Her arms stretch over her head, banging into the headboard.
"Dammit," she grumbles.

I shake her again. "You're going to be late."

She's quiet for a moment, lying perfectly still. Even the rise
and fall of her chest has stopped.

"I know you're awake."

"Fuck off," she grumbles.

I sigh. "I'll see you in the kitchen."

Candace is already up, leaning into the open refrigerator, wearing only boxers and a thin tank top.

"I see you're already dressed for whatever it is you do all day."

"Fuck off," she says, pulling out the milk and an apple.

"That's twice in one morning."

"You're off to a great start."

"Whatever. Did you start the coffee?"

"Am I a maid?"

I bite my tongue, and begin making the coffee. The rhythm of this ritual calms me, first the filter, two scoops of coffee, neatly packed, warm water, setting out three mugs. Candace sits on the counter, swinging her legs back and forth as she alternates taking bites of her apple with drinking milk directly from the carton. She's pushing so many of my buttons that I choose to tune her out rather than get riled up. As the coffee begins percolating, Ursula stumbles into the kitchen, her blouse partially unbuttoned, the hem of her skirt at a strange angle.

"What time is it?" she asks, her voice gravelly.

I look at my watch. "You should invest in one of these. Its 7:15."

She falls into a chair at the kitchen table, leaning her forehead against her arms. "I need a job where I can wake up after noon."

"Janitors are always in demand."

She raises her head only long enough to flash me a glare. "What is your problem this morning?"

I fill our mugs with coffee and set one in front of her.

She kicks me lightly, trying to reach up and ruffle my hair as I step back. "Answer me."

"Perhaps the better question is what was wrong with you last night?"

Ursula stares at me blankly. She doesn't even blink. "I don't know what you're talking about."

I take a sip of coffee, wincing as it burns my tongue. "Of course you don't."

Candace waves her hands in the air. "I am in the room. Maybe you could have your little tiff later."

"Maybe you could just leave the room."

"Don't snap at my sister," Ursula says.

"Are you married to her?"

Without waiting for her answer I grab my briefcase and adjust my tie. I don't even bother saying goodbye as I leave for work. Neither does she. After about an hour at work, I am calm. There is a reassuring and fashionable order to working as a lawyer for an insurance company. Denial of coverage claims come to me, and I decide whether or not to settle the matter or take it to court, and as with most decisions in my life, I never settle, because if I settle I might regret. Day in and day out I compare the havoc of other people's lives with the relative stability of mine. It is almost comforting. Today there are three folders on my desk. A twenty-one-year-old kid in Florida who's white 1996 Honda Accord was stolen but found less than a mile away, the inside burned to a crisp. Even the CDs were still in the car, the plastic deformed and fused with the char of the floor mats. The agent investigating the case believes the kid was involved, something about wanting a new car from his rich daddy.

Next, a woman whose jewels were stolen from her home while she and her husband were asleep. Nothing else reported stolen. And my favorite of the day, a banker's claim for the loss of his prize-winning and purebred Irish setter, who has run away to parts unknown. I make a few phone calls, take some notes, and hand a pile of paperwork to my assistant. I have to be in court in the afternoon, so we discuss a few pre-trial motions. When he returns to his desk I begin clearing my desk of everything. I have a file cabinet especially for my nameplate, Ursula's picture, the calculator, my calendar. This is another one of my rituals before going into court, cleaning my desk; an empty slate to think things over.

I briefly wonder what Ursula's doing at work. Ironically enough she's a divorce lawyer. I could never understand that choice, getting so intimately involved in other people's lives, watching day in and day out the end of something that was supposed to last for ever and has dissolved into nothing. But she loves it. We had a long conversation about it once, right after we had graduated and were studying for our bar exams. It was late at night, and we were the only two people in the law library. She was curled up in an armchair and I was seated at a nearby desk, wondering how she could possibly study sitting in such an odd position. I distinctly remember what she was wearing; flannel pyjama pants, a neon yellow t-shirt, and a dirty fisherman's hat pulled down low. Visually offensive, but adorable nonetheless – a reminder as to why she was good for me. I was wearing khakis and a polo shirt.

Fresh starts, she said. There's always potential when something ends. And that disturbed me, as I reminded her that when life ends that's pretty permanent but she had a two-part answer for that. Death is different, and no one knows what happens after death . . . that unknowing . . . that potential.

I don't know why I'm thinking about that night. I should be focused on work. I like to visualize the courtroom; the judge's bench, the court reporter, the jury box, usually empty for the cases I try. The bailiff standing in the corner, making sure everything runs smoothly. I once decided that if law didn't work out for me I would become a bailiff, my sole duty to preserve order and calm without the dangers of, say, police work. But realistically I know that such would not be the case . . . all that standing around, never being able to speak. It would drive me crazy.

Sometimes, though, silences are beautiful. On the third day of our honeymoon in Hawaii it began raining in heavy sheets. Ursula stared outside from our hotel room and suddenly decided that in that very moment we needed to be outside. We ran into the parking lot and stared upward, our clothes instantly soaked and clinging to our bodies. It was strangely still. All the other tourists seemed to have disappeared. Ursula grabbed my hand and pressed it against her chest and, looking into her eyes, I heard this peculiar silence that seemed to last for ever . . . for ever until we saw a bolt of lightning and ran back into the hotel lobby, leaving puddles of rain in our wake. We've never talked about that moment and I often wonder if it was as intense for her as it was for me. And I wonder about our marriage.

When I get home Ursula is cleaning out the refrigerator. I set my briefcase on the counter and loosen my tie. "How was your day?"

She shrugs, dropping a Tupperware container with week-old ravioli into the trashcan. "The same as any other."

"That's not telling me much."

She sniffs a bowl of custard she made over the weekend, wrinkling her nose as she empties it into the kitchen sink. "There's not much to tell. I got a new client. I was in court for hours. Same old, same old."

I don't know why, but I want to pick a fight. "I guess I'm as useless as those leftovers you're dumping."

She stops, wiping her hands on a dishtowel. Slowly she closes the refrigerator door and turns to look at me. "What would possess you to say something like that? It's so . . . melodramatic. You're my husband, not some crap I'm throwing away."

"Maybe that's how I feel."

"And somehow that's my fault?"

I slam my hand down on the counter. She jumps, surprised. I start to say something but change my mind and, grabbing my keys, I leave. I've never walked out before, but it feels good to leave the apartment, without looking back, imagining the expression on her face. I'm too even-keeled she'll often tell me. This should give her something to think about. I have no idea where I'm going as I get in the car, so I spend an hour driving around town wishing I had some place to go, yet wanting to be at home cooking dinner with my wife. When I return, Ursula and Candace are sitting on the couch watching television in the dark. The light from the screen flickers strange and shadowed patterns onto the walls and I am mesmerized until Ursula asks, "Where have you been?"

"Out driving."

"Out driving where?"

"Around."

"Could you be more specific?"

"There's nothing to tell, Urs. Like your day at work."

Candace shifts uncomfortably. "Do you two want to be left alone?"

Ursula starts to shake her head, but I say, "Yes, that would be great. We would love to be alone."

Candace stares at her sister for a moment, then heads for her bedroom, and soon we can hear loud music reverberating throughout the apartment. I sit down on the arm of the couch looking at my wife. "She could have just stayed in here for all the good the music is doing us."

Ursula looks away. "You really hate having her around don't you?"

I look at my hands. "What makes you think that?"

"You don't try to hide your exasperation very well."

"Under the circumstances I think I'm behaving quite well. She's still here isn't she?"

Ursula stands up. "See. I knew it. That's what this is all about. You resent the fact that she's staying here."

I rub my forehead for what feels like the millionth time in one day. "Baby, your sister is the least of my worries. Yes, she gets on my nerves, but it's nothing personal. It's that we're never alone and it hardly feels like we're married."

She turns to look at me, gently clasping her throat. "I feel like we're married."

"We both know that that isn't true."

"God, I'm so sick and tired of you acting all vague and cryptic. How do you know what I'm feeling?"

I crack my knuckles, and undo the top button of my shirt. I want to say the right thing here . . . as if our whole relationship is balancing on the next sentence that comes out of my mouth, and suddenly I feel tired, balancing something so heavy. My throat muscles go limp, suddenly afraid to push any words out of my mouth. I clear my throat but my voice cracks as I say "I see you crying at night. That's how I know what you're feeling. I don't know exactly what it is you're feeling, but I have a pretty good idea."

Ursula snaps to attention, her eyes narrowing in the darkness. "You've been spying on me?"

"No, I've been waking up, alone, in the middle of the night."

"Oh. My world doesn't revolve entirely around you, you know."

"I know that."

"Then why do you think that it is our marriage making me cry?"

"What should I think? You don't talk to me about what you're feeling. You hardly talk to me at all. In fact, I talk to your sister more than I talk to you, and you talk to your sister more than you talk to me. We might as well be married through her rather than to each other."

"Why haven't you said anything if you're this upset about it?"

"I figured you would come to me when you were ready. I thought that maybe you . . . I don't know what I thought."

"Maybe I don't know what's wrong with me."

"Maybe you should have shared that with me. It breaks my heart to reach out for you at night and find nothing, and it hurts even more to see you crying to yourself when I can do nothing but watch."

"It's not easy being green," she quips.

"So we're going to make jokes?" I run my fingers through my hair, clenching them into fists. "I'm going to bed."

"It's early."

"I don't care," I snap, stalking out of the room. It's the second time today, the second time in our entire relationship that I've walked away from her, but I don't know what else to do. I don't know how to do anything any more. I wish I could just fall into the floor until our lives reverted to the marriage I envisioned when I proposed to her. Later that night, she crawls into bed next to me. I can feel her body, cool, slightly damp from the shower, and I can hear her breathing as she tries to find a comfortable position. My throat is dry, so I swallow, again feeling the need to say something. Minutes pass.

"Are you awake?" she asks.

I roll on to my back, looking up at the ceiling. There is a long cobweb dangling precariously over the bed and I wonder if and when it will fall. "Yeah. Can't sleep."

"I fell asleep on the couch."

"Okay."

"I'm just explaining why I'm coming to bed so late."

I turn toward her and try to slide my hand across to her, but I stop mid-way, clenching my fingers into a fist. "I appreciate that." Then I change my mind and inch closer toward her, resting my ear against the flat of her back.

"What are you doing?"

"I'm listening to your body."

"Do you hear anything?"

"I can hear your stomach gurgling, and I can hear your heart, and I think I can hear your blood flowing."

"That's gross."

I rest a hand against her thigh. "It's beautiful."

"Michael, I don't feel like there's any potential left in my life."

"I'm not sure what you mean."

"It feels like there is nothing to look forward to. I'm too old to be a prodigy at anything. From here on in, my accomplishments will be unremarkable. And even with us. When we were engaged, we had the wedding to look forward to, and now there's only tomorrow."

I exhale loudly. I didn't realize I'd been holding my breath. "I'm not sure what I'm supposed to say to that."

"You don't have to say anything. I guess what I really mean is that I look forward to spending my life with you and realizing all the plans we've made together. I just don't know how to get through all the tomorrows that lead to those plans."

"I'm looking forward to tomorrow because I know you'll be part of it."

"Did you get that from a Hallmark card?"

I can feel tears welling in the corners of my eyes. I quickly brush them aside, reminding myself that boys don't cry and turn away from her. "I guess so. Good night."

"Michael," she says, grabbing my shoulder. "Don't be like that. I didn't mean to be sarcastic."

"Yeah, Ursula . . . you did."

"Fine," she snaps, also turning in the opposite direction. "You know everything, as usual."

Seventeen minutes later, I ask, "Why do we keep ending up like this?"

I wait another seventeen minutes for an answer, but she says nothing.

The day before we married, my parents called me because circumstances dictated that it was the right thing to do. It was an awkward conversation, not because they don't love me, but because none of us really knew what to say. They apologized for not being able to make it to the wedding, and I reassured them that I wouldn't be bitter about their absence. My dad said a few words about what it takes to be a good husband, reminding me that my wife will always be right. My mom told me to anticipate Ursula's needs. And then we three were silent, because we had exhausted our reserves of familial wisdom. It was then that I began wondering if it is possible to run out of words to share with the ones you love . . . if there's a limit to what you can say to another person over the course of a lifetime. And now, I'm starting to think that maybe there is.

Three weeks later, on a Saturday afternoon, Ursula and I are on the couch watching golf. It's not really her thing, but I enjoy it and she is humoring me. Candace is out with friends. For the first time in a long while we are alone. We haven't been fighting lately. It's been more of the same silences. Our conversations are becoming fewer and farther between, and I'm finding it hard to even pick a fight with her. It's like I can feel myself losing interest in doing something about whatever problem there is between us. I think that scares me more than the silences themselves. Part of me thinks that I should shower her with gifts and affection and weekend get-aways, so that all these tomorrows are more bearable for her, but the more sensible part of me realizes that she probably wouldn't appreciate the gesture.

In a moment of paranoia, I feel like I've forgotten the sound of her voice, so I ask, "Anything exciting happening at work for you next week?"

She shakes her head. "More of the same."

I smile to myself and nod.

"What about you?"

"Work? Nothing new. My work is very . . . predictable."

She sighs and I can feel the muscles in her shoulder tense against mine. "I think, of all the words in the world, I hate the word predictable the most."

I put the TV on mute. "Why is that?"

"It's so depressing."

"I gotcha," I say, but I don't really understand what she means. In my opinion there's a lot to be said for predictability.

I lean over and kiss her on the cheek. She arches an eyebrow and smiles. I can tell that she's forcing her smile because the little muscle along her jaw line twitches slightly. Shrinking away I turn the volume up on the TV. "I was trying to be unpredictable."

"You were? I mean, that's so sweet honey."

"That's me, babe. Sweet. Sweet and predictable, and basically what you're telling me is that you're bored with our marriage, only not in so many words. The constant sighing and the crying and the arguing . . . that's what it's all about."

She looks at her hands, and I glance downward. She has the most wonderful hands of anyone I've ever been with. I've memorized every line, every texture that her hand has to offer. When we hold hands, I fall in love with her all over again, because as my thumb brushes across the back of her hand and her thumb brushes over mine and our fingers clasp together, I feel larger than whole. I've never told her this, and now there seems no point, but more than anything I want to take her hand in mine so I can feel good again, so I can care about caring about us.

"It is not something personal against you Michael," she says softly. "I love you, and I know that. But I also know that we don't have a lot to look forward to and I can't get over letting that bother me."

I stand up and begin pacing across the living room. "Were you paying attention when we exchanged our vows?"

"No, I took a mental nap."

I can feel my nostrils flaring and my head is starting to pound. "This conversation is going nowhere."

"You started it."

"You're right. And now I'm ending it. Are we still going out with your parents tonight?"

She plays with the frayed cuff of her jeans. "We're supposed to, but I can call and cancel if you'd like."

"No, we'll go. I wouldn't want to upset your mother."

She sneers. "Of course you wouldn't."

Ursula hates that her mother and I get along. Two peas in a pod she calls us whenever she's irritated. I don't see what the big deal is. I thought I was supposed to get along with her family, but I think she sees us getting along and views it as a personal affront. She's also bitter about the fact that her mother pressured her for years to get married. My relationship with my mother-in-law is nothing but a reminder of that. Sometimes I think that the only reason we got married is so that her mother would leave her alone.

I toss the remote control into Ursula's lap and go to our room and, after I undress, I take a long shower. When I step out I slide across the bathroom tiles and stub my toe against the toilet. Yelping, I grab my foot and start hopping around, cursing up a storm. Ursula appears in the doorway and giggles.

"What's so funny?" I ask, glaring.

"You're all red and wrinkled and, well, it's funny from where I'm standing."

"I think I broke my toe," I huff.

"Let me take a look at it."

I pout slightly and hop out of the bathroom and fall down on the edge of our bed staring at my toe, expecting to find a protruding bone. She kneels in front of me and gently wiggles my toe back and forth. "Does this hurt?"

I wince and draw my foot away from her. "Yes."

She kisses the tip of my toe and massages my foot. "Does that hurt?"

I clear my throat and try to look tough. "Nah. Maybe it's just a sprain."

She smirks, but nods seriously. "That's probably all it is." She kisses my toe again and starts drying me off with a towel. It's warm in the room, from all the bathroom steam, but I shiver and look at the goose bumps rising across my collarbone.

"This was pretty unpredictable wouldn't you say?"

She stops, draping the towel over my head. "You don't have to try so hard Michael. This really is about me."

I pull the towel off and wipe my face. "Whether you realize it or not, it's about me too."

She pats my knee and stands up. "You're good to go. Follow up with my office in a week or two."

I wiggle my toe tentatively. "We should get dressed."

She starts chewing on her fingernails like they are a buffet. "You're right. Any thoughts on what I should wear?"

I stand up, wrapping the towel around my waist, before I hobble toward the closet. "Something totally trashy."

She laughs. It's the first laugh I've heard in months so I close my eyes and record the sound in my memory. "That will go over well with Barb and Richard."

As I pull a suit off the hanger, I turn around and grin. "A parent's love is unconditional."

She heads into the bathroom. "No one's love is that unconditional."

I toss my clothes on the bed and turn to answer her, but the door is closed behind her.

After dinner we walk her parents to their car and decide to stroll around the Haymarket, the old part of town. It's late and the sidewalks are empty. We head past the train station and along the railroad tracks toward the rail yard. We're holding hands and I'm full of steak and wine and I'm enjoying the sound of gravel crunching beneath my shoes.

"If you think about it," she says, "this is the most exciting place in Lincoln."

I look around at broken glass bottles and weeds between the rails and large, unidentifiable hunks of metal. "That doesn't say much for the city does it?"

She snorts. "What is there to say about this place really? But seriously . . . these tracks can take you anywhere in the country. When I was a kid, I wanted to spend my life hitching rides on trains, like a hobo, never knowing where the train would end up."

In the distance, I can hear the low wail of a train's whistle. "When I was a kid I wanted to be a bailiff."

She squeezes my hand harder. "Have you noticed that we never become what we thought we'd become when we were kids? It's strange, almost sad."

"Our needs change, I think. And when our needs change so do our desires."

"I knew I could count on you to have a logical answer."

I let go of her hand. "That's who I am. That's who I've always been."

"No, no. I wasn't being mean. I was just . . . never mind."

"You were what?"

"I was just saying that I know I can count on you for that . . . giving me answers to big questions. I like that about you."

She takes my hand in hers again and I feel a wave of satisfaction. "I love the way your hands feel," I tell her impulsively.

She leans into me, resting her other hand against the center of my chest. "I feel the same way. I feel lots of things, Michael, that I don't share with you, and I want to, I swear to you I do. But sometimes I forget how, and sometimes I'm so wrapped up in my own strange thoughts that maybe I do forget that I'm supposed to be building a life with you."

My back stiffens. "Do you need some time to yourself? Should I move out or something?"

"I don't think my pre-mid-life crisis qualifies for such drastic measures."

"I wish there was something I could do to fix you."

Ursula gives me a look that I can't quite read, and I am strangely uncomfortable because, in the past, I've been able to read her looks. . . predict her intentions. "I don't need you to fix me, Michael. Like I said, I don't know what I need, but I will work on figuring that out, and when I need your help . . . I'll ask for it."

"What should I do in the meantime? I need a task, as stupid as that sounds."

"I don't know. I've been saying that too often lately, but it's all there is to say. Just be yourself and be patient."

"Okay," I hear myself saying, but I'm thinking that I want to do more and I'm thinking, praying really, that sooner or later her heart will work its way back to me . . . to us. And I'm realizing that so much – maybe too much – is going unsaid and I'm hoping that this moment is the beginning of the end of the strange silence that has been living with us.

We've reached the train yard now, and it's a deserted maze of boxcars and train tracks. The wind is blowing – there's a sharp pitch to it, and it feels like only in this place does wind have a sound. Ursula stops and motions toward the nearest rail. On either side of us are tracks in each direction and again I can hear a train's whistle. I sit down slowly, looking up at her.

"Is there a reason why we're stopping here?"

She shakes her head and places one finger across my lips. "You think too much."

I open my mouth to say something, but she presses a second finger against my lip. She kneels between my legs, and clasping her hand around the back of my neck she begins kissing me softly, so softly that I can barely feel her lips against mine. Her other hand slides down my chest and between my legs. She begins unbuttoning my slacks. My eyes fly open and I look from side to side but she grabs my chin and makes me face her. "Look at me."

"We're in public," I stutter.

"Look at me," she says, very deliberately.

I breathe deeply and look at her. Carefully, she inches my pants down around my ankles and lifting her skirt, straddles my lap. I lean forward, resting my head against the small of her throat, moving my hands under her blouse until I can feel the weight of her breasts in my hands. I don't know why we're here, or what we're doing. As I feel her body wrapping around me the tracks begin to rumble and she makes a faint choking sound. She lifts my head and presses her forehead against mine, and it almost hurts to look into her eyes.

From the corner of my eye I can see a train approaching on the adjacent track, its headlight cutting through the darkness in a singular beam of light. Ursula covers her mouth with mine. Our lips are moving so slowly it's like they're still. But it feels like she's trying to swallow me into her body. I close my eyes for a moment and imagine my heart, lungs, liver, flowing from me into her. The palms of her hands are firmly pressed against my cheeks, and another train begins coming from the other direction, and here we are, between them. The closer they get the more the tracks rumble, and her tongue is inside my mouth now, roughly running over my teeth and my tongue and the back of my throat. Her hips are rising and falling against mine. My mind is almost blank, thoughts canceling each other out until I stop thinking and I let myself fall into the rhythm of our bodies. As the two trains pass by, a gust envelops us. My ears are ringing, but I swear, in this moment of silence and noise and flesh, I can hear her saying, "I love you."

Feel the Pain

Michael Bracken

I screwed the barrel of my .38 into the spot behind Jeremy Wilson's left ear where his jaw attached to his skull.

"Go ahead," I said. "Give me a reason to pull the trigger."

Jeremy slowly raised his arms. Blood dripped from his knuckles and down the backs of his hands.

"Get your clothes, Cassie," I said to the plump brunette with the pulped face.

She stared at me through eyelids nearly swollen shut.

"Now!"

Cassie Wilson pushed herself away from the wall and scooped her clothes off the bed, holding them against her naked chest as she hurried across the room.

As soon as Cassie stepped through the open door I drove my knee into Jeremy's groin. When he doubled over I introduced my knee to his face and smashed the butt of my revolver against the back of his head. He folded like a bad poker hand and I left him face down on the worn carpet.

Outside the motel room I holstered my revolver, then steered Cassie toward my car, opened the passenger door and pushed her inside. I walked to the other side and climbed in beside her. Then I keyed the ignition, dropped the Chevy into gear, and pointed it toward the highway. As the front tyres bucked up onto the two-lane asphalt road from the gravel parking lot, I glanced at my passenger. She hadn't spoken and she still held her clothes against her chest.

"Your father hired me," I explained. "He wants you home."

She didn't respond.

Half an hour later I stopped at a clean and well-lit convenience store/service station. I pulled the car around back next to the rest rooms. When Cassie made no effort to leave the car, I went into the men's room, wet a handful of paper towels and returned.

I dabbed them against Cassie's face and she winced with pain. After wiping away most of the blood, I saw the damage her husband had done. I walked around the building and inside, returning a few minutes later with antiseptic and bandages. I did my best to patch up Cassie's face, wondering how much her father would ultimately spend on reconstructive surgery.

I finally convinced Cassie to release her death grip on the wad of clothes in her arms and I slipped her blouse onto her. I didn't bother with her bra – I'd never been good getting one off a cooperative woman and doubted my ability to slip one onto an uncooperative woman – and I didn't bother with her skirt. When I finished buttoning her blouse, I slipped one of my business cards into her pocket.

Then I drove through the night, only the occasional pair of oncoming headlights and the two cars that raced past us reminding me we weren't alone on the nearly deserted two-lane highway. Two hours into the trip Cassie asked, "Why's he want me home?"

I glanced at her in the darkness of the car. Cassie hadn't moved since I'd dressed her.

"He didn't say."

She didn't speak again.

Dawn arrived in Waco only minutes ahead of us. I exited the interstate at Valley Mills and a few minutes later found my client's home on Austin Avenue. I pulled into the circular drive and stopped before the wide brick steps. Before I could climb out of the car the front door opened and Richard Masterson greeted me. He wore blue silk pyjamas under his blue silk robe. Behind him stood Carvel Casey, a thick-chested bruiser in skintight jeans and a loose gray sweatshirt.

By the time the two men had descended the steps I'd slid out of the Chevy. As they approached I jerked my thumb over my shoulder. "She's inside."

Masterson and Carvel helped Cassie from the car, up the steps and into the house. I followed, stopping in the foyer while they assisted Cassie up the sweeping curve of the staircase to the second floor. From behind and below I saw the holster at the small of Carvel's back, the one usually hidden by his sweatshirt.

I paced until Masterson returned.

He pulled twelve C-notes from a gold money clip, counted the bills twice before placing them in the palm of my hand, then said, "Send me a bill for your expenses."

I didn't count the money, didn't even look down as I closed my hand around the crisp green bills and stuffed them into my pants pocket. I said, "Soon as I get to the office."

Elroy Johnson sat at my desk, awaiting my arrival. When I opened my office door and stepped inside, he asked, "Where you been all night?"

"With a client."

"Fat little brunette?" he asked. "Face like a pomegranate?"

"Why?"

"Got somebody says they saw you walking out of a motel in Texarkana about six hours ago. Drove off with a brunette. Motel clerk says two people checked in. You wasn't one of them. The brunette was." He paused, pulled an unfiltered Camel from the pack in his shirt pocket and lit it with a silver Zippo. "So was the dead guy y'all left behind."

I'd hit Jeremy Wilson hard enough to knock him stone cold, but I hadn't killed him. I didn't react to Elroy's narrative.

"Single bullet, back of the head," Elroy continued after a long drag from his cigarette. "Somebody messed him up good first."

"The police?"

"My guy won't remember you by the time they find him." Elroy took another long drag from his cigarette, then tapped the ash off into a paper coffee cup from which he'd been drinking prior to my arrival. "The girl?"

"She's home."

"She say anything?"

I shook my head. "Nothing important."

"That's good," Elroy said. He took one last drag from the cigarette, then dropped it into his cup. The cherry died with a quiet hiss when it hit the coffee dregs.

Elroy stood, walked around my desk, and dropped the cup into the waste can next to the door. He gave me a two-finger salute then stepped into the hall, closing the door behind him.

Texas is a big state, made smaller by men like Elroy Johnson. With loose connections to families in Kansas City, St Louis and New Orleans, they laundered money, brokered deals with the Mexican Mafia, and shared news of important events across the state. I'd known Elroy since childhood when I'd played high school football with his nephew, and our paths crossed more often than I ever cared to admit.

I replaced Elroy in the chair behind my desk, feeling the still-warm leather against my backside. I booted up my Macintosh, prepared an expense report for Masterson, then prepared a deposit slip for most of the money he'd given me earlier that morning.

With nothing scheduled for the rest of the day, I thumbed through a couple of science fiction magazines my kid had left behind the last time my ex had let him visit, then filed all the paperwork associated with a workmen's comp fraud case I'd closed the previous week.

By the time Millard Wayne Trout – "Millie" because his family still called his grandfather "Millard" – stuck his head in to my office and asked about lunch, I'd been dozing facedown on my desk for nearly an hour.

"Not today," I told him. "I have errands."

Millie nodded his shaved and tattooed head. "Suit yourself, Moe Ron. We're getting wings."

He returned to his shop in the front of the building and I slapped myself awake. Then I grabbed the deposit and Masterson's expense report and stepped out of my office. Only two other businesses remained in the building. An empty suite across from mine had once been occupied by a finance company too legitimate for the neighborhood and I walked down the hall between Millie's Tattoos and Piercings and Big Mac's Bail Bonds into the blinding midday sun.

The rest of the week passed into history without another job landing on my desk. I felt every second tick away my bank balance, and I briefly considered looking for some kid's missing poodle in hopes of earning the fifty-dollar reward.

The following Monday, Cassie Wilson stepped into my office. Even though the swelling had subsided, and carefully applied makeup covered most of the bruising, she couldn't hide the bandage across her flattened and reconstructed nose.

I stood.

"This you?" She handed me my card. Neatly thermographed on the front were my name – Morris Ronald Boyette – and my contact information.

"Yeah."

"Father says you brought me home."

"Regular chauffeur service." I directed her into one of the two guest chairs, then settled into my seat.

"I don't remember much about that night."

"Wouldn't expect you to."

"You shoot Jeremy?" she asked.

"It matter much one way or the other?"

She thought about her answer for a long time. Then she shook her head.

"Then why'd you come?"

She pulled an envelope thick with cash from her purse and dropped it on my desk. "Your expenses."

I let the envelope lie where she'd dropped it. "Your father could have mailed a check."

"I wanted to thank you," she said. "For – for whatever you did that night."

I stood.

She stood.

I walked her from my office and down the hall to the street. A silver Mercedes idled at the curb, Carvel behind the wheel. He watched our reflections in the rearview mirror as I opened the rear passenger door and helped settle Cassie inside.

"I ever need anything—?" She let the question hang.

"Just call," I said.

I closed the car door and Carvel dropped the Mercedes into gear.

Millie stepped outside and stood on the sidewalk next to me as the Mercedes pulled away. "Nice piece of work that one."

"Too rich for my blood."

"What's with the nose?"

"She had some work done," I said.

"Just the face?"

"Far as I know."

Millie scratched the top of his head. He wore a wife-beater, exposing the tattoos covering his arms, hands and fingers. "Up for lunch?"

I thought about the envelope of money still lying on my desk. "It's on me."

When I returned with burgers, fries and sodas for both of us, Millie said, "Elroy's in your office."

"How long?"

"Ten minutes, tops."

I grabbed a fistful of fries and walked down the hall. I pushed my office door open and found Elroy sitting in my chair reading one of my kid's science fiction magazines.

"Get this," he said without looking up. "The Hansel and Gretel witch? A time traveler. Where do these guys come up with this stuff?"

I ate my fries and waited.

Elroy closed the magazine. "Got a problem in Texarkana," he said. "Good news, my guy, bottle of Thunderbird and he forgets his mother's name. Bad news, he's not the only one saw you there."

"Who else?"

"Doctor. He's at the motel boffing one of his nurses. He's married, she's married, still he does the Good Samaritan thing and steps forward."

"Identifies me how?"

"Make, model, and color of car. Partial plate," Elroy said. "Won't be long before you're questioned."

I knew the drill. Even though Elroy wasn't my client this time, I'd worked for him many times before – even taking a bullet meant for his nephew. By collecting Cassie Wilson from Texarkana, I had stepped into Elroy's shit and he wanted to ensure that I didn't track it all across the police department's carpet. I nodded.

Elroy stood, then picked up the magazine he'd been reading. "Take this?"

My son wouldn't miss it. "Sure."

He stuffed the science fiction magazine in his jacket pocket and stepped past me. He turned at the door and looked back. "By the way," he said, "they recovered the slug."

"Thirty-eight?" I asked.

"Yep."

Jeremy Wilson's family had his body transported home when the Texarkana coroner's office finally released it. The mortician couldn't reconstruct his face, so the family held a graveside memorial service in Crawford.

Cassie Wilson attended her husband's funeral, accompanied by her father and Carvel, and I met her upon her return home, arriving as they were ascending the front steps. I followed Cassie into and through the house, admiring the way her hips moved in her widow's black dress.

She settled onto a love seat in the garden room and motioned me into a seat opposite her. A moment later Carvel brought drinks, then backed out of the room and closed the pocket doors.

"The police visited yesterday," Cassie said.

"And?"

She tasted her wine, then continued. "They asked questions, wanted to know how I'd gotten home."

"What did you tell them?" I slowly spun my tumbler of Jack-rocks in my hand.

"I told them I didn't know." She sipped at her wine. "I must have blacked out while Jeremy was beating me. Next thing I knew, I woke up in my own bed."

"They buy that?"

A smile played across Cassie's lips. "Had to," she said. "It was the only thing I was selling."

Even though I had already seen Cassie naked, something about the way the black dress clung to her figure and the way she touched her hair and wet her lips with the tip of her tongue affected me in a way that her blatant nudity hadn't. I felt my body respond and I shifted uncomfortably in my seat.

"And what are you selling now?" I asked. I placed my tumbler on the table, then stood.

Cassie stood, too, and stepped close enough I could feel the heat radiating from her body. She placed one hand on my right biceps, feeling the muscles beneath my jacket. The hint of a smile tugged at the corners of her lips. "I never thanked you proper."

She stretched upward and planted her lips on mine. I felt her warm breath against my cheek, saw her eyes half close, and then I pushed her aside.

I wiped her lipstick away with the back of my hand, then opened the pocket doors and left her standing in the garden room.

Masterson stopped me in the foyer.

"You married, Mr Boyette?" Masterson asked.

"Once, long time ago."

"Kids?"

"One," I said. "A boy."

Masterson looked back toward the garden room, where Cassie now stood in the open doorway watching us. "Kids," he said. "They'll break your heart."

The next afternoon Lester Beeson had a job for me. He'd taken over Big Mac's Bail Bonds twenty-seven years earlier when a disgruntled client emptied a shotgun in Macdonald Pearson's face, and he called on me whenever one of his clients jumped bail.

He tossed a Polaroid across the desk and I stared at the scarred face of a biker who'd spent time inside.

"Assault and battery. Assault with a deadly weapon. Attempted murder. Discharging a weapon within city limits. Littering."

I looked a question at him.

Lester shrugged. "He dropped the gun when he fled the scene."

Lester gave me Delbert "Deadwood" Woods's last known address and the addresses of his known associates.

"Like to have this one back," Lester said. "His mama stands to lose her house, and she's in the church choir with my mother. Won't make Sunday dinner a pleasant thing if one of my mother's friends comes up homeless."

I took the job and spent the afternoon on the phone, calling around until I found a mutual acquaintance who knew where to find Deadwood. Then I walked down the hall and offered Millie a few hours of evening work.

Just before 8 p.m. we found Deadwood's Fatboy parked on the front lawn of a mobile home in Bellmead. The single-wide belonged to an anemic blonde stripper who earned extra money servicing some of the town's backsliding Baptists.

Millie stationed himself outside the mobile home's back door while I approached the front. I knocked but received no response. I tried the knob and found it locked. I stepped back, braced myself against the porch rail, and kicked.

The door crashed against an end table, knocking a lamp to the carpet and sending a gray tabby screeching past me and into the night.

From the back of the house, I heard a loud thud like a body falling to the floor and then a woman began crying. A door slammed open, heavy footsteps pounded halfway down the length of the mobile home, then another door crashed open and I heard the ringing sound of metal against flesh.

"Hey, Moe Ron!" Millie shouted. "Come on back."

I followed the sound of Millie's voice and found him standing over the half-naked body of Delbert Woods. Millie had found a shovel leaning against the back fence and had swung it like a baseball bat when Deadwood crashed out the back door, catching the bail-jumping biker in the face with the flat of the shovel and dropping him to the ground.

"He was carrying this." Millie handed me a Glock nine-millimeter and I tucked it into my belt at the small of my back.

We trussed up Deadwood, stuffed him into my car and drove him downtown. While Millie walked him into the police station and answered a few questions, I tossed Deadwood's Glock into my glove box. When Millie finished, he rode with me to the tattoo parlor and slipped into his own car – a 1965 Mustang he'd rescued from a junkyard. I went to my office.

"About time," a woman's voice said when I opened the door.

I snapped on the light. Cassie Wilson sat behind my desk, a half-empty bottle of Jack Daniel's on the desk and a nearly full shot glass in her hand. Her sheer white blouse had been half unbuttoned and she wore no bra.

"Why are you here?" I asked.

"Because I figured this is where you'd be," she said. "Sooner or later."

Cassie stood and stepped toward me. It could have been the drink or it could have been on purpose, but she stumbled and fell against me, her heavy breasts pressing against my chest as I wrapped my arms around her to keep her from falling. I smelled her shampoo, her perfume, and the Jack.

She tilted her head back. "I didn't finish thanking you."

I tried to stand her upright. Before I could, Cassie wrapped her hands around the back of my neck and pulled my face down to hers. At first I resisted, but when she covered my lips with hers, I surrendered.

She buried her tongue in my mouth and I sucked hard. As we kissed she peeled off my jacket, dropping it to the floor. I pushed Cassie away long enough to slip off my shoulder rig and hang it on the coat-rack behind the door.

A few minutes later our clothes were strewn around my office and I had her bent over my knee.

"I've been bad," she said. "Very, very bad."

I spanked her naked ass again and again, so hard I left red palm prints on her pale white skin.

I liked it and knew I shouldn't. She liked it and didn't know any different.

Then I turned her over and pushed her onto the desk, spreading her legs and taking her hard and fast, spilling Jack Daniel's on the carpet and sending paperwork flying all over the room.

Afterward, before I even had a chance to catch my breath, she dressed, finished the taste of Jack remaining in the overturned bottle, and left me sitting naked and spent in my leather office chair.

A moment later, light from the alley behind the building

brightened my entire office. I spun my chair around, lifted the corner of the window shade and watched as Cassie slipped into the back seat of a silver Mercedes. I continued watching as Carvel drove the Mercedes out of the alley and around the corner.

Early the next afternoon two plainclothes officers from the Waco Police Department visited my office.

"When's the last time you visited Texarkana?" the tall one asked.

I told him.

"Purpose of your visit?"

"Professional," I said. "Picking up something for a client."

"There's a .38 registered in your name," the short one said. "Still got it?"

I opened my jacket and showed them the shoulder rig.

"Could you place it on the table, please? Use two fingers."

I lifted the revolver from my holster and placed it on my desk, covering a science fiction magazine that now smelled of Jack Daniel's.

"There was a guy killed in Texarkana the night you visited," the tall one said. "Shot in the head with a .38."

"I heard."

"Why didn't you come forward?" the short one asked.

I shrugged. "Lots of people in lots of places get shot with .38s. Don't have a thing to do with me."

"Mind if we take this?" the short one asked. He didn't wait for an answer. He wrapped a handkerchief around the revolver's handle, then lifted the gun and slipped it into a paper bag.

His partner issued me a receipt. "We'll run a few tests and get back to you."

"You do that," I said.

Millie brought a late lunch and we sat in my office eating wings and fries. When Elroy Johnson pushed the door open without knocking, Millie quickly excused himself and returned to the tattoo parlor up front.

"Now the doctor's not sure what he saw," Elroy said after closing the door. "Turns out the nurse's husband is a divorce attorney. Suddenly the doc don't want to admit where he was, who he was with, or what he was doing there."

"Too late," I said. "The cops've already been here."

"Tell them anything?"

I shook my head. "Nothing to tell."

Elroy fired up an unfiltered Camel, took a long drag, then let the smoke out through his nostrils. He pointed his cigarette at the science fiction magazine still on my desk. "You going to read that?"

"Take it." I pushed the magazine across the desk and Elroy picked it up.

"Jesus," he said. "Smells like you dipped it in whiskey."

"Close enough," I told him, remembering the bottle that had spilled while I fucked Cassie Wilson on my desk.

Cassie hadn't finished thanking me. The next night we drove downtown for Mexican food, then returned to my little brick two-bedroom home just off of New Road. I'd barely closed the door when she began tearing my clothes off.

I carried her to the bedroom, where we had hard, violent sex that left finger-shaped bruises on Cassie's breasts and hips and thighs where I'd clung to her. Afterward, I pushed myself off the bed and paced the bedroom, stealing glances at her as I thought.

She sat on the bed, leaning against the headboard, the sheet pooled at her waist.

"You like being slapped around," I told her.

Cassie didn't seem surprised by my revelation.

"But Jeremy went too far, didn't he?" I asked. "He began to like hitting you as much as you liked being hit."

She shrugged.

"Why did your father really send me after you?" I asked. "Why didn't he send that lapdog of yours?"

"Carvel?"

I lifted one corner of the shade. "He's out there right now, sitting in the Mercedes, waiting for you."

"Carvel's harmless."

"Then why the gun?"

"To protect my father's interests."

I turned toward her. "You?"

She lifted the sheet and tossed it aside, spreading her legs. "Think you can do it again?"

For a few minutes I forgot about the man outside.

Two hours later, dressed and standing in my living room, Cassie asked, "You take anything else from the room that night?"

"Just you," I said. "That's all I was hired to do. Why?"

"My suitcase didn't make it home. The police didn't find it in the room with Jeremy."

"What was in it that's so important?"

"Clothes," she said. "Just clothes. Hate to have to replace them."

I didn't believe her. "Take you home?"

"Carvel's still out there," she said. "He'll take me."

I opened the door. Before Cassie could step outside, I pulled her into my arms and kissed her. She bit my bottom lip and I jerked away in surprise.

I tasted blood.

"I'm not the only one who likes pain," she whispered. Then she stepped through the open doorway and hurried down the walk to the waiting Mercedes.

"Jeremy was a bag boy, worked for her father," Elroy explained. We stood at Lion's Park, watching go-karts circle the track.

"Cassie know?"

Elroy shrugged. "Jeremy wanted a bigger piece of the action, but couldn't figure out how to get it. Their little sex games went too far and he took his frustration out on his wife."

I waited.

"Then you showed up," he said.

"And screwed the pooch," I said. "Somebody's plans went all to hell when I pulled Cassie out of that motel room."

"Whose?" Elroy asked. "I thought we had things under control."

Richard Masterson moved money through one of Waco's smaller banks, an opportunity Elroy had presented to him many years earlier when Masterson's inability to cover bad bets had jeopardized his position at the bank. Elroy had monitored the banker's activities ever since.

I'd been thinking about it for two days before I talked to Millie. "I need your help," I said, then explained what I needed.

I'd been fucking Cassie every night, and that night wasn't much different. We skipped dinner and went straight to my place. I slapped her around, getting her in the mood, then I stripped her and threw her on the bed. I had climbed on top of her when the phone rang.

I rolled off of Cassie and lifted the receiver. "Yeah?"

"I have it," Millie said. "How much longer?"

I glanced at Cassie. "Twenty minutes, tops."

"I'm on the way."

I dropped the telephone handset into its cradle.

Cassie pushed me onto my back and straddled me, her heavy breasts brushing my chest. "What was that?"

"Business," I said.

"Don't lie to me."

I grabbed her wrists, twisting until she grimaced in pain. Then I rolled her off of me and onto her back. She spread her legs and I buried myself deep inside her. Like before, the sex was hard and left us both bruised in places not usually shown to others.

Afterward, we dressed and I walked her to the door.

She stepped outside and hesitated on the front walk. Then she looked back at me. "Carvel's not here."

"I'll phone a cab."

She looked up and down the street.

"That's not like Carvel," she said. "He's never far from me."

Hours after the park had closed, I met Millie and Carvel at Lover's Leap, overlooking the Brazos River in Cameron Park.

"What the fuck is this about?" Carvel asked.

"Millie has the suitcase," I explained. I held my hand at my side, my fingers wrapped around Deadwood's Glock, the safety off and my finger resting lightly on the trigger. "He found it in your apartment."

"What suitcase?" Carvel stood next to the rock wall. He stepped back so he could watch both of us. He stopped when his ass touched the wall and he could go no farther.

"You were in Texarkana same time I was," I said. "You'd followed Cassie and Jeremy, protecting her father's interests. You saw me take her from the room. You saw how messed up she was."

Carvel's gaze darted from me to Millie and back. He wet his lips with the tip of his tongue.

"You knew we didn't have the suitcase so you went in after it," I continued. "So what happened? Did Jeremy surprise you, start to get up, what?"

Carvel shook his head.

"Doesn't matter why," I said. "You shot him."

Carvel charged.

I lifted the Glock and squeezed the trigger. A single bullet ripped into Carvel's chest and knocked him back onto the stone wall.

Millie walked up to the wall, pressed one boot against Carvel's side, and pushed. The body tumbled down the side of the cliff. Then Millie dropped Carvel's .38 over the side.

We left the silver Mercedes parked at Lover's Leap for the police to discover and Millie rode with me back to the office. Along the way, we stopped long enough to dispose of Deadwood's Glock.

Millie moved the suitcase from the tattoo parlor into my office, then he drove home. I drove up Austin Avenue to Masterson's house.

I leaned into the doorbell and waited until Masterson finally pulled the door open. He hadn't been expecting me and he wore gray sweatpants that he'd hurriedly pulled on before opening the door.

"Yes?"

Cassie appeared at the top of the stairs, saw me standing in the open doorway, and hurried down the steps to the foyer.

"Where's Carvel?" she demanded. She wore a red terry-cloth robe that she held closed.

"He's with your husband."

Cassie slapped me. The robe gaped open and I took one last look at her naked body, seeing the bruises I'd left on her during our sex only a few hours earlier.

Masterson's eyes narrowed while he considered the implications of what I'd said. "Know anybody looking for work?" he asked. "Someone trustworthy."

"I think of anybody, I'll let you know."

Police found the abandoned Mercedes about the time dawn arrived in Waco, and a few hours later a jogger running along the riverfront path found Carvel's body. Over the course of the day, the police found Carvel's .38 and the spent shell from Deadwood's Glock.

That afternoon, Elroy met me at my office and I handed him the suitcase Millie had found in Carvel's apartment.

"You clean on everything?" Elroy asked.

"Clean as I can be."

"The gun?"

"Bottom of the Brazos."

Elroy opened the suitcase and handed me a banded stack of hundred-dollar bills. "Finder's fee," he said.

"What happened?"

"Jeremy planned to double-cross his father-in-law," Elroy explained. "The money was for some of my associates in St Louis. When Jeremy didn't show at the meet, they knew something had gone wrong. They wanted me to resolve the issue so I had a guy lined up for the next day." Elroy paused, pulled an unfiltered Camel from the pack in his shirt pocket, and lit it with a silver Zippo. After a long drag, he continued. "Then you showed up, followed only a few minutes later by Carvel. Changed all my plans."

Elroy carried the suitcase to the office door, then stopped and turned back.

"And give this to your kid, next time you see him." Elroy pulled the latest issue of one of the science fiction magazines from his pocket and tossed it on the desk. "It's a good issue," he said. "Just don't spill nothing on it."

I counted the money later and split it with Millie – 30,000 for him, 70,000 for me.

The lab later confirmed that Carvel Casey's .38 had killed Jeremy Wilson. Texarkana closed their file on the murder of Jeremy Wilson. Waco's file on Carvel Casey remains open but inactive. Richard Masterson disappeared one day after an intensive interview with local police and I suspect that Elroy Johnson or his associates gave Masterson a one-way ticket to the bottom of Lake Waco. Cassie Masterson Wilson moved to L.A., where she started a members-only website for pain lovers. And my bruises finally healed.

Two days after finding Carvel's body, the police phoned to tell me the tests on my .38 had turned up negative and that I could retrieve the revolver at my convenience. They never did ask any more questions.

The Summer of Grant Lee Buffalo

Maxim Jakubowski

I was asking her, as you do, about other men.

I already knew about those who had come before she met her present husband. Three in all, a modest figure. I was number five. Or did husbands maybe count double?

But surely I enquired there had been temptations, infatuations, attractions, even if nothing sexual had actually occurred?

"Well," she hesitated, lowering her eyes with false modesty, "there was a man in Wales. He was a bit like you in looks. Just saw him staring at me in a strange, insistent way from across the room at a reading I attended. It was last year. October."

"Really?"

"The way it goes. A look in someone's eye and you think, it could happen, there could be sparks. Sort of wondering what it would be like to fuck him, be fucked by him . . . But we never even spoke."

"Oh . . ." somehow I was disappointed. "Anyone else?"

"Well," her eyes again avoided me.

"Come on," I insisted.

"The bass player from Grant Lee Buffalo," she spat out, her tone almost breathless. "It was at their gig, just last week at the ICA. I was toward the front of the crowd and he was on stage. Our eyes met. Jesus, he could have had me right there. It was crazy. I felt like a slut. I think Chris must have guessed, or something, because he wanted us to leave at the end of the set and wouldn't stay for the obligatory encores."

I smiled. The next day I looked up the American musician's name (and physiognomy – rough trade with an intellectual bent) in the CD liner notes. But never remembered it later.

"Was it the music?"

"No, just him, up there, it was his eyes, they just cut through me, I swear. He was deathly thin, even gaunt, not even my type of man. But I knew, and I think that he also knew that something was in the air that night. I even guess my husband had some second sense of it because he also behaved unusually at the end of the concert, annoyed, frightened maybe."

Frankly I couldn't see what she saw in him. Too American, too rock 'n'roll. But there was an element of danger. Forbidden fruit? But then I was still amazed that she was even having an affair with me.

Would I ever understand women?

Even as I slept with them, gazed voyeuristically at their features in repose as they dreamed next to me in the illicit beds of the hotel rooms we inhabited, I felt I could read in their soft breath the seeds of their future absence or betrayal.

This was the summer of Grant Lee Buffalo. After we broke up I discovered Counting Crows and ached with the knowledge I would never play their music to her or whisper into her ears the lyrics of a couple of songs on the CD which just broke me up inside. Much later I'd come across Matthew Ryan. And others. Singers, groups, musicians. Funny the way rock music punctuated the major events in my life, the women in my life.

This was Kate, of the tousled hair, the porcelain skin, the repressed anger, for whom I would buy a Leonard Cohen CD and prepare an assortment of compilation tapes she would only be able to play on her Walkman on her way to work near Goodge Street.

Was being the operative word.

A summer that lasted into early winter as lust made place for love and then desperation, as embraces grew in intensity and the fucking took on an aura of violence as I realized my days with her were numbered. It was already there, in her voice, in her eyes, in the subtle twist of her lips as she shied away from passion, her cold, cold heart drifting away from more serious involvement than sweaty copulations on office floors or adulterous hotel rooms, rented for the duration of the lunch break. Those things you feel inside, don't you? So, you turn the screw on your anger; you tighten your hold on her wrists as you hold her down and thrust inside her, and she feebly protests that you are hurting her. You thread out the belt from your black trousers and, one night, tie her hands and render her helpless. She does not protest. Lets you do it. You raise the ante. Order her to close her eyes, and circle her fragile neck with the dark brown leather belt. Just like a slave collar. You install her on hands and knees and forcefully take her from behind, watching in fascination as your thick, darker member breaches her openings and makes its savage way into her wet intimacy, all the while holding on to the belt and pulling firmly, keeping her head in a vertical posture. With every new fuck you feel her moving mentally further away from you. But in her silence she still submits to those perverted whims of yours.

She comes, again and again, under your ministrations, with a soft moan, a deep sigh and, torturing yourself, you imagine her being taken in a similar position by another man, maybe the bass player from Grant Lee Buffalo even. You have used a piece of black silk to cover her eyes and positioned her over the bed cover, spread open, obscenely gaping, then led him to the room and indicated to him she is his for the taking. You watch. Of course he is bigger, longer and thicker than you, and as he makes his way past her lips, his cock brushes the folds of her labia away inwards, and every in and out movement, shakes her whole, white body as he pumps into her, bruises her engorged skin, marking her for ever. And, God in heaven, he stays hard so long and never tires. The sweat glistens on her back, her breasts swing gently under the impact of his attack, and the animal sounds that rise from deep inside her are unlike any I have ever heard rise from her before. Or, at any rate, with me.

Ah, isn't my imagination vile?

Or had I actually shared her with another man, whored her for the sake of my madness, would she not have returned to her husband? Maybe it was something she actually craved?

Two years later, Grant Lee Buffalo, having failed to achieve greater commercial success, broke up and Grant Lee Phillips, the singer and songwriter of the group, would launch a solo career. But his music on its own somehow never recaptured the intensity and gut wrenching impact of that initial year.

I never discovered where the bass player went or what he did. Another minor casualty of the rock and roll wars.

The French Lycée in London's South Kensington was the first school I attended where the sexes were not segregated and my initial few months attending classes there proved highly distracting. I soon lost my fascination for the Tour de France and continental bicycle riders and discovered that new race: girls. Somehow they had never really meant too much to me before. They were just there, another gender, a mere curiosity.

To celebrate the end of the first term, the headmistress organized a small party where all final year students, of which I was one, were invited to sip soft drinks, mingle socially and even dance, albeit under the watchful eye of some of the staff.

Thinking back on the occasion, I reckon it must have been shortly before the Christmas break, when many of the students from France and overseas would return home for a couple of weeks or so. I was awkward, had no social graces, moving from group to group of students and not-quite-friends, making small talk and stealing furtive glances at Catherine, Rhoona, Elizabeth and the myriad girls who'd caught my attention during the course of the term. Some from my class, some from others in the same year. They were all supremely exotic, unreal in a strange sort of way, emerging from the cocoon of childhood into a chrysalis of womanhood, stirring new, unknown emotions inside me that I was irritated to find I couldn't fully control. Creatures I wished to befriend, but knew not how, or even what to do with after the first insignificant conversation.

The headmistress worked the room, dispensing biscuits and cakes, helping to thaw out our shyness. Sensing failure, she finally signalled it was time for music. This was the year of the twist. Chubby Checker reigned supreme.

I hadn't truly wanted to go to the school's party but my mother had convinced me a change of atmosphere would do me good. I had fervently argued I couldn't even dance, so she had given me a twist-made-easy lesson a week before and I had been practising my movements in the bathroom every day since, using a bath towel as the centre of gravity for my graceless movements.

Six months later, the cancer inside her would get the better of my mother and she would be dead.

But the Chubby Checker tune was the song I was prepared for that day and when the first strains of its melody sounded, I swiftly moved to the dance floor and studiously began dancing.

And, oh, how I danced, and Catherine even joined me, with a wry smile on her face which just melted me inside. We twisted again like we did that winter and it felt wonderful and at the old age of 16 I entered the world of women in earnest. For ever. Never to leave it again, for good, for bad, for joyful, for heartbreak.

Encouraged, I even invited Catherine out a few weeks later after classes resumed in the New Year. Short Catherine who looked like a bird and made my heart flutter. But that's another story altogether. A sad one, of course but then it wasn't Chubby Checker's fault so hey ho let's twist again in a circular motion, and close your eyes, and imagine you are drying yourself after a shower and your body gyrates against the soft contact of the bath towel against your skin. Oh yeah.

In Paris I finally drowned in the sea of sex.

It was a mixed soundtrack. There were the studious sounds of jazz my flatmate would play non-stop, making me feel so damn guilty I could find no pleasure, no celebration of the senses, in its arty tones. These blended together with the latest hits I would import from back home, early Beatles songs, the Stones' "It's All Over Now" which would start the adrenaline flowing inside me like few other rock tunes could. A feeling I would soon grow accustomed to, opening myself to the sheer emotional power of music and marvelling at the fact that some melodies could affect me inside so strongly and scar my soul for ever.

It was a time of folly, of foolishness and shattered ideals.

Lois had blonde hair the colour of straw and looked, to my inexpert eyes, like a svelte and beautiful model. Her breasts were slight but full and her skin the colour of porcelain and I would feel like fainting every time I entered her, believing it was all a dream and this was too good to last. Of course it wouldn't and she quickly tired of me. When I remember her these days, it's to the sound of the Four Tops' "Reach Out and I'll Be There", the Tamla Motown hymn that kept on being played at the party at which we met.

Nicole and I never even had sex. We spent hours naked together on my bed, but never crossed that Rubicon. Did we have a song, a group? I hate myself now for not remembering the soundtrack of our relationship. She had high cheekbones, short, thick, light brown hair and a compact body. Her nipples hardened under the mere breeze of my breath. She was the first woman ever to say "I love you" to me.

And then there was the time I even went out with a singer on the folk circuit. When her career hit a roadblock in England, she decided to move to Nashville from where she would send me occasional demo tapes. She later married the much older owner of a Greenwich Village club and settled down to have kids before we lost touch. I still have her albums, gathering dust with the rest of my vinyl collection up in the attic.

With Natasha, we spent hours together listening to the fey but exotic sounds of the Incredible String Band on my deficient hi-fi and slowly falling in love in a quiet, unassuming way, later setting the seal on our relationship with a bus ride to the Hackney ABC to watch Franco Zeffirelli's "Romeo and Juliet".

Elaine was a classical buff, dressed most conservatively and sucked me off with the zeal of a common whore.

Tabitha liked Duran Duran and most of the New Romantic bands and liked to have her hands bound when we fucked.

Leonard Cohen's melancholy tunes punctuated the long, on-off affair with Mimi, although she was also partial to Metallica and isolated opera arias, a woman of diverse tastes and moods and sexual cravings.

There is something about Cohen's music, I suppose, that strikes a resonant chord inside my heart and my loins, as I would include many of his songs on the various compilation tapes I would record for her-who-must-not-be-named, alongside music by the Walkabouts, Counting Crows, Springsteen, Peter Gabriel, Oh Susannah, the Handsome Family, Matthew Ryan and, again, Grant Lee Buffalo.

Music, sex and heartbreak or the Reader's Digest abridged (and expurgated) story of my life. The people at Sony, Virgin and other record companies must be laughing all the way to the bank at my excuses for keeping them in business.

But when I suddenly wake up at three in the morning in an alien hotel room in some American city or another, and the world outside is cold and silent, and the emptiness inside me is just too much to bear, random thoughts evoke faces, bodies and tunes from yesterday with uncanny poignance.

Mimi's so pale blue eyes.

A tune from "Aida".

Kate's cunt. Her gash like a blooming flower of blood.

"Truly, truly, truly."

Nicole's uneven teeth. A smile designed to launch a thousand ships.

Gainsbourg's "Melody Nelson".

And on and on.

Maybe I'm just a sexual romantic who's seen too many movies and feels that every life, every relationship requires a soundtrack?

Or a disgusting, self-deluded pornographer, who believes that the shocking intimacy of every act of sexual excess can somehow attain sheer beauty with the right musical accompaniment?

I can live with both theories I suppose.

And already my shameless mind is busy speculating on what Claudia's soundtrack will be. Forget the hotel room, the railway station we meet at or the foreign city that will shelter our bodies, the colour of the wallpaper, whether she keeps her eyes open or not when we fuck, what I want to know is how I will remember her when it is all over.

I vainly try to guess what sort of song will go with those breathless phone tones of hers, that unsaid longing, that sadness that is already bringing us together, despite all the obstacles.

A dance tune from Jamiroquai?

A melancholy dirge by Goldfrapp?

I do wonder if she's ever listened to Grant Lee Buffalo in their glorious heyday, and whether she might fancy the bass player? Not that I have a threesome in mind, I assure you . . .

Look at Me

Riain Grey

Nick and I met in his store, a small place, tucked away in a corner of the Village, stacked high with dusty biographies and art history books. Not really my kind of bookstore, but I was forty-five minutes early for a visit with my cardiologist and I had nothing else to do.

Nick was leaning against the counter, his arms crossed in front of him, talking to a customer. I went and hid in the history section and spent fifteen minutes trying to think of something to say. Eventually I gave up and decided to go for the direct approach. I wandered back toward the counter and took a deep breath.

"I just spent fifteen minutes in the history section trying to think of something to say to you."

His eyebrows rose.

"Come up with anything good?"

"No."

"Too bad," he answered pleasantly. "I think I would have enjoyed talking to you."

"Hmm," I said. "Well, if I think of anything, I'll let you know."

"Okay," he said, and I thought I saw a tiny corner of a smile on his face.

"I'll try Fiction," I said. "There's always a lot to think about in the Fiction section."

"I'm Nick," he said.

By this point in my life I had more or less given up on the idea of having a normal relationship. For the last three years I had been sharing company with a vague but life-threatening illness that left me exhausted and furious. My hospital stays became characterized by the intense, complicated fantasies I created, in which my body was the innocent but willing victim, and my illness the cruel, handsome lover who took me apart, piece by piece, only to put me back together again. As I drifted in and out of morphine-induced calm, I thought I saw shadows, felt them tie my wrists and ankles, felt my master pushing his way on top of me, a shining knife blooming in his hand.

Eventually I was free to go, though the doctors never figured out exactly what was wrong with me. They cautioned me against heavy exercise or sudden shocks, apparently unaware that sudden shocks had been the highlight of my hospital stays; just leaving the room slowed my heartbeat. I moved back into Chelsea and adopted a cat. I worked nights at Dino's and tried not to behave self-destructively. I went to bed every night at 2:30 or 3:00 a.m. and watched the shadows of passing cars flicker across my wall. I lay awake and thought about things. As soon as the first smudges of light crawled through my window, I would feel something give way, loosening inside me, and I would fall into a helpless sleep.

My days became drowsy, hazy things, but my nights flickered into sharp focus. I felt myself moving into a higher gear. Things that had never made sense before were suddenly clear, like when your eyes get adjusted to the dark. At Dino's I waited tables with an easy grace that I had never felt before: my body in smooth, constant motion, my smile flashing out into the darkness. I started walking home from the restaurant, some twenty blocks, and always late at night, but it felt good to be outside. The summer air was sweet and sticky and coated my throat like cotton candy. At home I closed my eyes and listened, stroking myself to the outside sounds, waiting for something to happen.

Nick was an unexpected surprise. The first time I saw him I felt the sleep crumble away from my eyes, leaving me fragile and bare. He made me want to tell him things. His gray eyes turned flashing silver when he smiled. He had beautiful hands and curly brown hair that tumbled around his face when he looked at me. I wanted to talk to him for hours and touch him for days. There was a silver ring on his left hand that left me hot with lust; when I looked at it, all I could think of was his fingers wrapped in mine.

Nick didn't like to talk about himself, as a rule. Even after repeated visits to see him at the store, I knew almost nothing about him. "I'm a pretty boring guy," he would say apologetically, though this was untrue, and while he avoided mentioning specifics of his life, he was fascinated by even the smallest details of mine. I would leave his store in the afternoons feeling dazed, like I had had too much sun. I spent a lot of subway rides speculating about his life, all the private time he kept hidden from me.

I tried to imagine Nick in his bedroom – what would he be doing? Reading? Writing? Jerking off to *Hustler* magazine? I imagined myself in his room, lying on his bed, listening to records and smoking endless cigarettes. I imagined myself kneeling beneath him, sucking him dry. I imagined him looking down at me, his cigarette burning away to nothing between his fingertips, a thoughtful expression on his face.

One night I surprised myself by allowing these thoughts into my head while I got myself off. Usually it was nameless, faceless men, doing unspeakable things to my body, but this time it was Nick, sweet Nick, kneeling over me with a beautiful, painful expression, watching my face as we fucked. *What the hell?* I thought to myself, but I went with it because I didn't want it to stop, and Nick was there, touching my face and hair, holding me tight, his face buried into my neck. I rubbed myself until I came, twisting in my sheets, almost moaning out loud, and Nick's name came rushing out of my mouth – *Oh Nick, oh Nick, yes* – and I fell asleep that way, with my hand between my legs and his name sweet on my breath.

We kissed for the first time almost a month after we met. I went to visit him at work and stayed until it was time for him to close up. We locked the door and shut the gates, and when I asked him what I could do he looked at me almost helplessly and pulled me down with him until we were both kneeling on the floor in the cookbook section.

"Can I . . .?"

"I wish you would."

He laughed as he kissed me, the vibrations deep in our throats. I leaned into him, feeling my skirt ride up against my thighs as I pulled my body closer to his. We kissed breathlessly and his hand reached for my breast, his thumb rubbing my nipple absently.

"Is this okay?" he asked, his hand pausing against my chest.

"Christ, yes. Isn't it?"

"Oh, yes," he answered, seeming surprised.

"Well, don't stop," I said.

"No," he promised, and bent to kiss me again.

The next time I visited Nick at work, I hung around trying to act casual and waited for it to be seven o'clock. Nick was full of secret smiles for me. I shelved books and helped clean up. We stole kisses in the narrow aisles. Looking at him left me shaking and lustful. His hands drew fire across my back. When Nick finally locked the door I felt a tingling rush of heat deep inside my belly. He turned to look at me and I felt something give way inside me. Holding his gaze, I walked backwards, step by careful step, until I was surrounded by bookshelves, covered in shadow and hidden from view. I dropped to my knees and waited.

When Nick knelt down next to me, I resisted the urge to kneel down even more. I wanted to lower myself, give my body up, give him everything. Instead I reached out to touch his face and we kissed, sweetly and then harder. My breath caught in my throat and he looked at me intently.

"I know what my girl needs," he whispered, and I felt waves pulling me down, pulling me under, pulling me in.

He put his hand under my skirt, running his fingers up and down my inner thigh. I looked at him, feeling hot and liquid. Eyes locked on mine, he reached his hand up higher until his fingertips just grazed against my cunt. His surprised look turned to a hungry one when he realized I wasn't wearing anything under my skirt.

"Did you walk around like this all day?" he asked, his voice low, one finger just barely touching me, flicking against my clit.

"Yes."

"Were you wet like this all day?"

"No."

"Wet for me?"

"Yes."

"I don't think I've ever touched a girl this wet."

I could feel the blood rushing through my head, pounding, leaving me dizzy and breathless. My face burned bright red as I stared at the floor.

Nick laughed a little.

"I like seeing you like this," he commented, "I really like you like this," and he pushed his finger up inside me. I watched his hand moving under my skirt and felt myself falling into an ocean as he played with me, his thumb on my clit and his finger sliding up, slick and hot. "Lay down," he said suddenly, and pushed me gently backwards. I leaned back until I felt the floor, hard and cool against my back.

Nick pushed up my skirt with one hand, his other still dipping and twisting in my cunt. He knelt over me, staring down at my face. I closed my eyes.

"No," he said, "don't close them. Look at me."

I watched him silently.

"I want you to come," he told me, "and I want to look at your cunt while you do." I gasped as he slid another finger into me. He turned his gaze to my pussy, fascinated. He fucked me harder, bracing himself with one hand on the floor, and I arched my back, trying to push his fingers in deeper. Nick glanced up at me to see my reaction. When he saw me watching him, he caught his breath, his eyes turning liquid and still.

"My sweetheart," he breathed, "my sweet girl," and with that I was coming, hard, exploding into his hand, all sea water and salt, waves crashing against rocks in the tide.

The first time I went to my monthly doctor appointment after things started with Nick, I was flushed and out of breath. The nurse noted my elevated heartbeat with raised eyebrows. I sat in the examination room, almost dizzy, waiting for the doctor to come. The next month I was late – those fifteen minutes spent instead in Nick's store, leaning across the counter, eyes shining. And the month after I told the doctor I didn't need to see him any more.

"What do you mean?" he asked blankly. "Melinda, this is a

serious illness. We need to keep an eye on you. What if you have a relapse?"

"I've got someone," I answered, buttoning my shirt. He didn't ask me what I meant.

A few nights later I knelt before Nick again, my heart pounding in my throat. He tried to pull me up, but I stopped him. I looked up at him but couldn't express it.

"What is it?" he whispered.

I couldn't seem to do it. He put his hands on my shoulders and squeezed.

"Tell me," he said, a commanding tone in his voice.

Something gave inside.

"I – there's something I like."

"Yes?" he prompted.

"I like it when you – well. When you sort of take control."

His grip tightened on my shoulders. "You mean like now?"

"Yes," I whispered.

"You mean like before, when I fingered you?"

Fingered. God. I was wet already. I nodded, not trusting my voice.

"Why do you like it?"

"Because – I don't know."

"Because it makes you hot? Wet?"

"Yeah," I muttered.

"Hmm," he said. "That's interesting."

"Um," I squeaked.

"What else?" he asked, grabbing my hands and twisting them behind my back. "You like that?"

"Yes," I managed, trying to hold in a gasp.

"How about this?" he continued, shoving me down to the floor. "Want me to play rough?"

He held me down, my hands pinned above my head. He put his hand across my mouth, gently. I moaned into it. He laughed and pushed one of his fingers into my mouth. I moaned again and started to suck it, as sweetly as I could. I looked up at him and tried to tell him everything with my eyes. He was so, so beautiful. I wanted to fall, drown, sink under with my Nick. He looked at me as if considering something. I pleaded silently for more, twisting under his hands.

"Shh," he suggested, pulling his hand away and resting one finger on my lips. "Don't move. Don't think. Just be here. With me."

Nick touched my cheek, slid my hair behind my ear. "I don't want to play around," he said, his voice clear and quiet. "If we do this, we do it for real."

I nodded.

"You understand? No games."

"I know," I whispered. My breath shallow and fast.

"Good," he said, his voice short and crisp. He pulled away from me, letting go of my wrists. I caught my breath when I saw how he was looking at me.

"Get up on your hands and knees," he ordered calmly.

I climbed up onto my knees, struggling awkwardly for balance.

"No. Hands. And. Knees."

This was a Nick I had never seen before. Still slow to anger, but with a cold, blue flame. I positioned myself as best I could, feeling clumsy. I bit my lip and stared at the floor.

I felt Nick move behind me, looking me over. "Good," he said, a satisfied tone in his voice, and I shut my eyes tight against sudden tears.

His hands were smooth against my back. He pushed my skirt up over my ass, his fingers catching in the material. He brushed the skirt smooth and rubbed his hand over my cunt. I felt hot indentations where his fingers pressed down. In one sudden motion, he hooked his fingers into the waistband of my panties and pulled them down around my knees. Cold air flooded my cunt and made me stiffen.

"I can smell you," he remarked conversationally, and pushed two fingers up into me. A pathetic noise escaped my mouth. Holding his hand there, he wrapped his other hand in my hair, grasping my neck with steady, sure fingers. I was tingling and tense, shivering a little. His hand stroked my neck, holding my head perfectly still.

"Is this what you meant?" he asked softly.

Yes, yes, yes, I thought. I wanted so desperately to look at him. I could feel my heart beating steadily, hot pulses in my chest.

"Yes," I said quietly.

"Yes, what?"

"Yes, Sir," I said.

"Good girl," he answered approvingly, moving his fingers in and out of my cunt, slipping into a rhythm, his other hand still on my neck. I could feel myself edging toward oblivion with every breath. "You're so perfect," he said suddenly, and I could hear the surprise and admiration in his tone. "So well-behaved. So beautiful. I think this suits you."

"It does, Sir," I managed.

"I think I could get used to this." He leaned over me and shoved two fingers into my mouth, hard. He let me suck them for a moment and then moved away, casually wiping his hand on his jeans. "I'll be right back. Don't move."

Nick walked away and I closed my eyes, feeling a rush of blood buzzing in my ears. When I felt him near me again I held my breath, trying to tell what he was doing from the movement in the air. There was a pause, and then the unmistakable sound of a lighter clicking into flame. I heard a tiny whoosh and then heard Nick exhaling, smelled the smoke drifting toward me. I felt something nudging at my lips and took a grateful drag of his cigarette.

He inhaled again. "Look at me," he said, the words circling around his cigarette lazily. I opened my eyes to find him kneeling above me, eyes narrowed and dark. The cigarette hung suspended in the corner of his mouth.

"When you look at me, I can see all the way in you," he said, smoke trickling from the corners of his mouth. "I can see all your secrets."

I looked up at him, my heart pounding like it might burst.

"I can see that you're a girl who wants to be held down and fucked on the floor of a dirty bookstore. I can see that you want me to own you."

Nick unzipped his pants, the movement of his hands making me sigh with pleasure.

"Now you know your secrets, too."

He pulled out his cock and guided it into my mouth, cradling my head with both hands. I relaxed into his hands as I sucked him.

"You're mine, now," he said absently, his fingers tangled in my hair, and I felt myself starting to cry. "Shh," he said again, and reached one hand between my legs. He stroked me carefully, teasing with two slow fingers, slipping in and out.

"Let go," he said urgently. "Let it go, Melinda." His fingers moved faster and I whimpered, trying to pull him deeper into my mouth and arching beneath his hand. "Let it go," he repeated, and I felt it happen, felt myself slide away into hot, dizzy streams, blood rushing through me, my heart hammering until I felt myself burst, hot and wet. Nick pumped his cock in and out of my mouth, his hand clutching at the back of my neck. Somehow I knew everything was different now. I reached up for him and sucked harder as he slid in and out of my mouth.

"Keep looking," he whispered.

Cashmeres Must Die

A.F. Waddell

Stuart Metzler sat in his 1959 Pontiac Chieftain on his Maple St driveway. Mmmm . . . that new car smell. One day they'll bottle and sell it, he thought. He pulled a small memo pad and pen from a suit pocket and made a note. "New car smell – replicate and market!" He took in the car's interior. "Dashboard needs more knobs! Bigger!" he jotted. As a Strategy Formulation consultant he had diverse information and ideas but felt occasionally envious as he watched clients succeed in their projects. He experienced random, uncontrollable urges to lie, and enjoyed gauging reaction. Stuart anticipated the day's work, and wondered what his secretary Vicky would be wearing.

Donna Metzler stood in her bedroom staring into a lingerie drawer. In a jumble were the panties: the 100 per cent white cotton high waist, the pastel nylon, the killer girdles, the Days-Of-The-Week undies. She consulted a calendar: Tuesday! She sometimes wore Sunday's undies during the week. Cotton felt best, softly clinging in her curves and nooks and crannies. Nylon felt strange, and smelled stranger when dirty. Girdles could be a bitch, but on occasion they helped achieve the ever popular iron belly effect. Brassieres with evil-eyed tips looked up at her: silk, cotton, nylon; underwire, torpedo, push up. "The breasts! The breasts must be controlled! *Control* the breasts! Mmmm ha ha ha ha HA!" She imagined a mad designer at Playtex.

Donna finished dressing in a pink-and-white checked cotton blouse with a Peter Pan collar, black Capezio pants, and flats. She grabbed her keys, purse, and sunglasses, and was out the door. She commandeered her Chevy Bel Air and drove the Springfield streets. The homes and lawns seemed quiet and perfect. A little too quiet. A little too perfect. She imagined chaos and pain behind closed doors: little pastel houses, like gawdy wedding cakes, poison under layers of frou frou and frosting. The whites were dingy. The soufflés were flat. The decanters were tapped. The one-eyed god droned, selling soap, lies, and subliminalism . . . Snap out of it! Donna told herself.

She pulled into the Texaco station on North Main. Donna smiled as Tony appeared at her driver side door. He grinned broadly. Was it her imagination, or did his eyes and teeth project sparkles of light? His uniform was always suspiciously spotless. His chronic perkiness was a turn-on. Men in service were a turn-on.

"Check your fluids, Mrs Metzler?"

"Please, Tony."

In his office Stuart pulled a magazine from his desk drawer. *Secretaries* boasted photographs of smiling women answering telephones, typing, serving coffee, bending over to pick up dropped pencils and more. A young woman sat behind an open-front desk in a grassy field. Her hair draped her face and heavy-lidded eyes as she chewed a No. 2 pencil and dreamily stared. She wore a sweater and skirt, but no stockings. Her legs were parted. She wore white cotton underpants, the whitest imaginable white, which contrasted with her freckled tanned thighs. *Debbie is a secretary who dreams of an acting career. In her spare time she volunteers at her local Senior Center, and as a Big Sister.*

Vicky Miller sat outside Stuart's office at her desk in a small reception area. She wore a twin sweater set, form-fitting skirt, nylon stockings, and heels. Her desk neatly displayed a front strike Remington typewriter, telephone, and intercom. She opened a desk drawer: it boasted nail files, polish, small cosmetic bag, perfume, hairbrush, extra pair of nylons, almost everything a young woman might need to look and feel her best.

Stuart buzzed. "Miss Miller, please come into my office."

"Be right there, Mr Metzler." Vicky grabbed a steno pad

and pencil, and entered the sacred chamber of dark, rich woods, shades of forest-green, wall trophies, and Men In Suits.

"Miss Miller, may I ask, what is that sweater you're wearing?"

"Why, it's cashmere. It's very soft. Feel?"

"But of course. Cashmere . . ." He hesitantly reached and slowly ran his hand over Vicky's left sweater sleeve. "It's amazingly soft."

"It's heavenly. But I've often wondered. What does a cashmere look like? They don't have to kill them, do they?"

"Vicky, I'm sorry. Cashmeres must die."

Her eyes slightly widened and her moist lower lip trembled. Stuart patted and rubbed her left shoulder. Warm sensation filled his palms and sent nervous vibration through his arms, shoulders, chest, belly, and cock. His cock! The world seemed full of teasing textures. His cotton pyjamas, his cotton flannel bed sheets, his starched boxer shorts. As he imagined being surrounded by its texture, his prick swelled against his cotton boxers and slacks. **Memo: Create and market cashmere bed sheets. Slash cost!**

At Wilson's Tailors, two men discussed a transaction.

"The styles, items, and material we discussed . . . how very unusual."

"Can you do it or not?"

"Yes, we can. But it will not be inexpensive."

"Very well."

"It will require fittings."

"Just do them in sizes eight, 38B, and medium. And make it snappy."

Stuart let himself in and marveled at his surroundings. "Honey, I'm home!" Minimalist Deco furnishings rested upon shag carpet. White tailored polyester drapes were drawn against the sun. Dark wood paneling and a faux stone fireplace helped to complete the decor.

After a dinner of hot dog casserole, iceberg lettuce, and cherry Jello, Stuart and Donna sat on the plastic-covered couch. Donna wore yellow baby doll pyjamas. Stuart wore a t-shirt and boxers. As he clicked the television remote, a dark, intense man came on. "Portrait of a little woman with big dreams, one Annie T. Zimmer by name. A housewife cursed to wander a physical universe where there is no end to dirt and drudgery. A woman for whom perfection is an impossible dream and who feels criticism like knives. A bitter woman who's never been able to capture realities more intangible than herself – respect, success, acceptance, and love. Up ahead, an intersection of her desires, an entrance that leads to opportunity and . . . The Twilight Zone."

BRRRVVVUP! As Stuart and Donna moved toward one another, their legs made moist suction noises as they peeled from the plastic. His hands fondled her cotton covered breasts as his mouth explored hers. Her lipstick was messy and waxy and smeared. She smelled of Ivory Soap. He was scented with Old Spice. His nipples rubbed his t-shirt as his chest buffed hers. He moved his knee from between her legs. Her transparent cotton pyjama bottoms clung in her splayed pussy lips, a thin sheath of soft yellow, bisecting moist pink underneath.

She gripped his tented cock through his shorts, pulling the cloth firmly over it. She could feel its unique shape as she squeezed and ran her hand up and down its covered expanse.

He left on her soft pyjama top. As she lay on her back, her breasts slightly drooped toward her prone arms. He put his fingers under her pyjama shorts waistband and pulled them down, peeling them from her and slipping them down her legs, and off. He cupped her and stroked her and slid his middle finger inside her. If not for the flange of his spread hand he felt he might be consumed by quivering monstrous wetness. She ground herself around him, hips rocking and heels digging into plastic. He guided his cock in and out of her, shallow to deep, shallow to deep, shallow to deep! As she arched her back, engulfing him, her moist backside slid forth then back. Her head against the arm of the sofa, they slid toward orgasm. *There! Yes!* Stuart's face froze as he pumped and stopped; Donna briefly cried out, before they lay in tiny pools of moisture. BRRRVVVUP! Donna rose and went to the kitchen.

Returning, she leaned over the sofa and cleaned it with a damp sponge.

Donna walked out of her front door, onto the walk and lawn. Cars gleamed in driveways. Sprinklers hissed in the dark. Plastic flamingos shone wetly. Drops of water splashed on her naked skin. As street lights sent their shafts, her form glimmered, face and breasts and belly and legs. A spotless sidewalk led her past her neighbors' houses, which seemed to be breathing, their surfaces slightly rising and falling, rising and falling.

"Check your FLUIDS, Mrs Metzler?" Tony the Texaco man was suddenly in her path, eyes and teeth sparkling, maniacally grinning. He had something draped over his left shoulder.

"What? . . ."

Tony quickly unrolled a large tarp and threw it over her, lifted her, and slung her over his shoulder. Donna struggled as Tony marched the sidewalk, whistling *I Get A Kick Out Of You*. Physically subdued and verbally stifled, she noticed that the material smelled of motor oil and auto mechanical chemistry. It draped and rubbed and chafed her skin, as her waist bent over the jut of Tony's shoulder, breasts flattening against his back.

"Mmmmmpppph . . . Mmmmmmppphhh!"

Wake up! Lucidity ruled; she awoke in her twin bed.

Stuart and Donna sat across from one another at the kitchen table. Stuart gobbled meat: sausage, bacon, and to insure adequate protein consumption, eggs. Toast, juice and coffee rounded off his menu. Donna nibbled boiled eggs and fruit.

"Need more butter, sweetie?"

"I'm fine, thanks," Stuart said, his mouth and chin shining greasily.

"Busy day today? Lots of clients scheduled?"

"Fairly busy. How about yours?"

"Cleaning. Shopping. Gassing the car. Nothing special." She smiled.

Stuart drove west on Oak. He loved his large formidable Pontiac, a veritable tank of a vehicle. He imagined almost effortlessly driving through fences and walls. The interior needed additional features, he thought: beverage holders. A small built-in television. A minuscule broiler oven. A tiny barbecue grill. . .

"Good morning, Vicky." He strode past Vicky's desk and into his office, sat down at his desk and opened his briefcase. He pulled a magazine from it. He lay the issue of *Goat World* in front of him and flipped it open. *The Himalayan Cashmere Goat is a ruminant mammal of the cattle family, with hollow horns, coarse hair, and a characteristic beard. It is closely related to the sheep. It has been bred for centuries for its highly valuable hair and wool. It can exist only in mountain regions of the Himalayan mountains and in Tibet and Mongolia, at altitudes of 15,000 feet or more. Himalayan cashmere goats live in herds and feed on grass and shrubs.*

Its long, straight, coarse outer hair has little value; however, the small quantity of the underhair, or down, is made into luxuriously soft wool-like yarns with a characteristic highly napped finish. This fine cashmere fiber is not sheared from the goat but acquired through frequent combings during the shedding season. Cashmere is a much finer fiber than mohair or any wool fiber. It is soft and lighter in weight than wool, and quite warm; however, because it is a soft, delicate fiber, fabrics produced from cashmere are not as durable as wool.

The intercom buzzed. "Mr Metzler? Mr Johnson is here."

"Fine. Send him in."

"Good morning, Mr Johnson. Please have a seat."

"Thank you. Mr Metzler, I understand that you suggest that Corp Inc. not proceed with the fast food idea?"

Stuart smiled. His eyes gleamed. "I do. In my opinion, the fast food business is a flash in the pan. It will never last. I'd recommend going into Specialty Retailing. It's all in the report."

"Specialty Retailing?"

"Yes. Specialty Retailing. Choose a single type of merchandise. Scotch tape, for example. Sell only that item. KA Ching! See?"

Donna sat at the cluttered kitchen table and read over coffee. She had a magazine jones. The paper was glossy. The colors were bright. The text was perky. Their pages called to her from newsstands and checkout stands. Their energy could be exciting. Comforting. Some of the information was practical. *Woman Today* offered advice. *A housewife should run her household the way an executive runs his business: with goals, schedules and plans. Plan for dinner, or at least shop early. Take time to rest and relax during the day so as to avoid exhaustion and depletion. With proper planning, one can have all home duties finished before noon. When he arrives home, greet him with a warm smile. Don't voice problems or complaints. Don't complain if he's late for dinner. Just count this as minor compared to his potentially rough day. Make him comfortable. Suggest he lean back in a comfortable chair or lie down in the bedroom. Have a cool or warm drink ready for him. Fluff his pillow and offer to remove his shoes. Speak in a low, soft, soothing and pleasant voice.* The last part made Donna warm and tingly.

She took a brush to her laundry after applying *Stain Be Gone!* White was the worst. Blood and food stains were tough. She held the cotton fabric in her left hand and agitated the brush with her right. White . . . whiter . . . whitest . . . goddamnit! Housewife. Housewife! What was she, married to a house? She might as well make love to it . . . embrace it . . . roll naked in its piles of silky laundry . . . straddle her vacuum cleaner and ride its vibration as she cleaned Cleaned CLEANED, her physical orgasm melding with a psychic one, her rocking grasp satisfied, her sanitary standards met − before slipping falling dripping into soft fragrant fabric folds, pulling their texture around her mounds and curves; around her neck and under her arms and between her legs . . .

BBBBBRRRIIIIIIIIGGG! The doorbell brought a flushed Donna to reality. Her friend Susie was at the door, sporting magazines, chocolate cake and brandy. Donna loved their occasional mornings together.

"Catch you at a bad time?"

"No, not at all. I'm ready for a break. Come into the kitchen." They took a seat opposite one another at the table and spread the goodies on red Formica.

"Fork for that? Or do you just want to use your hands?"

Susie smiled and sloshed St Regis into two jelly jar glasses. They sipped and gulped and dug into chocolate cake.

Susie thumbed *Women's World* magazine. "So, I was reading this article. The Yesnik Report says that 62 per cent of women masturbate, and that clitoral orgasm is natural and superior to vaginal orgasm."

"Really?"

"S'true, the article says. Donna, do you ever masturbate? Have you ever seen your clitoris?"

Donna laughed and swilled her slightly fiery brew. "I've touched myself, sure. But I've never really seen that part of me. My clitoris."

"Get a mirror."

"Susie!"

Donna leaned back on a vinyl chair. Through her parted robe, blue silk panties shone.

"S'okay. Go ahead and slip them off." She refreshed Donna's drink.

Donna lifted her hips and rolled her panties down, pulled them off and tossed them aside. She leaned back on the chair and parted her legs. Susie held the angled mirror inches away. With her right index and middle finger Donna slightly spread her labia and saw the mirrored reflection, a steamy pink jungle of curves and folds and bumps staring back at her from the small round mirror frame.

"The clitoris is at top center. S' hidden, like. Now, put your finger there and rub . . ."

Donna pressed a fingertip into herself and watched it slightly disappear.

"Hic! Oh shit. HIC! Now I've got the hiccups! I hate it when this happens!"

"Donna, first you need to take a teaspoon of sugar. Then hold your breath and drink 12 ounces of water. Hold your nose as I plug your ears. Always works for me."

"HIC!" She ate the sugar and gulped water – held her breath and held her nose. Susie stood closely behind and plugged Donna's ears.

Donna began to laugh as the doorbell rang. Probably another salesman, she thought. She choked on laughter and spat water across the kitchen. "HIC!"

"Just a MINUTE! Be right there!"

The garment bag hung in Donna's closet. She took it from the rod and laid it on the bed, unzipping it and flinging it open. Padded hangers were stacked between layers of hot pink softness. In front of the mirror she adorned her body with black pearls; bra and panties; shirtwaist dress; apron; gloves. She slipped on black high heels and walked to the kitchen. Her heels clicked and clacked on the black-and-white squared linoleum; her calves curved and bulged and protested at the assault of three-inch heels; spinal alignment threw her head and pelvis forward. Layers of cashmere trapped warmth; her kitchen trapped warmth.

Stuart entered the kitchen. Donna stood at the stove with her back to him. He was hit with a wall of odor: cooking browning bird, raw white onion, pungent spice, sulfurous vegetables; of moist rising yeasty bread dough in a cotton cloth-covered bowl; of Youth Dew perfume, and coconut shampoo. Had the scene been depicted in a cartoon, a cloud might have enveloped him.

He watched her cook. He smelled chicken juices steamily drenching sage stuffing in her hot Amana. She made gravy. In a skillet bubbled seasoned browned drippings. She added Half and Half, poultry seasoning and coarse ground pepper. As it began to boil she added a flour and water paste and turned down the heat. Fat, starch, moisture and heat chemically colluded, combined and expanded, its mass getting thicker and creamier and larger.

He approached and stood behind her, the molecular essence of her skin and clothing mingling in his nose and brain. His bare skin brushed the back of her dress; he stroked her breasts. His erection pushed against her buttocks, moving in soft cashmere folds; she loved the feeling of its stiffness against her; she yearned to envelop it. He untied her apron and let it fall. He lifted her clingy dress up and over her head; static electricity sizzled between it and her lingerie, between it and her hair. In a synergism of warm skin and fibrous fluff, she faced him and gripped his cock with a gloved hand. He watched her vivid, pink-fluffed fingers stroke his peachy-pink blue-veined cock. She gently, firmly grasped its head, then quickly slammed her hand down its shaft – slowly gently up! Quickly firmly down! She moved to the table and sat on its edge, leaning slightly back, legs apart, black high-heeled feet askew. The pink cashmere panties were to spec: bikinis with a slit in the crotch. Her pussy looked a study in color, a surreal blossom, flesh pink surrounded by hot pink fibrous softness, upon red Formica. He stood at the edge of the table and stroked the panty; he stroked her exposed pussy. She guided his hand. "Here . . ." His finger parted her and angled upward, flesh-hook rubbing her clit. He explored more deeply; he felt an odd texture. He seized slick round hardness and pulled. Out slid glistening black pearls. "Cashmere Cunt With Pearls, On Red" the painting might be named. He pushed his cock into her as she melted over the edge; she wetly slammed herself against him, around him. As she straightened her back, the angle of his cock pounded her more forcefully. Her clit was electric white-hot; he prodded her higher and deeper as forms of sensation merged and released in her screams. Faster he stroked her cashmere covered cunt as he tensed and came, shooting pearly white into pink, on red. White bodies sprawled on red. On the stove, rich brown gravy bubbled over edges of stainless steel and splattered onto a white surface, as it made its way to a drip pan.

The Arb

Nicholas Urfé

I'm neck-deep in trying to figure out how to squeeze Mircea
Eliade and the intersection of the sacred and the profane into
three pages double-spaced when the phone rings, so of course I
leap to answer it.

"Hey," says Jamie.

"Hey."

"I, uh, got some really good stuff. You know? From Chris."

"Yeah," I say.

"And Eva's here," she says, but I've already heard her
laughing in the background. Sounds like they're listening to
Tom Waits.

"I'll be there. Give me fifteen minutes or so."

"Okay," says Jamie.

"What's up," says John as I grab my jacket, my favorite
four-button, black-and green check jacket.

"Jamie's got some good pot."

"You hate pot," says John.

"Yup," I say, headed for the door.

I'm wrong. It's not pot, it's hash. Jamie pinches off a little
chunk of it, brown and glistening with oil like a crumb of really
intense granola, and puts it on a saucer stolen from Dining
Services. She sets it smoldering with a match, then drops a big
glass bell jar over it. The thick white smoke curls up inside.
Eva's shaved her hair back down to virulent yellow fuzz again,
which makes her face look harsh and delicate all at once. Her
eyes are swimming blue behind thick black-rimmed glasses.
She's lounging on Jamie's bed in anonymous grey underwear
and a grubby white V-neck T-shirt that says "Queen Dick,"

and I don't ask where her pants are. Jamie at least is dressed, in baggy jeans and a flannel shirt buttoned up enough to mostly hide her bra.

"Go on," she says, putting her hand at the top of the bell jar, and I stoop down so when she tilts it up I can suck the smoke billowing into my lungs. Whoa. Shit. I'm dizzy. I sit down heavily in Jamie's desk chair. I don't think I like hash much, either.

Eva giggles. It's Jethro Tull playing now, the mouse police, you know, never sleeps. Never sleeps. Now Jamie's giggling, breaking off another pinch.

"I never said I wasn't a cheap date." For some reason it seems important to point this out.

"More for us," drawls Eva. Jamie, having set up another chunk, flops back onto the bed to watch the smoke, thick and white, trapped and raging under the glass. Eva strokes her thigh. I'm not jealous. I'm not. I mean, Jamie's my girlfriend and all, but I'm not the jealous type, you know?

The mouse police never sleeps.

"Hey," says Eva, after sucking in another lungful of smoke. She blinks, thickly. "Hey. Let's go for a walk."

Back in January, it's two in the morning, we're walking back the three of us from a New Year's party at the Ministry of Truth. It was warmer than usual – there was one of those amazing fogs that's just thick enough to be beautiful, trees looming out of it in new and fantastic shapes, all the street lamps ringed by perfect circles of colored light. But Jamie was chilly nonetheless and Eva was feeling butch so it was Jamie twirling in Eva's leather jacket, buckles jingling, the cuffs swallowing Jamie's hands. Eva looked cold in her sleeveless T-shirt. Gooseflesh pricked her upper arms, the Celtic knotwork tattoo ringing one of them, a vaccine scar pocking the other.

Jamie stops twirling and dances up close to Eva. "You look cold," she says. And Eva shakes her head and starts to say, "No, I'm not," I think, but she stops suddenly and instead says, "Oh, fuck it," and kisses Jamie, and Jamie, arms outstretched in that leather jacket too big for her, is too surprised to do anything but kiss her back.

I looked away.

The thing that happened next, though – there was a crunch of gravel, a footstep, and then Eva's kissing me.

See, *that's* what practically knocked me on my ass.

May, and Eva's buttoning on, Christ, a skirt, though it's more of a kilt, really, pleated, but in a weird plaid, yellow and red and orange on black, that I don't think any Scot would ever claim. She throws on a ratty black cardigan. Jamie pulls on some muddy hiking boots. "Where we going?" I ask.

"The *Arb*," says Eva, as if this is self-evident.

I look at my thrift-store wingtips and sigh.

The Arboretum: it's, I dunno, fifteen? Twenty? How the fuck big *is* an acre, anyway? It's a considerable chunk of the north-eastern corner of the campus, laid out half-wild more through neglect than design. There are thick stands of trees mostly free of undergrowth, some open fields, a creek, and the town's two reservoirs, square lakes side by side, held back by tall earthen ramparts. Given that 3,000 liberal arts undergraduates hang out hereabouts, going slowly mad as they study literature and music theory and political science and the weird cyclic history of Yeats and Mircea Eliade and his sacred and his fucking profane, and all of them wrapped up in the soap opera hot-house of college sex, well – there's a lot of weird shit that's supposed to have happened here. It's one of Those Places, you know. There's the big house on the hill there, that's one of the tonier dorms now; supposedly, the stables were down there, at the edge of the Arb, and they burned down one night and now the ghosts of the horses roasted alive are supposed to go galloping through the Arb with the full moon. Or maybe it's the new moon. You can't hear jets flying overhead, they say, or the cars on the highway just past that stand of trees, and no one knows who owns the creepy dogs that seem to bark at any time of day or night from nowhere in particular. My first acid trip, I came here and heard the trees calling my name and danced with weird lights in the middle of one of the fields, and a friend swears he woke up in the middle of the night and came out here for no good reason he could name to find a bonfire, in that clearing down there, with no one around to have built it, and he sat and watched it burn itself down until morning. But he drinks a lot. Witches' Sabbats, secret trysts, handfasting ceremonies, stupid jock pranks, open-air Shakespeare, drugged-out cliques desperate to escape overdue papers and looming exams – the Arb has seen it all.

Eva is the Residential Advisor for my floor, and back in the fall semester we used to go for long walks here, me bitching about classes and being homesick and not being able to deal with my high school girlfriend two states away, and her doing the "mm-hmm" and "yeah" and "I understand" thing that good RAs are supposed to do. Her hair was a little longer then, long enough to coil into a little Kewpie curl at the top of her forehead, but it was just as yellow and her glasses were as thick and heavy and her T-shirts as grubby and cryptic (a black one, I remember, with an Indian on horseback printed in red, holding up a compound bow), her jeans as ragged and holey, her big black boots kicking up drifts of dead leaves. I was head over heels in crush. It was on one of those walks that I made my grand pronouncement: my decision. I would, I said, call Christine, and tell her this wasn't working. Not two states apart. I sighed, and felt, physically *felt* some provident angel swoop down and lift this heavy pack off my back, straighten my shoulders, pat my ass, whisper you *go* in my ear.

"You have to do what you have to do," said Eva, slumping down on a log. "I mean, if you're not happy – you can't stay in something like this out of some sense of obligation, you know. It's not fair to you, but it's also not fair to her. Not at all."

She was so – wise, you know? And so powerful. And beautiful. I sat down on the log next to her, looked at the late afternoon light gilding the edges of her face, touching her hair to a slow smoldering burn, glinting off those glasses, her lips, pale, uncolored, parted just so.

"You know," she said, without really looking over at me, "that I'm gay. Right?"

"Well," I said. "I mean, yeah," I said. "Duh."

So the sun is setting and there we are, the three of us, hand in hand at the gate to the Arb off the highway. A semi judders past, and Jamie squeezes my hand, and I'm still light-headed from the hash. I can't think on the stuff, you know? See, I start this thought, any thought, and I get maybe halfway through it, and I lose track of what I was thinking, so I figure maybe if I follow my train of thought back, I'll figure out what it was, and so I start to do that, and get maybe halfway through, and lose track, and . . ?

Which is maybe why I'm not asking any of the questions I ought to be asking, like, what are we all doing here, now, why is Eva on the other side of me, squeezing my other hand like nothing's happened, and why are we walking into the Arb when we all know, yes we do, what's going to happen?

Which might very well be the reason why I smoked the hash in the first place.

After that confused New Year's Eve, or rather New Year's morning, sloppy half-drunk kisses and chilly flesh tumbling over Jamie's narrow dorm-room bed, tits and lips and hands and cock and skin and legs and mouths and cunts and no one ever really quite sure who was doing what to whom – after that, Jamie wanted to buy Eva a Christmas present.

"It's a little late for that," I said.

"So it'll be an Epiphany present," she said. "That's not till January sixth. You know, the day the wise men actually showed up and gave him frankincense and myrrh and all that shit. That's why there's *twelve* days of Christmas, you know."

I knew, but I let her tell me anyway.

So we hop a ride on the shuttle bus to the only mall worth the name in a thirty-mile radius, and you've got to understand – I can be really slow, sometimes. I didn't figure it out till she pulled me to a stop outside the Victoria's Secret outlet.

"Oh, geeze," I said.

"You deserve it," said Jamie. "Besides, I think she'll get a kick out of it. Wait here."

See, for Christmas I'd gotten her a copy of *Long Dark Tea-time of the Soul* – but I'd also gone to Victoria's Secret, grinning like a goon at my daring, and blown fifty bucks on a lacy black teddy. She'd blushed when she opened that present, the night before we'd all flown to our various homes for Christmas break. And then, her long lean body cupped in black lace, she'd lain back in my arms and kissed me as I fingered her, gently, her hand on top of mine.

So, that night – she didn't wait till January sixth – they make me wait in the hallway outside of Eva's overheated dormer room. So I fold my arms and lean back against the wall. I couldn't keep the slap happy grin off my face. Somebody walking past to his own room gives me a look and I shrug. One of them inside giggles. "Come in," says Jamie, and I open the door and there's two tall blonde girls in black lace, Jamie striking a supermodel pose, her golden curls snaking down her back, Eva half-insolent, half-amused, one hand on a startlingly bare hip, crypto-sexy with her short, short hair and those absurd office-nerd glasses. "Get in here," she says. "Close the door." And then Jamie's kissing Eva, they're wrapped up in each other, bare legs twining around bare legs, arms wrapping around bare backs, hands on blonde hair, black lace, bare skin.

"I think," says Eva, "mm-hmm, I think he likes your Christmas present."

"Epiphany," says Jamie. And then they're reaching for me, Eva's tugging on my sweater, Jamie's unbuttoning my jeans, and between the two of them and me I'm laid out in short order naked on the futon that takes up half the floor. They knelt on either side of me, grinning, and on their elbows took turns licking up and down my cock and each other's mouths, my hands stroking lace and skin and long heavy curls and short, short hair like seal's fur. I start laughing.

"What's so fuckin' funny?" growls Eva, biting my thumb.

"It's a straight-boy thing," I say, giggling. "Y'all wouldn't understand. Ow!"

Eva stumbles down the steep slope into the dim little bower, already soaked in twilight. I follow, perch myself maybe halfway down the slope, my skin tingling with inevitability. I reach up and catch Jamie's fingers and I hand her partway down the slope into Eva's arms.

It's already begun.

They tumble back together into the grass, all the green in it washing away into night, and they're kissing like no one else has ever been in the world. Jamie already has her hand up under Eva's kilt, has yanked those underpants, pulled them down to her knees.

I stand there on the slope above them, wishing absurdly for another hit of hash smoke, thick and harsh. The first stars are coming out above us.

"It's not," says Jamie, lying back in my arms, "like that. No. But Eva . . ."

She's wet with cold rain still, the winter's morning rain that's lashing at my window.

"Eva was in my room last night. All night."

"I guessed," I say.

"You're not mad."

"I'm not mad."

"You're not jealous."

"I told you. It's just not in me."

"Because, I mean, we haven't really talked about this. At all. And to be fair it ought to just be the three of us, all together, you know? But."

"But."

"It was like," she says, squirming closer to me, "it was like I couldn't stop. I couldn't stop, you know. Coming. I mean, she would kiss me, and blam! Or I'd just be lying back on her bed, and she was lying there, half-asleep, and she would breathe on me, and I'd start to whimper. My legs, my legs were still quivering when I walked over here . . ."

I kiss the back of her head. "Should I call her?"

She tenses a little. "Why?"

"You said. It ought to be the three of us, or."

"That's different," she says. "You get that, don't you? This, this is just the two of us. We're still? – I meant, her. Anything with her. Except, last night."

"It wasn't."

"It wasn't. And that's okay?"

"Yes," I said, kissing the back of her head again. "It's okay."

And I hold her there, as she falls into a shallow sleep, and I hold her, not moving, for two, maybe three hours, till she wakes up, wanting coffee.

"Oh, fuck," says Eva, her knees up, one now-bare foot planted on Jamie's blue-jeaned ass bobbing as Jamie's mouth works its magic on Eva's cunt. "Oh, fuck. Hey. Unh." She hooks her glasses off, her eyes quizzical and blue, tiny now atop those cheekbones. "Straight boy. Get your skinny ass down here."

She's not the best kisser in the world, Eva. Too aggressive, too pushy, too straightforward with her tongue trying to climb between my teeth. Maybe she kisses girls differently, I don't know. Her tits are bigger than Jamie's and absurdly soft, like slowly deflating balloons. She shivers as I brush a nipple with my hand, and then I'm tugging her T-shirt up and over her head. Eva's lying back in the dark, color-leached grass, and I'm sucking one of those nipples cool and pebble-hard into my mouth, and Jamie is swarming up her body next to me, taking charge of the other breast. I reach down past Eva's rumpled skirt and stumble into Jamie's hand there. Our fingers tangle together, slicking themselves as they slip along the lips of Eva's cunt.

"Oh," she says. "Oh, fuck."

It lasts, what, most of January? And on into February, too. We all three of us went to the GLBT Valentine's Dance, Jamie femmed to the nines in a slinky black minidress and fishnets and heels you could kill somebody with, and Eva crossing more than a couple of lines with her engineer's boots and her tight black jeans and her "Some of my best friends are gay" T-shirt that gets stripped off almost immediately once we're inside, leaving her in a black satin bra with straps as wide as a thumb. A black heart's painted on her belly, dripping black tears past her navel to her big silver belt buckle. Me, I'm doing the delicate pretty-boy goth thing: black jeans and black Chuck Taylors and a black poet's shirt – yes, black; pride of my wardrobe – hair hanging loose, face paled with powder, lips lipsticked black, eyes rimmed with mascara by Jamie, who giggled at how squeamish I am about people poking about my eyes and cursed how thick my lashes are. "You don't need this

shit," she said. "You lucky bastard." The music loud and fast
and thick, Jimmy Somerville singing that unreal falsetto over
pounding gospel pianos, girls dancing with girls, boys with
boys, colored lights flickering and flashing everywhere in the
dark basement. But girls were dancing with boys, too, and boys
with girls, of course, and none of it mattered at all, we didn't
think, we just did. It was Eva danced up to unlace my shirt, it
was Jamie stood behind her, grinding against her, cupping her
crotch. It was me between the two of them, humping to some
dusty disco hit, it was some random stranger, boy or girl,
nibbling my ear as I watched the two of them dancing slow,
stumbling drunk, Jamie's hands wedged into Eva's back pockets. It was some boy named Craig or maybe it was Frank I
danced with, his butt in my crotch, my hands snaking along his
shirtless chest, skin stretched thin over hard ribs, tough tight
muscles with no soft tits anywhere to be found. His cigarette-
smokey mouth I kissed, narrow little lips nibbling at my
tongue, as Jamie and Eva cheered.

"Ah," says Jamie, "all he needs is a good fuck."

"And I'm just the man to do it," says Frank, or maybe Craig,
and what the hell, right?

Like now: like now, we aren't thinking, I didn't consciously
plan to be lying back in the cold grass, kissing Eva as she lies
back against me, she didn't have to think to sit in my lap, lie
back in my arms, Jamie isn't thinking as she kneels again to
finish what she started, her shirt's gone, her bra's gone, and she
didn't care about how her bare ass would be hanging out in the
night air like it is now when she unbuttoned her jeans and
shoved them over her hips so that I or Eva, I forget which,
could ease a finger into her cunt. Jamie's curls spill madly
down her back, glowing in the eerie twilight, and I'm not
thinking about how Eva must taste to her or what her knees
must feel like wedged into the not exactly muddy ground. I
don't care that one of my wingtips has already fallen off, that
burrs have snagged the sleeve of my jacket. As Eva begins to
shudder and come, one hand pulling out a clump of grass, her
head tossed back as I nibble her throat, as I look down across
her heaving belly to see Jamie's eyes peering up at me over the
sparse dark hatching of Eva's pubic hair, as Jamie's eyes

crinkle in a smile buried between Eva's legs, as all of this is happening at once all I'm thinking, I think, is *now*, and *now*, and *now*?

Me and Eva, hanging out alone, sitting on the fire escape outside the old Finney building, smoking cloves and drinking Jenny Creams. It's March, and unseasonably warm, and Jamie isn't feeling too well, so we aren't doing what we'd thought we'd be doing, which was seeing the 9:30 showing of *The Five Thousand Fingers of Dr. T*.

"Hey," says Eva, and I pretty much know what she means, so I kiss her.

We don't turn on the lights in her room and it's like it's the first time all over again, getting nervous as we undress each other with fumbling, frantic fingers. It *is* the first time, really. Because, you see?

"Did you bring a condom?" she asks, in my ear. "Christ." She snorts. "I never have to think about that crap."

. . . in all we'd done, I'd never actually, *well*. Not with her.

Lying back, half-lit by the lights out on the quad, glasses gone, vulnerable and delicate and – fuck! – *scared*, even, this amazing lanky force of nature, waiting for me, hunched over her, suddenly ashamed of my burning cock, shoved into a latex sleeve and pointed at her like a sneer. "Hey," she says. "Hey. You chickening out on me?"

She was hot and wet and I slipped so easily into her. She wrapped her legs around my butt and her arms around my back and said, "*Just hold it here, a minute, just a minute*," into my ear, and we lay there until it got to be too much, and I started to pull and push even as she started to buck under me. And then I was fucking her in a frenzy, slamming into her over and over and over again, her thrashing there on her futon, throwing her head back, growling and gasping and bellowing, raking my butt and my shoulders with her short and stubby fingernails, pulling my hair, me working one arm and then the other under her legs, lifting them up until her thighs were pressed against my chest, her knees over my elbows, her eyes wide open and stunned and grey in the dim light, my cock sliding in and out and in again, smooth, well-oiled, stroking deep and out again, and again, and again – I felt it, the orgasm, starting to build a wave in the back of my head, in my butt, in my ankles, and like a surfer I tried to swim out to meet it, not caring about where she was, what she was doing, trusting her to look out for herself, but something – the angle, the mechanics, the light, the moment, *something* – something went awry. The wave washed past me and left me flickering in its wake. As I slowed, dulling, Eva began to thrash wildly under me, grabbing the sheets, bucking as she yelled incoherently about something, fuck, fuck, goddamn, goddammit all to fucking *hell*. Hot pain lanced the head of my cock. I pulled out, and she nearly hit me. I caught her wrist.

"Fuck," she said, trying to yank her wrist free. Panting harshly. "Fucker."

"It hurts," I said, clipped. Holding her wrist. She trembled, and hearing that, her face softened suddenly, the scowl melting away.

"You didn't," she said.

"No," I said. "I didn't."

"Oh," she said, and I let go. "Oh. I couldn't. Either."

"We could," I said, and she nodded, "Maybe later." But we fell asleep and didn't wake up till morning, and Jamie had been calling my room all night, looking for me.

But now, now, now Jamie lies back in the grass, naked, breathing so carefully, very carefully so as not to disturb the orgasm we're building within her, patient tinkerers that we are, our fingers and our tongues playing together on the lips of her cunt, the tense little bud of her clit, the edges of her nipples, the rippling skin along her flanks, the shivering gooseflesh of her arms and thighs, the whorled pucker of her ass, the humid cups behind her knees. I can feel it, what we're building within her, me and Eva: delicate, intricate, interlocking crystals full of light, shutting out the night around us, swallowing us all inside it, this inhuman thing that doubles and redoubles itself, as shivery cold as the night breeze that runs over my bare back, growing on its own now with no help from us, spiking into her like salt, seen through a microscope, and she trembles at the hugeness of it all, oh, oh – and as she comes, her mouth is open, just, her eyes are shuttered, and as she comes, I look to Eva, who built all this with me, but she is looking at Jamie, and her face is closed, sealed up, unreadable in the light of this wondrous thing we've made.

The moon. If you stare at the moon, if you fix something, a tree branch that isn't moving in a breeze, that's still and hanging there, between you and the moon, if you fix your eyes on that, and concentrate, you can just barely see the moon move. The rotation of the earth under you, spinning you away from it, slowly but inevitably. You can see it, and feel it all. The stars, wheeling ponderously away.

"Did you bring any condoms?" asks Jamie.

But I've already come, I don't say. Standing, my pants around my knees, the head of my cock rolling on Jamie's lips, hot and wet, Eva behind me, her hands, only, cupping my ass, one spit-slick finger sliding inside, oh shit, oh. The come lost in the darkness. But I had brought them. Maybe John hadn't seen me slip them into my jacket pocket, but I had. I'd known. I fish one out, my lazing cock slowly shaking off its stupor. Eva chuckles there in the darkness, her hair silvered in the moonlight.

Jamie takes the packet from me and rips it open with her teeth, squats over me, unrolls it carefully down the length of my half-stiff cock, which is more than half stiff when she's done. I reach for her, my hand tingling, and she shakes her head, almost as if I'd known she would. And, "No," she says, before any of us can say anything else, "not me."

Eva sits up, in the grass. "I," she starts to say, but doesn't finish whatever it was.

Jamie sits beside her, and kisses her, gently, and they lie down together, Eva on her back, and Jamie beside her, stroking her thigh. Beckoning. I stand, lightheaded, as if the air at the bottom of that bower is richer somehow, funkier, as if I've suddenly been shot to the top of a mountain. But I can't see anything. It's dark.

"Here," says Eva, or maybe Jamie. "Come on," says Jamie. I'm pretty sure.

I kneel there, between her knees. I kiss her. She kisses me. Then Jamie kisses her as I feel for her cunt, where it is, where I am. Jamie's hand meets mine, and then Jamie's hand is on my cock as Eva's hands spread herself and I plant my own hands to either side of Eva, my arm brushing Jamie's belly, Jamie guiding me inside.

Someone starts to say something, someone else stops their mouth with a kiss. Someone's fingers are in my mouth and they have that tang, that musk, but for the life of me I can't tell whose, whose fingers, whose cunt. My legs, Eva's legs, Jamie's legs all tangled together, I can't tell whose is whose. Whose hand is clenched around my butt, whose breath is hot and thick in my ear. I'm kissing someone, and I don't know who it is.

But I know whose cunt surrounds me. I know where my cock is.

I try to find Jamie's cunt, try to reach for it with my fingers, to be inside her, too, but it's too awkward. I can't. Eva is moving under me, I catch myself, dig my knees into the ground I suddenly notice is cold and damp. Dirt grits under the heel of my hand. It's Jamie stroking my back, murmuring something I can't make out. It's Eva, moaning. Coming. Coming, even as I feel it swarm up from behind me and pounce, my muscles jerking as it all comes pouring cleanly out of me. It's over, all over. Almost before I knew it had begun.

March, and we're walking through the Arb, Jamie and me, along the narrow path between the two reservoirs, random wisps of fog steaming up from the grey unruffled water. Our winter coats hanging still in the still air.

"We can't," she says, resting her head against me. "Not any more, okay?" And I want to ask her why she's looking for my approval. None of this had ever been my idea, after all.

But I don't.

"It's just," she says, "it's so confusing. When it's just you, and just me, I know. You know? I know what you want. I know what I want."

I stoop down, pick up a rock, utterly fail to send it skipping across the lake. It sinks, and the ripples are swallowed in the slowly seeping fog.

"They say," I tell her, "that the triangle is the most stable shape there is."

"That's horseshit," she says.

"That's geometry," I say.

Eva ungainly, pulling up her underpants, her glasses already back on her face, a silvery sheen of moonlight masking her eyes. Jamie, naked, holding up Eva's kilt.

"That's it, then," says Jamie, as if answering a question.

Eva freezes. Then slowly takes the kilt and wraps it around her waist. Buttons it. "Well?" she says. "What do you have to say about it?"

And I realize with no little astonishment it's me she's talking to.

"Anything?" she says.

And I open my mouth and realize I have no idea what she's talking about.

"Shit," says Eva, to Jamie now. "It was never *him*, you know. I mean?"

"That doesn't matter," says Jamie. And I'm starting to think maybe none of us has any idea what any of us is saying. Or thinking.

Eva pulls her T-shirt over her head. I am uncomfortably aware that I am naked, and it is chilly outside in Ohio in early May, at night. She shrugs into her cardigan, kicks a foot into a boot. "Well?" she says, to me again. "Is this it?"

"It's not up to me," is what I say.

And Eva says, "All right."

And she walks away.

Back at the end of October, and what's trying to pass for a homecoming party is too loud and trying too hard and there's a whole bunch of white kids in expensive clothes dancing to "Fight the Power" and even though me and Eva are both white, and her jeans were probably a pretty penny at Unique Boutique, and I was wearing my magic four-button black-and-green check jacket, we're both sniggering at them. That's when the "Most Amazing Girl in the World" comes back from the bathroom, and shit, would you look at that? She brought me a fresh cup of beer. Damn.

"Look at you," she says, but I can't stop looking at her,

those amazing blue eyes, that hair, that unbelievable head of shaggy gold. "I leave you for a minute and you're already macking on somebody else," she says. You hear that? She says "macking on." Is that not Amazing?

"Naw," I say, "you don't get it. This is Eva, she's like, one of my best friends. She's a lady-killer, like me. Eva, this is Jamie, and I saw her first."

"You wanna fuck anyway?" says Eva, grinning sharply.

"Some other time, maybe," says Jamie, and that was that.

The Key

Sage Vivant

Of all the tourists who invade Santorini each summer, Americans are my favorite. They don't bother to learn much Greek before they get here, but they are friendly enough to make you forgive them.

My brother and I have run our restaurant, The Octopus, for nearly 20 years. Our sign is not in English but still the Americans come. Christos and I prefer the Greek customers, but in the end, everybody's money is the same.

Only half the restaurant is enclosed. It faces the narrow walkway through Oia. The east side is completely open and overlooks the clear, sparkling Mediterranean. Tourists usually gravitate to that side. Locals come inside so they can talk with me and my brother, hear the music, be close to the bar.

I was a little surprised when this gorgeous American woman sauntered in and sat at the bar. We do not have one of those fancy bars like you'd find in an upscale restaurant or hotel. There are only five tall chairs and they aren't even comfortable! Greeks sit, drink and talk for hours so, generally, they settle in at tables rather than the bar. It's more relaxing. But she came in, just as the dinner crowd was starting up, sometime around eight o'clock or so.

Her dress was the brilliant blue found in the Greek flag. We paint homes and buildings with that color, too. It represents valor, the sky, and the peaceful water.

I knew she had to be American because the dress hugged her body like any man's hands would have. Americans are famous for their blatant clothing, leaving so little to the imagination.

But in this case, I did not object to the lack of subtlety. Beautiful full breasts and a nice, round ass for balance. Greeks love shapely women and believe me, this one was a feast of flesh.

I greeted her because I greet everyone who comes to The Octopus. She had an easy, pretty smile but she had that dismissive air women put on to discourage small talk. For me, not talking was just fine. I could stare at her luscious tits more easily if I didn't have to pretend to watch her face while we spoke.

Everyone noticed her. Women shot wary, judgmental glances at her while the men stole furtive, hungry ones, when their wives weren't watching. She ordered a glass of the house wine after I told her it came from my winery.

She spoke to no one and pretended to be very interested in her napkin. A beautiful woman, alone, who speaks to no one – what is such a thing? I wondered. This woman intrigued me. She exuded warmth and sensuality but held on to it tightly, as if she might otherwise lose it. I decided she was probably meeting someone, so I shifted my attention back to running my restaurant.

No one spoke to her, probably for nearly half an hour. I gave her another glass of wine, my treat, to be kind but also to see if a little alcohol might loosen her up. The longer I watched her breasts rise and fall in that blue dress, the clearer the image became of my hands full of them. I offered her some *mezethes* but she refused. Without food, the alcohol would act faster and I was anxious to see that happen.

A tall man with a goatee came in, dressed nicely, also definitely American. He approached the bar and I thought, "Ah, here is the man she has been waiting for." Their eyes met but no words passed between them. The man sat at the bar, leaving an empty chair between them. He ordered my vineyard's wine, too.

He was only human, so his eyes kept roaming over her body. I confess I walked by her more often than I had to, just to appreciate the curve of her behind warming the seat of my very lucky chair. She ignored us both.

And then I walked by as she crossed her legs and pointed her toe at the man. She shifted in her seat to do this. Her eyes stared at her glass, but her foot was only a few centimeters from his leg.

I heard him ask her if he could buy her a drink. She looked at him, finally, but refused the drink. She didn't look away. Instead, she stared at him with such bold curiosity, I felt like an intruder in my own restaurant. His color deepened as she let her eyes travel from his face down to his crotch.

He spread his legs once her gaze settled on his lap. They were facing each other now.

"This is how people meet in America?" Christos muttered from behind me. His words made me realize I'd been staring, so I forced myself to visit a few tables. It was still too early for the locals, so I had to make conversation with a few Germans. If you know any German tourists, you know this is no easy task.

Christos caught my eye as I was telling some of them how to catch the bus to Thira. He raised his eyebrows in the direction of the bar. I looked over to see the voluptuous beauty with her wineglass in one hand while she traced her cleavage with the other. Her foot now slid up and down the man's shin. I could see his bulge from across the restaurant.

The man had that look on his face that every man, regardless of nationality, knows too well. It is the face that betrays desire, the look that says, "I await the tiniest sign of invitation." It is, sadly, the way we look when all we want is to fuck the woman who tempts us.

Every man wanted her, but he was the one with her toes near his thigh. She extended her leg fully so she could hover at his crotch. Her bare legs were smooth, well muscled with feminine slopes.

Nothing like this spectacle had ever occurred in The Octopus before. Customers stared openly because it was clear that the couple was aware of nobody but each other.

She put her glass down. Her lips parted and glistened, just like pussy ready for cock. The woman had cast a spell over every man in the room. I wanted her at least as desperately as the man she had chosen.

She stroked the inner curve of her breast. As her fingers

moved, so did her neckline. Lower, ever lower, inching with excruciating slowness to reveal more of her fleshy tit.

I was so hard I could barely walk. Why had this never happened to me at a bar?

The man's erection tented his pants. I felt a mixture of sympathy and jealousy for him.

She stared at him while she stroked her breast. As if she'd willed it, he rose from his seat. His movement did not faze her. In fact, she seemed to expect it. And why not?

He walked by the chair between them. As he approached her, he slid his palm along the outside of her bare thigh. He stopped when her dress bunched at her hip, unable to go any higher. I shuddered with lust at how close his hand was to her glorious ass.

Their eyes locked in some silent contest of wills. She stroked her breast languidly as he caressed her exposed thigh. She moved the fabric at her fingertips so that a full half-moon of titflesh rose up into view. He bent down to kiss it.

One of the waiters hooted with delight, which helped to break the thick, awkward silence. Some people laughed nervously, others made valiant attempts to look away. I made no pretense about my interest. I watched shamelessly from only a few meters away. What would she do next?

She removed his hand from her leg but her expression did not change. He returned to his seat with more dignity than most men would have been able to muster. Once he sat, he searched her face, obviously trying to read whether she'd lost interest.

She reached for her purse and my heart sank. Not that I expected them to fuck right there on my bar, but to have this interlude end now, so abruptly, disappointed me beyond words.

The purse was in her lap. She opened it and extracted a key. With the same unwavering gaze, she placed it on the bar and slid it over to him with meaningful deliberateness.

Once he touched it, she got to her feet and glided out of the restaurant. Her tits jiggled provocatively but so subtly as she passed the awed diners. And, oh, that ass. I could practically feel the flesh of her ass cheek against my tongue.

Sex is rampant on Greek islands. That any couple should

meet and fuck within minutes did not surprise me. But this
couple. This woman. She would have some kind of plan, I
surmised. My curiosity, among other things, needed satisfying. I turned and walked through the kitchen, out the back
door and down the alley that led to the street of the restaurant.
I emerged just after they passed before me.

I followed the man. Indeed, I felt I was the man. He, in turn,
kept a pace or two behind the woman. She stopped in front of
the Stromboli hotel and looked coyly over her shoulder at the
man, who nodded with understanding. She walked on and he
headed off into the hotel.

Her decorum pleased me. Most Americans did not concern
themselves with appearances of modesty or gentility. Most
would've just walked into the hotel, leaving the watchful
proprietor or other guests to see quite clearly that an assigna-
tion was in progress. But this woman knew the proper method
was to let him precede her to her room. She would join him
shortly, but to anyone watching, the man and the woman were
not so obviously together. Impressive, this woman.

Like a fugitive, I lurked by the foliage near her room after
the man let himself in. The rooms at Stromboli all open out
onto a different patio level carved into the island rock. All of
them face the sea.

It was dark, save for the brilliant stars and nearly full moon.
I didn't want to frighten the woman when she returned so I
crouched behind a small lemon tree and stayed immobile. She
arrived minutes later and walked, without fanfare, into her
hotel room.

I heard them dissolve into laughter. What was this? Another
strange American custom? Sex as comedy? I moved to the
window, whose shutters thankfully were open.

"I never thought you'd pull it off," the man said, holding
her around her waist as he chuckled.

She was giddy, a sharp contrast to her cool demeanor in the
restaurant. "What a show that was! Do you suppose they'll
ever stop talking about it? I was awfully good, wasn't I?" She
tossed her streaked auburn hair over her shoulder.

"You seem to think the show is over," he replied, running
his hands over her ass.

"Oh, no, my darling. I most certainly am not under that impression."

He raised his eyebrows expectantly as she unbuckled his belt and unzipped his fly. His cock popped out eagerly.

"Why don't you lie down on the bed?" she suggested.

Grinning indulgently, he complied. Pillows propped up his head and he watched her, waiting for direction.

The steely expression returned to her, although now it was tempered with the affection I could see existed between them. Standing at the foot of the bed, she slid her dress over her shoulders and pulled it downward. As she peeled it from her arms and breasts, I saw she wore a white, translucent bra that pushed her tits up and together. It was sheer enough to allow her nipples to show through.

The top half of the dress lay bunched at her waist. She traced the outline of her nipples with her fingertips and he reached for his dick.

"No," she warned.

"What?"

"I don't want you to touch yourself yet."

No Greek man would have permitted a woman to control what he touched in the bedroom! Her impertinence rankled me. And made me harder. But I did not bring a hand to my cock.

She wiggled out of the rest of the dress, letting it pool at her feet. She wore panties unlike anything I'd ever seen. A tiny patch of the shimmery fabric at her auburn triangle of hair, and elastic that crossed her hips and disappeared between her ass. I wanted to be that elastic, buried in her ass.

When she was certain he'd had a good look at her soft curves in that fancy lingerie, she walked, still in her heeled sandals, to a nearby suitcase. She pulled out short pieces of rope.

I thought to leave. I wondered if all Americans traveled with rope. I longed for it around my wrists and my ankles.

She attached him to the bed with expert knots. She looped the rope firmly but not tightly. His cock prayed skyward, to the gods, as did mine. Both of us remained clothed and at her mercy.

She crawled up on the bed and knelt between his splayed

legs. I wanted her lips on my hot tool. She swirled her tongue around his thickness a few times before she took him into her mouth.

"Oh, Keisha," he moaned.

Her head bobbed up and down in exactly the right rhythm. I pumped my fist with the same tempo, spreading my pre-cum over my shaft and imagining it was her saliva.

The man's eyes were closed and the muscles in his legs tightened. She stopped sucking and straddled him with remarkable agility.

She sat on him, impaled by his engorged cock. There was so little to her panties that entrance to her cunt was unimpeded.

She raised and lowered herself on his pole, moaning with pleasure. Her tits jiggled in the flimsy bra and I wanted her to take it off.

She reached behind her and unhooked the garment. She tore it off her and grabbed her own bouncing titties as she rode her lover. What powerful legs this woman had!

It was a small room. The scent of her pussy could not be contained by it. I breathed deeply to enjoy her aroma. My palm was her dripping snatch, enclosing around my cock, sucking it up inside her like a hungry animal. I listened closely and could hear the wet kisses from her juicy hole.

She fucked him faster, harder, landing on him with a force she must have felt all through her cunt. An intensity consumed her so completely that her lover watched her, fascinated.

Her cries came up slowly, as if they started between her legs. They burst loudly from her throat as she bucked and trembled, all the while still bouncing on his cock.

So complete a woman was she that he and I forgot our own gratification. We watched, admired, devoured this orgasmic goddess and let our fluid sit like nitroglycerin in our balls. And we were grateful for the privilege.

When she had let all her orgasms pass through and out of her beautiful body, she fell forward on his chest, nuzzling his neck. I imagined her hot breath in my ear. He kissed her hair, her cheek, her eyes.

"Untie me, babe. I need to look at your sweet ass while I fuck you."

Yes. Yes, that was exactly what I needed.

Dutifully, she freed him. He immediately sat up and took one of her big tits into his mouth. He sucked like a newborn calf and I licked my lips.

He held her other breast and pushed it up. She bent her head down, stuck out her tongue and lashed at her hard nipple. My knees were weakening at every moment, watching him suck one nipple while she licked the other. My cock swelled in my hand.

A few minutes later, he positioned her with her back to me, by the side of the bed. She bent over and dizziness overtook me. Her perfectly contoured ass was on display for me! The slope of her hips as they melded into her thighs remains a sight I will never forget. I could not decide then or now if I wanted my face or my cock buried between those rounded cheeks.

The man pulled her silly panties over her hips and down her lovely legs. She stepped out of them. When he positioned himself behind her, most of my view was obstructed. But he stuffed himself into her pussy quickly enough. He rammed her hard, making her gasp.

"Oh yes, Mark! Fuck me, honey. Fuck me, Mark!"

What I could see of her ass shook with each thrust. I was her lover, holding her full hips to steady her against my pounding. He fucked her; I felt her juices coat my balls.

We came at the same time.

With my cock no longer in control, my brain resumed functioning. I grimaced at the sight of my cum on the ground, my penis peering at the stars. I saw the American couple cuddle happily on the bed.

And I remembered I had a restaurant to run.

I hurried back to The Octopus, grabbing a tub of fresh marides from the back of the restaurant to bring to the front, as if that might explain my disappearance. Every table was full and several parties were waiting. Christos threw me a stern, impatient look.

I busied myself with customers. Business was so brisk that I didn't even notice that Christos had seated the American couple in the corner.

They wore different clothing, more casual and appropriate

for a beach climate. They were relaxed and smiling. Even Christos hadn't recognized them, and he waited on them throughout their meal. Oddly, I found I could not face her.

By the time they left, it was nearly midnight. They strolled out, arm in arm, before I went to their table to clear it off.

My heart stopped, then pounded wildly. A room key gleamed on the tablecloth.

Had she left it on purpose? Was this an invitation? Had they seen me and now wanted me to join them? I had no experience in such sophisticated sexual games. My mind raced. I picked up the key and twirled it slowly between my fingers, plotting my escape and my alibi to Christos, when I heard her voice.

"Excuse me."

Her face was before me, so young and fresh, invigorated by good food and good sex.

"Did you perhaps find a key on this table?"

Speechless, I held the small metal object up for her to see. She reached for it, smiling.

"Oh, thank goodness. We were afraid we'd lost it! *Kalinichta!*"

And she disappeared into the night, taking my wildest fantasies with her.

Too Bad

Cara Bruce

I enjoy my own company.
I am my own best friend.
I am unique and special.

Mira looks in the mirror as the words of the subliminal message CD float over her. She hates the first part of this CD, the part that says the stupid phrases out loud, grinding the fact that she is alone deep into her consciousness. She feels like a part of a *Saturday Night Live* skit, but this one isn't funny.

She is trying to get her life back together, to get over her obsession with boys, specifically bad boys. She hasn't been the best girl her whole life but the boys she has fallen for have been worse. They are the types of boys who started smoking when they were thirteen, lost their virginity at fourteen, shoplifted, drank too much, drove without licenses. These were boys she would see huddled on street corners, tongues flickering over bad teeth, hands balled into fists and shoved deep into pockets big enough to steal with. These were the boys she loved.

In a fit of rage Mira grabs a bar of soap and flings it at the CD player. It hits and slides down, not even skipping the CD. A siren floats by underneath her bedroom window as she lets out a half-yell and looks for something to punch.

Mira resides in a small studio apartment. It is the only thing she can afford in the city these days. Since her resolve to give up bad boys she has barely left it, feeling trapped and timeless like a junkie. Just without the momentary euphoria.

She stares out of her window onto the busy street below, the boys gathered like ants at a picnic, then scattering like roaches whenever a cop car crawls by, a single megaphone ordering them to disperse.

Mira's first boyfriend was named Tad. He had crazy black eyes, glittering with insanity. He was energetic, bustling, busy – overflowing with a contagious energy that made Mira proud. He dealt drugs, supplying people with ingested happiness and need. He bought her a car and occasionally gave her flowers – acts that Mira now saw as a way to shut her up. A few romantic gestures in a lifetime of cruel ones, and they had fooled her. She had thought she loved Tad and he had tried to keep her. He put her down, took from her, let her take care of him so she felt needed. This was a pattern, which hours with her therapist had helped her to recognize. She needed to feel needed. Needed to feel loved, important, cared for. And bad boys were the ones that let her do that. Bad boys seemed to always have secrets; she never knew what they were going to do next. It was the uncertainty of them that got her blood racing. Which is why she needed to be needed by them, if she wasn't she would be too uncertain, which made her crazy with lust, so crazy she wondered if this is how they always felt.

Sex with Tad was violent, unyielding. He liked to hurt her, back when she was against being hurt on principle. Maybe if she had given in to that one thing they could have reached an agreement and worked everything else out. But Tad was big and strong and Mira's refusal only made things worse. He knew Mira didn't love him. She knew she didn't love him. The only reason they stayed together was because of his reputation for being bad. But as soon as he started getting his shit together and stopped going out doing drugs she grew edgy, anxious, bored. When he calmed down and was ready to admit he needed her . . . it was then she left among a flurry of violence and crazy outbreaks – scared, guilty and confused.

Not understanding herself and too worried about how other people saw her she moved on to the next boy. A singer in a punk rock band whose ego clouded every chance she had to shine. He didn't last long but still did damage. After a while she noticed she was staying with him just because he had been the ultimate bad boy. Her lust for him was built on a faded reputation. But his bad boy behavior wasn't linked to fun things like breaking into churches and baptizing each other or driving down to Baja with nowhere to stay and sleeping in rest stops – some of the best moments of her life. No, his bad boy behavior was all about him, was fucking around behind her back, lying and occasionally snorting cocaine. Even though he never stopped being a bad boy he wasn't spontaneous, fun, or needy enough for Mira. But before she could leave, he did. Surprised at herself, she didn't really care.

At this point she should have been dating bad men. But there is a difference between men and boys, and these were perpetual boys. The next one was an ex-junkie. Or so he assured her until her roommate found a syringe under the bathroom sink. In her need and effort to help him she was pulled down with him, swirling deeper and deeper into that place with no air. She would fantasize about his death, exciting herself into a frenzy where she would become convinced that she would come home and find him stiff, a needle poking out of his arm. She drove herself crazy with this ultimate fantasy of not knowing, while he drove himself further into addiction. She was the perfect enabler. Yelling at him to do something while he hid in the bathroom for hours trying to find a vein. Yet she couldn't let him go, or maybe it was the comfort of the addiction that she craved. Either way, it took almost losing their lives until they reluctantly let each other loose. Although she still clung to him; not knowing where he was made her want him again. They still talked late at night, both scared of the future and afraid to be alone. Each picking up the pieces of their life slowly, two steps forward and one step back, going in tiny circles.

Mira's parents have tried to enforce something. They joke about the fact that they would be happy with a son-in-law who graduated high school, has never been in jail, and never does drugs. So far Mira has yet to accomplish that. Almost a year of therapy has only helped to reinforce what she has known all along: Mira simply has a fetish for bad boys. But it has gotten so bad that she doesn't even know where to meet good boys, much less men. The methadone clinic she goes to every day surely isn't the place, neither are her AA meetings or codependency support groups. She doesn't even know what good boys do.

She avoids people or they avoid her: the circle of money owed is too big to comprehend. She dresses and walks out of her apartment, turning off the CD with its stupid new-age music playing over the sounds of oceans and mountain streams. *The only thing the CD is good for is helping her piss*, she thinks to herself, irritated. It sure as hell isn't going to help her find a good man. Not that she thinks she needs one; in fact there are times, more often than not, that she wonders what she will do if she does find a good one. He will probably stifle her, bore her to tears. She will become demanding and out of control. They will end up hating each other. It seems like she can't fall in love unless it is a completely co-dependent nightmare. Mira's fear drives her into a heated, sexual frenzy, and she wants to be done with that.

The craving for something comes over her as she walks down Mission Street, the music from the CD stuck in her head. Her body is anxious, aching. The familiar feeling of being uncomfortable in her own skin overpowers her. She needs something – she thinks it could be drugs until she finds herself staring at a boy leaning on the bus stop. He has a faded black eye, a torn leather jacket and an unfiltered cigarette hanging out of his mouth. She reaches up absentmindedly to rub her own shoulder, straining her neck to get a little stretch. She can remember a time not too long ago when she was addicted to exercise, when she had to work out at least once a day so she wouldn't go insane. Now she is stuck on something easier – a quick fix, a valium, or a fuck with a stranger. She makes a mental note to call the psychiatrist to make an appointment to get on an antidepressant. She has never tried that before but she can't seem to pull herself out of this black hole and some of those mental magic pills help with addiction. Or so she has heard. Her life feels at odds, she has a good job, is smart and attractive, yet she stands on line every morning with the dregs of society to drink methadone out of a paper cup. She knows she could get off it for good but she can't seem to let the world of bad boys go.

Yet, it is precisely these early morning visits that prompt

Mira to change her relationship style. If it weren't for the last boyfriend she wouldn't be here in the first place, although he has taken no responsibility for that. The ageing punk rockers in the clinic are ghosts. Once bad boys in rock bands and disgruntled poets, they are now flickering patterns of light against the concrete walls of the city. This is what happens to young drug addicts, to all of the bad boys: they simply disappear. Once loved and cared for, they become a burden to those around them, or simply forgotten as they fade away into the background of daily life. But for Mira they represent the familiar feelings she identifies as want, need, craving: in short, sex.

But it is the realization that her last boyfriend could end up pushing a shopping cart that has set Mira on her goal to get rid of her bad boy obsession. She never thought that she would be the type of woman to end up with an ex that lives in a cardboard box. And she knew she had to separate herself from him in order to deal with that. She comes from the suburbs and still speaks to her parents once a week to check in. She takes yoga, goes to work, cleans her bathroom. She isn't the type to throw her life away, although she has come close many times now, each time, on account of a bad boy.

She goes to the park and sits on a bench, watching the different groups of boys: the Mexicans with their hair slicked back and shirts buttoned up to their necks; the black gangstas with big, baggy jeans and starter jackets; the punk rockers with rainbow hair, black leather jackets and worn jeans. Each group united in the economy of the drug trade. They have their own, private financial system. Trade, barter and petty robberies each feature brightly. Mira notices a few girls in each group, the loud mouths slashed with bright, pink lipstick, jackets too big that claim them as belonging to one, if not all, of the boys. The girls that hang out with these boys have to be tough, have to hold their own. They are the brassiest, most brazen, but they are also the ones that are usually the saddest inside, often they have made the mistake of having children, are walking the line between addiction and mild discomfort, or just wanting to be loved. She is familiar with that girl.

Mira watches the complex play unfold before her. Each group similar in the way they treat each other. Each group occasionally picking on the girl, until she defends herself with insults to the rest of them, before they ignore her again. It reminds Mira of being in high school – some things never change.

As she sits watching, a boy comes over and plops down next to her. Mira feels her heart beat and her stomach churn. He smells like sweat and cigarettes. He is good looking, in that rough, unkempt way that she likes. He wears a faded T-shirt of an obscure punk band, the scars on his arms tell the tale of where he's been. She bites her lip, promising herself she isn't going to give in to this one. She has stayed off drugs for a few months now; she can stay off bad boys as well. But fetish isn't an addiction – one can be broken, she knows that, she's not so sure about the other.

"Got a cigarette?" the boy asks her, looking at her only out of the corner of his eye. His lack of acknowledgment makes her cunt wet.

Mira huffs in response, yet begins digging around in her purse. She pulls out a battered pack, handing one to the boy and keeping one for herself. The boy pulls out a shiny Zippo and lights her cigarette first. Mira sucks in deeply, afraid to say thank you, afraid to look.

She thinks of a poem given to her by a friend, a poem about ex-boyfriends. She thinks how this boy looks like every one she has ever known. She remembers how lonely she is. She fights the urge to make something up, offer to give him something she has at home, a drink, a bong hit, anything to get him alone. She crosses her legs, tightly. His aura makes her hot.

"What're you doing?" he asks.

"Nothing. I don't know," she says brusquely, wanting to stop the conversation before it gets the best of her. Fighting herself with each breath. "Nothing."

"Well, 'Nothing', what's your name?" the boy chides.

"Mira," she says slowly, deciding whether or not to lie but then deciding that it is too small a city, that she will run into this bad boy again, at a club, a bar, on the street. She always does. Once you meet them it's like they follow you, tagging along like a bad afterthought.

"Figures," he laughs. "Do you know your name means 'bitter' in Hebrew?" She is taken aback. She considers herself a nice person. More than that, she's blown away that he knows this. A smart bad boy. She swoons, imagining him shoplifting books for her, breaking into museums to take her on private tours. She inhales deeply on her cigarette, a blush running up her cheeks. "It means 'marvelous' in Latin," she tells him, enraptured in their private game, this instant intimacy with a bad boy.

"Marvelously bitter," he says, laughing harder. She is turned on by his sense of humor, his ability to smile. She recalls reading that laughter actually is the best aphrodisiac; it sets off your dopamine neurotransmitters and really does make you feel good. Before him she had thought her dopamine was shot out.

The boy is still amused with himself and this amuses her.

"Are you Jewish?" she asks.

"No," he says, "I just like names."

They are silent for a moment until the boy says, "My name is Max. It means 'greatest' in Latin."

"We both do well in Latin," she says, trying to be funny, the pulsing in her clit tells her that she has given in already.

The boy cracks a smile and asks if she would like to take a walk. They get up off the bench, their simple movement attracting attention from all three groups of boys. He calls her "Nothing" as they walk; she is touched by the fact that he already has a pet name for her, no matter how degrading.

As darkness falls they end up at her studio, each of them carrying a 40-oz. bottle of beer. Mira thinks back to all the times she has taken home strangers; had great sex with bad boys. She presses her answering machine button and realizes that her ex-boyfriend hasn't called yet today. She doesn't care; it's not him, the ex or the one here now, it's what they represent.

Max has his arms around her in an instant. He is kissing her neck, his snake tongue rummaging in her ear, his hands everywhere at once. She wants to ask him to slow down but doesn't, instead she gives in to it, to the way he feels, his warm flesh, his thumping heart. She is sinking, unable to control herself around bad boys.

They fall onto the unmade bed and she wishes she had cleaned up. He pulls off his T-shirt and Mira lightly traces the tattoos that adorn his chest, she tries to imagine how proud they must have been once. He has been in jail, has been addicted to drugs, and he never finished high school. He is everything her parents' don't want, and everything she does. Mira gives in to his caresses, his unspoken promises. She can imagine him sitting on her bed, watching TV night after night as she works her boring job, coming home simply because he needs her.

He pulls her closer, as if sensing that she is pulling away, and whispers how beautiful she is. She feels these words as shallow; she hears the lies hanging off his voice. But it is exactly this that fuels her, the uncertainty of truth. She kisses him back. The room heats up and she takes off her own shirt. His fingers deftly unhook her bra, like one who has done this many times, before he leans forward to suck on each tit until she moans. He runs his tongue lightly over each nipple until they spring to attention. His hand is undoing the button of her jeans. She reaches down to help him, to speed up the process. Together they wiggle her free of pants and panties. She is naked on the bed and he is still wearing jeans, socks, and boots.

Their kissing is intense and she lets herself go deeper into it. His fingers move down to her pussy and begin to rub her clit. This always makes her happy. She loves to be touched there. Bad boys always know what to do. She moans and raises her hips in encouragement. He moves faster, harder. She bucks and grinds beneath him. Two fingers are now moving at lightning speed over her clit, she breathes harder, whispers for him *not to stop, keep going, I'm almost there*, and she is, almost there, teetering on the edge. He moves one hand into her, her pussy wet and dripping, his fingers moving upward, outward, as if he really knows where the G-spot is. His other hand contains the two fingers that dance rapidly on her clit and that's all she needs. She digs her nails into him and swallows his hand with her orgasm. Her thighs tighten around his hips, her head falls back and her cry fills the room.

He quickly pulls out a condom, ripping the tinfoil package

with his teeth. She likes the fact that he has condoms on him, thinking he probably fucks a lot. He pulls down his jeans until they rest around his knees. His cock is hard and thick. She's glad he can get it up, she knows too many bad boys that can't anymore. There is a fine line between bad and useless. He slides the condom over his dick and quickly pushes it inside her. She is so tight she gasps.

He moves against her, pushing in deeper, harder. She clings to him, pulling him closer with both hands. He fills her up, his face scrunched in a mixture of concentration and ecstasy. She closes her eyes and lets herself go, hoping for one more orgasm. He thrusts in and out, groaning with each movement, you . . . feel . . . so . . . good . . . She blushes, moans back, her hands reach behind her for the bedposts. He notices and moves one hand to hold her wrist, tight, the way she likes it, and she likes how he knows this. He pushes deeper as she yells, her cunt again spasming. He feels this around his cock and can control it no longer. He gives one final, massive thrust and seems to hang right above her, his feet turning, eyes squished, as one tiny bead of sweat drips, landing smack between her breasts. He falls over on her, his legs still trapped in his jeans. She lies there, staring over his shoulder at the water stain on the ceiling. She counts to ten, as his body grows heavy, wondering if he has suddenly fallen asleep.

"Hey," she whispers, nudging him with her elbow. "Hey, get up!"

Max doesn't move. Mira is trapped beneath him. She groans, *get . . . up . . .* as she pushes him to the side and slides out from under him. He remains face down on the bed, his white, pimpled ass shining; his legs still stuck between his jeans.

She shakes him harder but he doesn't move. "Fuck. Get the fuck up. Quit freaking me out," she cries. She grabs her bathrobe off the back of the chair and swats him hard across the ass. For a split second she wishes he had spanked her, like a bad girl.

She pinches his earlobes, something she had read in an OD pamphlet at the free clinic. She pulls his head up by his hair. His face is turning blue.

"Fuck!" she screams, suddenly afraid. This fucking bad boy, this good for nothing asshole, this stranger, has died in her apartment. She doesn't even know his last name. She crosses the room in hurried steps and dials 911.

"This guy, this guy, he's in my house, he's dead," she pants. She is panicking, afraid. Did she kill him? What will they do to her? Will she be in trouble?

"Is he dead or dying?" the operator asks.

"I think he's dead," Mira said. "I think so but I'm not sure."

The operator tries to calm her down. Mira rattles off her address and the few details she knows. She is wondering whether she should pull up his pants when the operator on the other end tells her not to touch anything.

She gets off the phone to wait for the paramedics. She wonders if they will send the OD combo – the short fire truck and the ambulance. The operator asked her if he was on drugs. Mira said she didn't know; that she didn't really know him at all.

Mira gets up and tiptoes over to him, half expecting him to jump up laughing. She thinks of how pissed she'll be if he does, but she expects him to be an asshole. She pushes him again, he still doesn't move. His body is getting cold; way different than it was just moments before. She thinks this is like a bad urban legend, she is now one of those women that kill men by sex. She wonders if this is a crime.

Mira rifles through his pockets. She pulls out a dirty syringe, a packet of cottons and a cooker, the complete package from the Needle Exchange. She also pulls out a wrinkled ten-dollar bill. She thinks about pocketing it. In his other pocket is a list of phone numbers, scrawled in bad boy handwriting, most of the numbers belong to girls. She wonders if her number would have made it onto the list. She also pulls out his ID card. Not even a driver's license but a California Walker's ID. His name is Maximus Pastorelli. It sounds familiar. With some quick math she figures that he is, no, he was, 38. Even dead he looks much younger. She sits on the side of the bed and pets his dirty hair. She is shocked that he was able to have sex. This makes her think he hasn't used yet, or hasn't been using that much.

She wonders if she should tell the EMT this. She wipes off her fingerprints and puts the drug paraphernalia and the ten bucks back in one pocket. The ID in the other. Before replacing the list of phone numbers she copies them down and hides the piece of paper. Then, it hits her. Maximus Pastorelli. He used to be in one of her ex-ex-boyfriend's favorite bands. She has even met him before at a party. He was rumored to be clean. For a brief instant she wonders if this will make her ex-once-removed jealous.

The paramedics come, ask her questions, write down her information, look at the syringe and take him away.

"So did he OD?" she asks.

The EMT points out track marks on his neck. "It could have been an aneurysm," he says and shrugs. He gives her a number to call for the autopsy report.

"You don't use drugs, do you?" the paramedic asks, looking right into her eyes like a high school principal.

She slowly shakes her head no.

"You're a pretty girl," his partner pleads, "you don't need guys like him."

She nods. She finally understands. Bad boys aren't filled with uncertainty. No one is. The ultimate uncertainty is death, which is, also, the ultimate certainty, the final frontier, the last hurrah, all that crap.

She unearths the phone numbers she has hidden and calls one of the girls, hanging up after listening to her say, "Hello? Hello? Fuck you." Her voice is raspy as if she has been smoking since she was 12. Mira puts on the CD of Max's band. She feels as if a huge burden has been lifted off of her. His music doesn't even sound good any more. But she still sits and listens to the entire CD, as if it is a eulogy. She wonders if she should tell anyone what has happened. She calls her ex, the fan of Max, but hangs up when his new girlfriend answers. She showers, dresses nicely, then calls an old co-worker, one who dates nice guys, and asks her what she's doing tonight. In mere minutes she has a plan. She applies makeup and brushes her hair. It's like the last time she shot dope, she knew she was done, it was out of her system, she no longer needed it.

Her co-worker picks her up and takes her to a bar. The woman has changed and no longer dates computer programmers and accountants. Now she dates girls. She takes her to a trashy dyke bar. Mira walks in and looks around. She is halfway to the bar when she realizes the place is filled with bad girls. She smiles widely. The air is electric; it smells like showered sex. Mira has never been with a woman before and the uncertainly makes her pulse gallop. She spots a heavily pierced woman smoking under the bright red NO SMOKING sign. Mira makes eye contact, and smiles.

Spring Pictures

Donna George Storey

"Please open it," Kimura said. He was smiling.

Anna fingered the knot of the old-fashioned wrapping cloth and smiled back. After a year in Japan, she knew it wasn't proper to open a gift in the presence of the giver. But some nights Kimura wanted her all-American side, impulsive and refreshingly innocent of the finer points of etiquette.

"Please." In his eagerness, he almost brushed her arm with his fingertips.

It was a book – she'd guessed as much from the shape and heft. The crimson cover was blank. Inside, the first page had characters she could read – "spring" and "picture" – but the next pages were all Japanese text, winding down the page in tendrils, incomprehensible without a dictionary. Still, she enjoyed the softness of the fine paper, the intoxicating fragrance of expensive book. She fought the urge to bury her nose in the crease of the binding. That would not be proper at all.

Then came the pictures.

At first, in the carefully crafted twilight of the hostess club, she saw only shapes: swirls of kimono silk, tangled limbs, caterpillar crescents of pubic hair against pale flesh, towering cocks, and conch-shell vulvas. Kimura had given her a book of *shunga*. Antique dirty pictures. Of course, some people would call such things art. Anna thought of herself as that sort of person and yet she was blushing.

She began to turn the pages quickly. She crossed her legs. She uncrossed them again. Had she been alone, she would have stopped for a closer look, but she was all too aware of the silvery glint in Kimura's eyes that seemed to cut through clothes and flesh to the warm ache of arousal growing inside her.

Only when the wanton figures were safely hidden away between the crimson covers did she have the courage to look at him. By then he was himself again: the kind, but slightly bewildered, widower who patronized the club every Friday evening. A yogurt wholesaler of all things.

"I hope this will prove useful in your study of old Japan."

She'd told him that she was hostessing to save money for graduate study in history. Unlike most of the things she said to men in this room, it was true.

Anna nodded, accepting the gift, although it meant she must give something in return. Kimura was a gentleman. It was probably enough, letting him watch her that way.

It came to be a ritual. Anna would get home from the club at one in the morning, strip off her tasteful working dress and lie naked on her futon to lose herself in Kimura's book. It was no longer foreign to her, this world of ochre and ivory, black and terre verte. She glided easily through paper doors and behind painted screens to spy on couples engaged in intimate embrace, men and women frozen in ecstasy for 250 years. She even grew accustomed to the mammoth sex organs, for that was what her body became as she lay on her stomach rocking her hips into the soft mattress – one huge cunt with grasping, ravenous lips.

When she could bear it no longer, she chose a pose: lying on her back with one knee to her chest, toes curled in. On all fours, ass tilted up in invitation. Sitting with her legs open wide to be studied by a samurai lover or passing serving wench or Tom Thumb Maneemon watching it all from under a kimono sleeve, or all three at the same time. It was for them that she stroked the fleshy folds the *shunga* makers so lovingly tinted rose or salmon, for them that she rubbed her nipples with a spit-slick palm. But it was for Kimura that she came, legs trembling with the strain of contortion, neck arched back from the weight of her elaborate coiffure. His eyes seemed to float before her still, affirming her hunger, feeding it.

At the club he was as courteous as ever, content to chat on

about censorship and sumptuary laws in the Tokugawa period, while she stole peeks at his trousers, half hoping to see his exposed member, thick as a tree trunk and brocaded with veins, arching up from the open fly.

Some weeks later, he casually mentioned he would like to guide her around the old post towns of the Nakasendô, where the daimyô stopped on the long journey from their fiefdoms to the capital. The trip would require an overnight stay, but it was far more appealing than the usual drunken proposition to meet after work at a rent-by-the-hour hotel. Still, Anna knew a clever hostess was expected to toy with a prospective lover first, and certainly lighten his wallet of more than the price of a book. She pulled out her palm pilot to set the date. She had a favor to return.

By dinner, she was convinced Kimura was toying with *her*. Why else would he bring her to a centuries-old inn deep in the mountains to share an eight-course meal in their bathrobes, then spend the whole time flirting with their maid?

It didn't help that the woman was handsome. She was older – Anna guessed late forties – but still elegant in a dove gray kimono and obi of midnight blue. It was her tongue Anna envied most, the way it swirled around those thorny honorifics, the way its music eased the lines of tension in Kimura's forehead. He was tired from showing Anna around the local sights all afternoon. No doubt he was tired of English, too.

When dinner was over, the maid laid out the bedding side by side, quilt edges touching, then bid them good-night. It was a promising sign. If they were a couple in that woman's practiced eye, Anna knew there was hope. All she had to do was nudge the shy Kimura in the right direction. She got the book of spring pictures from her overnight bag and sat down beside him at the table.

"I want to show you the ones I like," she said.

His eyes twinkled. "I would very much like to see them."

This time she turned the pages slowly. The amorous couples were good friends. She paused at her current favorite, a scene of a courtesan kneeling before a mirror to fix her hair, her kimono in artful disarray, while her lover reached from behind to fondle her exposed pussy.

"I see you prefer Harunobu, the most elegant of the *shunga* artists. He discovered much in his exploration of the multi-colored print."

Anna tilted her head in the saucy way she used at the club. "He certainly discovered what a clitoris is for."

"Yes, that is important knowledge." She'd made him blush.

"But it's more than that, don't you think? I don't know how he does it, but his figures seem alive in there. That woman in the picture knows she's being watched." Her voice trailed off.

They sat in silence.

"Kimura-san, I want to thank you for the book. I didn't do it properly before." She stumbled over the words, as if she were baring something more intimate than flesh.

He bowed. "I am glad it has given you pleasure."

She was sure she saw it in his eyes then: the tiny image of herself, masturbating furiously as she gazed down at the book.

Kimura stood up. "Excuse me a moment. I have something to attend to." Before she could speak, he left the room.

She rested her forehead on the table, shamed and confused. He probably just had to use the toilet at the end of the hall. It was like him to be discreet. But surely it was the height of decorum for a man to make amorous advances to a woman he'd invited to a secluded inn? Everyone knew couples came to places like this to screw themselves silly. Kimura would have to be blind not to see that she was more than willing to continue this venerable tradition.

Anna frowned. What if she were the blind one? What if the book was his subtle way of telling her he was "unable," that images and ideas were the only form of intercourse they could share?

He was back. Anna sat up and fixed her face with a smile. He walked over to the futons and pulled the closest across the room. He could not have made his intentions clearer.

"I think I'll go down to the bath now," she said briskly. It wouldn't do to let him see her cry.

He shook his head. "Come here, Anna-chan. Bring that book with you."

Her body took on a strange languor as she knelt before the old-fashioned mirror stand – for that is where Kimura placed the futon – and set the book down. He knelt behind her and eased the robe over her shoulders, arranging it at her waist.

"Now fix your hair. Like the girl in the picture."

Anna raised her arms and grabbed two thick ponytails of honey brown hair in each hand. The pose stretched and lifted her breasts, as if she were offering them – not to him, exactly, but to someone waiting in a mirror world beyond.

"Now, how was the man touching her?" Kimura pulled one side of the robe open like a curtain and began to tease her curls.

"I smell you, Anna," he whispered. "I could smell you when you were showing me the book. A most joyous perfume. I worried you thought I was nothing but an old fool. My English is too poor to say the things in my heart. My dream, Anna-chan, is to meet in a place where we don't need words." His finger inched closer to her clit. "*Senzuri* they called it in the old days. A thousand rubs. Do you think it will take a thousand tonight?"

She moaned and swayed back against him. Kimura wasn't impotent. The evidence was pressing into the cleft of her ass. If only he would touch her breasts, too. The starched cotton robe the inn provided had been chafing her sensitive nipples all evening. They needed soothing with hands and lips. But that wasn't in the picture.

And neither was the maid, now standing in the doorway with a tray in her hands.

With a yelp of surprise, Anna crumpled forward, scrambling to cover herself with her robe.

"You asked for more tea, sir?" The maid's voice was as cool as a mountain stream.

"Yes, thank you." Kimura seemed unfazed by her entrance.

The maid nodded and busied herself measuring tea-leaves into the pot.

Gently Kimura pulled Anna up and positioned her body before the mirror again. He tugged the robe down to her hips and guided her hands back to her head.

"Shall I wait and pour for you, sir? The young lady appears otherwise engaged."

"Yes, please. In the meantime do help yourself to a cigarette. You must be tired taking care of all of these troublesome guests." As he spoke, Kimura's hand wandered back between Anna's thighs.

"Thank you, sir, I think I will." The maid tapped a cigarette from the pack on the table. In the darkness, she seemed larger than before. Coarser. She must have put on makeup, too, because her lips were fuller, a dark glistening red. Her eyes swept boldly over Anna's body, lingering first at the breasts, then the exposed slit. A fine sweat rose on Anna's skin, as if she'd been rubbed with wet silk.

"I'm very impressed the young American lady enjoyed our dinner. Even the raw carp." The maid spoke in slow, careful Japanese. Anna was meant to understand. "She seems to have a taste for traditional Japanese things. Like *shunga*, I see."

Kimura laughed assent. His breath was warm on Anna's neck.

The maid puffed her cigarette. "Does she like mirrors, too?"

Kimura met Anna's eyes in the mirror. "Yes, I would have to say she does."

"I wonder if she'd like this one?" Smiling, the woman leaned over and took something from the mirror stand drawer. It was a hand mirror, round with a flat lacquer handle. "I've seen some interesting sights in my work, not that I mean to spy, you understand, sir, but once I saw a guest – a fine old-fashioned Japanese lady – kneeling right here fixing her hair and the gentleman guest came and took this mirror from her and began to caress her naked bosom with it. In little circles, round and round over the tips. Oh my, the sounds she made! I knew without asking they'd want their breakfast brought later."

Kimura hesitated. He bent closer to Anna and whispered, "This action sounds very interesting, but strictly speaking, it is not in the picture you chose."

"Forget the fucking picture. Do it," Anna snapped in Japanese, her breath coming fast. She'd picked up street slang from some of her less refined customers.

The maid chuckled her approval and passed the mirror to Kimura.

Anna watched as he brought it to her breast, watched her

nipple stiffen and reach toward the shiny surface as if to kiss its reflection in the glass.

Oh, it feels sooo good.

Carol Anderson pulled her pyjama top all the way up and pressed her chest to the glass of her bedroom window. Anna knew she'd have to try it next, because she made the mistake of confessing she was sore there, too. Which was good because it meant she was developing, but sometimes she wished it would stop, that burning feeling in her puffy nipples that reminded her of the quivering blue flame of the Bunsen burner in science class.

What's the matter, Anna-Banana? Are you chicken? Carol's eyes flickered in the March moonlight.

The squirmy feeling in Anna's tummy was indeed fear, but it was something else too, like she wanted to do it, like her body was telling her she had to do it. Blushing, she hiked up her top – covered with ponies galloping through a flannel forest – and leaned toward the fogged windowpane . . .

Kimura's glass was smoother and dry, yet it sent the same twinges of dark pleasure to her belly. And like the old-fashioned lady the maid spoke of, Anna was making sounds, soft, animal-like whimpers of need. Down below, at her other mouth, the flesh made wet, clicking sounds under his finger.

Kimura switched the mirror to the other breast. The sensation – hot twined with cold – made Anna cry out.

"I told you she'd like it," the maid crooned. "Look at her arching her back like a little pussycat."

"Indeed, I owe you many thanks for your help, but I mustn't keep you from your duties any longer. The young ones usually take a good while to reach satisfaction."

"Nonsense. She's going to finish soon, aren't you? Be a good girl now and climax for the nice gentleman who's working so hard on your behalf."

Good girls don't come while strangers watch, Anna knew that but, like an incantation, the woman's words transformed her, gave her image in that mirror a new tint of wantonness.

Now she had permission to do it. In fact, it was her duty. Like a courtesan in a brothel of long ago.

"Yes, madam, I will." Anna choked out the words in proper humble form. And then it was happening. Her cunt expanded, opening in swirls of hot, thick satin as wide as the universe, then clenching tight, as if squeezed by a huge hand. She dropped her head back against Kimura's shoulder, her jaw locked open in a silent scream as the orgasm seared through her. He rocked with her, cradling her in his arms. Gasping and shaking, Anna sank down onto the futon. He followed, covering her with his body.

"You may go now," he said into the air. The door slid open, then closed with a faint rattle.

In the cool silence, Anna lay floating, back from the dream of an artist 200 years past, back from a moon-drenched room of her own childhood. When she opened her eyes, she was on the futon with Kimura beside her. He was smiling. She smiled back. Anna owed him more than ever now, but she knew just what to do. Her eyes traveled to the book lying open beside him. In the dim light, the lustrous paper thickened and swelled and she saw, as if through a veil bedecked with fresh flowers, Primavera rise up from the pages and hold out her hand.

Nick/Nicola

Mark Ramsden

"Write something about me," says Nick/Nicola.

There are two of us here but this is a threesome.

Nick/Nicola is two different people; mostly male but also credibly female whenever s/he wants.

Nicola is bent over her dining-room table. On huge platform heels schoolgirls shouldn't really wear. With her silver disco skirt rucked up around her waist and translucent red panties hugging her bottom. Which is going to get six licks with this rattan cane before being kissed better. After which all heaven may break loose.

But first I'm sat at his/her computer, trying to preserve who s/he is for my amusement. Capturing who people really are – or at least the way they look to me – is an obsession of mine. *Probably because that is the only way you can control anything.* That's my inner shrink. A prissy little spoilsport who is also going to get a damn good thrashing in a minute. If I ever get tired of Nicola. And her taut, tight derrière. Which reddens up nicely. Yet always heals quickly. And is so clean inside and out you would think the little darling was an enema enthusiast. But no, she's just delicate.

Sugar and spice and all things nice. That's what this little girl is made of. Sweet as she is, it's often hard to have a relationship with a tranny. They are already deeply committed to an idea of themselves; who they might be – one day soon – when they have found the right wig and make-up. And should I mention relationships in an erotic context anyway? Especially when we are still hot for each other.

We have yet to die the long, slow death of marriage; life

without parole, in a cell that's always too small. Couples are, in theory, a union. In practice, they are usually like two dogs fighting over a bone. Or actors elbowing each other out of the spotlight.

"This is about relationships," says Nick/Nicola. "It's supposed to be about me!"

Or perhaps like siblings competing for gifts and attention . . . The comfort and cuddles brigade sometimes say it is worth getting old and fat together. I was ready for that – for the sake of the children. But I didn't have enough money for my greedy whore of a wife so I'm back on the prowl now – blade-thin, with an expensive sniffle that just won't quit. Although it's not all bad. I'm permanently excused family Xmases. And other people's parents.

Nick may not want Xmas but he is still a tranny; a cross-dresser with a hidden agenda. And I'm less interested in being someone else's mirror. Even if s/he is a pretty little thing. Nick has light blue eyes, blonde hair, soft clear skin, a delicate upturned nose and full feminine lips. He is a fine figure of a man. Driving round the countryside in his sports car he looks like the star of a sixties action show. Nick King; Private Detective. Cruising down the Kings Road in a white Aston Martin. While an acquiescent blonde in a fur coat simpers obligingly in the passenger seat.

Right now he is in his early forties although there are few signs of this on his face. Quite why his skin is so soft and silky is a mystery. No paid liar for the beauty industry would believe that this complexion is the result of a diet consisting of white bread and microwaved curries. He does not take vitamin supplements or use any grooming products. He washes in supermarket own brand shampoo, a substance also used as shaving lather and sexual lubricant – at least for the purposes of self-love. He's very cute but I doubt whether he has ever seduced anyone with a handful of cheap supermarket bubbles.

Nick could claim to be trans-gendered, although at an early stage on that confusing journey to two separate destinations – fulfilment both as a man and as a woman. As if those of us setting out in one of those directions ever got far along the road before the traffic got too heavy. Before unexpected diversions eventually sap the will to continue. Besides which, there is only one real destination on this journey, a dark eternal cul de sac that most refuse to contemplate. But why not focus on youth and beauty as Nick embodies both those qualities? And, as Philip Larkin demonstrated for far too long, wittering on that we are all going to die is not particularly helpful.

"This is about you again," says Nicola. "Or telling us about some gloomy old git. Write something about me! I'm here right now!"

A proper dom would have insisted on Nicola saying "Master" or "Mistress". But I can't be bothered taking myself that seriously, being a human first and a pantomime dom second. He may also be too damn strong to be subjected to real mental and physical torment. Which sometimes pushes people over the edge. I am the dominant partner in some sexual situations, but my hands are softer and gentler than Nick's. I never launched my forehead at the bridge of anyone else's nose. The one punch I ever threw produced a black eye, but it left me with a permanently crooked fourth finger – as no one had ever shown a softie like me how to box.

My grim face sometimes frightens people but Nick actually is hard. There have been times when decades of taunts about his prettiness caused a swift and decisive outbreak of violence. Times when ignorant and aggressive drunks found themselves weeping and writhing on the floor, their ugly faces now a little more rugged and manly than they might have wished. Some pretty boys could head-butt harder and faster than the average drunk might have reasonably expected. Maybe "reason" isn't the right word when discussing the tabloid-fed male, those who judge a sunburnt beer-belly a badge of pride. The media might be liberal these days but your average lad still wants to attack anyone who triggers their buried homoeroticism.

"Write something about *me*! Not *you*, again."

She's so needy. Just like me when I was a sub. I rub the twin tails of a tawse between Nicola's legs and watch her squirm as it stimulates some dangling equipment that real girls don't have.

The first time we met I had her over my knee, while others played in the same room. I didn't know her name or anything else about her. For once my dick broke through the drug barrier and a certain shyness during group sex, lurching up toward my belly button. It must have been her mingled earth and sex scent, as I dug my fingers deeper and deeper into her opening. Even though Will was with the gorgeous and beguiling Ritz, he couldn't keep his eyes off us as my hand burrowed into her past the knuckles. No lube and almost fisting. Scrupulously clean inside and out. Always gagging for it. There must be a flaw somewhere. Oh yes. We both prefer women – heaven knows why, but there it is. I suppose they do offer a better selection of textures and odours. If you can stand the grief.

We both had wives who threw us out although we didn't want to go. And we both didn't want to go for the same reason; the children, whom we love dearly. Neither of us yearns for the dumb dollies we married. Although perhaps Nick and I shouldn't have been dumb enough to listen to society's dictates. Get married! Have children! And if you don't agree you haven't "grown up". Although what is so "grown up" about the adult female search for Prince Charming women have yet to tell us . . .

"Why isn't this about me?" says Nicola, justifiably annoyed that s/he had opened so much of herself up and she was being ignored. So let's have some "back story", as they say in the movies.

His/her mother was still spanking her at a surprisingly late age. This was not exactly child abuse – teenager abuse, I suppose. But if the legacy of these dreadful childrearing techniques is these seven-hour whip and fuck fests, we shouldn't complain.

I can't figure out why some trans-gendered people are also tough guys. Did they toughen up in response to fear of being gay? Or did they learn to relax and let the feminine spirit come through as they grew to maturity? I have a shaven head, tattoos and muscles, but I feel feminine some of the time. And have always unconsciously chosen gay or girlie colours, fashions and styles of art. That's Mother Nature and her twisted sense of humour – always eager for a laugh at our expense. Why would she make a fit bloke like Nick then inflict several years' worth of surgery on his manliest organ during the crucial years of adolescence? I couldn't bear to ask why all that surgery had been necessary but the resulting organ eventually functioned well enough to produce two children. Perhaps Mother Nature couldn't make her mind up. Was she building a man or a woman? So she decided to do both.

For a handsome guy he certainly makes a good-looking girl. Especially when Nicola wears my old wig which looks much better on her – a red bob that frames her prominent cheekbones. Seen from behind, like now, as she shifts her weight from her aching knees, Nick is an attractive woman with a small, tight tush; a delicate little derriere that most women would do *any-thing* for. Anything other than give up alcohol, chocolate and chips. While reserving the right to bitch on endlessly at any other women's slightest gain in weight or the hint of a wrinkle. Oh dear, the writer's a "misogynist". No, just pointing out some-thing we all know but aren't allowed to say.

"Write something about *me*! This is just you going on and on again."

Sometimes Nicola reminds me of those perhaps illusory, easy-to-please girlies of my teenage years. Before feminism mobilized and the sex war became about as much fun as a real war. Perhaps I expected too much from women. (*Perhaps*? Chorus of many disgruntled ex-partners.) If Nick does some-thing annoying it's not like my mother betraying me yet again, or the pointless random opposition of women in general. It's just a man pleasing himself – which is something I can relate to.

Although it's harder to understand the need to be a woman. For me dressing is another fetish to be explored, another excuse for sexual debauchery. Whereas some find trans-gen-dered personalities within themselves that strengthen and develop. My female personae come and go, perhaps wilting for the lack of proper care and nourishment.

In my view, not hers, Nicola is sometimes too influenced by those a little too far gone round the trans-gender bend, a little lost in their own self-built mazes. He talked about hormones, a momentary madness, thankfully. For what could be sadder than going through years of gender reassignment to find you don't like your new sex? And you can't re-assign your mem-ories, can you?

Besides, s/he has yet to learn the walk. As for the voice . . .
well, few people get that right and I don't care anyway. The
male/female mix is exciting to me. Cross-dressing really is
more than an elaborate ruse to allow same-sex eroticism. Cue
snickers from lifestyle gay men here, although none will have
lasted this far. As this isn't a story about the hunt for the largest
cock or the prettiest boy they will probably have turned to
something more in tune with their needs and desires. Ooh. All
this cross-dressing must be making me bitchy.

"Stop all this . . . crap about what gay men supposedly like.
Write something about *me*."

But who are *you*? You don't even know yourself, for all this
talk about dressing being a path to "who I really am". And who
on earth are "we", this couple who come together every now
and again. We have wildly dissimilar backgrounds so it's hard
to see where this could ever go. Without the social glue of
ecstasy we would never have met.

"What do you see in me?" s/he once asked.

"You've got many cute habits," I might have said, if ecstasy
and ketamine hadn't reduced me to the usual catatonic trance.
"Your natural androgyny, that girly face and bum, the way
your left eye starts to droop and then stays closed the more
blitzed you get. It makes me feel like I must be doing something right. Look! She's winking at me again."

What would he see in me? As I'm not handsome or confident
enough. Hardly surprising as my life has just fallen apart. I'm
"decent", apparently. Which would be news to my wife or
anyone else I have hurled a lot of abuse at. Maybe I am a
contrast to the many gay men who just want to fuck anything
with a pulse. And then find another one. Having crossed the
first guy off their list.

"This is all about *you*. Write something about *me*!"

Vanity, thy name is Nick/Nicola. Without me you wouldn't
even get on the printed page. Without me you wouldn't have
that wig – instead of the foul curly perm you used to have. And
s/he gave herself the wrong name. As trannies sometimes do. I
know a posh t-girl called Sharon. And nobody terrestrial
should be called Chane (pronounced Shanay). Not that I'm
a control freak or anything. Not at all . . . Chane is a character

in a science fiction book and movie. The movie starred Sting. Sorry to invoke the anti-Christ but there it is. Science fiction and a faint memory of Sting. It's definitely the wrong name. So it's "Nicola" from now on. The name for the person I want to create. Nick may not agree. Couples often don't.

I could rhapsodize about the scent of his, sorry, *her*, body, or some of his cuter habits or just what s/he triggers in me. But men leching on about their own hunger for sex is not exactly a popular theme so let's stick with the romance. Suffice to say I make a three-hour journey each way to get her on my own over a table. Anyone who lives in London already knows that's a pretty strong endorsement. "Are you writing about me?" s/he asks, wiggling her bum. Which will have to wait for the moment. Fulfilment is transitory but frustration is eternal, my dear . . .

"Of course I'm writing about you," I tell her, with a fond chuckle. As if I would be going on about myself again. It's not as if either of us are *men* – selfish bastards concerned only with our own needs and desires.

S/he's right though. It's time Nicola got what she wants. What I want too. And if something doesn't happen soon the reader may well be back on the internet; where you can get anything for free. And there are few enough trans-gendered kink enthusiasts as it is . . .

"It's not that dragon cane again, is it?" asks Nicola. In a not remotely servile voice. You would never know that Nicola sees herself as a submissive. She's one of the many willing to be a slave, just as long as it doesn't involve any personal inconvenience. And as long as s/he gets everything she wants, when she wants it. Just like I used to be. Luckily I have evolved this Liberal Democrat style of domming. "You might like it if . . ." "Why not try this?" And I always leave multiple choice options. Perhaps I'm as hopeless at domming as s/he is at subbing. Or perhaps it's infinitely preferable to be who we actually are, rather than follow some tedious, granite-faced S&M script.

"It's the dragon cane," I tell her. "Rattan. The one with the scarlet thread. And you love it," I tell her, tapping the rod across the proffered buttocks to take aim, prolonging the wait for the first kiss of the cane. And it's another excuse to touch her many more times before the caning begins. Every now and again it's good to pinch her, to ascertain how firm her flesh is, to see how her bottom shifts and wriggles, the cheeks rubbing against each other, occasionally offering glimpses of the mystery in between.

Sometimes s/he yearns to be in a couple. As I do. Although distance conspires against us. And, let's face it, if we lived too close the heat would dissipate. We would have the same problem with monogamy that everyone else has. How often do you want to eat cold porridge? So, for the moment, and in the moment, it's going fine.

"Breathe deeply," I tell her. Although her pain threshold is high anyway. She sometimes complains but she's a pain-slut really. Maybe just an everything-slut, bless her. After a few minutes hand spanking to warm her up, it's almost time to begin. She would mark better without the warm up but a caning is a serious business, far too painful without a little preparation. But then she did leave me stranded on the station. In the dark. After I had taken rather too much ketamine, a seriously confusing substance. Especially when consumed on trains. For that she deserves a proper thrashing, never mind "safe, sane and consensual", the scene mantra which most people ignore whenever it suits them. It's a fierce joy to peel her red knickers down slowly, to bow down and plant a kiss on each cheek, to catch a hint of her clean but ever so slightly savoury scent. One more swish of the cane through the air, as hard as I would like to hit her for keeping me waiting. Which would be painful enough to make her leap up. But I can't do that. Having abandoned senseless cruelty some time in my youth.

"Oh, I'd got changed already," she said. She had "dressed", as trannies say, in order to tart around in a chat room. When a real person had dragged themselves across two counties to see her. Typical male sexuality, of course. Nothing is ever good enough. It's always the hunt for the next one. Even if, like me, you mislay valuable possessions in the process. Such as wives. Lovers. Careers . . .

There is a deep throaty laugh after the first stroke lands. Is it really going to be that hard? Well, yes it is, petal. She likes it, really. It's best when it's hard enough to feel the next day. When the glow from sex and the shafting with our various toys can still be felt. She likes to taunt her homophobic work mates with what a good time she has had. Although getting inside her tight, winsomely cute ass is not always easy it's heavenly when I do. But first, a disobedient little madam needs her rump reddening.

I stand back and take careful aim. You would never know that caning someone is such hard work, not from pornography often written by people who never do it. It's easy enough to miss and catch someone halfway down the thighs, triggering a searing agony with no erotic benefits.

Another stroke draws a long sigh and a shake of her hips. Then it's time to kneel down and kiss her along the red ridges left by the cane. During which time I lose my head and drift. Lost in the moment. Worshipping her. Pleasing myself. Groaning and grovelling. Sex, violence and religion in one package; how can you go back to infantile dreams of monogamy after this? Pressing her opening with the heel of my hand gets her whole body to rock, preparing her to open up for me later. And all through this my erection is aching. Hello, old friend. Haven't seen you much during the many recent ecstasy binges. We really must do this more often . . .

"Write about *me!*" insists Nicola. Aware that I'm drifting off-message. S/he always wants to be centre stage. Just as I did, when I was in her position. I lay on a few strokes, which are accepted gratefully. I compare this moment with the many images I have both real and imagined – a resource just as valuable to me as some monogamist's dreams.

Stroke number five falls right across the middle of her lovely cheeks and there is the satisfaction of hearing a genuine cry of pain, something to file away for later enjoyment. I lay on a few more punishing strokes and watch her wriggle. Then I kiss her and help her up. A hug, a cuddle, it's time for a rest. A pit stop to take on fuel before more circuits of the track. More drugs, more depravity. A hint of tenderness now and again. No arguing about sheds, shelves or parental visits. You could get used to this. It's sweet watching Nicola rubbing her bottom and smiling ruefully.

"It wasn't too hard for you?" I ask, past an age when I might want to use people or hurt them, a veteran of too many broken love affairs and one broken marriage. Which is the only broken marriage I am ever going to have.

"You look amazing," I tell her. "A true Princess."

There was a time when I might have wanted to say "Goddess" there. Although believing in a female deity that doesn't exist turned out to be no more fruitful than pining for a grumpy old male God.

At some point round about now, when he feels happy or positive about trans-gendered activity, Nick usually says: "I want to be *me*. I want to be who I really am." The tone is defiant. Perhaps he's addressing his wife or some other ex-partner. I still think that s/he is looking for a woman. As I am, despite it all. Except that she is looking in the wrong place. For real girls often tire of helping trannies find the right wig, the best eye shadow. There may well be women who will put up with not being centre stage: if there is a power imbalance, if there is a significant age difference or if they are doing it for money. Women looking for life partners tend to want raw clay they can mould into something they want. So cross-dressers had better get used to looking for that ideal woman inside themselves. Which may be a sensible strategy anyway. Tired of chasing genetic girls? Been hurt too often? Think there are too many design flaws in the original product? Well you can always come up with a better prototype yourself. Maybe you already know the love of your life, your own female persona. After all, if you want something doing, sometimes you have to do it yourself . . .

The Permanent

Catherine Lundoff

Run, my mind sings. *Run.* And I do. I am almost flying now, my heart thudding against my ribs like a rabbit pursued by hounds. My bare feet pound against the dirt as I do my best to outstrip whatever it is that hunts me. *Bare?* I glance down at a frothy lace confection of a nightgown, at my pale naked feet twinkling below me in the darkness. *Why am I wearing this . . . thing?* The thought jars me awake just ahead of the phantom grasp of my pursuer.

Just ahead of the alarm as well. I sit up, heart still pounding as I turn off the clock radio. When I look down, my nipples are gradually relaxing and I can smell the dampness like rust between my legs. I scramble for a tampon, coffee, and clothes, then drag my carcass out to catch the bus. It stops in front of a big redbrick building with high arched windows. Two large stone pots filled with scraggly brown leaves and twisted stems stand on either side of the doorway. I wonder what it was before it died.

I'd also wonder why they don't shell out for landscaping, but I've been inside. I know the answer to that already. Genteel decay doesn't begin to cover it. Once through the doors, I have to stop and blink for a while to adjust to the dimness and the dust. There are ancient red velvet curtains and musty old Persian carpets and dark, dark wood everywhere. I don't see Terese until I almost bump into her. Not that I mind that part. She and her brother Gerard are the best part about working here, besides the pay, of course.

"Hello, Magda," Terese purrs down at me, not bothering to step back. She's about five inches taller than me and round and curvy in all the right places. Her big black eyes come into focus as my eyes adjust and she flashes a bright white grin at me.

I love hearing her say my name. In her deep voice with its indefinable accent, "Magda" becomes an exotic Eastern European beauty with cheekbones to die for and yards of black hair. Of course, I do look just like that, except for the cheekbones. And the hair. Well, all right, and I'm not particularly exotic; can we drop it already?

Terese moves slowly away from me as Gerard comes in to the hallway. "Hello Magda. We've got some fun stuff for you tonight." He smiles reassuringly, teeth dazzling in the gloom. He is long and lean in contrast to Terese's abundant curves. They both have the same melting eyes though, and black hair that looks more like ravens' wings than ravens' wings if you know what I mean. Their hands are pretty similar too, all long fingers and slightly tapered nails. Just the right size to fit into all kinds of inappropriate-for-the-workplace things.

On the other hand, Samuels, the other employee, is more than a little creepy. He has eyes that kind of slide away before they really catch yours. I follow Gerard into the next room where Samuels wanders up to us. When I glance up it looks like he's trying to smell my hair or something.

I back up until Gerard speaks. "Didn't you say that you wanted to get started on the billing, Dick? I'll be in to talk to you about it in a few minutes." Gerard's voice has just the right authoritative ring to it and Samuels dutifully trots off without a backward glance. I hope the office lights are too dim for Gerard to notice my small sigh of relief. I wouldn't want him thinking that I don't play well with others.

He keeps the lights low and they work mostly at night because he and Terese are both light sensitive. I'm finally getting used to it; soon, like their general gorgeousness, I'll just take it in my stride. I tell myself that when he leads me over to his computer. His hand rests lightly on my shoulder. All of a sudden, I want that frothy lace horror I was wearing in my dream. I wonder if he'd like taking it off. Then he breaks the mood by taking his hand away and standing tantalizingly out of reach as he tells me what he wants me to do.

But I'm having trouble concentrating. The room is getting

warmer. Maybe it's just the dark red velvet of the curtains drowning out the setting sun's watery light. Maybe it's the rise and fall of Gerard's voice as he speaks to me. I reach up and unbutton the top two buttons of my blouse but he doesn't seem to notice and it doesn't cool me off at all. The room spins slowly around me and instead of listening to the wonder of invoices, I find myself imagining the touch of his lips, the feel of those long fingers on my skin.

"You're confusing her, brother dear." Terese slinks in to sit on the edge of the desk, as close to me as she can get. I turn my chair a little so my leg touches hers ever so slightly, just enough to send shivers up my spine. I am getting wet listening to them banter back and forth above me, soaking my tampon until I wonder if my blood will pool beneath me in a small sea. I contemplate throwing myself at both of them. But what if they say no? How humiliating would that be? *Coward* says the little voice inside my head.

Terese leans forward to point out something on the screen and I can see down the front of her dress. Round breasts glow like alabaster against the soft dark blue of the cloth and I long to bury myself in them. She reaches out and I feel her white fingers caress my face. I turn to kiss them. *Wait; that's not it all. She's reaching out to get a paper from Gerard. Damn, Magda, get a grip.* I drown in her eyes anyway and come up gasping.

My fingers play with the next button on my blouse. "Are you too warm?" Gerard purrs solicitously and from somewhere a cold breeze startles my flesh from its daydreams. Goosebumps run down my arms and my nipples leap erect and I gasp aloud at the sudden chill.

"Too much, I think." Terese stands up, her fingers now gently stroking the goosebumps from my bare arm. I chew my lip in a frenzied effort at self-control. I should go get a glass of water, take a break, do something, anything, so I don't make a fool of myself. Not here, not in front of them.

With a huge effort I make myself say, "I'm fine, really. Well, I should get started on this stuff." They both smile down at me and for an instant, I remember my dream and my body braces for flight. Then the moment's passed, leaving nothing but my pounding heart behind as they glide like panthers from the room. Terese gives me what I interpret as a smoldering gaze over one shoulder and my lips part in a soft pant.

The door shuts behind them and I am left alone in Gerard's office with its ancient wood furniture and red velvet curtains and a giant stack of invoices. When I look down I can see the rivulets of sweat run down between my breasts. *Are you showing enough cleavage there, Magda?* the voice of my common sense demands shrilly but I ignore it in favor of wishing that I had worn my good lace bra today instead of my sad nylon one.

I don't rebutton the shirt, but I do make myself work for a while, make myself pretend that the growing wetness between my legs isn't there. I try to squelch my new fantasy of being chased through the woods by both of them. And better yet, being caught. It works for a while. Then I give up and begin typing with one hand as I unzip my boring khaki skirt with the other. I stick that hand inside the waistbands of both skirt and underpants.

My fingers swim upstream to my clit and I imagine they're Terese's tongue, circling, stroking, then darting inside me. Heat washes up my thighs and I quiver against their touch. I abandon the keyboard to stroke my nipples through my shirt and bra, first one then the other, pinched into points with my, no her, free hand. My clit hardens beneath my fingers, her tongue, skin slick with my own juices, with her imagined softness. Her phantom fingers slip inside me and I ride the wave, cresting it with a soft moan, legs shaking against Gerard's chair.

I hear the click of the door before I open my eyes. In an instant, I am looking doggedly at the screen, both hands resting on the keyboard. Casually, I reach back and zip up my skirt. But when I look up there's no one there.

Dinnertime rolls around eventually and I go and eat my sandwich in the backyard, which is about the size of a postage stamp and overgrown with old rosebushes and morning glories. I can pretend that I'm Sleeping Beauty while I sit on the old iron bench and remember what summer looks like. Samuels glances out of the door at me, faded eyes sliding all around me, but he doesn't come outside.

I'm overjoyed when he disappears back inside. There's

something creepy about that wrinkled face with its weird eyes shifting and wandering but never quite coming to rest. If it weren't for the pay and the chance to lust after hotties like Terese and Gerard, I'd ask to be pulled from this job. Not that I think that way once I'm back inside.

I close the door behind me and notice Terese through the open door of her office. She's meeting with someone, perhaps an actual client. They don't seem to have all that many of those, possibly because of the evening hours. Or maybe it's that silly slogan: Forever Insurance Insures You Forever. I mean, who needs insurance *forever?* Lifetime total is usually enough for most people.

Terese leans forward, talking with her hands all the while and looking earnest. Definitely a client. I wander back to Gerard's office in time to find him sitting at his desk. He gives me a sleepy grin and ushers me back to his chair. The way he hangs over me when I sit down almost makes me wonder if he can smell my wet warmth and I squirm against the upholstery at the thought.

I wonder what would happen if I turned around and unzipped his fly and took his dick in my mouth. In my mind, it's just the right size and he groans at the touch of my tongue. I rock my head back and forth, then pull away to lick my way slowly down to his balls. His breath quickens into short gasps as I embrace him with my mouth once more. He clutches my shoulders in an effort not to ram himself down my throat. I can feel him shake with desire and I smile a little. I just love polite boys.

He reaches down to grab one of my hands and pulls it up to his mouth. I can feel his mouth on my fingers, then his tongue on my wrist: distracting, but not unpleasantly so. I work harder until I can taste his salty tang and, as he comes in my mouth, I feel his teeth sinking into my wrist. I groan in surpise and desire, panting as I watch him drink from me. His tongue pulls at my wrist like a tongue on my clit and I spread my legs, straining against the chair. My fingers stroke my clit until I forget where I am and come in waves.

When I'm ready to start paying attention again, he's gone and I've got nothing better to look at than the computer screen.

I remind myself sternly that there was no way Gerard was going to be doing the temp at work, not with the door open, anyway. The voice of my common sense takes over despite the imagined slight ache of jaw and wrist.

I type listlessly until it's time to go home. Terese's client is gone and she and Gerard are talking softly to each other when I say good night. They stop talking to smile at me as Samuels holds the door open for me. I wonder if he lives upstairs. He's always there when I get there and still there when I leave. I look up at the curtained windows of the second floor where I have yet to venture. They look deserted but my flesh crawls a little as my eyes meet their glassy blank stares.

The dreams are more intense tonight. This time, I worry that something serious will happen if I get caught and I run faster than ever. Still, something grabs me and I fall, tumbling not to the ground but into the afternoon and safety. The last things I remember seeing in my dream are the curtained windows of the second floor of Forever Insurance as I run past them, pursued by whatever it is. Terrific. I hate it when my subconscious works overtime.

I decide to take the proverbial bull by the horns, or any other available body part, and check out the second floor. Once I knew there were no dead bodies or whatever up there, I'd get over this whole thing. Or so I tell myself.

The groovy ghoul is the only one at the office when I show up. "Terese and Gerard are meeting with clients downtown," Samuels informs me in a voice like a damp fog. His bulbous, colorless eyes gaze just past me until I get impatient and slightly queasy. I flee to Gerard's office and my very safe invoices. Joy.

But at least I'm not working with him. He has his own office down the hall. As long as he's busy, this is probably my best chance for checking out the dreaded upstairs. I just need to know that I'm overreacting, then I can make it all go away. Tomorrow I'll go have lunch with some friends, maybe catch a matinée. Get back to normal, whatever that is.

I do remember being normal. That was the time when I wasn't having weird dreams about things chasing me and could enter invoices for hours at a time without even once thinking of fucking my bosses. Back then, I wasn't looking at little cuts on my wrist and wondering where they came from. It's not like anything actually happened yesterday so I really don't have a clue. I rub them a little and they fade under the pressure, disappearing into my skin like they were never there. Bizarre.

I wait a reasonable amount of time before I head out into the hall. I poke my nose around the door of Samuels' office and wave the universal signal for "see you later." He bares his teeth at me, whoops, no, that was a smile. Sort of. He goes on talking on the phone, so I move as quietly as I can to the big staircase, just out of sight of the door. It has dark wood banisters that curl at the ends and it's very dark up at the top. *All right, just go up, look around, then back down* I tell myself.

I'm shivering a little on the first step and more on the third. By the time I get to the seventh I know this isn't a good idea. But on step ten I know I might as well go all the way up. Five steps more and I'm on the landing. There's a little light coming in from somewhere, but not much.

The air is really still up here, like it's anticipating something, and it's a lot cooler than downstairs. There's a short hallway to my right and I walk down it, swearing to myself that I'll just peek into that open door on my left. Then I'll go back downstairs. Just one little look . . . the room is almost empty, except for the two long boxes on the floor and the hurricane lamp on the table above them.

I make myself open the boxes. I just have to know. They aren't sealed or anything but the dirt inside doesn't tell me much. Maybe they're into gardening. Or maybe, they're . . . *What?* My little inner voice demands. *Bloodsucking fiends from Transylvania?* Outside in daylight, I would have laughed. Up here in the dark, crouched over two big boxes of dirt, I start shivering.

I close the boxes as quietly as I can and stand up very slowly. Just a few steps and I'll be down the stairs and out the front door. Then all I have to do is call the agency tomorrow and tell them things haven't worked out. I don't see Terese in the doorway until I bump into her. "Hello, Magda. I see that I don't need to chase you this time." Her eyes are black pools and I fall in, drowning until I would crawl over broken glass to get to her. Or let her chase me through my dreams until she catches me.

Then she kisses me, with lips so cold they burn mine and a tongue that freezes the inside of my mouth. I kiss her back, trying to warm her with my breath, my desire. We move slowly down the hallway to another room, her hands busily unbuttoning my shirt. Tonight, I wore my good bra, the red lace one with the snap in front. She has both shirt and bra off in moments. Her cold lips pull away from mine and drop to my breast. She takes my nipple in her mouth and it hardens until it's almost numb.

I don't feel her teeth sink in, just the sense that she is drinking, draining me of something I didn't know I had. Something I hope I don't want. She unbuttons my skirt and it falls to the floor. My underpants follow after an expert tug. I am pushed backward onto a bed, an antique four poster with curtains. *Black velvet, natch*, the analytical portion of my brain notes, as my eyes adjust slightly to the glow of the single candle.

Terese releases my breast and looks up to meet my eyes at the thought. I whimper as I watch her lick my blood from her lips and she smiles knowingly and slides down between my legs. Her icy caress finds my clit and strokes it, first with fingers, then tongue and I shiver and shake with longing and desire. She tugs the tampon from me and I close my eyes as she slides her tongue over it. Then I come, bucking wildly against the glacier of her mouth, and she drinks from me like a goblet.

One moment, it's just us on the bed, with me writhing against the persistent pressure of Terese's fingers and teeth, then Gerard's there. His pale skin glows against the velvet of the curtains as he climbs in next to us. Terese lifts her face and bares her fangs at him, my blood staining the pale glow of her chin. "Share and share alike, sister dear," he responds as he kisses me and I know they've done this before. For an instant, I wonder what happened to the others: are they dead or what?

Then I find myself on all fours, my face buried between Terese's suddenly very naked thighs. I lick fiercely because I want to be the one they keep, the one they share between them and tell all their secrets to. I want them to want me like I want them: desperately, all barriers gone. Terese is very dry against my tongue, but I hear her breath hiss against her fangs, feel her body stiffen slightly.

Gerard slides up behind me, his fingers guiding himself inside me until he fills me with his biting cold. Terese pulls my hand up to her mouth and sucks fiercely on my wrist as he rides me, my groans muffled in her flesh. I try not to get too distracted, my tongue still coaxing her clit, begging her to lose herself in me. Gerard sinks his teeth into my shoulder and I whimper at the momentary pain. I want to surrender but my instinct for survival is too strong and I struggle, fighting against losing myself utterly.

Terese releases my wrist and slides down between my arms to kiss me. "Gently, little one. We will not hurt you. Much." Her voice purrs on the word and I relax into her arms as Gerard shifts position so his fingers can stroke their way up between my thighs. He is still inside me when I come again, howling against Terese's neck. As one, they drop their mouths onto both sides of my neck and begin to feed. My body shivers in arousal, in terror until I pass out.

When I come back round, I'm at Gerard's computer, fully dressed and very tired. It's the end of my shift. I notice that the stack of invoices is gone from the basket and I feel as empty as it is at the sight. Are they out of work for me? What if they don't want me back? The place is very quiet as I log out and get my jacket and there's no one around to ask if they have work for me to do next week. I crawl home, depressed at the loss.

I don't remember why I'm so tired or sore, at least not at first. But I don't have any dreams that night. Then Bob from the agency calls in the morning and says that Forever Insurance loves my work, but they don't have anything for me just now. He tells me about some other gig and I answer like a robot until I can get off the phone. Then I curl up and cry around the big empty space inside me. I wonder what used to fill it. My fingers find my wrist and I massage a sore spot, dully surprised that it hurts at all.

I get up to look at myself in the mirror and I look like I haven't slept for days. Bats could nest in the dark caves of my eye sockets. I wonder what Terese and Gerard would have seen in me, if they could see anything in me at all. The imagined touch of their hands thrills me for a moment, and I close my eyes, then open them and make myself head for the fridge. It wasn't real, none of it. I just have to get over them.

I'm insanely hungry this morning, for whatever reason. It's only after I rummage around for a while and the cold freezes my fingers that I realize that I'm supposed to remember last night as an elaborate fantasy. But what if it wasn't? Then I got used: a little blood, a little sex, and then put away like yesterday's news. The words hang there in my mind until I get good and pissed. *Who the hell do they think they are?* I wanted them to keep me, maybe even make me one of them, but what do they do instead but try to glamour it all right out of my head.

That night I will myself to sleep, thinking of nothing but my dream until I am back on the road. Nothing pursues me yet because no one knows I'm here. I lean against a tree in the dark, waiting, my own blood running freely down my legs. They will come, called to me by its rusty scent. My fingers toy with a small crucifix, then stroke the rough wood of the stake that I dream into being. They need a new employee at Forever Insurance. I just hope they can see that before I have to hurt them. Much.

No Solace for the Soul in Digitopia

John Grant

My wife Xanthe was standing naked at the counter in the bathroom brushing her teeth when I woke up. Still lying in bed, I watched her back with a voyeuristic frisson for a few moments, then I climbed out quietly and padded across the bedroom to creep up behind her.

Standing there, looking at her smiling eyes over her shoulder in the mirror, I ran the tips of my fingers softly down over her shoulder blades and then the length of her spine until I reached the lower curves of her buttocks. With my fingernails I repeatedly stroked gently outwards from the fork of her legs along the twin creases beneath the smooth swells, all the while brushing her back with the soft hairs of my chest and nuzzling my nose in among the sleepy tousles of coppery red that fell over the back of her neck.

She gave a sort of bubbling moan through the froth of toothpaste and relaxed her stance, moving her feet apart and bending at the waist, supporting herself with her left hand flat on the counter. I stopped my stroking and reached round her hips to let my fingers play among the tangles of her pubic hair, teasing the strands tenderly, then slid one forefinger down to the topmost fold of her sex.

Xanthe's a tall woman, taller than I am, so when my erection slipped between her thighs to find a harbour it was only the ripe bell of my penis that lodged between her labia, cupped in moist warmth. She carried on brushing her teeth, though her steady rhythm was by now becoming disjointed; stuttering vibrations caressed the head of my penis and transmitted themselves softly down its shaft. The movements of my hands, too, were becoming uncoordinated as I alternately cradled her buttocks and rubbed the rounded ridges of her pelvic cradle, leaning against her once more as I kneaded the sides of her small breasts with the soft skin of my inner wrists, touching the taut raspberries of her nipples and gripping them fleetingly between paired fingers.

She dropped the toothbrush into the basin and gulped, the gulp causing a muscular contraction that tweaked the top of my penis with a little kissing sound. Almost immediately afterward further delicate movements there told me that she was having a small orgasm.

She put her other hand down on the counter and, with a long low gasp, bent her legs, easing outward and downward and backward so that the full length of my shaft was slowly engulfed by her hotness and she was almost sitting in my lap as I took part of her weight.

"Good morning," I said in her ear, looking at our faces smiling side by side in the mirror, casting my gaze down a little to where my hands had settled on her breasts. Her skin was flushed pinkly down one side of her neck and over her chest, the pale tint spreading across the top of one breast.

"Morning," she sighed.

Supporting herself with just one hand once more, she reached with the other between her legs to couch my balls, rolling them lazily back and forward against each other, rubbing with her thumb at the base of my penis where it met the stickiness of her.

For a minute or more the motion of her hand as she fondled my balls was the only movement between us. I could feel a steady pulse building up in the lower part of my shaft and an almost painful tingling at its tip.

Then she began to sway herself against me, up and down along my penis, also giving a small swivel to her hips. In the mirror her lips were still forming a contented smile and her eyes were still dancing, but through my own closing eyes I could see my mouth was pulling into an earnest grimace. I dipped my head and began to cover her shoulders with my kisses, my own hips beginning to move now in counterpoint to hers, feeling her smooth buttocks squeezing down onto my lower belly and then pulling themselves momentarily away again. Grunting a little, I ran a hand back down to her sex and found her clitoris with my fingers; the first touch drew a whooping cry from her, and the speed of her movements against me quickened. She shoved backward, taking a small, uncontrolled step, making me nearly stumble, dropping her head so that now she was almost bent double, pushing me deeper and deeper and more and more forcefully into her, the wet sounds of us slapping the walls with muted echoes.

It was as if there were no longer two of us, just one single organism trembling and pulsing in a quest for unitary pleasure. I felt as if I were being absorbed entirely into her, so that her breath was my breath, her velvety morning skin-smell a warm cloud that embraced both of us, her twitching shoulder blades in front of my eyes a plain of flesh that was my own flesh.

Each plunge of her buttocks against me was now almost like a punch. With each thrust she was yelling – incoherent sounds, wordless cries. At some time she'd given up holding my balls, which were now rolling of their own volition, my scrotum beginning to tauten and shrink, above it the base of my penis seeming to swell as it prepared itself.

"Shall? We?" I could hardly keep my mind together enough to form the words.

"Do? This?" Someone else might not have recognized her noises as speech.

"Together?" I gasped.

An old joke between us. An affectionate little playful joke it had been at first, in the early days of our lovemaking, but now become so intimate that it was as erotically charged as anything else we did together.

"Yes!" she shrieked.

And began to come, this time not with one of the many little minor orgasms that had been tickling my penis all along but with full intensity, so that it felt as if firm hands were clutching at my shaft. Inside me a dam, held momentarily against the rush of my own orgasm, then was breached by a final powerful thrust, and my juices were surging in slow irresistible convulsions all up the length of me to gush into her in great viscous spurts that seemed to tug at the sensitive flesh of the meatus before launching themselves.

For long seconds my entire universe was just a haze outside the brilliantly glowing focus of our conjoined sexes. I was the smell of her and the taste of her and the touch of her and the breath of her. Then slowly I became conscious that my cheek was nestling against her spine and that I was moaning softly. She was still coming, her orgasms tumbling one on top of each other, my penis lovingly buffeted by their strength, her buttocks moving in spasmic little jerks. Mingled moistures seeped out of her, running over the root of my penis and down the tight fist of my scrotum; a couple of drips fell to the floor. The air was rich with the smell of our lovemaking.

Finally she stilled.

I held onto her with both arms around her belly, dizzy, needing her support. I was still hard within her, hard as stone, so hard I thought I would never, ever stop being hard like this, would never stop being in this embrace with her, would be making love with her for eternity and all the while be growing harder . . .

"I love you," I said.

"I love you," she replied.

Eternity is quite a lot shorter than you think it is, and so half an hour later I was showered and fully dressed and out on the street, walking to the bus stop where I could if I wanted catch the number 264 bus to work. My whole body felt satisfied, as if it had been given an extensive internal massage complete with sweet-scented oils. I kissed Xanthe goodbye when she stopped at the car, and watched her, waving loosely, as she drove away to join the streams of traffic toward the other side of town, where she worked as a marine architect.

Standing there in the warm morning sunshine, I was somewhat vague as to what precisely my own profession was, and so instead of carrying on toward the bus stop I turned up a small alley and was in bed with my wife Lyssa.

Lyssa is small and blonde and so petitely cute that it almost hurts the eyes to look at her, as if so much beauty shouldn't have been crammed into such a small compass, and right at the moment she was coming drowsily awake with her face burrowing into my side. I pushed silky near-white hair back from her forehead and squirmed around so that I was facing her and could kiss her into full wakefulness. Even as her eyelids pulled slowly open her eager little hand was tickling its way down over my belly to where my erection was slowly, then swiftly, mounting.

She wrapped her hand around the shaft, pressing her thumb down on top of the tip, grinning through the increasingly fervent kisses I was placing on her lips. Gripping a little more tightly, she began moving the thick satiny skin of the shaft slowly up and down.

"The kids are awake," I whispered, pulling my face back from hers. "I heard them moving around a little while ago."

She pouted, half-mocking, half-serious. "Damn," she said.

When Lyssa and I make love it tends to get noisy. The kids know better than to charge into our bedroom unannounced, of course, but they'd be bound to ask us later about all the creaking and yelling. We've tried making love silently, and it's kind of fun because it feels as if we're committing some sort of delicious naughtiness together; but at the same time inhibited lovemaking has its limitations.

"Still and all . . ." I began, leaving the sentence unfinished as I rolled her onto her back.

I kissed her again, harder this time, our tongues probing into each other's mouths, caressing within, our breath becoming loud in each other's ears. Then I ran the tip of my tongue around the edge of her cheekbone and down to her chin. She arched her head back as my tongue moved on to the crease of her neck, tasting her sweetly salty sleep-sweat there. In moments I was kissing her breasts, taking each of her small nipples in turn between my teeth, not biting, not even gently biting, rolling my lips over my teeth and pressing gently. She held my head in her hands, breathing more deeply now, her hips moving reflexively against my chest, her legs parting to either side of my torso, her furry little sex making small wet noises of its own against my abdomen. Between her legs, my erection against the sheets seemed heavier than it had any right to be, as if it were becoming larger than all the rest of me put together.

I lingered at her breasts tantalizingly longer than I knew she wanted me to, then my mouth continued its downward exploration of her body, pausing once more when I reached her navel, probing the tiny folds with my tongue, tracing damp circles around the concavity. Her belly is flat and smooth, even though she has borne our two children; through its wall I could hear her blood rushing and her insides making modest gurgling noises. Often enough in the past I'd held my cheek here and listened to first my son and then my daughter moving in her womb, felt their diminutive kicks and punches. I knew I was smiling broadly as I kissed her here now, sensing the tension building up in her loins, remembering those other moments of intimacy . . .

Half-kneeling, I pushed her legs gently yet farther apart and sank my head to rub my nose over the silky skin of the inside of first one thigh and then the other, breathing deeply the warm muskiness of her pinkly unfolding sex. Her fingers began clawing the sides of my head as she tried to force my face toward her vagina, but I deliberately resisted her just a little while longer, continuing to rub and kiss her inner thighs as her behind squirmed frenziedly against the sheets.

At last I relented, first placing a broad warm kiss over her wet opening, sucking slightly, tasting the juices; then I puckered my lips and, pulling her labia aside with my thumbs, very daintily kissed her clitoris. She jerked against me, even that brief and inconsequential contact bringing her to the brink of orgasm. Once more I kissed the little nub of her clitoris, and then I pushed my tongue between the warm folds of her vagina, blowing gently.

Her hands scrabbled through my hair. She mashed my face tight up against her tuft of wet pubic hair. Her hips jolted upward, clear of the bedding, and despite any resolves to keep silence she let out a long, soft cry as she came, her thighs juddering against my ears, her fluids pouring into my mouth, the muscles of her belly writhing and tautening. I slipped my tongue out of her vagina and ran it swiftly over the underface of her buttocks and in the groove between her sex and her rear, and she gave a great convulsive heave of aftershock, then another and another . . .

When she was at last done I pulled myself up alongside her, my penis, though somewhat smaller here than usual, still a dominating presence in my mind. I could feel the wetness of its tip where clear juice had escaped. I gazed at her reddened face, at the beloved crinkles of her ears, at those pale blue eyes still half-closed, at the parted pink lips, at the corner of her mouth where a trickle of saliva glistened, at the darling curls of damp-darkened blondeness flattened against her scalp around the back of her ears. I truly love this woman of mine – love every part of her, both spiritually and carnally. I caressed her cheek and jaw with my hand, feeling her heat and her perspiration, and, despite the throbbing of my erection, began to drift into a half-doze, cradling her in my arms against me.

But then her hand walked its way down to my erection again and clasped it.

"Wait here," she breathed.

Pushing back her hair with her other hand, she wormed her way slowly down the bed and took my left ball into her mouth, sucking it softly, easing and increasing its ache at the same time. Then she kissed the underside of my penis, working slowly up from root to tip, where she tickled with her tongue tip the tight cord of folded flesh that joins skin to head.

I shut my eyes and saw visions of rushing through space among the stars, my consciousness ebbing toward the tingle of her tongue tip's touch and the warmth of her breath on the bulging bell of my penis head.

The movements of her tongue grew broader, and then she was taking me into her mouth, almost coyly at first, as if her mouth were experimenting demurely, then more fully, her lips gripping the skin and sliding it backward and forward, a finger and thumb gripping the base of the shaft to steady it.

Within just a few seconds I felt myself beginning to come. Lyssa felt it as well, starting to press rhythmically with her thumb at the throbbing area near the base of my erection's underface. She speeded up the motion of her head, clamping my penis more firmly between her lips, her tongue dashing hither and thither across the meatus on each retreat of her head. She was stroking my balls with her palm, feathery strokes, just brushing the springy hairs on my sack, sensitizing the whole area there until it seemed I could feel the individual molecules of air jostling against that wrinkled flesh.

I craned my neck and looked down along the plains of my body at her. Just at that moment she glanced up at me, paused for a fraction of a second, her blue eyes alight with mischief, her cheeks puffed out. Her lips moved in a languorous grin, and I felt every last adjustment of her flesh against mine. And then I flung my head backward on the pillow, arching my back, staring at the grey ceiling, groping with my hands for her head, for her hair, running my fingers through it, feeling the play of her facial muscles and the subtler tectonics of her scalp, putting a palm to her bulging cheek and . . .

The breath rushed out of my lungs in a huge gust as I came, spitting semen over the roof of her mouth, the back of her mouth, feeling her swallow once, twice, her head now stilled as she accepted my offering.

Once she had satisfied herself that she'd drained me entirely, she fastidiously licked me clean, touching me gently with her lips and her tongue because she knew how close to pain any rough contact would be. Then, holding her body against mine, she slithered up the front of me, her breasts embracing my erection for a fleeting moment of mixed ecstasy and agony, until our mouths were together and I could kiss her deeply, tasting my salty semen on her teeth and tongue.

"I love you," I said at last.

"No more than I love you," she said, her voice hoarse, hardly more than a whisper. "Hold me tight, darling. Hold me tight."

I held her tight, pulling a sheet up over us in case the kids came bouncing in.

It was a Saturday, so the four of us breakfasted together in leisurely fashion as the sunlight spilled in yellow pools across the kitchen. Lyssa scrambled some eggs – daughter Karen's favourite – while I prepared endless relays of hot toast for Mark and myself. Every now and then Lyssa and I would catch each other's gaze above the industrious small heads of the scarfing kids and share a secret grin with each other. After a while I had to sit down at the table with the kids because those intimate grins of hers were making my weary, still slightly throbbing penis swell again inside my slacks. I diverted my mind by making earnest conversation with Mark about the iniquities of various of his schoolteachers.

After breakfast was over, the table and counter wiped clear of crumbs and smears, the dishes stashed safely away in the dishwasher and the kids safely out at play in the yard, Lyssa and I clung together for a long moment, feeling the familiar curves and angles of each other's bodies through the resented barriers of our clothing. If it hadn't been for the kids we'd have made love once more, there and then, on the floor or the kitchen table. My fingers on the crotch of Lyssa's pale blue jeans, I could sense her renewed dampness. My own excitement was far more obvious.

She touched a hand to my lips.

"Later, later," she said with a lopsided smile. "You've got a date for tonight, mister. Don't forget."

I kissed her one final time, and made for the door.

Whether it was the afterglow of love or whether it was carelessness, or whether it was simply an unexpected quantum event – as if that weren't a tautology – I do not know, but as I walked down the bright dusty street of our semi-rural small town, my mind anticipating eagerly a visit with my wife Isolde, my feet took a wrong turn and I was sitting in a cluttered one-room apartment listening to poundingly loud music that I eventually recognized as Bryan Adams.

Damn!

These things sometimes happen – in fact, probably more often than anyone quite likes to admit. The pathways through the interstices of the polycosmos are more than infinite in number, so it's hardly surprising that our instinct, being powered by neurons that are somewhat, if only slightly, less in number than those pathways, should occasionally lead us astray as we journey between the realities. Usually it doesn't matter at all, of course: you emerge to discover yourself with a partner of either sex who is, shall we say, similarly inclined, and whom you have always and for ever known and loved. Bathing in the mutual love, either alone together in bed or on a long country walk with the dogs or yelling and screaming with the kids on a carnival rollercoaster – or wherever, all the myriad ways there are in which love can be made – you establish your presence, your soul, your identity, so that the whole great machine of the polycosmos keeps trundling along toward its eternal futures.

But sometimes you're not so lucky with these missteps of the mind, and this was what had happened to me now.

I had landed myself in one of those realities I call digitopias.

If you're lucky or simply more stayathome than most of us, you've never encountered a digitopia. They're rare – *fortunately* rare. So let me explain.

Everybody knows that the totality of existence comprises the polycosmos, which is the sum of all the infinity of infinities of realities that there are or ever could be. Each of those individual realities can be considered as not just a universe of its own but also a microcosmic (if you can sensibly use such a term of entities that are so vast) polycosmos in itself, for it too comprises countless infinities of realities. And, of course, each of those realities is in itself a further polycosmos . . .

Every event, every action, every slightest shift of a quark will – and does – spark a new reality, yet there are also infinitely many and infinitely large *families* of realities brought into existence at the birth moment of each of the universes; these families are like the major branches of some unimaginably huge and complex tree, with the other realities serving as its twigs and buds and leaves. What distinguishes one family from the next is that the physical laws governing each are not quite the same as in any other family. At the birth-moment, the Big Bang, of each universe/polycosmos-in-the-making there springs into reality whole gamuts of possible sets of physical laws under the reign of which a viable universe might run, and *all* of those viable sets are reified.

The most important physical law that can be varied from one to the other concerns the rate of passage of time: as a second passes in one, a year might pass in the next, or a millennium. If you cared to, you could pick a pathway through the interstices between the realities of even just our own small universe so as to travel into realities where everything is many billions of times older; or, by going "the other way", you might enter realities (if you were fool enough to do so) where the Big Bang initiated itself scant milliseconds before. It's as if you could travel freely backward and forward through time, except that all the realities and subrealities are different existences – they've evolved independently and of course at variant rates, and some have been majorly influenced by trains of events that have never even touched others.

Still, if you move carefully among the interstices you can restrict your travels to realities – whether within our universe or elsewhere in the polycosmos – where the speed of time's flow is always much the same, and where the physical laws, too, are not so divergent from those you are accustomed to. The sun is still yellow-white in a sky of blue. When you drop a dish it falls swiftly enough to smash on the floor – or at least it does *fall*, rather than drifting off to the side or floating blithely up and away.

But some of the very tiniest variations in the physical laws can have the most profound consequences, and they can make two realities that should, on the face of it, be nearly identical in fact be strikingly different.

The behaviour of the electrons of the antimony atom is one area of relevance. In almost every reality where there exists such an element as antimony at all, which means 99.99999999 percent repeating of the realities within our own local polycosmos, the polycosmos that we'd regard as our universe's families of realities, the electrons squat lumpenly around the nucleus, unwilling to be dragged away from it. In a few realities, however, those electrons are prepared to be far more freewheeling, and in a tiny percentage of *those* miserably unfortunate realities it has been discovered that antimony can be used to "dope" silicon such that minuscule transistors may be manufactured.

The reason I call such godforsaken realities digitopias is that they have a science of microelectronics – tiny computers everywhere, gadgetry proliferating like a plague of locusts and devouring all the soulstuff of the people of the worlds.

The reason I knew I'd accidentally danced into a digitopia was that the Bryan Adams track that was filling my ears was being played by a small black machine with on its front a display of moving lights that served no purpose.

And so on.

Well, there I was, dumped like a beached whale into a digitopia. I could have turned straight around and left – I could physically have forced myself to do that – but it would have been to violate the rules of love that keep the polycosmos (and the polycosmos of polycosmoses, and all the tiny polycosmoses that swarm within and alongside every particle of us) evolving and growing and alive. I had to stay here for at least long enough to give whatever love I could to the partner who awaited me, and whom I had known and loved for a long, long time.

I was sitting on the floor of the apartment, fully clothed, my back against the wall beneath a curtained window. Opposite me, also sitting with her back against the wall and also fully clothed, was my long-time fuckmate (her term) Kath. I'd asked her several times if maybe, you know, we should get married, but her answer was always the same: that she didn't want to commit herself to anything too long-term that she might not be able to sustain. Only once did I try to explain to her that there was a way of having both permanence in love and yet also constant change and freshness. She'd looked at me as if I were crazy.

"You've seen it yourself," I'd said. "You must have. You know those moments when your gaze meets someone else's across a crowded room or on a train, and you all at once realize that, even though you've never met or spoken to this person and probably never will, you *recognize* them as somebody you've known intimately, body and soul, for as long as you can remember. And you can see them recognizing you as well in the same way."

"You fancy them, like?" said Kath, struggling to grasp what I was saying.

"No, it's not that at all. What the pair of you suddenly know is that you've spent a whole love story together, but not here, not now, not in *this* reality – so it's a love story you'll never be able to read with your lives, a love story that you'll never know."

Kath began to chortle. "You're just saying you sometimes fantasize about fucking other women, breaking it to me gentle, like. But that's OK. Sometimes I fantasize about fucking other guys, so we're equals. Quits. You hungry?"

(I remembered all these things, you see, even though I'd never been here before.)

"No," I insisted. "Sure, I sometimes wonder what it'd be like screwing pretty women I see in the street or meet at parties – I'm not a saintly monk, or whatever – but I'm not talking about that."

"What *are* you talking about, then? You keep saying what you're *not* talking about, but what you're saying doesn't make much sense. Not *really*."

"I'm talking about the encounters all of us sometimes have with our lovers, but our lovers in realities other than the one we happen to be in. Maybe we've been able to cross into those different realities briefly in dreams, or something, or maybe it's just that our awareness can seep through the boundaries that separate the realities – I don't know. But it's a fact. Those little instants of recognition – they're a *fact*."

"You've been watching too much *Star Trek*."

And that was as far as the conversation went.

Gazing across at my fuckmate now, I felt my heart lift with song and loving, because she was very, very beautiful. Her hair was a cascade of black curls surrounding her oval face. Her skin was grey with the weariness of existence, and I wished I could do something to change that; but for all that she was lovely.

"Kath," I said as the CD reached its end and the machine grunted and squealed softly, changing to another. "Kath, come here. I want to hold you."

"Nah, not right now," she said. "I wanna spend some time with the veerigogs. Wanna join me?"

I sighed.

Veerigogs. VR goggles. The latest craze in this dismal digitopia. Kath had bought (or, I suspected, stolen) us each a pair as soon as they'd started appearing in the highstreet electronics stores. Put on a pair of veerigogs and you enter a fake, or virtual, reality. If you have the right plug-in-and-play program chips you can choose any fake reality from the large palette of scenarios the manufacturers have devised. You can use a pair of veerigogs on your own and the illusion seen by your eyes and heard through microspeakers in your ears is so all-embracing, so entirely convincing, that your other senses are deceived as well: you can touch the surfaces, you can smell the odours, you can taste the tastes of the imaginary world. But the way most people use veerigogs is together, fucking with each other while their senses tell each of them individually that they're fucking someone else: a movie star, or a rock singer, or . . .

When Kath had teased me about fantasizing fucking other women, she was counting the use of veerigogs as fantasizing. But there's a difference between a fantasy and a fake reality.

"OK. I guess so." My voice sounded eager not because I was skilled at disguising my true lack of interest but because, by definition, I loved this fuckmate of mine and had done so for as far back as my memory would go: giving her pleasure, in whatever way I could, was to gain pleasure for myself.

She tossed me my veerigogs and began to haul herself out of her overalls. I caught the gadget and began myself to undress, staring at her body as it was unceremoniously revealed to me.

There's an old cliché that some people are more beautiful with their clothes on than off. It's not something that I've ever much subscribed to, because I always love my wives wholly, and find them equally beautiful however I might see them. But as I watched Kath I was able to distance a part of my mind and see her as someone else might do, and that facet of me saw that she was a woman who was startlingly more beautiful naked than even her lovely, adorable clothed self. Her legs were long – longer even than Xanthe's, and sleeker. Her entire body, had she ever learned to straighten it properly, had a dignity that was somehow chaste while at the same time deeply sensuous. I wanted to spend days just poring over each square inch of her skin, even the places where she'd bruised herself as a result of her habitual clumsiness. I wanted to lay my head in the small of her back and stare at the smooth, perfect twin drifts of her behind rising like hillsides, their foothills just inches from my eyes, the downy hairs on them making scintillating stars as the breeze blew across them in the sunshine. I wanted to try

making love with her through simple touching – the two of us
stroking each other's faces and flanks, gazing all the while into
the depths of each other's eyes and souls, until our sensualities
bubbled over. I wanted her to be astride my face so that I could
lose myself in the warm world of her sex, kept from floating
away into the ether only by the distant sensations of her mouth
on my own sex. I wanted to hear the loud pulsing music of
orgasm, see the wraithed colours it brings, like trails of illuminated dust clouds out where the stars are young. I wanted us
to dance together in our lovemaking to the place where there
are no longer two, but one.

"Who do you fancy me being this time?" said Kath, grinning. Her breasts were pale little apples, pink-tipped, framed
by brassiere creases, but she was unconscious of them as she
fiddled with the fastening at the side of her veerigogs. "Marilyn Monroe? Michelle Pfeiffer? Winona Ryder?"

All I want you to be is Kath, I thought, but of course I didn't
say the words out loud because to do so would have been to
hurt the one I adored.

"Natalie Marahat," I said at random. Marahat had recently
starred across from Richard Gere in a frothy little comedy we'd
seen at Loeb's. She has a grace and style and slow-moving
elegance and profound beauty, not to mention the most gorgeously appealing little smile – all of which were completely
wasted in that movie. Somewhere in the polycosmos, I'd
realized as I'd stared at the big screen amid the popcorn
redolence of the movie theatre, perhaps she and I had loved
or would love each other – in truth, *did* love each other, because
there's no past or future in real love, just an everlasting
present.

Kath chuckled. "In that case, then, I guess you'd better be
Richard Gere." She plugged the cord of her veerigogs into the
box and tapped in instructions. "He's a bit old for my normal
type but . . . yes" – reading the microscreen – "I can have him
when he was still thirty." She beckoned to me to plug my own
cord in. "And here's Natalie Marahat for you." All cosy.
There, that's settled.

Standing close to her nakedness, as I now was, I'd developed
a quite enormous erection. I don't mean just that it was hard as

a rock – although it was – but that in this reality I had a bigger penis than in just about any other I'd so far been in. My balls were pretty gargantuan too, dangling in a sack that seemed to stretch halfway to my knees, but my erection really was a truly impressive object. In fact, although not too impossibly huge for sex to be practicable at all, it was probably too big and thick to be a very satisfactory part of genuine lovemaking, so I was quite relieved that it belonged in a digitopia rather than be an encumbrance elsewhere.

Kath didn't seem to notice it, concentrating as she was on fine-tuning the physical attributes of Richard Gere as well as setting the controls to define the fake environment we'd find ourselves in.

"Now," she said at last.

We lay down together on our futon and carefully donned our veerigogs, trying to synchronize as nearly as possible our entrance into the artificial world.

I was on a very good imitation waterbed. Lying there beside me, naked in the candlelight, was a truly lovely creature, her body flawless and perfectly proportioned. Natalie Marahat.

A fake Natalie Marahat.

What made the fakery obvious was exactly that: the flawlessness, the absolute perfection of her every proportion. It was as if her body had subliminal erotic triggers implanted in every pore. The result, instead of making my mind blaze with desire, was an overload of eroticism that brought into stark blatancy the chill of her artificiality.

As this vision of loveliness put her arms around me, I thought as fervently as I could of the naked Kath I had left just moments before.

"Fuck me, baby," said Natalie Marahat.

And so I fucked her.

Later, after we'd taken the veerigogs off, I tried to coax Kath into lovemaking on the futon, but she said she was tired and anyway *The West Wing* was just about to start on television.

I left her during the first commercial break.

She didn't notice me going, of course, because there was still the familiar slumped male on the couch beside her, nibbling crackers as he watched a woman on the screen tell him how he could say goodbye to all his allergies with only a long list of minimal possible side-effects. I slipped on a pair of jeans and a sweatshirt and a pair of old, worn-down sneakers, and made my way out of the apartment and down three flights of stairs and out into the streets of a city that was a blare of light and sound. I sensed that everywhere around me there were people busily watching other people doing things that they wished they could do themselves, or plugged into one device or another that would effectively obstruct their every fortuitous leaning toward discovering the ways that you can skip through the interstices of the polycosmos, pausing wherever you will to fuel it with the love it needs to keep on living and becoming. All of these machines, driven by the properties permitted by the laws of physics to belong to the electron shell of the antimony atom in only a tiny percentage of the realities that make up the everness – all of these machines pretending to stimulate yet instead inhibiting the imagination from roaming through the infinite possibilities that the polycosmos reifies.

I stood on a street corner, listening to the clangour, and offered up thanks to the surly dark artificial orange sky that digitopias are so infinitesimally few among the boundless realities.

And at the same time I felt a great rush of pity for the individual souls trapped here.

Souls?

Half-souls, quarter-souls, shrivelled relics of souls, more like. Their only blessing is that they don't recognize their trappedness, believe instead that their undiscovery of love represents the fullest freedom of them all. They're prisoners who aren't conscious of the cage's bars, who look at the window of their cell and see just reflected grey light which they believe is the world . . . and see nothing of the riot of colours and brightness beyond the razor-thin imprisoning glass they could shatter with a touch.

I turned away from the scowl of the angrily uplit sky, took a few paces along the sidewalk and was in a field of bright green grass with my many husbands. I called out to them in merriment, and they grinned and waved at me, then began to walk toward me, singly or severally.

The insides of my thighs were already damp by the time the first one reached me.

I loved them, I loved my husbands, and they loved me, their wife. We always love each other.

And today, with the sun shining down upon us and the blue and yellow flowers bobbing their heads in the breeze that caressed the grass, we had a lot of lovemaking to do if the infinite realities of the polycosmos were to continue eternally to bring forth their blossom.

Swimmer's Body

Patrick Califia

Time for morning laps, Surfer Boy, Gary told himself. *No dawdling.* Well, maybe a few extra deep-knee bends, just to show our bronzed and god-like body to the stolid Swede in the far lane. Wonder if he can see the crack of my butt in this new suit – or do the leopard spots (which make Coach Bassett cluck his tongue) camouflage the dividing line between my buns, which have been unbuttered for far too long? He did an imitation of Coach Bassett's cluck. "A young man, so much promise, so little – what? Let's just say he wouldn't marry the boss's daughter."

The outdoor pool was perfectly smooth turquoise Jell-O™ in a white, Olympic-sized trough. Gary thought (peeking between his toes) that it might really be like diving into a thick gel, and he would simply flounder, unable to pull his smoothly shaved torso through it, no matter how long his reach. It would be a fitting end to these deadly dull two months (and two still to go!) at the Little Dixie training camp.

As always, he was in the water before he knew his body had decided to throw him into it. It was a good dive, and the shock of pleasure he felt at his own skill made him lose consciousness of the need to time arm-strokes, breathing and kicks. Instead, it felt as if a wave flowed down the whole, single muscle that was his body, propelling him smoothly, without thought or strain. Then he rolled (toes brushing the electric eye that timed his laps) and kicked harder, suddenly furious to be done with it. He had hoped, when he sent in his deposit, that the heat and isolation would make it easier for him to stay in the water here, building his peak for the spring matches.

But he hated swimming when he was only training, hated it as much as someone who wasn't any good at it. It was his ticket to college, to something other than obscurity and a desk job in a medium-sized city. He loved competing – the adrenaline rush, the knowledge that, win or lose, you didn't dare hold anything back. But everybody in the pool came ready to win. You had to train, and it never got easier for him, only harder, and he was so upset with himself that he took in a lungful of water instead of air and had to haul himself up on the rim of the pool, choking like a little kid in his first Red Cross swimming class.

The Swede finished before he did, and Gary passed him in the shower on his way to his locker. Larsen was bigger than Gary. His muscles looked like slabs of pale stone when he was in repose, but in the water he was a buoyant streak of speed. His impartial, careful hands applied soap evenly to his body, completely unaware of the beauty of what they touched. Gary made the clucking noise again. He couldn't imagine anybody snapping a wet towel at his ass in this locker room, much less waving anything more interesting around.

Back in the dorm, Gary saw a small stack of mail on his cot. He immediately cheered up. Under a letter from his mother and a letter from his "roommate" Aaron (the return address had only a discreet initial before the surname) was a thin plastic envelope. *The Advocate* had finally caught up with him. He had debated whether it was wise to notify the magazine about his temporary change of address, then figured he would go nuts without a little contact with gay life. Since nobody was in the dorm, he slit the package and skimmed the magazine. The letters (even Aaron's) would be safe to read at lunch. This was not.

They had sent him the east coast edition. He chuckled at the restaurant reviews for New York City and Washington, DC. No excuse not to have a swinging weekend now! It would take him – what – only a full day of driving to get out of the deep South? There was probably nothing in the classifieds either, but what the hell, he didn't want to read the opera review or a feature about gay involvement in the anti-nuke movement. There were four whole columns of ads from California. Unbidden, his eye picked out Aaron's post office box and flipped up to read the ad ("Straight-appearing young executive look-ing for summer fun, no strings, no games, no fats, fems or downwardly mobile types"). Well, they had agreed there was no sense in Aaron coming home to an empty apartment every single night . . . Feeling a little pain behind his sternum anyway, Gary flipped to the end of the classifieds. Well, what do you know – there was actually one entire ad running under his state. "Fine mind in a swimmer's body seeks same. Let's make a big splash!"

Gary couldn't stop laughing. He ripped the ad out, stuffed the magazine back into its envelope and, on his way to the cafeteria, as he buried it under a bunch of trash in a big oil drum, he was still laughing.

Over lunch, Coach Bassett stopped and handed him a thick packet. "What're these?" Gary queried rudely, around a mouthful of despised salad.

"Publicity photos. Pick out the three you like the best. You can keep the rest or pitch 'em." Gary had forgotten all about the photo session last week. Surely this was an omen. He fanned them out on the table and picked one of himself on a stand, with his arms up and tense (showing off the deep armpit, his beautifully proportioned lats). His quads stood out nicely. Unfortunately for the newspapers, so did his basket. But the anonymous advertiser (read "geek") would appreciate it. Be-fore he went to the track to run his laps there ("Are you a man or a merry-go-round, Surfer Boy?"), he stopped at the dorm again for an envelope and stamps.

"This is a real swimmer's body," he wrote on the back of the photo, "and if you can match it, drop a pic c/o," and the address of the camp. "If not, don't bother."

Three days later (three days during which training seemed less arduous), he had a snapshot of a man (still young, but older than Gary, with a nose that looked like it had been broken) treading water. Even wet, his dark hair curled. His thickly furred chest was so broad that Gary wondered if it didn't churn up too much water resistance to make good time. But those biceps and forearms looked burly enough to drag the Titanic to safety. He reluctantly conceded that in this case, the phrase "swimmer's body" had not been just a euphemism for "ninety-pound weakling." He turned the picture over and read, "All this, and *I* have my hair," and a phone number. Gary ruefully rubbed his shaved skull. He was so used to other swimmers' faces, he had forgotten how odd his pale blond eyebrows and bare pate would look to anybody who wasn't in training. Cocky fucker. Where was the pay phone?

It was a brief call. Something wrong with the connection. He even had trouble making out the guy's name – Marvin? Martin? No – Marcus. But it turned out he lived just a bicycle ride away. Gary explained his situation at the training camp – so many days of working out, followed by a break day – and received a standing invitation to come over any time during his "off-day." Tomorrow, as it turned out.

That night, in his sleep, the lumpy cot turned into the chest and thighs of the well-built stud in the photograph. He lay face-down on him, his hands pinned between them, searching for the other man's cock. He knew it would be thick, the foreskin like folds of silk, the balls heavy in a sac covered with crinkly black hair. The whole flexible, flaccid shaft could be cupped in one hand until he began to squeeze and massage it, then it would slowly add inches until it protruded beyond his fist.

Instead, Gary woke up, and realized it was his own cock that was thrusting in his grip. He took a deep breath, listened. Nobody else was awake. Then the urge to come was so sharp, a pain in his lower stomach, that he said, "So what?" out loud and took himself over the edge. The splashes of cum felt good on his knuckles, hot, and the tangy smell made him realize he had not jerked off since his first night here. When was the last time he had felt a pronounced need to spurt, instead of having to coax that good stuff out of his balls?

Aaron had been a real find, a business major he met in an economics class. It had been fun, in the beginning at least, to put the moves on somebody who pretended to be a little reluctant. Aaron turned out to be the oldest son of a conservative rabbi, and his coyness was not just flirtatiousness; he still was not out to his family about being gay or even living with another man. While Gary enjoyed the new side of himself that Aaron brought out, a more toppy, aggressive persona than even he'd realized existed, after a while he began to wonder if Aaron really wanted to have sex with him. He didn't mind pushing Aaron in the direction of the bed most of the time, all the while gently insisting that he really was going to fuck his brains out (and the front door was locked, and the oven was off, and no important phone calls were expected). But once in a while, he wanted Aaron to be the one doing the pushing and insisting.

Laying on his uncomfortable dormitory bed, Gary rubbed his hands over his own body, resenting the smoothness of his own skin, but needing the reassurance that he existed, he could feel, the envelope that contained his consciousness was still alive. He couldn't even remember what he looked like with his fur intact. There was something emasculating about shaving so often, as if he were stripping away any physical impulse that had nothing to do with swimming. He admitted that it wasn't just the training camp and the constant rejection of being surrounded by straight boys that made him feel extremely lonely. Didn't everybody need the passionate reassurance of a lover's uninhibited desire, the experience of being taken somewhere by someone else's touch? Maybe he wasn't attractive to Aaron. He could easily conjure up his lover's bespectacled, usually serious face, and see his kissable lips move in the fond phrase he repeated several times a day: "I love you, Gary."

Wasn't it sophomoric to want something more, something else, something more dirty, perhaps, even dangerous? Gary conjured up the photograph of Marcus, and realized that he wanted to see it again, to study it, to see if he could glimpse some hints about the rest of the big man's body beneath the opaque water. Did he have a big thatch on his lower belly? Were his balls large enough to hang low, two separate eggs in a fuzzy, crinkled sac? And did his cock have a slight curve to it, with a tulip-shaped head? Gary wanted to run his tongue along the rim between the head and the shaft of that cock, and lap at the little tangle of nerves at its base. He wanted to slip his tongue into the piss-slit of that cock and savor the thin salty clear pre-cum that would tell him the dark man lusted after his hungry mouth. He wanted two hands around his ears, to be lost inside another man's need, to be able to stop thinking and exist only as a tunnel for his cock, a hole that offered just enough resistance and response to give that cock the best ride of its life. Sucking and sucking as if he needed Marcus's cum instead of air.

The intrusive memory of Aaron's cold little personal ad intruded on the building tension of a second erection. It was out of character for Aaron to take the initiative like that, to put himself out there as a sexual actor. What kind of man would answer that ad? Would somebody else plow the tight, round little ass that Gary had marked off as his own? Would Aaron do things for the man (or men) who answered that ad that he refused to do for Gary? Would he swallow that shadowy stud's cum? Or lick his asshole? Would Aaron get down on his knees and beg to be taken? Could it be that Aaron might be the one who told his trick to get up on all fours so that he could plow them from behind? And did the specter of Aaron with his cock in somebody else's butt or face make Gary feel better or worse than imagining his lover's face distorted with discomfort and pleasure as he was penetrated by a stranger?

When they saw each other again, could it be that the bond between them, for all its faults, would be changed or even damaged? The rational part of Gary forced him to admit that it might be good for Aaron to loosen up a little, but the concrete picture of his boyfriend actually being loosened up by somebody else's hard dick made him unbearably sad.

By answering Marcus's ad, wasn't Gary going to put Aaron through exactly the same sort of sorrow and uncertainty? *No,* Gary told himself, *I will not feel guilty about wanting to get laid.* They had talked this over. He had Aaron's permission to get lucky. It would be distinctly uncool to take such emotional baggage to his encounter with Marcus, but in his cold and rough sheets, Gary longed to put his head on Marcus's big chest and receive absolution and comfort. He wanted to feel those hands rolling his cock back and forth, giving him a sort of sexual blessing, drawing him into a world where he didn't have to ponder such difficult questions. Eventually his imagination conjured up such a clear image of Marcus's red nipples, surrounded by swirls of bearish fur, and the sensation of that eager, arching cock sliding into the crack of his ass, that Gary's hard-on came back with a vengeance, and demanded some wrist-music.

Normally, Gary just needed to jack off and come once; it was easier to get it up again when another man was present to give him bad ideas and a raunchy second chance. He was curious about what this orgasm would feel like, and it was as ambivalent as he was. His second shot was smaller in volume, but the feeling was more intense, as if his urethra was on fire. Despite that, he wanted it to go on for longer than it did; he was abruptly dumped back into a damp, sweaty, soft-cocked state. How could you actually feel dissatisfied after coming twice? Gary fell asleep before he could answer this or any of the other big questions he had about the mysteries of Eros.

He made himself eat the next morning, made himself wait. He read a newspaper that was two days old and started a letter to Aaron that he knew he would not finish. But it was only 9:30 when he got his ten-speed out of the shed and pedaled away from the training camp, a note with directions he had already memorized tucked carefully into the pocket of his T-shirt. He was only on the macadam for twenty minutes before he peeled off and went down a dirt lane. A pheasant broke cover and beat frantically across his path. He swerved, then realized it was already safe in the brush at the other side of the road. The sweat between T-shirt and skin reminded him of the shape of his own body, how it had felt to rub his palm across his nipples last night, and pinch one of them gently, to make himself come.

Gary heard the creek before he saw it. The bike bumped across a wooden bridge. Then the road took a turn to follow the creek. Even when the water was hidden from view by thick growths of willow, he could hear it, laughing to itself. This charming, bucolic stream would eventually become one of the tributaries of America's largest river. On either side of the river were marshlands that had been set aside as protected habitat, a bird sanctuary. He wondered briefly about the existence of a private residence in the middle of a federal park. It must have been there for a very long time. The wild land and the free-running water was a reminder of how close Gary was to the gulf, to the salty father of all waters. But that ocean was not the lovely blue Pacific where he had learned how to swim and surf, where he knew a dozen beaches like the palm of his own hand. This was a land where water meandered, became swamps and sandbars. The Gulf of Mexico seemed to Gary to be older than the Pacific Ocean, more corrupt, and the way to it was treacherous, full of false turns and snags, alligators and other strange fauna. It was a place for a bayou boy, poling his pirogue, low and slow, silently blending into the background of drowned trees and Spanish moss. Death to a boisterous mob of young guys with California tans and freshly waxed boards.

According to the odometer between the handlebars, he must be almost there. Yep, the road forked here, and there was a lightning-struck oak, so he took the right-hand branch, away from the water (twinge of disappointment), and there was the house, "set back from the road a piece," as Marcus had promised, under shady trees. The yard was overgrown and the house looked uncared for. He knocked on the front door, got no answer, and walked his bike around to the back. A note was pinned there. "Welcome, Gary, I'm down by the lake. Just follow the trail. Hope you left your Speedos at the camp. Marcus."

He grinned, leaned his bike against the steps and loped down the trail. It was a few hundred yards down a slope, and there was the river again, feeding a medium-sized lake. A homemade dock ran into the water. This must be where the snapshot had been taken. But he didn't see anybody. Oh, well, the water looked good. He skinned out of his cutoffs and T-shirt and strolled to the end of the dock.

"Dive in! It's deep enough," somebody called. There was his host, treading water ten feet away. How had he gotten so close without making a sound? Gary shrugged and slipped into the lake. It felt good.

Marcus had been submerged when Gary arrived, but he felt the tremors in the water when his guest's feet hit the dock. He came up for air, and it took a few seconds for his eyes to adjust. Nevertheless, he got a clear and very appetizing glimpse of a tall young man who might have been blond if he wasn't completely shaved. The lack of body hair made his guest seem vulnerable despite his almost inhuman, peak physical condition. Gary had a face that was masculine but expressive. His features had not yet settled into the immobile and unreadable condition of an older, more disappointed and resigned man. He seemed enthusiastic, although Marcus was sure he had to be feeling some anxiety about meeting a stranger. Somebody who might be even stranger than you could guess.

Doubt surged in his chest. Had he been right to come here, to return to his childhood home? So much had changed since he left to enlist in the navy; his parents were both dead, and his brothers had scattered to South Carolina, even Tennessee and Texas, and one sister in Seattle. It was truly unsettling to feel like such an alien in this familiar place, one whose smells and sights conjured up a wealth of nostalgia and regret. (For even a happy memory can bring sadness, since that moment of joy has vanished, one bright bubble in a flock of malicious crows.) And what was he to do with this Yankee boy, someone who came from such a different place and time? But Marcus wanted what he saw. Sex, as it so often does, overcame any qualms he might have had about the consequences. He was bigger and stronger than Gary, and could control the encounter, keep his secret, just this once.

The silky cool water caressed Gary, noticeably more friendly than the dead, chlorinated water in a manmade swimming pool. It seemed to leach any trace of tiredness or pain out of him; the energy it infused him with as he did a shallow breast stroke was clean and light. Then he suddenly felt even better. A hand that was a great deal warmer than the water had circled his shaft, and was measuring him slowly, up and down. He was face-to-face with the man in the photograph, and the smell of his body hit Gary in the face like the first smack in a spanking. Marcus smelled like something that would be good to eat and never stop eating. Up close, he was even furrier than the photograph had shown. He was matted with hair, and Gary wanted to rub his face all over that big chest.

Taken aback by the lack of preliminaries, he tried to reach for the other man's body, but Marcus evaded him. "Let me take you out farther," he said, and had Gary in a towing hold before he could protest. Gary could have sworn they didn't stop until they were in the center of the lake. Marcus let him go, then began a weird game of sexual tag. He was swimming around Gary in amazingly quick, tight circles, and he would dart in just often enough to administer a caress (and keep Gary afloat). Sometimes it would be his mouth instead of his hand that would enclose Gary's cock. He trembled, trusting the hands under his buttocks to keep his head above water. It had been too long since he'd felt so good. He was eager to reciprocate, but no matter how hard he tried, he couldn't grab hold of Marcus's dick, although a couple of times he felt it brush his stomach or thigh, and knew it was as hard as his own.

"Let me touch you!" he finally cried, exasperated, near tears, and Marcus (behind him) pulled him close, wrapped his hands around Gary's aching, over-stimulated rod, and thrust his own cock in between the muscular cheeks of the other swimmer's ass. He timed the hand strokes to his cock thrusts, giving Gary the giddy sensation of simultaneously fucking and being fucked, though he knew Marcus's cock remained outside his body. He did not realize they were still swimming until he saw swirls of semen lost behind them and the familiar piers of the dock. He was pushed toward the makeshift wooden ladder before he could turn and kiss Marcus, who had darted away, back to deeper water. "You go inside, lunch is on the table. Don't wait for me to eat. I want to swim a little more."

Gary felt like he would collapse if he stayed in the water. The intensity of his orgasm was making his limbs shake as if he had hypothermia. How often had he fantasized about sex in the water – weightless, streamlined sex – with another athlete whose stamina and physique equaled his own? He dragged himself into the house. Just as he entered the kitchen, he saw the back of a departing older black woman. She wasn't wearing a uniform, but something about her neatly pressed dress and apron made Gary sure she was a servant. The table had been set with enough food for five people. He ate a lot of cheese and fruit and drank a couple of pints of water. He even made himself a thick sandwich out of forbidden cold cuts. This morning had made him feel better than months of coaching, lectures on nutrition, sprints and power-lifting. When he was done eating, Marcus still had not come out of the water. Gary wandered into the living room and fell asleep on the couch.

His dreams were disturbing. He had read about Vietnam

vets who had been injured by a particularly nasty kind of land mine, one that jumped to waist height before exploding. The men who survived usually lost their genitals as well as their legs. (In his sleep, Gary protectively cupped his drained, waterlogged and tender cock and balls.) These men had a powerful incentive to participate in a government experiment with human DNA that might restore the lost parts of their ruined bodies. While a carefully crafted virus went to work on their genes, the men sat patiently in vats of nutrient solution and antibiotics. Part of the experiment worked fine. With proper recombinant encouragement, their newly ambitious cells recreated perfectly operating cocks and balls. But from that point on, things went awry. Their leg bones fused, articulated like a spine. Where new legs were supposed to grow, large and powerful fish-tails sprouted.

The military was not apologetic. The experimental subjects were reminded that they had known they were taking a huge risk. The men (mermen?) were relocated to a larger, common pool, where they began to forge a team identity – although the purpose of that team remained vague, at least in the beginning. Sexual conditioning was used to reinforce that bond, and some of the methods used to break down the men's resistance to homosexual conduct were cruel. The Pentagon's liaison to the research staff hinted at the possibility of them re-enlisting, being formed into some kind of special services unit. The idea of being kept together, belonging somewhere (and the accompanying training in underwater communications, demolition, navigation, flora and fauna) kept many of them from going into shock. But there were some men who could not live in such a drastically altered form. Gary woke up before one desperate man in his dream figured out how to commit suicide in a tank with smooth aluminum walls.

The house suddenly seemed threatening, and claustrophobia propelled Gary outside, back down the trail to the lake. Where the hell was his friendly swimming companion? The hot afternoon sun was soothing, and made the goose bumps fade from his bare skin. Once more he scanned the lake and saw no one, until he went to the end of the dock. "Ready for another round?" leered the handsome face.

"I'm not sure. I had some pretty weird dreams."

"Come into the water and tell me about it."

Gary slipped nude into Marcus's element. But instead of talking they wound up sexing, even more frantically than before. Gary barely made it back to the camp by curfew. He left behind a thoughtful man who was far too captivated by the young swimmer. Had it been so long since he'd had really good sex with another man that he was a pushover for falling in love? Love had not been part of the plan. But maybe it would be okay to have a regular fuck buddy. Despite his skill at manoeuvring in the water, Gary had spent less time in that element than Marcus, so perhaps there was less danger in meeting again than the older man feared. The sincerity in Gary's voice when he cried out, begging for the chance to touch Martin was moving, more moving than Gary probably knew. And Marcus wanted to feel those hands and that mouth all over his body. But it couldn't happen. Ironically, to allow Gary to do the things that Marcus ached to have him do would ruin everything. The sex could only keep happening if it was strictly limited.

There was such a difference between having sex with a man who knew that he was gay and accepted it than a forced encounter with a heterosexual who knew he had no other outlet than to make use of male flesh. Marcus knew that many a straight man had a far greater capacity to enjoy gay sex than he knew. But still, in an institutional environment, such revelations were unwelcome. When a man like that got his rocks off, there was an undercurrent of regret, shame and anger that set Marcus's teeth on edge. He wanted the man he embraced to be thinking of his body, infused with desire for all of his virile attributes, not pining for breasts and the entryway between a woman's thighs. Gary's grace in the water, his quick intake of breath when Marcus supported his weight and almost fucked him, his hunger for more – these things were so seductive that Marcus put his face in his hands and tugged on his hair to try to get them out of his mind. He realized he would have a hard time waiting until Gary's next day off. A very hard time. Such a hard time that a cold shower (or a bath, of course) would not be much of an antidote.

The next off-day found Gary back at the old, empty house. The week of training had flown by. He had done better than ever before at meeting his goals, and didn't give a shit when Coach Bassett told him so. The troublesome images of Aaron's – adventures? Not infidelity! – lost their sting. When he wasn't with Marcus, he was still with him in the spirit, reliving each precious moment of contact, moving in his arms, panting to be put upon his cock, and coming despite the fact that it was denied him. He was there the next week as well. And the next.

The sex was *so* good, but Marcus would not allow Gary to touch him, nor would he engage in any kind of penetration. Gary accepted it after a while, assuming that since Marcus was calling the shots, he could change things if he wasn't satisfied. The brief heat of Marcus's semen jetting between the cheeks of his ass, before lake water washed it away, became an erotic trigger that always made him come too. Then Gary would get out of the water, go inside and eat, take a nap (always marred by more weird dreams), and eventually come back outside for more sex. When he left, Marcus would still be in the water. Gary would cycle back to the camp, alternately mulling over his sensory impressions of Marcus's body and the dreams.

His nightmarish visions of the military medical experiment were supplemented by dreamy visions of a blue, underwater world where silvery-scaled people cavorted in their strange cities, playing dolphin games with each other all day long, offering each other gifts of necklaces and sex and food. Their behavior with one another was so sensuous that it was difficult to tell where sex began and ended. There seemed to be no restrictions upon who or how they embraced. There was no obvious work being done, yet their playfulness was also creative. There were buildings, ornaments, art, and all of these things had a quality of buoyancy, with no sharp edges or corners. Gary loved these dreams. He sometimes found a trace of tears in his eyes when he woke up, exiled from that idyllic setting and those gentle, beautiful beings.

Over time, the underwater sex with Marcus was interspersed with more and more conversation. What little Marcus revealed of his personality fascinated Gary. He was a man who was apparently capable of violence, in the appropriate context, but was also burdened with a delicate conscience and a sense of compassion for human frailty. Gary had never encountered anyone like him before. Growing up in southern California with its emphasis on youth, novelty and pretty surfaces had not prepared him for the complexity of a southern gentleman's melancholy character, nurtured in an atmosphere where there was no escape from a tragic sense of history and abundant evidence of man's capacity for evil as well as good. Nobody would ever guess from looking at Marcus or listening to him that he was gay. But he accepted his own desire for other men as naturally as he accepted all of his other basic needs. There could be no sexual shame in his presence, only permission and – even better – skill. Despite Marcus's insistence on controlling their encounters, Gary sensed that he would respond to an equally assertive partner. The fact that he could not find the trigger that would allow Marcus to bring down that wall tormented and teased Gary into a frenzy. How could he turn kissing somebody into a sexual fantasy? Who jacked off to thoughts of doing nothing but kissing another man? It was weird, being this crushed out, but the elation of the crush sped Gary through the tedium of rehearsing for races.

One fateful day, the strangeness of the repetitive dreams made it impossible for him to respond to Marcus's light, familiar, but still achingly arousing, touch. Gary was also feeling a growing anxiety about the approaching end of his incarceration in the training camp. As the lusty grin on his friend's face was replaced with genuine concern, Gary knew he was falling in love with this man, and instead of making a joke about not being able to get it up underwater, he haltingly described the dark visions that troubled him. Eventually even Gary's muscles tired of treading water, and he relaxed into Marcus's tattooed arms, wondering how he could keep both of them afloat so effortlessly. Then he happened to look down, but off to one side, the way his father had taught him to look for fish in a brook. And he saw the lower half of Marcus's body for the first time. The two-fluked tail was muscular, dappled brown like a rainbow trout and undeniably masculine.

"It's true, then," Gary said thoughtfully, and wondered why he was relieved. Probably because he had known the truth for a long time, but had not let himself acknowledge it. Marcus was a mer.

"Yes. Do you want to hear the rest of the story?"

He did. Gary's body signaled urgently that he wanted something else, too, now that his tension and anxiety were gone, but he made himself wait.

"One of their own scientists betrayed them. She had spent years developing a way to communicate with dolphins, killer whales, and other intelligent ocean mammals. The military had gotten wind of it, taken over her project, and taught the pinnipeds to carry explosives and conduct underwater sabotage. A lot of the animals were injured or killed during carelessly conducted exercises. None of the stupid lifers in charge of this very hush-hush project could understand why this would traumatize her, or anticipate that she might turn against them because of it. She was supposed to teach each of us how to work with a dolphin partner. A weird variation on the K-9 corps. Somehow, she found out that the Navy intended to use us to staff underwater nuclear missile silos. She also found out how they intended to replace us. The mervirus is in our semen. Theoretically, we can make any man into a mer. But they never got far enough in the experiment to actually offer us a victim to see if that transformation would really take place. I think the woman who let us go was actually more upset about the prospect of the dolphins getting killed than she was about the way we had been treated. But one night she sneaked out to our tank, told us what the score was, and gave us the location of the underwater base they had already built for us. Then she let us loose. We found it, and moved in."

Gary postponed dealing with the full import of this by quibbling about details. "How do you live underwater? You still breathe air, don't you?"

"I'm breathing with my lungs now, but in the water my gills keep the oxygen coming." Marcus took Gary's hand and ran his palm over his chest, then farther down, to his hips. The skin began to change there, acquiring a slightly abrasive texture, the triangular pattern of large, hard scales. Marine armor for a new kind of warrior. Gary could barely feel the frilled edges of raised half-circles, rhythmically fluttering open and closed. "I'm a deserter. I left when I found out that there was another, hidden agenda to our creation that even the scientists didn't know about.

"Being a mer is really hard on your mind and soul, Gary. I can't ever go back to the land again, and I never lose my sense of loss about that, the fact that I can be so close to the shore, but never really return home. They wanted to exterminate those people you saw in your dream. After the worldwide boycott of the tuna industry, which happened because of all that graphic publicity about dead dolphins, they are running scared about what would happen if school children and little old ladies and all the members of the Sierra Club knew there were people down there. I don't know why they think they need a war to do it, though, because we're killing them already. All the poison that we pour into the ocean has already endangered them."

Gary was so excited to learn that his idealistic nap-time visions had a basis in reality that he couldn't stop himself from interrupting. "But you and your buddies, you could put a stop to that. You could fight back! You could save them!"

"Gary, you don't understand. How can you when you haven't been there? When we found these people, they were so different from us. I never thought I would encounter such innocence unless I was dealing with a child. But they're not children, and yet they don't know the meaning of violence. I don't think they even know how to get angry. Even when they knew we came from the same people who had hurt them, they still took us in and helped us, made it much easier for us to survive. They don't even know what it means to be dishonest, Gary. They can't even tell a lie. And by teaching them to fight back, we're already changing them. And I don't think it's a good change. I just couldn't stand to watch it. So I left. I decided to come back here, to this house that my mother and father had left me, and . . . I don't know what."

"Stop. You don't need to tell me any more." Gary felt like his head was going to explode. He could get away! Away from Old Mother Bassett and his satchel of vitamin pills. Away from Aaron, who might be relieved, although he would never admit it. A series of tricks would be much easier to conceal from his parents than a boyfriend. Away from his own stifling closet, the racing circuit. Away from the boredom of staying in peak physical condition for no good reason. He would never have to come out of the water, and he could be surrounded by gorgeous, available men all the time – and it would mean something besides a trophy or a scholarship. But was he ready to be a soldier in an underwater world?

"Give me that seafood," Gary snarled, laughing, and dove for Marcus's rigid cock.

Marcus tried to fend him off, but Gary had acquired a strength born of a drive to join the strange new world that had opened up before him. He ran his tongue up and down the fat vein on the underside of Marcus's cock, which was indeed shaped exactly as he had imagined. Marcus's hands found his face underwater and urged him to take the heart-shaped head into his mouth. He licked around, inside the piss-slit, his lips rolling back and forth across the coronal ridge. Marcus's grasp on his head grew tighter, and Gary's teasing was soon rewarded with a thick, slick dick opening his throat. Just as he was about to run out of air, Marcus rolled onto his back, his wet erection glistening in the failing sun, and one of his arms closed around Gary, holding him above water so that he could complete his mission. The first dose of semen spurted into Gary's mouth almost immediately, and he swallowed every drop of the salty, sticky cream. Lost in the crisis of his own orgasm, Marcus let go of him, and Gary was unexpectedly dunked into the lake.

"All I can say is, I hope we have to do this a lot to change me," Gary sputtered, surfacing. Marcus shook his head at the two-legged swimmer's giggling face. How could he joke about something so dire? How could he be so eager to abandon the dry world – wild flowers, museums, movies, music, crowds in shopping malls and bars? "I told you, man, I have no way of knowing if their crazy theories are going to work. We shouldn't have done even this much. What if the way that they fucked me up messes you up in a bad way? I don't want to be responsible for screwing up your body or your life. You need to really think this through. Even if you do change and become like me, I don't know if I can go back there. I love the sea-people, Gary, but by the time I returned, they wouldn't be the way that I remember them anyway. I don't think I can stand to witness any more suffering or death."

"But how can you refuse to help them? Look, you and the guys in your outfit, you didn't choose this war. It came to you. Fighting back is better than just giving up. How often do you get a chance in your life to do something really good? To be a hero?"

Marcus shook his head. "Listen to you, child. 'The guys in your outfit.' You haven't even been to basic training, and you're trying to talk like an old soldier. Have you even been on a hunting trip and had to shoot a deer, youngster? Yeah, I didn't think so. War is not some happy adventure, Gary, even if you honestly believe you are on the right side. Terrible things still happen. Things that you can't ever get out of your mind. I'm sick of it. I'm sick of killing and death. And I'm tired of being a pawn in somebody else's game. They want us back, and I never want to be their prisoner again. I don't imagine the punishment for escaping is going to be very pleasant, do you? And I just don't think we can pull it off, honey. How can a few dozen ex-Seabees and thousands of pacifistic, day-dreamin' mermen and mermaids who can't stop having sex long enough to finish looking at a map bring the entire US military to its knees?"

"Well, we didn't exactly win in Vietnam, did we?" Gary challenged. "Guerilla warfare is very damned difficult to defeat. And you have the advantage of dealing with an enemy who is entirely out of his element."

"They don't need to put on diving gear and come down to fight with us hand-to-hand," Marcus said wearily. "They can shoot us down with missiles. They can stay up on top of the water and beat us to death with huge sound waves. They can use chemical warfare or germ warfare. They prefer to kill at a distance."

"Yeah, well, they also don't want anybody to know this is going on," Gary said. "And I know who could tell on them. The two of us, right here. With you here to show them that it's no joke, no story out of the *National Enquirer*, we'd be on every news program from here to Sunday."

Marcus laughed. "I can't argue with you any more, honey. I'm tired of talking. Why don't you go inside and get something to eat?"

"Okay," Gary said. "But then I'm going back to the training camp, and I'm going to pack up my stuff and come back here. I'm going to stay with you. After all you've been through, you shouldn't have to be alone. And you won't be. Never again. Whatever we decide, we can do it together."

Marcus looked at him thoughtfully, nodded once, and then swam away. Gary wondered if he ever got to stop swimming. Did he sleep? With those gills, he supposed it would be possible for Marcus to simply drift off underwater. *I want to sleep with this man*, he thought, and realized, with his heart so full of feeling that it was about to burst, that this was no euphemism for "fuck him to pieces" but was instead a softer desire for contact with his body, for affection and intimacy.

Someday I will, he resolved. *When I have a real swimmer's body.*

Communion

Lisabet Sarai

When the first flames taste my flesh, I feel no pain. Eyes closed, I attend to the summer dawn: blossoms mingling with the wood smoke, birdsong greeting the sun. Ecstasy wells up inside me even as my robe ignites. Grace, gratitude, glory. I open myself to the agony, let the pain wash over me as the Master taught me.

The memories come unbidden, seasons of my life passing before my mind's eye. I did not expect these recollections, but I welcome them as I welcome the fires swirling around me. My father's keep, hung with brilliant tapestries to block the winter winds, and my mother's hands, slender and sure at her needle-work. My older brother, swinging a wooden broadsword with his groom.

When my brother's life was spared by the wasting fever, my father consecrated me to the Church as his thanks for answered prayer. This was seven years ago, just after my first monthly bleeding. I did not mind being sent to the abbey; I was thus saved from the rough and grimy hands of the neighboring lord, to whom my father originally planned to wed me. "The claims of the Lord overrule the poor intentions of men," he told me when he left me with the sisters at Thoronet. "May your virginity be a gift that for ever glorifies God."

When I was a girl, I found the simple, orderly life of the convent a comfort. The sisters were strict but never cruel. There was always work to do, but it was the sort of labor that satisfies: tilling the garden, tending the vineyard or the convent's goats, baking bread. I slept well on my straw pallet, in the dormitory with the other novices.

Seven times daily, we knelt on the cold stone floor of the chapel and prayed. I loved the stark bareness of that sanctuary. The flickering light of the altar candles scarcely reached the shadows of the vaulted roof. The gold-encrusted crucifix on the altar shone as if lit from within. You are the light of the world, Christ had said, and there in the chapel I was suffused with that light.

I especially loved the Compline service, though sometimes it meant a rude awakening and a stumbling through midnight corridors. In the heart of night, the chapel was full of mystery. With the other women, I raised my voice to sing the hymns of praise. The soaring melodies made me ache with joy.

Our songs came, the superior told us, from Mother Hildegard, whose abbey on the Rhine was one of the centers of our Benedictine order and whose visions blessed us all. As I sang, I dreamed of mystic encounters, of being tested in my faith like the virgin saints.

As I grew to full womanhood and approached my final vows, however, I changed. I grew restless and distracted. I daydreamed instead of attending to my tasks. The midnight service still had the power to move me, but I approached my other devotions mechanically, as duties to be executed rather than as the joys they had been. I slept fitfully; my slumbers were racked by vague, distressing dreams from which I woke with racing heart and damp brow.

I had not lost my faith, but I knew that I was full of sin. As one of the few novices who was literate, I was often asked to read from the Scriptures as we sat in the refectory over the evening meal. I began to feel prideful of my knowledge, to sneer inwardly at my less learned sisters and view them as inferior.

I was also vain. Though my hair was cropped short and hidden beneath my veil, though my body was swathed in voluminous homespun robes, I knew that I was beautiful. On the occasion of my brother's marriage, I was allowed to return home for the festivities. In my drab brown habit, I sat among the bright, bejewelled ladies, and I knew that despite their velvets and furs, I was the most lovely woman in the company. There were no mirrors in convent, but when I bathed, my own hands told me that my limbs were well-formed, my waist slender, my breasts smooth and full.

And here, perhaps, was the root of all my sins. When I touched myself, I could not help that touch becoming a caress. There was an ache in my loins that I knew was carnal desire, and it drove me mad. For that desire could never be satisfied; I was doomed to endure it, silent and unfulfilled, for the rest of my days.

Who knows what might have happened, where my waywardness would have led me, if the Master had not entered my life.

He came first in the winter, an itinerant priest seeking food and shelter. It was late afternoon, just before Vespers. I was sweeping the rear courtyard and opened the gate to expel the dirt and straw. My mood was darker than usual as I looked out over the yellowed fields, dank and bare in the chilly drizzle. A heavy mist hung near the horizon, obscuring the bulk of the massif that rises south of the Argens valley. No heights were visible, only the flat, featureless February landscape.

I was about to shut the gate when I saw him coming up the path, a slight, gray-robed figure in a wide-brimmed hat. "Good afternoon, Sister," he called to me. "Might I impose upon the hospitality of your convent for a few days?" He entered the courtyard without waiting for my permission.

I recognized the marks of his vocation, the heavy crucifix around his neck and the tonsure that was revealed when he removed his hat. His hair was dark with moisture but nevertheless he covered it almost immediately with a black skullcap retrieved from his bag. He gazed at me with disturbing intensity. I noticed that his eyes were a bright, crystalline blue.

"Welcome, Father," I said, dropping my own eyes in confusion and an attempt at modesty. For when he looked at me, I had the strangest feeling that he was looking through me, into those black depths of my soul that I tried to hide from my sisters. "I am sure that the Mother Superior would be happy to have you reside within our precincts for as long as you desire. If you follow me, I will take you to her."

"Thank you, Sister . . ." He paused.

I curtseyed. "I am called Sister Ursula, Father. Though I have yet to make my final vows."

"Thank you, Sister Ursula." He seemed to linger over my name, savoring it on his tongue. I blushed. "I am grateful for your hospitality. I am called Jerome." In my confusion, I did not answer, but led him silently to the superior's chambers.

We were not a cloistered order. Occasionally, we offered shelter to a weary traveller who found himself in our remote corner of the land. These voyagers provided welcome relief from the ordered monotony of convent life. After the twilight orisons, we all gathered for the evening meal. Instead of my reading, Mother Superior asked Father Jerome to select a passage.

"With your permission, Mother, I would rather tell a story. A parable if you will."

"Of course, Father. Whatever you wish."

The priest settled himself in his chair and surveyed us with those unsettling blue eyes. I do not know what the other sisters felt, but when his gaze lit on me, I began to sweat beneath my robes, though the stone-walled refectory was chill as it ever was in winter.

"You all know Christ's parable of the talents of silver," he began. "This tale is it's companion, though it was never recorded in any of the Gospels.

"A prosperous merchant called his steward to him. 'I am going away on business for a short while,' he told the servant. 'Here are the keys to my treasury and my wine cellar. I expect that you will manage my house, my affairs, and my other servants as I would, until I return.'

"The servant was honored by his master's trust. 'Of course, Master. I will keep all in order for you.'

"For the first two weeks, the steward meticulously fulfilled his promise. The great mansion was spotless. The staff went about their duties, efficient and content. Tradesmen were paid; provisions were ordered; the tasks of the changing seasons were all accomplished simply and promptly. The steward was pleased and proud.

"When his master did not return after a third week, the servant began to be concerned. The house still ran smoothly, but there was often a frown of worry on his face. 'Perhaps his ship has been wrecked,' thought the servant. 'Perhaps my master has been waylaid by bandits.' These thoughts chilled him for, in truth, he loved his master well.

"A month went by, and then another, and still the master of the house had not returned. The servant was on edge, nervous and short with the staff. Several of the household resigned after he upbraided them for imaginary shortcomings. There was dust on the furnishings, and mud on the floors. The steward's fear and concern turned to despair, and then to anger.

"'My master has deserted me,' he thought. 'Well, I will at least take advantage of his wealth.' He opened the vaulted room that held the master's treasures. He used the gold he found there to buy himself rich attire and lavish jewelry. He spent it in the taverns and in the brothels, carousing and wallowing in concupiscence. Each dawn he would stagger back to the mansion and open a bottle from the wine cellar, gulping the rare vintage until he fell into a stupor.

"The staff fled. The servant wandered alone in the mansion, alternately cursing his master and bemoaning his fate. His debaucheries affected his health. Finally, all he could do is lie abed, sweating and shivering by turns, his vision blurred and his tongue thick with thirst.

"He lay there, moaning, ill and nearly blind. 'Master!' he cried out into the night. 'Why did you forsake me? Oh, how I have betrayed you!'

"A hand touched his, curling his fingers around a goblet of wine. 'Drink, my son,' whispered a voice. 'I know your thirst is terrible.'

"The servant knew the voice as well as his own. He raised himself with difficulty, peering through the shadows closing around him. 'Master! You are safe! You have returned!' He fell back onto the bed, exhausted.

"'My faithful servant, I never went away. I have been here in the house the whole time.'"

The priest paused, allowing the silence to lengthen until we squirmed on our benches. "Who can tell me the lesson of this parable?" he asked finally. None of us dared speak, not even elderly Sister Marie or Mother Superior.

He laughed, a strange ringing laugh that sent a shiver up my spine. "Well, I would ask you to meditate on this tale, which provides some insight into the nature of sin." He stood and shook out his robes. "It is late, Sisters. I will retire now, if you will excuse me. Tomorrow morning I will hear your confessions, and tomorrow at midnight, I will celebrate the Mass."

He gave us one last look as he headed down the corridor to the guest cells. "God be with you," he said.

"And also with you, Father," we responded in automatic unison. His odd manner seemed to disturb the other sisters as much as it did me.

I was terribly nervous about confessing to this Father Jerome. Still, I could hardly forgo the opportunity. In our remote abbey, it might be weeks or even months before another priest would visit, with his promise of absolution and his gift of the Sacrament.

He set up his curtain in an alcove of the chapel. I tiptoed into the sanctuary an hour after Matins, hoping to find him available. Cold winter light poured through the arched windows. I could see his feet behind the drapery; I knelt on the floor before him.

"Bless me Father, for I have sinned. It has been forty days since my last confession."

"I know your sins, Sister Ursula. You need not recite them."

I was shocked. "Father . . ."

"Be silent, Sister. I will tell you your sins. You are proud and vain, knowing that you are gifted with beauty and intelligence beyond those of your sisters. You are rebellious against the discipline of the Order, wishing another, worldly life for yourself. Do I speak truly?"

I bowed my head in shame. "Yes, Father."

"Furthermore, you have unclean thoughts and desires. Your young body burns with need. You dream of many hands, stroking and caressing your flesh."

I never recalled my dreams but, as he spoke, I remembered, or imagined, the scenes he described. I felt dampness on my thighs beneath my habit. The ache there was a hundred times stronger than I had ever felt before.

"You feel that you have been abandoned here in the abbey, left to languish here, unnoticed and ultimately alone, for all your days. That is the worst, is it not?"

His perceptiveness astonished me. I had not consciously realized how much I missed the feeling of belonging that I had enjoyed when I was younger.

"Yes, Father. Can you forgive me, Father? Can you give me absolution and peace?"

"I can, but only after you have done penance. Meet me at sixth hour in the stables."

"I will be there, Father. Thank you. Should I say any prayers?"

I could swear that he laughed to himself. "I will teach you to pray this afternoon."

The air in the stables was cold, but ripe with animal and vegetable smells. Father Jerome was waiting for me. In his hand was a whip of braided leather. He ran his palm over its length as he watched me approach.

"Kneel before me, Sister Ursula."

Puzzled but strangely pliant, I followed his instructions, my eyes cast down. The straw tickled my nostrils.

"Sister, the heart of sin is the feeling of separation from God. The remedy is total surrender to His will and a return to communion with Him. Do you understand?"

I nodded, though I hardly grasped what he was saying.

"No, you do not, not yet. But you will. Remove your habit."

Once again, he shocked me. I looked up, into those azure eyes of his. "Surely, Father, this is not proper . . ."

"We are all born naked. The flesh is glorious, not shameful. Do as I say."

He spoke with such authority that I could only believe and obey. Unknotting the cords around my waist, I pulled the bulky wool robe over my head, then folded it neatly and placed it beside me. Now I wore only my rough linen shift, my crucifix, and my wimple and veil. I shivered in the February chill. Yet at the same time my cheeks, my earlobes, my fingers and toes, all grew warm, pulsing with some inner heat. My breasts felt heavy; my tightening nipples scraped against the homespun fabric.

Father Jerome paced a circle around me. "How do you feel?" he asked me.

"Embarrassed," I replied. "And strangely free."

He nodded, apparently satisfied. "I will beat you now. Not as punishment for your sins, but to teach you to surrender. When you surrender, your sins will evaporate like dew in the morning sun."

Before I could respond or even comprehend his words, he stepped behind me. He tore open my shift. There was cold air on my naked back, and then, the searing trail of his whip.

I cried out, in surprise as much as pain. He lashed me again. The leather bit into me, teeth of a wolf tearing at my flesh. Sharp, deep, prolonged: the pain echoed through me long after the leather left my skin.

At first, Father Jerome's strokes were slow and measured. He gave me long moments to reflect on the way the pain flowed through me, ripples of anguish spreading from my back through all my limbs. Soon, though, he increased his pace, stalking back and forth behind me like a tiger, slashing at me with all his strength. I was panting and moaning under his assault; I could hear him panting, too.

"Live in the pain, Ursula. Revel in it. Welcome it. Let it wash through you. Let it drown you."

His words were a chant, soothing and hypnotic. The sting and burning ebbed, transformed themselves to something quite different. Dimly, I realized that the familiar throbbing between my legs was more intense than ever. Each time the lash cut into me, something swelled inside, pulsing with a power that I did not understand.

"Give yourself to my lash. Release yourself. Let the pain release you, open you, free you."

My breathing changed, became deep and regular. I sensed his rhythm, knew before the leather touched me where and when it would land. I felt his crystal eyes on me, stroking my bare flesh along with his whip. I heard his voice, all around me in the flame-tinged darkness behind my closed eyelids.

"Ursula," he seemed to whisper. "Sweet sister, surrender. God. Blood. Peace. Power. Pain. Surrender. Now."

Something tore through me like a whirlwind. That constant

ache shattered into a million shards of pleasure. I heard my own voice, keening, as I shook in the gale that emanated from my own flesh. I felt the leather kiss of the whip again, each stroke a new convulsion of delight. I breathed a silent prayer of gratitude.

Moonlight streamed, glorious, into the chapel that night, as Father Jerome celebrated the Mass. The familiar Latin words of the liturgy, intoned in his strong and resonant voice, held new power for me. I thought that I understood the true nature of the Lamb of God.

I was pure and free, full of light again, as I knelt before the rail and received the Body of Christ between my lips. My back was raw and sore, but my spirit soared as never before with Hildegard's melodies.

My master Jerome left the next morning, but the peace he brought me stayed for many weeks. I was kind to my sisters, meek and obedient, and took joy from the smallest things. I felt an urge to do service, and so with the convent's permission, began to visit the sick and the destitute in the nearby village, bringing them material and spiritual comfort.

Mother Superior sensed the change in me, and we spoke about my final vows. We agreed that I would make them at Easter.

The days warmed and lengthened. The fields were green with fresh growth and sometimes one could see the purple bulk of the massif rising in the distance. My heart was light as I went about my work, anticipating the day when I would belong wholly to Christ. The village folk whispered about me, saying that I had the spirit of a saint. My pride was not completely vanquished. I felt sharp delight when I overheard such things.

The Master came again on Maundy Thursday. I was returning from the village with my empty basket, and found Sisters Madeleine and Louise huddled together in the herb garden. "What news, good sisters?" I asked.

"That strange priest, Father Jerome. He has come back. He has promised to stay and officiate at the Easter Mass."

Something flared in me at this news, totally consuming my tranquility. I had to see him. Shame and excitement warred in me as I recalled my punishment in the stables. I understood that I wanted it again: the pain and the glory of surrender.

"Where is Father Jerome now?" I struggled to keep my voice calm and even, though my heart was beating so hard I could scarcely speak at all.

"In his cell in the visitors' quarters, meditating. He asked that we not disturb him until Vespers."

He was my Master. I should have obeyed, bowed to his wishes. But my need to see him, to look into those luminous eyes, was too great. I knocked softly on the rough plank door.

"Who is there?"

"It is I, Father." My voice was so soft, he must have barely heard. "Sister Ursula."

I half-expected him to send me away. Instead, he opened the door. I was astonished to see that his torso was bare, and criss-crossed with the raw stripes of a whip. "Come in, Sister," he said shortly, and swung the door shut behind us.

Without being told, I knelt before him. "Father, bless me, for I have sinned." He smiled a bit grimly, and raised me up.

"No, Sister, it is I who have sinned. I should not have come back to this convent."

"It is Easter-tide, Father. You do us honor and service by spending it within our walls."

"True. I came for Easter, because I heard that it was then you would seal your vows. I came to see you, one last time."

My heart leaped in joy. My master had returned for me. He loved me. The traces of the lash on his chest were the badges of his love.

"Punish me then, Father, for I have tempted you. The Bible tells us that man's flesh is weak, and susceptible to the wiles of women."

Father Jerome laughed. There was a desperate edge in that laugh. "So, you would have me beat you again?"

"Yes, Father. Master. Teach me more of the joys of sur-render."

His eyes searched mine. I smiled up at him, modesty abandoned, burning with desire.

"Very well, Sister Ursula. Remove your clothing. All your clothing."

I did not mind baring my body for him. I reveled in the thought that he would find me beautiful. I hesitated, though, in removing my veil. Somehow, being bare-headed made me feel more naked than being bare-breasted.

"Stand by the cot, with your palms against the wall." The stone was cool despite the April sunlight streaming through the slit-like window.

"Breathe," he whispered, and then I felt once again the glorious bite of his whip.

This time, he concentrated his attack on my buttocks. He did not begin slowly as before, but immediately began to thrash me with all his strength. Each stroke sizzled like a lightning bolt, straight to my swelling loins.

"Oh, yes," I moaned. "Beat me, Master. Teach me."

I could sense his passion, and his agitation. His lashing hurt far more than the first one, and yet, I would have endured it for ever. Just as the throbbing in my sex rose to crescendo, however, he stopped. The whip clattered on the slate floor.

"I will teach you indeed, Sister, a new lesson," he growled. He grabbed my hips roughly. Terror shot through me. My virginity was for God, not for man, not even for my Master.

As if he heard my thoughts, he laughed, mocking.

"Fear not, sweet Ursula. I will leave your maidenhood intact. You will consummate your vows a virgin still."

He pulled my globes apart and without a moment's hesitation, plunged his maleness into my bowels.

I thought I knew pain before. That was like a mild itch compared to this agony. I felt myself stretch to breaking as he worked his organ inside me. Blood trickled down my thighs from my torn flesh. The smell rose, hot and shameful, blood and excrement, as my Master plowed my rear hole again and again.

"This is the ultimate surrender, Ursula," he growled. "Open yourself, your most hidden and secret self, to me. Receive me, honor me. Now, Ursula!"

I felt his member swell and burst within me, spattering my bowels with burning seed. Until that moment, I had felt nothing but the pain of his ripping violation. Yet when I sensed his climax, my own body convulsed in answer, muscles contracting to grip him and hold him within me.

Later, I lay with him on his pallet, aching inside and out. He stroked my cropped hair out of my eyes.

"I must leave, Ursula. Right away."

"Do not forsake me, Master. I need you to teach me."

"I am not the Master, Ursula. I am no more than His representative, and a poor one at that. I have given you my last lesson. I have nothing more to teach."

He stood up and donned his robe, wincing as the rough fabric brushed over his welts. "You will never see me again. But I will always be with you. Remember what you have learned."

I fell to my knees before him in tears, circling his knees with my arms. "Please, Master, do not go. Or if you must, leave me some token. A piece of your clothing. A lock of your hair."

He looked down at me for a long moment. Then he sighed. Reaching into his bag, he extricated a short leather-sheathed knife. He removed his skullcap. I was astonished to see that his hair was a fiery red, the color of maples in autumn.

Roughly, with no concern for his own comfort, he hacked at his tonsure until he had a thick lock in his hand. He placed it in my palm and closed my fingers around it. "Here you are, girl. Keep it safe, and remember me."

He slipped his feet into his boots, donned his wide-brimmed traveling hat, grabbed his bag, and was out of the door before I could even rise from my knees. Looking out of the narrow window, I saw him striding away.

As if in a dream, I dressed myself. The bells called me to chapel. Detached, but strangely at peace, I knelt on the stone with my sisters and asked the Lord to bless me.

On Easter morn, I made my final vows and became a bride of Christ. The sisters whispered together about the strange priest's sudden departure. As far as I could tell, no one connected this event with me. We had no Mass, but we sang our hymns to the Risen One, songs so lovely they seemed to pierce my heart. There were tears in my eyes. Yet I had never felt such joy.

After my consecration, I wandered through my days in a kind of peaceful trance. I felt no shame and, strangely, little longing for my Master. He was with me, I knew.

My sisters sensed a change in me, though. I was as pliant and obedient as ever, but there was a new distance between me and them. The people in the hamlet sensed it too, though I still brought them bread from our ovens and apples from our orchard, still asked them for news of their children and their crops. I made them nervous, with my deep quiet and my bright eyes that seemed to look into their souls. I overheard no more discussions of my saintly spirit.

In May, the wasting fever broke out in their cottages. Many died, most especially, it seemed, in the houses that I had been wont to visit. There were whispers then, rumors of witchcraft and evil spells. I went about my work, strangely immune to the gossip and the danger.

Mother Superior called me to her. She asked me about incantations, potions, contracts with the Evil One. I smiled and told her I knew nothing of such things. Then she sent Sister Marie to produce the lock of red hair they had found pressed between the pages of my breviary.

The bishop came, all the way from Avignon, to try me as a sorceress. The inquisition was held in the chapel. The golden light of summer streamed through the narrow windows, lighting the concerned and frightened faces of my sisters. I found it difficult to concentrate on the proceedings; I wanted to walk barefoot in the newly green fields and rejoice in the sun.

Again and again the bishop questioned me about the lock of hair. I was silent. What could I say? I could not speak false-hoods, yet I would never betray my Master. The sisters stripped me in order to confirm that I was still virgin. They found me intact. However, the lingering traces of my last beating they denounced as the mark of Satan's talons.

So it is that I came to this pyre, condemned for sorcery when all I sought was peace and service. I do not blame the villagers, the sisters, or the bishop who pronounced me guilty. My soul is clean of sin. My heart is full of love.

The flames lick at this vessel of flesh, reminding me of my Master's lash. There is a smell of charred meat, now, but I ignore it, focusing instead on the flowers. I feel His eyes upon me, luminous and powerful, and I release everything to Him, knowing at last the full truth He was trying to teach me. I am incandescent with joy.

Like Christ Himself I am a bright torch of sacrifice, burning for my Master, and his.

Contented Clients

Kate Dominic

Andre was more than a little miffed. I'd been quite specific letting him know that the matronly outfit he'd designed for me was about as sexy as a burlap sack.

"I want to show boobs, dear," I snapped, dumping the custom-made 1950s style housedress on top of the naked mannequin's headless neck. "Mother's 'naughty little boys and girls' need to be squirming in anticipation of a nice, comforting nipple to suck on, even before I turn them over my knees."

"As Madame wishes," Andre sniffed, his beautiful green eyes flashing with righteous indignation as he tossed his short blond curls. In a flash of dramatic pique that only a former runway model could master, he turned and swept up the yards of atrocious yellow floral print. He froze in mid-pirouette when my hand snaked out and gripped his slender, denim-covered butt cheek. Hard. I wasn't sure what Andre's problem was today. His costumes were usually exquisite. But I was in no mood for an artistic temper tantrum when I had clients scheduled for that scene in less than a week.

"Madame damn well wishes," I said quietly. "And if Andre has a problem with that, perhaps Madame should call Andre's sweet, smiling lover over to give dear little Andre an attitude adjustment."

Andre looked nervously over his shoulder, his eyes locking on the large, bearded man hunched intently over the computer screen on the other side of the room. The only time I'd ever seen Bedford's lips so much as curve upward was when he was paddling the bejeezus out of Andre's ass. Bedford clicked on to a new screen, leaned back, and carefully stroked his chin. The latest design appeared on the web page he was updating, and Bedford nodded once, so slowly that the long, brown hair tied back at his neck barely moved over the flannel shirt covering his thickly muscled shoulders.

"That won't be necessary," Andre said primly, almost hiding a shiver as he carefully turned and set the discarded material onto a side table. He glanced once more in his bearish lover's direction. "Shall Madame and I sit down at the other work station and discuss alternative design options?"

"The operative word being 'sit,'" I snapped, releasing his ass-cheek. I managed to control my smile as Andre politely escorted me over to the computer, offering me a chair before he called up my profile with even more efficiency than usual. From the way his ass was twitching, I gathered that sweet, pouty little Andre's entire snit had been staged purely to let Bedford know that he was hungry for a good, old-fashioned ass-warming. Despite Bedford's apparent lack of attention, I had no doubt that he'd heard every word – and that a very sore and well-fucked Andre would be working standing up for the next couple of days.

It wasn't the first time I'd been an unwitting prop in one of my friends' private little scenes. I doubted it would be the last. I shook my head and bit back a grin as my voluptuous cyber model filled the screen and a nervous, eager-to-please Andre and I got back to designing the perfect costume for my stable of submissive little boys and girls.

Overall, I'd been quite pleased with PFA, Inc. Personal Fetish Attire had provided me with my first dominatrix outfits with almost off-the-rack speed – no mean feat, given my well-endowed size 2X proportions. As my clientele had grown, Andre and I had worked together to design some very chic leather teddies and harnesses that emphasized my Rubenesque curves for my hardcore "mistress" clients, as well as the flowing drapes of satin and lace that highlighted the ample padding so comforting to my naughty adult children. When I'd branched out into less traditional fetishes, PFA had quietly made some introductions – to other clients, for whom they then also supplied costumes. Several of my fantasy scenes had even been Bedford's idea.

"We got this guy who's really into horror flicks," Bedford had said one fall afternoon. He was lacing me into my new black corset as Andre put the finishing touches on my Hallowe'en vampire costume. "Cleavage" didn't begin to describe the size of the valley developing between my boobs as Bedford cinched me into place. Andre had somehow managed to build in a truly comfortable support bra, without losing the sleek lines of the corset. "This dude would think he'd died and gone to heaven if you had your way with him in this costume, Ms Amanda, especially if you bit his neck a couple of times. Hell, if you let him nurse on these mamas, he'd pay whatever you wanted. And honey," Bedford winked at me as he tucked the lacing ends under the intricately tied knots, "he can afford to pay whatever you want."

In short order, I'd found out that Timmy could indeed afford my services. Frequently. From there, it was a short step to a half-dozen men who wanted to be spanked and diapered and fed a cup of warm milk, then held on Mama's large, comforting lap to nurse contentedly on her huge ol' boobs while they went to sleep. That costume was easy, too. I set the scene to be one of "baby" waking up at night, so the seductive peignoirs that, along with leatherwear, were the mainstay of PDF, needed only a complementary pair of feathered satin mules to have "baby's" hard, horny dick drooling into the neatly pinned cloth cotton diapers Andre had custom-made for them. At the end of the scene, I'd sit in the oversized rocker Bedford had built and unhook my specially made "nursing bra," one cup at a time, and let "baby" suckle my huge, dark red nipples until the heavenly stimulation – and the ben wa balls in my pussy – made me explode in orgasm. The sucking, along with my usual expert wrist action, usually had baby creaming into his diaper as soon as he'd sucked me through my climax. My submissive and infantilist clients were an excellent match for me, as my breasts were about the most sensitive part of my body. After a good session of nipple stimulation and roasting naked backsides, all it took was a few quick flicks to my clit or a well-placed toy to make my cunt gush.

Although my clients paid well enough that I only needed to have a few regulars, I was interested in branching out again.

For the first time, I also had a couple of women clients. Both they and a couple of new "boys" that I'd taken on were hot to do a Teenager Gone Bad scene.

One of the girls, Cherise, had had serious problems with bulimia. I'd had a long talk with her doctor before I accepted her as a client. Cherise, however, was not into infantilism. Spanking, yes. But at twenty-six, she saw herself more as a naughty high-schooler who needed someone to take her firmly in hand and teach her to be good and do right – and to help her gain a healthy dose of the self-esteem she was fighting so hard to achieve. After her last visit, I'd told her that next week "her mother" wanted to discuss her report card with her – most specifically, her citizenship grades. She was to be sure to wear her best school clothes and saddle shoes. Cherise had shivered, her face positively glowing as she kissed my hand and whispered, "Yes, ma'am. I'll be here right after school." Which meant 6:30 p.m. sharp, after she'd finished work and eaten exactly as the doctor's regimen directed.

Part of the success of our session, however, hinged on whether Andre got off his butt and got me a sexy enough "loving but stern 1950s middle-class Mom" costume. I knew Cherise's costume was done. Although Andre hadn't shown it to me, he told me I'd be pleased. He also assured me that my costume would most definitely not be lacking by Thursday evening when I picked it up. I assured him that it had better not be, or I'd be lending Bedford one wicked fucking Lucite paddle.

Of course, Bedford had heard the whole exchange, despite how engrossed he'd appeared to have been in the website updates. As I walked toward the door, I heard him growl, "Drop yer pants and get over my knees, boy!" followed by the sound of a chair being pushed back, the clink of a belt being unbuckled, and Andre's plaintive "I'm sorreeeee, Bedford!" I smiled and turned the "closed" sign to the window on my way out, locking the door behind me.

Whether it was the hiding Bedford gave him for "sassing the customers," for which Andre tearfully apologized into my answering machine, or just his usual desire to create gorgeously sexy attire, Andre outdid himself with the new and improved version of my happy housewife ensemble. The soft, full, autumn-colored skirt brushed just below my knees, a wide leather belt cinching Mother's ample waist in just enough to show her well rounded hips. A simple beige silk button-down blouse tucked into the waist, veiling but definitely not hiding the cream-colored peek-a-boo satin and lace front-hook bra that was, again, wonderfully supportive and comfortable. Since it was a warm fall day, Mother wasn't wearing underwear per se, just a butterfly vibrator in a thin-strapped thong-type harness, a lacy garter belt that matched her brassiere and held the tiny control box for the vibrator, and thigh-high seamed nylons. Whether or not my errant daughter was going to discover what was beneath my skirt remained to be seen. I'd made plans for several contingencies. A pristine starched white cotton apron that tied at the waist rounded out my attire, along with low brown leather heels and a pearl necklace and earrings. By the time I took the hot rollers out of my hair and sprayed my period hairdo into place, I had just enough time to spritz on some White Shoulders perfume before the front door quietly opened.

I walked to the stove and lifted the lid on the pot of thick hearty vegetable soup that was cooking, picked up the long-handled wooden spoon and started to stir as I heard Cherise come into the kitchen. I looked up at her and smiled.

"Hello, dear. How was school?"

Andre had outdone himself again. Cherise wore a poodle skirt and a soft pink angora sweater that softened the angular planes that were slowly filling out as she grew healthier. When I nodded appreciatively, Cherise blushed and slowly turned around, the careful draping of the thick skirt flowing with her as she moved to show off how her pretty bottom was finally rounding out. Her legs were bare except for ankle socks and saddle shoes, and her fragile, usually pale face was suffused with a happy blush. The three textbooks she carried under her arm added more to her teenage look than her blonde ponytail held in place by a charming pink satin bow.

"School was fine, Mother." Cherise smiled, one of her truly happy smiles, even as she quickly lowered her gaze. I was surprised to realize how much I'd come to anticipate that quiet, shy look. "I got all my homework done, and I had lunch with my friends."

But Cherise was studiously concentrating on the pattern in the linoleum. Her deliberately averted eyes told my "mother's intuition" that something was up. I cleared my throat and set the spoon down on the counter.

"Cherise, are you wearing lipstick?!" I asked sharply, clucking a feigned disapproval. "Young lady, someone as naturally beautiful as you does not need artificial enhancements!"

The creamy, dark pink ribbon of color would have been impossible to miss. Andre had no doubt spent hours ensuring it would complement the natural blush that slowly suffused Cherise's face. She obediently looked up at me, her blue eyes sparkling.

"I wanted to look pretty today, Mother," she said shyly.

"Cherise," I said, shaking my head in mock exasperation. "You are always pretty. This," I pointed sternly at her lips, "is like adding lipstick to a rose. I am sorely tempted to turn you over my knee!"

"Oh, no, Mother." She reached back quickly to protect her bottom with her free hand. I wasn't sure how much of that was an act. Cherise loved the catharsis of a long, hard, tear-filled spanking; she wasn't satisfied until her backside was blazing sore and she was sobbing like a baby. "I'm much too old to be spanked."

She moved to the table and set down her books. A bright yellow folded piece of paper fell out: REPORT CARD. Quickly she tucked it under her algebra book. I bit my lip and very deliberately wiped my hands on my apron.

"Nonsense, sweetheart. A pretty young lady like you is definitely still of an age for a good, sound dose of Mother's hairbrush when you need it. I hope you're hiding that report card because you want to surprise me with your wonderful grades, and not because of bad citizenship marks again." I carefully unfolded the card. A "B," three "Cs," and a "D" were marked in heavy black letters in the academic columns – right across from five bright red "Fs" in citizenship.

"Cherise!" I said sternly. "What is the meaning of this?!"

"Um, I don't know, Mother," she said nervously, shifting

her weight from one foot to the other as she peered over my shoulder. "Maybe the teacher made a mistake?"

"Have you been doing your homework?" I demanded, giving her bottom a quick, sharp swat.

"Yes." She stepped quickly back, out of the line of fire, lowered her eyes again and stirred her foot in a nervous circle. "Well, most of the time. Sometimes I forgot."

"I see," I said icily, tapping the card on my fingers. "And the tardiness, talking in class and lack of participation were also caused by forgetfulness?"

"Um, sometimes." Cherise licked her lips nervously, highlighting the bright color of her lipstick.

"Yet you could still remember to put on your makeup."

Cherise clamped her hand over her mouth and stammered, "Just today!"

"Give me the lipstick." I held out my hand. "It had better be almost unused."

Andre knew me well. Cherise reached into her purse and, as she drew out the well-worn tube, I could see that the contents had been carefully honed down so that only half a stick was left.

"So, now you've started lying as well, young lady?"

Cherise hung her head in shame. Her pert little nipples were hard under her sweater. My labia started to tingle.

"I'm sorry, Mother," she whispered. "I won't do it again."

"You certainly won't," I snapped, tossing the report card on the table and turning the soup down to simmer. "You've earned a good, sound bottom roasting, young lady."

"Mother!!" Cherise wailed, reaching back to cover her backside, this time in earnest. She backed up against the cupboard. I shook my head sternly at her.

"Not in here, Cherise." I took off my apron and carefully folded it over the back of the kitchen chair. "I'm going to be taking down your panties. If your crying draws the neighbors, we can't have them looking through the window and seeing your bare, red bottom wiggling all over my lap. We're going to your room."

"Mother!!!"

Ignoring the increasingly loud protests of innocence and the promises to do better in the future, I took my errant "daughter's" hand and marched her resolutely down the hall, hurrying her with a few well-placed swats when she dawdled. We entered "her" room, and I locked the door behind us.

For a moment, Cherise just stared at what was behind the door. I'd taken the room that usually doubled as Mama's bedroom for the infantilists and changed it into a teenaged girl's dream, complete with delicately flowered chenille bedspread, turntable with rock and roll records, vintage movie posters, and a neat study desk, complete with dictionary, sharpened pencils and a new, lined notebook. As Cherise looked around the room, I purposefully strode to the window and lowered the blinds.

"It's too hot to close the windows, Cherise. So don't even think to complain that the whole neighborhood is going to hear your spanking. You should have thought of that beforehand. Neighbors or not, I'm going to spank you until you're crying at the top of your lungs. Maybe it will do you some good to realize that everyone knows your mother loves you much too much to let a good girl like you get away with such nonsense."

"Mother!" Cherise seemed shocked, but I knew she could hear the air conditioning running, so she'd know this room was as soundproofed as the rest of the house. But Cherise's low self-esteem in public was a big source of her problems. The instinctive shiver that ran up her spine told me how much she was enjoying the idea of "public" proof of her value to me. I walked over to the nightstand and moved the thick maple hairbrush to the front edge, within easy reach. Then I sat down on the bed and pointed in front of me.

"Come here, Cherise, and lift up your skirt and slip."

"Motherrrrrr," she wailed, stomping her foot and backing against the closed door. I'd learned on our first visit how much Cherise enjoyed losing the battle to avoid her spankings. "I'm too old to be spanked bare!"

"Right now, young lady," I snapped my fingers, "and for your insolence, you will now take your skirt and slip OFF!"

With a loud sniffle, she shuffled over to stand beside me and slowly unbuttoned and lowered her skirt. The delicate white satin slip that hugged her hips was a work of art. But when she removed that as well, I needed a moment of reprieve while she carefully folded her clothing onto the nightstand. Andre had outdone himself: pristine white satin tap pants, bordered with Irish lace and decorated with dainty pink butterflies, framed the softly swelling mound between Cherise's legs and clung to the new fullness of her bottom. I slipped my shaking fingers into the waistband and slowly lowered the exquisite panties, exposing the neatly trimmed soft blonde tufts covering her vulva.

"I'm too big to be spanked bare," she sniffed, reluctantly lifting first one leg, then the other.

"Nonsense." I smoothed my skirt and patted my thigh. "Mother's lap is quite big enough to hold you." Cherise slowly lowered herself across my legs, reaching forward to grab a thick handful of the plush chenille bedspread as I pulled her into position. She stiffened as I situated her so that her angular bones were cushioned comfortably over my full thighs. I wanted all of Cherise's attention to be focused on her bottom.

"This is going to be a very serious spanking, Cherise." She whimpered as I slowly slid my hand over the smooth, creamy curve of her bare behind. "I'm going to paddle your bottom until it's so red and sore, you won't be able to sit down for the rest of the week." I caressed her until she was squirming. I wanted every inch of her backside awakened and hungry to be touched.

"You will give your best effort, Cherise, in everything you do." I brought my hand down sharply across her right cheek. She yelped, jerking, and I brought my hand down hard on the other side.

"Ow!" Cherise arched her bottom up to meet each slap. "Mother! That hurts! Ow! Ow! OWWWW!!!"

A dozen sound hand spanks later, her bottom was pinkening nicely. After another dozen, she was sniffling loudly, though she didn't try to move out of the way. I knew that would change the moment I picked up the brush.

"By not doing your best, you're only hurting yourself, dear." I quietly lifted the cool-handled maple brush and, with no warning, smacked it loudly over her right bottom cheek. Cherise howled, and her hand came up to cover her behind. I firmly held her wrist against her waist and spanked her again.

"We'll have none of that, young lady."

"It hurts!" she wailed, her legs flailing on the bed as I began to paddle her in earnest. She twisted and bucked, yelling at the top of her lungs as I covered her entire bottom with sharp, hard swats, up one side and down the other, with the steady rhythm I knew she so enjoyed. "Ow, ow! It hurts!!!"

"Of course it hurts," I snapped, stopping just long enough to pull her tightly to me. "Mother is punishing you, dear. I want your bottom good and sore."

Cherise's ensuing howls told me she was really feeling each swat. She kicked her way through another half-dozen sound, hard cracks. Then I paused and set the brush down, cupping her heated bottom and sliding my fingers between her legs and over her labia. Cherise's whole cunt was drenched. She arched into my hand, crying out as my fingertip slid forward to caress her swollen clit. Cherise spread her legs, sniffling loudly. The smell of her arousal filled my nostrils. My own pussy clenched in response.

"Good girls are always doing their best." I gently pinched her swollen nub, my nipples hardening as she cried out and pressed back into my hand. "They take care of themselves so they are strong and confident." I slid my hand back and squeezed her hot, red flesh, first one side, then the other. "You will remember to always do your best – for yourself, dear, but also because you know that Mother will spank you if you don't."

I picked up the brush again. "Do you hear me, Cherise? You . . . will . . . always . . . do . . . your . . . best!" I punctuated each word with another blazing wallop.

"I will, Mommy! Ow! I will! I will! Mommy!!!!" After another ten scorching smacks, Cherise's screeches suddenly dissolved in great, heaving sobs. "I w-will, Mommy! I w-will!!!" Her body shook as the cleansing tears finally started flowing into the soft, fluffy threads of the bedspread.

I set the brush down and gently pulled Cherise into my arms.

"There, there, dear," I murmured, holding her tenderly to my breast. She clung to me, sobbing, as I unbuttoned my blouse. I'd barely finished when Cherise pulled the fabric aside and immediately began rubbing her tear-stained face against the soft, creamy lace. Without a word, I unhooked the front catch. My breasts fell forward and Cherise nuzzled her face against my nipple, taking deep, gulping breaths as she shook and licked. Sensations shuddered through me as her cat-rough tongue dragged over the first side, then the other, outlining and laving the areolas. My pussy throbbed. I lifted a shaking hand and gently stroked her cheek.

"My bottom hurts, Mommy," she whispered, her tongue never missing a beat.

"It's supposed to hurt, sweetie." I shivered as she tickled her tongue over the sensitive tip of my nipple. "That's how you learn. Suckle Mommy's breast if it will make you feel better."

Cherise opened her tear-filled blue eyes to meet mine. Then she smiled, and with a long low sigh, wrapped her lips around my areola and sucked the entire nipple into her mouth like a lonely, frightened child. She inhaled deeply and started to nurse.

I held her close, panting hard with pleasure. Each tug brought exquisite sensations. For a while we just sat there, the only sounds the hum of the air conditioner and Cherise's contented suckling, and my occasional moan. When Cherise's fingers slid down to her vulva, I moved my hand to her thigh.

"Would you like an orgasm, dear?"

When Cherise nodded, I eased her legs apart. She slid farther down, spreading wider for me, and sucking hard. She winced as her full weight rested on her well-spanked bottom. My hand slid into her slick folds.

"Don't fight the pain, sweetheart." I stroked my fingers up and down her slit. She whimpered, her legs stiffening as she inadvertently leaned more heavily on her tender behind. "The soreness will remind you to listen to me, dear one."

Cherise wiggled uncomfortably a few more times, then looked at me and smiled tearfully. She kissed my nipple slowly. Carefully I slipped my middle finger into her quivering pussy and caressed her clit with the pad of my thumb.

"You are truly beautiful, Cherise, from the inside out." Her eyes filled again as I pressed my finger deep, curving up toward her belly. She trembled against me as I found the sensitive spot deep inside her vagina. "Only a healthy body can feel this intensely."

With my finger still inside her, I started massaging her juice-slicked clit with a slow, rolling motion. She cried out, sucking ferociously.

"Take care of your body, sweetie, so it can enjoy the pleasure of a healthy, happy climax." I kept up a steady rhythm, pressing deeply. Cherise's skin started to flush. "That's it, beautiful. Let your wonderful, young body come like the strong, lusty animal you are."

Cherise sucked so hard that my whole body quivered. Then with a loud cry, she arched into my hand, bucking and thrashing as her body convulsed with an orgasm that shook her from her toes to where her lips latched tightly onto me. She clutched me fiercely to her, sucking her way through a long, rolling climax.

She left me shaking with need.

Cherise slowly caught her breath, her lips falling free of my swollen breast. My nipple was a deep, bruised burgundy against her pale cheek as she lifted a shaking hand to my face. Her fingers traced the outline of my chin.

"Thank you, Ms Amanda." Her face glowed with an almost luminescent blush. "I feel so good all over, even where my bottom's so sore." She stared at me, slowly brushing her hand over my cheek while another flush burned suddenly deeper and darker over her face. "Um, ma'am, I was just curious, but . . ." she took a deep breath, but this time she didn't look away as she blurted out, "do you get turned on by my, um . . ."

Even the skin beneath her ponytail seemed to be blushing. I laughed and hugged her tightly.

"Yes, love," I kissed her hand. "Pleasuring you is intensely arousing to me."

"But you didn't . . .?" Her eyes stayed intently on me as she stammered out her question.

"No, dear," I smiled. "I'll take care of it later."

Cherise nodded and snuggled back into my arms. Her breath was cool over my wet nipple as she sighed contentedly and whispered, "In two weeks, I get my report card from my Greek and Latin tutor. Do you want to see that, too, ma'am?"

The possibilities for those costumes were mind-boggling.

I kissed the top of her head and settled in for one final bit of cuddling. Andre was going to be very busy.

The Lessons

Nola Summers

I'm sitting here alone on the dock, waiting for Jacob, the heat from Lesson Two still warming me against the early morning chill. I've been good. I want Lesson Three; I want all the lessons.

The Canadian Shield whizzed past the car, changing from farmland to rocky outcrop with every passing mile. We were headed to Ranger Lake – two weeks in the great outdoors. I'd complained bitterly before we left. I'd known it was coming for months but I still sulked. Ranger Lake Lodge: mosquitoes, fish guts, boredom, misery. My husband could do what he wanted. I'd play along, but I was never coming again.

Go straight, I chanted silently at a highway junction, but we turned north, taking the Sault Ste Marie bypass. Straight on would have taken us out of Ontario and into Michigan, the long way home to Detroit, but at least I would be in the right country.

I waved my husband off to fishing heaven the next morning, then canceled the canoeing lessons he'd booked for me. No one told Jacob, the instructor, though, and he came to collect me for Lesson One. I followed him to the water, my disinterest displayed like a shield. I was unnerved by his dark eyes and somber manner, but when he told me to get in the boat, I did.

Jacob sat behind me as we paddled up the shore. It was hot. I could feel him watching me, sure he could see the sweat running down my back and into my shorts. Other than a few paddling instructions there was no conversation.

The lake darkened to black just off the shore, a contrast to the smooth, steep granite that fronted the lake: pink and gray with an occasional white stripe. The rocks were dotted with wind-carved trees, overgrown bonsai, their roots anchored in the tiniest of cracks. The solitude, broken only by an occasional eagle's cry, was hypnotic. Hidden here and there were small sandy beaches.

I was taken by surprise when Jacob spoke: there was a place we could stop for lunch, he said. He steered the canoe into a secluded cove, beached us, and helped me out.

I moved up onto the rocks, then turned to look at him. Jacob was Native, tall and bronzed, with dark eyes, chiseled features, and long black steel-cut hair that he wore loose. He had taken off his T-shirt and shoes, leaving just a faded pair of shorts. He was well-muscled, but his chest was baby smooth, his nipples like hard brown buttons. Just a trace of hair peeked out above the button of his fly.

He turned toward me and slid his shorts off. This unexpected nakedness neither frightened nor intimidated me; in fact, it amused me more than anything else.

"Come here," he said, extending his arm. I felt like I was in *The Last of the Mohicans*, when Magua reaches out to his young captive as she stands on the edge of the cliff. The edge that I stood on was different, though I don't think I realized it then; I could say no, and just continue with my ordinary life.

There was no real hesitation. Something in his voice, his eyes, his outstretched hand, drew me toward him. Jacob turned me, knelt and undid my shorts, hooking his fingers in the elastic of my underpants and pulling everything off at once. His long hair brushed me as he slid his tongue up the cleft of my ass. I turned to face him again and his tongue made a wet trail around my hip then down between my legs. He held my arms at my sides and teased me with the tip of his tongue, gently pushing apart the soft folds and burrowing between them. When I pushed back, Jacob stopped. He stood, pulled my top off, and left us both naked under the noon sun.

There was a ledge in the rock like a seat and he lifted me onto it, the granite sun-warm and smooth against my skin. Jacob looked in my eyes as he spread my lips with his long bronze fingers. He was silent as he probed me, and I was unable to speak.

His tongue covered me with long wet strokes, like a mother cat cleaning its kitten. My face, neck and breasts were left cool with his licking. Jacob worked his way down to my core. When he began there it was as if there were two tongues instead of one. I felt his hands on my hips, easing me forward. The lap of water against the shore matched his tongue, stroke for stroke. Steady, strong, relentless. I came with a fistful of Jacob's hair in each hand.

I had barely caught my breath, still wondering why I was doing what I was doing, when he lifted me down and turned me to face the rocks. I braced myself. He slid all the way in on his first thrust.

"How do I want you?"

I wasn't sure what he wanted for an answer.

"How?" His grip tightened on my hips, pushing me away, pulling me back sharply.

"Hard," I said.

He withdrew.

"How do you want me?" he asked.

"I want you hard. I want you to fuck me hard, Jacob."

"Good," he said. "Because that's what I'm going to do."

I could barely stand as he pounded into me. I acknowledged the surrender of power. I was going to give it, and Jacob was going to take it.

When I started coming he stopped and pulled me firmly against him. He played me with his long lean fingers, controlling my orgasm to match his own. My insides contracted, milking him as he spurted. His come ran down both our legs into the sand.

He carried me to the lake, washed me, then took me out to deeper water, lifting me and wrapping my legs around his waist. My breasts bobbed in the lake, the cold making my nipples harder and more sensitive.

"You shouldn't cover these," he said. "They should be seen. Touched. Sucked." Jacob drew a nipple into his mouth. He bent me back with one hand, cupping one breast, then the other, rolling the nipples between finger and thumb, increasing the pressure until I gasped.

He moved toward the beach and let me slip down his body

till my feet touched solid ground. He walked to the stone shelf, sat down and spread his legs.

"Come here."

I did. I sucked the tip of him first, running my tongue around the head and probing the eye. I held his smooth shaft with one hand and cupped his balls with the other, licking him from base to head.

"Take it," he said.

I opened wide, sucked him in. He was big for me: by the time my nose was buried in the black hair at his crotch he was hitting the back of my throat. He tasted of the lake and our come. His hands held my head, controlling me.

He made me look at him as he came. When I didn't manage to swallow all of him and it ran from the corners of my mouth, he wiped it off with his hand and I licked each of his fingers clean.

Jacob got me dressed then and took me back to the lodge.

"Lesson Two. Tomorrow, same time."

I was sunburned in places that had never seen the sun before. I was in the bathroom when my husband came back to the cabin, wondering what I had learned.

"There's a lot more to it than I thought," I said, catching my breath. "It's kind of interesting, but the canoe guy doesn't say much. I'll probably try again tomorrow; there's not much else for me to do." I spoke from the safety of the shower, washing sand out of all the little folds where sand wasn't meant to be.

Next day, Jacob was as silent as before. We had only gone about half the distance to the cove when he pulled to the shore and told me to get out.

"Lesson Two. Get undressed, face away."

He pulled my arms behind my back, tied my wrists with leather, and helped me back in the canoe. I tried to get him to untie me. No, he said. We were going to the cove. If I didn't sit still and be quiet he would gag me.

He told me that he knew I had tried to cancel the first lesson.

"That was wrong," he said. "Very disobedient."

I tried to explain, but Jacob wouldn't listen.

"You need to think about your mistake. And be thankful that I will consider forgiving you."

We went the rest of the way in silence. When we reached the cove he carried me up the shore. He laid out a blanket and told me to kneel. His eyes never left me as he took off his clothes.

"You must learn to obey."

He smoothed the hair from my face and slowly pushed his thumb between my lips. "Your mouth is mine," he said.

His cock was touching my cheek, moving in slow strokes, leaving a wet trail on my face. It came to rest on my lips.

"Open."

I did and he slid in. He held the back of my head and slowly worked himself in and out of my mouth.

"Your body is mine." Jacob said. He knelt, massaging my breasts – pinching and rolling my nipples before bending to suck them into his mouth. I watched as he pulled at one tip with his teeth. It was still tender and swollen from the day before, but I couldn't stop my back from arching to accommodate his punishing mouth; I couldn't stop myself from offering the other nipple.

Jacob reached between my legs. "This is mine," he whispered, as his fingers wormed inside me.

His hand twisted and pushed, then slowly withdrew. My knees spread in response to his careful movement, and when they did, he took away his hand.

He eased my head down to rest on the blanket, my knees spread and my backside completely exposed. He tongued me from behind. "Your ass is mine too." Jacob said.

He plunged into my own wetness to slick himself before easing his cock into my rear. I had never been stretched this way before.

Jacob waited for me. Not moving.

"Do it," he whispered.

I knew nothing except my need. Not the lake, not the sky, not my husband. I begged him to move.

"No," he said. "You take it."

With my face buried in the blanket and my hands tied, I fucked myself on him. Jacob pulled out as I was coming and untied me, pulled me to my hands and knees, and told me not to move.

I rocked back and forth, anticipating his re-entry.

The noise and sting of the first slap shocked me upright.

"Learn to obey, or be punished," he told me, as he walked round to face me and knelt to slip his tongue between my lips, kissing me tenderly. "And maybe sometimes, you'll just be punished," he whispered, lips still touching mine.

He eased me back down and spanked me. When he stopped I though it was over until I felt him tongue fucking me from behind, but each time my legs began to quiver the licking stopped and the slaps returned.

If he was spanking me then he would be licking me soon. If he was licking, I would be close to coming. I was beyond sniveling and begging, my pleasepleaseplease muffled in the blanket.

At last I felt a hand snake between my thighs, manipulating me as the slaps continued, steady and controlled. He wanted me to come. He wanted me to feel the pleasure with the pain, and I did, unable to distinguish them any longer.

As he dressed, I lay sprawled on the blanket, my insides still contracting. He knelt and rubbed my tender backside. Today's lesson, he said, was about control. It was about giving and taking. He had taken, I had given.

"It is a good day to give," he said. He laughed. "My ancestors said something like that."

He stood and eased the canoe toward the water. "Tomorrow," he said, "is Lesson Three."

Nude in Magenta

Debra Gray De Noux & O'Neil De Noux

Through the viewfinder of his Nikon, James Steele watches his wife sit in her red miniskirt on the finely-trimmed lawn of Jackson Square. Her skirt is so short her white panties are plainly visible. James focuses on her semi-sheer underwear and takes a picture. He feels an immediate rush, his wife sitting this way in public.

With her short brown hair, striking blue eyes and model's face, Helen looks stunning on this bright, Saturday morning. She's never looked prettier, especially with only a hint of make-up and that brown lipstick, which draws out her creamy complexion. She still looks much younger than thirty-two, although that's what her Louisiana driver's license says.

James takes another picture, then sits next to Helen to re-load his Nikon. He catches a whiff of her light perfume again, which increases his turn-on.

The calliope of a steamboat starts up, its shrill notes bouncing off the roofs of the French Quarter. James looks toward the seawall protecting New Orleans from the Mississippi and sees the steamboat's funnels over the top of the concrete wall, recalling the view before the wall was built, back when it was all wharves along here.

"Someone's out on the balcony," Helen says, turning James's attention to the Pontalba House Apartments across narrow St Peter Street from the square. A man stands leaning against the railing of the intricate, wrought-iron balcony running the length of the block-long, redbrick Pontalba House.

"I think it's him," Helen says quickly, "and he has *bino-culars.*"

Helen raises her right knee, revealing even more of her panties, as James moves in front of her to take another picture. Beneath the brilliant sunlight, James can see his wife's dark pubic hair through her panties. He feels his heartbeat rising.

Helen leans back on her hands and raises her face to the sun, eyes closed. James moves to her side to give the man with the binoculars an unobstructed view up her skirt.

Three minutes later, as James snaps yet another photo, he spots their quarry hurrying through the iron gates of the square. Carrying his own camera, the Honorable Frederick Newman, associate justice of the Louisiana Supreme Court, heads straight for them. Helen raises both knees high, revealing the panty-covered lobes of her ass for James to photograph. Moving to his wife's side, James spots Newman pull up his camera to take a hurried picture up Helen's skirt.

In his mid-sixties, Judge Newman is a thin man, a good five inches shorter than James Steel's six-foot linebacker frame. Newman has intense green eyes, a hawkish nose, and sandy hair showing only a hint of gray around the temples. Like James, Newman wears a sport shirt and jeans.

James's sport shirt, worn out, covers his 9mm Beretta, tucked into his beltline at the small of his back.

"Hope you don't mind if I take your picture." Newman flashes a warm smile at Helen. Turning to James, he adds, "I'm a professional photographer and she looks so pretty. Hope you don't mind."

"No problem," James says as Helen sits cross-legged, like an Indian, the entire front of her panties exposed. Strands of her silky pubic hair stick out the sides of her skimpy underwear. James focuses and snaps a photo as Newman does the same. Helen leans back on her hands again.

Two men pass behind James and he sees them ogling his wife. A mischievous glint comes to Helen's eyes as she smiles at her husband, her face flushed. She's getting turned on.

Helen stands and pushes down her skirt. "Let's go to the Moonwalk," she says, taking James's hand.

"Mind if I tag along?" Newman smiles again.

Helen smiles back and Newman sticks out his hand, intro-

ducing himself as Fred Newman. Helen takes his hand as
James introduces them.

"Such a gorgeous day for pictures," Newman adds as they
cross Decatur Street and move up the steps to the top of the
concrete seawall. Over his shoulder, James notices a young
man checking out Helen's rear as they climb the steps.
He's probably getting a good view, James thinks and feels a
rush again. They cross the streetcar tracks to the wooden
moonwalk atop a smaller levee next to the river. A warm
breeze, smelling of coffee from one of the nearby wharves,
tousles Helen's hair and lifts her skirt momentarily. Moving to
an open bench, Helen sits. Even with her knees together, James
can see her underwear. He and Newman snap a photo and
Helen goes into model mode, moving her feet up to the bench,
showing off more of her panties.

James feels his heart pounding in his chest as several men move
closer to watch. Helen drops one leg off the bench to show her
crotch to the peering eyes. Smiling broadly, she playfully toys
with the buttons on her blouse, unfastening the first two to reveal
most of her cleavage. James and Newman both take pictures.

Suddenly, Helen stands and buttons her blouse. James turns
to see a cop slowly approaching. Thankfully, he's looking at a
passing ship on the river. James takes his wife's hand and leads
her back up the moonwalk.

"James, Helen," Newman calls out as he follows, "would
y'all like to go up to my place for some wine? I live in the
Pontalba House."

"The Pontalba House, huh?" Helen smiles again. "Never
been in there." For an instant she remembers watching the
workers build the old apartment house, laying the red bricks,
hoisting the pieces of the lacework balcony.

"It's the oldest apartment house in North America," Newman adds.

"What kind of wine?" Helen's flirting now. James squeezes
her hand and she squeezes back, smiling even wider.

"I have a wine room."

Once a small closet, Newman's wine room is at the end of the
long hall just inside his second-story apartment. He pulls out a

bottle of French cabernet and motions them into the wide living room with its french doors opening to the balcony overlooking Jackson Square.

Pulling out the bottle's cork, he lets it breathe while he shows off the living room, neatly decorated with a mix of antique love seats, a modern sofa, an oriental screen, mahogany tables, oil paintings on two walls, the third with floor-to-ceiling bookshelves of leather-bound books. James catches a scent of lemon polish in the immaculately clean room.

"Delicious," Helen says, sipping the wine.

"The light in here is nearly golden," James says. Helen takes the hint and sits on the sofa, posing for the men. She kicks off her sandals and pulls her feet up on the sofa. Lying back, she spreads her feet apart for the photographers.

James feels a growing hard-on and is forced to adjust it. He sees Helen catch him, winking as she does. Newman lets out a long breath as Helen pulls her skirt up to show her dark mat of hair plainly visible now through her sheer underpants.

"You are truly beautiful," Newman gushes as he moves in for a closer picture.

Finishing her wine, Helen poses in different positions, always showing her panties, her face getting more flushed as James and Newman hover around her, snapping pictures.

Refilling her wineglass, Newman asks, "Why don't you finish unbuttoning your blouse?"

Helen takes the glass from him and sips it, her eyes lingering on his as she shakes her head. Stepping to one of the mahogany tables, Helen poses next to it, lifting the back of her skirt to show her ass. Away from the golden light of the french doors, James turns on his strobe unit as Helen continues moving around, posing for the men.

Returning to the sofa, she glances at her watch, then looks expectantly at James.

"Well," James says, "guess we're running out of poses." He tugs up his jeans, feeling the reassuring weight of his Beretta.

Newman quickly refills Helen's glass and hands it to her with a gleam in his eye. "Y'all want to see something truly exquisite?"

"Sure." Helen takes another drink of wine.

Newman leads them back into the hall to the far end where a pinkish red daybed sits beneath a large mirror.

"Nice." Helen shrugs, her heart suddenly pounding. She masks it with a calm question, "What's exquisite about this?"

"I'll show you mine if you show me yours." A smirk crosses Newman's face as he reaches to the side of the mirror and pushes something. Hidden lights illuminate the mirror and James hears a whirring sound. Slowly the mirror moves downward behind the daybed to reveal a painting in a gold frame. James keeps his face from reacting to the color of the painting as shades of magenta are revealed by the slowly descending mirror. He sees Helen's face is also expressionless.

The face in the portrait comes into view. James feels the hairs stand on the back of his neck as he stares at the long-missing Degas, the *Nude in Magenta*. It has been so long since he's seen the portrait and that familiar face and even more familiar body captured by the master. The critics who call Degas' work *icy objectivity* are certainly wrong with this painting.

In tones of pinkish magenta, the nude woman reclines on a magenta daybed, much like the daybed lying beneath the picture here in Newman's hallway. She lies on her back, her legs extended, and looks longingly to her right as if her lover stands there, just off the painting. Typical Degas, James thinks, as if he's peeking at this woman, instead of her posing for him.

"It's . . . magnificent," Helen says, stepping closer to the portrait. Her face softens as she relives the pleasant memory of when she had lain on the daybed and the intense look on Degas' face as he painted her during that long, steamy summer of 1872 when he lived in that wonderful mansion on Esplanade Avenue with his mother's family.

Degas was a shy man but a keen observer of people. Helen remembers him taking her home, not by cab, but by streetcar. "I love to ride the streetcar," he told her. "I can look at people. We were created to look at each other, weren't we?"

This is the Degas she remembers, the great insecure man whose paintings were sometimes painted as if the subject did not know he was there, as if they were not posing, as if he were looking through a keyhole.

James stares at the portrait. The hairstyle is different but Helen's face hasn't changed. Her lipstick is darker today.

"Truly magnificent," James says.

"She's not so bad herself," Newman answers as he leers at Helen's backside. James smiles.

As if mesmerized by the texture of its strokes, Helen unbuttons her blouse and tosses it aside. She unzips her skirt and drops it behind her, then climbs out of her panties to stand with her back to the men. James takes a picture of Newman taking a picture of his wife's naked rear.

Newman moves frantically, snapping pictures, as Helen whispers to herself, "Oh, Degas. You always liked me best when I was naked." A vision of the great artist peeking at her from behind his canvas. Such a determined little man, he showed much more imagination in his art than in bed.

Running her fingers through her hair, Helen turns and faces them, her face nearly glowing with the big turn-on, being naked like this again. Both cameras bathe her with white strobe light as the men focus and photograph her.

Reclining on the daybed, Helen assumes the same position as the magenta nude. Her breasts more full than the woman in the portrait and her skin more tanned now. Back then a woman's body was rarely exposed to the sun. Helen looks to her right, directly at James as he carefully focuses and takes a picture. Her nipples are erect, her pink areolas so inviting.

Both men hurriedly reload their cameras and take another picture of Helen posed as the woman in the portrait before she starts moving around on the daybed. Opening her arms and legs, she lies spreadeagled for them, then curls on her side, then rolls on her belly. Kneeling on the daybed, Helen poses, then climbs off to pose on the carpet.

James hears his own heavy breathing as he moves behind Newman to take a quick picture of the *Nude in Magenta* without Helen in the frame. He takes another to be sure he has it, then returns to photographing his nude wife.

Helen crawls away from the daybed, then rolls on her back as Newman stands between her legs. He snaps a picture and James snaps one as Helen inserts a finger into her pussy. Her hips rise to her fingering as the men photograph her.

Helen rolls on her belly, rises on all fours, and continues crawling away.

James turns around, carefully focusing on the Degas, and squeezes off another picture. Suddenly, Helen scoops up her clothes, stands, and begins dressing.

Newman looks at James, then back at Helen as she zips up her skirt and puts on her blouse.

"How about some more wine?"

"We have to go." Helen's voice is deeper, filled with passion.

"Whatever for?"

Helen reaches for James and pulls him close for a long French kiss.

"We have to go!" Helen is nearly breathless as she steps into the living room for her sandals. Passing Newman on their way out, she adds, "We have to go home and take care of this. This *turn-on*."

"Y'all can do it here." Newman waves to his sofa, camera still in hand.

Helen turns back to Newman and brushes her lips across his. "See ya around," she says as she leads her husband out.

Bounding down the ancient stairs, James tells her, "That was so damn hot!"

"You're telling *me*?" Helen fans her blouse and exhales loudly.

Driving straight home, James rubs Helen's breasts and fingers the wet lips of her hot pussy. Helen sighs and grinds her hips to his fingering. He keeps her high and hot until they get home.

They fuck on their sofa. Frantically at first, then in long, penetrating, loving strokes. Helen comes quickly, as usual, bucking against James, pulling the orgasm from him. He gushes in her and lies atop her for long moments.

Then slowly, they start a second round, the way Helen likes her seconds, very softly. He moves his mouth down to her breasts to nibble each pointy nipple, to run his teeth across them, to suck them. He kisses his way down to her navel, rolling his tongue into it, then kisses his way down to her bush and round to the softness of her upper thighs. He can smell the scents of their sex, her pussy juices mixed with his semen. He flicks his tongue across her clit and she shivers and starts grinding her hips again.

"You like that, little girl?" He rubs her clit with his thumb, slipping his middle finger deep inside. She shudders and pumps her hips to his fingering.

"He took pictures of you fingering yourself," he reminds her, and she gasps. He reminds her how yet another man has seen her naked, how she caused yet another stranger's erection to throb in his pants. Then he reminds her of the other spectators and how they gaped at her.

Helen pulls him up and inside and they go for long seconds, her face enraptured in pleasure, James working hard, and it's magnificent.

As always, once she's properly stimulated.

They fuck again, later that evening, after returning from their favorite one-hour developing center. The young man behind the counter grins mischievously as the pictures come out of his developing machine, starting Helen's juices flowing again, causing James's dick to stir and harden.

The following Saturday morning, Helen presses the buzzer below Judge Frederick Newman's apartment.

"Yes?" Newman's voice echoes through the intercom.

"It's Helen."

"Oh! Come on up."

The door buzzes and James pulls it open for his wife, two uniformed New Orleans police officers, a crime scene investigator, and Detective Nelson Dante, a huge man with mahogany skin, a shade darker than the fine tables in the apartment upstairs.

As the column of people moves up the narrow stairs, James watches Helen lead the way in her extra-short, denim mini-dress, so short the full rear of her pink panties is exposed to the men behind her.

Detective Dante, pulling legal papers from his coat pocket, moves next to Helen as she taps on Newman's door. James can't see Newman's face when he opens it, but watches Dante hold up the legal papers.

"Police! We have a search warrant for this residence." Dante moves straight into the apartment, followed by one of the uniformed officers and the crime scene man. James and Helen go in after them, leaving the second uniformed officer to guard the door.

Dante moves down the hall to the mirror. Newman, standing in a T-shirt and shorts in the doorway of his living room, stares owl-eyed at James as the couple passes. He couldn't look more innocent.

"The button or whatever is on the left side of the mirror," Helen explains as she and James arrive behind Dante. It takes the big detective less than a minute to find the switch and James hears the motor hum as the mirror descends.

Dante lets out a long whistle as the Degas is revealed.

Footsteps behind James turn him around to see a bespectacled man carrying a small silver case approaching. The man's gaze is locked on the portrait. He nods and says, in a thickly Italian accent, "I think so."

Dante waves everyone out of the new arrival's way.

"This man's the curator of the museum in Florence, Italy," Dante tells Newman. "This painting was stolen from there thirty years ago."

Newman doesn't react.

As the curator pulls an electronic magnifying glass from his case, Dante asks James and Helen to accompany him into the living room.

"I'd like to see that warrant," Newman says through gritted teeth.

Dante hands him the legal papers.

"What judge signed this?" Newman flips through the papers.

"You're instructed to remain in the living room," Dante tells Newman. "Officer Jones will stay with you." Stepping back into the hall, Dante adds, "We got an ad-hoc judge to sign the warrant. Barely knew who you were."

Jones, in his crisp N.O.P.D. uniform, grins at Newman and points to the sofa. "Make yourself at home, Your Honor."

Newman's shoulders sink and he steps back and plops on his sofa.

Helen sits in the love seat facing the sofa and crosses her legs. A small triangle of her panties can still be seen and James sees Jones looking. James sits next to his wife.

When Newman turns their way, Helen crosses her legs like a man, knees spread to give the judge an open view.

"What kind of cops are you?" Newman snarls.

"Cops? We're not cops." James shoots the judge a cold smile.

"We're private investigators," Helen adds quickly as she pulls the sides of her miniskirt up to show even more. Jones smiles in appreciation.

James points toward the hall. "The museum hired us. They didn't want to go through N.O.P.D. with you being a supreme court justice and all."

"Good idea," Jones agrees, folding his large arms as he stares between Helen's legs.

"The museum sent in a plumber and an electrician earlier," James explains, "but they couldn't find anything."

Newman closes his eyes and leans back.

"It took us a while to find your weakness," Helen says.

Newman's eyes open.

"Everyone has a weakness." Helen shrugs.

"What weakness?"

James cuts in. "That's where your ex-wife came in. You should never have hidden so many assets from her in your divorce."

Newman is suddenly pale.

Helen uncrosses her legs. "Your wife told us you're a voyeur."

James points to the hall again. "They'll be searching for the Mozart original score you picked up on the black market in Vienna. Your wife was more than helpful."

Newman's face reddens and he growls at Helen, "I still have those pictures of you, little lady."

"Good." Helen raises her right knee and plays with the side of her panties, revealing most of her pubic hair to Newman and the smiling Officer Jones.

"Don't feel so bad," Helen purrs. "We're your perfect foils. I'm an exhibitionist and my husband's a voyeur."

James looks at her with admiration.

They've come a long way since stumbling across each other in Hyde Park on that bright spring morning, the first day of April, 1700, both spotting that fancy-pants pickpocket at the same moment. Catching him red-handed and returning Lord Bristol's gold watch was a thrill, but not as thrilling as looking into Helen's eyes for the first time. She was a governess back then, he a common copper, a constable on patrol.

Over the years, they've had so many adventures, have been able to right so many wrongs graduating from pickpocketed gold watches to tracking down the burglars who lifted Queen Victoria's emerald necklace to recovering the legendary crown of Alexander the Great. And now a long-lost Degas to go along with the van Gogh recovered in Vienna and the Renoir they pilfered from that old lecherous general in Buenos Aires two months ago.

He took in a deep breath. Doing what they do, for as long as they have, hasn't been hard at all. The hard part was finding each other.

Well, James thinks, *it's time we got back to Kashmir to pick up the trail of the lost jewels of Amthor. It'll be so nice seeing them around Helen's neck again.*

Doing the Dishes

Rachel Kramer Bussel

The first time I did it, I did it for love.
The second time I did it, I did it to seduce.
The third time, I was ordered to do it.
And I loved every minute of it.

No, it's not something filthy at all. In fact, it's the opposite of filthy. I'm talking about doing dishes. I know, you're thinking, *how crazy is that?* but please understand. I get off on doing dishes. I cannot pass by a sink filled to the brim, or anything but empty, and just keep going. I'm lured to it by some force that draws my hands under the water, into the depths of the suds and spoons and discards. Sometimes I even do it with my eyes closed.

But, just as with people, all dishes and sinks are not created equal. While I'm a pretty equal opportunity dishwasher, only certain people's dishes can affect me in *that special way*.

It all started with Alan. Before him, I was never much of a housekeeper and the farthest thing from a housewife as you could get. I reveled in my slovenly ways, thinking I was exerting some backward feminist statement by being just as messy as the guys.

But in Alan's apartment, something changed. When I saw that huge pile of dishes soaking in his sink, something stirred inside of me and I was drawn to them, almost magically, like Alice, but instead of mushrooms my intoxicant was dishes. They weren't really soaking, most of them; they were piled so high that some spilled over onto the counter and stove. I could tell they'd been there for ages and I just wanted to get started

on them. I stared at them, entranced. I was ready for my first
fix. But when I asked, he told me not to do them. "I couldn't
have you do all those dishes, there are three weeks' worth
there! Don't go to all that trouble, I'll just put them in the
dishwasher."

I didn't bother to point out that if it was that easy, he'd have
done it already, or that so many dishes wouldn't even come
close to fitting in his dishwasher. I didn't say anything, just
nodded, fingers crossed behind my back.

Now, if it were up to me, all the dishwashing companies
would go out of business and start making microwaves or
something. We could give everyone with a dishwasher a free
microwave and be done with it. Who'd want a cold, impersonal
machine to do this special, seductive job? Not me. In fact,
anyone dissatisfied with the policy could come to me for a very
personal dishwashing. And whoever invented the dishwasher
should just be banished to some island and forced to eat only
with their hands.

So even though he'd asked me to leave them, I ignored him.
It wasn't easy, let me tell you, to wait two whole days for him to
leave the house. I didn't want to look too eager about him
leaving, but when he was finally gone, and I'd made sure to
hear him head down the stairs and slam the door, I did a little
dance of glee before racing over to the now obscenely piled
sink.

I first turned the hot water on, holding my hands under the
heated spray. I let it wash over my fingers for a few minutes,
getting them used to the heat. I don't use those icky yellow
gloves either; they make my hands smell like rubber, and if I
were going to do that, I might as well delegate the dishes to an
evil dishwasher. No, I like my dishes hands on.

I then went to fetch my shoes; at my height, I wanted my
heels so I could reach everything more easily. Also, something
about this act just calls for heels, it looks much nicer than
balancing on the tips of my toes. I felt almost like I was being
filmed and wanted to look the part. Some of the plates and
utensils needed soaking, so I let the sink fill up with water and
poured the liquid green soap into the mix. I lifted one plate,
relatively clean, and lightly ran his purple sponge over it.

I smiled when I noticed the days-old coffee in a mug next to the sink; he'd probably been in too much of a hurry to finish it. I ran the tip of my index finger around the edge of the mug, thinking of his soft lips sipping the steaming brew, then probably slamming it down on the counter before rushing off to work. I lifted the mug to my lips and gently licked the rim, wanting to stay connected to him for just a little bit longer. I'd been making progress with the dishes, and only about half a sinkful were left.

In another mug, I found fresh remains of hot chocolate, and smiled. How adorable. I dipped my index finger into the sweet sludge, then slowly ran it across my tongue. I felt the first shiver pass through my cunt at the taste. Mmm . . . I took many more dips before plunging the mug under the water, erasing all remaining traces of chocolate.

As I got to the dishes, mostly steel pots, at the bottom, I really got into it. For these, I'd have to work. I opened the cabinet under the sink, looking for a thicker sponge. I found a heavy duty one, unopened, and ripped the plastic with my teeth. I then attacked the first pot with as much vigor as I could. I had the water on full blast and was scrubbing away, so I didn't hear the door open.

Then all of a sudden, he was in the kitchen doorway, a scowl on his face. "WHAT are you doing?" he screamed.

"I know you said not to do them, but I just couldn't help it. Please, please don't be mad. Actually, well, I didn't want to tell you this, but it turns me on. I've been doing your dishes for half an hour and now I'm all covered in water and turned on. Don't you want to come over here?"

He stared at me for a good minute, taking in the way my nightie clung tightly to my chest in the many areas where water had splashed onto it. I still held the purple sponge in my hand. He came toward me and pressed my back up against the sink. The sponge fell to the floor but I didn't care. He lifted me up so I was sitting on the edge of the wet counter. "So this gets you turned on now, does it?" he asked as he stroked me over the wet fabric of my panties.

"Yes, it does," I said, leaning back with my arms on the side of the sink. I knew I'd be able to get him to see dishes in a whole new way, and I was right.

The next time, dishes helped me get the girl, at least that's what I told myself.

We'd been having a pleasant enough date, but one that looked like it was going to end with a sweet kiss on the lips and an "I'll call you soon." She was going to drive me home, but said she needed to take a shower first. Well, that was a weird sign but, short of asking to join her, I couldn't figure out how to spin that into her bed.

So while she turned on the blast of the shower spray, I turned on the tap. I rolled up my lacy long sleeves, knowing they'd still get a bit wet. I didn't mind. I let the hot water run, no gloves, feeling its heat course through my body. I plunged my hands in, soaking them as I scrubbed. I thought of all the commercials I'd seen as a child, talking about "dishpan hands," the dreaded disease of mothers everywhere. But I liked the way my hands felt after a good scrubbing, all wrinkly and used.

I went slowly, savoring each dish. I rinsed the bowl we'd used for the salad, removing traces of oil-covered leaves. I found the knife that could only be hers (I only use forks and spoons), and slipped it into my mouth, feeling the ribbed edge and tangy metal against my tongue. Finally I slid it out and washed it properly, wondering how it would feel inside me.

I was nearing the end when she stepped out of the shower, wrapped in a robe with a towel atop her head. I could feel her stop on her way to her room and just watch me, but I didn't turn around. With the next knife I found, I again opened my mouth and slid it in, pushing it back and forth in a fucking motion that she'd have to be completely dense to miss.

She walked closer, dropping the towel to the floor. She walked right up behind me and pressed herself to me. She reached for the knife and slid it into her own mouth, then pushed my head forward and trailed it over the back of my neck. I gave a startled jump, and she pressed it tighter against me. She led the knife down the ridge of my back, slowly, while I tried to stand perfectly still. As she reached closer to my ass, I couldn't help but move, and I spread my legs a little wider. She was now standing a few inches away, focused on her kitchen knife. She tapped it lightly against my ass and I moaned, and she did it again, harder. I lifted my ass into the air to give her better access, but she was past that. I felt the knife about to enter the place of my fantasy from moments before. She'd turned it around, but I could feel the heavy end of the knife slowly entering my slick pussy. I moaned and gripped the edge of the sink tightly.

She slid a finger in alongside the knife handle and I felt like I would explode. She didn't move the knife too much, just a slow back and forth, but the whole experience pushed me over the edge. My body shook and I had to hold on to the sink ever harder as well as pressing my feet firmly to the floor.

She handed the knife to me and steadied me against the counter. "Keep washing, we're not done yet."

I took a deep breath and turned the water back on. I held "our" knife under the hot spray for a moment, ignoring the ecological implications of this act in favor of watching it splash off the silver metal. She reached around me and fondled my nipples. "Keep washing, remember," she reminded me as she twisted my nipples. I kept the water going, moving slowly, not in any hurry to have her torments end. She kept on twisting my nipples, occasionally rubbing my clit as I did my best not to drop the dishes. Then she'd grab a utensil and fuck me with it, making a never-ending cycle of dishes that I was more than happy to play my part in washing, and getting dirty.

I smiled happily. Maybe tomorrow I'd start on mopping the floor.

About a year later, my dishes fetish had gained me quite a reputation. I was frequently asked over to friends' houses after dinner parties, and they'd covertly imply they wanted me to wash their dishes or outright ask me.

But this time, I was caught off guard. I'd spent the night at a kinky party flirting shamelessly with Alex, a dyke top who'd before now seemed totally aloof and unapproachable. But even while she whipped several other girls into nicely streaked creatures, their marks proudly shown off for any interested bystander to see, she kept sneaking looks at me, and I could feel them even across the room. I couldn't even look at anyone else, just kept crossing and uncrossing my legs and wondering if my mid-thigh length black leather skirt was too short. I drank so much soda that I started to get jittery and had to keep passing by Alex to get to the bathroom. Finally, near the end of the night, she grabbed me on my way back from the bathroom. "Are you coming home with me tonight or what, you little tease?" Then, I don't know what came over me, but in response I kissed her, pushing my nerve-bitten lips up against hers and rubbing the rest of me against her as well. "I guess that's a yes. Go wait for me by the door." I gathered my things in a fog and waited at the appointed spot.

We drove silently to her place, with her hand on my thigh for most of the trip. If we didn't get there soon, I was going to have to move her hand up a bit higher to get some relief. After the longest ten minutes I could remember experiencing, we pulled into a driveway. I didn't really take in the scenery, just followed her up some stairs and into a large living room filled with a thick white carpet and plush leather couch. I moved to sit down on the couch, but she grabbed the waistband of my skirt and steered me in another direction, to the kitchen. What I saw took my breath away. It was like Alan's but much, much worse. This woman owned more dishes than I'd ever seen in one place, ever. And they were scattered all over this room, on every possible surface. It was like some surreal art exhibit, with honey and chocolate sauce and spaghetti sticking to each item. It looked like a food fight had erupted amongst the foods in her refrigerator, each one battling for the title of "able to do the most damage to a single kitchen."

"I've heard about you, missy, so I had some friends make a little treat for Miss Dishes." She reached her hand under my skirt and pressed her fist against my cunt, the hard edges of her knuckles making me even wetter. "Now I know you're just dying to have me beat the shit out of you; I thought you were going to pass out from watching me at the club. And as much as that hot little body of yours definitely deserves it, you're going to have to make this kitchen sparkle before you get any of my treats. Do you understand? Now, I'm going upstairs to rest for a while. Don't bother me unless it's an emergency. When I get back I want this kitchen perfectly clean, okay?"

I sucked in my breath and nodded, because as she'd been talking she'd been kneading my pussy in a way that brought me oh-so-close to orgasm, but then she took that fist right with her up the stairs. I stared longingly behind me for a minute, before trying to figure out how to tackle this mess. Well, the first thing to do was strip. I threw my clothes into the only clean corner of the place I could find, and set to work. I brought all the dishes over toward the sink and stove, placing them in like order.

I started with the silverware, even though conventional wisdom says that with any major project you're supposed to tackle the larger items first. Well, that's never worked with me. The silverware is like foreplay. I can go quickly, stacking the shiny spoons and surprisingly sharp forks, and I get to hear them jingle together. I like to build up the anticipation before I get to a really huge pot, one I can linger over and fondle.

But before I got anywhere near the pots, Alex came back. She stared at me from across the room, barking orders, telling me to work faster or to go back and redo a certain plate; how she could tell the state of its cleanliness from ten feet away I don't know, but apparently she could.

As soon as she'd come downstairs, I'd started getting wet (again), and was nervous that some of my juices might dribble down my thigh in excitement. But her voice would brook no argument, and truth be told, that's why she made me wet. She started marching closer to me. I felt like we were at boot camp or something when I noticed she had a miniature alarm clock. She set it for five minutes. The sink still held an overabundance of dishes, plus the kitchen itself looked like a war zone. There was seriously no way I could get it all done.

"Bend over, right here," she instructed, next to yet another pile of dishes. "Since you don't seem to be doing too well the traditional way, I'm going to have you lick these plates clean. Go ahead, I want your tongue on that top one there." No sooner had my tongue reached out than she lifted up my skirt and started spanking me, first with a light hand and then much more firmly. She meant business. My tongue lapped and lapped, wishing it was her pussy, working frantically to get through even one dish. I did somehow get it to look relatively clean, though who she'd get to eat on a licked-clean plate I didn't know.

"Good girl, now, let's move along." She placed the clean plate in its own new pile and presented me with more. Some had chocolate sauce, but even that was hardening. She took pity on me, reaching up to a shelf and pulling down some whipped cream, then covering the entire plate with it. "Knock yourself out." I plunged my face into the cream, not caring about making a mess (what difference did that really make in this environment?), and eager for her next strokes. This time, I went at it with gusto, and the more I licked, the harder she spanked me. Then she slipped her fingers inside me, not starting with a delicate single digit but pushing three fat fingers inside me. I could barely keep up with my whipped cream but I knew I had to if I wanted to keep getting fucked. Just as I was about to come, the alarm went off. Had five minutes already passed?

"Okay, darlin', you're off the hook for now." She blew a whistle that had been hidden in her pocket and two sexy women in French maid outfits appeared out of nowhere. I guess I'm not the only one with a cleaning fetish. Alex led me upstairs and fucked me for the rest of the night, whispering dirty words about suds and sponges and silverware in my ear the whole time.

Avril's Name

Thomas S. Roche

I thought I had her figured out. I thought she'd be an easy fuck, a casual lay to rinse from my mouth the too-fresh taste of a broken love. I thought we'd fuck, I'd go home, I'd forget her. And she'd forget me. No harm, no foul, no long goodbyes.

"Once," she told me, leaning against me in the bar. "I'll sleep with you once."

I'd seen her so often, looked at her body with lust in my eyes. She tended at Markers, the bar I frequented, a hip bar filled with young tattooed punks and staffed entirely by women. She knew what all the other bartenders knew – sexy clothes spelled big tips. But she didn't go the route the other girls did – tight, low-slung jeans showing off their hips and the fact that they wore no underwear; short skirts and knee-high leather boots that made their thighs more tantalizing than a pair of high heels ever could have; belly-baring T-shirts showing off sexy tattoos and pierced navels.

Instead, every inch of Avril's flesh was always covered, except her hands, her face, and – just occasionally when she bent forward within sight of me – the small of her back. Her tattoos were dense, indistinguishable; they adorned the small of her back so tight and finely woven that I couldn't make them out. The tight leather pants she always wore kept them hidden most of the time; her long-sleeved, tight black turtlenecks forbade any real view of her slender arms, her flat belly, or her ample tits. But that didn't make her any less sexy; on the contrary, the clothes she wore were so form-fitting that no contour of Avril's body was unfamiliar to anyone who went to the bar. She was a frequent source of discussion among male patrons, speculation often centering on how the hell she could have gotten into pants so tight they looked sprayed-on, how she managed to make her breasts stand so firm like that when it was clear through the tight, stretchy material of her turtlenecks that she wasn't wearing a bra. Nobody knew, but it titillated them to speculate. It titillated me, too; it made me want her more than I already did.

The bar girls at Markers were notoriously slutty, most of them recently out of college and moved to the city to be hip and be seen, to get high and get laid. A joint, a hit of E, or a baggie of Ketamine tablets, it was said, would get you pretty far with one of these girls. But Avril was different – no older than the others, probably, or at least no more than a few years. But her reputation was pristine despite her provocative clothes. Rumor had it she'd never gone home with anyone. Not men, not women – not anyone.

But she flirted with me. When I dropped in for a drink near closing time, when she was the only bartender on duty, she would kick everyone out, lock the door and chat with me while she cleaned up. She wanted to know about me – my interests, my dreams, my desires. She avoided all the like questions I sent her way. Even after a month of regular flirtation, I knew only a few things about Avril, all of them relevant but none of them terribly illuminating. She was straight. She was single – had been for some time. She was from Nebraska, but had lived in dozens of towns since running away from home at an early age. She was of mixed Italian–Dutch parentage. And she never, ever showed off her skin.

But I knew one more thing, just a rumor, murmured by one of the bar girls I'd taken home one night: Avril's mother had been a tattoo artist, had died young, of a broken heart.

As she finished counting out her drawer one Thursday night, I sat at the end of the bar watching her, smoking cigarettes – another testament to the fact that she liked me, for the health department could have fined them even while the bar was closed. She glanced over to me between stacks of ones and clanking rolls of quarters, her eyes hungry, her lips full and red with lipstick.

"I was thinking I might stay up for a while," I said. "My

place isn't far away. Would you like to come over for a drink?"

"I have to work," she said nervously.

"Friday's your day off."

"Oh, yeah," she said, and blushed.

"One drink," I smiled. "I promise I won't try anything."

She turned to me, her face washed with sadness. She ran her hand up the length of her sleeve, as if it itched.

"I want you to try something," she said.

"Then I will," I told her, fixing her dark eyes with my stare.

She came around the end of the bar, put her arms around me. She smelled like a mix of flowers and Johnnie Walker. Black Label; maybe even Gold. We kissed, and I felt the press of her body against mine, the slick rub of a tongue piercing as she explored me. The taste on her tongue was definitely Gold label, a brand Markers didn't carry.

"Once," she told me. "I'll sleep with you once."

I smiled, shrugged. "Who said anything about sleeping together? I'm talking about a drink."

"Once," she told me. I opened my mouth to protest – if we liked it, couldn't we do it again? She put one finger across my lips, finding them still moist with her spit.

"Once," she told me. "I'll sleep with you only once."

My apartment was a few blocks away, and as we walked she leaned against me, seeming to need support. Perhaps she'd been single for so long that the thought of being with me scared her. I wanted her so bad I knew once wouldn't satisfy me; perhaps if I was good enough, she'd be open to a repeat performance.

I slipped my hand down the waistband of her pants, feeling that she, like the other girls at Markers, wasn't wearing anything underneath. She cuddled up next to me as we walked. I took a deep breath of her – Scotch and flowers, fear and fire. I fumbled with my keys and let us into my apartment.

We tumbled onto the bed without turning on the light, and her mouth was insatiable. She pushed up into me, her back arching as my swelling cock found her leather-clad cleft. She moaned and pulled me hard against her. She kissed me like a savage, like a cannibal. She slipped her hands under my T-shirt and massaged my back, pushing her hands into my jeans to cup my ass. Her pussy rubbed firmly against my hard cock. She pulled her mouth from mine and my tongue worked eagerly after it, seeking. She grabbed my hair and forced my head back. I stared into darkness, Avril nothing but black, not even a shadow.

"Undress me," she said.

"Let me light a candle," I said. "I want to see you."

"Not yet," she told me. "Take off my clothes first."

Kissing her tenderly, I unfastened her belt, peeled the moist painted-on leather pants down her thighs. I could smell her bare cunt the moment I exposed it; her musky tang was thick and hungry. I unzipped her boots and pulled her leathers off. Then she put up her arms and I pulled off her top.

My mouth found her tits and I felt the smoothness marred by tiny, almost imperceptible lines. They were barely there at all; my tongue could feel them, but my fingers couldn't. Her nipples were pierced, which I'd known ever since I'd first laid eyes on those perfect orbs in their stretchy silk prison. I suckled her tits and teased her metal-cool rings with my tongue. She moaned softly and as I slipped my hand between her legs I found her wet. One finger slid easily into her; two made her tighten around it and moan louder; three, with a thumb on her clit, made her arch her back and gasp.

"Fuck me," she said, her voice hoarse with desire. "But I need you to see me first."

I got up in the blackness, fumbled for the candles in my nightstand drawer. I'd done this often enough with enough women to know the procedure without being able to see. Before I lit a match, I stripped off my T-shirt, kicked off my shoes, dropped my jeans and stepped out of them. My undershorts joined them on the floor, and I lit the match.

Avril stretched beautiful and pale on the bed, her white skin crisscrossed with black lines from the top of her throat to her wrists, from her shoulders to her hips to the lengths of her slender legs, all the way to her tattooed feet. Only a dead white spot at the top of her left breast remained unadorned, her natural skin color without benefit of ink.

"What the fuck?" I whispered.

"Light the candle," she told me, and I did, snugging it into an old whiskey bottle.

I joined her on the bed, bending close to inspect her body. My eyes wide, I ran my fingers over the black lines, disbelieving.

They were names: hundreds of them. Written tiny in ornate script, large in dripping blood horror-letters, medium-sized in faux-typewriter. And a hundred other variations, two hundred, more than I could count. I ran my fingers over her, eyes wide, reading.

Richie. Darius. Mac. Jonah. Jerrold. Roland. Frederic. Quinn. Jeremy. Sean. Stanford. Walker. Mikhail. Tobias. Saul. Lawrence. David.

And on and on, in swirls and slants and grids around her naked body, leaving only her heart untouched. Names repeated, but were they the same names? Or simply echoes of past loves?

She looked into my eyes, her dark orbs flickering in candlelight.

"Men," she told me. "Men I've been with. Every one of them. Even a kiss," she said. "Even the smallest touch. Every one of them."

"You're crazy," I said. "Is it your . . . your mother?"

"You heard," she said.

"I heard," I told her. "Is it true?"

"That part's true."

"Is it why you do this?" I asked.

"I don't really know," she told me. "It just happens. Every time. It's too late now," she said. "We're here. We've kissed. You're mine." Her hand moved to mine, took it, pressed it to the blank spot in her breast.

"I'm running out of space," she said.

I kissed her, hard, and her tongue swelled against mine as her back arched and she pulled me onto her. My tongue traced a path from her mouth to her heart to her nipple, then down her belly to her pussy. I could barely see with the dancing shadows from her body writhing on the bed, but there were names there, too. Even on her lips; even on her pierced clit, so tiny I couldn't read them. But the names above it I read; Anton and Val and Conrad stitched on the shaved, smooth mound of her sex. I closed my eyes and listened to her moan as my tongue worked her clit. When she came, she begged me to enter her, and I did, climbing atop her and sinking into her pussy so smoothly I almost came, myself, right away. But I held back and fucked her, my fingers tangled in her hair, each strand parting to show names written there, too, on flesh that must have once been shaved. I kissed her hard when I came, and she pulled me down onto her so hard I could feel her pubic bone against mine; she bit my tongue, drawing blood in the instant my orgasm peaked. When our lips parted, her lips were glossy with blood. "I love you," she said, shuddering. "I'm sorry. I love you."

Deep into the morning, I rested, Avril clutching herself against me, sighing almost sadly and murmuring in her sleep. The candle burned down to a ruined mass of wax, leaving acrid strains of smoke curling through the apartment, illuminated by the slanted light of the rising sun, segmented into improbable patterns by the Jolly Roger hung in my window.

I stared into the smoke and asked the question all men ask, or perhaps only most – how many? Hundreds, clearly, but how many more? Were names written in names on Avril's body, the writing so dense that the names of new men had covered those of long-lost ones, the kind of cover-up you get when they throw you out of the street gang?

And what of the blank spot on Avril's left breast – virgin white over her heart? Untouched, unspoiled, unknown?

Avril lolled to one side, dozing fitfully. She rested in a hot band of sunlight shooting molten from the window. I looked down at her and froze.

There it was. Written large, in block letters the color of blood: My name.

I might have thought I'd only missed it before; my name is not uncommon, and Avril could have had one of me before. But there was no mistake. My name was written on her breast, in the spot that had been blank.

My name was written on her heart.

I shook her, softly, whispering her name. She stirred and

shivered. She looked up into my eyes, and saw the question there. She looked down at her breast and her mouth dropped open slightly.

She turned her face to mine, sad, and shook her head.

She curled up onto me and whispered into my ear, her breath warm and Scotch-scented.

"I'm sorry," she said. "I'm so sorry."

When I woke she was gone. She'd left no trace except for her discarded leather pants and turtleneck top, her discarded boots. Perhaps she'd borrowed clothes from my drawer; smaller than me, Avril never could have fit in my jeans or my boots or my turtlenecks. Nonetheless, she was gone, the only trace of her the scent of her cunt on my body, the smell of her Scotch and her sweat and her tears on my bed. I went into the bathroom to wash her from me.

I stopped.

Staring into the mirror, I drew my hand to my breast. An inch above my left nipple, it was written in letters the color of blood. In feminine script, but shaky, fragmented, as if rendered by a tattoo artist being forced to do so at gunpoint.

The tattoo was fresh, as if she had rendered it while I slept, without waking me. Blood oozed from the fresh marker, trickling down my chest.

I knew she wouldn't be there when I went back tonight after work. I knew she wouldn't be anywhere that I would find her, ever again. I knew she was gone, vanished into the wind, roaming the planet wearing my name on her heart – touching it sometimes, late at night, whispering into the darkness: "I'm sorry . . . I'm sorry . . . I'm so sorry . . ."

I stood there in the mirror and ran my fingers over the bloodied script of Avril's name carved across my chest like the notebook scrawlings of a very small girl, lovesick and alone.

I could smell her in my nostrils, taste her on my lips.

See her named on my body, rendered by a lovesick girl in the middle of the night.